NIGHTFALL IN THE FOREST OF DESTINY

A TALE OF MAGIC & LONGING

THE NIGHTFALL SERIES BOOK 3

LOREN TUXFORD

by Loren Tuxford

Content Warning

The Nightfall Series is an epic fantasy tale featuring multiple POVs. It contains mature themes such as mild violence, coarse language, and romance (MF in Book 1, MF & MM from Book 2 onward).

Dedication

For little Loren.
To the monsters who watch from within,
with eyes of starlight, cold and eager.

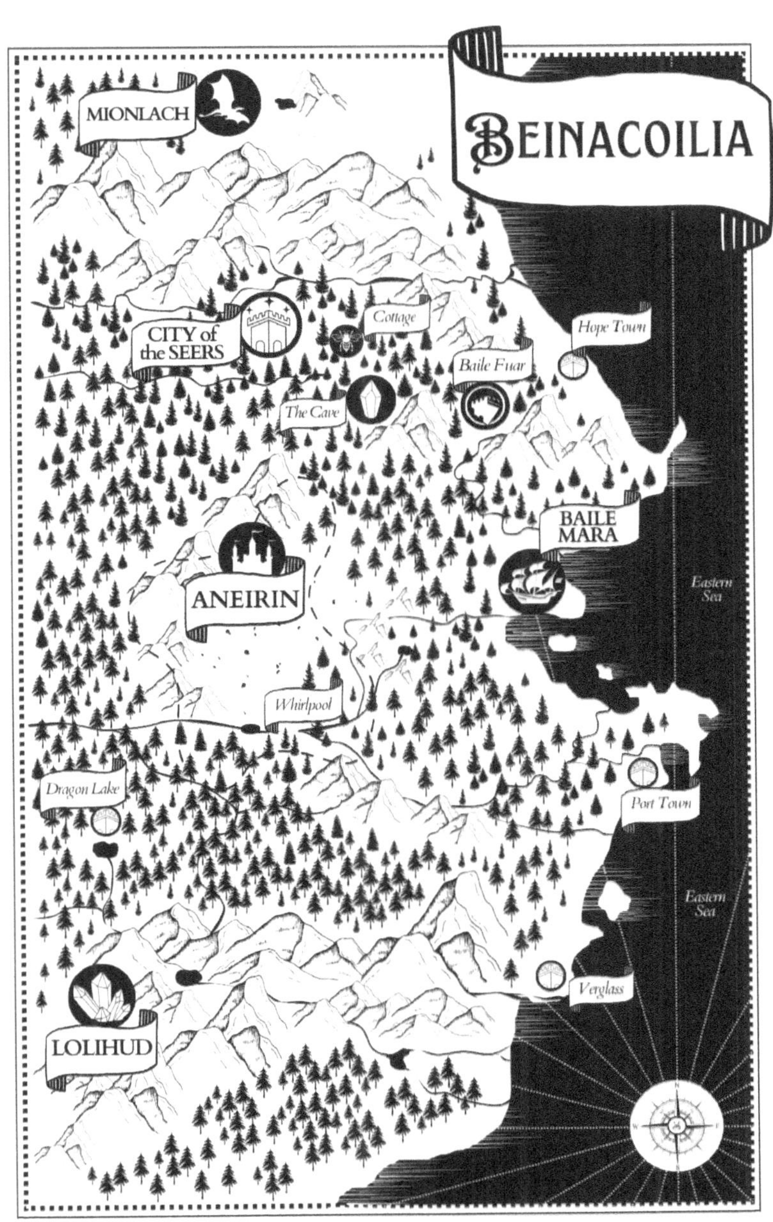

BEINACOILIA
MIONLACH
CITY of the SEERS
Cottage
Hope Town
Baile Fuar
The Cave
BAILE MARA
Eastern Sea
ANEIRIN
Whirlpool
Dragon Lake
Port Town
Eastern Sea
Verglass
LOLIHUD
N

Contents

PROLOGUE

Germination

"Seeds across various species may remain dormant for some time. When certain environmental conditions are met, a seed bursts forth, growing after a period of near desiccation.

In this way, the right combination of light, water and dormancy may allow a tiny spark of life to bloom, seemingly from nowhere and nothing, after biding its time within quiet depths."

Taken from 'Plant Lore on the Continent of Beinacoilia' by Hypatia Carter, commissioned for the Library of Seers.

Added underneath in an expressive scrawl:

'My dear wife, am I mistaken, or is the eldest of our two terrors exhibiting changes, like some long-dormant seed? Not the changes that we hoped for, however. It is most unexpected. Unsettling, even. I fear that we were... wrong.

x Illarion'

Underneath lies another note, written with tightly restrained form:

'Husband.

I am never wrong.

Hypatia.'

Morgan

Year 240
Baile Mara, City of the Sea

"That's not a book."

At the unwelcome voice, the librarian's hand stalled over the sword.

Swallowing a sigh, Morgan Rose eyed the impeccably crafted weapon before her. The weapon lay across sheets of yellowed parchment on the central worktable. Small fists tightened around the soft polishing cloth, freckles rippling across pale knuckles. Heat crept up the back of the librarian's neck, all the way to her aching forehead. Yet she refused to turn around.

Instead, Morgan glared at the ridiculously high stacks of books requiring attention to her left. She scowled at the precariously stacked scrolls to her right. Annoyingly, the uninvited visitor was correct. She wasn't working on a book.

Because books...

Well.

In the clifftop library of Baile Mara, City of the Sea, the pungent aroma of metal polish mixed with the sweetness of beeswax candles. Morgan eyed the towers of bound parchment, important words requiring cataloguing and care.

The librarian snorted.

She wasn't working on a book, because books could fuck right off.

A single storied building of native black stone, the library of Baile Mara was built a short walk from the cliff's abrupt edge. Like a log of dark rock and old wood, the building crouched along the ridge, weathering the fierce sun and even fiercer winds. Inside, hundreds of years' worth of histories and scientific research were housed. Outside, the strong winds had created twisted, ghostly shapes out of the native eucalypts. But despite its exposed position, the library's contents were safer up here. The old scrolls and dusty books were purposely kept away from the salty fog and mineral tainted air of the steep, ocean side city below.

Hugging the curved shore of the peacock blue bay, the city of Baile Mara was a maze of winding streets, warehouses and public houses spread out in sloped terraces, much like a jagged upturned clam shell. Visitors became easily lost. Along the upper terraces, plots of greenery, open fields, official buildings and grand houses circled the city's outer walls. Tall spires jutting up from various temples spread throughout both the upper and lower districts, made of the same black rock on which the extensive city had been founded.

From the library, the view of the volcanic island in the bay, with its haze of sour gas, was usually spectacular. Today being overcast, the view was about as interesting as soggy parchment. A brine-scented storm had blown along earlier, lingering grey daylight at odds with the golden glow of lanterns and candles inside.

Morgan's lips pursed. The library wasn't much, but at least she was left alone here. Usually.

A faint draft accompanied the unbidden bastard who had entered and disturbed her peace. The cool air shifted the layers of parchment and frayed books that, yes, Morgan should have been cataloguing. Deep rows of bookshelves rose to the heavily beamed roof. Amongst them, shadows loomed like black shrouds. Tiny dust motes flaked off of old scrolls, her long red hair ruffling as the heavy doors closed with an arrogant thud.

The visitor cleared his throat. "That's not a scroll either, little librarian."

Eyes firmly focused on the sword, Morgan pursed her lips, resuming carefully wiping a soft rag along the cross-guard.

Newly in her possession and something she admittedly had no use for, the sword was magnificent. Morgan smiled at the faceted red depths of the large ruby in the pommel, the jewel catching the flickering light with a bloody wink.

Perhaps the blade agreed with her distaste for their unwelcome guest.

"Or is it a fancy new quill, little orphan?"

"Piss off, Rook." Morgan added more polish to the rag from a battered tin before buffing the cloth back along the brilliant metal.

"But, my bloody Rose," Rook drawled, smirking at the wordplay, named as she was for the flower left with the babe on the doorstep of a backstreet temple, "from the dreamy look on your face, it could be just as interesting."

Lips in a thin line, Morgan raised her head, brushing a loose lock of her red hair back from her freckled cheek. As she met Rook's mocking stare, an enormous wave crashed violently onto the black rocks below. The dark regrowth on his chiselled jaw shifted, and his smirk widened.

Tall and finely muscled, Rook Harbour looked like an unassuming scholar or artist. Usually the man dressed in robes of crisp white linen, sometimes flecked with delicate spots of the paint he used to create strange works of art on washed up driftwood. Rook did not look at all like the drug lord of Baile Mara's terraced alleys and laneways that he was. All sorts of games and fights were under his wayward jurisdiction, at odds with his hobby of supporting local artists. He currently lived above one of the Inns that he owned along the lower terraces, one that was frequented by sailors. Shiny black hair hung down his back in a long braid tied with a leather cord.

With his striking appearance, he might have been attractive if his black, almond-shaped eyes weren't full of malicious promise.

The deep shadows beneath them didn't help either.

Morgan snickered. Perhaps some disgruntled customer had added to their bruised appearance. Rook was always picking fights, loving the chance to throw his power around.

Both as a man *and* as a dragon.

As a man, he was a bastard.

As a dragon, he was a hundred times worse.

"Prick," said the librarian.

Rook snapped his perfect white teeth at her.

Disgusted, Morgan broke their stare first. She had no desire to possess the amount of magic he had hoarded within. All that she needed was just enough to break the chains of her current life.

Her mood darkened at the thought, her already throbbing head protesting further. Where was that flask? Discarding the cloth with a curse, Morgan poked about the uneven piles of scrolls.

Rook laughed as she swore under her breath.

"Fine, fine. I'm fully aware of your distaste for this place." He flicked a glance at the musty stacks around them and approached her worktable in the centre of the warmly lit space. "But why a sword? I thought you put up with this shithole only to hoard coin and someday get out of this city. How did you even afford it?"

"I traded."

"Ah." Rook sounded put out. Glancing up, Morgan glared at his pouting face. His lips turned up into a sly smile. "I am aware that you can trade your poppy milk with customers directly," he mused, eyes flashing. "Just save the best for me and my customers, hm?"

"Whatever. Fuck off." She shifted the sword by its sparkling ruby topped pommel, the long, straight blade flashing a warm silver. Setting it aside with a grunt, Morgan resumed sifting through the work she should have been doing. Where the fuck was it?

"Tsk tsk, Morgan," Rook teased as he poked around the scrolls beside her with a dry rustling. "Where did you find it?"

"A pub this morning."

"Pirate?"

"Perhaps."

"That was brave of him to come ashore." The rustling beside her ceased. "That blade is finely made, Morgan."

"It is."

"I find it curious."

"What?"

"Why a sword you can't use? Why now?"

"Go away." Her flask should have been right there. It wasn't. "Go paint another naked sailor for your gallery of dicks."

"I will. You should come visit again. The new gallery above The Stiff Mast is coming along rather nicely. Not bad for an underworld crook, hm?" Rook's white teeth flashed under her green-eyed scowl. "So. Was it a dream that told you so, little thing?"

Unable to hide her flinch, Morgan hissed. "Don't speak to me of that *affliction*."

Green eyes glared at black, wide with innocence. The bastard had breezed in like some unwelcome float of rancid kelp on the black shores below, and the peace of her day was gone.

Fuck, she mouthed, pink lips enunciating clearly, *off*.

He laughed, raising scarred hands in surrender, battered gold flashing.

Morgan swore.

In one of his hands was her flask.

Chuckling under his breath, Rook sidled along the table towards her. The faintly sweet aroma of poppy smoke accompanied him.

"Alas, I cannot fuck off just now. I'm meeting someone here."

"How wonderful. If you don't hand that over —"

"Peace viper, peace." Rook licked his lips as he waggled the flask suggestively. "So while I'm waiting, kindly tell me what you know about Nolan's Sphere."

"What?" The offensive taste in her mouth sharpened. Hating him and herself a little more, Morgan stretched up and yanked the flask from his grip. "That's oddly specific. And concerning," Morgan muttered, green eyes narrowing at the towering man. "It's not real."

"Some say dreams that foretell the future aren't real either." Rook's head tilted to the side, black eyes unreadable. "Even with common rumours that some of the royal family suffer from your same *affliction*, as you call it."

As Rook studied the librarian's stony expression, far below, the unsettled sea crashed onto black sands in thunderous waves. The force of the oceans could be felt as well as heard at high tide. Morgan tore her glance from the man, unscrewing the flask's clasp. Strong fumes mixed with the fragrant beeswax of the library's candles and lanterns.

Last night's dreaming had been especially intense, leaving her with a splitting headache on waking. None of it made sense, the various panoramas chaotic and disorienting. A river of magenta sparks, flowing like liquid rock, cut across a black landscape stinking of dying animals. Rippling waves of magic twisted about like diseased arteries of energy. Large, jagged blue crystals bound with flashes of quicksilver bursting forth from thick shadows.

And amongst it all, a sword cleaving through the chaos like a silver blade of starlight.

The exact weapon before her now.

Within hours of the dream fading to a dull ache behind the librarian's eyes, the sword had appeared in real life. The ruby had caught her eye first. Appearing in the hand of a desperate sailor at the pub where she'd shot back a steadying drink on waking, the jewel had glimmered with a teasing flicker from amongst pale cloth bindings. At the bar, Morgan had choked on her liquor. With a weight like basalt in her guts, Morgan had traded a pouch of fine poppy paste for the blade. No one else at the pub had coin enough to compare to the value of her product. Almost immediately, after the deal was done, its former owner had made a hasty exit. A thief, most likely.

She hadn't cared.

Morgan blinked, attempting to clear her vision, struggling to drag whirling thoughts back to the present. Tipping back the flask, Morgan welcomed the sour wine with a long swallow. Rook edged closer, ebony eyes intent on her face. She bit back her revulsion, draining the rest of the wine.

"Share your dreams with me," Rook urged, his voice velvety. Morgan's skin itched at the oily feel of it so near. "Join me in Dragonhood. I told you I'd get you more power, pretty thing. I'm on good terms with —"

"Oh, Rook. What did I already tell you? Let me think."

"Now, wait —"

"Ah, yes. I told you 'I'd rather fuck a scorpion than accept a favour from you'. Selling you opium is enough. Now piss off."

"Tsk, tsk." The shelves of aging parchment muffled Rook's laugh. "So much venom for this late in the day. Magic can do many things for all of us. It could do more for you."

"Magic," Morgan hissed, "can indeed do many things. Like helping the elite members of this once-shining city lord it over the rest of us. Fuck off. I'm fine with my allotment as librarian, and what Dawn shared with me more than makes up for it."

"Dawn? Pfft. A mere weakling. But..." Rook let the word hang in the thick air between them, his eyes glittering, "it could all change soon."

At his careful tone, the back of Morgan's neck prickled.

"What could change?" Dropping the flask and grabbing the cloth, she worked it in tight circles, pale green eyes looking anywhere but at Rook's face.

"The way magic is shared from dragon to person for services owed to this city..." Rook's dry voice curled about her like grey smoke. "Some of us are working on how to make magic equal for all. Releasing it from control by the Elphin royal family and the city council. Integrating into new bloodlines, where it can be…" he paused, "managed more appropriately."

Morgan's snort was abrupt.

As if.

Lifting her head back to glare at the wooden beams overhead, Morgan pursed her lips. The quickest way to get rid of him would be to help.

"Fine." She threw down the cloth. Rook blinked, excitement rising in his gaze. "I know of a book by —"

They were interrupted as the library's heavy ironbound doors burst open. Both of them flinched.

With the gush of fresh ocean breeze came the sweet aroma of fresh honey and the bitter tang of old ash. At the combination, dread pooled like vinegar in Morgan's chest. Shifting on her wooden stool, worn leather boots hanging above the floor, Morgan took her time turning around.

In the doorway stood Hypatia and Illarion Carter.

Baile Mara's prized alchemists.

Behind them, the horizon of the endless sea shifted moodily, like the bile rising in Morgan's throat.

"Ah, fuck, no," the librarian hissed. Scholars like these were the reason libraries of useless words like this place existed.

"Hypatia," Rook drawled, elbowing Morgan in her ribs. "New look?"

"You're here? Good. Yes, it was a neat little experiment with carnelian and iron," Hypatia said briskly, charging in. She was startlingly tall for a woman, the same height as her lanky husband. To top it off, the alchemist's shoulder length hair, normally a mousy brown, was now a startling shade of pink. The odd combination of scents grew stronger as Hypatia reached them at the central table.

Parchment fluttered and stirred as ocean air danced past.

Standing right next to Morgan with blue eyes wide with barely suppressed eagerness, Hypatia slipped ringed fingers into the pocket of her brown apron, resting them over the curve of her pregnant stomach.

Morgan frowned.

A stain of reddish brown splatters spread across the apron's brown leather. Averting her gaze, Morgan examined Hypatia's intense grin. Despite the climb to get to the cliff top building, the alchemist was barely breathing hard. Her husband's cheeks, on the other hand, were flushed as he joined them after closing the library's heavy doors. The blonde man struggled as he was holding a bulky cloth bundle in his arms.

"Rook," Illarion puffed, his green eyes flashing with mirth. His normally deep voice was ragged. "Morgan. Remind me, why did they build this blasted place up here?"

Rook laughed. "You need more exercise, oh mighty scholar. Why didn't you take the bridge across the clifftop from your estate?"

"Ha," Illarion wheezed with an amused glance, wiping sweaty blonde hair back from his forehead. "We had to swing by the lower city, visit the temple."

"Temple?"

"An offering needed to be made." Illarion shrugged at his wife. Hypatia ignored her husband. Rook chuckled.

"You made an offering? Ha. What offering for those dead rocks did you take?"

Illarion scoffed. "We took honey for the priests, not an offering for the statues, you twit."

"Why?" Rook sounded bored and amused. Morgan began covertly wrapping up the blade.

"We will need good tutors in all the arts and magic." Hypatia patted her belly.

A dry laugh filled the musty space as Rook flicked a lock of long hair off his shoulder with a shiny nail. "Hm. Very organised of you."

"Why shouldn't I be? There is much to do. Great things are happening."

Morgan bit her lip, eyeing the door. If she stood, would it be obvious she was about to dash away?

"Besides," Illarion added happily as he wandered over to join them. He was still breathing hard. "The midwife said something about fresh air being good for expectant mothers."

"And how is that," Rook jutted his chin at Hypatia's stomach, "coming along? Motherhood at age... hm, what was it? One hundred and ten or so?"

"One hundred and twenty," Illarion corrected smugly. "Or so."

"My, my," Rook crooned. "Share your secrets with the rest of us."

Illarion laughed. "You've had enough power for ten citizens! Your extended years are guaranteed."

Black eyes glittered. "Are they?"

While Illarion laughed, Hypatia's smile brightened. The sword was wrapped, and Morgan was judging the steps required to extricate herself from the situation. As she weighed her options, Hypatia's apron snagged the librarian's gaze once more. Blue eyes bore down on Morgan. A long finger pointed to the mess over the leather.

"I hit an artery," Hypatia said thoughtfully. "It was a mess," she added.

Morgan's jaw dropped. Hypatia wasn't a Healer, working with patients requiring care.

"Mm. We didn't subdue it properly." Illarion shrugged. Rook looked between them incredulously.

"'It?'" Rook asked, his tone exaggeratingly polite. Morgan bit back the bile rising in her guts.

"Latest clutch of hybrids with warm blood," Hypatia said. As if that explained anything.

"It was a lovely colour too," Illarion added, nodding. His arms tightened around the cloth-wrapped bundle in his arms. "Pity."

"Lovely to see you all," Morgan interrupted, straightening the mess before her. "But I've just remembered I've got to go and... do something, somewhere that isn't here." She attempted to hop off her stool but didn't get a chance. Hypatia brushed past Rook, grabbing Morgan's shoulders with firm hands.

"Stay," Hypatia commanded, blue eyes intent on Morgan's.

"Me? Why?" Morgan asked. The dread in her guts thickened.

"She did it," Illarion said eagerly, his voice sounding more normal. He nodded, as if his contribution explained the fuck out of anything.

"Did what?" Rook asked. Morgan scowled at his leering face over Hypatia's shoulder.

"I've had an amazing idea." Pink hair shifted as the woman beamed, oblivious to Morgan's frown.

The dread in Morgan's guts spread to her spine.

"I'm sure I'm right." Hypatia laughed with an airy wave of a hand, her other tightening on the librarian's shoulder. Morgan winced. "It could go wrong, but I doubt it. I've got the coin from the city's latest investment and now we can proceed. But I need help. I can pay," the alchemist continued, eyes shrewd, "those who help with my idea."

"Help?" Morgan pulled away from Hypatia's hands. Rook coughed into his hand at the librarian's sour expression.

"Help me find what I need," Hypatia pushed, her pale eyes at odds with the shocking colour of her hair. "We can pay."

"I get paid," Morgan protested weakly.

"Pah." Hypatia smiled and waved her hand again. "I am going to help you break free of the priestesses, and their charity that barely keeps you above the poverty line here in this place. How about an extra infusion of magic, beyond your allotment as librarian? To keep you young as you spend your gold, perhaps?" Hypatia's eyes glinted.

Morgan's hands clenched in her lap.

Hypatia's smile grew.

"What —" Hating herself, Morgan licked dry lips. "What do you need?"

"I want you to take something home tonight and dream with it by your side. Tell me tomorrow what you see."

"D-dream? With what?" Morgan croaked.

No longer wheezing, Illarion held up a bundle the size of a person's head. As her husband shifted its weight with care, Hypatia pulled the covering away.

Beneath the thick wool sat a dark blue crystal. Its surface was covered in ridges that flashed green as Illarion tilted the iridescent object to catch the light. Morgan stared at it, glittering like the jagged sapphires from her dreams. The dread in her spine shot up to pierce her skull like a brand.

Rook whistled.

"Fresh from our trader in the Eastern Isles," Illarion explained proudly. He stepped closer to his wife. Morgan blinked. The crystal seemed to throb brightly for a moment as it came into proximity to the alchemist's pregnant stomach. Illarion beamed. "I was burying an amethyst amongst my beehives when the courier rode in with two of these beauties."

"Veszelyite, with a jagged shell of vivianite," Hypatia explained, her gaze fixed intensely on Morgan's wide green eyes.

"So? I can't help with that —"

Oblivious, Illarion shifted excitedly from boot to boot as Hypatia leant down towards the trembling librarian. The alchemist lowered her voice, each word clear and direct. The scent of ash intensified.

"Yes," the pink-haired woman interrupted, "you can. Rook here tells me you have very interesting dreams. You speak about them when you are..." her blue eyes darkened, "not quite yourself."

Rook coughed into his fist once more as Morgan tore her gaze from the sizeable chunk of veszelyite to glare at him. Illarion nodded expectantly, green eyes wide. At last, Hypatia's unsettling grip released Morgan. The pregnant woman straightened.

"Your dreams will help confirm that I've figured it out. So I can proceed."

"Figured *what* out?"

"About how to appease the council elite and the common folk. I wasn't always so well situated, Morgan. It's long been my dream to share magic more easily with those that don't work higher up in the service of the city. There is a sickness to the way this city functions, a lacking. We need more magic, shared more easily, not the painful process of the now. So more people can experience the benefits." Hypatia's finely shaped lips twisted into a chilling smile. "I'll do anything to achieve this."

"How?" Thinking of coin and freedom, Morgan sucked in a ragged breath.

"Like I said. I've had an amazing idea." Eyes glinting with a strange light, Hypatia patted her protruding belly. "I'm going to change the world."

PART ONE

Humus

"The forest floor is made up of the most basic elements: decaying leaves, twigs and deceased animals. Humus forms, this layer being key to a fertile forest, whilst also preventing disease amongst the growth above.

Without this rich, pungent layer of rotten things, new life simply cannot grow."

Taken from 'Plant Lore on the Continent of Beinacoilia' by Hypatia Carter, commissioned for the Library of Seers.

Added underneath in an expressive scrawl:

'My dear wife, do you see? Despite his lack of progress, he is determined to make something of himself. The truth is there in his strange eyes. He could yet surprise us.

x Illarion'

Underneath lies another note, written with tightly restrained form:

'Husband.

The strangeness of his eyes is the only surprising thing about him.

Hypatia.'

1

The Watcher

Year 367
Aneirin City

"**F**uck the Elves."

"Yeah! Fuck 'em."

"They bewitched our king!"

"That bloody bitch! Have you seen how she looks at us with those strange, bright eyes?"

"Aye! All of them! With their unblemished skin, looking like they've never worked an honest day in their lives, filled with dark spells and curses as they are."

"Here, here…"

"Elven scum!"

"Animals!"

"Now we can't meet in the holy temple of our own city, now that it's being used to house their bloody elder council! How insulting is that?"

"At least there's ale here —"

"That's not the point, idiot!"

"Oi. Keep your bony elbow off me, mate. That hurt, my wound is still bleeding —"

"Well, don't be daft then."

"The Elves came to wipe us out, and yet we are expected to welcome them with open arms?"

"Too right!"

"We need to wipe them out instead."

"It's only fair… and our new king wants us to be fair, doesn't he?"

Riotous laughs and slurred catcalls erupted from both men and women. As the noise settled, a single, low voice spoke with quiet determination.

"So we deal with them."

Thoughtful silence filled the room beyond the inn's back wall, laughs fading to assertive murmurs. After a moment, a throaty belch joined the thrum. The wooden screech of chair legs scraping along the stone floor set the Watcher's ears into a flinch. A young woman called out, her voice laced with scorn.

"We *will* deal with those pretty fuckers. Permanently."

Laughter and jeers resumed, louder, as tin mugs clinked.

"Here, here!"

"Permanently!"

"We kill them all!"

"Yes!"

"Exactly." Satisfaction laced the low voice of the man who had spoken earlier.

Wyll's voice.

The Watcher's hands clenched.

"I think, ladies and lads," Wyll continued, as the private back room of the inn filled with quiet expectation, "that is exactly what we must do."

Ear pressed resolutely to the outside back wall of The Wet Oak, a middle-class inn of good repute, the Watcher bit their bottom lip. The rear alley, exposed to the chill air rolling down the jagged red slopes of the mountain range above the city, meant their legs were cramping, face numb. A cloak was pulled up high about their neck, but as night fell, the temperature followed. With no clouds obscuring the sky, bright stars blazed crisp and clear after the day's icy rain. It stank of stale wine and fresh piss amongst the mossy cobbles and dank puddles. Yet the Watcher stayed put, crouched in the same position for some time.

Occasionally, hearty aromas floated past from both familiar and foreign foods cooking nearby. The Watcher's mouth watered, yet they didn't move. They had come for one purpose, one that hadn't panned out. But they stayed as slurs and curses had risen in pitch and fervour, aimed at the foreigners residing in Aneirin.

The Elves.

The Watcher was both fascinated by and furious with them. Heart thumping with sickening irregularity, they slumped against the damp wood at their side.

With only the occasional cat hissing from a roof nearby, it was still here, at odds with the heated exchanges beyond the wall. The atmosphere had turned from drunkenly bitter to sober and serious, the slurs darker, meaner. Now, after one voice cursed another for making a drunken pass at the server bringing more ale, the voices hushed.

A door closed with a dull thump that the Watcher felt through the wood and plaster against their icy cheek. Voices cheered again, mugs clinking as a fresh toast was made.

"To the fucking Elves!"

Riotous laughter reverberated through the walls. Someone hiccupped with coarse abandon. The scornful girl said something that the Watcher didn't quite catch. Wyll must not have either.

"The king?" he queried, voice clear above the din.

A clank of what may have been a tankard slamming onto the table shut down all other conversations. The Watcher held their breath, sour aromas thick in their chilled nose.

"Yes." The girl raised her voice, her tone dripping with resentment. "What of the king, and his misled, sympathetic heart?"

Malicious undertones seeped through the thin cracks between wooden planks. These finally died down as a throat cleared.

"The king?" Wyll mused with careful consideration amongst the expectant hush. "Hmmm, what shall we do?"

2

Aurelia

Year 367
Aneirin Farmlands

"Aurelia."

"Bindy."

"Are you sure you want to do this?"

"Yes."

The single word stung like a bitter barb on her tongue, and Aurelia struggled to set it free. Beside her on the bridge that joined Aneirin to the Forest, Bindy eyed the ornately carved wooden bow clutched tight within Aurelia's hands.

"Do you want me to stay?"

Aurelia's knuckles whitened. "I need to be alone for this."

Beside her, the tall Elven woman hummed, the soft sound a wistful sigh. "I understand." Bindy eyed their ponies grazing amongst the frosted grass at the far end of the bridge. "Shall I take your pony back for you?"

"No." Aurelia smiled, a grim twitch of lips. "That would only alarm Rhydian."

"Fair enough. But I'm taking the rest of your arrows, at least. Can't let my handiwork go to waste."

"Sure. Fine."

"Oh." The Elf hesitated, tugging on her braided hair. "Which colour did you use for these?"

Out of the corner of her eye, Aurelia could see Bindy was pointing with the end of her long silver braid at the handrail.

A brace of dead rabbits hung over the wood, cooling blood draining into the wild churn of the currents below. The rabbits were coloured in various mottled greys and earthy browns, each one large enough to be mistaken for a baby deer.

Shot by her dragon-cursed bow that Aurelia had wanted to use one last time, they were spread out along the gnarled wood like offerings for some troll out of Elven folklore.

"Red." White knuckles jerked, fingers pressing into finely carved wood. Aurelia swallowed. "I used red."

With a grunt, Bindy nodded. "That's good." Her shoulder bumped fiercely against Aurelia's, their thick cloaks barely softening the action. Bindy laughed as Aurelia hissed. "But black would've been better, a way to close this cycle of events. A veritable 'fuck you' to this chaos."

Aurelia didn't bother to reply, rubbing at the numbness spreading along her arm.

What more could be said? Chaos was a suitable word as any for the accumulation of lies that had dogged her bootsteps from icy caves to giant trees. Lies that had led her to a kingdom built of reddish stone on the side of a mountain range, overlooking the wide valley of ruined farmlands behind her. Change, irreversible. A black arrow had caused enough ripples of change for a lifetime, even an extended Elven one.

Freeing one hand from its deathly grip on the bow, Aurelia adjusted the purple cloak around her shoulders, her breath a white mist. With a gentle sigh, the icy breeze scattered flakes of ash around her. The once lovely material of the cloak was now soiled by dirt. By blood. Salty tears likely stained the lush velvet, too.

Hers.

Rhydian's.

Perhaps Fox's.

Inside her chest, the beat of a weary heart stuttered against chilled ribs.

He's turned them back, she'd said to Rhydian, *into us*.

So was Fox really a man?

Or a dragon?

Did it matter? No. But there was more to what she'd been told. She knew that, felt that. Fox's happiness may well depend on it as they moved on in the aftermath of revealed secrets and lies.

And what did that mean of Flare, the dragon she had knowingly grown up with? Exactly what or who was he, besides a traitor?

Aurelia stared at the rush of water flowing out from the eastern side of the bridge. After using the bow for one last time amongst the outer edges of the farmlands, now scorched fields that stank of soot and blood, she had come to the bridge. It seemed fitting to close a cycle here, to acknowledge all that she had lost, all that she had learned. Blinking against an icy flake of frosty ash settling amongst her eyelashes, Aurelia sighed for the beauty of the present.

Glancing up, her heart caught at the vista of the human kingdom of Aneirin. Despite it all, the scene was a beautiful sight. In the wan light, the walls, buildings, and winding streets grew up along the reddish mountain like fungi along the trunks of the ever present mass of trees behind her. Occasionally, a weak slash of sunlight broke down from the thick clouds to paint the city in lingering washes of colour. The rest of the mountain range spread out on either side of the sprawling city, the rare sun rays passing over steep peaks and stumpy ridges. It was a foreign place, but captivating nonetheless.

If one ignored the battlefield.

Churned farmlands stretched in blackened drops and gentle rises between the bridge and the steeply terraced city. Sharp Elven eyesight could just make out the city's major gateway. The gates were open wide, great doors of iron and weathered wood pulled apart. From here, the tiny gap in the ringed lower wall of the terraced city was only the size of a thumbnail at arm's length.

Since her black arrow had arched over the field, they had remained wide. Humans and Elves were now working together, mere specks at this distance, continuing to make sense of the now decimated fields sprawling along the valley floor. The bodies of friends and enemies had been cleared. Grim work was underway to make some sense of the farmland beneath the carnage. Aurelia's nose twitched. Tumultuous aromas of damp soil, charred wood and acrid smoke drifted along the river's banks, mixing with the spicy pine and eucalyptus blend from the crowded forest nearby.

On the far side of the bridge, to where the thick planks of wood met rocks and carpets of jewel-green moss, tree tops towered above. They stood high enough that if one felled a single tree, it would more than easily span the wide reach of the river.

Aurelia shifted in her soft boots and glanced down. That's likely what had built the planks on which she stood. The recent traffic of hooves and boots had cleared the moss from the centre, leaving only patches of growth amongst the gnarls along the outer planks under the handrails. The bridge was clearly made by master carpenters, but parts of it looked like it was part of the forest itself. Inhaling deeply, Aurelia lifted her gaze to beyond the bridge, beyond the ceaseless rippling river.

The line of trees resembled a cliff if one lowered their lashes. Not of rock and stone, but of greens and browns soaring into ominous grey clouds. The massive forest seemed a fitting symbol for the life she had emerged from. Darkness, shadows, hidden figures, roots amongst the moss ready to trip the unwary off their chosen paths. Fragrant pines of dark green, with individual fronds longer than a tall Elf, crowded close in patches, bark rich in texture and mottled patterns.

"Beautiful," Aurelia sighed, caverns of ice seemingly another time, another life. "A blessing."

"What?" Bindy coughed, adjusting her cloak about her.

"Nothing." Aurelia dropped her elbows to the rail, green eyes drawing in the life of a quiet day, one of few after too much turmoil.

Other trees of golden green, whose type she had yet to discover, soared broad and high, the reach of their immense boughs wide enough to capture hundreds of shrubs and plants in thickly arrayed colonies of emerald, sage and shadowed greens below. So close to the water, the creak of branches and giant trunks, the shush of endless leaves rubbing against one another and the wild bird song was muted here. Even for her slightly enhanced hearing, the river washed most noises of the day away.

Beneath her scuffed boots, beneath the thick planks of rippled wood, the river sang with its deep hum, flowing, sure and unstoppable. Aurelia's nose ached with the mineral cold fragrance of wild water slowly turning from clear to milky, frost forming around the banks on both sides, green moss dying, brown spreading along the wet rocks like mold. Exhaling slowly, Aurelia's hands relaxed. With the fall of whatever magic Rhydian's parents had cast, as the energy faded, warmth seeped away, a chill encroaching along the kingdom's fragile edge.

Aurelia turned to face the valley of Aneirin. Winter had arrived, swift and abrupt. The kingdom was experiencing a descent into the chills like it hadn't known for years, perhaps decades. On her ride down through steep streets, the city folk had red noses, wide eyes and icy hands clenched together as they stared at the thick clouds hanging close. As her pony had picked its way along cobbled streets, Aurelia had to hide a bitter laugh, Rhydian's oversized wool top under her cloak almost too warm for her in the deepening chill.

Aneirin folk thought *this* was cold.

Give them a day in the icy haven of Lolihud, where ice was a constant companion, the lush green and temperate nature of the Aneirin Kingdom a fanciful dream. A dream that had hung over them with the threat of war for years.

A tapestry of lies.

Enough deceit for a lifetime, truly.

Bindy made no comment as Aurelia spat over the handrail with a vicious hiss. She straightened, readying herself for the task ahead, and turned around.

Aurelia watched a flock of dark birds glide overhead, soaring over the half-ring of reddish mountains that cradled the kingdom. Their wings and calls losing out to the hum of the river and its whirlpool beyond. The birds turned as one, wheeling over some part of the field that had possibly yet to be cleared of battle detritus and debris. One bird, faster than its flock, raced ahead, breaking formation as it sped towards the ground.

A rat, perhaps?

The two Elves watched silently as the bird glided with precision towards the ground, head and sharp beak focused on its prey. It barely touched down before it rose, a great swooping attack of wings, ash and speed that the small animal in its talons wouldn't have heard coming.

As the bird flew off, its mates racing to catch up, Bindy laughed her approval.

"Good hunting, little friend," Bindy called over the river's churn. She bumped into Aurelia once more. Her rich turquoise fur cloak was at odds with the ruined glory of Aurelia's faded purple. The tip of Bindy's silver braid pointed at the rabbits. "Same for you. Better than the fungus and bats of home, hm? Didn't see enough rabbits back at Lolihud."

Green eyes shifted from the expanse of fields where farmers and soldiers toiled together to bring some semblance of order back to the scarred landscape. Aurelia eyed her bow. As a chilled gust lifted the loose hairs from her neck, it was hard not to be taken back to another river, not far from here when one counted the distance she'd travelled.

When a tiny purple dragon murmured in her ear.

When a young man offered to help a lone traveller, despite the arrow pointed at his heart.

The prince.

Aurelia swallowed around the dry lump in her throat.

That wasn't right.

King.

Aurelia tilted her head back, eyeing the grey clouds. Thick, boiling and full of the promise of something Rhydian and his people would likely lose their shit over. Snow. No hint of blue peeked through with the sky ready to blanket the Kingdom of Aneirin with winter's kiss. The blue sky still reigned over the lands, though hidden now from view.

It seemed fitting that the different shades of blue were concealed behind a frozen veil. Like blue-ringed-blue eyes that had once been full of light. With their darker ring of blue around the irises, Rhydian's eyes hadn't lost their kindness, or their care. Yet now they carried the shadows of betrayal, a haunted sheen that lingered from the events of recent weeks.

As the purple cloak flapped around her leather riding pants, Aurelia bit her lip, wondering at the part she had played, and how she had been played in turn. Inhaling, she prepared to spit again, but a delicate fragrance from somewhere nearby broke through the shadows of her thoughts. Shifting, Aurelia inhaled deeply, tracing the soft notes of aroma amongst the ash and frost. Her green-eyed gaze rested upon Bindy's cloak pocket.

With a line marring the flesh between her eyes, Aurelia eyed the obnoxiously coloured fur.

"Bindy," Aurelia murmured. "What were you doing out here before you found me?"

"Huh?" The tall Elven woman's tawny eyes shifted uneasily to the side in too-casual avoidance.

Sniffing dramatically, Aurelia indicated Bindy's cloak with her chin.

"Ah." Bindy's cheeks pinkened.

Aurelia's eyebrows rose. "And?"

Peeks deepening to flushed rose, Bindy slipped a scarred hand into the deep pocket of her cloak. A bundle was carefully extracted from the turquoise folds, neatly clipped stems poking out from cloth the colour of dirty sulphur.

With a sheepish grin, the taller Elf unwrapped the item with care.

"I was looking for white, a symbol of life, found yellow." Bindy held up a wilted bouquet. "Fitting I guess. The symbolic colour of hidden things. Sulphur yellow, like the hot mineral within the deep, twisting tunnels of old rock flow back home."

"Flowers?" Aurelia asked, wonder in her voice. It was wonder at both the humble blooms and Bindy's poetic words.

"Well. I..." Bindy coughed. "I've got my eye on someone."

Aurelia's lips parted. "Oh." She cleared her throat. "I see."

"Hey." Bindy's flush faded, strong shoulders straightening under her cloak. "It's not just you interested in these brave, if magic-less, little warriors."

"That's not... I mean..." Aurelia bit back her protest, wondering at the crumpled yellow bouquet in Bindy's powerful grip. Ignoring Aurelia, the silver-haired Elven warrior meticulously re-wrapped the tiny flowers. Her orange and brown eyes rose to meet Aurelia's in a challenge, lips twisted in a smirk after the bundle disappeared into the folds of turquoise fur and wool.

"That's good," Aurelia hedged. It sounded lame, even to her.

"I hope it will be better than good," Bindy grinned. "I hope it to be fucking amazing, hot and —"

"Okay, okay, I get it."

Bindy whistled. "Here's hoping."

"Hm. Hey. Did they find Gavin?" Aurelia asked, her tone abrupt, leaning the bow on the rail, fingers aching from gripping it tight. She flexed her hand. "Or his body, at least?"

"Fuck no," her companion replied with a loud snigger. "I guess he's buried in the mud like the little shit he is. Was." Bindy paused. "What made you think of him?"

"Ugh." Aurelia bit her lip, smoothing the bloodied fur of the rabbit next to her hip. Calloused fingertips traced its back, the grey fur soft to touch. "He tried to give me winter blossom once, without telling me it was in the wine."

"Ew. Did you punch him?"

Aurelia's teeth flashed. "No."

"Shame."

"Yeah. He was... the opposite of Rhydian..." Aurelia began. She cleared her throat. "Rhydian showed me a new flowering bush yesterday. One I'd not seen before. 'Roses', he called them."

"'Roses'?"

"Mm. In one of the smaller courtyards of the older part of the castle. Someone had planted a garden a long time ago." Aurelia's smile faded. "But when he took me there, the roses were dying."

"That's a bit shit."

"This cold change doesn't bode well for them. But the half dead blooms, a lush, blood red, had the most lovely perfume I've ever encountered."

Green eyes narrowed into slits as Aurelia reflected on their stolen moment alone. The young king was busy pulling loose threads together amongst the frayed souls of Aneirin's people. Rhydian had stared at the roses as he'd pulled her against him, hip to chest in a fierce embrace. Warm lips had tickled her ear.

"Rose was my favourite scent until recently."

"Was?" she'd replied.

"Recently it's changed," Rhydian had admitted, his voice shy. "Honey and snow blossom, I think you called it."

Aurelia had smiled into his warm neck.

Honey and snow blossom, the fragrance of Aurelia's soap.

Bindy poked a rabbit carcass, tied to its limp companions with a strip of leather by limp hind paws. She pressed a long finger into the hole in the animal's neck. The wound was neat, with no torn flesh amongst the reddened fur.

"I taught you well," Bindy said, her voice barely audible over the hum and churn of the river. "Well enough to kill a king."

Aurelia said nothing, gaze steadfast on the rush of water flowing downstream. A fingertip trailed patterns in the ash on the wide handrail.

"At least the new one is alright to look at."

Aurelia closed her eyes. "He... is."

"That was unexpected for you, huh?"

"Yes."

"Considering your recent choice of bed partners," Bindy smirked, "I guess that fits." She coughed into her fist, a cough that sounded suspiciously like 'Fox'.

Green eyes snapped open and Aurelia tossed her hair over her shoulder, the long, dark strands catching on purple velvet. "You think you know —"

"I know enough," the taller woman interrupted. Her voice softened. "I know you'll be struggling with how things are back to front. You've always been the perfect, matter of fact little Elf. But you had to put on your big girl pants and make some tough choices."

Aurelia couldn't disagree. "Were they the right ones?"

"Do you even have to ask?"

"Flare... he..." Aurelia's voice faded to a bitter hiss of breath between clenched teeth. Bindy turned to face her, her hip resting against the wooden rail while the river churned below with undulating ripples of flowing milky blue.

"For fuck's sake, Aur." Bindy reached out to stroke Aurelia's loose hair down her back. The movement ended with a sharp tug. Aurelia winced. "Snap out of it. You're overthinking it. You killed a king and scored one in your bed. I'm impressed. We all are."

"But —"

"No buts!" Bindy snapped, stomping towards the far end of the bridge to where their sturdy ponies were steadfastly ignoring one another. Her heavy boots were loud and obnoxious. The Elf halted, whirling, her cloak a brilliant blue green amongst the wood and grey light. "Unless it's a *kingly* arse —"

"Get lost, Bindy," Aurelia called, turning back to the river.

"See you on the other side, Aurelia."

Aurelia didn't watch as Bindy mounted up and turned her horse back towards the fields, the city beyond. She wished Bindy well and said an ironic prayer under her breath to anyone listening for whomever Bindy's heart was set on.

A movement by her hip caught her gaze. One rabbit was still alive.

Perhaps she should have used black after all.

Ignoring the flashbacks of soaring black arrows that haunted her dreams, Aurelia pulled out a knife from her belt. The rabbit's throat gave way beneath the sharp blade.

"Like the exquisite roses, all things die. Thank you for your meat, little cousin."

Bright crimson blood spilled with careless grace to the churning river below. Calloused hands caressed finely made carvings of the bow beside her, tracing the subtle curve, following symbols that likely meant something to a cowardly purple dragon.

But not to her.

Fingers tightened in an instinctive flinch. Intricate carvings along the bow and her fingerprints merged with fresh blood. The weak magic in her bones flared for a fleeting moment, and sensation lingered on her damp flesh. The ghost of delicate, curled slivers of wood, shaved away to make such a fine tool.

Weapon, Aurelia corrected herself.

It wasn't a tool any longer.

Had Flare seen that somehow? That she'd need the bow? Not for sustenance along their silent trek into the human kingdom of Aneirin, but to end a pointless battle that should never have happened?

It was unlikely. But she'd never know, would she? That useless purple beast was now off with the strange man who had been pulling threads together behind the tapestries of how many events for the gods only knew how long.

Shifting the richly made purple cloak over her shoulders against the cool and damp mid-morning air, Aurelia leant a hip against the railing beside her fresh kills. The damp air had turned the layer of ash marring the wood into a thin coating of grime. It had been fine black dust, different in origin to the bonfires that had laid fallen warriors to rest in fierce flames.

"Curious." She wiped the grime off, onto the cooling, damp fur.

Aurelia and the other Elves had been surprised to find there was no official burial site for the dead of Aneirin. Members of the royal family, and those close to them, ended up in the crypts. Everyone else had their remains returned to the earth via burning, their bones and ash scattered to the farmlands that fed the people who lived there. Some Elves had been horrified, others unmoved. Elves usually left their dead to the snowy mountains.

Elves from Lolihud anyway.

Surely there were more? Survivors from whatever had happened in the City of the Seers? For now, until Fox returned, Aurelia's questions would remain tucked behind her heart while she dealt with the chaos in her mind from all that had happened. From all that had been revealed.

Her clear green gaze shifted to the wall of trees. As ever, it was dark below the canopy, the undergrowth thick and lush. The dirt road left the bridge and meandered its way between the near trunks and roots, to disappear into a dim, dappled place of mystery. The canopy was so tall that the trees scraped the low clouds and mist that threatened to turn into rain. Icy droplets gathered amongst the ash on her lashes, but Aurelia kept them open, welcoming the sting. She blinked, eyelids swiftly beating against the chill.

So many tree species that she didn't have names for grew there. Yet as her focus sharpened, Aurelia sighed, a long exhale of pent up fear and bewilderment.

"Mayflower," she whispered. The name was lost to the chaotic rippling of the icy waters of the river, a dull undercurrent to the various sounds around her. At the end of the bridge, her pony snorted, its breath a hot puff in the chilled air. A hollow scrape accompanied the animal as its hooves shifted on the planks.

"A Mayflower tree."

How had she not noticed it before?

There weren't many Mayflower trees close to Lolihud, it was too cold. But if one ventured far enough beyond the line over ever present snow, the trees could be found. They weren't quite as tall as the giant pines, but their height was still impressive. With wide canopies of deep green foliage and pale whitish pink flowers, they were treated with respect. Their fine twigs, blossoms and fruit made up a substantial part of an Elven diet, the fruit aiding in the digestion of many of the fungus that was harvested deep within the caves for food.

Aurelia scuffed the toe of her right boot along a gnarled plank. Each tree could be useful for many reasons, including for its medicinal qualities.

But the wood from the heart of the tree itself?

Never.

It was ill luck to cut one down.

"Rhydian," Aurelia murmured, blinking against the drops of light rain landing on her eyelashes, "how many Mayflower trees were felled by your family to build this bridge?"

And what of Fox? What had he done to bring about misery and deep trauma to himself? To cause him to rip magic away from the most powerful creatures known to the continent and whatever spanned beyond the fabled sandy shores to the east.

As if the gods had some dark sense of humour, the surrounding light dimmed for a moment. Glancing up, Aurelia watched thickening clouds gathering low over the valley. Fox was much the same, sucking the light from those around him, unless you knew the depths that sprung from whatever deep well he possessed. A well of magic, yes, but also of feelings. The likes of which she'd one day hope to be the object of. But on seeing Fox's eyes soften and light up, to near pure gold, at the face of his beloved, Aurelia had almost been embarrassed to witness their love for each other.

Tasting the smoke and pine on the rapidly cooling breeze, Aurelia turned back towards the river. Leaning right over to stare down, she wondered how deep his love ran. Considering whatever horrific chaos had caused him to basically destroy the dragon race, was his rage just as deep? What did that mean for her, the Elves, the Humans, and for Rhydian? Considering the man called Caspian was off gallivanting around with Flare, and the object of Fox's love was none other than Caspian's brother, Owaen.

"Am I the same?" There was no reply to her quiet murmur, only the churning of the river, the falling cool drops of rain, and the occasional snuff of her pony. "I fell in love with the son of my enemy. Am I the same as Fox? There isn't anything I wouldn't do for Rhydian, is there? I already proved that."

For a moment, it was hard to catch her breath, and the river seemed to agree, its twisting, rippled surface of smooth curves and clear bubbles calling out its reply. Her hands tightened along the wood of the railing, the ghost of a crystal dagger in her palm. Blinking away salt water as well as rain, the drops thicker now, Aurelia half laughed, half gasped. All she knew was gone, and what she had to learn was on the horizon like the clouds above, ready to burst with thunder and things she wasn't yet sure she could handle.

Right now was a rare moment away from the castle and the wide eyes of those in the same position. Elves and Humans alike, those waking from dreams held at bay by magic and false pretences while their so-called 'Elder' and a Human king waged a silent war. A years-long battle fuelled by resentment, old wounds and magical power that belonged to neither of them.

"I want... I want to go home..." Aurelia admitted to the fast-flowing river.

But was that true? Could home ever be the same, after what she had seen, learned, experienced? Would her parents have had word by now of what had passed, and her hand in it? What had yet come after?

Releasing her trembling grip from the rail, Aurelia rubbed her right wrist. Despite the faint buzz of magic in her blood, it still chaffed from being bound for so long, despite that being days ago. Yes, she could have had it healed. Fox surely would have seen to that. Yet the poignant reminder was better left to heal on its own, while her mind, and heart, came back to the ground to process all that had happened. It would take time. The sluggish fog in her mind from that strange blonde man had cleared. Fog had faded to shock. A numb wonder had her heart reeling in further thought, examining who Fox was, a relic of the past, someone who was not all that they once seemed to be.

Aurelia bit her lip, swallowing down the stormy feeling rising from her guts. As hard as that truth was to swallow, she was lucky in a way to remember after what she had been through. The oldest Elves, refugees from the fall of the City of the Seers, sometimes forgot the names and faces of their families due to shock. Something about magic making their bodies strong, but their minds weak. The Healers of home didn't speak of it openly, but a faint trauma lingered down the generations, of which had yet to heal.

Home.

If she couldn't be there, at the very least, Aurelia would rather be back amongst the forest. Not the once comforting and cavernous womb-like spaces of Lolihud. Or the historical grandeur of Aneirin Castle, with its endless hallways of worked stone and rich if faded tapestries. It had been a wonder, but after all that had happened, the shine had faded. She'd rather be under the trees, where the forest was wild and potentially dangerous, but true.

There were no lies in the forest, the trees and the undergrowth had a purity and honesty about them that the caves and city nearby no longer carried, for her or for Rhydian, she assumed. That's why the Elves and the inhabitants of Aneirin had wide eyes. If all they had known was mostly false, then what was true? A quiet anger fuelled both races, uniting some in one way. But dividing others as well.

Inhaling carefully, Aurelia closed her eyes. She focused on the cool air, the spicy aromas of trees, smoke, and churned earth. She didn't envy Rhydian at all. He was still a beloved figure of hope to some, but also a symbol of waylaid power to others. Thankfully, most still worked together to clear the battlefield, but the undercurrent of unease was obvious to anyone with a pair of eyes, Elven or not. A quiet anger that ran underneath day-to-day life. While two enemies with false leaders struggled to balance their broken dreams with the bitter taste of betrayal.

The trees of the forest were nothing compared to the lies that made up the dense woods of truths and falsehoods left to navigate.

With only a young, innocent man to guide them.

Elven elders that hadn't taken part in the battle were having endless meetings with Rhydian, accompanied by his soldiers and what little staff remained in the castle. As of yet, it was unclear what the future of both races would look like moving forward. Was it better that Fox was absent? Considering that Jessikah, another disguised creature once held in thrall by Fox, was one giant fateful error of his judgement, causing harm to them all.

Through it all, Rhydian had sat through most of the endless talks, silent, blue-ringed blue eyes dull, bloodshot and brooding.

"Fox," she breathed, solemn. "Are you coming back to take care of things? Or is that the last thing we want? Should you concentrate on Caspian instead?"

Thinking of Fox's startled pout at something Owaen had said not long before her rescue from the City of the Seers, saltwater welled in her eyes. A dark laugh bubbled from her lips.

Fox *pouting*.

Of all the strange things that had happened, his behaviour towards the tall blonde Elf and his dark green eyes was one of the most startling.

And one of the most welcome.

Perhaps there was hope yet for her and Rhydian, despite all the obstacles of race, parentage and recent events piled in their way. An unsteady cave in, with the potential of further disaster.

The first time she had seen him, with that traitorous dragon by her side, had been at a river deep within the solemn, watching trees. There had been a late snowfall, strange for how far north it had fallen. It had been a beautiful, wild place, and the prince had been a handsome and startling sight amongst it. But not a monster like she'd grown up believing the humans would be, just a humble, sweet man wandering along a rocky river bank, talking to his rather pretentious horse.

Unwillingly, her thoughts turned back to Flare, and the abandoned city of massive proportions with its abandoned silence. He had been what she had thought of as a friend once, who had been nearby since she was very little, the only dragon that still knew of the caves, the others gone by then, never to return. Not even Flare had talked of it. That made more sense now, knowing what little she did. Something the dragons had done had been unforgivable, and Fox had lived there amongst them, black and gold eyes on Flare whenever they happened to cross paths.

Aurelia had been six or seven winters old when Fox had first arrived at a Lolihud. With a warmly wrapped, frail figure and silent yellow haired woman in tow. Along with the only dragon to have visited the caves in years. A flighty, polite and chatty shining purple creature by the lofty name of Flare Shining One.

Her fascination had won over her awe, and Aurelia had been one of the few Elven children brave enough to introduce themselves. Even Bindy, fearless and full of fire, hadn't quite managed that.

She'd always wanted a dragon, ever since she was little. A wild creature from the stories, both old and recent, until their numbers had stopped visiting the icy caves of Lolihud.

A dragon of her own, but not to own.

A dragon to call a friend.

Deep lines of anguish formed on her brow. Aurelia tugged at the hood of the cloak, fingertips drifting upwards to idly brush thick hair from her forehead. Green eyes, flinty with barely contained rage, dropped to the bow.

"Fuck you, Flare," Aurelia hissed to the river. "I hope you're enjoying yourself."

3

Flare

Year 367
The Cave

"Did you know that, Flare? When Owaen was locked up in here, *I* was locked *out*. When his bleeding heart was most likely dreaming of saving more refugees or stray kittens or some shit. The gods only know why Skye shut him away like some holy artefact. He's such a *sap*. The stupid fuck broke my fucking sword! Fuck. Morgan's going to kill me. We've been through so much, that sword and I. I truly believed it was my destiny to put the world right with that blade in my hand. Shit. So anyway, I tried to get back in here and find out where the fuck Skye went, from my dear, perfect little brother —"

As Caspian's breathless tirade broke off in a hacking cough, Flare thought the haggard man had finally run out of puff. But across the eerie cave, a dry snort followed by a deep inhale indicated that Caspian wasn't finished.

"But Skye's magical seal was beyond my reach, beyond any dragon's reach. Otherwise, I could have ended Owaen right then and there. But now that he's out… fuck. Seeing him in the City of the Seers threw me, that's all. When I see him next… I'm going to squash him like the annoying little turd he is. I will." Another cough. "I *will*."

Munching away on the finest quartz he'd ever sampled, sparkling fresh with a cooling mineral aftertaste, Flare watched, silent, as Caspian rambled on. Words had been spilling from Caspian's pale lips for some time now. In much the same way that fine, glittering powder cascaded from Flare's massive jaws.

Curled up in his larger size, Flare crouched as far across the cave from the dishevelled man as he could. With his wings folded tight against his sides, tail curled around his hind claws, the dragon took up as little space as he dared.

The cavern was vast, with massive, glowing quartz crystal points as tall as Flare, soaring upward from the natural rock floor. From the ceiling, clusters of smaller quartz hung like natural chandeliers to meet them. Stalactites of the clearest crystal hung long and low, glittering with sparks reflecting the omnipresent green and blue glow.

Cool, ambient light and layers of crystal gave the impression of being underwater. The ambient glow was thick, glassy like seawater, inter-spaced with brighter shafts of light. The temperature felt the same too, cool and fresh against his scales. Through it all, the faint metallic aroma of rich veins of minerals drifted about on the gentle draft, meandering around the columns of shimmering quartz.

Sprawled against a large and rather splendid point of quartz near the tunnel entrance, Caspian sat facing him. The man had been alternating between silence, incoherent mumbling, and loud bursts of chatter. Occasionally, he grimaced at his ruined hand, as if offended by its brokenness. He'd stopped himself from rubbing it against his torn shirt multiple times, gritty with dust from the ruined city they'd left behind. His normally perfect blonde hair, with its odd grey streak looking green in the spectral light, was a spiked mess about his head. Eyeing Flare, Caspian leant forward, resting his chin on the... *thing* pressed against his chest.

Finely scaled nostrils rippled.

Flare had seen the thing long ago. It was about the size of Caspian's head. But instead of reflecting light, like the dirty man's white blonde hair, the thing absorbed it. Until it was moved, that is. The rugged surface was made up of jagged, crystalline features, deepest blue and flashes of sea green, just as dark. Yet a fine spray of sparks reflected off of it in a brilliant cascade as Caspian adjusted it tenderly against his chest.

"When I'd been here before, it was before Shadow Light fucked up a fine plan. Well. Mostly fine. All we were supposed to do was put our heads together, away from the City and that council of fucking clowns, and talk about the misuse of magic. How to fix it. Skye had her own endless well of power. I simply needed... I needed her assistance to put me into contact with my own. But then she disappeared."

Flare's heavy eyelids rose a fraction as Caspian took another deep breath. Resigned, the dragon took another bite of quartz, his pupils dilated with pleasure. Despite the circumstances, his feast was *incredible*. He felt rather pleased with himself, too. Rather than spoil precious clusters of quartz rising from the floor and cascading from above, he'd thought to rip chunks of quartz out of the glistening walls.

"When I finally made it back here after all that shit hit the trees, my brute of a brother had been locked safely away. Pfft." Caspian's expression darkened for a moment. "Behind a newly created wall of rock, I could feel him. My brother alone but for being surrounded by these crystals, all of these luminous tasty treats. Waiting for his lover…" His tone light, Caspian paused, a faint smile on dry lips. Wide and innocent, his bright gaze closed the vast distance between them. "With the crystals waiting for *you*, my shining one."

A ripple shuddered down the dragon's spiked back, all the way to his horned tail as Caspian's silver and blue gaze speared the dragon. Feigning indifference, Flare glanced away, sharp teeth pulverising quartz over his toughened tongue. His magic-fuelled body drained the power released from the crystals he loved. His digestive system worked eagerly to break down the chunks into particles, and finally the particles into the energy that his cells craved.

Crack.

Sharp claws broke off another sizable chunk of radiant quartz straight off the cavern wall, the thin echo bouncing off the clusters of luminous crystals. Slitted eyes drifted towards the narrow entrance.

The passage that led outside to the deep forest was big enough for a full-sized dragon to pass through. But where the tunnel met the cave, a black stone wall had been erected. Clearly artificial, it was smoother than the various natural black columns that peppered the cavern. A small, partially collapsed opening had been made in the lower half of the smooth wall, leaving the edges jagged with no finesse at all. Gritty sand spilled out into the tunnel from the glowing void beyond.

Thunder shook the trees and tunnel behind, a sign of the rain ready to burst from above. Inside, it was silent.

Earlier, the magical transformation from his larger size to small had been a most embarrassing occurrence. Flare had attempted to break the opening wider instead, but Caspian had stopped him with a hot lash of pain along Flare's tail.

"No."

"Wh-what?" Flare had screeched in shock, desperate with hunger to reach the throb of unspoilt crystal within. He'd felt their call even before landing awkwardly on the rocky shelf at the far end of the passage.

"Leave it," Caspian had commanded with a smirk, streaks of dust highlighting his handsome features.

Flare had stared at him for only a moment before turning away. Knowing Cas was daring him into vulnerability once more, the dragon had bit back a sob.

Gathering his thoughts to transform, Flare closed his eyes. As he let his energy and matter shift, shrink and change with a drift of purple haze, Caspian's amused laugh followed his transformation. Dreading that thing that was now accompanying them, transforming under watchful eyes, was like showing Caspian the soft scales of his belly. Vulnerable and hating it, once small, Flare had darted through the entrance in a mad dash.

Once through, he'd had some relief. The inner cavern was large enough for a dozen full sized dragons to fit comfortably, perhaps more. It was hard to see around the quartz clusters. The eerie glow distorted odd angles and played with perspective. Flare had transformed back to his colossal size speedily, scurrying for the far side of the cave. Having Caspian close by for so long, especially after his insane stunt back in the City of the Seers, had been more than enough contact for the rest of Flare's currently miserable life.

The thought had his tail jerk in anxiety. Was there any way to break free? Free from the fiery line of power that bound him to the insatiable man across the cavern? Without losing his tail in the process? Even as Flare sighed in pleasure at the thick flow of power expanding within his guts, there was much to digest within his mind.

What were the choices he had made to get here? And would he end up like that red, meaty mess back in the City of the Seers? A mess that was formerly an ambitious dragon of powerful magic and dark plans. Unseeing yellow dragon eyes would haunt Flare's dreams for ages to come, yet his wings twitched as the dead eyes morphed into green eyes.

Small, Elven eyes.

Gazing at him with the bitter disappointment of betrayal.

Flare swallowed, guts quivering, uneasy.

He hadn't wanted to leave things like he had...

But.

There hadn't been a choice.

This was all about *survival*.

As the tower collapsed in the City of the Seers, the bond between Flare and Caspian meant that Flare had to keep the maniac alive to save himself.

Once inside, ravenous with the hunger for magic, Flare hadn't waited for Caspian's permission. Frantic claws had broken pieces of pristine quartz straight out of the walls. Quartz so clear, like smooth windows of the purest glass, with ambient, mysterious lights pulsing deep within. And the *taste!* The flavour was —

A chunk of quartz bounced with abrupt violence off Flare's purple snout.

The dragon flinched, jaw hanging open.

Across the cavern of glowing blue and shifting green light, arms wrapped across his middle, Caspian peered at Flare intently.

"I said, 'aren't you grateful?'"

"Wh-what?" the dragon hiccupped around his current mouthful.

Blue eyes, one dark, one pale, flashed silver as they narrowed. Caspian pointed his long index finger at Flare, the littlest digit hanging off his hand like a tiny sausage protruding from a dog's maw. Flare winced at the sight. Not only did it look incredibly painful, the skin of his hand had an unnatural sheen. Caspian seemed not to care. Legs stretched out before him, Caspian tapped the toes of his scratched boots together as he spoke.

"Am. I. Not. Good. To. You. Flare. Shining. One? Aren't. You. Grateful?"

"Um, yes, yes..."

Caspian continued to stare at him, an expectant look upon his grimy face. Mismatched blue eyes glinted, reflecting the eerie glow in silver sparks. A long time ago, Flare had seen phosphorescence bloom along the shores of a black beach, so long ago that his limbs had ended in fingers and toes instead of dragon claws. The incredible sight of millions of twinkling sparks had looked much the same as the way —

The sound of a throat clearing interrupted the dragon's trail of thought.

Flare blinked, sharp teeth exposed around his mouthful of quartz.

"Oh, Flare," Caspian sighed. "What do we say to express gratitude, hmm?"

They stared at each other for the space of three slow, dragon-sized heartbeats. Potent crystal, so good it fogged his mind, rumbled in his stomach. Gods, it was simply the best he'd had, better than the temple —

Silver-blue eyes narrowed.

Ah.

It was Flare's turn to clear his throat.

"Th-thank you Caspian," Flare mumbled, crumbs of sharp points of quartz dripping from his lips, bouncing around like wasted jewels.

Caspian licked his pale lips. "How do they taste?"

"Um. Good." Flare's wings shifted minutely against his sides. "The b-best."

"Mm, really?" Caspian appeared to be holding back a snigger. "How about the seasoning?"

"The... what?"

"*Who*. Not *what*, pretty thing. The Elves." Caspian cocked his head to the side, eyes wide. "Are they to your taste?"

"W-what?" Flare choked.

Caspian blinked, an innocent flutter of lashes.

As Flare coughed, confused, a barely there flavour tickled his tongue.

Not mineral fresh.

Stale.

Meaty.

Ravenous hunger forgotten, Flare's spiked head reared back. His sharp claws scratched desperately on the jagged floor, the movement causing part of the wall beside him to collapse in a glowing, crackling cascade of quartz. Shards shifted and pooled around him.

And amongst it all-

Smooth skeletal shapes spilled forth, bouncing and cracking onto the floor at his clawed feet.

Even as the rich crystal in his guts was absorbed greedily, the dragon stared wordlessly as the chiming chaos settled into heavy silence. Flare's slitted eyes widened, unable to move, unable to look away.

Bones.

Each one was clean and clearly formed, leaving no doubt about its heritage.

Slowly, as if dreaming, Flare glanced up at Caspian. With his horrific broken finger flapping bloodily, Caspian pointed towards his own smirking mouth. His tongue, a dark wet mocking thing, poked at his upper teeth, exposed with a malicious grin.

Flare took a shuddering breath, realising what the blonde madman was indicating.

The dragon's own great tongue poked at something stuck in the between two of his dagger-like fangs. His stomach heaved as a rogue point of quartz poked back.

Along with something else.

Something that wasn't crystal.

Large amethyst dragon eyes locked with silvery blue, one light, one dark.

A small, tortured sound escaped Flare's throat.

"You look like you're enjoying them, so I hesitated to interrupt. But I thought they looked a little dry," Caspian said conversationally. He held up his shimmering hand, broken finger hanging, blood spraying about, black in the eery light of the cave. A faint scatter of drops landed amongst the grime on his cheek.

Caspian beamed across the deathly silence of the cave.

"Would you like some sauce?"

The horror wasn't just the fact that Flare realised he'd been munching on the bones of fallen Elves. The horror was exacerbated by Caspian's thrilled expression.

"What are you going to do, dragon? Right now, you can't do much."

A wordless moan filled the eerie cave, desperate and thick.

"You do have a choice," Caspian continued, eyes bright. "Make yourself tiny and try to flee your shame. At the risk of your tail." This statement was highlighted by a fierce tug along the part of Flare's anatomy in question. "And your glorious guts, as pretty crystals in your belly rip you open from the inside, in much the same way that cheeky fox ripped open our dear Shadow Light. Or you can wait until they digest. Then we shall get down to business."

Eyeing the cave entrance, Flare inhaled carefully around his mouthful of horror.

Caspian snorted at the frozen dragon before him. Looking pleased with himself, the man's muttering resumed. High cheekbones flushed, Caspian stared at Flare through lowered lashes, the *thing* clutched tight in his arms. Flare had been desperate to ignore it. As Caspian's muttering morphed into a mocking song, despite his current shock, Flare realised Caspian wasn't talking to himself.

With a spike of rising anxiety, Flare's gaze lowered.

Caspian was talking to the egg.

Mouth full of bone dust and crystal shards, the dragon breathed carefully through his snout.

The man was whispering, his lips against the textured curve. Even though it wasn't smooth like a chicken egg, its shape was reminiscent of one. As Caspian shifted, its glittering ridges of blue and green glinted darkly, contrasted by the diamond-like flashes that the cave's eerie light picked out. Almost like it had been rolled in shards of another type of gemstone. The claws on Flare's right foot twitched.

The wretched thing was both equally captivating and disturbing.

"For hundreds of years, I've put up with the disappointment of others," Caspian mumbled. "Far too long —"

"It hasn't been that long," the dragon whimpered through the shards in his mouth before he could stop himself.

Immediately, silvery blue eyes flashed his way. As Flare trembled, Caspian said nothing, his gaze narrowing.

"You're not that old," Flare mumbled.

"I'm not?" Slowly, Caspian's eyes widened. His expression clouded over as he blinked once, deliberately like the process of adding up the years caused him discomfort.

"I'm s-sure," the dragon replied thickly, his voice fading to a whisper as the bones shifted on his tongue. "I r-remember when you were born."

Caspian stared at the dragon a moment longer until his attention returned to the egg.

"Anyway. When my charming parents alchemized crystals with biology, Flare," Caspian said loudly. "I bet you didn't know *how* they'd done it. I bet you were simply glad to have been a part of the first chosen few to get wings." A sigh. "Wings. Not just some pleasant buzz from magic that could prolong your life, shine your teeth or make your prick a pretty colour. Oh, no. Magic *evolved*."

Jaw frozen once more, Flare's heart beat strangely, slow thumping pulses. The muscles of his tongue rebelled at being held still, his mouth half-full of what his body craved.

"Mm-hmm," the blonde man mused. "Despite the risk, you were so grateful to be part of that first batch of crystal-infused dragons. Being powerful, thriving with that extraordinary feeling of all that came with fancy wings, pretty scales, pointy teeth."

The dragon's shining spikes twitched, his hopeless mouthful of crystals a tantalising example of what Caspian was talking about.

Energy and power.

Flare had left his whole life, including his family, behind. He had embraced all that Dragonhood entailed. It had been like awakening from the mundane into a world of possibility. Hypatia and Illarion, brilliant visionaries, had surpassed the studies and research of the most prominent scientists, past and present.

Magic had evolved. Therefore, so had Humans, becoming magically infused creatures.

Elves.

Flare had never questioned the why of it, either. He'd been an older man by the time his opportunity had come. So he had taken it. With little hesitation. Some guilt remained, however. The indiscretion of not consulting his family beforehand was a subtle sting, but barely anything compared to the line of fire that threatened to ignite along his tail at Caspian's displeasure.

"*But.*" The hissed word broke the silence of the cave.

Tempted to swallow, Flare caught himself in time. The ache for the energy ready to be sucked from the quartz was like a sharp tugging deep in his guts. A dull spasm rocked his throat.

"But," Caspian repeated, annunciating the word sharply against his teeth with his tongue, "during all of these exotic new experiments, the brilliant Hypatia Carter had an even *better* idea."

With a laugh under his breath that could have been mistaken for a sob, Caspian dropped his forehead to the egg.

"After maturing Elven magic users into Dragonhood by a singularly painful process, the city folk wanted *more*. More magic. More energy. More life. More, more, *more*. But there were simply not enough willing participants to become dragons who, in turn, could share their magic with others. Not all those humans who went through the initial, rough stage of energy absorption of human to Elf to dragon survived. It was an unpleasant, risky process. As you know."

Hardly daring to breathe, Flare closed his eyes. The fear of having to go through that process of alchemy from Elf to Dragonhood had prevented him from leaving his scaled form behind for two legs, as some did now and then. He would never.

Ever.

"So another way was needed to share magic with the populace who sang for more, more, *more*."

A dark laugh bounced around the glowing cavern. Flare's amethyst purple eyes fluttered open. Caspian raised his head, eyes narrowed under his matted, white-blonde hair.

"So, the greatest alchemist to have ever lived became pregnant." Caspian cleared his throat. "With two perfect, innocent little darlings."

The dragon's scales twitched in shimmering purple tremors at the shadows in Caspian's voice.

"Her focus was on *birthing* Elves, popping them out like pips from some ripe peach. Not simply creating them from mere humans, wanting wings and power, those who risked death by initial energetic absorption." Caspian's eyes dimmed briefly, before brightening again to take on the wild, eerie glow of the cave. "Whilst simultaneously working on how to create a magical creature from nothing. Hm. Or rather, from the jewels of the earth itself. In effect, my dear mother ran two experiments at once. There were two sets of twins. One set from the fertile loins of a woman, the other from the loins of the earth.”

Caspian lifted the egg with care, holding it suspended before him. Despite the tension, Flare was struck by the faint tremble in the man’s hands as sparks and flecks of light caressed Caspian’s face. Catching the glow as he rotated it carefully, its curved surface sparkled with shades of mysterious blackened sapphire and precious, ominous emerald.

Mismatched blue eyes shifted to glare at the frozen dragon. Brushing his lips against the shimmering surface as he lowered it, Caspian settled the egg in his lap, his broken hand caressing it with tender devotion. Expression unfocused, lids heavy, his eyes closed.

“And so. With the fearsome vision of reckless alchemy, two sparkling, impossible miracles were created from the earth and crystal. While two little boys were born. One whole.” Caspian exhaled, his voice a strained whisper. “And one broken.”

A single bone rolled out of the wall beside Flare. It landed with a loud *crack*, the sounds from outside muted by the thick tension inside the cave.

Neither of them moved.

“So much potential,” Caspian sighed dreamily. “So much power.”

One eye opened, dark and gleaming, and then the other, pale and silver. The whimsical expression had gone. Instead, a blinding fury expanded from the blue depths.

Taking a shallow breath through his nostrils, Flare very carefully shook his head, tongue scraping against quartz, recoiling from shattered bone. He may have moaned. Caspian’s top lip curled, his expression losing some of its rage as his gaze lowered.

“Shall we tell this dear little egg a pretty bedtime story?” Caspian spat with quiet violence. He bent forward, lips brushing against jagged crystal ridges.

Flare’s wings rustled, another tortured sound escaping him, loud in the stillness of the glowing cavern. Dragon eyes, wide open, filled with mineral-rich tears.

“Your twin,” Caspian whispered to the egg, “cracked open the world.”

No! Flare wanted to cry.

Yes, his shameful heart whimpered.

Hanging his head in shame, Flare stared at his claws, mouth full of the crystals that fuelled him, and the bones of the countrymen that had likely been refugees from the chaos that reigned after.

Caspian opened his mouth to speak, then shook his head with a grimace instead. After licking his lips, he tried again.

“When was it? Centuries ago? Or more recently? The years are mixed up in my mind. Either way, my sweet little thing, Skye was hatched from the same green depths in which you dwell. The first *hatched* dragon! Born, like me.”

Caspian glanced up as Flare’s head rose. The wild-eyed man bared his teeth. The dragon’s eyes spilled over.

"A glittering gold and green scaled beauty of almost limitless energy. Born. Not a dragon that began life on two legs with a life and family of their own. Oh no, no, no. Hatched from whatever strange alchemy Hypatia had wrought with all that she had learnt in the extended life she enjoyed from all her magical experiments. You saw it with your own slitted eyes.

"And once the world caught her breath from the hatching, my beautiful birth city, Baile Mara, once shining and perfect on the black shores of the Eastern Sea, cracked open. Half of the city's inhabitants gone in a delightfully violent series of events not long after. In one giant, salty gulp of a boiling ocean."

Flare closed his eyes, swallowing the howl threatening to break free. He had been doing well to refuse memories of this time, memories of the cost of wanting more magic.

Because Skye's hatching had been *catastrophic*.

Like a thunderstorm below the earth, the lava pools had overrun, the land had heaved. It was as if the gods themselves protested the hatching of the first true dragon as some kind of crime against nature. Thousands had perished beneath the boiling sea, crushed amongst the collapsed city, or disintegrated like ash when the air itself had reached shocking temperatures.

Most of those that survived were Elven magic users, capable of some protection, or at least healing themselves from the point of death. Those that had no magic only survived if they lived further from the epicenter, away from the lava lakes that spilled from blackened caves into the bay.

Chaos had followed. Countless more died from starvation and disease, and those that could make the trek as refugees went to Baile Fuar further inland. Or to the City of the Seers, much further inland and north. During the time of chaos in the years that followed, Caspian was thought to have died, not long after his parents had perished of some unknowable disease that no magic could cure.

"Incredible, wasn't it? That you and I survived. That any of us did."

At the wryly amused voice, Flare opened his eyes. For a moment, he had no words, no thoughts. Only fear, draped like a veil of ice over his trembling heart.

Because the other egg, twin to the one whose hatching had wiped out a city, was before him now. Clutched in the arms of the man who held Flare tightly by a leash of that same deadly power. Caspian, one of two of the most unpredictable magic wielders Flare had the displeasure of knowing.

The other was one who simply called himself Fox. Cold, calculating, detached from the world.

A man who had been born as a dragon named Skye.

Twin to the egg in Caspian's arms.

Caspian stared at Flare, his expression peculiarly blank. A ringed finger tapped the sparkling surface. A blonde eyebrow rose.

"It makes you wonder though, doesn't it?" The dishevelled man snickered, a hysterical bubble of unexpected mirth. "My brother was born whole, and I, alas, born *broken*. Are the eggs the same? Then which one was Skye? Was the chaos of her hatching the *least* of what could have happened?"

Jaw aching with strain, Flare didn't dare move a muscle as Caspian beamed.

"Which one is this, Flare?" He shook the egg like a trophy before him. "Whole or *broken*? Isn't it exciting to just... not know?"

Exciting?

No! That's not the right word to describe this at all!

"Poor Skye," Caspian sang out, head tilted back to eye the faceted stalactites above. "Taken to live with you scaly, crusty old fucks in the north. And there in Mionlach, amongst the hot, dry black sands of the volcanic ranges, that innocent little golden dragon grew up into a fierce creature with cold eyes. Hilarious! You were friends with that Elven woman, weren't you? After you fucked up later with that Queen? But Skye, hmmm, that clever fox, took better care of her than you did. Ha." A dry cough followed Caspian's snigger. "You fucking coward."

As guilt wrapped painfully around Flare's heart, Caspian lowered his frightful gaze and shifted his legs, a small smile playing upon cracked lips. Flare ran his tongue over mineral shards that teased, teeth both dreading and eager to crunch down, his heart a horrified witness to the bones within.

Closing his eyes and hating himself a little more, Flare gave in.

He relaxed his jaw.

And swallowed.

The sharp points could be felt all the way down his throat, horrifying accusations of the dead. Eyes welling with bitter tears, Flare cringed, knowing they were going to come right back up. But it seemed less horrific for them to come back involuntarily, rather than spit them out at will.

"It's just so fucking *exciting*!" Caspian shouted.

Not from across the cave.

From directly in front of the dragon.

Flare's eyes shot open. The remaining shards shifted amongst his teeth like tiny wasps as he shrieked.

Right below Flare's head stood Caspian, swaying but upright, smelling of stale sweat and fresh blood. Dark circles hung heavy under wide, mismatched eyes. Pressing the egg to his dusty cheek, Caspian flicked out his tongue, licking one sparkling ridge of the vivianite crystal. From lowered lashes, a silver blue wink flashed up at the petrified dragon.

"What's the matter, Flare? Elf got your tongue?"

4

Cas

Year 367
The Cave

*"*F *riend or foe?*
Nobody knows.
Either way,
Let's run away..."

Cas paused, licking dry lips whilst searching for the words teasing him just beyond the tip of his consciousness. Tremors wracked his ruined hand as a finger tapped random patterns against the crystallised egg clutched to his chest.

"Let's run away... hm." He cleared his throat. "And... *and ignore all the warnings..."*

Cas smiled, teeth flashing, as he sunk back down to the uneven cavern floor. Across the cave, Flare remained motionless. His spiked head rested on forelegs that trembled occasionally. Purple slits shimmered as fresh tears continued to fall.

"What shall I call you, dear one?" Cas murmured, hoisting his prize to his lips.

At the far side of the glowing cave, a purple slit twitched.

"Tell me what you want to be known as. Your twin is called Skye. Shall you be her friend or foe, my glittering emerald pumpkin, hm?"

Cas tapped the toes of his boots together as he lowered the egg to his lap. He was in quite a state. His mess of a hand throbbed like a demon's arsehole. Stone and cave dust covered him in all sorts of uncomfortable places. Landing outside the cave tunnel had caused them to stir up a layer of freshly fallen ash from the cloud that occasionally peppered the continent. Even as his mind registered the disturbed tracks amongst the ash on the rocky shelf, Cas' nose had scrunched up. His clothes were ruined. The purple cloak came to mind. During its purchase, Cas had stumbled on a man back in Aneirin, a man desperate enough to stir up trouble.

Trouble that just might be a boon for later plans.

"What was that idiot's name?" Cas mumbled, frowning. "Bill? Wilt? Dill?"

Either way, that cloak had been wonderful. Perhaps he should have kept that for himself? Except... hm. That green-eyed Elven woman had looked miserable, hadn't she? Sometimes his own actions surprised him. Rarely, but they did.

What had her name been?

"Areola..?" Cas sniggered. Surely not.

Ever since they'd stopped here to catch their breath, it became harder to focus his thoughts. A sharp spike of pain occasionally lanced through his head. He also needed to take a piss. Even with the king's magic fueling him, he was bone tired. Feeling defeated. Even when there was still so much to do. More so now.

He'd been so sure only days ago, flush with the king's magic, that he'd had what he needed to get done what was required. But now? Seeing Owaen had taken his breath away, all Cas' magic lost at the memories of a brother whom he'd never measured up to.

Hard earned magic.

Cas shuddered.

Images of the dead king's sweaty thrusting left Cas feeling as sick as the great scaled creature across from him looked.

Fuck.

"I'm sorry about that, Morgan," Cas whispered uneasily. "But there's been no one else..." He swallowed and pushed the thoughts away. It would be fine. Everything would be fine. Gaze lowered, he grimaced.

The sight of his little finger hanging off at its unnatural angle was one more worry on top of everything else. He *should* fix it. Although, it was a nice reminder of the events in the City of the Seers, and the sight of his perfect brother's annoying face. A reminder of how not to get thrown off course again.

Ignoring the pain, Cas lifted his hand to inspect it more thoroughly. A faint sheen covered his palm. The dusty man frowned. An odd kind of shimmer had bloomed over parts of his skin. It was hard to tell the true colour in the blue glow of the cave, but the sheen could have been gold or green. Almost a nice reminder of Skye.

Hand dropping to the top of the egg, Cas sighed. Skye, who was now a cold-eyed man, a man who had somehow caught the affection of Cas' gods-be-damned youngest twin.

Owaen.

Despite the intense wave of anger in his guts that thinking about his sibling created, it was hard not to be impressed.

"Well fuck you, little brother," Cas hissed. He blinked at a giant quartz point, as tall and wide as a chimney to his right. "Owaen didn't deserve the power of our endless Skye then, and you don't deserve her now. How did you win her over when you finally met, and not me? I see absolutely no reason for that."

Rolling his head lazily to the side, Cas eyed the sullen dragon at the far side of the cavern. If one looked closely enough, you could see the faint tremble of folded purple wings, or hear the occasional rumble of indigestion. Flare had eventually retched some of what he had swallowed. The faint smell of bile had added a sour note to the mineral breeze of the cave.

But his beast had been fed and watered, yes?

Cas glared at the dragon.

"I see no reason Skye would prefer Owaen over me at all. I look after what's mine."

Inhaling through his teeth, Cas rested his head against the crystal wall behind him, feeling the grit in his hair catch on the fine points of a small cluster. It was annoying as fuck to be this filthy and tired. Yet he'd had to lie low for a few years, so it wasn't a new feeling. His hard-earned magic had once been ripped away by a fucking martyr of a copper dragon, while Shadow Light made work of Skye all by himself. Tapping the toes of his boot together, Cas surveyed the scatter of bones around the far side of the cave. Some were whole, some were shattered, mixed with chunks of quartz.

"It's fitting," he licked dehydrated lips, nose scrunching at the bitter grit, "that the bones of Elves lost to Shadow Light's failures are now becoming one with the most un-dragon-like creature of all."

Leathery wings jerked with a flash of deep amethyst. Smiling a little, Cas spat to the side. Reaching up his good hand, Cas stroked his hair, wondering at the grey streak. The man's magic was potent. But the flavour was... wrong.

"And now I'm back, with King Dickhead's magic, no less. I would have preferred Skye's, though. But I am back, nonetheless, with this precious little poppet."

Wincing at the pain behind his eyes, Cas examined the egg. He tapped its jewelled surface and absentmindedly brushed his fingers together, examining the odd shimmer of his skin. Morgan might know what it is. She'd always looked after him.

Until she hadn't.

He pursed dry lips. Cas didn't blame her for her unfortunate reaction to the first stage of his plan.

"But I freed us from them," he mumbled into the quiet, glowing cavern. "I freed *everyone*."

Now it was the egg's turn to be free as well.

"I'm going to look after you. Morgan too," Cas whispered. "All of us. No more alchemists. Just a few magic users who don't destroy cities. Who don't destroy the lives of innocent people going about their day, eating, shitting, fucking and living however the hells they choose. That is their right. Or it was…"

The fact that he had partially ruined what was left of the City of the Seers, and a few lives along the way, was merely an unfortunate side effect of what must be done.

One must sacrifice for the overall cause, surely?

He paused at the thought, a faint shiver of unease brushing across his shoulders.

"No matter, I'll fix it. We'll make it right, hmm? After we get that pretty little map. We need to know where to take you, after all." His smile was dreamy as he casually scraped a dirty fingernail across a particularly jagged ridge. The egg remained silent, as always. Cas' exhale was a melodramatic huff of amusement. "I started a rebellion for you, little thing," he added. "Back in Aneirin."

The sharp inhale from amongst the quartz over the far side of the cave thrilled him.

"The sparks were there," Cas added, louder now. "I just fanned them a little. What's that, little egg? Not just for shits and giggles, no. A distraction is always handy."

But what was next? He had come to the cave, fed his pet, and now…

No.

He knew what was next.

The *how* was the perplexing part.

"The egg. Morgan. Mara," he mumbled, eyes closing. The first had been retrieved. Morgan had resurfaced, her flare of power a spark of hope in his heart. So it was about time to head back to where it all began.

"Dear one," Cas said, his voice quiet. "My *other* dear one. Morgan. I like her name, do you?" His tone was conversational. Opening his eyes, he glanced down.

The egg sat as a heavy weight in his lap, the jagged edges of vivianite a blue tinted green in the surrounding glow. Was it listening? Was Morgan listening, too? Awake yet dreaming, eyes closed, red hair fanned like a copper pool of blood around her beautiful, ageless face?

"Morgan," Cas said, smiling faintly. "If this fails, and I am pathetic enough to die, your name will be on my lips as I go."

Across the cavern, large dragon eyes blinked at him, sullen, fatigued.

Afraid.

The mix of emotions pleased Cas. What did not please him, however, was the faint thread that occasionally wound its way across his vision. That was confusing. A silver thread, almost a trick of the light. It began from somewhere he couldn't see and ended somewhere else. Cas couldn't explain it, yet it flashed across his vision on and off nonetheless like some ethereal cobweb.

Flare's wings twitched at the expression on Cas's face. He expected some kind of rebellion soon from the dragon. For now, the great shining purple creature simply stared, leathery, talon-tipped wings settling back against his scaled flanks with resignation.

Cas sniffed. Things were as they should be then. Things were as they —

He sniffed anew.

What was that?

Cas inhaled deeper, tasting a wet freshness beneath the layers of dust that covered him. The scent of rich earth before rain fell reached his partially clogged nose, clogged with filth from the city in the north that they'd not long left behind.

Delighted, Cas laughed, a loud bark that broke the solemn quiet of the glowing space. Flare raised his immense head, startled, purple eyes blinking rapidly.

"Petrichor," Cas sang across the cave.

Lower lip quivering in a ripple of finely shaped scales, Flare gawked at Cas, naked fear in his shining eyes.

"I once saw a spider dancing with a gold ring," Cas laughed, even as pain lanced his brain. Images and sounds drifted through his consciousness, barely felt threads of light. "A spider... it ended up looking like some kind of tiny fairy prince..."

"Wh-what?" The dragon's alarmed gaze widened.

"It was quite spectacular," Cas said, serious now. He winced as the ache throbbed sharply behind his eyes before fading to a faint weight at the base of his skull.

Across the cavern, the great purple dragon cleared what was likely to be a sore throat from all his retching. Purple eyes flicked down to where his hands, one aching, both dusty, clutched the egg. "Caspian...ah... I think there's something wrong... with your hands..."

"Wrong?" Cas scoffed, head tilted to the side, odd blue eyes blinking rapidly, throwing off silver sparks. "With just my hands?"

Flare stuttered, his delicate, scaled eyelids fluttering over slitted eyes. "Um.. perhaps with... ah, all of you..."

"Yes." Cas' eyes widened. He held up the egg, marveling as the sharp ripples and ridges of the dark crystalline outer surface caught the eerie glow. "That's the whole fucking point, you giant amethyst twit. That's why I need Skye to help me. To help all of us, rotted away inside by the poison that contaminates us all. I can't believe how fucked up all of this has become... Fucking, fucking hells. Our home city was completely destroyed, Baile Mara gone back to the sea like the gods dropped a cursed anchor back into watery depths. And then the City of the Seers falling to ruin not long after. How many more will follow, hm?"

Flare opened his mouth wider, seemed to think about it, and then slowly closed his jaws. Dropping his head back to his folded legs before him, Flare kept his eyes fixed on Cas' face. Ignoring the dragon, Cas traced a sparkling valley that curved over the top of the egg with his fingertip, the odd shimmer of his skin almost pearlescent. The way the sheen was spreading across his hands was indeed alarming. But there were other things to worry about first.

"Skye, I needed you. How could you choose him?"

There was so much at stake, so much to weave back together after his parents' mess had torn apart the fabric of his world. A gentle draft of cool air reached his face, fresh and promising. Cas inhaled carefully, the scent of gathering rain reaching him from the tunnel. He loved that smell. Growing up by the salty sea under a sparkling sun, incoming clouds and the scent of fresh rain filled him with the promise of something else.

Something unpredictable.

There was a name for that aroma, wasn't there?

"Magic, magic, low and high,

Yet not enough for me.

Magic, magic, where are you, Skye?

I am your destiny."

Eyes barely open, he noted a lengthy shudder rippling along the purple dragon's spikes. A smile spread across parched lips.

"Morgan. Cas. Petrichor," Cas hummed, loving the dull echoes caressing the massive quartz points that rose from the cavern floor. Drawing the egg back into his chest, ruined shirt catching on the jagged ridges, Cas dropped his head. His chin scraped the rippled crystal, skin tingling at the rasping caress.

The aroma of rain coming filled his senses, coating the inside of his being with a tranquil light. It was the unmistakable scent of life, gifted from the heavens, blessing the waiting earth below.

"A blessing," Cas purred, pressing his chin deeper onto the crystal surface of the egg, "usually followed by a storm."

5

Karlien

Year 367
Baile Mara, City of the Sea

Karlien assessed the cock in his face with a shrewd stare.

Its pleasing, glistening hue brought to mind the perfectly ripe apricot he'd consumed earlier that evening. A hiccup tasting of crisp wine escaped his swollen lips. Kneeling on the floor next to the bed, his warm breath caused the ripe flesh to shudder with a gentle ripple.

"Not as pretty as mine," Karlien sighed. "But it shall do."

"What?" Bloodshot eyes blinked rapidly above his head.

Rising, Karlien shrugged. He pointed a dainty finger at the young man seated on the edge of the bed. "Hands and knees."

"Sure, but —"

"Hush. Turn around."

Hazel eyes narrowed. Yet the young man obliged, uncapping a vial of oil whilst getting into position. The young man's short blonde curls bobbed as he shoved a soft toy owl to the side.

"Be careful with that," Karlien scolded with a dainty sniff.

The velvet toy had barely any sheen left. It looked terrible, really. Even so, Karlien watched closely as the young man set the snowy owl to the side of the pile of pillows. A word was muttered with a mocking twang, sounding suspiciously like an insult.

Karlien didn't care. He was naked and alone with a young man of an age close to his own seventeen winters. Tonight's current activities would be a perfect escape from the council sponsored dinner taking place in the old estate, a couple of floors below.

Earlier that evening, after sharing a few covert glances, Karlien had grabbed the young man's silken sleeve. Unseen, the youth had laughingly let himself be dragged out the door with crafty steps, close behind a crowd of servers leaving with empty platters. Now, here in his room, white wine flowed freely for just two. Lightly fizzing and perfectly sweet, it dulled the annoying labyrinths of delirious dreams that lingered in waking hours.

Nothing else mattered except this perfect moment. Everything could wait, family, duty. Especially his bodyguard, Baek Hyeon, wherever the hell that brooding barbarian had slunk off to. Probably searching for more sweets from the obliging cooks, to be chewed angrily as he watched over his wayward charge.

Karlien snorted, carefully mispronouncing the man's name in his mind. There was a great pleasure in saying it exactly how he pleased. Karlien was well aware that *Hyeon* should be spoken similar to *young*, but so what?

That silken-haired brute could glare all he wanted. Because right now Karlien was perfectly content doing exactly what he wanted to, with no one who thought they knew better telling him otherwise.

Do this.

Do that.

Read this.

Memorise that.

What?! All of it?

Yes. All of it. It will come in handy someday. I dreamt about it. Didn't you, Karlien?

His great-grandmother's twinkling blue eyes contained the shrewd light of one who knew exactly what Karlien thought about that.

Yes, my lady, Karlien always responded with a bow.

He would then go off and do what he was told, rolling his eyes at the injustice of endless lessons. His closest friend Torres, a distant cousin in the Hart branch of the family, made jokes constantly about Karlien's eye rolling. Apparently, one day he'd roll them so far back he'd 'shit them out like some all-seeing turds'.

Ugh.

But right now, away from the bustling function at full swing within the crumbling expansive home, now was *his* time. Here, in one of the few rooms not needing extensive repairs after the chaos of over a century before, Karlien did what he liked. Who he liked.

Glancing down from the glimmering frescoed ceiling, tiny patches of black stone visible because of missing tiles, Karlien flicked a glance at the heavy curtains pulled across the closed window.

From behind the rippled glass, faint laughter drifted in from one of the candlelit courtyards below. Apart from the crackling fire that kept away the ever present damp that seeped in on salty tides, inside it was quiet. The estate had been built with the same black stone on which the city sprawled in once majestic terraces, lending a safe, womb-like feel to his room.

Yes, the bedchamber's angles were off the tiniest amount. Yes, faint cracks split the ebony walls like strikes of lightning, frozen in time. Yes, the floor was uneven and dangerous, the underfloor pipes of years gone by no longer carrying heat from the burning-stone fires deep within the estate. Again, yes, jewelled tiles fell occasionally from the frescoes above when faint tremors shook the land. But rich, scenic tapestries covered the cracks that travelled from floor to ceiling. And as for the floor, Hyeon had finally done something useful, procuring carpets the very same day Karlien had tripped, bruising a bony foot on an uneven slab.

With the addition of those carpets, his room had finally become the insulated retreat he'd longed for. Sleeping next door to his grandmama as a child, Karlien had grown up enough to demand his own chambers at the rebellious age of fourteen.

Now he had a sprawling series of chambers connected by open archways. Actually, his bedchambers were more of a small suite than one room. There were lacquered cabinets full of curiosities he'd found exploring abandoned houses as a child, soft cushions for sprawling amongst, and shelves full of old diaries and ancient maps. A heavy old oak desk was reserved for lessons, complete with silver inkwells, fresh quills, a large pearlescent sea conch and a large quartz sphere resting on a delicate three-pronged bronze stand. There was a lovely little makeup table with a gilt mirror and drawers for his pots and brushes, with a matching velvet covered stool. A massive vase of white porcelain in one corner by the desk held a collection of driftwood pieces, interesting shapes of bleached wood, twisted and sea-washed smooth.

Capped with a domed ceiling, the lushly furnished space carried the aroma of the sweet beeswax candles, made from wild hives spread across the city, accented with fragrant flowers that a servant installed fresh each day. So when Karlien escaped the eyes and expectations of those outside, in his wooden bed of four heavily carved posts and slightly threadbare silken sheets, here was a sanctuary in which to catch his breath.

Except at night.

Karlien's body would be fast asleep. The magic in his blood was not.

It remembered things.

Vivid dreams conjured the once glorious estate back into life and perfect symmetry. In the dark hours as he slept, the expansive building was intact again. Full of right angles, expertly cut and fitted ebony stone. Exotic plants in golden pots, pretty birds in massive cages, and fragrant, coloured smoke emerging from the great room at the heart of the place.

The old study.

A place once filled with magic and mystery would be proudly on display for his subconscious mind in all its glory.

Then it would slowly come apart.

Every night.

Karlien would wake with a hand over his heart, eyes wide, eyelashes fluttering, Hyeon's grey wolf staring intently from its white fur rug by the door, amber eyes intense.

"I'm fine," Karlien would proclaim with lofty indifference. Each and every time, letting whatever words would come to mask a racing heart trying to find respite in the waking world. "D-don't you dare wake your master!"

The wolf would lower its noble head onto long forelegs tipped with massive paws, amber eyes unblinking. Karlien would repeat to himself that he was awake, that the sad echoes of chaotic years were just that, echoes. The past was simply an annoying inconvenience that his unconscious mind snared with the little magic that still laced his family's blood.

Everything was fine.

It was merely caution that here in his sanctuary a fire was always lit, or a candle always flickering. By that single light, Karlien could tell that this was Baile Mara, surviving in the aftermath of catastrophe.

Crooked, cracked.

But persevering like the few that remained here, stubborn and still standing, still here.

"My family is still here," Karlien breathed, blinking at the curtains that hid his broken city beyond. "We have not been destroyed."

Throwing off the memories of broken nights, Karlien climbed upon the bed, adjusting his hardening flesh against a freshly slicked, bare offering. A resigned sigh spilled forth from a dimly lit corner of the lushly carpeted bedchamber to his right. Turning his head just enough to eye the massive grey wolf, Karlien bared his teeth.

Stretched out on its side, amber eyes on Karlien's flushed face, the wolf's bushy tail wagged once with a lazy twitch.

Rolling his blue eyes at the frescoes, Karlien turned his mind back to the task at hand. Hiccupping, tasting the sweet wine a second time, he enjoyed the faint spin of the tapestries that covered flawed walls, the hiss of the lit fire at his back in the crumbling grate.

The young man in front of him leaned to the side, lips parted to blow out the candle.

"No!"

His partner paused, twisted around with a mocking lift of one eyebrow.

"Leave it," Karlien snapped as haughtily as possible.

Considering his erection was at full attention before him, it was difficult. His partner merely smirked, turning back to press his face into the mound of pillows. Karlien chose to ignore the taunting smile. The satisfied gasp as his cock slid into oiled heat was reward enough. As his crown found that hidden, inner spot of spongy flesh, the young man arched his back, lost to pleasure.

Karlien tossed his head with an airy sniff.

Everything was fine.

He slapped one half of the buttocks pressed to his groin, enjoying his partner's flinch. "Move," Karlien ordered.

A disbelieving laugh, muffled by the pillow, shook the youth's slim body. Karlien slapped the other cheek, harder. His partner began to buck backwards against him, the muted grunts as the youth adjusted to his size soon turning to gasps of pleasure. It *did* feel good. Better than being stuck in his mind thinking about — Karlien bit his lip. He focused on the bare flesh that teased his gaze, blocking out the nightmarish images of last night's broken sleep.

He leant over, sliding one hand around bucking hips. Delicate fingers grasped the young man's stiff cock. He squeezed. The youth faltered against him, a surprised gasp reaching Karlien's ears. Smirking, he began a pace of his own, lazily thrusting against his partner while working his hand up and down on his front. It took some coordination, but the tightening of the heat around him was worth it.

"Oh my *gods*," the young man impaled on Karlien squeaked. "Don't stop, *please...*"

"What? This?" Karlien thrust once, long, deep.

Then stopped. He waited, a smirk twisting his shiny lips.

His partner turned his head to the side, eyes wide and incredulous, as he glared at Karlien. "Are you kidding?"

Karlien bit the sweaty shoulder at his chin hard, then drew back. He slapped the young man's cheek again, his palm making a satisfying smack on flesh starting to sheen attractively in the low light.

The man flinched, the pleasure exquisite around Karlien's cock.

"Move," Karlien repeated.

Cursing into the pillow, the young man obliged. Karlien's smile was a brittle thing. He eyed the lone candle, inhaling the aromas of his chamber. Rose oil, salt air from outside. The familiar scent of home.

Of safety.

Where everyone was fine.

Everything was just perfect.

From its fur rug in the shadows, the grey wolf sighed again.

The next morning, excited shouting outside broke through the unpleasant fugue of faded dreams. The usual images had only been dulled by his nocturnal activities, as much as he'd hope to dim them completely.

Excited shouts broke into spontaneous cheers.

"What the heck?" Karlien groused, mouth tasting of old wool.

Eyeing the heavy velvet that covered the window, Karlien poked the naked figure beside him with a toe. Hazel eyes cracked open, bloodshot and unfocused.

"Go see what it is," Karlien announced airily.

"Go see yourself," the young man yawned, pale hair a mess. He rolled over, taking the sheets and blankets with him. The lush fabrics were nice enough, but not nearly as soft as those reserved for his grandmama.

Pouting at the bare back in his face, smooth skin marred only by fresh scratches from manicured nails, Karlien turned back to the window. Grumbling, equally annoyed and curious, he roused himself to investigate.

Bare feet landed on thick carpets, cooled by the black stone beneath. He grabbed an embroidered shawl draped across one of the bedposts. The embers in the fireplace had died, and the chill was biting. The single, thick candle on its golden stand by his bed had burned low, the lone flame doing little for warmth, only keeping the nearest shadows at bay.

Pausing as he passed by the freshly polished bronze mirror in its gilt frame, Karlien examined his reflection. The mirror displayed a slim, petite, flushed-faced teenager, gold and copper curls wild, eyes heavy lidded, eyeliner smudged. But considering the wine and last night's carnal activities, he was well pleased. Even the bite marks across his abdomen, tiny red blooms of passion, barely gave him pause. Karlien was proud that his creamy skin had fewer freckles than others with the same colouring, so the small bruises were an unwelcome blemish. Except, luckily for him, the faint magic still contained within his family tree was enough to have the marks gone by evening.

Tiptoeing past the sleeping wolf, Karlien smirked to himself. It was time to send his bodyguard out for more supplies of the slick, rose-scented oil he preferred. There was still a bountiful stash in the red lacquered cabinet by the ornate chamber door. But Hyeon's blush would be worth it.

Shawl pulled tight over toned shoulders, the young man padded to the window. His delicate nose scrunched with disgust at the faint dusting of ash and scattered mouse droppings on the cracked sill. Someone needed to control the mouse problem once and for all. Pulling aside the curtain, once a royal navy but now a faded grey, Karlien pushed hard against the old ironbound frame. A resisting screech bit at his eardrums as he pushed, the patterned shawl slipping off one arm. Finally, he got it open far enough to stick his head through. Tousled curls blew wildly in an icy, salt tainted breeze as he squinted at the late morning light, the ocean air bright and clear.

The voices below had died down, yet they were still chatting amongst themselves. Surely it was far too early to be up after such an indulgent dinner?

Glancing down, Karlien spotted a small gathering of sunlit figures in one of the few courtyards that were still relatively flat. Most other yards and gardens were unsafe, with uneven flagstones treacherous to cross, cracked with the violence of a chaotic past. Ignoring shallow chasms and uneven ridges, a few jewel-bright peacocks crooned directly below, parading and poking about on verdant grass paths amongst the estate's native rose bushes.

It was hard to believe that the peacocks were protected by law, declared sacred by some long gone relative. As a child, he'd been terrified of them, attacking him for simply trying to collect charming feathers.

Karlien bit his lip at the memory.

It hadn't been his fault the feathers were still attached.

He still hated the birds, territorial beasts that they were. Only last year, a whole glittering pageant of the feathered shits had charged him when he'd been minding his own business, well with a young woman, in the gardens. Hyeon, bound to protect Karlien and thankfully lurking nearby, had appeared at Karlien's screech. The man had laughed at the scene he had stumbled upon.

Until Karlien burst into terrified tears, gold threaded trousers around his ankles tripping him over as he scrambled backwards, away from the peacock's charge.

So Hyeon took care of the beast while the young woman consoled Karlien to the best of her rather skilled ability.

That night, the chicken dish had been rather gamey. It was hard from across the table, but Karlien had pointedly ignored Hyeon's satisfied glow. Karlien had gotten good at ignoring the man's ridiculous face.

Nose scrunched, Karlien sighed and was about to turn from the sweeping view when, in the courtyard below, one of the warmly cloaked figures finally mentioned something interesting.

Aneirin.

"That backwater town?" Karlien scoffed. Aneirin had been cut off for longer than Karlien had been alive.

An exchange between two women, one in burgundy robes, the other in sea green, had him stretch further over the disgusting windowsill. He missed the start of what one of them was saying.

"...fallen?"

"Yes," her companion replied. "Apparently, they're both dead."

"What? Who?" This was a fresh voice, an older man in grey robes rushing outside from the hall.

As he leant out further, loose hair caught on a rusted hinge. Karlien jerked back.

He screeched.

Not only from the pain of his caught curls. But from the fresh mouse droppings that one bare palm had just squashed into the cold black stone of the windowsill.

Karlien gasped, the feel of tiny turds smeared against his bare palm as horrifying as the pain in his scalp.

Below, curious faces turned to the window three floors above. Swallowing his nausea, Karlien's answering smile was watery. He waved a shit-smeared hand with as much dignity as he could summon before carefully withdrawing inside. Blue eyes glared at golden copper strands of hair, left behind in the iron hinge, undulating in the salty breeze.

Another noise joined the faint laughter below, a high-pitched cacophony. With his tainted hand held away from him, Karlien very carefully peered out, not daring to lean out. Two of the peacocks were circling each other at the far edge of the expansive courtyard. Their jewel-toned hues were bright against the black terraced walls behind, leading up into the ridge above the city. They were beautiful birds. He wished they'd all die.

"Go shit somewhere else, you filthy pests," Karlien hissed, cheeks flushed pink. "I am *trying* to *listen.*"

The peacocks ignored him. With the conversation over, the gathering moved inside. Pouting, Karlien glared at the shimmering turquoise birds, tails proudly on display.

"Damn all of you to the kitchens," he sniffed.

Idly fiddling with his shawl with his clean hand, Karlien remained at the window, observing the bright morning. The salt breeze tickled his nose as he tried to ignore the gritty, greasy feel of his marred palm.

This high in the terraced seaside city, the sight was as impressive as ever. The shoreline was black sand, and the crashing waves were almost invisible against them. Yet further off, the saltwater turned into sparkling turquoise. Truly, the shifting of blues of the bay and the contrasting black sands along the coast made for an engrossing view. An island consisting mainly of a fog laden mountain, a half cone with a sheared off tip, loomed offshore. Karlien was happy here, despite the weight of future responsibility. He'd be content to lounge about in silks, sipping cool wine, gazing out over collapsed tiled rooftops and crooked, cobbled streets.

"Everything can be just fine," Karlien murmured, catching his lower lip between his teeth. The faded line of the horizon where the Eastern Sea met the sky was much more graceful than the city spread out before him.

It was a challenge sometimes, to see the beauty of his home. The terraced levels of the city were uneven, deep fissures opened up between ruined buildings and shattered temples. Despite years of repatriation, half the city was still missing or crumbled into chunks and shards of black obsidian.

The docks were no longer fully operational. They'd been the first to disappear beneath a devastating wall of seawater that hadn't receded to the same level as before. Much of the rubble that had been cleared from Baile Mara had been carried, rolled, or carted to the wide ebony beach. A long, low break wall of black rock extended from the south edge of the city by the beach, into the waves to allow ships to dock away from the old harbour. Apart from the missing wooden docks, the bay was filled with entire buildings, homes, and streets that had fallen away into the waiting sea.

The city still traded, and some craftspeople remained. Baile Mara, City of the Sea, had connections to Verglass, Port Town and even inland to Baile Fuar, City of Stone. The light coloured rock from Baile Fuar had been quarried for the City of the Seers.

The soft shawl rustled on delicate shoulders as Karlien exhaled, wistful.

What had happened to the continent? Why had so many things gone wrong? Weren't those in power supposed to prevent this chaos? Or at least foresee it with dreams and magical gifts, and mitigate the fallout?

All he could do was cover up the cracks and the ruins with a clever eye for detail. He could see what newly woven tapestry would cover the most broken fresco. Or what imported wool carpet would look best when rooms were gradually opened up at the old black castle along the clifftop. No one lived there yet, even after all these decades. The royal residence had seen a lot of damage and was more skeleton than building. Grandmama had insisted throughout her years, growing up amongst repatriation works, that the lower city should be where the endless repairs should focus.

Thoughtful eyes lowered from the ruined beauty of the city along the sea, his gaze honing in on the lush rose beds. Grandmama had insisted they were replanted each year, roses to pepper the black terraces with pops of colour and a heady fragrance. When the earth trembled occasionally, Karlien imagined the blooms calmed the wary eyes of the city, and that the aromas covered the sour gases that arose from fissures. It wasn't always the case.

More importantly, the blooms were his tribute to the bones of the people who never made it out. Bones, scattered amongst the stinking rubble, buried amongst the black broken stones, submerged beneath icy waves.

"Ash, not bones," Karlien murmured.

There weren't many bones left after the City of the Sea split open, according to his grandmama.

"Chaos," he whispered.

Two syllables, easy to say. Over and done with in a breath.

Nothing compared to the devastation of magic gone wrong, a lived experience of horror and years of struggle for the ancestors of the stoic people of this once great city. Thin shoulders rose and fell. Stoic people, who saw him as a flippant, promiscuous fool, as they prayed for his grandmama to outlive them all.

He turned back to the quiet chamber, filled with unease that felt like boredom but was likely better compared to a feeling best described as *where do I fit amongst all of this?*

Karlien shook the words out of his mind with a toss of his hair. Restrained words that barely disturbed the fragrant air of his chamber slipped from lips that refused to tremble.

"Everything is fine."

He shook himself with a toss of curls and intentionally set his mind to other things. A line appeared between perfectly shaped eyebrows.

"Hmm."

His bodyguard hadn't yet interrupted the morning. Just where was he?

The towering, tattooed man was likely glaring at people somewhere, his brown eyes deep enough that the prince fancied they had a crimson tinge to them in warm light. Rolling his own at the absurd thought, Karlien wandered over to his marble basin and let the water run from copper taps turned green. There was no longer any magic to heat the water, but it ran clear nonetheless. He scrubbed vigorously with rose petal soap. After rinsing, he reached for a towel decorated by a family crest embroidered on its corner with fraying, golden thread.

Without warning, a cold nose poked the back of his bare thigh.

Karlien squealed.

Whirling to face the wolf who had approached on silent paws, Karlien opened his mouth to curse. The placid amber stare had the words dry up in his throat. Tail wagging low, the wolf tilted its head. With his clean hand pressed to his fluttering heart, Karlien broke their stare and spun towards the bed. A quiet snore indicated the boy was half asleep.

"Get up," Karlien demanded loudly. "Go down. See what it is."

There was no answer.

"Hey...ah, you." Karlien cleared his throat. "Wake up."

"Fuck off," came the muffled reply.

"Just who the hell are you?" Karlien snapped, moving to stand over the bed. He eyed the form burrowed in fur blankets. "And is that any way to speak to me?"

"My apologies." A carefree yawn came from the mound as it shifted. One limp hand emerged, middle finger extended in salute. "I meant, of course, 'fuck off, my prince.'"

6

Morgan

Year 241

Baile Mara, City of the Sea

"At least one of them is fine, even if the other is damaged."

Morgan glanced up from the scroll she was copying, ink-stained fingers tightening around a worn out quill. It was an effort to blink away the images of magma chambers and sulphur gas drifting through her subconscious, nauseating echoes of last night's dreaming.

"The eyes are interesting, but the rest? A shame," the woman's voice continued.

The librarian's shoulders drooped.

The two alchemists were back, their voices loud along the cliff top as they made their way towards the library, deep in conversation.

It was tough to decide where she'd rather be. Even with the help of poppy smoke, peaceful sleep seemed beyond Morgan. But here, in the place she hated for its useless words and histories dictated by old men best forgotten, a kind of peace could be found.

Except when disturbed. Especially by this pair, considering what Morgan had been doing for them over the past few months at night.

Gods, she needed to get out of here. Not just the library, the whole sorry excuse of a city. Where fairness was the motto, but the balance of power was tipped to those who worshipped dragons and magic like the gods and miracles they weren't. Would what she had done helped in any way? It didn't seem like it. Whatever idea Hypatia had come up with, the plan was long, without instant change. Not that the librarian expected it.

Feeling sour, she lowered a hand to run ink-stained fingers against coins in her purse. Hung between her breasts, the purse contained fresh-minted reddish gold coins of a sort that she'd never seen before. From the royal coffers themselves, apparently. Either way, the coins were welcome, but the effort she had made had cost her.

Morgan chewed the end of her quill as she slipped off her stool.

Would it be worth it?

The voices outside grew loud. Peering between the shelves, the librarian watched as the two alchemists breezed through the great doors that faced the cliff's edge. Behind them, a blue, yawning horizon gave a tantalising glimpse of the world beyond.

Hypatia entered first, carrying a wailing bundle. Her tall form was dressed in soft linens, a tunic and pants under her leather apron, long hair tied up in a loose bun, pink with a crown of brown regrowth. Following her into the library, her husband Illarion carried the crying baby's silent twin. Illarion's green gaze was soft as he glanced down at the sleeping baby in his arms. He was dressed for the outdoors. His outfit of thick woollen pants and sleeves was a protection against the hives he loved, in the same pale straw colour as his silky blonde hair. As always, his cheeks were pink from the steep climb to the library.

Clearly on a mission, Hypatia's bright blue eyes lit up on catching sight of Morgan, who had unsuccessfully ducked between stacks of the dusty tomes that rose higher than her to the beamed ceiling. Of small stature, most things were taller than her. Gritting her teeth, Morgan stepped back to the main work area. Acting as if she had not tried to hide, she hopped back up on her stool.

"Lord and Lady Carter," she murmured, biting back her distaste at the honorifics the Elphin Royal family had bestowed upon them.

Hypatia smiled, a faint curl of pink lips, at Morgan's resigned expression. Illarion was rubbing noses with his silent son. Lips pursed, Morgan met Hypatia's stare steadily.

"A failed test?" Morgan queried above the sound of the crying child.

Illarion's expression darkened, glancing at his wife. Hypatia shrugged as she reached Morgan's work table. The tall woman sniffed, patting the wailing child with a firm hand. The baby's cries grew in volume.

"Even with the blood of the Elphin family, things didn't —"

"Wait," Morgan interrupted, astonished, eyeing the flailing bundle. "The Royal family let you use their blood for this?"

"Yes." Hypatia nodded, head tilted in annoyance. "But even with their immaculate bloodline, was it too much to expect both of my children to be born as intended?"

Speechless, Morgan glanced at Illarion. His clear gaze was neutral, directed across the desk to one of the thick candles he supplied to the city. Morgan raised her eyebrows at him, catching his attention. Illarion rolled his eyes in return and turned his back, wandering away. He rocked the baby with tender movements whilst examining a dusty shelf of used quills and other odd ephemera Morgan had collected over the years.

"One of them is disabled," Hypatia added, holding the screaming baby away from her.

"Disabled?" Morgan grimaced, eyes watering at the noise.

"Unfortunately, yes." Hypatia flicked a glance at the quiet bundle in her husband's arms. Morgan stared at Hypatia.

"This one shows no spark of magic whatsoever."

"Oh. I see." She didn't. It was all Morgan could do to offer up a weak smile.

The woman's answering grin was rueful. As if to say, Oh well, we can't have it all.

"Anyway, it's an opportunity to study them as they grow," the alchemist added, her tone proactive. "To refine my techniques. Because the other is," she said as she held the distressed child further away, "perfect."

Illarion was still studiously examining the shelves across the musty room.

"Um," Morgan muttered. "Sure."

"Moving on," Hypatia said, her tone bright. "I've got another idea."

"Another one?" Morgan muttered, frowning as Illarion knocked over a stack of black rocks that had previously been balanced with precision. They tumbled apart with a racket.

"Shit!" he cursed, wincing, green eyes wide.

"Leave it," Morgan said. Turning from the shelf, Illarion smiled, a guilty dimple forming in one cheek under the blonde scruff on his jaw.

"Oh, yes." Undeterred, Hypatia tapped a palm on the work table until the wriggling baby in her arms started to slip out of her other hand. She shooed away Illarion when he appeared at her side, trying to stop the bundle from landing on Morgan's bench.

Morgan stared at them both, unsure of what to say.

"Shall we swap, my wife?" Illarion gestured with his chin at the quiet child in his steady arms.

"It's fine. Anyway," she said, brightly. "So. We ended up using quicksilver and a tiny scrape of the vivianite, while both fetuses were gestating. I realise now it should have been a combination of both gold and quartz, with a larger portion of the vivianite, perhaps veszelyite too, instead."

"We didn't know that until now, however," Illarion added helpfully. "But after experimenting with my bees, we have a clearer idea. And we need heat."

"A *lot* of heat," Hypatia added, nodding.

"How much?" Morgan asked, dread lacing her tone. Her small, ink-stained hand moved to cover the scroll she was copying without her having to think about it. With her other hand, she smoothed a stray lock of red hair away from her cheek.

"Liquid rock." The words rolled off Illarion's tongue like stones dropped into an empty well.

Liquid rock, Morgan mouthed, not daring to glance down.

Her dreams last night had been dizzying.

Strange sapphires, light and dark, touched with the flash of deadly quicksilver, had circled her subconscious. Those sapphires, one deep blue and the other more transparent, like a cross between sapphire and aquamarine, had felt ominous. They gleamed like wicked jewels that should be smashed to dust lest they cause harm from whatever power lay within. Red hot magma and an ill-fated event on the horizon of time, perhaps even more than one event, had caused Morgan to wake covered in a sheen of sweat, heart ready to tear through her chest.

Despite the confusing events and images, the sights and smells were so vivid it was, without a doubt, a true dream. One so intense that Morgan had no hope of preventing its coming to pass. If it wasn't her that pushed them to find what they needed, it would be someone else.

So it was fine to take what she could, wasn't it?

Money, magic, steps closer to freedom from the library, the priestesses and the poppy smoke that she ached for even now. Gods, she'd kill for a pipe right now.

Perhaps it would shoo the new parents away, the smoke deemed a risk to the babes?

Unlikely. Hypatia would most likely want to see the effects.

Shit.

Breaking away from Morgan's uneasy stare, Hypatia shared a glance with her husband. They seemed in agreement about this new idea, at least.

"What is it, Morgan?" Illarion asked, eyes worried.

"Nothing." She swallowed, thinking of the gold in her purse, the wine and her pipe in her shabby home, not nearly enough to deal with these unhinged scientists.

"Nothing? Mm." Hypatia nodded, and shrugged. She flicked a glance at a lantern hanging from the heavy wood beam above the desk. "Anyway. Extreme heat for both the crystals and biological tissue will be necessary."

"Biological tissue?" Morgan shuddered. "Will that much heat for a baby be... safe?"

"Oh no, Morgan." Hypatia smiled, eyes gleaming. "Not babies. I'm aiming much higher than that."

Illarion nodded his agreement, a faint wash of pink colouring his cheeks. It was clear he felt more affection for his children than his wife, yet the idea of further experiments was clearly affecting him, too. The baby in Hypatia's arms paused its wailing, and they sighed as one.

"It's going to be incredible," he admitted, green eyes wide. "Life changing. We are almost there, almost ready to change the way magic works."

"If it works, husband," Hypatia added, demurely. "If it works."

"Gold is more precious. We should have used it before. But quicksilver, it seemed more potent," Illarion mused.

Morgan sucked in a breath. "It sounds more lethal, too."

This earned a laugh from Illarion. At this, the babe in his arms wiggled for the first time. He cooed down at it. He wandered closer to Morgan. The baby in Hypatia's arms started crying anew.

Unconcerned, Hypatia made for the shelves that contained the oldest notes on crystals. "Lethal? Yes, but the effects are superbly interesting."

Morgan almost laughed out loud at Hypatia's lack of maternal instinct. "And volatile?"

Hypatia's voice called from behind a deep stack of shelves full of yellowed scrolls. "Yes. That too."

Morgan shivered. Right.

"Do you want to hold him?"

Startled, the librarian looked down. Not waiting for an answer, Illarion pressed the baby into her ink-stained hands before she had a chance to protest.

But as the tiny thing's gaze met hers, Morgan froze.

Eyes of two different blues stared back.

Sapphires, one light, one dark, both laced with a quicksilver flash.

The ill-fated gems from her dream. Jewels that carried doom, jewels that should be smashed into tiny pieces rather than let loose upon the world.

"Oh, fuck me," was all she could manage.

Illarion glared at her coarse language, pale eyebrows drawn together in admonishment. Morgan didn't notice, staring down at the babe in her arms. With odd blue eyes wide, a tiny, pink fist reached up to yank fiercely on a stray lock of red hair.

At the sharp tug of pain on her scalp, Morgan cursed once more.

The baby laughed.

7

Cas

Year 367
The Cave

*O*utside, a storm had turned midday to unnatural dusk.

Wild rain crashed against a rattling window. The onslaught of water meant it was hard to tell the chilly drops and the bubbles of air in the thick glass apart.

Ornately crafted stone pillars spanned the lone window, giving the room the feel of a well-built prison for noble offenders. Despite the raging weather outside, inside the room was cosy, a warm haven from the elements raging in the clouds above and the ocean far below.

Cas blinked.

But the light was wrong.

He was having trouble focusing his gaze, yet he could see that the room was lit in cool tones, not the gentle flicker of yellow flames. That was a surprise, considering the warmth against his exposed skin. Instead, the light was a confusing shifting of rays, in shades of blue and white glimmers.

Cas narrowed his gaze at the storm beyond the glass, unable to work out why it was so bright inside. Flashes of lightning, close to the cliff top, arched across the sky in silver sheets amongst roiling clouds.

The storm's violence was increasing.

Whilst confused at the contrast of warmth amongst the cool light surrounding him, Cas laughed at the sight of the storm. The fingers of one hand twitched in anticipation.

He flinched.

Startled at a strange sensation against his skin, Cas peered down. Blonde eyebrows rose at the black feather quill clutched tightly in his left hand.

When had he picked it up? He'd forgotten, but was pleased to see that his hands were clean of ink. That was curious, though. He hated writing; he hated letters and... his smirk disappeared.

Seated at a simple wooden desk, Cas' lips twisted on realising what he was doing. Dressed in simple linens, a long-sleeved shirt and loose pants of white linen. One hand clutched the quill. Beneath his other lay an open journal of deep red leather and thick parchment. More loose sheets were heaped haphazardly nearby.

"Ugh," Cas scoffed. "Homework is fu —"

The scent of beeswax and ink reached his nose.

A scent that stopped his heart.

"Don't whine, you beast. Keep going," murmured the owner of the aroma that filled his dreams. "Here you go."

Unable to turn around, and not sure why, Cas sat up straight. He shifted in the uncomfortable chair, toes curling. His bare feet felt damp, as if the floor was wet sand instead of the grey slate it appeared to be.

It was just so gods-damned hard to focus, sensations and sights not making sense.

"M-Morgan?" Cas asked, hating the slight catch in his voice. "I can't see you."

"Then turn around."

He tried. "I can't. Something is preventing me. Where are you?"

"I'm right here."

"Where?"

By will alone, he tamped down the spark of panic flaring within his chest. Cas strained to move, but to no avail. His feet now splashed amongst the warm water pooling under the desk.

He truly was stuck, facing the window, head only able to move up or down.

The spark of panic eased a little when a small shadow spread over the edge of the desk. The scent of beeswax, bitter ink and dusty books increased, the familiar perfume of the one he loved easing his wild heart and racing mind. Breathing deeply, his nostrils filled with the air that he needed to live. Below the desk, at the same time, his cock swelled. This was why he endured, why he survived, for this sense of rightness, of wholeness. Yet, frustratingly, Cas could not look away from the seething storm and the violent horizon beyond.

"Morgan," he repeated, straining against the force that held him. He swallowed a pathetic noise at the back of his throat. "Where have you been?"

"Baking."

Baking? He hadn't expected that.

With a soft rustle, a petite, freckled hand appeared before him. Delicate fingers stained with black ink set a fine porcelain plate next to his right arm. A single slice of cake, plain with the barest wisp of pale icing, sat upright in the middle of the dish. Next to it lay a silver fork. A tiny crumb was stuck to one prong, as if the fork had been used to position the slice just so.

Uneasily, Cas' bare feet splashed in the rising water under the desk. Outside, lightning lit the sky and the room's cosy glow brightened for a heartbeat. A moment later, thunder boomed. A fresh scent joined the heady aroma of salt rain and beeswax.

Was it the cake?

Burning filled his nostrils.

"I've missed you," Cas admitted, warily eyeing the dessert.

"I was baking." There was an amused snort from lips he could not see but yearned to taste, to feel pressed against his own. "Can you imagine that, Caspian? Me, baking for you."

"Is this your apology?" he asked.

"Apology? Whatever for?"

"You left."

"Hush. I was only gone for a moment," Morgan replied, her voice calm.

He couldn't turn to see, but her presence was a warm sensation against his back. Gentle fingertips brushed a lock of hair off his forehead and adjusted something soft attached to his left ear.

"It was a moment too long," he sulked. Cas flicked the quill towards the cake. "Take that away."

"Beast," said Morgan with an amused snort. "Why?"

"There is nowhere near enough icing." He sniffed. "A cake is only there as a stage for the sweetness that graces its crown, my love."

Her muffled laugh caused his hard cock to jump. Maddening him further, lips pressed into his blonde hair, gentle and soothing, lips like butterfly wings.

"I thought you were going to say take it away because it was made by me."

"Because you made it?" he asked, confused.

His feet ached to rise from the wet floor. Yet, he could not shift them. With a frustrated growl, he strained against the invisible force. Cas glared at the endless display of the boiling clouds and rain outside, breathing fast through his nose. Something else caught his eye. Inside, the light, wrong as it was, was changing.

A new light source was growing.

Was it yellow?

Or green?

He couldn't tell. It hurt his head, a new ache forming behind his eyes. The light made no sense, and was getting worse as the ache spread behind his cheekbones. Morgan sighed against him, fingers like cobwebs travelling down both his chest and his back.

"I thought you may refuse it because of me," Morgan answered, fabric rustling as he sensed her crouch down. "Because I made it." Another clap of thunder boomed. "Like I helped your mother make you."

In the silence that followed, Cas' lips formed a delicate Oh.

Swallowing down the bitter wave that threatened to rise from his guts, Cas stared at his immobile hands. He'd known that already, though, didn't he? Why did it twist his heart to hear it again?

As Morgan's soft kiss found the tip of his arousal through his pants, the spell that bound him broke. He grinned as she lifted her head, still kneeling before him. It seemed he could move now. Cas stayed where he was.

"Hello," Cas murmured. The situation was odd, confusing, yet a smirk spread across his face in spite of it all. Cool green eyes, directly in front of his wide blue stare, sparkled with mischief.

"Hello," replied Morgan.

Morgan.

The one he burned for.

Morgan's flawless face, sweetly heart-shaped, filled his vision. Or half of it, at least. It wasn't just the eerie light that was odd. His vision wasn't quite right either. Cracking his neck, Cas dropped the quill to slide fingers into the flaming red hair that framed Morgan's face.

"Morgan," he said, as the scent of burnt cake tickled his senses. He tugged. "Morgan, why can't I see you properly?"

A small hand reached up and fiddled with the thing attached to his ear again, brushing against sensitive skin. The dull ache behind his face spread to his skull and neck.

He blinked. Morgan, with her face so close to his, wore an incomprehensible expression.

She looked... sweet?

That was wrong, too.

Morgan was many things.

But never sweet.

"What is this? Where are we?" Cas said belatedly. He shifted his hips, wrapping fiery hair around his fists. Her sweet expression didn't change. "It's been so long since I've seen you. Why aren't we fucking?"

Her expression didn't change.

A trickle of unease slid down his spine like thin honey.

Lightning burst outside the window. The illumination backlit the stone pillars that crossed the thick glass, long twisted shadows bursting into stark relief across his desk for a fleeting moment. Exactly what was this place?

"Morgan?"

The scent of burning filled his nose in heavier wafts, accompanied by the sound of splashing water. Not rain outside, but within the oddly glowing room. Cas peered down. The water at his feet was draining away. He blinked, attempting and failing to make sense of the nonsensical. The shifting glow of the room hurt his not-quite-working vision.

"What the fuck is this place?" Cas spat.

Morgan pressed close, cheek to cheek, her warm lips teasing the sensitive skin of his ear. "In this light, your eyes would be the colours of my dreams that fill me both with dread and longing." A kiss was pressed to the side of his head, firmer than the kiss on his cockhead, with enough force that his head tipped to the side.

"Dread? Why —"

Words were lost as a powerful gust of salt air blew in, the lightning breaking what seemed like right outside, the window glass abruptly gone. In a violent rush, salt water drenched the table, the parchment, everything.

Including Cas.

Fuming, he spluttered curses, unable to kick back from the desk and work out what the hells was happening.

"Oh dear," Morgan sighed. The wild gale still engulfed the room, yet her soft voice still reached his ears. Hair whipped past his face, blonde and red strands mingling like fire and snow.

Cas grabbed uselessly at the loose sheets that flapped around his face. Before him, the red leather cover of the journal flapped over, showing a lovingly designed script.

Amongst the chaotic bluster of overwhelming sound and lights, he froze.

A pattern of ornately formed words in bright yellow gold leaf caught his gaze.

It said —

Wait.

What did it say?

Cas cursed at the strange affliction affecting his vision.

All at once, the gale inside died away, the rain gone as if it had never been. Loose sheets of parchment, miraculously dry, fluttered down around the two of them to settle on the desk.

"What the actual fuck?"

Even as he dripped with icy rain, the floor was bone dry. The silence that followed the gust was as loud as the wind that had gone before it.

The light brightened, golden words on the journal's red cover glinting.

"What does..." Cas began, his pale brows furrowed. He blinked. "What does that say?"

Morgan reached across him, covering the quill held tight within his white fingers with her petite hand. Cas stared at the leather cover, its deep red and yellow gold letters, trying to make sense of the stupid thing, but it was fucking hard to see, like one half of the blinding light was missing from his vision as the light became painful in its intensity.

As the words formed into meaning, the saliva in his throat dried in shock. The blue light, tinted green and gold, brightened until Cas couldn't see at all.

"Morgan, it says I d —"

Cas woke with a startled cry, quickly stifled.

Something gritty and unpleasant pressed against his cheek. Vision groggy, his mind churned with the last vestiges of a dream. Silver and blue sparks faded into the eerie glow of the cavern as a dull throb began at the base of his skull.

"Gah," Cas groaned, inhaling something sour. He blinked.

He was sprawled on his side, drool leaking from his parched lips, merging with the glassy sand of the cavern floor beneath his cheek. The grains near his eyes sparkled as he roused. Cas blinked once more, his cheeks feeling oddly damp. He wasn't sure if he'd imagined it, but not far off, a massive quartz column the size of a grown man brightened for a moment, before settling back into the ghostly blue green.

"What in the actual fuck was that?" Cas muttered, teeth catching on the mineral grit coating his tongue. His cock softened at the disgusting sensation.

He shifted his hips, muttering a prayer to the gods that at least one part of him still worked as it should. The thought earned him a wry laugh. Until a cough wracked his lungs. The throb in his skull sharpened. Gagging, Cas pushed up into a kneeling position with his good hand, his throbbing hand wrapped around the jagged surface of the egg.

How long had he been out?

Cas swallowed against the wave of nausea the throb in his skull was bringing forth, disorienting him, his inner magic a chaotic tide of energy within. He sent out an abrupt tug along the magical binding to Flare. It was faint, but still there, an invisible leash, a thread of pulsing power between them. The great purple lizard whimpered. Across the cavern, Flare crouched low, wings hunched and immobile, amethyst eyes wide.

Cas smiled.

At least *that* was as it should be.

Spitting out dust with a dry mouth did little to help his situation. Frustrated, Cas grabbed the hem of his shirt and wiped at his face. Fuck, the dust and grit were all over his hands as well. He worked to wipe the crap off of his clammy skin, swearing under his breath at the fiery lash of pain from his torn finger.

The dishevelled man paused, glaring.

The dust wouldn't come off.

"What the fuck?"

Holding his messed-up hand up to the eerie glow of the crystal by his side, he tilted it back and forth. The knuckles of mangled fingers ground sickeningly against each other. He ignored the agony, eyeing his stained skin. Yet it wasn't dust from the cave or powdered crystal.

Bringing his hand close to his face, Cas squinted.

It was as if he'd plunged his hand into pearlescent ink. He sniffed. He smelled nothing other than blood and something sour from across the cavern. Torn flesh was swelling and weeping, it was dirty, yes, and required attention. But that wasn't the cause of the shimmering rash affecting his hands, front and back. It was hard to tell its colour in the unnatural light, but it appeared transparent, more iridescent than pigmented.

He'd seen a lot of shit, but nothing quite like this. Turning his hand over, Cas stared. No explanation came to mind.

"C-Caspian?"

Startled, Cas glanced up.

Like some enormous armoured feline amongst the towers of quartz, Flare had risen. Cas hadn't heard him edging closer. Wide, slitted-pupils focused intently on Cas' face.

"Are you... ah, alright?"

"Fuck off." Furiously, Cas used the corner of his torn shirtsleeve to scrub the annoying dampness from his cheeks. "How's my hair?"

The dragon gawked at Cas, massive jaws of swordlike teeth hanging open.

"Flare."

The dragon swallowed.

"Flare. I said how —"

"Fine!" Flare huffed, his claws curling with an irritating screech into the cavern floor. "It's just f-fine. You look fine enough for your plan of... revenge... or whatever this is..."

It was Cas' turn to gawk, mismatched blue eyes wide with disbelief.

"Revenge?" he mumbled. Remaining on his knees, Cas tipped his head back. He snorted at the clusters of ornate minerals hanging from the cavern roof. "Oh, no. This has nothing to do with something as simple as that."

Flare's jaws snapped shut, a meaty clunk. Eyes narrowed, Cas lowered his gaze. The dragon was clearly at a loss for words. Well, after whatever the fuck that dream had been, so was Cas. It had come from nowhere and knocked him unconscious. Right when he needed to get back up and moving. Surely that was more than enough rest? He was dead tired, but didn't want to risk slipping back into whatever the fuck that had been.

Besides, the place stunk.

The sour tang infiltrating Cas' senses appeared to be wafting over from the fresh pools of dragon vomit. Even worse, Cas shuddered with realisation, was the sweaty aroma of his unwashed body. It was definitely time to go.

Inhaling shallowly, he could just sense the fresh scent of rain from outside, falling in earnest by the gentle sound of dripping water echoing up the tunnel. The yearning to be amongst it was rapidly becoming a physical ache, like the throb in his skull. So that was the next step, to wash away the dust that clogged his throat and his mind. Ignoring the unease in his guts left behind from the disorienting images from the vision or dream or whatever the fuck that was, Cas fought to focus on the tasks directly ahead.

Once he was back to himself, then he'd attend to tasks that had almost come to fruition.

"Fuck you, Owaen," Cas mumbled, stumbling to his feet.

Everything had nearly been his. Surely Skye would've helped him, if Cas had been able to show her the egg, without his righteous twin around? If Owaen, that worthless do-gooder, hadn't shown up like an uninvited guest.

His brother would never approve of Cas' grand scheme.

But a dragon that had gone through what Skye had experienced?

Absolutely.

Admittedly, Cas had a little something to do with how things had gone poorly for Skye. But he had never intended for how things had ended up.

Furious with himself and Shadow Light, Cas hissed under his breath. Morgan's soft touch would be required, no doubt about it, to get Skye on board and his brother out of the way.

Somehow.

He needed to get back to Aneirin, back to where he had felt her special brand of magic bloom. Right before shit had hit the trees. Along with what was left of that bitch queen.

"Morgan. I'm trying, I'm trying..." said Cas tonelessly. He looked down at the sparkling egg, with its surface of craggy ridges. His gaze was almost trapped amongst the maze-like patterns of darker veins of green among blueish ripples.

"I don't feel so good," he admitted, simultaneously coughing and inhaling more grit. "Are you doing okay in there, dear heart? I'm going to make it right. All of it. Everything."

Cheeks feeling damp once more, Cas wiped his face.

Red stars crossed his vision.

"Fuck! Fuckity shit fuck!" he howled into the echoing cavern. "Fuck. Ugh. Just fucking die and drop off already, you fucking useless little things!"

He'd wiped his cheek with his crippled hand. The little finger, hanging by its flap of skin, had got caught in a knot of the hair stuck to his cheek. The result was that his finger went one way, and his dirt encrusted palm went another.

Fresh blood welled in his mouth. He'd bitten his tongue as agony had spread along his hand and up his arm. Purple eyes flashed with fear. Cas glared at the dragon. He waved his offending hand at the scaled creature. Flare was retreating to his far side of the cavern.

"As I was saying," Cas hissed, slumping against a stretch of smooth crystal behind. "This is not about revenge." Bitten lips formed a terrifyingly beatific smile, his teeth stained with blood that appeared black in the strange glow about them. "This is about *survival*."

Flare's wings twitched. "W-whose?"

"Everyone's." Cas paused. "Well. Mostly mine, of course."

"Of c-course." Flare's whisper was barely audible.

Cas ignored the trace of sarcasm. "I refuse to die like some pink worm on a beach, discarded as unfit to catch a fish by some opinionated bastard who doesn't know any better."

Gritting his teeth against the pain that threatened to choke him, Cas held up the egg in his good hand. It was as heavy as a man's head. But he had a point to make. Feeling his gorge rise, he held up his other hand, the ruined digits flapping about, red, swollen. They were supremely disgusting.

"In the eyes of the world, this is me and my family, Flare." Cas rested the egg against his cheek. A rush of energy welled within his heart, warring with the agony of his ruined hand as he turned it about. "The egg is a bright well of magic like my family. And this smallest, broken and useless digit? This is *me*."

"I don't under —"

"And what can a broken digit do to repay that tightly puckered bunch of fucking magical arseholes? Arseholes that spew magical shit like it's going out of style?"

"Oh, I really don't —"

"We fucking repay them in kind." Cas coughed. He spat out a gob of blackish blood. Lowering the egg carefully, he made sure to use his good hand to wipe the remaining spit off of his chin. "Anyway. Are you sure my hair is okay? I need a wash."

By the droop of his wings and lowered head, the dragon appeared to be as miserable as Cas was feeling. Flare opened his mouth, then hesitated, his scaled jaw working silently.

"What now?" snapped Cas.

"That grey streak..."

"Does it make me look wiser?" Cas stood straighter. "Do you think Morgan will like it?"

"N-no."

"*No?*"

"No, I mean no... It's gone. Or a-almost gone. In here, the light... it's hard to tell. But I've been watching it fade all day."

Gone?

Huh.

Tossing his blonde hair back, Cas pressed his fingers into his temple, under where the grey streak of hair was apparently fading. That was definitely beyond his understanding. He felt confident that Morgan would likely know. Perhaps even Shadow Light might have. That bastard had been the one who'd taught Cas how to syphon magic off of others, after all. He shifted the egg in his grip, its weight feeling more of a burden than earlier.

Despite the alarming need for a bath, a weight suddenly eased from his shoulders. He may have imagined it, but a familiar burst of magic had spiraled along a faint chord from far off to the southwest. Surprised, Cas inhaled sharply as the fingers of his injured hand jerked. He cursed as fresh agony made its way along his arm.

Interesting.

Amongst the iridescent shimmering stain that graced his skin, a faint tingling arose through the agony of his ruined fingers for a fleeting moment.

What?

That was interesting too.

Packing that away for later, Cas ignored the excitement in his heart. He cleared his throat and changed the subject.

"I expected better of you, Flare."

"What?" Flare's head rose, his long neck straightening.

"That's why I gave you the surviving shard from Skye's egg for safekeeping."

"Oh," Flare inhaled sharply, blinking stupidly at the change in conversation. "I didn't want to hold on to it... I c-couldn't use it even if I wanted to, but an Elf? I saw a need... the queen you see, her son... I wanted to protect their kingdom from harm..."

A pale eyebrow rose. "Harm, you say? You went and fucked that right up."

"I'm s-sorry," came the thick whisper, "I didn't mean —"

Throwing Flare a dark look, Cas scoffed. "That fucking spell! Ha. It became a fucking curse. You're useless. It fucked the city up, and more importantly, hid Morgan from me for too long. She... I know she's there now. We've been apart too long. It's time. That's why you owe me. I gave you the shards for safekeeping, you fool. But you bloody gave them to that so-called queen." Cas glared at Flare, unable to hide the incredulous expression blooming across his face. "I explicitly said it was for *saving the lonely son from dark magic.*"

Flare rustled his wings. "I thought Morgan had a dream. That the shard would help evolve the dragon race. I heard her at the same time you did! The son of the rulers, she said, the queen, Sophia, and her son —"

"You dumb fuck!" Cas shouted. He pushed himself away from the crystal with an elbow, boots slipping on the gritty floor. "The son was *me!*"

The dragon stared at him in shock.

"Me!" Cas repeated as he found his balance, his head full of aches and fog. "I am the son of the rulers. Rulers of magic, not the prince. *Ugh.* I'm still pissed at that. Stop talking."

Clawed feet clacking as he rose as well, Flare blinked rapidly. Cursing under his breath, Cas turned away. He wanted to rip those giant eyes out of the dragon's head and kick them across the cave. Except, he still had to get to Aneirin. While avoiding Owaen, wherever the heck he was.

Fuck.

"Now we just need the map of our home."

"H-home?"

"The good old City of the Sea. Home," Cas murmured, eyes unfocused. He kissed the egg, pulling away sharply.

His lips were tingling.

Had he imagined it? Most likely. The throb at the base of his skull probed him like a lead spike dipped in salt. It was hard to focus.

"The City... Baile Mara?" Flare gasped, aghast. "Why there? It's in ruins!"

Ignoring Flare's whining, Cas stared at the egg. "The king, his death, I thought it was a good thing... and yet... I think he did something to me." Eyes bright, Cas glanced back at the dragon. "Is there anything you want to share about that?"

"About what?" Flare whispered, eyes wide.

Cas allowed a feral grin to widen across his face.

"The map."

"M-map?" the dragon stuttered, throat working as if he was going to retch again.

"Tsk tsk, swallow it down," Cas admonished. "What a waste of your fellow country folk."

Flare shrieked, a wail of horror and loathing.

"Don't look at me like that!" Cas shouted in protest. "It wasn't *me*. That was Shadow Light's handiwork. So think of it as clearing away the mess your friend left behind."

"No," Flare whined. "He wasn't my... no... my friend was... A-Aurelia," Flare finished with a sob, his left wing grazing a squat cluster of clear quartz. "Oh gods, Aurelia..."

Cas' lip curled in disgust. "Puh. Friends. She might have been one once, but you fucked that up, didn't you? Heh."

Wincing, Cas adjusted his groin *very* carefully with his broken hand. He tilted his head to the side, beginning a slow stalk towards the dragon. Flare recoiled, his tail spikes quickly butting up against the far wall. There was nowhere else to go.

Holding up the egg, Cas beamed at Flare, halting his stalk midway across the cavern, the eerie glow washing them both in ghostly light as they stared each other down. "We are the only friends you need. Or at least, the only ones you have."

Flare swallowed.

Eyes twinkling with silver, Cas began cautiously picking his way over the crystal shards and the puddles of dragon vomit. He was mindful to keep his breathing shallow. On reaching Flare, ignoring the throb behind his eyes and balancing the egg in his good hand, Cas lifted it up high, mindful of its weight. Flare shook his head, eyes widening, the slits themselves expanding into black pits of fear.

"No, no.. Caspian... p-please... take it away..."

By his will alone, Cas toughened his magical grip on Flare's tail, giving it a sharp, maddening tug. It took most of his concentration. Pleasingly, the dragon cried out. Flare scrambled sideways, claws slipping and sliding on flakes of quartz and shards of bone.

"Friends don't shy away from friends in need, my sparkling amethyst, so where are you going?"

Resuming his stalk, as the dragon wedged himself into a convergence of three massive points of glowing quartz, Cas laughed. Wouldn't it be hilarious if all his plans were unnecessary? Perhaps a kiss from a dragon, like some raunchy tavern fairy tale, told at night by bards, would wake his treasure? Not just the molten fire of Baile Mara?

"You can't leave yet," he crooned, eyes wide. "Come on Flare. You know you want to..."

"No! No... p-please..."

"Flare."

"Nooo..." The word broke apart into a pitiful moan. Cas could hardly contain himself. *What if..?*

"Come on, cutie. Pucker up."

"No," Flare whimpered.

"*Flare*," Cas warned, sending red hot pain along the leash to the terrified dragon. Flare cried out, freezing from the agony. Cas edged closer, struggling against the weight, his ruined hand a glove of torture, a challenge he refused to throw down.

"Argh... C-Caspian, it hurts —"

"FLARE."

"No —"

"KISS IT."

A loud whine escaped the dragon's trembling maw and his eyes snapped shut. Trembling, scaled lips edged towards the jagged green curve.

Eyes wide, silver blue and wild, Cas held his breath, fiercely expectant.

There was a final moment of hesitation.

Then Flare's lips touched the egg.

Oh!

The dragon's eyes flew open.

8

Flare

Year 367
The Cave

Nothing happened.

The egg was just a rock.

Or more precisely, it was simply a crystallised rock.

A rare and potent crystal, yes, but if there was anything else expected of it, disappointment would follow. Because, on making contact, the magic Flare had expected simply wasn't there.

Reeling his head back, Flare blinked rapidly. His massive jaw snapped closed. Directly in front of him, Caspian's eyes darted madly between Flare's finely scaled snout and the innocent-looking lump of glittering blue green crystal.

"That's disappointing," Caspian murmured.

Flare said nothing, he simply trembled. He could not halt the little involuntary muscle spasms rippling throughout his body. A lot of terrible things had happened, but this..? The relief was as potent as the insidious crystals he'd consumed.

Lowering the egg, Caspian turned it in his hands, wincing a little. Eyes flashed silver with sudden hope, odd blue eyes looking up to meet the dragon's fixed stare. "Let's try again, shall we?"

Flare backed away. Caspian eyed Flare shrewdly, noting the dragon's immediate reduction in panic.

"What?" Caspian asked, suspicious, drawing the egg back to his chest protectively.

"What?" Flare squeaked.

Silver blue eyes blinked, an innocent flutter of long blonde eyelashes. "Flare. Tell Uncle Cas what's going on in that giant amethyst brain of yours."

"The e-egg," Flare hiccupped. "It's..."

"Go on." A fingernail began tapping against the jagged egg clutched to Caspian's chest. Apart from the sound of gentle rain echoing along the cave tunnel, that soft tapping was the only sound.

Aside from Flare's racing heartbeat, loud even to his own ears.

"It's..."

"It's *what*?" Caspian snapped.

Flare swallowed as blue eyes, one dark and one light, narrowed into flinty slits. The tapping halted.

"By the gods," Caspian hissed, "if you don't tell me —"

"It's dead!" Flare shouted, startling them both.

As the echoes of Flare's outburst faded amongst the glowing quartz towering around them, the blonde man, sweat-streaked and covered in dust, blinked swiftly.

Neither of them spoke for a while until dry lips formed a tight smile.

"Excuse me, oh mighty dragon. Would you mind repeating that?" Caspian drawled. The exaggerated patience had Flare's scales itching. His sore tail from Caspian's last magical tug still felt as a blazing ache, all the way to the quivering, pointed tip.

"There's n-nothing inside, Caspian," Flare gushed. The spikes along his spine rippled.

Nothing? Caspian mouthed slowly.

Flare nodded emphatically.

The dragon carried on, his relief rendering him almost unmindful of the storm brewing before him. So great was his relief that the thing was dead inside, that he didn't notice the mismatched gaze in front of him turning dangerously blank.

"The egg, it's simply a w-wonderfully sizable chunk of vivianite, yes, and quite a pretty one too, ha ha... I'd never seen the size of it, apart from Skye's egg, of course, right?"

Of course, Caspian formed the two words with cracked lips, no sound escaping.

Flare gasped for another breath, eyes closed. The spasms of his muscles had halted. It was just his wings twitching uncomfortably now. "But I'm r-really sorry to say there's nothing special about it. I think Hypatia got it wrong, you see? Oh my. We might have had another disaster on our hands!"

"Dis.. aster?" Caspian said softly enough that Flare opened his eyes to check the man had spoken at all.

Caspian stood before him, frozen to the spot, his eyes on the egg. His mangled fingers looked disgusting, yet both hands carried a weird, iridescent sheen. Flare swallowed, forging ahead, desperate to get out of this place. As words tumbled from his scaled lips like the shards of quartz had only a couple of hours before, the tense atmosphere inside the vast cavern turned smothering.

"At least one egg h-hatched, I guess in the same way that she expected both you and Owaen to be born with magic... oops, ah —"

Flare's voice screeched into silence as his wings ceased their twitching. Actually, he couldn't move at all.

"C-Caspian?"

The taste of the mineral scented air of the cavern had changed, like a static charge building up before approaching thunderheads. Flare gulped, the air tasting both sour and rain-fresh on his tongue all at once. Staring at the chunk of dead crystal in his hand, Caspian had absolutely no expression on his face. Flare was overcome by the sickening expansion of energy before him.

Uh oh.

Wincing as sharp shards, of what Flare knew wasn't only crystal, shifted under his claws, the dragon edged along the glowing wall with tentative steps. Holding his tail off the floor took some concentration, as it was still aching from Caspian's last tug along their connection.

"Caspian...?"

With an abrupt movement and without another word, Caspian whirled around and stalked off.

Slipping on shattered crystals and cave dust, the dishevelled man headed towards the tunnel. There was the indistinct murmur of muffled curses as Caspian sought to rid himself of his shirt. He got stuck halfway. The once white but now ruined material was half over his head and half off his chest, one shimmering hand tearing at it in vain. The egg was still gathered against his chest. Hating himself, the dragon picked his way over the crumbs of crystal and, retching a little, Elven bones. Past the shards, he followed Caspian with caution, eyes scanning left and right for vomit. There had been a shameful amount.

Flare yelped as his forefoot touched something soft. His gaze jerked down.

A man's boot, scratched and wrecked beyond repair, lay under his claw. He looked ahead.

Not far beyond was its twin.

Eyes wide, Flare peered up. He was just in time to see Caspian, still stumbling and now barefoot, fling his shirt away with an awkward curse. It landed on a low cluster of incredibly transparent quartz to his right. With the egg tucked under one arm, Caspian ducked into the tunnel. The air in the cavern was getting thicker, the static charge feeling like tiny bugs crawling along Flare's leathery wings.

A sharp curse echoed from the dark opening.

The dragon ducked under a low hanging quartz stalactite. He halted at the tunnel's mouth, claws sinking into the piles of collapsed rubble and sand. While weighing up the for-and-against arguments about breaking the gap wider and staying in his larger form, the dragon noticed another item discarded just inside the tunnel.

Flare gasped.

"Caspian! Are those your *p-pants*?"

The dragon emerged from the tunnel, pushing against static that pressed into his scales, claws digging into hard black rock.

Around him, the high cliff trembled. A low pulse of sound that was more felt than heard reverberated from beneath the dragon's claws. Loose pebbles from the rock face above bounced with sharp whiplike cracks, larger stones shattering on impact.

A stiff breeze was growing in intensity, and Flare was caught in a strange vortex of merging temperatures, humid coolness from outside, and dry heat from behind. Before him, the great green wall of the forest groaned and swayed as the breeze turned into a gale. Leaves and twigs bit at his scales.

Flare squinted through the rain and chaos, heart loud in his ears, loud enough to be heard over the rush of the massive trees, trunks twisting, and the dull moan of shifting rock.

The lonely figure of Caspian stumbled to the edge of the rock shelf, his pale backside naked as the day he was born. His pale hair and skin were slick with thick drops of rain. At the sight of the flesh across the man's bare back, Flare flinched.

"Don't worry, don't worry," Caspian cried out, desperate, mangled hand held up to the voluptuous, roiling mass of clouds circling above. "I know you're okay, everything is going to be just fine!"

Who was he talking to?

"Don't listen to the cowardly dragon!"

What?

Facing outwards to the surrounding forest, the canopy reaching past even the lofty height of the cave, Caspian tilted his head back. Taking a deep breath, he yelled into the storm of cyclonic leaves, stinging twigs and roaring wind. Lightning cracked, thunder boomed, once, then twice. With the sharp, fractured taste of ozone, it happened again.

Flare sneezed, cowering by the tunnel opening.

"Are you listening, Mother? I'll wake it yet!" He held the egg above his head, the grey light showing its startlingly deep blue colour, emerald green facets flashing brightly. "You *need* to wake up. The dead of Baile Mara demand it! And so do I! Just wait until you meet Morgan! She's going to —"

The dragon sensed it before he heard it.

Boom.

The mountain rumbled with a violent shudder, an unearthly flinch of stone and rock, the movement of deeply shifting strata felt from the tips of his claws to the tops of his spikes. Scattered pebbles became falling boulders, crashing with enough force to kill a person. The tearing wind beat at the leather of his wings. It was a struggle to keep them tucked against his sides.

Loud shattering reached his overburdened ears. He tilted his head up, neck twisting painfully, ears bleeding from the discharge of energy that was, incredibly, building again. A massive slice of black rock was falling, twice his size, from directly above. With a lurch and a screech, Flare barely twisted his bulky body to the side. The giant sliver missed him by a scale. Wings lifted of their own accord at the brutal impact. The piece was so massive that only the base of it shattered; the bulk of it settling amongst the other haphazard chunks of rock.

Terrified, Flare cried out.

The tunnel, and potential shelter, was blocked.

Trying to find purchase amongst the desolation, he dodged falling boulders, thankfully less deadly than that blocking the tunnel. It wasn't over yet. Cracks were appearing on the black shelf under his claws, patterns below mirroring the burning-white lightning flashing above.

A man's delighted laugh reached Flare's ears just as the charged particles of detritus around him froze, suspended in midair.

The shelf of rock beneath him shuddered.

Oh no —

White light blinded him first.

Not even a moment later, the violent impact of freshly discharged, wild, and uncontrolled magic caught Flare off guard. Pain filled his snout, his ears full of agony. Rain, heat, and potent waves of energy beat against him, over and through him. It stole his breath, his thoughts, along with his footing as the shelf tilted in a sickening, stomach dropping jerk.

Flare cried out.

His ears popped at the sudden change in air pressure. Unable to fly off in the violent storm of lightning and wind, talons dug into hard stone as the straining dragon fought to stay upright against the cruel onslaught. As the rock shelf shook and tilted, he closed his eyes, sobbing. Horrific, tearing and ripping sounds, colossal trunks exploding, reached his bleeding ears, the scent of burning eucalyptus and pine assaulting his nose.

The waves of energy, sound, and light pulsed on and on and on. Flare, hardly able to breathe, vomited his half digested meal into the wildly bucking shelf of precarious rock.

It was an onslaught of sound, smell and sight, waves of bitter magic and uncontrolled power rendering him into a blubbering, whimpering mess.

With another groaning tremble, the shelf beneath him tilted further.

The dragon fainted.

Amethyst eyes opened with the reluctance of one who knew that no good could come of facing what lay ahead.

Tears fell, along with a cherished name from scaled lips. A name that Flare felt he no longer had the right to utter out loud. A sob wracked his lungs, nostrils twitching, a bitter sensation like burning coating his tongue.

The dragon lay amongst the tumbled ruins of the buckled shelf of rock, no longer flat but severely tilted and unsteady, listening to his heart. The beats of his tortured organ were loud, fast, desperate. Flare sniffed. It was difficult to see. His eyes were gummed with grit and fresh tears. With no idea of how long he'd been out, the shivering dragon eventually got a hold of himself.

"Get up, you old fool," he coughed, wincing at a dull pain in his side.

Claws slipping and scraping against new piles of rocks and dust, Flare wiped the chunky globules of vomit, containing both undigested crystal and bone, off of his jaw against the closest boulder. He hiccupped and his bloody ears popped.

The following silence was clear.

All-encompassing.

The wind had fallen; groaning under the mountain had abated.

Clouds still gathered, rain falling in such a fine mist it was almost no rain at all. It felt gritty against his wings. He swallowed, tear ducts working to clear his vision. There was a crimson aura across his gaze. Had he cut himself?

Straining his senses, unable to focus, Flare realised even the great forest of trees was silent, no leaves or birds marred the eerie tranquility of the day. Only the wretched sound of Flare's gasping marred the stillness.

"C-Caspian...?"

There was no answer. Amazingly, the dull light seemed to grow brighter.

Coughing, choking, Flare grit his jaw and pushed up. Pebbles scattered and gave way. The red hot leash, the binding along his tail, was fading with the daylight behind the clouds. Blinking rapidly, his pupils tried to make sense of what he was seeing.

His eyes *hadn't* been bleeding.

Shame wasn't the reason for the bitter taste in his mouth.

It was the light that was crimson.

It was hot ash coating his tongue like years-old lies.

The dragon raised his scaly head, spikes quivering.

Slitted eyes widened.

Flare was witnessing the afterglow of rapidly spreading fire. Not around him, but above.

The clouds were burning.

No longer deep shades of threatening grey, the clouds were aflame with red, purple, and shifting gold. Fading heat painted his snout, wings, and back spikes with radiant waves of a deadly caress. He stared, entranced. From the epicenter above, circular waves of flame clouds boiled away in massive ripples.

And utterly silent.

As the clouds burned and boiled, Flare had a moment to thank the gods he didn't believe in, that he had been in his gigantic form when the discharge of magic and energy had erupted. As he stared, mouth agape, the colours faded from red and purple, to peach and pink.

"Holy, holy gods," Flare breathed, horrified.

Behind the impossibility of the scorched clouds, the bare evening sky peeked through the gradually widening aperture. Innocent stars shined down, ash still falling, rain still drifting from the clouds continuing their silent burning. It was a sky of nightmares, his nightmares. It was an echo of the chaos from when the first true dragon hatched long ago. A tiny, golden green and shimmering thing. An innocent soul. Not a thing of nature, but a creature born from the minds and dark determination of two careless, resolute alchemists.

A creature who had grown up amongst dragons evolved from Elves, not hatched like it had been. A creature that likely had something to do with the fact all the other dragons Flare had known were gone. Twin to the thing —

A sickening, wet thunk sounded beside him.

He jumped.

The corpse of a bird lay beside Flare. A small, thin whine escaped his throat. Thankfully, the creature was dead, eyes unseeing, long, thin curved beak open, its black tongue half out. The feathers of its body, once mostly white with patches of black, were singed to charcoal. It may have been a sacred ibis. He wasn't sure.

Another wet thunk sounded behind. This time, Flare didn't flinch. Fortifying his heart, he directed glazed eyes elsewhere. At the precarious edge of the shelf, there was movement, the flash of a blonde head, washed red and pink in the burning light, tilting back to face the unholy sky.

Caspian stood by the steep drop, facing away. His mangled hand twitched by his hip, the other had that infernal egg tucked by his side. Caspian's bare back, covered in hundreds of tiny scars, heaved, the skin tight over muscles were blackened with soot. The dragon's eyes slid past the lone figure.

His jaw dropped, ready to cry out.

No sound emerged.

Not at the third dead bird falling to his right, but at the vista before the cliff face.

For a horrific distance around them, the forest was gone.

A great expanse of skeletal trees had managed to survive a fair distance away. But close by, there was bare earth. Grey puddles of soot and rain were already forming amongst blackened shapes and mounds of ash into the depressions of naked earth.

Also naked, skin washed with red light as the clouds rolled away in copper flames, Caspian turned around. Quicksilver blue eyes, wide and unblinking, calmly examined Flare from claws to spikes to snout. He paid no attention to the shimmering rash spreading up both arms, copper coloured in the light of the clouds of flame.

The shimmering stain glinted for a moment, an unnatural brightening for a single pulse before fading to the wicked lustre of before. Ash tickled Flare's snout and quivering tongue. He sobbed once, swallowing it quickly, wings quivering.

"Oh, Flare," Caspian said. His voice cracked. The naked man took a step towards the shivering dragon. "Don't worry. I'm alright."

And without another word, Caspian collapsed.

Eyes unfocused, he fell first to his knees before folding into an ungainly heap amongst the rain and ash. A dull thud hit the rock; it was the egg trapped underneath him. As the unconscious man lay still, the hot thorn of his stolen magic wavered along Flare's scales. It was the energetic chain that bound them, rippling like the tale of a strip of silk in a brisk breeze.

The chain flickered.

And faded.

Not daring to breathe, Flare took a step.

Then another.

He needed to get away *now*.

One more step.

Throwing a glance at the cliff face behind, Flare grimaced. It was too close. Even with the wide radius of now smoldering, broken and missing trees, he'd need to reach the shelf's jagged edge to get clearance.

He swallowed dryly. The last vestiges of crystal shards and vomit in his mouth irritated and sickened him. Gathering his courage, he pressed on, the silence of the surrounding ruins not even broken by his breath this time.

Flare lifted a massive clawed leg.

Only a step away, a single blue eye opened.

It was the pale blue one, a glowing opal, in Caspian's soot-streaked face.

"Oh, Flare." A damp cough slipped from chapped lips. The magical leash that bound them twitched.

Flare gasped, claw frozen in midair, clearance to fly off only a quick hop away.

The spikes along his tail and spine rippled with revulsion as the chain flared back into its strictly pulsing binding of before. A low laugh reached the dragon's aching ears.

"Too slow, my precious jewel."

Too slow, indeed.

Miserably, Flare lowered his foot to the wet stone. The surface was quickly being covered by wet, sticky grey and black ash, along with the still occasionally falling charred birds. Paper thin layers of what may have once been leaves or even trees floated down, landing on the rock shelf like burnt butterflies. There *had* to be a chance to get away, but now was not the time.

A sharp tug along his tail had the dragon arching his spikes in terror.

"Argh! You're so m-mean!" Flare wailed.

As burning wisps drifted by, Caspian's face paled under the dirt and grime. He blinked slowly, as if in pain, shifting weakly on the exposed rock.

"What did you," another cough, "just say to me?"

Swallowing, Flare backed up a step, tail haphazardly pressing into the fallen boulders. He gulped, spluttered and gasped all at once, his senses sharpening from trauma to fear.

"I said, what did you —"

"You're so m-mean!"

"Mean?" Caspian croaked. "I am not."

"You are!" Flare wailed, the shock of recent events leaving him in an unchecked rush. "You're a b-bully!"

A gasp. "You take that back right now."

"You are a bully with no home or friends!"

The expression on Caspian's face was *almost* laughable. Until it faded into a cool assessment. Mismatched blue eyes narrowed. Flare hiccuped under the speculative appraisal.

Smirking and tilting his head sideways, wet hair fanned around him, Caspian made a show of peering lewdly at the dragon's underside. His sour laugh was followed by a wet choke. But the dishevelled man kept staring, his expression rather leering. Sooty blonde eyebrows lifted suggestively.

"What are you looking at?" Flare shrieked. He scrambled sideways along the rock shelf, wings scraping the sheer cliff face towering behind and above them.

"Usually you can't see them when you're in dragon form." Caspian licked his lips. "So when they're tucked away, it's hard to know what's what, hm?"

"What?!"

"Your balls. It seems like you finally grew a pair."

Flare experienced a moment of acutely embarrassing horror as Caspian raised a limp hand. As silver-blue eyes gleamed, Flare's entire body shuddered, a great wave of fearful anticipation. He knew exactly what was coming.

The dragon closed his eyes.

His shivering grew violent, teeth clacked, his jaw aching. But no pain followed.

One giant slitted eye opened, prepared to slam closed straight away. Caspian merely looked at him, eyes flashing, a wry smile twisting his lips.

"What are you waiting for?" Flare pleaded. "Just do it!"

Caspian's smile widened. "I will."

"Why are you waiting?!" This time, Flare's hoarse voice was a dry sob.

"I," Caspian drawled as if he had all the time in the world, "wanted to wait until you were ready..."

The limp hand made some kind of unnecessary motion that was deadly, nonetheless. Red hot pain sliced across Flare's scaled breast, a cruel flick and twist of sickening, carefully aimed energy. Scales cracked. The dragon howled into the mockingly gentle rain. Caspian howled in solidarity, like the maniac he was, a guilty commiseration that was as bad as the severing of Flare's flesh.

Gasping and trembling with the aftershock of fresh trauma, Flare hung his head, sobbing while his magically refreshed cells began the work of advanced repair. Spikes couldn't grow back, but at least scales could close over a gaping wound.

A wound that had been carved onto Flare's breast in a familiar shape.

Flare didn't even have to glance down to check it. He had felt the cut's precise formation. Caspian had carved a perfect 'C' into the dragon's scales, right into sensitive flesh underneath.

"Flare. Good on you," chilled words broke the spell of pain around Flare. "But don't speak to me like that again, or else I'll fucking rip your tail, and your scaled balls, right off."

A rivulet of dragon blood joined the rain and the falling ash, as Caspian eyed Flare calmly from the ground. Lips a thin line, their stare was broken only when Caspian flinched, raising his head to stare down at the crystallised egg still held steadfast by his good hand against his naked chest. Rain had washed some of the grit and grime from his hands. The tinge to Caspian's hands and arms was indeed a deep, iridescent copper.

Aware of Flare's silent, heated gaze, Caspian spared him a glance. It appeared he wasn't quite seeing the dragon, though. His mismatched gaze was unfocused.

"I am not a bully," he mumbled, blinking rapidly, turning his face away.

"A-are too," Flare sobbed, head hanging low as his wound throbbed.

"Am not," Caspian sniped back with a pain drenched hiss. "I had a friend once, a good friend... he told me... uh, fuck... what happened to him?" A pause. "I forgot..." Flinty eyes, wild and wide now, speared Flare with barely suppressed rage. "But he told me! I am not a bully. He said so..."

"No." Flare gulped as Caspian's gaze held his. "I was wrong." Flare took a breath, unable to hold the words back, as if he watched himself from afar. "You're not a bully. You're a m-monster."

Another moment's shocked silence passed between them.

Astonishingly, despite the chill, a smile bloomed across Caspian's face. He held Flare's stare evenly, his gaze eventually dropping to the now-healing slash across Flare's breast. But instead of inflicting another wound, Caspian sighed, dropping his head back to the rock.

"Monster? Is that the word?" He huffed a wry laugh. "Actually, I feel that I'm just liberated, liberated from feeling any regard to be good towards those who really don't deserve it."

Groaning, prone on the ground, eyes shut tight, Caspian winced. "Fuck, my head hurts. I can't use the crystals here. Shit. Flare. As much as I hate to say it, we need to get to Baile Fuar."

"W-where?"

"The quarry town, you dumb f —"

"I know what it is!" Flare interrupted recklessly, heart still pounding from recent events. So the cut across his breast had been awful. He hadn't lost his tail yet, had he? Caspian obviously needed him. Perhaps Flare could use that.

"Why there? Tell me. P-please."

Ignoring Flare's demand, Caspian was back to muttering under his breath. "Now there were some magic users! Those priestesses, ha! I'd worship at their altars any day. But the priests?" He snorted. "Cowardly leeches. All of them."

Blonde hair a sooty mess, his pale skin like charred wood with rain splattered ash spanning his exposed flesh, Caspian grimaced.

"The same as you. What a waste of dragonkind you are. You're so, ugh, fuck. You're so small even when you're big." From the ground came a sound like a choked sob. "Fucking lizards. You all suck. All you magic users. Maybe me. All of us. Except Morgan."

There was no retort Flare could think of, nor any he'd likely feel willing enough to share.

"I made sure I ended up with magic to help Skye and Morgan both, to help rise above the evils that bring us down. And do you know *what* those evils are, Flare? *Whom* those evils are?"

"Who, Caspian?" Flare mumbled, his heart doing odd flips in his chest. The scales along his neck twitched as black spots of ash landed and disintegrated in the puddles gathering around the boulders and slices of stone.

"All the fucking other people with magic that manipulate the world, like damned pieces on a grandly scaled game of tiddly-fucking-winks."

"Oh."

"'Oh'? Is that all you've got to say?"

"Y-yes…"

"Of course. You think I'm on that fucking board playing as well? Fuck it. Even if I was, it's only fair! Owaen got one of them. It's only fair if I get the other."

"The other?"

"He got Skye," Caspian declared, raising himself away from the rock shelf with one arm, his other clutching the egg to his chest like it was still the prize he'd schemed for. "I'll have this one," he turned his head slightly, squinting at Flare as if in pain, "maybe there's still a chance for both… for me, for Morgan…"

"I don't think," Flare croaked out, his incredulity winning over his fear, "that is ever going to happen."

Strangely enough, there was no explosion of expletives or rude gestures. Instead, the sodden mess of a man dropped his forehead to the now sooty and muddy surface of the rock shelf he was sprawled along.

"Morgan, wait for me," Caspian mumbled, his faint voice full of longing.

Around them, rain continued to fall, cold water plastering them both as the light faded, burning clouds gone to wisps along the horizon. With soggy ash covering the land below, the brutalised evening sky above remained a heavenly witness to the desolation of barren ground.

"Flare…" Caspian groaned, sounding even more dejected. "Flare, I don't feel so good. Get me out of here. Help me."

The dragon didn't move.

Caspian, naked and in a mess, pushed himself weakly onto his back. His ruined hand, copper tinged and trembling, reached towards the dragon.

Flare stared at it.

Caspian stared back. A muscle twitched along his finely shaped jaw.

"Please, Flare." His voice held the barest trace of vulnerability.

Flare let out a slow, shaking breath, aware the danger was not anywhere near past.

What was worse than a man like Caspian with power?

Nothing.

There was nothing.

So perhaps…

His nostrils gathered the scent of ash and charred forest. The trembling dragon peered unseeing through the sluggish mist, his mind drawn inward to his trembling heart.

Perhaps I deserve to lose my tail.

Green eyes, shining with betrayal, filled the dragon's soul.

I have nothing left to lose.

"What now, Caspian?" Flare whispered.

Mismatched blue eyes shone silver. Their iridescent depths shone with pain, but also with secrets, of wistful innocence and supreme cunning.

The dragon swallowed.

"Flare," Caspian replied. "Get me to Baile Fuar. I need a priest."

9

Morgan

Year 367
Aneirin Castle

"**M**organ Rose, get your fucking shit together."

Wiping at the vomit on her chin, the librarian eyed the bile decorating the floor beside her bed. Intense dreams had left her sweating and delirious, hanging over the edge of her mattress, shivering uncontrollably. The faint sliver of light from underneath the single door to the hall was barely enough to see the sour puddle splattered across the ancient flagstones.

"Shit," she hissed.

Leaning further over the edge of her bed, Morgan retched anew, an aching heave of filth. It was a blessing her chamber was far removed from the crowded halls of Aneirin Castle, the walls stony, broad and off a side passage hardly used.

Flopping back onto her back, Morgan scrunched her nose to the shadows above. Her tiny chamber, a room both windowless and stale, had barely enough room to move about in, so the air was thick. Yet the sour smell wasn't a bother. After all the wine and other crap she'd drowned herself in over the decades, she was used to it. It was the sharp cramps from a stomach protesting at bringing up watery bile that left her wincing. She needed to eat, but food left her feeling worse. Snorting, Morgan wiped long, red sweaty hair from damp cheeks. Avoiding eating hadn't helped her cramps one bit.

Not this time.

Not when there was so much at stake.

"Caspian."

Three syllables slipped like warm honey from her lips.

Honey with the risk of a sting.

"Caspian."

There was no answer, of course. He was to the northeast. The tug of awareness that he'd bound around the pair of them rippled with a caustic pang of longing behind her navel.

From her, from him.

Did it matter?

No.

What mattered was time and distance imposed by her, much to Caspian's dismay. Yet it had to be endured. A type of penance. For both of them.

Lately Morgan's nights had been filled with wide, watching eyes trailing that idiot of a man stirring up unrest. The twit, Wyll, had no idea of what unrest was, really. Coddled and cut off as the Kingdom of Aneirin had been, the innocent humans were completely without experience of what true disorder entailed.

Eyeing the walls that she couldn't see, Morgan rolled her lips over her teeth, biting hard against the cries of the long dead wailing in her ears.

They all had no idea.

But last night, Morgan had dreamed of Caspian instead of that subversive arsehole. It had been the first dream featuring the one who had haunted her lonely heart for quite a while.

Thinking back to the shifting images, a new prickling of awareness entered scattered thoughts.

"Caspian. I was there with you," the librarian mumbled to the castle wall. Morgan kicked the sweaty linen sheets away, trying to hold on to the fading images.

Blonde head tilted forward, Caspian had been seated at a writing desk in a stone chamber. Morgan had been pressed to his side, inhaling his musky aroma, along with the scent of something burning. The delicate ink-stained tips of her fingers had moved in a ghostly, barely there curve down his cheek. His soft skin was the same as she remembered, velvet covered pearl.

Morgan.

Amongst the delirium of her dream, he'd asked her a question about a journal. About words in yellow gold that teased her eyes. Alone in her bed, the cloying silence helped her think. The images of what had happened had a glassy quality to them, uncertain and vague. Unable to decipher them, Morgan let them turn over in the back of her mind.

One thing was obvious, however.

Caspian Carter was closing in.

Not in her dreams, but in the awakened world. A world of loss, lies and disappointment.

Caspian, with his vision of how things should be, a grand plan that eerily echoed the dark desires of his mother, was closing in on Morgan.

What had she expected, though? Under the castle, in the wake of the tremors which shook the land with increasing frequency, she'd used magic. After ignoring her powers for decades. She'd known Caspian would sniff it out, like some kind of deep sea predator scenting a drop of blood hundreds of leagues away.

A beacon like the lighthouses that dotted the eastern coast.

Stay away, those tiny points of light said to all who sailed close.

Or for others, they might say *come find me*.

Follow the flickering flames if you want to experience being broken apart against the jagged rocks of a lonely coastline.

In much the same way, Caspian would come. They had both been broken by others, and were quite adept at breaking each other further apart, where no certainty of a stable future could be predicted. Not even in her dreams. Inevitably, a day of reckoning would come.

"Caspian."

The lonely word hung densely in the sour air.

Sighing, Morgan turned to the wall featuring a small, tiled hearth. Letting her magic out like a whip, half-burned logs burst into bright flame. Feeling the radiant heat paint her cheeks with a reassuring caress, her shivering decreased. It was barely enough to reach the corners of the tiny chamber, and yet the warmth was welcome. Warm light flared as the flames crackled. Shadows danced up the walls.

Morgan's pale green eyes rose from the grate to blink slowly at the stone around her. Yes, the warmth was welcome.

Despite bringing her sins to the light.

Each crime was written in ebony ink across the bare stone walls. Anyone coming across the words would never suspect a classically trained librarian had left them there. Shaking hands had transcribed them along the smooth stone, from memory into ink. The words were tiny, precise, but at chaotic angles. Irregular lines had left thousands of letters and shapes at a slight tilt, offending an eye that preferred symmetry. Yet she welcomed their presence, every single letter.

Small hands flinched, freckles shifting as white knuckles clenched the rough texture of the bedsheets. As a faint spark of awareness flickered far off, Morgan snorted.

It had been a surprised burst of pleasure to the northeast. Coupled with something harder, the sensation spiraled along the connection. A joining of energy to the one who worshipped the air she breathed. But as she untangled the feelings reaching her across the continent, a line formed on the freckled skin between her green eyes. What else was she feeling there, besides Caspian's dark delight at sensing her presence? It was almost an ache, like the sharp cramp in her empty stomach.

Morgan closed her eyes, separating threads of invisible light, pulling apart the tight weave of sensitivity that caressed the area behind her eyes.

Copper eyelashes fluttered. Her eyes snapped open.

Pain.

Caspian was in pain. It was physical and deeply sheltered within his soul as well.

Curious, but not yet alarmed, Morgan sat up, stuffing some dishevelled pillows behind her. A travel journal, a worn out thing of brown leather and yellowed parchment, was tossed on the low table by her bed. Would she take it with her when the time finally came? Or leave it here with the other inscriptions that adorned her chamber? Either way, she cared little. The physical words meant nothing. It was what they represented, those that were gone forever, that disturbed her soul.

Ignoring the sour stink of recent vomit, Morgan inhaled with forced sluggishness. Her mindful exhale was even slower. She repeated it a dozen times. Eyes on the wall before her, the librarian let her mind go.

Images from the fresh dream drifted through her state of near trance, the shapes from the journal's front cover forming into crisp lines that didn't quite make sense.

What had it said?

Her lips formed words without disturbing the silence.

Letting her mind settle, Morgan sank into a greater trance. The sour smell of the room faded, the orange glow from the hearth dimmed. The walls, filled with thousands of words in black ink, morphed into the images of her dream, until gold letters on red leather popped into crystal clear shapes.

"Oh," sighed the librarian, the chamber claustrophobic and unyielding. "Of all the things... that is... unexpected."

Eventually, the words faded. Black letters on grey stone replaced them, the modest chamber coming back into focus. Morgan sank back into the pile of pillows. Her startled mind carefully pronounced each syllable with gentle respect, as if each collection of letters was a mystery that could wound the reader if they dared to speak them out loud.

Well.

She dared.

"*The Life and Death of Caspian Carter,*" Morgan whispered.

Embers flared. Propped in the shadowed corner next to the fireplace, the ruby at the tip of her wooden staff glinted.

"*Co-written,*" she continued, green eyes wide on the red jewel, "*by Morgan Carter.*"

The librarian bit back a hysterical laugh.

Swallowing, Morgan glanced down at the bare ring finger of her left hand. Caspian had once joked about no jewel doing her beauty justice. He'd admitted he would try, though, one day when she finally said '*yes*'. A ceremony wasn't necessary. Their souls were intimately joined, by events beyond their doing, but also by choice, no matter how unexpected.

Forever.

"*The Life and Death of Caspian Carter*," Morgan repeated.

How could that dream be a true one, a foreshadowing of the future?

Considering what else had yet to take place?

Nostrils flared, the stink of vomit mixing with the bitter aroma of dried ink.

What *must* take place.

The librarian gnawed at her bottom lip, teeth working the soft pink flesh. Recently her focus had been on keeping an eye on Wyll and his band of clueless followers, sensing the unrest building. At times, her dreams showed her glimpses of their useless plans despite not wanting such knowledge. Her curiosity had led her to mingle within their unsuspecting numbers during the past week. They were getting serious, which was a bother. There could be interference with plans that had been laid for decades.

The penance was nearly over. What had to happen, *must* happen, at all costs. Her heart skipped a beat with a sickening lurch.

Fuck.

Moving with reluctance, Morgan unlaced her thin linen nightdress and pulled the material apart. A scar marred the freckled skin of her left thigh. It was a scar she'd refused to heal, left by sharp teeth in a moment of absolutely wild passion. Her shriek at the time had been matched only by Caspian's boisterous laugh.

The Life and Death of Caspian Carter.

Reaching behind, Morgan dragged a sweat-damp pillow from the pile at her back. She dragged it up her chest, past small breasts and a madly thumping heart. Morgan took a shuddering breath in before positioning the pillow over her face.

She screamed.

Tasting sweat and musty linen, Morgan heaved her suffering into the pillow. Hunched over in her soiled bed, she screamed until her lungs gave out, sobbing into the damp fabric. The wake of her torment reverberated in her ears. Shoulders shuddering and guts twisting, the librarian inhaled the vapors of anguish, ready to set free another burst of rare emotion.

Tap tap.

The stricken librarian paused.

Tap tap tap.

It was the sound of someone hesitantly knocking on the wooden door. Morgan withdrew the pillow from her wet face. Compared to the violence of a moment before, the noise was almost lost amongst the deep thumping of her tortured heart. A muffled voice coughed.

"My lady?"

Morgan stared at the material in front of her eyes. Fresh spots of salty eyes and hot mouth had made a mocking impression of her face. She sniffled.

"Lady Hywel, is that you? Are you back..?"

Another slight cough. The voice called again, stronger.

"My lady, are you... well?"

Petite, freckled hands flinched.

Was she?

No.

"Yes," she croaked. Morgan cleared her parched throat. "Yes, I am quite well."

There was a pause, a pause heavy with anxiety, felt through the thick planks of old oak. "I see, but —"

"Go now," Morgan announced, weary, feeling all her decades of age.

Magic kept her appearance youthful, only faint lines marring her speckled skin. Yet the burdensome weight of the decades was carried on slim shoulders, with every step taken towards an inevitable reckoning.

"Are you —"

"Fetch fresh bread," Morgan interrupted the servant's query. Green eyes blinked at the twinkling ruby across the chamber, the smooth white wood of the staff covered in pulsing warm light from the low flames. Morgan inhaled, letting the fragrant smoke fill her lungs, joining the fuzz of her mind. She grimaced. "And wine," she added.

Another pause from beyond the door. "Yes. Of course, Lady Hywel."

Footsteps faded down the lonely passage. Someone must have spotted her return to the castle after her absence for so long.

Morgan lifted the pillow back to her face. The pathetic thing captured a hot puff of air, a hiccup that may have been either a laugh or a sob. Or both. She didn't care. There was no one else to judge. The pillow slipped from limp hands and landed with a soft thump in her bare lap.

"Get," she hissed through clenched teeth, "your shit together, Morgan."

Throwing back the covers completely, Morgan placed her socked feet on the flagstones. Avoiding the puddle of watery bile, she rose, wandering over to the fireplace. A trembling fingertip reached out to trace the tip of the ruby in her staff. Wood smoke filled her nostrils, further cleansing the stink of vomit from her senses.

Glancing at the metal bucket beside the hearth, she realised the dry wood pile was just about depleted. She'd been away so long that the job had been deemed unnecessary, as so many had left during the previous king's ominous reign. Magic had been banned. Afraid of his curse-stricken wife, the suspicious king had been able to sniff out most of those that carried it in their blood. If one was able, like her, it had been wisest to leave. She had no part to play in such petty games of power. Others, despite less magic than her, also had enough of a knowing to realise suffering was afoot. Those same folk that had enough to break free and leave. Leaving Aneirin a town of missing persons, as families fled to wherever they could to escape a threat felt in the blood, if not understood in the mind.

The librarian's finger drifted lower to trace the staff. Her magic was a fickle thing, an energy that filled her with capabilities she had no use for. Never depleted in its efficiency, as she hardly used it, Morgan had no doubt she could snap the staff into pieces. The shaft was as thick as her arm, but careful concentration could lash out a red whip of energy. In the same way as an innocent man's head had been separated from his shoulders, not long ago on the stones of the courtyard outside.

The staff would give way easily. Idly tossing her long red hair over her shoulder, Morgan wondered if the ruby would shatter. Would there be any flames from the dry old wood? Or just cleanly sliced edges glowing with the violence of ill-used magic?

"But you would only light this room for a moment," she muttered to the object. "And I need to burn brightly for now, with you close by for support."

The expiring embers in the hearth throbbed, the once bright orange fading to black. Opposite to the colours of a gaze that filled her equally with passion and despair. Eyes of blue and silver, eyes that would scoff at her unease.

Eyes that filled with longing each time they found her running away.

"Caspian." His name was a plea of both agony and desire. "My Caspian."

She turned from the staff and crossed the cramped, windowless chamber to a low table. Morgan stopped at a large bronze basin of water. An unseen spark of power flicked from her finger to the thin ice that sealed the water beneath. Pushing through the sharp edges of the ice, she plunged freckled hands beneath the cold shards. The icy liquid pained her flesh immediately.

"The agony will fade," she announced to the endless loops of black script blanketing the stone wall near her face. "The pain will fade to numbness."

While the librarian's hands protested at the brutal temperature, the wall stared back, impassive, inert. Lines, lines, and more lines of text in no particular order, letting her remember. Sins recorded in dried ink on ageless stone. A reminder that life was brutal, life was pain, with very few rays of light intersecting each regretful decision.

Or indecision.

An indecision of not taking steps to... Morgan grit her teeth. Of not taking steps to... *extinguish* the threat of one who held too much power to remain stable and in control.

"Who was I to decide, back then?" Morgan asked. "Or now?"

Chilled hands jerked under the shattered layer of ice.

She held them there, arms trembling. Dreams of knowing, magic and power. Both blessing and curse.

Rhydian was back from his mission to save the one he loved, the new king likely feeling the full unwinding of his father's brutal curse. And what it meant for him, for his family's bloodline. Would he understand her pain? Morgan bared her teeth, her hands completely numb.

Was the man's mind, or his young heart, strong enough to bear the newly revealed betrayal of his family?

Time would tell.

"Time."

It came out as a whispered syllable. A single sigh before a sharp inhale, as Morgan plunged her face into the basin of freezing water.

This time, her anguished scream was more insulated to possible listening ears. It went on for some time, eyes tightly shut, long hair stuck in her mouth as she wailed.

When her lungs gave way, cheeks protesting with cold, Morgan pulled away from the basin. Icy water and hot tears travelled down her face, scattering the tabletop with wet splotches. Numb hands gripped the edge of the table. Taking a single step back, Morgan lent over, pressing her forehead to the thick planks of old wood. The dust and grain of the past pressed into her damp skin. Long red hair dripped in a sodden curtain, sliding over trembling shoulders, pooling at her feet on the frigid floor.

Morgan blinked through the wet veil of her hair. The ruby winked back. Bloody, rusted crimson sparks gleamed over facets that appeared black in the shadows. A fine symbol of her love for a man who shone brighter than anything she deserved.

Shivers ran down her spine, ghostly fingertips of the man that awed her, the man who she ached for. Morgan's voice was as subtle as the ripple along her bones, a dusting of delicate words in the seclusion of her chamber.

"It's time."

10

Cas

Year 244, Cas at age 3
Baile Mara, City of the Sea

The little boy raised the sphere of clear quartz crystal in his tiny fist, prepared to launch it at his younger brother.

Wane's lower lip trembled as he watched his older brother raise the sphere. "Waney wants!"

Across from Wane, blue eyes blazed with silver.

Fed up with the balls constantly being snatched away, Cas had grabbed the last crystal ball from Wane. Cas didn't understand how Wane could roll them from Cas towards himself without touching the shiny things. Even the shapes that didn't roll like a sphere slid to Wane when his brother wanted them, cubes, pyramids and even the pink crystal heart. Moving objects like that was *another* thing Cas couldn't do. Stubby fingers barely made it around the smooth, curved surface as Cas held it, ready to throw it in a fit of pique. Thankfully, before any damage was done, a large hand clasped his firmly from above, preventing what would surely have ended in tears.

"Cassie, no. Don't be a rascal." His father's voice held a note of resignation. After a beleaguered sigh, Illarion smiled at Wane. Deep green eyes twinkled from beneath his white blonde hair. "And as for you, my clever little boy, remember that magic is for emergencies only."

"But —"

"Shall I put you outside for a while, Caspian? Like the sick plants taking the sun and a time out?"

"I am not a plant!" Cas huffed.

A delicate laugh, quickly stifled, sounded from the far end of the work desk. He was *not* in need of a timeout, and he wasn't sick. Both things made him irritable. Cas yanked his hand free from his father's grasp. Illarion let him go, smiling serenely. The oldest twin sat back, little arms crossed over his chest, mismatched blue eyes shimmering.

The siblings had been left to play on a soft, multi-coloured wool rug near the main workbench of the big place that smelled musty. Father had given them a collection of coloured crystals to play with. They were shiny, smooth, and pretty when the lantern flames caught the shimmering flecks within their depths. It was fun watching them make shapes as they rolled about.

Each time Cas picked one to play with, his brother took it away from him.

Without using his hands.

The first time it had happened, Cas had stared, fascinated. Wane appeared shocked as well, green eyes wide and startled. Then he did it again. So now, each time Cas tried to capture a ball, Wane did something without moving, and the ball was no longer in Cas's possession. Sometimes the musty, stuffy air of this place made Cas' eyes water. This time it was the frustrating, gleeful grin on Wane's face that made Cas's throat hot and his eyes sting.

So this time, Cas had intended to give the last one to him.

With force.

Until father put a stop to that.

Sighing, Illarion gave Cas a flat look, his blue eyes narrowed as he made a show of handing the sphere to Wane. Wane chortled to himself and gathered the balls together, laughing at the clacking sound they made as they tumbled between his feet.

Cas screwed up his nose, but said nothing. His father went back to work, leaning over the big table he was seated at.

Maybe it would be better to get up and explore? Long rows of shelves and rolled up papers made for lots of nooks and crannies to investigate. In previous times, when the little boy had managed to toddle away from scrutiny, he had seen lots of interesting things. Giant books were stacked on the lower shelves, their bindings mostly cracked. Cas liked to peel away the gold leaf off the spines, enjoying the slow giving away of dry letters from thin, splitting leather.

Until father's firm hand had reached out that time too, his father's exclamation followed by a word that Cas wasn't allowed to use.

So he had been banned from exploring beyond his father's line of sight. The smacks on the back of his hand when caught wandering off didn't bother him. The sting didn't hurt. But the last time he'd received a smack in here, he'd caught a pair of pale green eyes, set in a sweetly freckled face, coolly assessing him.

Cas had never wandered off again.

Well.

Not where she could see him get a smack.

That in itself confused him. Why did Cas get told off? If Wane did naughty things, at worst he got a shake of the head.

The elder boy's gaze grew thoughtful. Either way, he was over playing with the lovely sphere. Wobbling a little, Cas stood up. The boy smiled at Wane's pouty lip as Cas teetered over him. The siblings looked almost the same. But Cas was taller, tall for his age too. Cas gave his brother a wide grin. A line formed between Wane's eyebrows, but a noise had them both peer into the gloom along the rows of shelves.

The lantern light didn't reach all the way into the long and narrow building. Usually, it was the bare minimum of flames illuminating the space. Those who came and went mostly sat by windows that faced the sea, or forested grove behind, unless they needed the big central desk to work on.

Cas peered into the shadows. A tall figure was striding towards them, returning from the furthest shelves stuffed with their endless books and splitting scrolls.

A towering woman emerged, hair long and golden, eyes the same colour. Dressed in layers of rust and orange, the woman winked at Cas as she passed. He got a close look as she stepped over the twins. One hand rested on the ornately decorated heavy sword at her hip. Her other waved a tightly rolled scroll at the adults seated at the desk. Not waiting for a response, the gold woman headed for the library doors.

"Don't lose that, Dawn," a delicate voice called from the central workbench.

Cas turned towards the one who had spoken. He liked that voice.

Behind the little boy, the golden-haired woman's noncommittal reply was cut off as the heavy door shut with a thud.

"She thinks rules don't apply to her," a deep voice commented. From where he stood below the top of the desk, Cas couldn't see who it was. Three figures sat there. He guessed it was the tallest one.

"You think the rules don't apply to *you*, Rook." That voice belonged to the petite woman with the flaming red hair. Cas thought her voice was pretty. Rook made no reply to her comment.

Sticking his tongue out at his brother and ignoring Wane's reddening cheeks, Cas wandered to the desk. He stopped at his father's leg. The man was seated at one end, the other two figures further along.

Overhead, coloured and clear glass lanterns painted the work area with bright shapes of light. Which is why the far corners of the library seemed dim and mysterious. The boy gave the nearest gloomy passage a wistful look. Not looking at his son, his father patted Cas' head twice before resuming his reading. Ignoring his father in turn, Cas grabbed the edge of the bench, standing on his tiptoes. He was just tall enough to get a look.

Mismatched coloured eyes peered over the top, his nose pressed against the thick wood of the edge.

The surface was covered with piles of paper and stacks of books. There were shiny metal things the little boy didn't have names for, and the occasional potted plant, their fresh fragrance at odds with the musty aromas of the place. Another man was seated beyond his father, a tall man with hooded eyes that filled with mirth when Cas approached.

Cas examined him now. Unaware of the appraisal, the man shifted on his stool. He was frowning at one of the plants by his elbow. Cas peered at where the fronds appeared to be covering the sheets before him. Peculiarly, as Cas watched, the plant twitched. Then, with a quiet scrape, the pot slid away from the dark-haired man. It inched along the table, enabling him to unroll the sheets before him further.

Cas blinked. So others could move things too? Not just Wane? The little boy shifted on his tiptoes.

While wondering about that, a sharp, green aroma met Cas' nose. He sniffed.

Rose, he mouthed carefully, *Rosemary*. Like in the garden of his family's home.

Whatever it was, it smelled far better than the stale air that filled the rest of the building. The boy inhaled deeply. He caught a whiff of beeswax candles, along with something delicate and soothing.

Blue eyes, one pale, one dark, glinted at the third figure seated at the desk.

It was the slender lady with hair like the setting sun. Her eyes didn't look at him with mirth, like the tall black-haired man. Cas didn't know why, but she hardly looked at him at all. Apart from that time when she'd seen him get told off by Father.

With his toes aching, the boy dropped back onto his heels. The tall man leaned to the side and peered at Cas' father's work.

"Ship building? A new craft for the bored alchemist, hm?"

"Funny Rook, funny."

Cas peered around the corner of the table. The lady kept silent. He could see the tip of a quill darting before her, the faint scratch reaching his straining ears. Dark circles under her eyes, at odds with her creamy, speckled skin, only added to the little boy's fascination. Her pale green gaze avoided looking in his direction. They remained lowered while his father and the tall man continued talking.

"It's for a ship," his father was saying.

"How interesting." Rook's tone was dry. "Off hunting lost treasure?"

"A *toy* ship."

"Even better, Illarion. How expansive of you."

"Wipe that smirk off your face. My children need a lesson on sharing. Hypatia is too busy, so it's fallen to me."

Cas liked the idea of a toy ship. Not the sharing part. He shuffled along the table's straight edge, closer to the woman. The soothing scent was greater here. Not looking up, the woman altered her position on her stool, turning away from him ever so slightly.

Cas took another step.

"How is it going?" Rook drawled. "Your two *other* children?"

His father laughed, loud and merrily. "*Other* children? Ha. I think they're gestating quite nicely, thank you. It will be a long, winding road of challenges to get them where we want them. There are so many fine details to weave into the process."

"I can only guess."

"I bet you can more than guess. I heard you had some sport with the wild bears recently."

"I do what I can. Those wild beasts have been hassling the small shipping villages around the heads towards Port Town."

"Dragons are meant to help, not destroy," Illarion chided.

Cas shuffled along, a smile playing about his lips.

"I did help. Those bears were a menace. They needed to be culled."

"Help, you say? Shredding them into strips and discarding them for the seals seems a little..." his father paused. "Against nature."

"Illarion," Rooks said, clearly amused.

"Yes?"

"Against nature, huh? That's a bit ridiculous coming from you, hm?"

"Well." His father cleared his throat. "There are reasons for what we are doing."

"Making lives easier and all that. Spare me the heartfelt poetry. It's simple. Magic equals power."

"It can —"

"For those that have it," the man interrupted. His voice lowered. "Unlike your eldest. Cas is clever for his age, yes. But not magically talented, like his brother. How's Hypatia coping?"

Not hearing what the grownups were talking about as he was close to where he wanted to be, Cas paused his advance. He was right next to the red-haired lady now. Perched on a big stool, her petite boots swung free from the bottom rung. Long hair framed her face, spilling over her shoulders and down her dark green tunic. When the flickering lantern light became trapped amongst the strands, it looked like a river of molten fire.

"What?" Cas' father protested at whatever Rook was saying. "She's fine —"

"Sure. I'm sure she is. The perfectionist with an experiment not quite going as planned, huh? What does that spell for the next lot?"

"They are coming along nicely, like I said."

"I heard you, Illarion. I also think you could do better."

"What?"

"I think you could do better by the eldest lad. He's smart. Anyone can tell by looking at the way he observes and absorbs the world. I was reading, right here in these scrolls actually, about theoretical crystal use, without the energy overload —"

"Rook."

"Yes?"

"My son is fine the way he is."

"Your wife think so too, hm?"

"I've got work to do," his father said stubbornly.

"Sure. Have fun with that." Rook laughed. "Illarion Carter, gardener, beekeeper, alchemist, boatbuilder."

"Ha. Now shush."

From the far end of the table came the sound of Wane clacking the spheres together. A merry laugh followed a loud crack. Almost right by the lady, Cas' lower lip protruded. Why did his brother have to take everything? Unsure, and with one hand fiddling with an ear, Cas stepped forward. His other hand reached out.

He tugged on the lady's dark green pants.

"Fuck!"

The lady surged up from the table, one arm knocking an ink well over. Cas leapt back out of the way as ink splattered about. He glanced down. A few drops had spoiled his clean shirt.

"Morgan!" snapped Cas' father while Rook burst into howls of laughter.

"Shut up, Rook," the lady hissed, her face covered in black spots amongst the scatter of freckles. Grabbing at a cloth from her tunic, she wiped up what she could. Frowning at the material, she sighed. There was a big stain in the centre of her chest. Cas bit his lip. The black ink sort of looked like a heart.

"Sorry," Cas mumbled. He wasn't, but she seemed upset.

"Apologise," Illarion said loudly, rounding the bench. Both Morgan and Cas stared at Illarion, unsure as to whom he was referring. Shaking his head, Illarion pointed at Cas, his deep green eyes resigned.

Morgan straightened. "He already did. It's not his fault." The lady's gaze never once reached Cas. "He startled me, that's all. No harm done."

"Apart from your tunic," Rook said with a smirk.

"It's fine," the lady snapped. Eyes straight ahead, she stepped lightly past Cas to disappear around a bookshelf. The tall man laughed and bent back over his work after darting a wink at Cas.

"Cas," Illarion said, pinching the bridge of his nose. "Don't disturb the librarian, okay? She has important work to do."

Rook laughed as the librarian returned to the table and glared at him.

Wane appeared from behind his father's leg, staring with wide, curious eyes. Cas crossed his arms over his chest. His younger brother had one of the crystal balls in his grubby fist. Illarion reached down and caressed Wane's head.

"I'm doing something important too, for you and Wane, okay? I just need a few more plans. I'll be ready to take you home soon. Okay?"

Cas stared at the ball in Wane's hand. Wane clutched it to his chest. Cas glared. But he nodded.

"Cas," his father waved a hand at the back wall of the stuffy room, "please stay out of trouble. Don't wander off."

Nodding again, Cas waited for his father to take Wane back to the rug with the rest of the crystals. When his father's back was turned, Cas immediately wandered off in the direction the lady had taken.

Following the line of bookshelves, the little boy ended up in a section of the long, stale smelling building he'd never been in before. Most walls had shelves stacked with rolled up things, the occasional coloured ribbon trailing out to denote important words.

But not here. Between a row of long narrow windows of thick, rippled clear glass, a section of the wall had been left bare of shelves. The space was being used to hang images and drawings. From the floor all the way to the beams, metal plaques and framed parchment spanned the wall. Most were crude, made of line drawings and flat shapes.

"What are they?" Cas murmured. They were beautiful. He reached out to touch the closest one, a metal one almost the same colour as the librarian's flaming hair.

"Maps."

Startled, Cas spun around. It was the lady. Not looking at him, one of her stained fingers pointed at the wall.

"Maps," Cas repeated. The little boy touched the closest one, stubby finger tracing the reddish metal. "Pretty."

Sighing, Morgan motioned towards him. "Please come away."

His small finger continued to trace the etched lines. A cobweb covered part of one corner. The boy flashed his missing two front teeth at the librarian.

"No."

"What?" the lady replied, eyebrows raised, her gaze focusing past his blonde head. Cas' grin widened.

"Pretty," he repeated.

Loose flaming hair shimmered with the shake of her head, lips a thin line.

"That's Baile Mara," the librarian reluctantly explained. She shifted in her brown leather boots. "Where we are." She pointed to each of them, and then at a nearby window. "Home."

"Home?" Cas asked, his blonde head tilted to the side. He pointed at the wall.

"Home," said the lady. Her pale green eyes examined the metal plaque.

Chortling, Cas held out both hands to her.

"No," she said firmly.

Ignoring his outstretched hands, the lady stepped towards the wall. Slender fingers traced the same plaque that had fascinated Cas. A stained fingertip landed on a wide shape that reminded the boy of the blue bay below the cliffs. Underneath the pad of her finger sat a cone shape that looked like the stinky island offshore.

"Home," murmured the librarian. "The heart of the chaos in my dreams."

The spicy sweet aroma of beeswax and parchment filled the boy's nostrils. He liked it. When he had first come here, the place had that smell, something that had been familiar. Comforting. Unlike the strange bitter smells from home.

"Up," said Cas, turning from the wall. He waved his hands.

"No."

"Hug."

The lady reached inside her tunic, searching for something amongst the folds. The dark circles under her eyes appeared blue here in the shadows. Pulling out a small silver container, she turned away. After taking a long drink, she retraced their path along in the direction of the main work area.

Before she reached the end of the musty corridor, Morgan looked back to examine the little boy. Cas had trailed after her, sure enough. Her gaze finally made contact with odd blue eyes, wide and insistent. Cas blinked. Hers were dull and completely without expression.

"Hug!" A little boot stamped the chilled slate floor.

"No," said the librarian, walking away. "Never."

11

Aurelia

Year 367
Aneirin Farmlands

"**F**uck you, Flare," Aurelia hissed to the river. "I hope you're enjoying yourself."

Under the bridge, the wintry water rippled in agreement, the whirlpool a deadly snag of humming currents downstream. Aurelia closed her eyes to the sights and sounds of Aneirin's frigid valley, to the wall of colossal, shifting and creaking trees, and strangely bubbling clouds.

As a young child, Aurelia had finally spotted the purple dragon by himself. He'd been sunbathing in a rare patch of weak sun, at the mouth of the Funnel, the vast half-open tunnelled entrance into Lolihud. Both of them newly arrived in the caves, the mysterious Elder One rarely let the creature out of their sight, even for a moment.

Gathering her courage, the little girl had seen her chance, and taken it.

In the main cavern of Lolihud, the curved natural rock ceiling above echoed with squeals and high-pitched laughter. The extreme winter was long past, the weak sun not quite making it from Elven-made skylights to the tiled floor.

About a dozen Elven children raced across the immense cave. Dead twigs and branches collected from a frozen forest stood in for swords, spears, bows, and arrows.

Aurelia had swindled a bit of leather cord in place of a true bow string, but that didn't matter. She had used her expensive paints, gifted from her father, to paint the bow. Red for luck in the hunt. All the arrows had their special meanings, too. An old miner's cap, hung upside down over her shoulder, made do as a quiver. She was proud of that piece of innovation. The bundle of coloured sticks with broken fletches, some without feathers at all, rattled and bounced on her narrow shoulders.

Feeling wild, the little girl whooped and howled after the kids who had been nominated as the 'baddies' for that day.

Fed up with the mad echoes from the gaggle of children, the adults had shooed them away from the inner chambers. That made little sense to Aurelia. In the lower levels, sounds were dampened by the twisted tunnels and fungus-insulated walls. Echoes increased the closer they got to the Funnel, the black basalt passage a natural feature that exaggerated sound.

Aurelia, going her own way even then, had opted to split off from the "goodies" doing the chasing. She ducked around a red faced Elder male Elf and found a higher ledge to aim her homemade arrows from. She needed to follow it up and almost outside, before she could race with balance along a higher ledge inside. While halfway along the tunnel wall on the unworked basalt steps, she came to an abrupt, hopping stop.

The little girl had come face to face with the massive dragon.

The creature raised his head with an abrupt rippling of great purple spikes. He blinked at her, his purple slitted eyes wide. He was in a feeble patch of sun, out of the wind, just inside the wide opening or arching basalt rock. Despite the weak daylight, the snow was bright. Aurelia's young eyes needed time to adjust to the glare. It was hard to distinguish the dragon's bulk from the rock formations around him.

"Oh!" said the dragon.

"Oh!" said Aurelia.

"Um," the dragon added, his sharp teeth appearing as his finely scaled lips formed deep words. "H-hello."

"Hello, Mister Dragon."

The dragon and the child examined each other in silence, the whoops of the other children fading away. Aurelia didn't mind one bit. She pointed her bow at the dragon's tail, curled around one scaled hind leg.

"You're curled up like a big snow leopard."

Shining purple scales gleamed, and pointed teeth flashed anew. "I guess I am, little one."

"I'm not little."

The dragon dipped his dazzling crown of spikes towards her. "Ah, my apologies. Um. I meant it in the same way that, like today, I am not always little, either."

"Oh. That's okay then." Aurelia tossed her dark hair over the multicoloured feathers poking over her shoulder. The little girl had the feeling that the dragon was trying not to smile.

Lowering his head, the dragon snuffed gently as she edged closer, booted feet shuffling along the basalt ledge towards him.

"Please call me Flare."

"Hello Flare. My name is Aurelia."

Amethyst eyes wandered over her crimson bow. "Um. So, what are you doing?"

"I'm winning battles against the scourge of the north." Aurelia turned in a circle, to show him her quiver of coloured arrows. They made a nice rattle as she came face to face with the dragon once more.

"Scourge?"

"Humans, of course!"

"Oh." Purple eyes blinked at her briskly. "But aren't you a girl?"

"So?"

"Don't you want to be a princess instead of a hunter? What about babies?"

"Blech! No!" Aurelia frowned. "Why? Do you have a family?"

The dragon's gaze shifted to the bright snow outside. "I had some once."

"Oh! Baby dragons? Ooh, I would rather have one of those."

"What? No, not a dragon... My chil — Ah, never mind. Ahem. Why a bow and arrow?"

"I can get the stinky humans from afar when they can't see me. I'll protect you, Flare," Aurelia proclaimed, puffing out her chest.

"Will you need to, dear child?"

Flare stood, stretching. Smooth purple spikes rippled from neck to tail. Leathery wings rustled as they spread wide to catch the last of the fading light. Aurelia laughed at the pretty rainbow shimmers reflected over the black basalt on either side of the Funnel. The make-believe bow pointed at Flare's scaled chest, the overlapping scales rounded and even.

"I might! They won't see me coming, Flare. I'll fight for the Elves and keep us safe from the humans, before they get a chance to try their luck in the snow and ice. We're friends now. I'll protect you."

Did Flare remember that ridiculous conversation?

Was that why he had gifted her such a beautiful bow before she had set out from the caves only weeks ago? Aurelia had traded the finest pyrite from her collection for the arrows to complement it, each one fletched in feathers of the purest colours. Hues that her younger self could only dream of.

Even a single black arrow, just in case.

Aurelia glared at the soggy sky, her mouth a hard line.

On the eve of battle, Flare knew that black arrow would be used in an attempt to end a pointless conflict that should never have happened.

Looking back now, the shock on his face at her declaration of not wanting babies wasn't disgust. It had been fear instead. Perhaps a strong woman had scared him. At that stage he had been part of the Elder One's confidence, hadn't he? One he had known was Rhydian's mother, the disgraced queen on the run.

Fighting the stormy rise of unpleasantness in her throat, Aurelia hissed. The ash and rain on her lips were more welcome than the bile roiling in her guts.

"Fuck you, Flare," Aurelia whispered.

Angrily wiping her cheek, Aurelia blew her nose with angry spite on the once beautiful cloak. The repercussions of Flare's role in the curse, along with the Elder One, could be seen in the desolated farmlands along the curving valley.

Whatever that man, Caspian, was planning, she hoped Flare lost his spikes along with whatever shred of dignity he had left. She'd felt stripped of hers, treated as she was. Both under Flare's ashamed eyes and the watchful, hateful gaze of the one who had been called Jessica.

Calloused fingers caressed the rich embroidery along the edge of the cloak. It was strange that the blonde man had cared for her comfort one moment, then discarded her the next. Was he an Elf? His magic didn't seem native to him, like he'd resented it rather than relished its gift. Caspian had been changeable like a storm, calm but full of coiled violence, ready to break over them all.

Wondering if Bindy and her slightly squashed flowers had found their target, Aurelia frowned at the churning river, green eyes unfocused. When was the last time she had felt free from the anxiety of those who wielded power for their own nefarious needs? Yesterday, but only for a moment. Even then, the air had ended up charged, tainted by prejudice.

Rhydian and Aurelia had been in the stables, helping Merion and Kyle, one of Chase's younger brothers. The horses clearly had a soothing effect on Rhydian, the boy too. Although the king was obviously pining for Blackthorn. Each careful stroke of his brush along the flanks of a stocky grey was followed by a forlorn sigh.

"He'll be back soon," Aurelia had said over the stall's low wall, nose scrunched at the powerful odour of horse. "He'll smell you from way off. The way you stink of stables won't cover it."

That had earned her a tired smile. "Ha. Perhaps he'll scent your strange flowery aroma first, my love. Are you sure you came from lands of ice and not the meadows of the gods?"

"Shut up. Bindy gave me hers, it's our favourite. Flowers from a vine, a creeper that lives in the snowy pines."

Merion's head had lifted from his bench at Rhydian's loud laugh, a rare sound these days. The groom's beard twitched over the saddle he was polishing. "Your soap is made from creepy flowers, you say?"

Placing the brush back on its hook, Rhydian had emerged from the storeroom, hay in his golden brown hair. Aurelia chucked her brush at him. He caught it with ease, and in turn, threw it with care to Kyle. The boy caught it with a solemn twitch of his lips. Merion's cheeks rounded under his beard. The groom nodded at his king before he went back to scraping mud, and the gods only knew what else, off the saddle before him.

"I am allowed to miss my horse," Rhydian declared. He had lost a little colour in his face from the strain of recent events, a headache plaguing him on and off. The unshaven growth on his chin lent him a little toughness, but thankfully, the sweetness was there. His blue-ringed-blue eyes gleamed under his waggling eyebrows. "Perhaps you can take my mind off it though, yeah?"

A shocked silence followed this statement. A horse whinnied. Merion blushed over the top of his beard. Aurelia tilted her head to the side, mouth hanging open.

The young king blinked. "Huh? What?"

The groom cleared his throat. "Ah... perhaps the lad and I shall leave you to it, then?" He stood up.

Aurelia burst into laughter as the light of realisation dawned on Rhydian's face. His blush was equal to the red-faced groom's.

"Wait! No... I meant we could go for a ride —"

Aurelia's laughter grew louder at his fumbled words, her sides aching.

Rhydian had groaned, then stalked over to her, pulling her close for a rough embrace. His whispered words against her ear had left her blushing as bad as he. Merion pretended not to notice. He sat back with the boy, pulling a fresh cloth from his thick apron, explaining the in-and-outs of the right saddle polish.

With the scent of fragrant wax peppering the air, Aurelia had wrestled Rhydian down to the filthy slate stable floor, both of them laughing and cursing. They had been free for just a moment, without worry and responsibility. They were just two young folk, being silly.

The moment hadn't lasted long.

A shadow had fallen across the stable doorway.

Both Rhydian and Aurelia looked as one, laughter dying on their lips. Rhydian had been facing the open doors. Wrapped around him and facing away, Aurelia had caught sight of Merion's deep frown at whomever had arrived. Disengaging from the warm embrace, she resisted his arms as they tightened to hold her in place. Shifting around, Aurelia faced the door. By the stale aroma of beer, she'd guessed who it was.

Sure enough, it was Wyll. He stared at his king in the muck with Aurelia, his face a mask of open disgust.

The silence gathered thickly, broken only by the occasional hoof stamp along the stalls.

Watery brown eyes glared at the scene before him.

Against her back, lips on her hair, Aurelia felt Rhydian open his mouth to speak.

Wyll got in first.

The man spat on the floor at his boots, spun on his heel, and left.

Merion's soft curse broke the shocked silence left behind.

Without a word, Rhydian pushed to his feet. He helped Aurelia up. After dusting them both off, Rhydian headed for the stable doors. The light in his eyes had gone.

Aurelia grabbed his wrist. "Leave him stew in his own prejudice. We all have to. He'll grow out of it."

Both of them glanced at Merion, who had risen to come stand by them. He smelled of wax. His cheeks were pale beneath the bush of his beard. The groom stared at the stiff back of Wyll, stalking across the cobbles.

A muscle in Rhydian's jaw had clenched. "And if he doesn't?"

"Of course he will, sire." The groom's hard expression was at odds with his words of reassurance. "I'm sure he will."

Aurelia had made no comment as Rhydian jerked his wrist free of her grip, stalking into the cold, heading after the bitter man.

Aurelia had a lack of comment and answers for too many things at the moment.

For example, the nature of Fox's magic. Or his dragonhood. Other Elves had appeared equally enthralled or jealous of his power. Mysterious glances followed his easy manipulation of matter when he deigned to assist in certain tasks back home. His power was breathtaking, earned somehow when off helping refugees from the fall of the City of the Seers. But he wasn't the same Fox who had left to help, was he? He was someone else, one who had come to the caves with the face of Gavin's brother.

Someone with power enough to put some Elves to shame, while inspiring awe in others.

Someone who had turned out to be a dragon.

That explained his great magical abilities, but not his origins. As a man, Fox was crotchety at the best of times. As a dragon... well. She wished Owaen luck. That muscled blonde Elf seemed to have more power than most, too. Aurelia sniggered at the dead rabbits along the handrail. Or was it just Owaen's dogged stubbornness that appeared as magic instead?

Her own stubbornness aside, Aurelia could manipulate some minerals, or sense them at least. Yet compared to Fox, and perhaps Owaen, she was just a bug.

Was that one explanation for Wyll's heated expression? Humans compared to the Elves were a step down, if one valued magic as currency or power.

For the first time in her life, Aurelia was fully aware of being alone, perhaps with Rhydian, alone between the inevitable collision of two cultures.

There were the old ways of the Elves with deeply seated resentments against the humans. All of it based on lies. Then there were the humans living out in the open, away from the caves, away from the trees, under the open sky. But who had lived in the shadows left by the rule of a deceitful king.

Even her time with Flare and Caspian had left her with more questions than answers. Aurelia had tried her best to pay attention, and despite what she'd overheard, there was a lot she didn't understand.

What did make sense was that she had the freedom to step away from everything she had known, into something new. Without expectations of anyone else, even Rhydian.

Even the intimacy she had shared with him was based on shaky foundations. He knew she was there on a quest to break a curse. A nefarious binding that his family was responsible for. But despite what she had done to him, what he knew she would do, he expected her to go through with it for the sake of both of their peoples.

Well.

There was no quest now, there was no dagger to find. There was no target to take down inside a curse, no dragon watching over her shoulder, no black and gold eyes watching her progress. There was only herself, the sky above, the churning waters below what she thought had been an answer, in the form of a seemingly bottomless whirlpool that hummed down stream even now.

What could she choose now? What choices were there? There was no going back to wild oblivion. The paths forward were full of uncertainty, with little guidance from anyone qualified to rule.

Aurelia reached for the bow. Her hand tightened around its beautiful surface, knuckles white, calluses scraping over the intricate designs, damp now with mist that had formed into a light yet skin-chilling rain.

"Fuck this thing," she hissed. "Fuck this fucking bow."

A bow, given to her by a shining, amethyst coloured dragon whom she had once called a friend. A friend who had snatched her from the sky one moment, only to leave her plunging towards oblivion the next.

Before Aurelia had come to the river, deciding here was best to end it, she'd tried to break the damn thing. Bindy had found her, holding back angry tears, trying to snap the bow in half. The wood had resisted, bound with a part of Flare's magic that she hadn't quite realised was ingrained within its decorated form.

In a way, she was similar to Rhydian, growing up with layers of magic around, with no knowledge of the lies that followed every step. But while Aurelia had grown up surrounded by a community of Elves who lived and breathed magic without fear, Rhydian had not. He had grown up isolated, cut off from other people, and the truth of how and why.

How long would he be reeling from his family's betrayals? Would he be welcome in the caves if he ever made it there, to see magic could be a natural part of life? He seemed happiest amongst the massive trees of the forest, with their deep green glades, paths of fresh emerald moss, and clear air. Perhaps the caves could do better, with magic to help, not wound. Could he be helped by the gentle magic of the Healers? They had ways to help young Elves who have trouble coping with a life lived mostly underground. Maybe they could help Rhydian adapt to life on the other side of being a king.

For her part, Aurelia was focused on working a little magic of her own.

Cycles began, cycles ended. It was best to mark them. For her, for the young man who had entered her life so unexpectedly and in the most dire of circumstances. She would do this for him, too.

Aurelia placed a boot on the lower railing and hoisted herself up. A shout sounded from the battlefield.

Unwinding the coat from her shoulders, she glanced up to see Rhydian far off, mounted on a chestnut roan horse, galloping towards the bridge. Smiling at him through the gathering rain, Aurelia balanced on the top railing, proving to herself despite it all, she had the power of choice even now.

Leaning down, she hoisted up the bow, wrapping it with the purple cloak.

Words formed in her mind, a weaving of grief and resentments that needed to be set free, let go, washed away.

"It's alright," Aurelia called to Rhydian. He was too far off to hear over the river, the distance too great. She continued anyway. "I'm sorry about all of this."

Aurelia waved and turned to face the ferocious river under the bridge.

She let go.

12

Rhydian

R hydian examined the ornate pair of wooden doors. With the outside world a muted buzz down the hall, the whorls and patterns of faded letters and symbols in the wood grain shifted as tired lids lowered over weary blue eyes.

He didn't want to be here.

With a sigh, Rhydian rested his forehead against the worked gold inlaid into the oak. Another headache was forming again behind his temples, sharp and dull all at once. An unwelcome parallel to the pang in his heart.

Was this his life now? A life of duty, full of things he didn't want to do, in the place he didn't want to be?

If he was being honest, there were only a few things he wanted. As king, peace must be had for the folk of Aneirin. As a son, he wanted answers for the devastation his parents had left with their fruitless push for revenge, power, whatever they'd seen as the ultimate end for the shit they'd been through.

But as Rhydian?

He wanted Aurelia all to himself, to be left alone with her intense green-eyed gaze, dark hair of delicate scent, her untamed floral aroma that filled his soul with ease.

Bracing himself, Rhydian turned the golden handle of the left door, proud of the fact the tremor in his fingers was invisible.

Mostly.

The heavy wooden door, stained a dark chestnut to offset the yellow gold, gave way with a muted creak of worn hinges. A familiar scent met his nose. Sage, along with something woodsy. Blue eyes opened, their dark ring of blue almost black in the gloom that spilled forth into the empty hallway.

His father's chambers were the same as he remembered.

Gods. When had he been here last?

Boot steps made no sound as he stepped into the empty royal chamber. The thick woven carpet of maroon and sapphire wool saw to that. Without looking, Rhydian shut the door behind him with a gentleness that may have looked born out of respect to anyone if they were here to witness.

It wasn't respect that had him close the doors with a modest *clack*.

It was reluctance.

Resignation.

Yet, as with most things these days, there was no choice. He'd not leave this task to anyone else. With a sigh, Rhydian surveyed the series of alcoves in silence.

A gentle puff of air kissed his right ear.

"Shit!"

He spun around.

A silver moth fluttered away, darting off to land on the back of one door. Swallowing, he watched it settle into a shallow crevice amongst the whirling lines and shapes. Heart barely contained within his chest, Rhydian expelled a hot breath of air. The powdery insect had chosen a small abstract dragon to rest upon, the scaled creature's horned head topped by a simple outline of a crown.

So.

His people wanted a coronation, didn't they? Some kind of ridiculous celebration, hoping for a new page of renewal, like turning a rotten leaf over in some old dusty book. Perhaps a book from the locked library a few chaotic floors below. A muscle in Rhydian's jaw twitched.

He wasn't here to think of books.

"Where's the fucking crown, father?" asked the grieving king.

In the otherwise empty room, there was no reply.

Swallowing the unease swelling within his chest, Rhydian straightened his shoulders.

He kicked aside a pile of floor cushions. Noting the dust that rose in the gloom, Rhydian wondered if the things were a leftover embellishment from his mother's time here. The idea of his father lounging around on floor cushions seemed utterly ridiculous.

With a dry cough, he wandered further in. Apart from the layer of gathering dust, the chambers were surprisingly neat. The furniture was rich and ornate, yet only the occasional flash of gold or flicker of jewel caught his eye. Most of the wood was left bare, polished with aromatic beeswax instead of gilt, like some of the old formal rooms elsewhere in the castle complex. The ceilings were high, the stone bare. Each separate area had a different vaulted ceiling of white stone, a nice contrast to the polished red stone walls. Hanging keystones in the cross points of each set of stone ribs were carved in elaborate shapes. Each one was unique, some pointed, others rounded.

Rhydian examined them, head back, lips parted slightly. As a child, he wasn't in here much, but he was sure one of the decorative keystones was flattened, fashioned in the shape of a shield. Unable to spot the shape he vaguely remembered, he moved deeper into his father's deserted rooms.

This suite of chambers was situated in the primary residence of the castle, higher up and on the other side of his tower. How had that come to be? He'd moved in there as a young teen, on his own, his father's silent disapproval louder than any spoken words. But as the prince, Rhydian had gotten away with it.

Had he known something was off with the state of affairs in Aneirin, and wanted to distance himself?

"Who am I kidding?" Rhydian sighed. He brushed golden brown hair off his forehead. "I was just a rebellious teen that wanted some privacy when I discovered my... ah, well. Anyway. Crown, crown... where do you dwell?"

The layout was grand, as befitting a monarch, much grander than his simple chamber. Thick tapestries of various mythical scenes spanned a couple of walls. Their jewel-toned colours had faded, yet they were much newer than the tattered relics in the castle proper. To his right, flanked by tables of pewter candle holders, a towering blue velvet curtained bed took up a sizable portion of the room. Beyond the bed, behind a curtain in matching blue velvet held back with a gold chord, sectioned off a separate chamber for dressing.

Rhydian stood at the foot of the bed, hands slack at his sides. The deep blue velvet and dark wood made the bed appear inviting, ready for wonderful dreams and other things, with one you loved.

He'd never sleep here.

There weren't very many memories of being in here at all, and those he did have were neutral at best. There were no cosy family gatherings by the massive red marble fireplace across the carpeted floor. In fact, the last time he'd been here, Rhydian had been about eight or so.

"A bonfire?" the little prince had queried, head tilted to the side.

In the royal bedchambers, Rhydian stood in his finest new boots and warm fur cloak behind his father. The king was clothed in shining brocade and shining boots before a tall mirror inside the dressing area. In readiness for some seasonal ceremony to be held that evening, the crown of Aneirin royalty rested atop brown hair only faintly streaked with grey. The object was a creation of solid yellow golden spokes, like a wild sunburst frozen in metal. Ice-blue eyes glinted in the bright light of six fat candles set around the dressing chamber, assessing his son's reflection.

"Yes."

Wide eyes shone with youthful curiosity. "To bring luck to the farms?"

His father's manservant approached with a cloak of nut brown fur.

"Yes," his father had murmured, arms held out as the servant, a black-haired man younger than the king, held up the cloak.

A fire to ensure the farms would do well, that the sun would come up each day? Of course it would. The boy had frowned, unfocused eyes on the stonework above.

Or would it?

"So it's magic?" wondered the young prince.

Out loud.

The following silence was marred only by the king's cloak dropping to the floor, a benign pooling of fur.

Startled, Rhydian's gaze met the servant's. The man's mouth hung open.

"You," the king began, then cleared his throat with a mild cough, "may go."

The servant swallowed at the king's dismissal. Then the man had backed out of the room, face pale, not meeting Rhydian's eyes. Rhydian's gaze slid to his father's. A trembling part of the boy's mind assessed the reflection. The bronze mirror added a warmth to the king's face lacking from the real man.

Smiling in the way lichen stuck to wet rocks along the river at the end of the wide, curved valley, the king turned from the mirror to face his son. Rhydian tried to take a step back, feet shifting with futile tremors.

The boy couldn't move.

"Rhydian."

"Yes, father?"

"Use that word again," his father's smile tightened, "and I shall have your horse fed to the street dogs of Aneirin."

Frozen in place, eyes wide, Rhydian nodded.

The prince knew which word the king had meant. But despite the many questions burning his tongue... To risk his tender old pony? He'd never said that word out loud again.

In fact, for the rest of the evening, the young prince hadn't said anything at all.

"Ah shit. My parents were a matched pair, weren't they?"

No answer came from the hushed space.

At least he'd turned out alright, hadn't he?

Idly, Rhydian rubbed his chest, ignoring the deep ache spreading a little further outwards from his heart each new, challenging day. He advanced deeper into the royal chamber, boots leaving the lush, if dusty, carpets behind for slate tiles.

In the furthest part of the primary space was access to two others, via a pair of painted screens. Both carried depictions of brightly coloured birds intermingled with purple flowers and leafy green shrubs. Behind the left panel was a narrow bathing chamber of pale marble and windows of thick glass. The panel to the right covered an opening into the windowless ceremonial dressing room.

Rhydian slipped behind the latter.

With the ache in his heart deepening, and the strain in his head making it hard to focus, the young king halted in the centre of the inner room. Fists clenched at his sides. Blunt fingernails dug into the faint sheen of sweat forming on his palms. He had yet to touch anything with his bare hands.

The light here was faint. Details were hard to make out. His eyesight was better than most, yet he cursed, realising he should have brought a lantern. There were no windows in this inner space, lest the daylight fade the splendid fabrics of all the dress robes hung under and around the circular expanse. There was no need for tapestries here, all walls covered in open shelves or supporting hooks and stands for the royal wardrobe. Here was a room of wasted cloth. Rhydian would never wear these clothes. His nose crinkled as he surveyed the packed room. A spicy aroma permeated the enclosed area here, an attempt to ward off moths, perhaps. Thinking of the powdered wings that had brushed past earlier, a sardonic grin twisted his lips. All of this could rot.

"Or is this an opportunity to create something out of this waste?"

Perhaps he could have these items dispersed amongst those still seeking refuge in the castle below. Even the townsfolk who hadn't taken part in the chaos on the ruined fields beyond the castle walls might benefit. His father had hardly worn these items, preferring to dress more simply in later life.

Almost daring himself to do it, Rhydian reached out a hand. Hesitant fingers caressed the opulent fabric of a deep, rust-coloured piece of cloth peeking out from layers of protective yellowed linen.

Even young Kyle's family might want some new fabric. The young boy was wearing his same patched up clothes, refusing to wear any of his older brother's clothing. Rhydian didn't blame him. So even if these fabrics were deemed too expensive by some to be used for playing in the mud, he didn't care.

It had been a wonder yesterday, rolling in the stable muck, laughing wildly with Aurelia under the vaguely amused glances of his head groom.

Until Wyll had appeared.

A deep throb of barely quelled anger in his guts pulsed. Wyll was clearly struggling to understand the fact that the army that had come for them in war was now welcomed into the castle with peace.

Rhydian had chased Wyll down.

"Why?" Rhydian had demanded of his friend, grabbing Wyll's arm and spinning him around.

"Why?" Wyll had laughed, eyes bloodshot, his normally shining hair matted with grease. He'd staggered back, pulling away. "Because you entertain monsters in our home!"

The man's shout had echoed across the courtyard, earning them the attention of dozens of pairs of eyes and ears. The burning anger in Rhydian's heart blazed for a moment, then died down almost immediately.

"Wyll," he said, clearly for all present. "The monsters were my parents."

It was the wrong thing to say.

Even as Wyll's cheeks flushed white, then red, Rhydian knew what the man's retort would be.

"Yes. And so, my *liege,* what does that make you?"

A flock of cawing crows had passed overhead, a shit poor omen if anyone read into that. A sad smile formed across Rhydian's face as a single charcoal black feather drifted on the chill breeze behind Wyll's scowling face. He had nothing to say to that. Wyll offered a mocking bow before striding off into the city. Guards snapped to attention as he passed, before sliding guilty glances to their king, left alone in the centre of the frigid courtyard.

Rhydian understood the man's venom.

He truly did.

But his people wanted him to be king, and in his heart he knew as king he *had* to welcome in his so-called enemy. Because he was acutely aware, more than any of them, about how both the Elves and the Humans had been deceived. Led into a war of lies by two magic wielders, both with violent and underhanded intentions.

The rust-red fabric felt oily to his trembling fingers.

"The last couple of decades," he whispered, "we've been cut off. An endless nightfall of lies, the lost dreams of something *better*."

It's like the people of Aneirin had lived in the dark while the rest of the world moved in daylight. What else was out there?

That question had been on his lips when he'd woken that morning. Rolling over, he'd been about to voice it out loud. But the far side of his bed was cold. Aurelia had left quietly without disturbing him. He appreciated that, letting him find rest where he could. It was a thrill to have her share his bed. Except after all that had happened, along with the troubling dreams that plagued him since, it made his heart race to wake to her absence.

Tousle-haired and groggy, Rhydian had lain there, face pressed into the sheets where Aurelia had lain against him for the few hours they had to spare together.

He inhaled with care, breathing in the remnants of her presence, eyes damp. Yes, along with shadows, the young Elven woman with magic had given him an unexpected gift.

Her love.

Against all odds, they had faced each other across layers of deceit, a cultural divide. And they had shared their love.

Aurelia had done the unthinkable for her people while on a mission ordained by a ruler filled with bitterness and lies. Hesitating at the last, Aurelia had gone through with it at Rhydian's behest. Not understanding how their hopeless situation could come good, he had risked everything for his people.

For her.

And somehow, it had worked.

Magic.

A force of power to be wielded for good, when a sacrifice was called for at exceptional risk. His life, for his people to wake up from a curse that held them separate from the rest of the continent.

Or a force to be wielded for evil, when the sacrifice should not have been called for in the first place. When a woman and a man filled with fear or greed had laid plans for a binding to insulate them from harm, that might never come.

Truths had been revealed, the curse had fallen. So had his father, his stranger of a mother, and too many innocent lives in the process.

But it had brought him Aurelia... Which in his heart of hearts only added to his guilt at being the son of monstrous magic users. A pair who had created the divide of their races to begin with.

The sudden ache for Aurelia's embrace hit him with such force it left him gasping.

The crown be damned for now.

Rhydian yanked on the rust red fabric, an abrupt tug that had the cape, jacket, whatever it was, pooling to the slate floor. The thing settled in the dust like his blood had lined the icy floor of his chamber only weeks earlier. The spicy aroma filled his senses. He wanted light and flowers instead. It had been a mistake to come here so soon.

"I don't want this," Rhydian hissed. His heart constricted painfully, head throbbing. "I can't do this."

Pushing blindly past the wood panel, he didn't give a shit about the fact a crash was left in his wake. The thing could shatter to sharp splinters for all he cared. He burst out of the royal chamber with the same disregard for the heavy doors, ignoring the loud heaving *thunk* they made as they slammed into the stone walls.

He ignored voices calling for him as he descended through the busy castle, food smells and voices assailing his senses. Rhydian dashed past an older servant in robes of pale blue, one hand raised to flag him down. He gave a wide berth to a group of young Elven warriors sorting a pile of armour on the grand steps in the main courtyard outside.

Aurelia.

The name pulsed like a provocative drumbeat in his heart.

Gods, where was she?

He hadn't seen her since last night. It was midday now, judging by the weak light and wet air below grey clouds as he rushed across the damp courtyard. His nostrils flared. The wide open space had a scent of ash about it. He wanted to wipe out the stench of old burning with fragrant blooms and towering pines instead.

Skidding through the stable doors, her favourite haunt of late, Rhydian's eyes adjusted with swift focus to the lantern light, a welcome glow compared to the wan daylight behind.

"Groom!"

Merion's head popped up over a stall door down the aisle, a twist of hay in his bushy beard.

"My liege? Are you —"

"Where's Aurelia?" asked the young king, lungs heaving.

Merion blinked, one hand reaching out to unclasp the stall door. "Gone, sire."

"Where?" Rhydian demanded, already backing towards the closest occupied stall. The pain in his head bit sharply now.

As sharp as the dagger that had slit his throat.

Aurelia!

Where are you?

Merion stepped out of the stall, palms held out as if dealing with a startled animal. The groom licked his lips, a frown marring his broad forehead.

"Sire, please —"

"I said gone where?!" It was a shout. Rhydian squinted, unsure why it hurt to breathe, why it hurt to think.

"She took a horse, sire, much earlier —"

"For fuck's sake! *Where*?"

"I don't know!" Merion exclaimed, beard trembling.

From the stall behind the bewildered groom, a second head popped up. It was the silver-haired Elven woman. Rhydian halted, the horse he'd urged from the nearest stall tossing its head with a concerned whinny. The Elf's chin rose as she said something he couldn't hear.

Disoriented, Rhydian blinked, the stable seeming to tilt around him, shapes and angels closing in. He didn't hear what she said. His ears felt like they were stuffed with soggy linen. But he read each word, words of dread dropping from the Elf's pink mouth.

"What?" he breathed, wanting to be sure.

The Elf examined him from top to toe. Tawny eyes squinted.

"The river."

What?

Gods, no!

Rhydian mounted the horse with an ungainly leap, without bridle or saddle. Man and beast left the castle at a gallop, soggy ash blowing on the frigid breeze in their wake.

The horse's hooves were swift as they thudded along the churned up road out from the city to the flattened fields, once lush farms. The beast was fast, but not fast enough.

He was close to the wide sweep of flowing water at the south end of the valley, close enough to catch the falling pop of purple fabric with his frenzied gaze.

Ahead, plunging like a dagger through the rain, a flash of purple released from the bridge, tumbling into the frigid currents of the river below.

He was a sobbing mess by the time he reached the bridge.

Pale blue eyes with their outer ring of sapphire blue were wild, clouded.

The lone figure on the bridge turned to him, frowning, mouth agape. He rode the horse right up to her, tumbling off the foaming animal, both man and horse heaving for air. It took only a moment for his arms to find her.

Too long, too long, his heartbeat pounding in his ears.

Firm arms pulled him close, lips pressed into his cheek as he wept. Aurelia was saying something. He couldn't tell what. He collapsed to his knees; the strength leaving him in a rush all at once. The floral scent of her hair calmed him only slightly. It wasn't enough, mixed as it was by ash and fresh rain.

"Aurelia," he wept, kissing her hair, her cheeks, her neck, "Aurelia…"

"Rhydian?"

"I saw the cloak!" he exclaimed, voice thick with tears. "Like in that ruined city, you fell… my dreams…"

"The city? Oh, hush —"

"I'm fine," he gasped, "…fine, you're fine, too…"

"Oh Rhydian," Aurelia said, her voice sweet against his ear, "Rhydian, it's okay, you're alright…"

She continued to hold him, leaning over and around him, as both their hearts made a kind of frantic dance within their chests, pressed to each other as if letting go was impossible. He squeezed harder, feeling the fabric of her thick wool shirt give way, the rain dampening his flesh.

"The cloak," he choked. "I saw it."

"Yes," said the sweet voice against his hot ear, "but not me this time."

Pulling away, Aurelia disengaged one arm from their tangled embrace. She pointed through the wooden supports, finger aimed downstream.

With the rain falling around them, they watched the once splendid cloak of amethyst, dark and sodden now, make its way towards the whirlpool downstream.

"I've given all I can…" voice barely audible above the water above and below, Rhydian hiccupped. "I thought I was ready! But…"

"But?"

"I… I don't think I've got anything left to offer…" he inhaled, snivelling, reluctant to speak. Knowing he must in order to let her inside his heart. "I gave them my life…"

Aurelia stiffened against him. Chilled hands grabbed his face. Green eyes bored into his. "I'm so sorry."

"Don't be. This isn't your fault. I panicked —"

"But I *am* sorry. I never said that about that fucking crystal dagger. It was cruel to use your help to find the blasted thing."

"I think I knew, though. Didn't I? What you could use it for, not how it would work, but what it could do?"

"But cruel, nonetheless. You can admit that."

"Cruel," Rhydian repeated, catching his breath at last.

A velvety nose nuzzled his neck. He swallowed, hiding from the curious beast. He shut his eyes tight against the wide expanse of ice blue waters, cloudy in parts as the temperature dropped. Trembling, he shut his senses to the wall of majestic trees past the bridge as they bore witness to his weakness.

"So much about this chaos is cruel," Aurelia said, wiping her cheek across his forehead. "My family isn't like this. Magic isn't strong in our blood, like your father and mother." Her voice was tender as she mused. "Is this what power does if you have too much? Wipe the board clear of all pieces until none but your own is standing?"

Rhydian was silent for a moment. "I think that's exactly how it is for some."

"Poor you," she murmured.

"Poor Fox," was his easy response.

There was a moment of thoughtful silence.

"Poor Owaen," they said at the same time.

Sniggering on the bridge together, they shivered as the wintry air blew past them in a sudden gust. His thin shirt did little to protect him against it.

"Crikey," Rhydian laughed, his cheeks damp as his heart slowed to a pace halfway normal. "How will Owaen cope with him... I mean with... that..." his voice faded, at a loss on how to describe Fox after all the recent revelations.

"Insufferable creature?" Aurelia supplied with a snort.

At that, Rhydian opened his eyes. He nodded with a weak laugh. At the sound, the tension in Aurelia lessened. She didn't let go, merely relaxed her arms a slight amount around his shoulders. Swallowing, he pulled away, him kneeling, sprawled on his boot heels. One foot was going numb. He winced, but didn't move. Aurelia was risen on her knees, wrapped around him, his shield for a little while at least.

The forest watched them from nearby. Even with the gloomy weather, his lips turning blue from the cold, the towering pines and their majestic companions filled him with quiet awe. The fear of losing Aurelia had calmed, leaving behind the dull thud in his head and the ache in his chest.

It felt like a shadow trying to worm its way from his guts into his heart, and from his heart into his throat.

Fuck.

He was beginning to suspect what the unwelcome, aching shadow may be. The idea of which scared him far more than all that had happened.

Gods, no.

Withdrawing one arm from around Aurelia's lower back, Rhydian pressed his shaking hand over his heart. He wanted to hide from the ache, from everything. He'd been cautiously optimistic once he returned home with Aurelia by his side. But along with those that demanded his time and attention, steely gazes followed him through the long days as well.

Red-rimmed blue eyes glared at the forest, the canopy lost to low clouds, and wondered if it were possible to get lost amongst their shadows, if the kingdom would carry on.

"Excuse me a moment, please." Extricating himself from the floral embrace, Rhydian stood up and turned away from Aurelia's questioning expression.

Tasting the forest in his senses, Rhydian faced his homeland. He considered the broad curve of the valley ahead, the rolling hills throughout, the red mountains of raw rock and the sprawling city built into the side of the highest peak to the left, the shallower cliffs and hills of shorter carpets of trees to the right. Rhydian's gaze drifted to examine the foregrounds, once lush farmlands that fed his people. A land now watered with their blood, along with the blood of the people of the one he loved.

He stepped away from Aurelia.

And roared.

In one great exhale, Rhydian cried his frustration, rage and grief to the valley, the sky, to the rivers beneath his boots. Breathless, he yelled, lungs gasping, throat raw. When he was done, the echoes of his pain disappeared into the churn of the frigid waters below. Heart heavy and lighter all at once, Rhydian sighed, shoulders heaving, hands clenched. He gazed straight up at the damp sky, head tilted back as far as he could go. The chilled air, rain and sticky ash landed in the lines of his face, lines he was sure had never been there until now.

Eyes stinging, he closed them to the threatening sky. Then, and only then, did Aurelia come forward behind him, her warm arms sliding around his waist, her face tucked into his neck. As one, they sank down together, dropping to their knees on the moss covered wet wood. He frowned at the fresh blood on the side of the bridge, but Aurelia spoke before he could enquire about it.

"Rhydian," Aurelia said tenderly, the sensation a soothing hum against his damp flesh. "Come to Lolihud with me."

He laughed, a bitter grimace twisting his lips as he blinked at the seemingly impenetrable forest. "Let's go."

"Ha. Not now. But one day."

"I'd like to see it," Rhydian said, turning on his knees. Wrapping his arms around her, Rhydian dropped his head to press his cheek against Aurelia's breasts. The fierce beat of her heart helped soothe his.

"I'd like to show it to you."

Rhydian nuzzled against her, his face rubbing against the floral spice of long, dark hair. "Could we run away? I know Owaen's brother is out there… but I am weary and I have only been king for a couple of weeks, no more."

Aurelia sighed against him. "Isn't that cowardly? Could you live with yourself?"

Fingers numb with chilly rain wiped damp hair from her creamy cheek. His foot was tingling. Rhydian pushed himself up and shook himself off. He offered Aurelia his hand, as well as a weak smile. She allowed him to pull her up.

"To get away from this place? And what my dear father and mother left us with?"

Aurelia pulled him to the rail, leaning a hip against it. She nodded, examining his expression, a calloused thumb wiping his right eye of its lingering tears. As she tended to him, Rhydian noticed a line of grey, limp furry shapes strung over the rail beside them. He blinked at the rabbits, his stomach rumbling.

"When I was a child," he said instead of answering her question, "the librarian, Lady Hywel, used to read me stories when father was away. Once, at the end of an epic featuring lost warriors, she told me about a secret, dark place. Where only brave kings dared to tread. She would tell me it was likely I'd need to be the most fearless king of all one day."

Rhydian paused. Aurelia kissed his neck tenderly in encouragement, the gentle bouquet scent of her clean hair filling his senses, grounding him.

"I used to think she meant going to a dark place, a physical place."

"You think she didn't?"

"Perhaps she did. But I feel like..." he rubbed the palm of his hand over his chest. Turning from the forest, Rhydian swung his gaze to the destroyed remnants of the fields that used to soothe him after strange dreams. "I feel like she might have meant something else instead."

Aurelia shifted against him, her lips finding his as he faced her once more. Her wandering hand found his hip, his belt, and stopped.

"What's this?"

A light tap marked one pocket of his leather riding pants.

"Oh, I was..."

There was a light pressure, as Aurelia freed the item from his clothing. She held it up between them. It was the head of the black arrow that she had used to strike his father down. He had thrown the shaft away, choosing to keep the point as a reminder of how *not* to be.

"Ah."

"I'd like to hurl this off the bridge, too," Aurelia declared, her green eyes grave.

"I'd like it if you didn't."

Large eyes questioned him coolly, fine eyebrows raised.

"I can't forget. About any of it. My family. Asking you to... and magic. How it can mess people up."

Green eyes softened. "I imagine you won't, even without this."

She slid the arrowhead back into his pocket with care, considering the tip was still sharp. Unable to answer, Rhydian held his forehead to hers, fighting the dread spreading within.

Please, no.

Not that.

13

Merion

Year 367
Aneirin Castle

"*Would you kill to save your life?*"

The troubling words had haunted Merion all day. They followed the groom like a quiet sigh amongst the icy drafts swirling through the royal stables. Today, and every day since the battle, the soothing and familiar comfort of menial tasks was nowhere to be found. Merion could not leave them behind since running into the young king that morning, with his sober words whispered in an otherwise silent place.

"*Would you kill to save your life? That's what we did.*"

With lengthening shadows falling across the cobbled yard beyond the open stable doors, Merion's beefy hands paused in their careful work. The pony against his side snorted. The groom's serious gaze stretched out over the stalls to the stable's main entrance.

It was a frigid afternoon. A rare patch of sun barely warmed the cobbles outside the stables. The main doors had been wedged open to allow stale air to escape, a fresh draught to replace it. The dismal weather that had settled over Aneirin since the chaos of the battle and subsequent aftermath had left the people both shivering and sour. There was talk of a feast being prepared now that the wounded were being rehoused from the hall into the many abandoned rooms of the ancient parts of the castle. Or, if they had another evening without rain, Merion had overheard the cooks talking about a series of spit roasts to be set up outside.

Unsure how he felt about that, Merion had continued his work as always, amongst the musk of horse and leather polish.

The groom's attention shifted from the doors to across the aisle.

A few well-shielded lanterns were lit to dispel some, if not all, of the shadows of the extensive building. With an occasional hiss, a charcoal brazier gave off an acceptable amount of warmth near the workbench filled with the tack waiting to be cleaned and refinished.

Bridles caked with mud.

Saddles caked with blood.

"Would you kill to save your life? That's what we did."

Merion's beard twitched as he chewed his lips, only half aware of a shadow obscuring the pale light at the doors for a moment.

His mind circled around the dried blood waiting to be wiped away from worn leather. The blood of two races. A symbol of life, either fresh crimson or flaking brown, blood that was the same colour and flowed equally, no matter if one had a little bit of magic infused amongst it.

"Master Groom?"

Leaning over and peering into the velvety mouth of Aurelia's pony, Merion stared at the row of blunt teeth, forcing himself to focus.

"Which stallion could we use, my sweet?" he murmured. "Surely Aurelia wouldn't take you away if you were in a delicate way. Hmm. When Blackthorn returns, perhaps —"

A throat cleared directly behind him.

"By the gods!" Merion blurted.

Jumping away from the stocky animal, he reeled around to face the stealthy visitor. His head tilted back.

And up.

Tawny eyes danced with amusement.

An imposing Elf, the tallest one he'd met so far, loomed over him. Her intensely verdant fur cape was thrown back off wide shoulders, with tanned, bare muscled arms crossed over the dark shirt covering an impressive chest. Merion brushed his hands across his oil stained apron, wondering how she'd slipped into the stall without him hearing.

"So I came to ask for a favour," said Bindy. White teeth flashed in a surreptitious grin. "But methinks I should ask you what you're up to first."

The groom swallowed, unable to explain what she had undoubtedly heard.

"Are you perhaps looking to expand your royal breeding stock?" she sniggered.

The blush spreading across ruddy cheeks from behind a twitching beard was impossible to miss.

"Ha!" Bindy clapped the speechless groom on his upper arm. "I *knew* it."

"I was simply —"

"Now, now," Bindy crooned as Merion stammered while rubbing his stinging arm. "Don't mind me. Good choice, by the way. This animal is a fine specimen of hardiness that your pampered city mares can only dream of."

The Elven woman gave the pony a resounding smack on its speckled rump. The animal's eyes rolled to Merion. His beard twitched in solidarity at the Elf's energetic greeting.

"Ah," Merion blustered. "Well..."

"Don't worry. I won't tell if you won't."

Merion blinked. "Won't tell what?"

Bindy stepped close. Merion's nostrils filled with the fresh scent of wild things.

"If you don't tell on me, that I'm asking for a good word," she said, her dappled eyes blazing.

"What?"

"Put in a good word for me, yeah?"

"A good word?" The groom repeated, not following.

"Yep. I won't tell Aurelia you're going to put a foal in her filly, right? And in return, you'll put in a good word for me."

A frown crossed Merion's face as the stocky pony's ears flicked back.

"With whom?" he asked, suspicious. It was the groom's turn to cross brawny arms over his stout chest.

The Elf glanced briefly at the open stable doors down the aisle, then back to Merion. Her silver braid, a weighty plait that could be the envy of many a horse, brushed against the groom's elbow as she leant over.

A name was whispered directly into Merion's ear.

"Oh!" The groom coughed into his fist, cheeks turned pink once more. "Well! Ah. I see."

Bindy took a step back. Her confidence faded, gathering into apprehensive expectancy. That alone, the earnestness of her request, released a little of the sadness that tugged at his heart.

All at once, Merion grinned.

He nodded.

With a crow of victory, tawny eyes sparkling, Bindy smacked his arm, the other one this time. As Merion spluttered, Bindy dashed out of the hay-strewn stall and back along the aisle, past curious horses as they snuffled about, out into the fading day. Merion had seen her about and knew her strange beauty would catch the eye of even the most resentful human soldiers, as she cut across the cobbles. It was unexpected of her to ask such a thing of him. But pleasing. Chuckling, Merion bent back over the pony.

It eyed him with its ears flicked well back.

"Hush, beauty," Merion soothed, running his hands over its flanks. It really was a superb animal.

What would Blackthorn's reaction be when the opinionated animal finally made it home?

At that, Merion's smile faded. Thinking of what strange things the king's horse might have seen, the groom's mind wandered anew to that morning.

Back to the words spoken with resentment, sadness, exposed softly to the stale air of the royal crypts.

Rhydian had been standing over the silent resting place of his beloved young friend when the groom had arrived to pay his own respects. A single lantern flickering at his boots lent a series of shadowy shapes playing across his listless face.

Freshly cut slabs of red stone were scattered nearby. They had been stacked ready for Chase's sarcophagus, but the pile had spilled during the deep tremor that had shaken the kingdom a week or so ago. A few cracks had appeared in the upper parts of the castle, but no major destruction had yet been reported.

After a cautious glance at the ceiling, lost in ancient shadows above, Merion surveyed the slabs as he approached, tasting dust on his tongue. Only one seemed to have sustained damage. One corner had broken away. He was struck silent at the sight of the deep red stone amongst the silence of the cavernous underground space, with its gloomy rows of sarcophagi leading off in all directions like a miniature, if morbid, stretch of city blocks.

"Would you kill to save your life?"

The gentle words spoken by the king caught Merion off guard as he set his own lantern down amongst the glittering dirt.

How the young man had heard him approach, Merion wasn't sure. Perhaps his boots crunching over the fresh off cuts of red stone and chips dropped from the soaring cavern roof. On reaching Rhydian's side, Merion chewed his beard. It was hard to sift through the confusing mix of emotions roiling in his guts.

Swallowing back the anger that simmered amongst it all, the groom cleared his throat.

"My king?"

"Would you, my dear groom," Rhydian said without looking at him, "choose violence to bring about an uneasy kind of peace?"

Pulling his wool cloak around him, Merion observed Chase's small body, wrapped in layers of linen. Unable to answer, he chose instead to recite a prayer to any of the gods who were listening.

A prayer for Chase.

For his king.

For all of them.

"My thoughts exactly," Rhydian murmured. "Although, Aurelia would likely tell me to harden up and —"

"Would she?" Merion interrupted, wiping his eyes with a stray twist of linen.

The king finally shifted his gaze to Merion. The young man's blue eyes were solemn, their normal bright hue blended with their darker outer ring in the wavering light at their feet.

"No." Rhydian hung his head as he exhaled, chin pressed to the matted fur at the collar of his cloak. "She'd tell me to feel. To do only what I can. To be my true self."

"Aurelia is an extraordinary woman," Merion chose his words carefully. "She cares deeply for her people. For you."

"She cares for all of us," Rhydian snapped, head rising to glare at the small body before them. But only a moment later, he drew in a shallow, trembling breath. "My apologies, I... I... She truly cares for all of us," he finished softly. "And she has certainly done more than her fair share to break open the shadows that cloaked us here for so long..." As the king's voice faded, one hand rubbed his throat with an absentminded gesture.

Far off across the cavern, the clack of small rocks dropping into the crypt broke the heavy silence.

Merion inhaled, the stale air laced with burial herbs, along with the fragrant oil from their flickering iron lanterns. He examined the rows of stony resting places, the shapes indistinct as they spread out into the gloom, people long lost to history and a curse that had made the kingdom's people forget.

Exhaling, the groom chose his words with care.

"Yesterday, Wyll should not have spoken so harshly, my king."

Merion almost missed Rhydian's flinch. The groom pressed on.

"You're a good man —"

"A good man could have stopped a battle," Rhydian interrupted, his voice thick and as bitter as the dust that drifted about the stale air. He used the edge of his cloak to wipe his nose. "A good man, a worthy king, could have found a way through. Without bloodshed."

"You *are* a worthy man, sire. There was little time for aught else."

"A better man could have prevented this," said the king, resting a clenched fist on the edge of Chase's resting place. "How did we miss such a snake in our home?"

"That blame appears to lie at the hands of Aurelia's friend... the, ah." Merion shifted awkwardly in his boots. "That mysterious man who was... also something else," he finished lamely.

There was magic in Merion's family. The few that remained in Aneirin kept the old lore alive at night by the fire.

But to say it out loud?

Dragon.

"Yes." Rhydian's gaze met the groom's as he spoke. A hand swiped through tousled golden brown hair. "Fox truly has a lot to answer for. And yet..."

Merion sighed, head tilted back as he chewed his beard as if he could make sense of the shadows that loomed above.

"That creature helped us, too."

Unable to speak for a moment, the king nodded in agreement.

"Yes," Rhydian's head bowing in a heavy sigh. "That creature truly did."

"From what I hear," Merion added, halting a little, "at significant cost."

"Yes." This was a whispered choke. "That's why I left when I did. I know it was wrong, but the magic that plagued us couldn't have been purged without him."

"Magic might be used for ill, but it can be used for good, too, sire. Your parents —"

"You speak to me of good magic, then mention my parents in the same breath?" Rhydian hissed. His eyes snapped to Merion's. "Magic exacerbated their selfish hearts. I am not worthy of this kingdom, offspring as I am of their ill-fated union." Rhydian snorted, tossing his head, a muscle twitching in his jaw. "I've never seen an example of a worthy king or queen. All I know now is unworthiness. So whose example shall I follow?"

As Rhydian rubbed his chest as if it pained him, eyes clouded and mouth set in a bitter line, Merion's hands tightened into fists. He didn't envy the young man at all. Merion had his own grief and loss to deal with.

But the king?

Indeed, whose example could he follow for the tasks that lay ahead?

Two races, recently at war, had lost their leaders to lies and magic.

Pieces had to be picked up and reassembled into some kind of unifying order.

Merion reached out gingerly, resting a hand on the king's tense shoulder. Together, they eyed the rows of silent dead, kings and queens long gone, their histories faded with the magic that had bound Aneirin for so long. Even with a little hoarded magic in his family, the groom couldn't quite remember who had come before Rhydian's parents.

"I remember you as a young lad, chasing after your father," Merion said quietly as the king fought his own inner turmoil. "He wasn't right in the heart. You were born with the unfortunate destiny of being his son. But by blood only, not by heart."

"But I *am* his blood. And I've got to make this right. For all of us."

"You will."

"Will I? I'm certainly trying." Rhydian made a strangled sort of noise. His voice dropped to a parched whisper. "But how can anyone forgive me? I can't forgive myself."

Merion looked up.

My king, he mouthed, his voice lost to an anger that was fading to the despair of their shared grief and loss.

A loss that was nakedly mirrored in the young man's tortured eyes.

"Merion."

"M-my king?"

"I'm wholly undeserving of this role."

"Oh, Rhydian," the groom sighed, giving the king's shoulder a firm squeeze before dropping his hand away. "We all feel that at some stage, lad."

"Lad. Huh." Rhydian cracked his neck. "Are you that much older to call me lad?"

"Ha. We are both man and lad, I think."

"Speaking of men and... lads." Rhydian sniffed, his voice thick. "I want to honour those fallen in battle. An honour roll, like those old inscriptions in plaques of bronze in the great hall."

Merion nodded, not trusting his voice to speak.

"The first name shall be Lord Cyrus," said the king, the words clipped, calm. Yet his hands trembled as he lay them palms down onto the cold slab before them. "Alongside him shall be Chase, son of Lorna and Dane."

Eyes on the unmoving, linen-wrapped figure of his murdered nephew, Merion nodded.

An honour roll was a gesture perfectly fitting for healing from the chaos.

Something a worthy man would do.

Proof that the young man in the frigid crypt was nothing like his father.

Letting Aurelia's pony be for now, Merion headed back to the main work area just inside the stable doors.

Outside, the frigid air had brought with it a fresh dump of freezing soot and ash. Expecting snow instead, something Merion hadn't seen in the kingdom of his birth since he was a lad, the ash added a curious dreariness to the wan afternoon. He grabbed a rag and a tin of polish, eyeing the piles of tack waiting for a turn to be cleansed.

Without a word, the groom grabbed the closest item and settled on a low three-legged stool.

Finished with his chores, Kyle had made himself a cushion of hay on the flagstones just inside the doors, close to one of the glowing braziers and its warmth. The solemn lad played a game with stones and lines, some complicated pattern that Merion was too old to comprehend.

Pressing a rag into a tin of thick oil, Merion spared a thought for his sister. The boy's mother hadn't left her cottage much at all, her youngest boy not far from her side as she lay in bed.

Furiously rubbing the pungent rag into the crease of a burnt brown saddle, the groom shook his head.

Why hadn't he made them all leave before the battle? Many of the townsfolk had. Not just in the recent weeks. Any families left with a spark of magic in their blood had sensed a shadow across the kingdom and left for the gods knew where. He knew by rumour there were some villages scattered along the valley, all the way to an ocean he had never seen with his own eyes. There was also talk of small settlements in the forest of massive trees, too. Aurelia's pony had come from one far to the south, near to where the snow and ice were a permanent fixture, apparently.

Even if it was too late, perhaps he'd take what was left of his family there?

Oil stained hands slowed, then stopped. As he listened to the gentle snuffles and snorts of the stable full of quietly munching horses, Merion grimaced.

No.

Despite the horror that had struck down his nephew, the king was still here, still trying to make amends.

Swallowing past the lump in his throat, Merion's brown eyes rose from the tarnished leather before him.

Kyle's mousey hair had fallen across his forehead in a messy flop as the lad shifted small, circular stones around. The pieces slid across lines on the parchment held down at the corners with three horseshoes. The fourth corner was held down by an old bread knife. Its time-worn point had been blunted to a nice curve that the groom sometimes used for scraping under hooves that carried too much muck.

Realising he'd put off the conversation long enough, Merion rose from his squat stool. Hefting the saddle onto one of the benches against the wall, the groom made his way to Kyle.

With a groan, Merion sat down on the flagstones by his nephew, wincing as he crossed his legs. After adjusting his apron with a dry creak over his thighs, he raked fingers through his beard.

"Kyle."

"Uncle." Not looking up, the boy continued to shift pebbles, adding them to the growing pile by his muddy boot.

Watching the stones move with graceful slides and shapes, the soft grey pieces ground smooth, Merion bit his lip. It was an effort to unclench his hands. He took a considered breath after clearing his throat. Twice.

"It's not your fault, lad."

A pebble slid out of order to its fellows as the boy's hands froze.

Ah, gods.

Merion's heart twisted in his chest.

"I know you were supposed to be helping Chase that day. There was naught you could do."

The stones began shifting in their neat lines once more. But their easy pattern was lost. Kyle gulped, and when he spoke, Merion had to lean forward to make out the words.

"Maybe I could have fought."

"No, lad," Merion said with a shake of his head. "Then your mam would be grieving you both. If you need to blame anyone, blame the king."

"The king?" The game ceased again.

Brown eyes, pained liquid gold by the lanterns scattered about, shone up at Merion's. The groom's heart twisted.

Chase had the same eyes.

"Is Rhydian really to blame for what happened?"

"No lad! No. The old king."

Understanding Kyle's wide-eyed devotion to Rhydian, Merion shook his head. He ran a hand through his beard again, the polish a pungent aroma in his nose.

"He showed us one face, but wore another behind closed doors," he added grimly.

Kyle blinked, absorbing this in silence.

Merion broke from the lad's intense stare only when a clatter from the cobbled yard outside interrupted.

A cart with four heavy duty wooden and iron-bound wheels had rolled to a stop outside the stables. As its two workhorses snorted from beyond the door, Wyll cracked his neck from his seat atop one of the many wooden barrels that sloshed in the back. Heavily armed with weapons, including a long sword and two knives at his hip, another was sheathed along at his thigh. The silver scabbard shone weakly atop his dark leather pants. The man's shoulder length hair, normally shiny, was a greasy kind of dull.

From his seat on the cold ground, Merion glowered. Wyll tossed his head and stood, grabbed the handrail, and swiftly hoisted himself over the side.

A flash of spectacular crimson caught Merion's eye. The driver had jumped down and was opening the back tailgate of the cart. He called out to Wyll. Wyll ignored him. Merion inwardly cursed.

Why had Wyll, of all people, been paired with an Elf for communal duties set by Rhydian and the Elders?

As if aware of Merion's inner dialogue, Wyll winked at the pair on the stable floor, an arrogant expression matching his overdone display of blades.

"Show me how to play this, yeah?" Merion said to Kyle, stopping beside the lad.

Kyle flicked a glance at his Uncle, too brief for Merion to read the emotions within. Innocent eyes that had seen too much for their tender years narrowed. But to the lad's credit, he bent back over the game and began to explain with words and gestures.

At a curse from the crimson-clad cart driver and a mocking laugh from Wyll, another stone missed its mark.

Merion ruffled Kyle's unruly hair.

"Don't worry about them, lad. Show me that move again?"

Instead of repeating his throw, Kyle set his handful of pebbles down. Uncle and nephew stared at each other over the complicated star pattern.

"Teach me to fight."

"What?" Merion blinked at his nephew with a wince. His bones protested at the icy stone below. His eyes found where Kyle's focus had gone.

At a frayed corner of the unrolled parchment, a short finger tapped the blunted bread knife.

Kyle shifted on his knees. "To protect my family."

Speechless, Merion swallowed. "Why, lad? I'm here for you. The soldiers are here for you."

It was the wrong thing to say, of course.

The lad's serious gaze met his uncle's with an even stare. "Like for Chase?"

Merion reeled back as if slapped. "Oh, Kyle —"

"Uncle." The lad's lower lip quivered. "I want to learn —"

"Learn what?"

Wyll had wandered over, leaving his partner to unload the barrels by himself. Merion grit his teeth. Wyll's tone was light, but his eyes bored into the groom's. He crouched down beside them.

The line between Merion's brows deepened.

Merion glanced at the cart, catching the Elf struggling with a barrel by himself. Water was sloshing over the top, and the Elf cursed.

Shaking his head, the groom stood up with a beleaguered sigh. Copying the groom to stand and hooking his thumbs into his weapons belt, Wyll repeated the question. His eyes stayed fixed on the groom.

"Learn what, lad?"

"To fight," mumbled Kyle from beneath them.

Wyll's appraising gaze shifted to the boy. Merion chewed at his beard, realising the boy had swept the pebbles to one side. The game was clearly over.

Wyll spared a bright smile for the boy as he crouched back down to rest on his haunches once more. He tucked a lock of Kyle's stray hair behind one ear.

"I'll teach you," Wyll said with more enthusiasm than was necessary. He slid a quick glance at the door and the lone Elf, then back to Merion over the boy's head with another irritating wink. "How about that? You never know when you need a worthy skill like that."

Merion schooled his face into a bland smile as Kyle whispered something.

"What was that, lad?" Wyll asked, leaning forward.

Sombre brown eyes glanced up, not at Wyll, but at his uncle.

"Okay," the boy mumbled.

"Hey, Wyll," called the Elf. Merion broke his nephew's stare and squinted at the door. The young Elf stood at the door, hands on his hips, beside two freshly unloaded barrels. "Are you going to help or what?"

"Or what?" Wyll mocked, his voice higher pitched. "I'm gonna teach my young friend here something. Surely your fancy blood can help you finish that yourself?"

In the uneasy silence, Merion inhaled with a deliberately long breath, attempting to let the familiar scent of horse and hay calm him.

It didn't work.

There was danger here. Merion had refused to go back to the city's temple, but perhaps he should have stayed to keep an ear out for things. He shifted in his boots, openly glaring at Wyll now.

"Are you sure you can teach that lad anything good right now?" Merion hissed under his breath.

"What do you mean?" Wyll asked, eyebrows raised in challenge. He pushed up, smirking at the Elf who was back to unloading the cart by himself. The young Elf was clearly strong, but the way the barrels of what appeared to be water sloshed about it was clearly an unsafe way to unload.

Before Merion could think of any way to call Wyll out in front of his nephew without troubling the lad further, light footsteps ran up to the stable doors.

"Feast tonight in the courtyard," puffed one of the two young women.

They were both dressed in thick layers of Aneirin's traditional grey wool. The shorter of the two, a bright eyed lass with golden hair poking out of her winter cap, smiled shyly at the Elf in the crimson cloak. Standing by the newly unloaded barrel, he bowed his head. The girl blinked at him. Then returned the gesture with a shy smile.

"All welcome," the golden-haired girl announced to the Elf. She turned back to the trio inside, not sensing the tension from the yard. "Courtesy of King Rhydian."

Sinking back to crouch by Kyle, Merion got in hastily before Wyll got a chance to disgrace them all.

"Thank you both," he said, loudly. "We'll be there."

Bobbing their heads, the lasses waved at them all, and left with a shared laugh.

"When we finish *our* work for the day," the Elf by the door muttered as he climbed back onto the cart to wrestle with another barrel. His words were muttered just loud enough for those inside the stable to hear.

The effect was immediate.

As a horse whinnied in greeting behind them from down the aisle in the shadows, it only half registered in the groom's ears. He was watching, aghast, as Wyll took a quick step towards the cart and cleared his throat with a sickeningly wet gathering of saliva.

The gob of spit spattered across the flagstones. It landed right under where the Elf was backing towards the tailgate with his latest haul. It was a sickening, petty insult, laid bare for the world to see.

Except, the Elf in the cart didn't.

"Awww," Wyll drawled. Shoulders raised, he held his hands out and palms up in a sarcastic gesture. "He missed my greeting."

The aroma of wild flowers reached Merion's nostrils. He had a moment to think *oh shit* as slim, leather-clad legs appeared in Merion's field of view.

As the groom peered up, a wool cloak was dropped amongst hay and scattered pebbles beside him.

"Don't worry," said Aurelia, the cheerful tone at odds with the ice in gleaming green eyes. "I didn't."

Spinning, Wyll balked, his eyes widening, mouth hanging open.

Striding straight past Merion and Kyle, the Elven woman halted directly in front of Wyll.

Then head-butted him in the face.

Wyll staggered back with a muted expletive, clutching his bloody nose.

Aurelia followed, step for step. Cursing, Merion sprung away, pulling Kyle up with him. Horses shifted in their stalls with an occasional whinny. They were joined by Wyll's thickly obscured cursing.

"Elven bitch!" he gasped, his voice thick, strained.

"I knew someone like you once," Aurelia hissed over the stream of profanities from Wyll's bloody mouth.

Teeth stained, Wyll sneered at her.

"And?" he choked out in a spray of crimson droplets, backing away as Aurelia circled him. "Where's your mate now?"

Retreating to the closest stall wall, Merion turned away, the boy struggling in his arms, as the Elf's shoulders rose and fell in a nonchalant shrug.

Aurelia's voice was cool. "We never found his body."

"You witchy cun —"

Aurelia charged.

Grabbing Wyll around the waist, head-butting him in the chest this time, Wyll's breath left him in a rush. Shocked eyes bugged as he was thrown back against the workbench. Merion winced. Not for Wyll, who deserved to be taken down a peg, or three, but for the saddle that got knocked to the floor. More horses neighed, calling out to each other. Hooves stamped and thudded with hollow booms against their stalls.

Wyll had mostly found his feet. Aurelia and he were brawling now, the Elf pummeling him while he shielded his face with one forearm, the other landing a sharp jab here and there.

On the cart outside, the Elf in crimson was staring at the brawling pair, his mouth open, eyes wide. Dragging his nephew away as the tussling and cursing pair edged closer, knocking over a large broom, Merion whistled loudly.

The Elf eyed him in surprise over the fighting duo.

"The king!" shouted Merion.

After a startled pause, the Elf sprang off the cart and sprinted toward the main hall.

The groom could only watch as Aurelia landed blow after blow. Her gaze had cleared, the anger gone, replaced by disgust.

Now that she had calmed down, it was clear from her precise, targeted punches that she knew what she was doing. No matter how many times Wyll tried to draw one of his knives or sword, Aurelia would trip him, so he had to fight for his balance.

Merion said a fast prayer to the gods that she kept it up until Rhydian arrived. The gods only knew what the king could do, but at least, Merion thought without shame, that it just wasn't his problem. He had Kyle to think of.

The boy had managed to wiggle down to the ground, and stood transfixed but close to his uncle, the groom's heavy hands on his shoulders, keeping him in place. The lad was trembling. So was Merion.

Aurelia's fists were bloody now, but her breathing was measured, her grunts quiet as her flesh connected with Wyll. On the other hand, Wyll shouted and cursed, frantic now, as Aurelia inflicted the superior amount of damage. Merion swore under his breath. Balanced and calm, Merion realised the Elf was causing as much damage as she could. The focus of her gaze showed she was holding back just enough so as to not knock the red-faced man out.

She was obviously toying with him.

Wyll slipped on some straw, landing on his arse with a thud. Green eyes met the groom's for a fleeting heartbeat as Aurelia smiled at Merion. He flinched. Her smile widened as she waited for Wyll to stagger to his feet. Then went back to taking the piss out of the huffing, wild man who could barely stand up. Two pairs of boots ground against stone and loose hay with a dry scraping that set Merion's teeth on edge.

"Elven," Wyll panted, "bitch —"

A bloody tooth landed on the slate with a muted clack as she landed her hardest blow yet across his jaw.

Eyes wide, Wyll gaped at the tiny, bloody thing. His horrified, animalistic gaze rose to Aurelia.

She hit him again.

He wobbled back. Then it was his turn to charge. A helpless one, everyone knew it.

Including Wyll.

At long last, while the fighters circled each other, the loud clanking of armed soldiers running towards the stables cut above the chaos. The shadows of about a dozen folk suddenly filled the door. At the sight of who was fighting whom, all of them stopped.

Except for one.

Rhydian dashed inside as Wyll, fury in his eyes, hair a mess, raised a bruised hand. Aurelia danced back with an ungraceful hop, half-shoved by Rhydian's desperate push, as he shouldered himself between them.

Which allowed Wyll's fist to connect with Rhydian's face.

In the shocked silence that followed the meaty smack, Kyle cried out, and Merion jerked him back from rushing to the king's aid. The bloodied man paused, swallowing as Rhydian stood there unmoved.

Then, without warning, Wyll erupted in a craze of fists and spat words of hate.

Two of the guards rushed forward, grabbing Wyll from behind about the waist and arms. Past reason, the red-faced man was swearing, his nose bloody and both lips split.

Eyeing him with distaste, Aurelia pushed her wild hair away from her face, wiping her mouth with the back of her hand. Apart from the inflamed skin of her forehead from her head-butting, she looked winded, but none the worse for wear.

"She's bewitched you!" Wyll shouted as he kicked about, the guards hauling him backwards towards the yard. "You are the king of Aneirin! Of the Aneirin *people!*"

The king, a mark blooming on his cheek, stood still amongst the kicked up hay and pebbles. Only his heaving shoulders betrayed the emotions at war within.

"Take him away," Rhydian hissed, his eyes shut tight.

His words were almost lost to the cursing of both Wyll as he struggled and shouted, and the guards pulling him out into the courtyard.

"Elven witch!" Wyll screamed, eyes red and wide. "All of you —"

"Shut him up and take him away," Rhydian ground out through gritted teeth. A fine layer of sweat had broken out on his pale cheeks, washed with the faint glow of the lanterns and orange brazier, which flared up with a crackle and hiss. Merion blinked at the sudden light until the struggling man found his voice once more.

"You traitor!" yelled Wyll vehemently as his boots slid about, fruitless in their quest for traction on the cobbles. "You —"

Pale blue eyes ringed with darker blue snapped open.

"I SAID TAKE HIM AWAY," roared Rhydian, clenched hands trembling.

At the thundered words, Wyll gave up the fight at last. With narrow eyes full of murder, he went limp. A guard shoved a cloth in the man's wide open mouth as they dragged him out of view.

"Rhydian," Aurelia murmured. She hoisted up her discarded cloak and shook it out with a flap. "I'm sorry, but your friend is a fucking dickhead."

"Aurelia, could you just…" said Rhydian, shaking his head and not looking at her, "just… please give me a movement."

The king shifted to face the aisle of concerned horses, one hand pinching the bridge of his nose, his other pressed flat over his chest.

Green eyes shot to Kyle, then to Merion. Breathing heavily, Merion shook his head at Aurelia. Stubbornly, she ignored him.

When Aurelia approached the king, her gaze unapologetic, Rhydian dropped trembling hands to his side. He refused to look at them. Still staring into the depths of the stables, his next words were unexpected.

"I need Lady Hywel," the young man mumbled, his voice raw. "I need that gods-cursed crown."

The groom's hands twitched on Kyle's thin shoulders. So much so that the lad twisted from staring at the king, to aim a wide-eyed stare up at his uncle.

Merion avoided the lad's gaze, his mind spinning at what he had just witnessed. Also from the king's abrupt remark.

Lady Hywel?

Merion chewed his beard. "The crown, m-my liege?"

"I need answers! I need the fu —" The young man broke off and spun to face them. His traumatized blue eyes blinked at Kyle. "That *blasted* crown," he corrected.

"Rhydian?" Aurelia queried, her flushed face full of concern for the anguished young man before them.

"The crown," Rhydian repeated. He shook his head, hands dropping away from his face. "A symbol to get everyone's attention to just… get along."

"Lady Hywel, you say…" Merion mumbled.

Halting her inspection of a torn sleeve, Aurelia frowned at the groom. Merion's beard bristled under her intense, green-eyed observation. Shifting in his boots, he glanced from Aurelia to the king.

The groom swallowed.

"The librarian?" he hedged.

"Yes." Rhydian's weary eyes met his.

"Um." Merion uttered one more prayer to any of the gods who might be listening whence they had disappeared. "About that…"

14

The Watcher

Year 367
Aneirin Castle

"**Y**ou can fight well. I saw it. But you're shit at that."

Davyn, his hair tinged with ginger in the early morning light, snorted at the Elven woman's blunt assessment. He waved a paint brush, dripping with pinkish paint, at the scrap of wood on the wonky easel in front of him.

"It's not that bad, is it?"

The Elf's laugh filled the out of the way, cobbled corner that Davyn had set up in.

Next to Davyn, with her long silver hair draped across her shoulder in a thick braid, the Elf looked like a mythical warrior. Dressed in a fur coat of shifting rich tones of turquoise and emerald green, she towered over Davyn by a full head like a colourful bird. There was no weapon at her hip or bow across her back, but a sturdy hilt protruded from the top of her fur-topped knee high boot.

Cheeks turning pink above his newly shorn off hair, Davyn shrugged.

"Your hair is different," the Elf commented, appraising him intently.

"Yeah." Davyn fiddled with his paintbrush. "I cut off my braid."

"Why?"

"It seemed right."

"For your fallen soldiers?" guessed the Elven woman.

"Yes. I chopped it off with my sword. Then buried it."

"You buried your sword?"

"My hair." They stood together, not speaking. After a while, Davyn held up the brush. He stared at it. "I don't feel like wearing my sword, though."

The tall Elf nodded. She tugged on her own long braid of hair.

"Maybe I should cut mine —"

"No!" Davyn exclaimed. He cleared his throat. "No. Your hair is a beautiful thing. We need more of that now."

Ignoring the Elven woman's gaze, Davyn set his paintbrush down. He produced a bronze flask from his own thick cloak of dark green wool. The flask was offered to the Elf first. A lean, muscled arm reached out to receive it. She took one swig, pulled the flask away to stare at it, eyebrows raised, shrugged, then took another long pull. As she wiped her mouth with the back of her hand, she examined the splotchy artwork with a thoughtful expression. Davyn shifted in his boots, taking the flask back and having a drink of his own.

The pair stood in a golden shaft of light that shone down into one of the castle's smaller inner wards. The air had a chill quality to it, the sky grey but for a few patches of bare sky allowing the weak daylight through. Positioned between the junction of a pair of thick walls, Davyn had set up an easel, a cracked flat fragment of wood on its shelf, with a few jars of paint on the cobbles at his boots. From the Watcher's lonely position on the wall above, it looked like Davyn was attempting to capture one of the castle's towers in the early light.

"Is it a dick?"

Davyn spat out his drink.

Above the figures, the Watcher's eyes widened at the Elf's question, while Davyn spluttered.

"What? No!" Davyn waved the flask at the stone buildings around them. "It's the castle. That's a tower."

"Sure." The Elf sniggered.

One long fingertip touched the tip of the phallic-looking shape on the plank of wood. Her muscled arm, bare under her cloak but for a brown leather greave, pulled away. Her fingertips rubbed together.

"It isn't finished," Davyn protested. His cheeks had changed from pink to bright red. "And it will take as long as it needs."

"A longer race to the finish can be more satisfying." A devious smile lit up the Elf's face. "I'm Bindy. Bindy Falkland."

"I know."

"Do you?" Pale eyebrows rose once more as she stared down her nose at the gaping man.

Clearing his throat, Davyn hastily tucked the flask away.

"What I meant was, Aurelia spoke of you. We haven't met properly yet." He held out his hand. The Elf eyed him for a beat before extending her own. Davyn winced as they shook hands, flexing his fingers as their palms parted. The Watcher tilted their head at the awestruck expression on the man's face. "I'm Davyn Blackwood."

The Elf's smile widened. "I know." After a cheeky wink of one tawny coloured eye, her bright smile faded. "You're friends with Wyll, yes? The sulking bastard who spits at our feet?"

To his credit, Davyn, for all of his clear infatuation with the taller woman, stood up straight, shoulders squared. "Well, considering the Elves came to wipe us out, that's a likely enough reaction, surely?"

Bindy nodded, tossing her thick braid of hair behind her shoulders. The Watcher was preoccupied for a moment with the way the tip reached beyond her waist. They dragged their eyes back to her face at her next words.

"Fair enough, painting warrior."

"I have never painted before," Davyn offered. He picked up the brush and scratched behind one ear with the handle tip. "But I found this stuff when cleaning out rooms for your... ah, friends."

The Elf stepped closer. Their shoulders touched. Her gaze was intent on Davyn's.

"I'm not ashamed of coming here, Davyn. Aneirin was trapped..." She pursed her lips, eyes narrow. "Aneirin still is, in a way. But I *am* ashamed of *how* it happened."

Unable to meet her gaze, Davyn fiddled with the paintbrush. "Good people died. At both the hands of your... ah..."

"Crazy bitch of a leader?" Bindy supplied, her tone helpful. "Clever cow. She had me fooled. The recent dead were denied an honourable end."

"Um, yes," Davyn allowed. The Watcher couldn't quite see his expression as the man gazed across the cobbled yard. A young girl was leading a cart laden with hay in the direction of the rear stables. "Good folk died at the hands of our previous k-king," his voice caught on the title, "as well."

The Watcher concentrated on not making a sound. The same raw emotions as heard in Davyn's voice twisted in the Watcher's guts, hot and constricting.

Man and Elf stood like that for a while, Davyn clearing his throat a few times. Without a word, Bindy fished for something in the pocket of her leather trousers. When she handed a small piece of rich, shimmering green cloth to Davyn, he wiped his eyes.

Allowing Davyn some semblance of privacy, Bindy slunk down into a crouch, squatting on her boot heels. She crossed her arms over her knees. With her chin resting on her forearm, her voice was muffled. The Watcher leaned out from the stone crenel to catch it.

"The things that are black-and-white choices for everyone else, the things we are supposed to reach for, the steps we are supposed to take before us," Bindy murmured, "that has never been my path."

His voice thick, Davyn dropped the green cloth from his face. "What was it like?"

Bindy tilted her head so her cheek rested where her chin had been. "What was what like?"

"The caves."

"Is that what you wanted to ask me about, the caves?"

Davyn's voice was soft. "Um. What was it that you were told about us...?"

Blowing out a hot puff of air that misted before her, Bindy blinked at Davyn, her gaze shrewd. Her nose scrunched as she pondered what to say. Her words surprised the Watcher. They weren't what they expected at all.

"Lolihud is a mining colony, Davyn. Did you know that?"

"No. I didn't."

"Our families have mined crystals down through the generations. Crystals for the dragons. And for us."

"There are more dragons?"

"Perhaps." Bindy's eyes opened one at a time. "Perhaps not."

"Oh. I see," Davyn said. But his pensive tone made it sound like he didn't see at all. The Watcher didn't understand Bindy's answer, either.

Bindy's fur-covered shoulders rose and fell.

"A while back, something happened, something violent that shook the earth and destroyed the origin of our magic, the glorious city of Baile Mara. Our dragon companions insisted we kept mining, so we did. Who were we to argue? But after a while, word came of more calamity. The great City of the Seers had also fallen."

Davyn remained silent. He shifted in his boots on the cobbles; the sun changing from gold to light honey across his hair and scruffy beard. The Elf went on.

"Word from the north died down. We sent warriors. None returned except for two. A brooding hero, clearly disturbed by the experience, his petite but vicious yellow-haired companion in tow. Both changed from the experience. They returned to the caves with some helpless guests, the Elder and a purple shit of a dragon. Two guilty souls who ended up leading us here." Bindy's voice grew bitter. "Lucky for Aneirin, it took us a while to get organised. Instead of mining crystals or hunting with Aurelia further south, I found myself training the youngsters. We were told, by those with power that was to be respected, that there was a deadly threat up north."

"Deadly threat," Davyn repeated "Us?"

"Mm."

Davyn crouched next to Bindy. He held up the damp cloth. Bindy waved it away.

"Keep it. A gift."

"Oh. Thank you." Davyn considered the cloth for a bit before sliding it into his shirtsleeve. He rubbed his thumb along his jawline, leaving a smudge of paint behind. Bindy smiled a moment before continuing.

"The Elder appeared with stories of those at fault for the chaos reigning beyond our icy home. Unfortunately, before the lies crumbled, we arrived."

"Aye," Davyn mumbled, "you sure did. And good folk died. Innocent folk."

Bindy had the integrity to look ashamed. The Watcher wiped their own eyes with their sleeve.

"People died," she agreed, fiddling with the tip of her silver and gold braid of hair. "The lies were exposed too late, and now the ashes and bones of both our people fertilise the farmlands that will feed you next time the seasons turn."

A choked noise escaped Davyn's throat. The Watcher couldn't tell if he was angry, or moved. The Watcher held their breath.

"I'm sorry," Bindy said quietly.

Davyn dropped his head to his chest. His head shook. The Watcher missed what he said, but Bindy leaned over and wrapped her arm around him, pressing her forehead to the side of his head.

"We are all sorry." Her words were muffled.

When she pulled back, her tawny eyes had turned solemn. The Watcher sniffled, then swiftly ducked down behind the crenel as those sad eyes flicked a glance to the Watcher's hiding spot. Bindy's voice was louder as she broke the morning silence.

"We realised we were wrong. A single Elf on a crazy bitch's fool errand, along with her human Prince, did what they could to expose the lies. But at significant cost."

There was silence for so long that only the sound of the cool breeze made any sort of noise as it whirled the stray wisps of hay into the corners of the yard.

Peering around the corner of reddish stone with caution, the Watcher blinked.

Another figure stood nearby. They stood within a shadow, far in the depths of the furthest arched gateway under the broad stone wall. The Watcher took a breath, then peered around the great stone that had maybe, or maybe not, shielded them from sad but shrewd tawny eyes.

"I doubt I will ever be sorry for coming here." Bindy said, pulling away from Davyn. "Only how."

Sniffling, Davyn raised his head. "I don't envy our young king."

"Hm. No. There are no short-term solutions to the chaos left in the wake of power hungry magic users." Bindy snorted. "Why do some folk need more than enough to live longer, see further, fuck better, and aim truer?" Spreading her arms, the Elf mimed knocking an arrow into a bow, releasing it.

"There really isn't a short-term way out of the trouble brewing here," Davyn agreed, rubbing his chest.

"I know of a fun way to cope, though."

"Oh?"

Bindy licked her bottom lip.

Davyn dropped his brush.

The man packed up his easel and paints with as much dignity as he could muster, despite the fresh paint down his chest. Bindy patted him on the back with a firm hand.

"Davyn." Her voice was soothing.

The man straightened, the easel clutched awkwardly against his chest.

"Y-yes?"

"Let's go get drunk."

With the pungent aroma of old horseshit in their nose, the Watcher crept along the stone wall towards an angry voice. They had followed the shadow as it slid off into the courtyard beyond the arch.

Not far off, a man cursed with startling vehemence. From a tucked away courtyard off the main forecourt of Aneirin Castle, words reverberated off blocks of stone.

Abruptly, the cursing culminated in a loud crack.

The watcher paused.

They had reason enough to be here, but they were sure their expression would give them away. Swallowing, the Watcher stepped around a pile of dried manure to creep forward another step. Holding their breath, they peered around the wall, ignoring the furious beat of a wild heart.

It wasn't from fear.

The sickening twist in their guts was from all-consuming rage.

Wyll was slumped against a low wooden shed, red faced and wild-eyed, his heavy black boots half unlaced. His hair was pulled away from his face in its usual plait, but its normal bright sheen was gone. Instead, Wyll looked greasy, tense. With his flushed face pointed to the sky, Wyll appeared to be a man of barely contained despair.

"Fucking Elves," he hissed, eyes closing. "Bastard scum. All of you will pay. Soon,"

Hands tightened into fists as the Watcher's breath caught at the words.

So the man was going ahead with whatever he and his drunken mates had planned?

But hadn't their king decreed a truce was now in effect? That the battle and death was a result of his own ill fated royal parents?

Such a thing was unthinkable, shameful, to let an enemy in the gates. But the king had stood before them all, and promised he would do better.

That he expected them all to do better.

They all had to do better in order to prevent any more needless deaths, like all that had happened in the chaos of war.

To prevent those that had died afterwards as well.

Unable to bite back the grief and rage that bubbled upwards from their guts, a choked sob escaped the Watcher's lips.

Wyll's eyes snapped open.

Finding the source of the desperate sound, Wyll's expression cleared.

"Oh, hello," he said, a sickly smile forcing its way across his face. His assessing gaze swept over his observer up then down. The man's dark gaze settled on the wide eyes that stared back, unflinching and focused. "You're angry too, huh?"

The Watcher shuffled the rest of the way around the corner. They nodded, a single, tentative bob.

Wyll tossed his head in solidarity, assuming the Watcher felt the same. Well, the Watcher *did* feel all the gut-wrenching emotions that were running across Wyll's face without restraint. But for entirely different reasons. The main reason was staring back in mistaken unity at the Watcher now.

Furled fists twitched with impotent fury.

"I'm going to do something about this mess. I'm going to make it right," Wyll announced, eyes clouded by anger.

The Watcher cleared their strained throat. "Me too."

15

Cas

Year 248, Cas at age 7
Baile Mara, City of the Sea

"I don't want magic."

Black sand seeped between Cas' bare toes. The gritty flow felt disgusting, yet Cas forced himself to remain where he was.

The scowling boy stood in the shallows of the southern beach, grimacing as chilled, frothy water lapped against his ankles. The combined scent of salt and ash coated the inside of his nostrils. He blinked, eyes irritated by the bright sun reflecting not off the shimmering black sand, but the sparkling, shifting waves. A fair way off the black shoreline of Baile Mara was the vast island with its perpetual veil of gaseous vapor, proudly rising from the deeper waters. Beyond that stretched the endless horizon, full of pirates, myth and possibilities.

Cas lowered his lids against the glare. The tips of his blonde lashes arched across his vision like minute silver sparks.

"I don't need it."

Overhead, seagulls called out to each other, with other shorebirds bobbing in the shallows offshore. The clear sky shone blue and gold. It was a perfect day to be down at the beach.

Cas' grimace showed otherwise.

The boy wondered if Wane had seen a giant squid yet with his friend's back at the docks of the city, far up the beach to his left. Small hands clenched, his feet sinking further into the ebony sand. He thought of his brother's green eyes, filled with pity, his father's blue gaze brimming with hope, then extinguished just as quick. Cas had nearly burned down one of the barns on their sprawling estate. Dismayed with the lack of magic in his blood, the angry little boy wasn't the least bit sorry that the stupid thing hadn't been razed to the ground.

After taking care of the barn, his father had found Cas throwing crumbs purloined from the kitchen to one of their peacocks in the formal garden. Approaching with caution, Illarion had appeared from a side gate to stand by his eldest boy. A tanned, muscular hand patted Cas' head.

"Cassie," father had said, voice bright with encouragement. "Don't worry lad."

Cas had eyed the magical quality of the bird's feathers, glittering and mythical. Like his eyes. But inside, there was no magic or special powers.

"I am not good at anything, even normal things, especially mathematics. I hate being different, father."

"Hush, now. Different can be good. Besides, you've got so much other potential, son."

Cas had chucked the rest of crumbs at the shimmering blue bird. The great tail of the bird shuddered, but the bird kept eating. Blonde head tilted up, Cas stared at the blonde man towering over him. "Like what?"

Startled by the intensity in his son's mismatched eyes, Illarion had taken a step back. The wide smile on his face turned brittle. He opened and closed his mouth a few times.

"Oh, you know," father had mumbled, his deep voice uncertain. "You... draw well."

After a moment, the young boy's eyes narrowed. "Thank you, father. I feel so much better now."

On the ebony beach, the boy stared at the haze of sky and horizon merging as one. Wane hadn't yet returned from his adventures in the city with his friends. The boy's lower lip quivered.

Escaping Evreth's supervision, Cas had slipped away to the crashing shore and lonely horizon.

What other potential did he have? The priests yelled at him for getting bored. But their lessons were things he already knew. Well, most of the time. Cas had overheard a prune faced older priest telling another that Cas was too smart for his own good.

What else could he do?

Drawing?

How could father say that, when the things he tried weren't received well at all?

Cas' latest creation, carved with an iron spike into the soft, pale sandstone of one of the estate's many fountains, had caused eye rolls and uproar all around. Mother had retreated to her greenhouse, father had shaken his head.

"I don't need magic."

His pitiful mantra was lost to the mild breeze that flapped at his shirt, a low mutter at odds with the grating cry of the gulls wheeling and turning above.

"I," Cas took a deep breath, letting it out in a rush, "do not need magic!"

The seabirds scattered. The boy smiled at this, pleased that his sudden yell had sent them screeching in all directions.

"But," he shouted, "I want it, if only to shut up every —"

Cas' voice died to a startled choke.

The brilliant day darkened with an abruptness that startled him.

A fantastically massive shadow blocked the sun for a beat, the jagged shape passing directly overhead with a great rush of displaced air. Accompanied by the deep thrum and thwack of expansive wings, the day went from calm to chaos in an instant. Staggering back, Cas shielded his gaze from the burning sun, trying to follow the shadow's path. Tripping on a washed up log, the boy landed on his arse in the damp sand. He attempted to scramble up, but the shadow caught him.

A dragon wheeled above.

Pushed back by both air and a wave of pressure beyond words or explanation, Cas was forced down into the sand, into the crashing waves. The back of his head hit another snag of driftwood with a *crack*. Waves hurtled over him as the shallows churned with the force of the dragon wheeling right overhead. Salt water burned his eyes, but he forced them open. The winged creature was a vision of shining scales, deadly talons, and bared teeth.

All in deep shades of darkest black.

Cas had never seen this dragon up close before. But he knew the man who was the two-legged version of the winged nightmare above.

"Stop it —"

His pitiful plea was drowned out by both the choking ocean as it bubbled over him, combined with the volatile pockets of shifting air. The weight on his chest increased and spluttering, Cas fought to stay conscious as oxygen became harder to find.

Heart racing and mind whirling in confusion, the boy pushed himself onto his stomach with great effort, pushing up onto his knees. Lurching upwards, he got to his feet as the dragon swooped above, taunting him with great gusts as the massive wings beat at the surrounding air.

The creature couldn't have been too close, could it? It felt like it from the crushing pressure bearing down on him. Cas had no idea why he was being targeted. All he could do was set off towards the cliffs. His bare feet sunk pathetically into the soft, damp sand as he ran for cover, a rocky shelf overhanging the beach.

He didn't make it.

The dragon circled back.

Cas was knocked flat into the sand once more.

The air thinned, and the loud beat of wings and a deafening roar filled his ears, his mind almost bursting with the pressure. Covering his head with thin arms, Cas pressed his face into the black, gritty sand. He wasn't afraid.

Fear didn't come close to the chilling, burning fire in his guts.

He was *furious*.

As the pressure at his back increased to pain, Cas roared into the damp sand.

The absence of what others had without effort, filled the chambers of his little boy's heart with a misery that he had no bearing to navigate with. His roar went on. Frustratingly, the closest he could comprehend out of the burning inadequacy that choked him was rage.

Small hands curled into the ebony grit that bit at his skin.

Magic should be a joy, a means to so many things, a way to adventure, discovery and unique ability.

Instead for him, magic was an absence that beat about his heart and mind with wings of resentment and despair.

Feeling the slightest decrease of crushing force, Cas flopped to his back and hollered at the sky. As if in answer, and all at once, the pressure on his chest ceased. With a mocking roar, the dragon soared away, heading south.

Panting, sobbing and extremely confused, Cas stared at the expansive dome of endless, desperate blues. The sun burned his eyes. He kept them open, blinking only when the sting became too great. How long he lay there, halfway between the crashing waves, now back to their normal outgoing tidal behaviour, and the soaring onyx cliffs, he didn't know.

It was only when a shadow blocked the sun directly above him that Cas came to.

The boy blinked, mismatched blue eyes swollen, lower lip refusing to tremble.

This shadow, now man sized, chuckled.

"Hello, Caspian," said Rook. White teeth flashed within a satisfied smile. "Enjoy your swim?"

The towering man was dressed in a tunic and long trousers of soft, colourless linen. A satchel of grey leather was slung over one arm, a way to carry clothes while travelling in his winged and scaled form. A piece of meat jerky was being chewed with contented amusement between evenly spaced teeth, while the boy glared.

Cas had sat up when Rook had found him, but refused to say anything. Crouching down close by, Rook tore off another bite. He glanced at the city beyond the boy, whose blonde hair was plastered to his skull. As his gaze lowered, he smirked at the boy's protruding lower lip.

Rook held up the twisted slice of dark red meat between them.

"Want some?"

Cas' lips thinned.

Rook snorted. After chewing and swallowing, the man grinned.

"At first I thought you were Wane," he said conversationally. "But then you shot me that flashing silver glare and I said to myself 'ah, here he is, the boy who everyone ignores'."

The boy in question said nothing. Resting his chin on folded knees, Cas wrapped soaked arms around wet shins. Recoiling at the sodden fabric, he flinched.

Rook laughed. "Am I wrong?"

Turning a little so the back of his head was facing Rook, Cas rested a damp cheek on his knees. The sensation was awful, sodden grit between two layers of skin. He swallowed the bile in his throat and concentrated on calming down his racing heart. A long sigh sounded from behind.

"I'm sorry for scaring you. I've had a day spent in my studio and needed to stretch my wings. I was only teasing —"

"I wasn't scared!" Cas snapped, spinning to face the smirking man.

"Sure, lad." Rook calmly took another bite of the jerky.

"I wasn't."

"I believe you."

Lower lip quivering, Cas eyed the man's hooded stare. Rook's long dark hair was reminiscent of the pirate folk, the eastern islanders, with their long shining locks of blue black. Yet his facial features were more similar to the people of Baile Mara.

The pair of them watched the tide crashing onto the beach in silence. With the threat gone, the shorebirds reappeared, gulls and even what looked like a great winged sea eagle soaring further offshore. Cas wondered if any of the feathers from the quills held in small freckled hands were ever from such a magnificent bird. Most likely not. He wondered what the librarian was up to, and if she'd find out what he'd done.

I don't care, he said under his breath.

Not far beyond the waves breaking on the shore, a gull landed on the calmer water with a landing far from graceful.

Small hands clenched the soaked fabric of his pants.

Actually, he did care, which confused him greatly.

"Are your parents here today?"

Pale eyebrows drew together. It was obvious that the beach was empty apart from a few tiny figures setting nets out, far off towards the city to their left. Cas shrugged and waved a hand at the deserted black sands.

"Thanks for that, Caspian." The sarcasm in Rook's voice was thick. "I meant up there." He pointed the last of his stick of dried meat at the cliffs behind them.

Cas rolled his eyes.

"Dragon got your tongue, lad?"

"No."

"Don't be mad. I was showing off. I'm sure you'll be the same one day."

"Ha."

"No?"

"You know I can't."

Rook considered the boy for a while before he spoke. "Are you sure about that?"

A trickle of unease ran along the back of Cas' thin neck. Turning to face Rook, Cas glared.

"Stop it."

"Stop what?"

"Teasing me. I don't like it."

"I'm not. I swear by all the old gods that there might be a way."

"How?"

Rook flicked a fleck of paint off of his knuckles, then waved his snack at the sheer cliffs of basalt and obsidian. "I've been here to research it on and off for years. It's going to be a long process, but I expect great things to come."

"How?"

The man grinned. "Because I'm smart. Greedy too. I want more."

"More magic?"

"Yes. Does that offend you?"

"I..." the boy shrugged. "I don't know."

"Magic isn't just a way to look young for longer or extend your life, lad. There's more to it."

"I know that!"

"Do you?"

Cas shrugged. "Magic might keep you young for a few extra decades, but I bet you'll age like a shriveled worm overnight once it runs out."

Choking back a laugh, Rook cleared his throat. "That *is* possible, hm. That's why I am looking for a way to increase the potency of the current process. Magic is more flexible than your esteemed parents realise, little shrimp. Perhaps there is hope for you yet." He pointed the last twist of dried meat at the boy. "Are you interested?"

"I'm not that smart." The boy tore his gaze from the breaking waves and narrowed his eyes at his unwelcome companion in challenge. "Or talented."

"I think you are." Hooded eyes shimmered. "Although not in the way your parents would hope."

"My parents..." Cas began. He swallowed. "Mother and father have no hope for me. None compared to Wane."

"See. You are smart. What you say is true. I think you are brighter beyond any other lad your age. I don't think they missed the mark with you at all."

Cas kicked some of the gritty sand around with his toes. He wondered where his boots were. He also wondered what the imposing man, with a heavy aura of secrets and dry amusement, wanted with him.

"I think Wane got magic in his blood," Rook continued under Cas' shrewd gaze, "and that you got something else."

The boy turned away from the man's sharp profile, biting back his smirk at a stray drop of green paint on the man's neck. He examined the horizon before them, navy meeting azure in a hazy line. Yet for all of his feigned indifference, it was impossible for Cas to ignore Rook's statement. The shame of it rang in his heart like a lead bell, dull and heavy, weighing him down.

Something sharp touched the little toe of his left foot. He flinched. It was a small crab, its shell a pattern of orange and pink splotches. Forcing himself to withstand the awful tickle of its exploratory poking, Cas hissed.

"I didn't get anything," he said eventually.

"You did."

"What."

"Cunning."

"I don't know what that word means."

"Yes, you do. Don't play coy because you want me to leave you to whatever sulk you have gotten yourself into out here."

"Get lost."

With an amused grunt, Rook didn't protest. He shoved the last of his jerky into his mouth, shouldered his pack and rose.

"Do the two special crystals glow when you see them?"

The question was so unexpected, Cas squinted up at the figure towering over him. "Huh?"

"When you are summoned to Hypatia's workroom, and those jagged blue-green eggs are out of their heated little nests for some fresh air," his mouth curled upwards at the corners, "are they glowing?"

Cas thought about it. "Yes."

Rook nodded. "Good."

"Is that important?"

"It is. They don't always glow."

"I…" Cas shrugged. "I like to look at them. But I don't know why they glow. It's something to do with the significant experiment about magic for everyone."

The tall man's smile was more of a baring of teeth. "Your parents aren't as interested in the common folk as they say they are, Caspian."

"So?"

"Your parents are interested in magic and knowledge for the sake of it. But their vision is so narrow, they've not realised something very important." Rook set off towards one of the carved sets of cliff stairs that would lead him to the top, far above. "Which is why I am on my way back here to find out how to make what your little boy's heart desires most."

Cas tossed his head. "I want toffee."

Rook's sharp bark of laughter startled a pair of seagulls wrangling a crab. They flew off for a beat before settling back to fight for their angry prize on the shore.

"Is that what you tell the pompous visitors from the castle when they come to check your mother's progress? To see how those two sparkling creations are coming along?"

Cas thought of the visitors that had been gathered last week.

"When who comes?" he muttered, feeling sullen.

Rook snorted. "The Elphin Royals, lad. Don't get cocky with me. You know what I'm talking about. The eggs."

Did he?

Turning to face the city, Cas wiped his nose. The castle along the highest terrace, not far from his family's estate, was a mass of spires and glinting gilded roofs.

Before he'd burned the barn, the rulers of this city had flocked to the Carter Estate for the alchemist's latest update. Cas didn't know how many there had been. All had stood around amongst the plants, workbenches, cages of animals, *oohing* and *ahhing* over the two chunky green crystals, decanted from their hot, smoking clay jars especially for the occasion. It had been noisy and stuffy.

What he did know was that he'd had to push through a crowd dressed in lush velvets and silks to get close to spot the glittering objects.

Before they were packed away once more to 'incubate'.

Whatever that meant.

A small man, auburn-haired and dressed in burnt red, had gasped as one crystal had gleamed for a moment. Cas's mother had laughed.

"They do that now and then," she mused. "They are quickening."

Wane had grabbed Cas by the wrist and pulled him away through the crowd, off to play pirates, before Cas had more of a chance to investigate.

Incubate.

Quickening.

Would his tutors tell him what those meant if he asked?

Here on the beach, a salty, slight breeze ruffling his hair, the boy stared at the black grains under his nails and grimaced. Likely not. Cas hardly paid attention, bored as he was by the histories he was forced to learn instead of battles and adventure. As back then, here too with Rook, the conversation which had been getting harder to follow was now almost indecipherable to the boy.

He knew what cunning meant, however.

Cas narrowed his stare at Rook's broad shoulders. "Why did you land down here?"

Rook paused a short way off. He glanced back, long hair shining as he tossed his head. "What?"

"Why didn't you land up there?" Cas pointed to the top of the sheer cliffs.

A slow smile spread across Rook's face, his eyes glinting in the burning daylight.

"See? Cunning."

"Why?"

"To let you know it's possible. One day, I will need your help."

"What? How?"

The man laughed, the sound a chilling, smug purr. "Someone saw it in their dreams, and their overflowing cup spilled it all to me."

"What do you mean?" Cas frowned, shielding his eyes from the glare. A gull passed overhead. A white splotch landed wetly on the black sand nearby. The boy's forehead wrinkled.

Rook pointed, with his finger now, to the cliffs. "I mean that your parents aren't the only alchemists out there. They *are* the ones with the most resources thanks to the royal family, yes. But others came before them. That rude, waspy little librarian knows —"

"Don't talk about her like that!" Cas jumped to his feet, lower lip trembling now. "If you say that again... I'm... I'm not going to help you!"

Rook eyed him in surprise. "Like that, is it? Hmm." He shrugged. "Whatever, lad. This is going to be a long process, so let's talk about the details in a few years, yeah?"

"I..." Cas rubbed his chest, unease rumbling his guts. "I don't need to talk to you."

"Not yet, true." Rook set off, laughing over one shoulder as he headed for the black stairs cut into the sheer black rock face. "But you will."

The boy didn't watch the man make his way to the steps that switched back and forth to the summit. Instead, he knelt in the damp sand, and picked up the crab that was investigating the impression left behind by Cas' bare foot.

The creature fit into his palm nicely.

It also made a pleasant crack as he crushed it, wincing as the shell bit into his skin. Opening his fingers, Cas scowled at the twitching remains.

He thought of Rook's words, that there might be a way for him.

No.

Mother was always right.

Father was, most of the time, too.

With a violent jerk, Cas flung the crushed crab away. It landed quite far off with a muted plonk. All that was left in his hand were grains of black sand. The boy grimaced at the ebony crescents left beneath ten neat fingernails.

"I'm sorry, little creature," he mumbled, "for you, there is no hope either."

Curiosity got the better of Cas.

Bored with his sulk by the beach, the boy had lasted about half an hour before stomping up the steep stone stairs.

Not because he wanted to see her, but to listen. Rook's words had been fairly simple, yet even then Cas had sensed a deeper meaning beneath. Feelings that went beyond words. An ache felt in the heart for things that would likely have been frowned upon if shared with Wane. Magic was for emergencies only, his father often repeated since Cas could remember. Usually when Wane had made things happen without warning.

Yet by the time Cas was crouched amongst the roots of a giant, twisted pine behind the library, the boy was rethinking his eavesdropping. First, he was bone-achingly cold. Normally not bothered by low temperatures, Cas was covered in a layer of sweat from his fast climb and evaporating seawater. The chilly breeze at the cliff's peak felt ten times as cool as sea level. Despite the scattered pines and other salt-weathered shrubs, the location was exposed to the elements.

Second, his feet were numb from the climb, his boots still either on the beach or in the waves as the tide was creeping in along the onyx shore. A trio of pinch-faced priests had emerged from one of the library's heavy wooden doors when Cas had peeped his head over the top step. Each one of them, dressed in long purple robes, had eyed him stonily. He'd rested on the steps before making a dash for the rear of the building, to catch his breath and rub the soles of his feet with numb fingers. On seeing the priests, he'd frozen. Then waved uneasily. Three sets of eyes had narrowed. Cas had taken advantage of a sudden gust of wind, blowing up three sets of purple robes, and made his dash past six pale legs while the priests had used words Cas wasn't allowed to.

Third, and this might have been the worst, was the fact that a giant owl was perched right above him. At the only rear window where he could finally hear indistinct murmurs from within, Cas was situated under a thickly foliaged pine. Trees were usually a significant source of delight and exploration. The massive splotches of bird crap and scatter of bloodied, iridescent blue feathers underneath this one said otherwise.

Cautiously peering up through the branches, Cas had spotted the well camouflaged culprit after a minute of searching. Large yellow eyes stared down at him from amongst wonderfully patterned feathers of brown and white.

"*Powerful Owl*," muttered the boy.

This rare find would, on most days, be a fantastic source of wonder.

However, the owl was in the process of digesting its previous evening's meal. Any little boy could be forgiven for whooping with delight at seeing a pinkish snake dangling from wickedly large yellow talons. Cas had nearly given himself away before he'd put two and two together. It wasn't a snake.

It was a strand of entrails.

From a peacock, most likely, considering the pretty blue feathers amongst the pine needles the boy crouched amongst.

"Ew," Cas breathed, both horrified and fascinated. Mindful of the disgusting detritus, he gathered a few feathers and stuffed them into his damp trouser pocket for later inspection.

One good thing about his position was the fact that the resinous pine needles were pleasantly fragrant, a pleasant change from the stinking natural gases of the city that reached the library on certain days. There was also a strange patch of what looked like red flowers further back from the cliff's edge amongst the trees. But he'd have to investigate those later. Perhaps with Wane, perhaps not. There was no time now as the murmurs beyond the thick glass grew louder.

Inside, near the back wall of maps and illustrations, Rook and Morgan were arguing.

Cas flicked one last suspicious glance at the brown and white owl overhead, watching as the yellow eyes closed.

Swallowing a snigger, Cas pressed closer to the stonework, the window's edge a mere finger's width from his cold shoulder. The bird's casual observation and subsequent dismissal reminded him so much of his mother that Cas almost burst into hysterical giggles. He shoved his hands over his mouth to stifle it. Cas pulled them away immediately, retching at the resinous taste of pine and bitter bird shit on his fingers. He would have to plunge back into the ocean after this. Spitting out a section of plant, the boy gagged.

Almost subconsciously, his ears pricked. Inside, the librarian hissed something about the temple and all the priests and priestesses. Rook's response was a dry laugh.

The boy risked a glance around the edge of the window. The pair of them were not far off inside. It was hard to judge how far along the library's back hallways they were, through the rippled glass and thick imperfections. Thankfully, neither figure faced the window. Cas hoped that neither would notice half of his face if they did. He was in the shadows more than they were, despite the golden glow of lanterns within.

"...scrolls," Rook was saying.

"No." Morgan shook her head, red hair turned burgundy from the low light.

"But we —"

"I said no. What you're proposing is madness, even for you. I've shared enough. Besides, I don't dream clearly any more —"

The tall man brushed his long hair back from his face. "I'm sure your wild field of poppies out there doesn't help much, hm?"

"Fuck off, Rook," the librarian hissed. She was carelessly shoving parchment into a niche on the closest shelf.

Cas grinned.

"Not today, little viper." Cas' grin vanished at the insult. Morgan didn't seem to care as Rook continued. "I am here because the Carter boy can be of help to us. Illarion himself had believed that, perhaps one day, there might be hope for the lad."

"What? And 'of help to us', you say? There is no us."

"Are you sure about that? Some of the other dragons and I know there is more to share, and you could certainly do with more. Why are you still here, librarian?"

Finally done with stuffing the parchment on the shelf, Morgan turned to face Rook.

"It doesn't matter."

"Why not?"

"Hypatia knows there is no hope."

"Hypatia isn't always right."

"Have you ever said that to her face, hm?"

Cas chewed on his bottom lip. Morgan's expression seemed to mirror what his own expression must have been.

No, you wouldn't say that to Hypatia Carter's face.

Grabbing a piece of cloth from a tunic pocket, the petite woman and tall man made their way closer to the window. Cas froze, instinct telling him movement would catch their eye, more than a sliver of a little boy's face. As he held his breath, a fresh mass of bird shit landed near his right foot. Stifling a scream of shock and disgust, Cas bit his tongue. Tasting blood amongst the resin on his lips, he winced. He concentrated on the conversation, not the bile rising in his dry, hot throat.

"Why are you so sure we can't help the lad at the same time?"

"Rook. Really, why are you doing this?"

Cas wanted to know, too. It sounded like Rook was pleading for help, for Cas? That couldn't be right, could it?

"You told me," the man drawled, leaning back against the shelves facing Cas, "that your dreams about the lad made you afraid."

What?

Morgan had dreamt of him? Why would that matter? Morgan muttered something under her breath, too quiet to hear. She put her cloth to work, angrily wiping the brass plaques along the wooden bookshelves.

"Morgan —"

"Rook," she said, voice louder and filled with ice. "Just leave him alone. He's been through enough, born to parents like that."

"Even if he wants it?"

"He's *seven*!"

Rook ignored the librarian's shout. The back of his head shifted against the scrolls as he stared at the beams above. "He reminds me so much of myself at that age."

"That's even worse, you sick fuck. He's just a boy."

Cas crossed his arms over his chest.

"Like I said, I know his type. Him and I are the same, born to brains with no heart. Don't blame me for the lack of nurture. Besides, after all you contributed, don't you think you should make amends —"

"I've done enough!"

Morgan's roar was so filled with desperation that Rook's head snapped down. He stood up straight.

"What is the real problem here, Morgan Rose?"

Dropping her forehead to the closest shelf. flaming hair swept over the librarian's cheeks to hide her face from view.

Cas held his breath.

What was happening? They were talking about magic, for those that didn't have it due to some immunity like himself. He'd figured that much out. But Morgan seemed set against it for reasons unknown.

"This..." Morgan's voice was soft. Ears alert, Cas heard every word. Not looking up from her hopeless pose, she waved a hand aimlessly at the scrolls and ephemera around them. "This is all going to..."

"To what?" Rook insisted, stepping close to her.

"...end."

Heart pounding, Cas closed his mouth.

"That bad huh, dreamer?" Rook murmured. He reached out a hand, as if to pat Morgan's shoulder.

Cas tensed until the hand dropped to the man's side. Morgan didn't realise or didn't care. Breathing shallower than normal, the boy ignored the blood in his mouth and the bird shit near his foot. He pressed closer to the glass, the uneven surface touching his nose with a cool caress.

"Everything here could be torn apart..."

Rook absorbed that for a moment. "So why haven't you left yet, hm?"

Turning her head to the side to stare at Rook, the librarian shrugged.

"You've got money and magic. Why stay if all is lost?"

Morgan mumbled a few words and pushed away from the shelf. She stared at the scrolls, running a dainty finger along the edge of a yellowed twist of parchment.

"Feeling guilty?" Rook said maliciously, eyes hooded and hidden from Cas' view.

"Fuck you and your scheming. I'll ..." Morgan's voice faded.

"You'll what? Tell them?" Rook sneered. "Go on. I dare you. The scientists and elite of Baile Mara are so far up their own arseholes they won't guess the scope of what they've missed. Both of us need to relocate to the City of the Seers by what you're saying. Energy transference goes way beyond the vision of this city. This city is a forest of magic waiting to be harvested, and yet we are dealing with the council and layers of half truths. They lord it like they own the trees of knowledge, towering above the common folk instead of really helping them."

Cas swallowed, trying to keep up.

"And you can?"

"Yes. There's a better way than creating a race of magic users by birth."

"How?"

"The ingestion of crystals, not just a vibrational therapy of being in close relation to them, is what we need to look at."

Morgan snorted.

Rook shook his head. "With their energy being directly absorbed, we can change how power is divvied up amongst —"

"You're madder than I thought. That will kill someone." Morgan stepped back from the shelf and headed towards the main workbench area. "Mad," she muttered until Cas couldn't hear her anymore.

"Undoubtedly." Grinning, Rook stepped up to the window. Too slowly, Cas whipped his head back. The man's voice was heavy with amusement. "But the risk of one desperate enough, well, who knows?"

Rook's laugh faded.

But not before a sharp nail tapped the glass.

Cas, with his back pressed against the library wall, tried to catch his breath. His heart was beating at what felt like a thousand wing flaps for every shaky inhale. The boy glanced up at the owl. Both yellow eyes, with large pupils of hollow depths, were fixed on his face.

He was only seven, as Morgan had rightly known. But Cas knew enough. He was desperate, wasn't he? Cas pictured Wane and how easily his little brother had lit a candle and run off without a care. His brother, loved by all, ending up with everything.

The boy closed his eyes.

"Maybe I won't show you those red flowers after all, brother," Cas muttered, bitterness choking him.

Cas loved his brother.

What he didn't love was how they differed.

Something slippery landed across his foot. Expecting to see more thick, white bird crap, Cas opened his eyes.

He yelped.

A long twist of peacock guts lay across his bare foot like a pink, fleshy rope.

Eyes bugging with horror, Cas kicked it away in a mad panic, racing for the stairs. A wordless scream remained trapped in his throat by will alone.

He'd never let a sound like that free.

Not where *she* could hear him.

16

Karlien

Year 367
Baile Mara, City of the Sea

Against the odds due to her ailing bloodline, Bathsheba Elphin had reached one hundred and seven hard lived years of age.

Notorious for blood sickness, short lives, accidents and basic ill-luck, a long life for an Elphin Royal was a celebration. Even more uncannily, Bathsheba woke early and toiled for the people still surviving within the crumbling city of Baile Mara.

According to stories handed down in hushed tones by relatives before they died, all far too young, Bathsheba was yet another rebel of the Elphin family. Along with being sharply clever that, even now, you couldn't get a trick past her, she was tenacious.

As soon as she was old enough, Bathsheba had worked the ruined farmlands of Baile Mara herself, to keep the populace alive after the chaos a little over a century ago. Her twisted hands finally prevented her at the age of one hundred and one.

'These useless fucking things' she had remarked of said appendages the last time she had tried, and failed, to hold a shovel.

Still salty about that, Bathsheba inspected the terraced land every month herself, nostrils flared at the indignity of watching from her golden litter while others toiled fertile ground. No one minded. Because while she was demanding, she was loved.

Bathsheba was a diligent leader, fair when the courts demanded justice, and extremely proud of that. A woman of short stature, silver hair, and lined face that only added to her regal beauty, her bright eyes were legendary. They were startling when first encountered.

With a halo of darker blue surrounding a paler iris, their piercing gaze brooked no fools. Bathsheba was also a wild flirt and could drink most robust men under the table.

Head spinning from honey-based liquor, Karlien pressed his lips to the column he'd wrapped his arms around. Bathsheba Elphin's outrageous statement at dinner that evening whirled around his mind.

In her own words, she was *'well respected, yet certainly not respectable.'*

"Not respectable," Karlien slurred, attempting to not slide down the stone column to the fissured flagstones of the lower ground hallway. "And not fair."

All week, Bathsheba Elhpin, Regent of Baile Mara, Karlien's great-grandmother, had refused to see him alone to discuss what had everyone in a tremendous tizz.

It wasn't unusual that Karlien and his grandmama went days without being able to talk privately. The indifferent prince would sit with scholars, taking *lessons* on running the city, while Bathsheba actually did.

Why did he never actually get to put into practice what he'd learnt? He had a few ideas about reorganising the deep-water docks, allocating them to oversea traders. But no, almost lost to the depths once, Baile Mare clung to tradition. So the deepest docks went to local ships who had no need of the deeper channels.

And people wondered why it had been hard to re-establish trade?

"That's fine. I don't care," Karlien said to the stone in front of his face.

He also piped up during one outdoor exercise, when city folk had been invited to comment on the wound that marred the rocky cliffs above the central city. Under the original royal residence of Baile Mara, a once impressive castle of black towers and golden domed roofs, lay a great gash in the hillside city. It was a gaping eyesore. When the capital had broken apart, half the royal castle had collapsed. Falling boulders of horrific size had caused the streets and buildings below it to fall away as well. Part of the castle grounds remained a jagged escarpment. Below that, lay a terrifyingly wide swathe of rock, earth and crushed buildings.

The mess, still very much present, was known as The Scar.

Above it, the only major part of the old royal castle that remained intact was a single black tower of polished stone, its golden roof a pretty mockery to the original complex of soaring halls and domes.

Most wanted The Scar to remain, a memory of power hungry scientists and how not to be. Karlien thought a memorial was fitting. But turning the area into a protected garden of wildflowers, shrubs would be much nicer. Perhaps even a vast wall of the destroyed rock, carved with the family names of all who were lost, would be a pleasant touch too.

"A park? Flowers? Ha!" had been the general consensus by the members of the city. The idea was panned, quickly forgotten. And so the scar remained.

"That's totally fine, too. Everything is fine. I don't care," Karlien repeated to the column he clung to.

What he *did* care about, was that it had been an entire week since his grandmama and he had some time to themselves. With her swollen hand caressing his curls, soothing his fears, whilst Bathsheba mused on what the previous night's dreams had borne.

So why the silence now, when the excited chattering and furtive glances of the courtiers and city councilors had only grown with the passing days? To make matters worse, a note had been delivered by Karlien's grumpy bodyguard, the silent grey wolf at his side. The prim handwriting grew a little more skeletal with each passing year, yet the words were perfectly clear.

'*Not yet, sweetheart.*

Keep dreaming.

See you at the garden party!

All my love,

Grandmama xoxo.'

"What the heck?" Karlien spluttered to the cool stone column. He stamped a silk-slippered foot. "I am the prince! I am her blood. Everyone else seems to know. Why can't she tell me?"

The stone didn't reply.

Karlien blinked, his glazed eyes unfocused. With the sound of running water in his ears, he noticed the stone seemed to be moving upwards. Or was he moving down? His soft, golden slippers were getting closer too.

"Hey! I'm talking to you. Stop moving."

"Princess."

"Oh. What happened?" Karlien mumbled, the hallway less focused. Somehow, he was now rather close to the cool floor of the central hallway of their estate's ground floor. The golden glow of a flickering beeswax candle in a gilded, recessed alcove to his left, hurt his eyes.

"Ouch! How *dare* you."

"Princess Karlie."

Ignoring Baek Hyeon's resigned sigh and poor understanding of the common language, the prince let go of the column. His rump made contact with the floor with a muted *thump*. Blearily, Karlien peered around to spot a girl peeking from behind Hyeon. The girl, about his age, was attractive, clad in a pretty, flowing dress of rich pinks and cream.

"Oh," said the drunken prince, pleased. He rose to his knees. "There you are. I'm going to have a drink from here, then we can go get naked, hmmm?"

'Here' was the little indoor fountain beneath the *rudely* flickering candle. The marble basin had seen better days, the golden spout bent, but the water was clear. Sometimes when ash fell outside on strong winds from the north, the outdoor fountains that still worked became clogged with soot. Indoor water sources were much better.

Most of the time.

"Don't drink that," the girl exclaimed as Karlien shuffled towards the fountain. With a breathy laugh, she emerged from behind Hyeon. "The pipes in this wing are dirty. It tastes weird."

"Hmp," Karlien sniffed. He plunged his fluttering hands into the basin, splashing equal amounts of water over his chin as into his open mouth.

The water was cool, but *did* smell strongly of minerals. Karlien flicked some water at the damaged flagstones under his knees, watching the drops seep into hundreds of minuscule fissures. Karlien halted from spreading sparkling drops around the recessed alcove and stared at his damp palms. The water hadn't hurt anyone.

Well, not as far as he knew.

Slicking down the wayward curls around his forehead, Karlien frowned. Should he have worn his little crown today? It was pretty, if somewhat lacking in glory. Yet it helped tame the unruly bangs about his face. Perhaps next time.

Smiling and feeling rather pleased with how the clear liquid tasted better than it smelled, the prince beamed at his two companions. He wobbled, but managed to stand up. Proud of himself, Karlien flicked the remaining droplets off his fingers onto Hyeon's pristine leather vest. The only response was a resigned exhale.

"See? I'm —" a hiccup interrupted his proclamation, "— just *fine*."

The girl, tall and willowy with lovely, long auburn hair, glanced sideways at Hyeon.

"But the water smells like the yellow smoke from the lower city."

Nostrils flaring, Hyeon tilted his head back with a long, suffering sigh. It looked like the man was rolling something around his tongue, jaw working hard.

As he wiped dripping lips, Karlien studied his 'bodyguard.'

Bodyguard.

Hmm.

That wasn't quite the right word, but his current state of inebriation couldn't quite make sense of the situation. He knew the man was serving a blood debt to the Elphin family. Which made him a sort of indentured servant.

From an island across the Eastern Sea, a place of fierce warriors, Baek Hyeon certainly gave credence to the myths and stories that circulated about the wild place. Along with the populace who lived between arid plains and icy mountains, strange creatures, like Hyeon's nameless wolf, were said to live amongst them.

Early on, when the young man had appeared at the royal residence to honour his family's debt, Karlien had asked if the missing dragons dwelt amongst them.

The expression on Hyeon's face had stopped Karlien from asking it again.

Although Karlien wondered, studying Hyeon's tattooed throat, perhaps the man hadn't understood? He still struggled with basic concepts. Especially when it came to dealing with his 'owner', for want of a better word, Karlien Elphin, Prince of Baile Mara.

Karlien continued to appraise the man before him, openly running his gaze over the man's golden skin, with its intricate cover of tattoos.

Chewing his lip, Karlien wondered why he still had to put up with the towering oaf. Baek Hyeon's kingdom of pirates hadn't attacked for years.

Was it still necessary?

"Yes." Hyeon's expression didn't change. Head tilted back, he remained glaring at the hall's lofty, shadowed ceiling. Only his interestingly full lips moved.

Karlien straightened.

Oh.

Perhaps he'd spoken out loud?

Just how drunk was he?

"Very."

It happened again!

The man's face remained as stony as the black rock that Baile Mara was built of. But his lips, they made lovely shapes. Karlien licked his own, wondering what other shapes they could make.

Hmmm.

Karlien concentrated on his next two words carefully, making sure he enunciated them clearly enough for Hyeon to understand.

"Blood debt," said the prince.

Hyeon's gaze dropped like basalt anchors, flecks of red clearly visible. From glaring at the frescoes above, shining, rich brown eyes sank to capture Karlien's wide blue stare, freezing the prince's gaze within unknowable, stormy depths.

The bodyguard stepped forward.

Karlien swallowed a squeak.

With the top of his golden copper head barely coming up to Hyeon's shoulders, the prince stepped back. The hallway spun slowly, his inebriation didn't quite explain the sudden flipping over of his stomach. Yet he didn't look away. Some sober slice of Karlien's soul, deeply hidden, was recklessly enjoying the open stare he was giving the normally intimidating man. With his imposing height and long black hair, worn loose but for a few delicate braids, his bodyguard cut an impressive figure amongst the brightly robed, shorter natives of Baile Mara.

Tonight, Hyeon was dressed in his usual dark grey wool vest, leather pants and heavy boots, his exposed skin covered in black tattoos. Some were thick, solid lines, like on his wrists and forearms, others small and intricate designs emerging above the laces of his collar. Karlien had never quite worked out what the patterns were. The skin beneath the black ink was an interesting dark, golden hue. Sun-touched warmth was set off by two twisted, rose gold torcs around the man's neck. The heavy decorative open ends of the metal rested just above sculptured muscles peeking through the man's white shirt.

Lost in contemplation, Karlien rose on his toes, swaying and exhaling honey-flavoured breath, to get a closer look.

Eyes closing for a brief moment, the tattooed man cracked a piece of candy loudly between his teeth.

"Prince Karlien? Are you okay?" The girl tossed her hair over one shoulder. "See! I told you the water wasn't good —"

"No," Hyeon interrupted. "Water... good."

Karlien and the girl glanced at him, two pairs of eyes wide.

"Agree with princess," Hyeon admitted eventually, dark brown eyes on Karlien's face.

Startled, the prince sank his backside to the edge of the basin, pretending to faint. His backside was damp, his sleeves too, but he didn't care.

"You agree with me!" Karlien laughed, delighted. The back of one hand pressed to his forehead, jewelled rings glinting. "Oh, that's rare. Thank you."

Hyeon spared a glance at their amused companion. "Water good. Tiny particles... ah, good for bones."

"Hang on," the girl said, eyes wide. "Forget the water."

"What?" Karlien sat up, shaking off water from his voluminous sleeve.

"I said forget the water. 'Princess'?" The girl queried, looking between them with less inebriated vision than her prince. She blinked, a smile forming on her red painted lips. "He still calls you that? Does Torres know? Oh, this is *fantastic*."

Karlien pouted, and the girl slapped Hyeon's shoulder. The bodyguard's eyes darkened immediately. Wordlessly, he glanced at where she touched him. The willowy girl stepped back, smiling more shrewdly now. Karlien sat up straighter, confused. Not far off, he caught sight of the wolf, seated calmly on sleek hind legs, watching with ears pricked forward. Shaking his head, Hyeon glared at the prince.

"Finish here."

"No."

"Princess is drunk."

"I am," Karlien said with a delicate hiccup, "not drunk."

A low growl rumbled from the man or wolf, the prince couldn't tell.

"By the old gods, princess —"

"Old gods? All the gods are old." The prince listened to the jitter of faint laughter drifting along the hall from the gardens outside. "Hey! Let's have a party on the beach."

The bodyguard crossed his arms over his chest as he spoke.

"Hyeon will escort Karlie alone to bed."

"No. You shall not."

"Ah, sure," the girl agreed quickly, interrupting them, with a curious glance between them. She tapped a pink-lacquered fingernail to her lips. "Huh. Who knew?"

"Who knew what?" Karlien shouted. Laughing, the girl turned on her heel to skip down the hall on silken slippers, back to the garden party from which he had snuck away. "I certainly don't! No one will tell me!"

"Come, princess."

"No."

Moving slowly because the long hallway seemed to grow longer as he watched, Karlien pushed himself up off the basin with exaggerated care. As he straightened, he caught sight of something carved into the inside rim of the marble. He shooed away the powerful hand that appeared from the side to prevent him from toppling over.

The prince bit his lip, studying the mark. Behind them, a group of servants were passing, carrying fresh jugs, the tallest young man steadying an ornate tray of cheese and fruit.

It was hard to see because his eyes couldn't quite get over the annoying dancing movements of the naked flame. Squinting, he bent over, hands holding tight to the other edge of the rim. There was a symbol etched without finesse. It looked like...

What was that?

"A dick and balls!" Karlien shouted, proud of deciphering the childlike rune.

Down the hall, a servant dropped one of the jugs. Beside him, Hyeon swore.

"Clumsy," admonished the prince, swaying slightly. He squinted along the passage.

The servants were frantically cleaning up spilt wine with barely suppressed laughter in their wake. The tallest boy was making a joke about a drunk whore with high-born partners all over the city. Louder laughs accompanied this, and someone dropped another item with a loud clang.

"Hmp. They shouldn't hire people who can't carry out simple tasks." Karlien straightened up, pointing at the hilarious carving. "Hyeon! Look at this!"

As Hyeon glared at the servants at the end of the hall, the wolf approached, a cold nose snuffling over Karlien's damp trousers.

Ringed fingers idly stroked the gigantic head, thick fur soft against his hands. Hesitantly, the wolf pressed closer, both of them not used to any shared affection between them. The giant beast was too wild, too foreign, but... Huh. Its fur was softer than expected. His fingers stoked deeper into the warm fur. Glancing up, Karlien examined Hyeon's profile. The man continued to scowl at the laughing group until they left. Once the chattering group had exited into the softly illuminated gardens, Hyeon's gaze slid back to the prince.

Karlien hiccupped.

Hmmm.

There really was a wash of crimson shifting amongst the rich, stormy brown impassive glare. Under his left eye was a minute brown mole Karlien had never noticed before. The prince smiled as he spotted something else. On the shining surface of Hyeon's eyes, two tiny reflections of Karlien's own face stared back.

"Oh," Karlien murmured with a slight tilt of his head, copper curls slipping over his shoulder. "I didn't realise. Your eyes are beautiful."

A sharp crack, candy shattering into even smaller pieces between his bodyguard's teeth, echoed around the hallway. Beside them, the trickle of water continued merrily, a pleasant accompaniment to the fresh evening air flowing in from open doors at the far end of the way. The wolf shook itself, backing away to sniff the base of the column the prince had slid down.

"Bed now." Another crack. "Princess drunk."

"Hm?" Karlien's eyes dropped to Hyeon's lips. As he watched, they thinned into a firm line.

"Now."

Karlien blushed, catching a whiff of boiled sugar. Blinking, he roused. His gaze rose to meet Hyeon's.

"Hm." He tapped a slippered toe to the flagstone. "No."

Very slowly and very calmly, Hyeon took a step forward. With nowhere to go, the prince stayed where he was, the marble basin's cool edge pressing into the back of his thighs. The prince lifted his chin. Unmoved and looking down his nose at Karlien, Hyeon smiled slowly.

"Here, I saw..." the bodyguard whispered, pausing just long enough for the prince's heart to miss a beat, "*mouse.*"

"What!" Karlien shrieked. "When?"

"Here. Today. Likely came for water."

Karlien's second screech had Hyeon's right eye twitch. "You let me drink it!"

"Mmm." Hyeon shrugged, blinking thoughtfully. "Could be more."

Gasping, Karlien grabbed Hyeon's hand and dragged him away, head spinning from both the liquor and the thought of drinking mouse water.

He sniffled. "Get me out of here! I'm going to be sick."

"Okay."

"Really sick!"

"Okay. We go quick."

"Wait!" The petite prince halted, his giant bodyguard crashing into him with a pained grunt. A heated word was hissed into Karlien's left ear.

"What."

Karlien bit his lip, turning his head a fraction. "I want more wine."

Nostrils flared close to the prince's wide-eyed stare.

Hyeon didn't let go of Karlien's arm the entire journey to the prince's bedchambers. He remained silent the whole way as Karlien pointed out in a cascade of hiccups that the wine cellars were in the other direction.

The wolf trailed after them, its dark, bushy tail wagging, ambling on broad paws that made no sound.

"Toxic blue," the girl whispered, smooth lips tickling the sensitive hollow behind his ear.

"What?" Karlien, panted in way of reply, grasping hands twisting her hair into sleek ropes. Beneath him, her laugh was a warm shudder.

He'd known the girl's name earlier at the feast. But like his past lovers come and gone for a brief interval of vague thrills, her name had slipped into the pile of forgotten names, a barely noticed mist within his mind.

With her long legs wrapped around his narrow waist, they were joined as one on his bed, sheets around their feet, the blankets somehow under their heads. Biting his lip in pleasure, Karlien wondered at that. Had the blankets moved, or were they the wrong way around on the bed? Also, how the heck was she here? She must have snuck to his chambers late in the evening.

Not bothered, Karlien traced her throat with his tongue, tasting jasmine and honey. Undulating his hips against her, the moan of their combined breaths added coiled patterns to the sweetly scented incense hanging about the chamber. The fire was out; the night was dark beyond the curtains, the single candle by the bed a lone spark of light in the gloom. Small, square tiles on the domed ceiling above glittered as the candle twitched with exhalations of pleasure.

"Your eyes," breathed the girl, drawing away. The candle's flickering slowed, stopping until it had become a frozen amber flame.

Karlien blinked, head turned to the side. The flame was the same colour as the amber eyes peering at him from a fur rug in a corner by the gilded door.

Curious.

"Your eyes..." the soft voice purred, "they look like the burning mist down by the northern wharves, all those tiny, twinkling blue lights... a blue sunset..."

"Ahh! Oh, move like that again... Wait, what? You're talking nonsense. Oh! Yes."

A soft laugh tickled his neck as Karlien pressed deeper, infinitely slowly, as she twisted around him with sensual stretches. The surrounding fur shifted. His restraint was rewarded with a pleased moan, blankets finding themselves pushed into tighter bunches against their passion-mussed hair.

"Blue lights... Where the earth is cracked and the seawater laps against toxic, luminescent shades of turquoise, sapphire and aquamarine, my little prince..."

"Oh," Karlien groaned, slowing his pace further still until their slick bodies ceased their slide against each other. Damp flesh melded together, tasting of salt and oil.

Despite the thick quality of the honeyed light around him, some clarity remained to the prince's thoughts. He knew his eyes *were* lovely. They were similar to his grandmama's, blue with an exquisite azure halo. The vague thought registered like a soft chime, deep beneath the pleasure spiralling up from his balls to flutter along his spine. He was enjoying himself, that was certain, his flesh never failing at the moment it was required, yet he wasn't as consumed as he always hoped to be. A hollowness remained within, despite the fun that kept disturbing dreams at bay.

Everything is fine, Karlien repeated to himself, refusing to let any unwelcome thoughts ruin his current activities. This was fun, not completely 'lose your head fun', but a nice way to spend an evening, nonetheless.

Laughing as the languid gratification built in intensity, Karlien captured the sweet lips of his bed partner, long hair sticking to damp flesh. He rolled from his side onto his back, pulling her along and holding her waist above. He was petite, but surprisingly strong. Yet as soon as the pleasant thought crossed his pleasure drunk mind, he was rolled over in turn. The room tilted, shadows shifted, and strange lights bloomed behind his eyes.

Laughing with surprise at being on top and not sure how it was working, Karlien threw his head back at the unfamiliar sensation, a strange morphing of pleasure from both his throbbing front and sensitive back. Lowering his head, he attempted to capture his partner's sweet lips. Toying with him, the girl hid her lips from him with a playful laugh. Beside them, the single flame's bright light faded, becoming only a faint glow. Newer lights, shifting jewel-toned colours, began forming from everywhere and nowhere.

"Gods," Karlien sighed as the room spun, his partner beginning to move beneath him with focused thrusts. "I'm more drunk than I thought. The room is full of jewels, haha..."

Firm hands pressed into his shoulder blades, blunt nails dragging down his back. Continuing to slide down, one hand kneaded his buttocks, the other drifting lower still, fingers probing along his crease.

Karlien gasped, surprised.

"Don't worry, little prince," the nameless girl murmured as his lips sought her peaked nipples, lost in the confusing lights and sensations. "I've got you."

"Little prince?" Karlien mumbled. "That's rude... I'm not little, I'm...ah!"

"Little..." she crooned, bucking beneath him in an oiled slide.

"Wait," he gasped as the sensations deepened, the eerie glow around them changing.

Where were the coloured lights coming from? Pressing an ear to the sweaty chest under his head, Karlien peered at the curtains. It was far too late for his crumbling city to be partying, wasn't it? Hyeon had dragged him to bed after scaring him with talk of monstrous mice and weird water hours ago, the girl running off, mirth in her eyes, back to the party.

Karlien's bloodshot eyes blinked.

The girl had gone.

A hand, powerfully firm yet exquisitely gentle, reached to cup his cheek.

"Little princess," Hyeon murmured, "stay with me."

Eyes wide, Karlien drew back, lips parted.

Below him was the flat, bare chest of a man, with a faint mat of hair scattered across black tattoos. A young man spread beneath him, slick with sweat and the evidence of their night's passion. Glowing in the candle's golden light, reddish brown eyes stared back, wide and unblinking.

"Oh," Karlien said, heart drumming wildly against his ribs.

"Karlie," Hyeon said, his unmistakable voice deep, heavy.

His bodyguard sat up with a pleased grunt as their flesh pressed close, melting against the other. Delirious, Karlien didn't know where or how or why or when. He laughed, eyes wide and shocked, the deep spaces within him taking notice of how his elation rose to meet his racing heart. This was fine! Really fine.

Actually... This was better than fine.

This was... what was this?

He'd never felt like this before at all.

"Hyeon," the prince groaned, lost to wonder. He was falling, his heart left somewhere above the clouds. He loved it. "Please. Don't tease me."

"Please?" Warm lips pressed against Karlien's closed lids, making their way to his flushed cheek, damp neck and the salty hollows of his throat.

"Hyeon, please..."

"Mmmm?"

"Please help."

Karlien's eyes snapped open.

He hadn't said that. Neither had Hyeon, moving with care and tenderness beneath and inside of him. It was wonderful, it was heavenly, and it was everything he needed and didn't know he craved.

An animalistic sniff from across the room indicated the wolf had raised its head.

"Please help us."

The single candle flame extinguished.

A rushing sound filled his ears, his breath, or his partner's breath, he wasn't sure. It may have been the roar of an ocean, the gust of a fierce wind.

"Move for me, Karlie," the voice urged, heavy with pleasure against Karlien's nape.

"What?" the prince asked, eyes heavy, head lolling, supported by thick fingers entwined within the hair at the back of his head.

"Anyone, please help us."

Confused, aroused beyond measure, the prince rolled his head to the side, his gaze coming to rest upon the heavy desk in the far alcove of his room. It was hard to understand at first how he could see it until his eyes focused. The sphere, normally a clear thing of inert quartz, was glowing.

Bright, flaming flames of blue illuminated opaque depths in waves of light.

"Hyeon," the prince breathed, hands sliding along tattoos to pull the man close. "Baek Hyeon... look."

"Karlie, Karlie," Hyeon said through tender kisses on the prince's sweating flesh, pressing into him from below, one hand sliding to grasp the ache in his front. Karlien gasped, pleasure and shock a sobering blanket of stillness settling over him, as tightness formed at the base of his spine, waves ready to crest.

"Please..." the prince choked out, room spinning, chamber full of voices, lights, sounds of pleasure.

The wolf pushed to its paws, eyes shining, reflecting blue, hackles raised as it surveyed the chamber. Its amber gaze stopped at the desk.

The prince, eyes thin blue slits, twisted to follow the animal's gaze.

What the heck?

"Hyeon, please, oh wait, ah, Hyeon..."

"Anyone! Are you there? Gods, if you're listening, help us —"

"Karlie, are you okay?"

Somehow, for some reason, Hyeon didn't seem aware of the sphere or what was happening. The quartz sphere, normally an inert pretty bauble, was alight with blue shapes and mist.

"Wait!" Karlien moaned, unsure what to do, his pleasure about to crest.

At his plea, the sphere glowed brighter in an intense burst, a fiery blue like when glittering minerals were thrown over open flames to change their colours, crowds gasping during festivities of gratitude under open skies in the summer.

The burst didn't last long.

"Please... given enough..." the voice pleaded, fainter than before, the sphere's frenzied colours dimming.

There was an urgent noise outside the chamber's ornate door.

The wolf whined, a soft noise of uncertainty as it stalked towards the desk.

"Stop!" Karlien shouted and gasped at once, pleasure frothing forth within and without, Hyeon beneath him with his head thrown back, silken braids stuck to his arms and chest, lost in his own release. "Wait! Stop! Oh, Hyeon, I'm —"

Outside the door, the noise became a deep thudding.

"Hyeon!"

As Hyeon's name burst from Karlien's lips, the ornate door burst open, the iron latch hanging off like a broken twig.

Armed with a sword in each hand, Hyeon stood in the open doorway, frantically taking in the room with a wild glance around. His eyes, not glowing, were wide and dark. His long hair fanning over his shoulders like a black, silken curtain, Hyeon's wild gaze settled on Karlien, kneeling in the centre of the bed.

Karlien, naked, freshly spent, Hyeon's name like a fresh wasp sting on his swollen lips, crouched there, unable to move. His fogged mind couldn't make sense of anything.

Except...

He looked down.

There was no one there.

Only twisted blankets, his nakedness, and the evidence of his passion over his bare thighs. A pink flush crept up Karlien's chest, warming his creamy cheeks to a bright crimson.

"Um," said the prince.

Carefully, Karlien dragged a corner of the nearest blanket to cover himself. He swallowed. His heart was skipping in wild, erratic beats.

"I..." Hyeon began and stopped. He cleared his throat and tried again. "I heard you say..."

Not looking up from the blanket, Karlien pointed to the desk, watching the sphere's dying, blue lights fading across the folds of fur in his lap. Unlike the wild, sensual moans branded into Karlien's memory, Hyeon's outburst was cutting.

"What the fuck?"

As they watched, the blue glow of the quartz sphere faded to naught. They were left in the dark together, the prince, the bodyguard, the wolf. Karlien shook his head, although Hyeon couldn't see.

"The voice... it wasn't me."

"Not... you?"

"It was... someone else," Karlien mumbled, glad for the darkness, his cheeks aflame. Was he going to vomit? His racing heart made it hard to tell if his guts were about to revolt or not.

"Has that happened before?"

"What?"

"The sphere."

"Oh." Karlien's shoulders slumped. "Yes. Once, I think. When I was little."

"Ah. Shall I remove it?"

"No. I... no. Leave it. It won't happen... it shouldn't repeat... Um, just leave it, please..." his voice faltered, disappearing on a trembling breath.

There was a metallic sound, the swords being propped against a wall. The soft change of cool air at Karlien's back had gooseflesh ripple along his arms. After a quiet murmur at his side, the candle by the bed reignited.

The lone flame lit the room with an intimate glimmer. Two pairs of eyes, faces with flushed cheeks, avoided the other.

"Um," said the prince, simple words suddenly hard to come by. "Is there magic," Karlien said, trying to think of anything to say, "in your family too?"

The pause was long and uncomfortable. Karlien peeked to his side. Hyeon was sharing a look with the wolf, who had retreated to guard the open door.

Eventually, the tall man swallowed, inhaling gently. He eyed Karlien with a complicated glance.

"Magic? A little."

"I see."

Another awkward pause filled the softly lit space between them. Hyeon cleared his throat.

"I'll sleep outside your door."

Normally, Hyeon was in the chambers across the way. Sparing a glance for the ornate door and its broken lock, Karlien nodded with one delicate bob of his chin.

"Okay."

Eyes straight ahead, Hyeon strode to the door. One hand dropped to gather his swords from an exposed portion of the cracked stone wall, the other to point behind him. Without hesitation, the wolf leapt across the room, landing on the bed with a heavy thud. Speechless, Karlien stared as Hyeon exited without another word, pulling the door behind him. It closed with a dull *whoosh*.

Struck dumb, Karlien stared at the back of the door, heart and mind consumed by what he had seen before it had closed. Shaking his head, he turned to the wolf. Amber eyes calmly watched for his reaction.

"Just for tonight," the prince allowed, heartbeat changing from apprehension to something else.

With an excited yip, the wolf flopped onto the mattress, one paw extended before it. Clearly it was in full agreement that, yes, this was a good thing if only *'just for tonight'*.

"Hmm," murmured the prince, eyes narrowing. A furry tail thumped the twisted sheets and furs.

Carefully maneuvering around the bulk of the grey beast, Karlien grabbed his discarded shirt and cleaned himself up as best he could without getting off the bed. Rearranging the sheets and blankets, it was with a disoriented sniff that Karlien slid into bed at last. The room felt hollow, emptier than usual.

He eyed the sphere, its shining curve of clear crystal only just reflecting the lone flame.

"I'm going to drop you into the sea," Karlien hissed. "Wicked thing."

As he knew it would, the sphere did nothing.

Wiggling beneath the blankets, the prince stared at the shadowed frescoes above. Who knows what would have happened if Hyeon hadn't arrived when he did? Would he have seen the man's face, if only in his imagination, as he came apart beneath? The idea was as frightening as it was fascinating.

With a thoughtful sigh, Karlien wiggled further down, settling only when his feet touched a warm, heavy weight at the foot of his bed. A soft, rhythmic thumping filled the silence. A happy canine sigh mimicked his.

Karlien, hair mussed and blue-ringed-blue eyes only just exposed above his blankets, peeped at the door.

"If I get lost in a dream, the wolf is here. Everything is fine."

Putting the strangeness of the evening's events aside, he no longer had to wonder about what designs Hyeon's tattoos comprised. Karlien bit his lower lip. With no clothes at all to obscure the magnificent view, they had been on full display, lit by the fading blue light of a mystical artefact, later by a single candle reignited with foreign magic.

The prince stretched his toes, the warm body at his feet shifting slightly with a contented huff. With his mind full of fierce waves, ornate ships, sea monsters and bizarre symbols outlined in midnight ink, he spared another glance to the ornately gilded wood.

"Blood debt," said the prince, loudly.

The door stayed firmly shut.

17

Fox

Year 367
The Forest

Cool fingertips fiddled with fragments of green crystal hanging from two metal chains.

The shards had been bobbing against Fox's shirt in time with the horse's gait along the forest path, a kind of syncopated rhythm to his own slow heart. Earlier, he realised he had forgotten to check the horse's name. It was certainly a pretty animal, with a warm chestnut coat, but so much had happened that a simple name had slipped his mind. The past week had certainly passed by in a blur. So Fox had nicknamed it Willow, for its graceful legs. That was good enough for now.

Other things were not so favorable.

Beneath trees that covered the overgrown dirt road with low-hanging branches, deep green foliage heavy with crisp morning dew, Fox inhaled with contrived calm. Black eyes flecked with gold were thoughtful under heavy lids, reflecting the dappled light as they passed through shafts of light. The scent of damp ash and flourishing moss filled his senses. Fond memories of wildfire in the north accompanied the intense bouquet, comforting Fox in a way that a young Elf might find solace in an old blanket held close at night. The forest path held a kind of soothing balm against the frustrating events of the past night and day.

But it wasn't enough.

Further along the path ahead, Owaen cursed under his breath.

Glinting black eyes opened fully, one lid rising at a time.

Owaen sat hunched in his saddle as his horse passed under a lichen covered branch sagging low over the uneven road. The fur of his cloak, almost the same colour as his white blonde hair, was pulled high. The Elf was riding the least sensible of Rhydian's two horses, the opinionated battle trained horse.

Fox gnawed at his bottom lip. Blackthorn was a beautiful animal. There was no doubt about it. But that horse was too highly strung for his waspish lack of patience. The horse actually reminded him of someone. He just couldn't think of who.

The more important matter for now, though, was that his lover wasn't talking to him.

After a day of brooding, it had only been while packing up their rough camp that morning, that Owaen had broken his extended silence.

After relieving himself against a tree, one of the many welcome conveniences of being a man, Fox was passing the black warhorse.

Blackthorn had seen a chance and taken it.

Sensing the snapping of horse teeth, Fox had cursed and whirled around.

Thankfully for one of them, Owaen had turned up in time to grab Fox's raised hand. Jerking Fox to face him, Owaen's pale eyebrows were bunched low over deep, forest green eyes.

"Don't," Owaen had snapped.

"Blackthorn bit me!" Fox yelled, dark eyes flinty, furtively masking how easily he leant into Owaen's warmth. Yanking his arm free, Fox flicked a lock of black hair off his forehead with a cavalier toss of his head. "I wasn't really going to —"

Only a fraction away, green eyes narrowed.

"Weren't you?"

"So." Fox's nostrils flared, dismissing the question. "Are you talking to me now?"

Owaen had glared at Fox first, and then at the arrogant horse.

Muttering under his breath, the blonde Elf turned and stalked into the rustling trees.

Now, with Willow following Blackthorn's prudent trail over moss and tumbled rocks along the old road south east, Fox let his breath out in a huff.

An obnoxious one.

In front, shadows flashed across blonde hair as Owaen shook his head. As if sensing his rider's mood, the black horse picked up the pace.

Releasing the shards of crystal, Fox let his hand fall to his thigh. It could have been a pleasant ride, here, far from worry, from intrigue, from people. If the world wasn't at risk of Owaen's mad brother running loose with stolen magic.

That was one reason Owaen was keeping to himself.

The other was that Fox had known for a while, a *long* while, something he knew would break Owaen's heart.

He'd withheld the fact that Owaen's parents were directly responsible for the loss of Owaen's childhood home, Baile Mara.

So, yes, Owaen *did* have things to be upset about. But he'd refused to pay any attention to Fox since finding out what despicable people his parents had been. And truly, the actual time they had spent together was rather short. Fox had worn another face when he'd realised who Owaen was, and where he fit into the mystery of Fox's own past. Yet it had seemed the right time to share his knowledge about Hypatia and Illarion Carter. Owaen certainly deserved to know and had asked Fox directly. But the Elf had gone into a kind of shock when Fox had obliged to share what he knew.

Their passionate reunion in the Carter's cottage had been exquisite, but far too short-lived because of more crazed magic users who couldn't just leave things be.

"I should have kept my mouth shut," Fox muttered as a hand rubbed his thigh.

His broken leg no longer ached, but the bone was still sensitive. Since snapping it not long before when moving too fast to realise what he was doing, catching Aurelia from yet another ridiculous disaster, Fox had healed it as best he could.

It hadn't always been possible to bind his magic with flesh and blood in the art of healing. Being able to mend a tiny Owl's wing was an unexpected cause for concentration. Far easier was tearing apart muscle, bone, scales and wings. The past few years of relative solitude in the caves of Lolihud had been interesting. Perhaps that's why the dragons had invested so much time clucking over his youth like watchful hens, pecking away to mold him into their desired form.

Blinking at the dappled light overhead, Fox tilted his head back, lost in thought.

They had wanted so much from him. As if he'd had no heart or will of his own, and would simply be a vessel of magic to use how they wished. It seemed likely they wanted to spend his magic on whatever they desired if he hadn't broken free of their claws. On creating a perfect world for them, without answering to anyone. Spending his magic like coins from a purse, but not a bottomless one. Shadow Light had certainly tried to push how much magic Fox could contain to the limit. Unlike their own limited crystal infused energy, as a young dragon, his power had been considered unlimited by the others.

Letting Willow find its way over a slippery patch of barely there road, Fox eyed the dense, rippling canopy overhead.

Unlimited.

That wasn't true at all, though, was it?

Thinking of how good it felt to force his way into Shadow Light's chest, like a frantic parasite digging for fertile tissues and flesh to feast upon, Fox grinned at Owaen's broad shoulders ahead. The memory of ripping out a still-beating heart, severing arteries, sinew, fat and muscle, with hands and ribbons of unleashed magic, would never leave him.

His smile faded, pale pink lips thinning to their usual unimpressed position.

As pleasant as that memory was, it would never replace the recollection of the wails of Elven innocents. Poor souls sacrificed so that a dragon, who once went by the name of Skye, could be forced into some kind of ideal creature that other dragons could use as they wished.

Black and gold eyes narrowed.

Ripping out Shadow Light's heart had at least allowed Fox to present it to his lover as both revenge for himself, and as an apology of sorts. For the way he had treated Owaen, for realising that what Fox knew about Owaen's parents would come to light one day. Unfortunately, that day had come far too soon.

He wasn't really sorry for his actions, of course. Yet as Fox had hesitantly shared what he knew of how the once revered alchemist's of Baile Mara had caused the death of their city and countless lives, Fox had to wonder. Perhaps, just maybe, he could approach certain challenges with more care. The shock in Owaen's eyes had humbled Fox, acutely aware of his own cold, reactive nature. Fox had reached out with a futile hand, but the Elf had simply stood up, blinked down at Fox, before quietly slipping inside the cabin to be alone.

It wasn't Fox's fault that he kept matters close to his heart.

There was simply too much to share.

When Owaen, shocked into silence by Fox's news, had got up without a word and gone inside, Fox had followed after a while. He was still naked from dozing in the weak sun, but the sound of crashing and thumping had him rise, expecting to see his lover amidst a pile of broken furniture. He had paused on the step leading into the cabin's open door.

Instead, Owaen had canvas sacks laid out, chests and cupboard doors thrown open.

"What are you doing?" Fox had asked cautiously from the doorway.

"What does it look like?" Owaen had bit back whilst wrestling with a fur blanket.

The fine fur was at risk of losing tufts as he pounded it into a vaguely folded mess. With a frustrated grunt, this was chucked into the pile. Black and gold eyes followed the mist of floating dust motes as other objects were thrown haphazardly into a couple of sacks on the floorboards.

"So soon?" Fox insisted.

"Yes. There is nothing left for me here."

After an iron kettle was dropped with a clunk into the closest sack, Owaen strode towards Fox. He stopped at the door.

"Excuse me," said the Elf with deceptive politeness.

Fox blinked, stepping away and off the shallow step, thinking the Elf wanted to pass.

Instead, the door had been slammed in his face.

Dropping his face into his tingling hands, hands that wanted to turn the wonderfully solid door into even lovelier little splinters, Fox had counted to ten.

Then twenty.

Turning, he had slunk back to their blanket on the grass to dress. Afterwards, he had sat down to wait, long legs crossed, one hand under his chin, mind twisting, heart numb.

He had remained like that, a statue of marble in the cold light until Owaen had curtly announced their horses were ready.

It was time to go.

To Fox's surprise, they hadn't headed south. Owaen had ridden ahead along the narrow path towards the City of the Seers.

"Ah... shit," Fox had mumbled.

And sure enough, once Fox had caught up with Owaen as the path opened to the main approach toward the once shining metropolis, he had found Blackthorn idly nibbling on damp grass. Owaen stood on the road nearby, hands clenched at his sides. As Fox dismounted next to him, his shock at Fox's ill news was replaced by another blow.

"I didn't notice before..." Owaen mumbled.

Not looking at the city, Fox rested a hand lightly on Owaen's broad shoulder. His cool fingers assessed the trembling beneath the Elf's thick fur cloak. He didn't need to ask why Owaen was barely holding it together.

The main tower was gone.

"How did I not notice?" Owaen whispered. Dark green eyes turned to Fox, their gaze wide and unfocused.

Swallowing, Fox attempted to keep his voice calm. "Well, we wanted to collect the horses, get to your cottage and then fu —"

"I know," Owaen interrupted, his cheeks slightly flushed. His deep green gaze focused back on the ruined city. "But the tower... our tower. It's gone. Did *we* do that?"

Fox frowned at the gap amongst the remains of the other buildings.

Other towers dotted the skyline above the collapsed section of the outer wall, but the tallest one was gone. He'd seen what remained, an uneven mound of shattered rubble, from above when wheeling overhead on golden green wings upon their arrival back here from Aneirin, a day or so ago. Focused on the meadow below, Owaen hadn't seen. As Fox glided low, the Elf was intent on rounding up the horses that had wandered close to the forest's edge despite their hobbled legs. It had been a risk to leave them like that, hence their haste to return and fetch them for the young king. Owaen still hadn't noticed on the journey to his family's cottage, his gaze fixed on Fox's bare backside ahead of him along the overgrown path. So Fox had kept the news of the tower to himself, more interested in spending time alone with Owaen at last.

"I don't know," Fox finally admitted. "Perhaps."

"I was atop that tower when I first laid eyes on you," Owaen whispered.

Fox remained silent, cool fingers sliding from Owaen's shoulder. When Fox had worn another face, he'd spotted the Elf there, felt his presence, their eyes connecting, hearts somehow already joined.

The Elf shut his eyes to the city. Owaen's voice, deceptively gentle, squeezed Fox's heart with an iron grip.

"Now it's gone."

Adjusting his seat in the saddle, Fox cracked his neck.

The colours and patterns on his back rippled with the movement, felt as a living presence. In moments like these, too much introspection was confusing. Perhaps more care could be taken with the scars that were invisible, deeper and more twisted than any ruined limbs or sinews. That seemed like something he should work on, considering the amount of time together he'd actually spent with Owaen was very little. They had met years before, but calamity had struck soon after.

Sighing at the clouds beyond the thick branches that weaved overhead in the frigid morning air, Fox squeezed his knees together. Without needing a word, his chestnut horse picked up the pace, coming alongside Blackthorn. The dark horse ignored them.

So did its rider.

Fox cleared his throat, a surreptitious croak amongst the whispering of damp leaves. "Owaen."

Rather than ignoring him like Fox had expected, Owaen observed him from the corner of his eye. The Elf remained silent, but a white eyebrow rose. Fox edged Willow to the side, as close as he dared. He licked his lips.

"Kiss me," Fox said, keeping his voice even. Owaen's own lips parted, but his gaze snapped away from Fox's mouth to the curve in the unmaintained forest path ahead.

"I don't feel like it," Owaen huffed after a while.

"Well." Fox sat up straight in his saddle. "Fuck you."

"Nope." Owaen's tone was as dry as the beef Fox had chewed for their crude breakfast. "Don't feel like that, either."

Closing his eyes, Fox exhaled with a focused puff of icy breath. "My apologies. I... I take that back."

"I don't."

Black eyes with barely a glint of gold opened.

This wasn't going to plan at all.

"Well, fuck you for real, my love. Do you want me to apologise for sharing ill news?"

"Yes."

"Even if I don't mean it?"

"Yes."

"Then I'm sorry," Fox groused.

Apart from the rush and ease of the brisk breeze that flapped their cloaks and rustled the surrounding forest, a stony silence weighed heavily between them. Fox flicked his reins and urged Willow to push into Blackthorn. Both horses snorted, and Owaen's knee pushed back against Fox's.

The Elf threw Fox an incredulous glare.

In response, Fox bared his teeth.

"I'm not really sorry," Fox hissed, "as you know. What did you want me to say? You asked me, and I told you!"

Drawing Blackthorn to a halt, Owaen stared at him. As their gazes clashed uneasily, Fox's horse shook its head as it followed its companion's lead and stopped. Blackthorn snorted once more, pulling back at his bridle.

Not breaking eye contact with Fox, Owaen blinked.

"Yes, you told me. But, my love, you knew. *Long* before I asked." The Elf's voice was tight with a strain that had Fox's toes curling in his boots.

Fox averted his gaze, following the trail of a silvery moth as it flitted past Owaen's shoulder.

"You knew, didn't you?" Owaen pressed.

Biting the inside of his mouth, Fox eventually nodded, a brusque gesture of his smooth chin.

Doing the last thing Fox expected, Owaen smiled. He reached between them and cupped Fox's cheek with warm, firm fingers.

"Exactly," Owaen said, calmly. His smile faded as his grip tightened for a heartbeat before dropping away. "So don't talk to me."

Hardly needing the command, Blackthorn walked on with a toss of his silky mane. Fox let them pull ahead. His cheek, held only briefly by his lover's touch, stung as frosty air replaced the warm caress.

"I'll..." Fox hesitated, at a loss on how to deal with this uncertainty. He grimaced. "I'll lock you up again," Fox called eventually as Owaen approached a bend in the wide old road. He was hoping for a reaction.

For attention.

For anything.

Twisting in the saddle, Owaen glanced back with eyes that should have spat fire.

Fox knew he deserved that, in a way.

Instead, his lover's gaze was filled with something worse.

"Oh," Fox breathed. Realisation dawned like the sun behind thick clouds. "Oh, he's... hurt."

I'm sorry, he mouthed, abashed.

Without responding, Owaen faced the road ahead and urged Blackthorn into a trot.

They disappeared around the bend, hidden from view by the wide berth of two sprawling old oaks twisted together, their roots partially exposed amongst the jewel green moss.

Fox contemplated the pair of trees, their two forms twisted into one organism, supporting each other out here in the seemingly endless forest of shifting green and moist, sparkling shadows.

With a delicate gesture, Fox lifted a pale hand and patted the leather pouch tucked into his shirt. Contained within, against his heart, rested the crystal dagger.

With a gentle snort, Willow resumed their progress.

"Caspian Carter," Fox murmured as they passed the twin oaks, "for my unhappy reunion with your brother, I am going to skin you alive."

By the time Fox and his horse had caught up to the two arrogant creatures riding up front, the day had expended its last rays through the canopy above. While nowhere near as staggeringly tall and wide as the forests between Lolihud and Aneirin, the forest here was a dense spread of ancient oaks and wise old beech trees.

Owaen remained slumped like a sack of grain in the saddle, jaw tight as he stared at an opening. Amongst the web of Old Man's Beard across tightly interwoven branches, through a creeper with silver green drapes, a break could be seen amongst the crowded, twisted trunks. Willow's ears flicked forward, the horse lifting its nose towards the break.

Fox tilted his head.

Where..?

Ah. There.

Not giving the brooding Elf a chance to rebuff him, Fox dismounted. His boots landed with a squelch on the side of the uneven road.

"Let me," he said.

Black hair flopping over his eyes, Fox flashed what he hoped was a sweet smile up at Owaen. Ignoring the stony grimace, Fox used both his strength and pulsing magic to widen the route into the trees, toward the faint bubble of running water.

They hadn't seen anyone through where they had passed, no sign of domestication anywhere along this stretch of the continent. But by unspoken agreement, camping and resting the horses away from the road was best. It would be obvious that someone had come by this way due to the freshly cleared trail, but they'd hear anyone coming.

Owaen's deep sigh followed as he dismounted behind and led the two horses into the forest along the opened up path.

When Owaen reached the little clearing about a five-minute hike down a steep hill of spiked ferns, Fox dropped a pile of rocks into the moss. After he kicked them into a rough circle, he headed over to Owaen, indicated the little area under a drooping cedar tree with a wave of a muddy hand behind him.

"Sit down," Fox offered, flicking away a wisp of delicate lichen from Owaen's slightly damp hair. "I'll make camp."

Without waiting for a response, Fox extracted the reins from Owaen's firm grip. He pushed the Elf into the clearing against the cedar, urging him down into the moss in a nook nicely protected by two low hanging, thickly leaved boughs.

Deep green eyes narrowed at Fox, yet Owaen stayed where he was.

After seeing the horses to the crisp little rivulet of water that could barely be called a stream, Fox returned with their packs and loaded sacks. Dumping them in a pile, he poked about them, a line between his dark brows. When he had travelled aimlessly with *Jessikah*, Fox had naturally made her do all the work. Eyeing the untidy spread of items, Fox hesitated. Eyeing a tuft of fur poking out from one sack, he went with that first.

Owaen kept his mouth shut as Fox settled the fur blanket around his broad shoulders.

Turning to the pile of goods on the ground, Fox grimaced at the jumbled mess of wrapped parcels and cooking implements.

He snuck a glance at Owaen.

The arrogant bastard was reclining back against the trunk. Broad arms were crossed over his chest beneath the fur wrap, long legs crossed at the ankles of his boots. Blonde eyebrows were high above eyes sparkling with barely suppressed smugness.

Nostrils flaring, Fox spun on his heel.

Fuel.

He needed to fetch fuel for their fire.

After stomping about amongst the trees, Fox returned with a massive, hollow log that had him staggering a little. Bits of splinters dropped from his hair as he settled the ridiculously sized chunk of wood amongst the ring of stones before his lover. With a showy toss of black hair, Fox uncoiled a spark of energy from within.

Unlike in the City of the Seers, his magic once depleted, no encouragement was needed now.

The chunk of wood, still damp and covered with moss, burst into immediate, searing flames.

As various bugs flew off in a frenzied scurry from the inferno, dusk spread amongst the forest undergrowth around them. Owaen remained silent. Fox wondered if one of the bugs might land somewhere sensitive and wipe away the Elf's amused expression with sharp pincers.

Mentally slapping away the satisfying image, Fox sighed. When he could put it off no longer, Fox grabbed their pouch of dried bread and beef. Folding himself primly next to Owaen, he held up a stick of meat.

"My love, are you hungry?"

Green eyes, flecked with amber sparks reflecting the merrily burning log, shimmered as Owaen opened his mouth.

His own eyes widening in disbelief, Fox was about to ram the dried meat down Owaen's throat when he checked himself. Shaking his head a little, he snapped off a mouthful of beef and placed it with care against Owaen's lips. Ignoring the insufferable Elf's satisfied smirk, Fox took a bite for himself and chewed noisily. He searched for something to say. His gaze dropped to a suggestively shaped piece of bark peeling away from the crackling log as it burned.

"You're wrong, you know," Fox said after swallowing.

"What." Owaen's voice was flat.

"You said to Rhydian I'm not a 'he'. Yet here I am, cock and all."

Fox glanced to the side, pleased to see Owaen's smirk fade.

Until a new light filled the Elf's eyes.

"I'm dealing just fine with that," Owaen purred.

"Are you sure?" Fox scoffed, taken aback by the change in the tension between them.

"*That* will never matter." Owaen's gaze roamed down and then up Fox's body. Fox shifted, glad he was dressed in quite a few layers of wool and linen.

"Then talk to me," Fox insisted, ignoring the lick of interest curling about the base of his spine.

"I will."

"Will you? Now might be good."

Owaen exhaled slowly, joining the sigh of the tree above them as a frigid evening breeze rustled the canopy.

"It's..."

Pale pink lips in a thin line, Fox waited.

When Owaen wasn't forthcoming, Fox pointed his stick of beef at the Elf's forehead.

"It's *what*? What is this? Explain what is happening in there, right now," Fox demanded. "I know you're hurt... and I'm sorry... for..."

Head tilting a little, Owaen blinked. Swallowing, Fox searched for something, anything, to close the distance between them. He *knew* the Elf deserved some time to process things. But the Elf's silence and distance was too much when they should be joined instead.

"You're sorry, huh?" Owaen enquired, his voice deceptively mild. "What exactly are you sorry for? You made it clear only a little while ago that you had no regrets, my little dragon. So, explain your apology. Tell me why."

Speechless, Fox stared at Owaen, the stick of beef held limply in his hand.

"Your parents and Baile Mara..." Fox began, then coughed into his fist. "I only knew later, more recently —"

"Recently?" Owaen interrupted. Sitting forward, he grabbed the beef from Fox's hand and threw it to the side. "What the fuck is *recent* for you?"

"Don't raise your voice at me, Elf," Fox snapped.

"I'm not!" Owaen yelled.

Down by the gurgling rivulet of icy water, Blackthorn snorted.

They glared at each other until Owaen slumped back against the tree, hands clenched in the soft grey fur draped around his shoulders.

"*Recent*," Fox proclaimed icily, "can mean many things to those with magic."

"Well, we have my delightful parents to thank for that," Owaen grunted. Resting his head against the rough bark behind him, he closed his eyes.

Fox sat up, shifting onto his knees.

This wasn't great, but it *was* progress.

"I'm listening, Owaen. Please..." Placing his hand on Owaen's knee, Fox kept his voice as gentle as he could. "Please talk to me."

Sagged against the tree as the fire crackled nearby, Owaen remained still for so long that Fox thought he'd drifted off to sleep.

"Owaen," Fox hissed, his patience thinning. "I am still talking to you —"

Without opening his eyes, a large hand snaked out from the fur blanket, grabbed Fox's shirt, and yanked him down to Owaen's chest.

"Give me a moment to work out what to do next, Skye,"

Struggling, but only a little, Fox twisted until his face was free of the fur blanket.

"Don't call me that," he sputtered, spitting out wet strands from his mouth. "You know what to do next. We need to take care of your brother."

"Why?"

"Why what?" Fox tipped his head back, gazing up at the jaw in his face with confusion.

"Because Caspian's a threat, yeah? To me? Or..." Eyes like burning emeralds narrowed. "To your girlfriend? Or to your boyfriend?"

Fox pulled away from Owaen's grip so fast that the Elf swore under his breath. Fox was about to slap Owaen across the face, but he stopped himself in time as realisation slid along his spine like a curl of curious magic.

Owaen stared at Fox's raised hand, his eyes sliding over the pale flesh to meet Fox's incredulous stare.

Today was a day of many lessons.

Patience being one of them.

The other...

"Ah." Fox dropped his open palm to Owaen's leather pants, squeezing the dense thigh muscles underneath. "I see."

"You see what?"

Fox patted Owaen's leg.

"Not only are you in shock, you're *jealous*."

Owaen's eyes flashed, lower lip rolled back between his teeth.

"Am not," the Elf muttered, eyes like a snow covered forest narrowing.

"I'm fucking right, aren't I?" For all the tension, Fox felt the urge to laugh. "Oh, you brute. You're jealous of my *friends*."

A muscle in Owaen's firm jaw ticked.

"They have spent more time with you than I ever had the chance to."

The words were simple, their implication was not.

Abashed, filled with both shame for his cursed pettiness and belated understanding, Fox collapsed in Owaen's lap, legs twining together. Squirming until he was pressed against the Elf's chest, Fox curled close, pressing his face into the heart that beat for him. That thought had his eyes stinging.

Angrily, Fox wiped his face against Owaen's shirt.

"Owaen, I'm sorry for some things, truly. I am trying to be... less mean. I'm sorry for not sharing."

A deep sigh rumbled in his ears, the deep vibration a pleasant buzz against Fox's cheek.

"You should be. How long did you know they caused Baile Mara to break apart? Fuck." Finally, *finally*, the arms that Fox craved drew tight around him. His eyelids lowered at the blissful sensation as Owaen continued. "All those people... my home. Don't hide me from something like this, not ever. I can't..." Owaen's voice cracked. "I can't win against you."

"You don't need to," Fox whispered, inhaling the musk that he'd dreamt about on lonely nights for too long.

He angled his head so he could meet Owaen's searching gaze. They stared at each other for a while, deep green eyes reflecting the fire, black eyes lit with golden stars. After a moment, blonde and black hair mingled as the Elf dropped his forehead to Fox's. Shadowed from the night, they simply looked at each other, the forest hushed, two pairs of eyes unblinking.

"Don't I?" Owaen whispered back.

The flickering radiance beside them flared, shadows playing across the Elf's grizzled jaw.

"If you ask nicely," Fox breathed, his pulse picking up speed, "I will let you win anytime you want, little Elf."

"*Little*?" A new light entered Owaen's gaze. He pressed his lip to Fox's, speaking directly into Fox's open mouth. "Exactly where am I *little*?"

"Ask me nicely," Fox sniggered, "and I shall tell y—"

Owaen swallowed the rest of Fox's words with a searing kiss.

Going limp with relief, Fox smiled, eager to pretend for just a little while that nothing else required their attention. Allowing himself to be lowered into the damp moss, Owaen lifted Fox slightly, shuffling the fur blanket beneath him.

"Thank you," Fox murmured around Owaen's tongue.

"You're welcome," Owaen replied with a low rumble.

He disengaged from their kiss to run his lips down Fox's exposed neck, tasting the salt from their travels, the dew from the damp forest. Lids closed to the cavern of branches above, and Fox melted into the sweat and musk scent that filled his senses, the heat that warmed his bones.

All he wanted was right here, against him, around him.

As Owaen bit and sucked his collarbones, grizzled jaw searing Fox with interesting textures, one of his hands snaked into Fox's hair to hold him in place. The Elf's other hand went deftly for the ties at the front of Fox's trousers. Owaen's fingers were broad and not quite suited for delicate work, but they knew what they were doing. Soon enough, Fox's aching length sprung free.

Owaen raised his head a moment, a wicked grin on his handsome face.

"This bit here that I am dealing with just *fine*," Owaen expressed with an emphasising squeeze as Fox panted beneath him, "is a fun, extra piece to play with..."

"Nngh..." was all Fox could reply as calloused fingertips roamed over his tip, his shaft, exploring lower.

There was some shifting about, fur and fabric rustling. Owaen's mouth moved further south, his breath hot through Fox's shirt. Not bothering to unbutton it, Owaen kissed his way down the material until his mouth replaced his skillful fingers.

As pleasure pooled in his groin, Owaen shifted once more, coating every intimate part of Fox with kisses, pulling his trousers to his ankles, lips softening, making cool skin slick. At last Owaen pulled away, sliding back up to meet Fox's open mouth, his cheeks, his nose, his eyelids. Black and gold eyes fluttered open as Owaen kissed Fox back to the present. Their hearts were loud between them, the night a cool mystery in the dark beyond, water trickling, an owl hooting with gentle urgency.

"May I?" Owaen purred, his gaze smoldering.

Fox slid both his hands over Owaen's front, finding the Elf's pants unlaced, his own hard length sprung free.

"You may," Fox breathed, twisting, turning and presenting himself to make it easier for them both, considering Fox's boots were still on, his pants shoved down to the top of his boots. As the cool nighttime air caressed his bare flesh, Fox shivered. "Quickly, now —"

Owaen didn't need any further encouragement. With his face caressed by warmed fur, Fox closed his eyes with eager anticipation. There was the sound above of a gentle gathering of saliva, then hot, slick fingers replaced the night air. Fox cried out at the sensation, the silky fur of the blanket tasting of smoke and crisp wilderness.

"Am I beautiful to you?" Fox breathed through the stinging pleasure that pierced him.

A languid laugh sounded above.

"Your beauty is endless..."

"Mmm... But...?"

"But also deadly in whatever form you choose, my love."

"Deadly for whom?"

Another chuckle. "Me."

"Hurry," Fox mumbled with a muted laugh, deliciously pleased by Owaen's admission while his once ordered thoughts faded to overwhelming sensations, "Owaen, please..."

"I am not going to hurt you, little dragon," came the amused reply as fingers worked Fox open with delicious probing undulations.

At last, fingers were replaced by something larger, something hot and firm, and Fox moaned at the feeling of being stretched open, smiling through the sting, relishing the gasp of wonder in his ear. Owaen lowered himself, his full weight to Fox's back, a feeling Fox had never thought he'd ever want, but knew he would crave until the end of his days.

"Is it... ah... all the way in?"

"Sure."

And with an amused huff, Owaen slid all the way home with a none too gentle thrust.

"Bastard," Fox gasped. "You l-lied..."

"Did I?" Owaen kissed Fox's ear, teasing with his words and his tongue. "Hm, lying, withholding information doesn't feel nice, does it—"

"*Shut*," Fox hissed as Owaen commenced moving, tears welling, "*up*."

"Are you crying, my sweet?" Owaen murmured, his voice a rumbling tease as Fox sobbed and cursed underneath him. "It's far too soon for that. I haven't quite started *yet*."

With that ridiculous proclamation, Owaen's teeth found the back of Fox's neck. The Elf laughed through his teeth with an arrogant snort as he held Fox there, with his hot mouth, heavy weight, tight arms, and lazy, focused thrusts.

Unable to surrender to anyone else, Fox allowed himself to relax, to give himself over to the pleasure of Owaen's love and urgency. It was like being held by the sun. Fox wanted to be burned to the bone.

"More," he gasped, "more, more, more..."

With a wicked growl, Owaen ceased the teasing roll of his hips.

"Owaen, I swear to —"

"I am not going to hurt you," Owaen whispered directly into Fox's ear. This earned him an uncontrollable shiver. "Not now, not ever."

"I will heal." It was pathetic, Fox knew it, and beyond reason.

Owaen seemed to agree. He placed a delicate kiss between Fox's shoulders, over his shirt, the wild tattoo a chaotic pattern on the slick skin beneath.

"You might heal, little fox," growled Owaen, "but that's not the point. I'll never intentionally cause you pain."

"I'm dying right now," Fox pleaded, "so make good on that promise... ngh..."

With an amused laugh, Owaen obliged.

Recommencing his deep glides, Owaen changed the angle of his hips. It was too much for them both. Words were muted, the world faded away. Their combined gasps and moans broke free anew for only the woodland to witness. Before long, far too soon, Fox cried out as his release left him, Owaen spiraling into bliss not long after. The fiercest heat that Fox craved filled him, and tears left his eyes, quickly absorbed into the dampened fur against his flushed cheeks.

"A gift..." Fox moaned, unable to help himself, unsure of what he was saying due to the fever and the pleasure that swept through him.

"Mmm?" came the lazy query against his neck.

"You are," Fox panted as he pushed back, "a gift to me..."

"That's interesting," Owaen purred, "I was just thinking how much I enjoy unwrapping all of your layers..."

It was hard to speak, to think, for quite a while. Fox, limp and sated, let Owaen love him as he wished, as they both wished. It was rough; it was tender at times.

It was all he wanted.

Ever.

"I need you, I want you, don't leave me again, promise me. I waited for you for so long..." Owaen mumbled, helpless, a heavy, spent weight draped over Fox's sweaty back. He held Fox close, arms wrapping around Fox's heaving chest.

"Owaen, my Owaen," breathed Fox. Disengaging with a wet slide, he twisted around. Owaen's warm lips mapped his face. "You're the sunshine to my night."

Owaen smiled into Fox's mouth. He pulled away, green eyes sparkling, lazy and unfocused. After planting a final kiss on Fox's nose, he sat up for a moment, stripping off his grey wool under-shirt. Underneath rested his gold chain, golden topaz and tiny golden wand, against his damp chest. Fox shimmied about until he, too, had the top half of his clothes stripped away.

"Come here, my love," Owaen purred, clever hands wandering once more. Fox arched to meet him.

After their second round, when Owaen had finished wiping him down tenderly with a damp cloth, Fox lay awake. Owaen had fallen asleep almost as soon as laying down, Fox's back held tight against Owaen's chest, wrapped by arms that no one would dare to move. The Elf's satisfied snore started not long after.

Smiling to himself a little, Fox blinked as something cool and wet dropped into his eye.

Squinting, he peered up through the dark shapes that crowded above. Another splash met his cheek. The patter of drops soon increased.

With a little twist of magic, the air shimmered around them, the particles twisted into a clear cocoon that would keep some of the damp, if not all, away. Pressing close to the one who held his heart, Fox wondered at that. He had wanted to shield Owaen since their first meeting. From dragons, from the greed that lurked in most hearts. Yet magic had made them both who they were. It had brought them together, while also wrenching them apart. Even now, skin to skin, in effect, they were still a leathery wingspan apart by race and the damage by people passed years ago.

Not just the dragon race, but also Hypatia and Illarion Carter.

Fox's glittering eyes glanced at the half-burned log, glaring at the flickering flames, flames that for him held nowhere near enough heat.

Magic was an unnecessary evil, and he needed it gone from the world. He needed to remove it from everyone who wielded it, lest their temptation to accumulate even more led to ever more chaos.

He needed to take it.

All of it.

Owaen's parents might be gone, but Caspian, apparently following in their wake, was still around to experience the frustration that ached within, like a bottomless well of ice, a chasm that was almost impossible to fill.

With that, Fox fell asleep, content, sated, at least for a little while.

We should have smashed that thing, a dragon roared as she melted away, revealing different flesh and bone, claws dropping off to reveal bleeding fingers, bruised toes.

Words thundered into nothingness across the sky, lost above a heaving landscape of black plains, dotted here and there with craggy peaks rising from the earth.

White smoke, hot ash and sharp cries filled the world, as a man fueled by rage and grief let his fury out on those who deserved it the most.

Above, the night sky burned crimson, white points of bright stars obscured by rolling gusts of smoke-filled, gritty wind. The heat seared his face; the desolation soothed his heart.

The Carters should have sent them both back...

Not understanding and uncaring for their pleas, Fox bent over, catching sight of a ghastly pale face reflected in one of the countless shimmering scales left behind. Cold joy bubbled up within his chest, racing to overcome the madness that threatened to consume him.

"I am not a monster," he said. "I am angry."

The haunted face didn't move. Black eyes simply stared.

"I have every right to be," Fox insisted.

As the earth groaned and the sky heaved, Fox peered up. Clouds boiled away in rings of flame, dragons falling from the sky to land amongst the piles of scales. The noise burst his eardrums, the scales scattering and cutting into him as they slid against each other, the rasp lost to the booming of great winged creatures making contact with the heaving ground. Ears bleeding, Fox let the cold joy be replaced by pain as he was crushed to the earth, under scales, under claws, under the desperate wails of justice being served.

I am lost.

I am lost to their greed —

Gently, almost too gently considering the content of his garish dreams, Fox woke. Glittering eyes focused on the darkness before his face, on the warm, bare chest, smelling of musk and salt against his cool lips. In Mionlach, long ago as a young dragon, things didn't make sense that maybe should have. Longing for more, he had learnt so much from venturing into the outside world.

But that had been brief, painful.

He had lost so much, had been lost.

Am I found?

His mouth formed the words without sound, lips and tongue tasting the skin of the one who had found him, who had seen him simply for being a soul, not a means to an end.

Fox's viscous thoughts drifted to ponder his tattoo, the greed and the loss it represented, not just in imagery, but its physical nature. After all, the tattoo ink had been made from the few scales Fox had carried with him as mementos, ground up and needled into his flesh.

Fur blankets shifted as Fox rolled over, his lazy gaze observing the last vestiges of red and orange from the cooling embers. Calm blanketed the wilderness of trunks and leaves around them, and Fox yearned for the calm to permeate within. Behind him, hard muscle and the impressive length of Owaen's nakedness pressed into Fox's cool flesh. A soothing finger traced the desolate shapes along Fox's bare back.

Eyes shut tight, Fox wondered if Owaen had yet spotted, amongst the shifting colours and lines, the tiny figure with long, green hair, holding a sleeping blonde man in her arms as she cried.

18

Owaen

Year 367

The Forest

"I'm still mad at you."

Fox shared a careless sigh in response to Owaen's matter-of-fact statement. "I know."

"I might be for a while," Owaen continued, examining the raven haired man seated beside him from under low brows.

"How long is a while?" Fox enquired through a lazy yawn, his finely sculpted jaw widening extravagantly.

The pair were breaking their fast as the dawn attempted to shine down from the damp branches above them. Only thin spokes of verdant light reached the dew-bright moss around them. It was a frigid morning, the different textured surfaces of bark, rocks and branches glistening with moisture. The sharp aroma of ozone permeated the air, faint tendrils of mist pooled in low pockets of moss and toadstools.

Owaen couldn't see the sky too well from their basic camp on the lush forest floor, but the few clouds he'd glimpsed when taking a piss down stream were oddly tinged, almost pink. A storm, perhaps? Surely he would have woken if thunder had rumbled overhead. He spared a glance at the moss next to his knee. Had it rained? It was damp, but not saturated. Maybe the cedar tree, its lowest fronds tickling his hair, had kept away most of it?

The forest certainly smelled like it had rained. A rich, living aroma of moist earth and cool mist permeated the morning, pleasant and reviving. It was a pretty dawn, a welcome way to start the new day, comprising another long ride.

"I asked how long?" Fox insisted from next to him.

"Let me see." Owaen sat back against their cedar tree. He pretended to think, tapping a piece of yellow cheese against his chin. "How long was I asleep?"

"Just now? You snored all night, so about—"

"Oh no, my love."

To Owaen's pleasure, Fox's eyes widened, his pale lips parting slightly. Owaen smiled.

"How long did you lock me away?" Owaen inquired mildly. Then took a bite. "Mm. Delicious," he said through his mouthful of crumbly cheese.

While he nibbled at the hunk of cheese, Fox stared at him, his own jaw working silently.

As the silence between them lengthened, Owaen tried to feel a meagre slice of guilt at his pettiness.

He couldn't.

With a dry cough, Fox stood up, avoiding Owaen's assessing stare. Brushing damp bits of twig and leaves off his black riding pants, he stepped past Owaen, heading for the horses. But halfway across the uneven ground of moss and rock, Fox stopped. He held up his right hand, staring at it as he flexed his fingers, curling and extending them back and forth.

"Are you alright?" Owaen asked, pettiness forgotten, a faint line forming between his blonde eyebrows.

Fox stared at his hand a moment longer before answering.

"Yes." Black eyes glinted at Owaen. Fox dropped his hand to his hip. "Tell me about your parents."

Owaen blinked.

His parents?

Swallowing the cheese, Owaen used his tongue to clean the softened crumbs from between his teeth, allowing his mind to catch up with Fox's change of subject.

Honestly, he hadn't expected Fox to bring them back up so soon. To talk about them after what he'd learned was just as difficult as to think of Caspian. To think that their parents were the cause of much more suffering than he wanted to examine, that felt as if he were standing before a wall of ice. With no end in sight, and no top either.

But it was a wall he had to pass through, wasn't it?

Our mother and father, Owaen had said to Fox only a day or so before at the cottage, *they didn't try as hard as I did.*

Had they tried too hard in other areas, separate from their sons?

Too hard in taking magic... too far?

At the cost of his home... and countless lives.

Mind shying away with a kick of panic, Owaen locked that chasm of new grief away for another day.

"What do you want to know?" Owaen said cautiously, unable to hide his wince as he shifted on the blanket.

"Tell me what comes to mind," Fox murmured as he toed the remnants of the arrogantly sized log he'd set fire to the night before.

"About them as people? Or scientists? They studied the natural world. They studied us, born of their experiments —"

"Your mother experimented on you? How?" Fox asked sharply, head tilted at a slight angle.

"She..." Owaen rubbed his arm with an absentminded gesture. "We were born different. I was born with magic. Other people had to go through a process to obtain it. Mother tested how I reacted to things."

"Tested how?"

"She compared our healing time. But it was alright," Owaen added hastily. "I healed rather fast."

"Lovely." Fox's top lip curled. "And your brother? Did he heal too, different as he was?"

Seated on the fur blanket and reluctant to rise, Owaen continued to rub the pad of his calloused thumb in circles over the shirt sleeve of his left arm. His skin beneath was smooth. The marks had faded from Hypatia's careful study of his flesh, and the way it worked with the magic that had been born into the world within him. Avoiding Fox's keen observation, Owaen slid his palms together.

Had Caspian's cuts ever healed?

The scar on his right leg never had, the result of some acidic substance that his reckless brother had spilled one day.

"Um, no." Owaen coughed past the dry lump in his throat. "Maybe?"

Fox was studying him curiously. "I would have loved a sibling. But not a mad one."

Owaen allowed his keen hearing to soak up the soothing trickle of water where the horses munched on their dwindling bags of grain. Dropping his gaze to his entwined fingers, broad shoulders shifted as he shrugged.

"He wasn't always... how he ended up." Owaen flicked away a rogue crumb of cheese at a brown beetle with iridescent green splotches, poking around the moss near his boots. "I loved him, but then he... changed. He finally came into possession of a kind of magic. It brought out his worst traits. His best ones too."

"Which are?"

"Loyalty. Focus." Owaen glanced to his right as one of the horses snorted. A brilliantly coloured bird had landed on Blackthorn's mane. The warhorse tossed his head, and the startled bird flew off with a piercing cry. "A unique style of justice."

In the centre of the rough clearing, Fox tilted his head back, eyeing the faint spots of grey sky through the layers of greenery above. He inhaled slowly, a pensive expression crossing his handsome features.

"Is that where you get it from..." Fox asked, his voice fading as he frowned at whatever he was seeing. His nose twitched as he sniffed.

Owaen followed Fox's gaze, eyeing the swaying treetops, wondering if Fox had spotted the curiously coloured clouds.

"I don't know if I got anything from..." Owaen licked his lips, hesitating. "From... him."

It was still difficult to speak his brother's name. He had only said his name a few times in the hush of a broken city, to explain the threat of calamity ahead. With Fox, it was easier as time passed. The further they moved away from his family's cottage seemed to make it easier, too. Fewer memories to haunt him, memories that perhaps had more to them.

If he cared to examine them.

The expression on Fox's face, as Owaen had briefed over his mother's experiments, seemed to show there was more to his childhood than he had ever cared to think about.

But did that explain his brother's chaotic path across the continent?

He wiped his palms together, allowing the last of his breakfast to fall away into the moss between his thighs, watching Fox head down to the water. In whatever form that his lover appeared, Fox had caught Owaen's attention. As both man and woman, Fox moved with a grace that wasn't quite fluid, but seemed part of whatever landscape he inhabited at the time. That seemed to stem from his own awareness of himself. His nature was intense and loyal, yet supremely unpredictable.

Much like Owaen's twin.

"Cas... Caspian," Owaen whispered as he ran a hand through his hair. "What the fuck are you up to?"

His older brother had been Owaen's only friend growing up. Intentional or not, the twins were kept separate from other children in the city of their birth. When Owaen had finally found his passion, travelling with Father through to the City of the Seers, Cas had moved on from spending time with his younger twin. He had become not quite a rebel, but jaded, perhaps? There had been questionable circumstances throughout Caspian's younger years. Owaen had never shared some of them with Mother or Father. There was *some* loyalty between the brothers, even as teenagers growing apart.

By their fifteenth or sixteenth year, Owaen was used to the fact that Caspian seemed happiest, or most content at least, with flames and chaos. Once, after hearing of a terrible incident concerning the group of bullies who plagued the twins when younger, Owaen had realised Cas had been absent for hours.

That wasn't unusual.

But the dread that lurked deep within his chest certainly was.

For some reason, the prickly librarian who assisted their parents had given Caspian a sword.

Mother hadn't realised or cared when her oldest son began to wear it. Father had made a joke about the boy finally settling on 'something to catch his attention'.

"Yes, Father," Caspian had agreed, odd blue eyes glinting. "Something has indeed."

"Use it well," Illarion had cautioned absentmindedly, his green eyes sliding back to observing his jar of golden honeycomb by the light streaming in the study window.

Owaen hadn't asked about the sword. Instead, he was more concerned about the hundreds of tiny red wounds all over Caspian's torso. It had been later that day when the twins had shared a rare icy dip in the frigid ocean, that Owaen had noticed them.

"Aren't they wonderful, Brother?" Caspian had said with a laugh, salt water running over the countless welts. "They helped me catch someone's long sought after attention."

Owaen didn't understand, and wasn't sure he wanted to.

After that, whenever Owaen had needed to find his brother, Caspian could often be found practicing swordcraft in one of Rook's smoke-filled public houses. The young man would pester anyone with any reputable skill, the rest absorbed through whatever written works on the subject he could find. Sometimes Owaen discovered him being instructed by the pirates that they had loved to spot on the docks as boys.

But one day, when Caspian had been absent for a night and almost a full day, Owaen had given in to the dread that had spiked on hearing an uproar amongst the servants. Something had happened in the city. Searching Caspian's usual haunts, Owaen had finally tracked his brother down.

Owaen had been aghast at what he'd discovered.

Stopping at the edge of the cliff top forest behind the city's lonely library, his heart temporarily forgot how to beat.

Caspian was kneeling amongst the meadow of ripe red, yellow, and orange poppies. His sword was stuck in the ground next to him. Its ruby hilt was upright, the blade below it stained crimson where it had been plunged into the dirt.

Green eyes, wide and unblinking, snapped to the delicate bright red splatter on Caspian's beaming cheek.

"What did you do?" Owaen breathed.

He pointed a trembling finger at the sword. Its faceted red jewel sparkled innocently in the blaring sun as a salt wind tousled the locks of two blonde heads of hair. Odd blue eyes flashed, wickedly brilliant in the bright sunlight.

"I used it well," Caspian announced with a serene smile.

Dropping his gaze to the bobbing meadow of flowers where Caspian was kneeling, Owaen eyed the half a dozen severed hands with fingers pointing up, planted amongst the happily bobbing poppies.

He spun around and violently brought up his afternoon tea over a low shrub of coiled leaves.

While Owaen wiped his chin of its sour juices with the sleeve of his shirt, Caspian had wandered over. His twin had patted Owaen's back in what was surely meant to be a soothing gesture.

Caspian's voice tone was matter of fact as he spoke.

"Don't worry, brother. If we let those with power push the rest of us around, we're just as guilty as they are for the injustices of the world."

Owaen had vomited once more.

Not sure why he'd never told their parents as the outcry continued to spread through the city, Owaen wasn't sure why the bullies, each left with one hand, had never reported Caspian either. And while he had to admit Caspian wasn't exactly wrong to punish those who preyed on the weak, his methods were..?

Owaen watched another beetle join the first and grapple long pincers for the right to a large crumb of cheese in the moss next to his leather clad thigh.

His methods were extreme.

Calculating.

Ruthless.

Like Mother, a small voice at the back of his mind whispered.

A muscle in Owaen's jaw ticked until he willed his shoulders to drop, and his neck to release. To re-examine these events, it was like rubbing fingers down spikes of grain, the fine hairs prickling with not pain, but an unpleasant sensation, nonetheless. There had been so much chaos, from Caspian's shenanigans, and later the devastation of their homeland.

It was like the loss of childhood, experienced anew as an adult, the memories tarnished by too much examination.

Which, he supposed with a dry snort for his own arrogance, was why he had not really cared to do it before. Pieces that made sense no longer made sense. Absentmindedly, his fingers rubbed at his arm again, watching Fox poke around their camp, arranging things for the next leg of their journey.

Towards Caspian, maybe.

Did he hope for that reunion?

Honestly, he wasn't sure.

What he was sure of was that he was leaving things behind, pieces of his past. Pieces that didn't really exist, whether a ruined city, or memories of a happy time that perhaps wasn't so happy after all, in a cottage used while the once great City of the Seers had been built. A cottage where he had spent some good times that would never change? Playing with his twin amongst the hills and valleys, stealing their father's honeycombs.

Had all of that meant nothing to his older brother?

Watching Fox struggling to stuff their blanket into a sack, Owaen sighed.

Caspian deserved to meet some kind of justice, for all that he'd had his magic-tainted hands in.

But what hurt most of all, if Owaen was being honest, right now, at this moment, was the loss of a once soaring tower.

Their tower.

Remembering the day before, Owaen had stared without words at the newly opened space in the grey sky. Where there hadn't been a gap since he could remember. Owaen had stood there when he had first laid eyes on a woman, a creature so beautiful he'd forgotten how to breathe.

How long ago was that?

Did that moment in time still mean anything if the place of its experience was rubble?

It was like everything he'd known had come to dust. Pieces that once made a whole structure had broken into odd shapes that would never fit back together.

Alone under the cedar tree, Owaen blinked. The morning had become a green, misty blur.

One of the blurred shapes moved, grew larger.

A cool fingertip stroked his face, cheek to chin, wiping away a lone, salty drop.

"Owaen," Fox murmured. After wiping his fingertip with his soft pink tongue, Fox shared a wan smile. "It's time to get going. I've packed up, my love."

Owaen nodded. He tried to speak. It took him a few goes to clear his throat before he could.

"Yep." Standing and stretching, he faced away. Not saying anything, Fox nodded and rose. He grabbed the last sack to be tied to one of the horse's saddles.

Glancing at Fox from the corner of his eye, Owaen laughed under his breath, his heart eased for a moment. His lover, dressed all in black but for his slightly soiled white shirt, a creature powerful beyond useful measure, was cursing loudly while attempting to get the final sack secured.

Owaen crossed his arms.

"Come on, my lusty dragon. Hurry up. We need to get these horses back to your..." he paused, unable to prevent the smirk forming across his grizzled cheeks, *"friends."*

Owaen had no time to be thankful the sack contained their bedding, and not the iron kettle, before it smacked him in the face.

"Waney."

A child's voice, piping, mischievous.

"Wake up, Wane."

A man's voice, deeper, sarcastic.

"Caspian?"

Laying on his back, Owaen twisted about, squinting in vain through the thick darkness that held him still.

"Of course." His brother's face appeared before him, the deadly gaze shining silver and blue. "Why did you break my sword? Morgan gave that to me. You were supposed to bury me with it—"

Owaen's eyelids cracked open.

They had travelled all day, resting the horses only twice. At their next stop, a grove of willows by perhaps the same stream as earlier that morning, they had finally camped.

Owaen helped this time. Fox had said nothing, but allowed Owaen to take the lead as previously. Both of them were weary after a long day of uneven road, the once bustling highway joining major towns now a mess of pebbles and stones sinking into mud and moss.

He blinked away the lingering fog in his mind, feeling both groggy and disoriented. Shadows from his fitful dream seemed intent on following him into consciousness. Because as the half imagined conversation with his brother faded, it took Owaen a while to realise that a hand a few degrees cooler than his own was down the front of his trousers, wrapped around his thickening cock.

Cool lips brushed Owaen's ear. "Are you awake? I'm *so* sorry..."

Owaen wiped his eyes with the back of his hands. Beneath their blanket of soft fur that was pulled up past their heads this frigid night, he turned to Fox, who lay half over him. Their lips touched, caressing, tasting for a lazy kiss. Pulling back a little, Owaen brushed away a lock of black hair from the pale forehead close by his. It was almost completely dark under their bedding, yet Fox's eyes glinted like the dark sky full of gilded stars.

"Are you really?" Owaen sighed, their breath mingling.

"No," Fox whispered back, unrepentant. "You know I'm not."

With reluctance, Owaen pulled Fox's hand from his pants, kissing Fox's pouting lower lip in apology. As much as he'd like to spend another hour, or two, wrapped around and within the cool beauty of the man by his side, with the trees arched overhead, now was not the time. Sleep was needed. Yet, images from his troubling dream lingered like faded snatches of conversations in the shadowed, forested twilight as night fell.

Why did you break my sword?

"I know you tried to keep me safe," Owaen mumbled, seeking to disperse the unsettling images and sensations from his subconscious.

He twisted a little, face breaking free of the blanket to stare at the nighttime forest. Their fire had died down, the last wisps of smoke mingling with the low rolling in of white mist over moss and ferns, green turned deep black in the darkness.

Fox exhaled as he shifted his own position. Silky hair brushed against Owaen's chin as an elbow pressed into Owaen's guts with a not-so-subtle jab. It seemed like an accident. Perhaps it was. Although if Fox was as hard as Owaen was, as the forest stirred about them with evening bird calls and its raw breeze, it was more likely the result of a frustrated pique.

"I *did* keep you safe, didn't I?" Fox mumbled into Owaen's chest under the layers of fur that encased them.

"You did. But to be clear as we head into..." Owaen squinted over the edge of the blanket at the lowest branches a few feet above his face, "whatever we are heading into, you can't make those decisions for me."

From under the heavy fur, Fox's reply was immediate.

"I fucking well think I can."

"Hmmm." Owaen wasn't sure whether to laugh, curse, or groan.

"Hmmm?" With another painful poke, to Owaen's ribs this time, Fox's head popped out from the covers by Owaen's, his normally silky black hair a spiked mess.

As he draped himself fully over Owaen, Fox rested his head on folded hands over Owaen's chest. Black and gold irises gleamed through thin slits as Fox narrowed his gaze. Entranced by the soul that peered out, Owaen slid his hands up and around Fox's bare waist, gliding along toned muscles, ever cool. Fox stared at him without speaking, but Owaen was pleased to note the man's beautiful eyes widened a little. Ignoring the hardened member that grazed his groin, Owaen forced his fingertips to trace the horrific shapes and colours that he couldn't see, but would never forget.

"The depth of your love overwhelms me," Owaen said quietly. "It scares me."

To his amazement, instead of another blow from a sharp elbow, Fox smiled. Even white teeth flashed in the faint orange light beside him. Spots of firelight tinged with golden rainbows from the last embers illuminated the spike of wild ebony hair.

"This pleases you," Owaen continued, his gaze searching, "doesn't it?"

Fox, for all the mischief gathering in his gaze, took his time to think it over. Owaen waited, letting the crisp night air fill his senses with the aroma of damp earth, while the soft gurgle of the stream echoed the call of some lonely night owl high above them.

"Yes," Fox eventually admitted.

Owaen's melancholy laugh earned him a snort from one of the horses.

"The way I feel about you, after what you've done, and what you're still keeping from me..." Owaen's voice drifted to silence as he examined Fox's expression. Black eyes didn't blink. Owaen sighed and continued. "This is messed up, isn't it?"

"It is."

"Will you and I ever find peace together?"

The words fell from Owaen's lips like coins from a cut purse, but Fox didn't flinch. Instead, he wiggled up and forwards until their foreheads, eyes, and mouths aligned, as if they shared one body.

One heart.

"Know this, Owaen Carter, keeper of my love," Fox vowed with an intense urgency that sent Owaen's skin prickling with unexpected gooseflesh. "I will burn the rest of the world down to keep you safe and prevent others from keeping us apart. I will burn it all."

Owaen swallowed against the fierce lump forming in his throat.

"I know," Owaen mumbled. Dark green eyes searched black and gold, back and forth. "But I can't... I'm not worth that —"

"Hush, Elf." Fox interrupted Owaen's desperate words with a fierce kiss. "To me, yes, you are. That's all that matters."

"But —"

"Open your mouth, stubborn fool. I want to taste you."

Letting the cool lips and smooth caresses wash away his worries, Owaen gave in to pleasure, surrendering to the storm barely contained within the creature above that held him down.

For who knew how long this rare moment of stillness, of peace, would last?

As Fox sighed with pleasure, coaxing Owaen's tongue into his greedy mouth, Owaen closed his eyes.

That's what worried him.

What would happen *after*?

Trembling fingers traced Fox's spine, travelling up past visions of chaos painted on his smooth back, digging into his shoulders to pull him close, allowing no space between them.

Would their time together ever find the even keel that this unique creature deserved?

It wasn't simply Caspian, unhinged, fueled with wild magic, along with a mad plan beyond understanding, that concerned Owaen.

It was also Fox himself, bound to Owaen by love and something deeper, filled with the unquenchable desire for revenge.

The travelers were back on the overgrown forest road the next morning, Fox filled with visible anticipation to get going.

They had been riding for only an hour or so, both brooding about what had happened, about what was to come.

Overhead, the clouds had gathered with another threat of rain. No sharp ozone smell lingered here, just the green smell of living things, each pocket of undergrowth of tiny lives lived in the shadows and loam, amongst wet moss and curled ferns. It was an entire world within a world. The morning was cold, the wind brisk and the daylight a dismal grey. A perfect setting for deep thoughts. Tucked in a hooded leather cloak, he examined his memories. Caspian had shown signs of his chaotic vision as a young man. Yet Owaen couldn't help but feel a pang, for the loss of the odd but bright blue-eyed brother that he had once considered his closest friend.

His heart heavy, Owaen shifted in the saddle. It wasn't quite broad enough for his rear, but thankfully the black horse was behaving today.

Well, mostly.

Blackthorn had deigned to let Willow ride next to him on the wider stretches of what was left of the rocky thoroughfare. Unless there was a branch that hung too low for both riders to pass under.

Blackthorn made sure he always passed first.

Each time it happened, Owaen had to cough into his fist or look ahead to disguise a snort.

Perhaps Fox was on the wrong horse.

When Fox came alongside Owaen's left after their latest walk in single file, Owaen inhaled deeply. He had always had a strong sense of smell, and the forest was a place of endless aromas, scents that were so thick in his nostrils and lungs that they almost had colours to them. Moist loam, dripping ferns and spicy pine filled his senses, along with the wild tang, reminiscent of a storm that Fox carried about him, whatever form he chose to embody. Owaen was pleased to note that his own scent, minerals and musk, whatever mixture it was, now permeated his lover's skin, blending to make something that was the scent of *them*.

"What are you smirking about?" Fox muttered.

Startled, Owaen avoided staring too keenly at Fox's swollen lips, damp with the gulp of water just taken from his leather flask. Instead, Owaen stared ahead at the moss and the draped beard-like vines drooping from one twisted branch to another. He chewed the inside of his cheeks, wondering whether to make something up, but chose honesty instead. It's what he'd asked for in return, so it seemed only fair. Dark green eyes filled with a wicked light as they examined Fox with a sly sideways glance.

Owaen was unable to help his serene smile from forming.

"I was thinking about my lover's cock, actually."

On his horse beside Owaen, Fox spat out his mouthful of water.

Laughing while Fox spluttered, Owaen tilted his head, observing the line of the outermost parts of the canopy. The edges shifted, rippling leaves not quite touching. A thin line of grey clouds was visible between the oceans of green foliage, the tips teasing against each other as the frigid wind moved through the forest with bracing gusts.

His airways and voice back under control, Fox glared. Owaen didn't need to look over to know it was there. The man's ire grazed his cheek like a shard of ice.

"Would you care to elaborate?" Fox asked, his tone about as easy as the dried beef Owaen had choked down for brunch.

Patting Blackthorn's silky ebony mane as the horse side-stepped a golden beetle crawling across the mossy road, shimmering in the dappled light like a discarded coin, Owaen gave the question more thought.

"I was wondering. How do you do it?" Owaen lifted a hand and traced pretend curves down his chest.

"What?"

Looking up from the glimmering bug as his horse passed by it too, Fox stared at him, disgust marring his pale face.

Owaen bit back another laugh.

"I've never wanted magic to rule my life," Owaen offered. His shoulders lifted and fell with a contented shrug. "I was born with an amount that does me well enough. But you, you have so much that you can change... woman, to dragon, to man and back again. *How do you do it?*"

"How?" Fox repeated, his dark eyebrows rising.

"You know." Owaen pointed at his own crotch. Black and gold eyes narrowed, but Owaen went on. "We never had that conversation. I knew some dragons..." his voice faded. "I knew it took a lot of energy. But I never asked the *how* of it."

As their horses navigated a spongier stretch of road, their hooves muted by the thick moss, Owaen waited. He snuck a glance at Fox occasionally. The man's expression appeared calm, so Owaen held his tongue.

"Matter," Fox finally began after the next dappled bend along the winding forest road. "All of us are made of tiny, tiny pieces. And each of those pieces has a... charge to them."

"Like lightning?" Owaen guessed, their knees almost touching.

"No. Like the air *between* the clouds and the earth, right before lightning strikes," Fox corrected. His eyes were almost closed as he thought about what to say. "That's what I... that's how I change myself. Using my will. Following that potential."

"With your will? But using your mind?"

"Yes." Fox shivered. "Although it feels uncomfortable. The further the distance, the worse the discomfort gets."

Owaen mulled that over, observing Fox's shuttered eyes.

"Yet you don't need to consume crystals to fill that potential." It was more of a statement than a question.

"Correct." Fox licked his lips. "I have been... depleted... of that potential only a very, *very* few times."

Mutely, Owaen nodded. Scarred fingers tightened on the reins. He had seen Fox during such a time. Recently, on their way to the City of the Seers.

Along with *before*.

When Fox had been in another body, captured by Shadow Light, held in the very same cave that Fox had locked Owaen away afterwards.

Steadying his breath, Owaen cleared his throat.

"Are you happy with how your matter is arranged now? Don't get me wrong." Owaen held up both hands, the reins dangling. "I'm here for you, however you come to me. I'm simply curious."

"This form..." Fox tilted his head back, staring at Owaen down his nose. "You know whom this body is based on?"

Owaen nodded, solemn.

Skye, still reeling from her captivity, had run off after Owaen had rescued her. Owaen had found her, stunned in the aftermath of what she had done, while fleeing into the forest. One of the figures dead at her feet had been an Elf, his pale skin and inky black hair just visible beneath the blood and gore.

With his blonde hair sticking to his forehead, Owaen shivered. The air was chilled, but a damp veil of humidity permeated this stretch of pines and cedars. But the sweat that beaded over his skin was mostly from the disturbing memory.

"When you are depleted," Owaen rolled the word over his tongue with caution, "you slowly come back to your original state by resting? Is that all?"

Fox hummed, his gaze on the dense woods to their left. "I feel like I'm drawing in from what is around me."

"'Drawing in'?" Owaen repeated.

"Hm. It's like I tap into the potential from the," Fox gestured vaguely to the trees with one hand, "surrounding environment." Glittering eyes shone at Owaen, wide now, sparkling with gold even in the wan, pasty light. "How is magic for you?"

"For me, it is a faint spark *inside*. While you look *outside* of yourself. That's curious."

"Yes. No." Fox raised his hand to indicate the trees and sky with pale fingers. "It's both. Like I'm part of everything for a very, very tiny moment in time I'm connected. Like a hive."

Owaen swallowed thickly. "A hive..?"

Fox nodded slowly, avoiding his gaze. "Mm. Like all of us are joined, or in unknown communication, connection. Like a swarm of bees."

"Oh. Bees, huh?" Owaen cleared his throat, a ripple of unease along his broad shoulders like leathery wings.

"What?"

"Um. Nothing." The current tension between them had settled, for now. To think of his parents was to invite back confusion and distress. Owaen simply wasn't ready. "Um. Perhaps we should have stopped at the sacred grove after all —"

"No," Fox said instantly. He was looking at Owaen oddly.

Green eyes blinked rapidly.

"Not even to pay our respects to the ancient heart of the forest?"

"No."

"How about I go?" Owaen offered, unsure why it seemed a good idea. Caspian was loose, but the closer they got to him, the closer they got to... No. Owaen cut that thought off. "Perhaps you can wait here if you don't want —"

"Are you stalling? We need to get back to Aneirin and then make plans with my *friends*. No."

"You're being heavy-handed, don't you think?"

"I'm sure it appears that way."

"Sk... Fox."

"Yes?"

"You're being a cold bastard. Again."

"I don't care."

"Ah," Owaen sighed. "Ah, fuck."

He peered at the overgrown mess of a road ahead. Blackthorn was doing well considering the shoddy state of it, dislodged pebbles and lichen, making stretches of its curves and dips quite uneven.

Swallowing through a throat suddenly hot and thick, Owaen licked his lips. He spat a moment later, the faint tang of bitter ash an unpleasant flavour on his tongue.

"Whatever we do," he said, his voice firmer. "We're going to need more grain for the horses. The supplies we could bring with us won't last us if the weather gets worse, if we simply headed straight to Aneirin. I expected more villages nearby to have some, but if their crops are as meagre as they always have been, Rhydian will strangle us *both* if we starve his prized horse."

Owaen let Fox chew on that for a while. Under his flop of damp, black hair, Fox's mouth was a thin line as he examined the crowded trees ahead.

"So, you mean to continue to head east first," Fox finally murmured. "To that stony town?"

"Yes." Unsure of Fox's mood, Owaen swiveled in the saddle to face him. "You've been there?"

"Hm. Once."

A blonde eyebrow rose. Dressed in layers of dark wool and linen, Fox's cool beauty stood out, but not out of place. The woods here were wild and just as cool with clouds obscuring the sun, the fierce breeze shaking the sea of trees. Fox eventually blew out a puff of air.

"I was newly reborn, with a yellow-haired mute beside me."

Owaen held his breath as Fox went on, the thickness in his throat becoming more uncomfortable. This was a story he'd never had a chance to hear before.

"We stopped there on the way back from Mionlach, looking rather worse for wear." Rather than concerned in any way, Fox looked pleased with himself.

Gritting his teeth, Owaen kept his mouth shut.

"I was numb, pleased, yes, but in a kind of shock. When I made it to the town, I saw some of the nomads that frequented the lower plains of the dragon homelands." Fox cracked his neck, his gaze straight ahead. "Their checked robes were few and far between amongst the homespun cloth of the locals. I had seen them both as a young dragon, so I knew who they were. They didn't recognise me, of course."

"Of course," Owaen muttered. He imagined Fox had been in quite a state after taking his revenge on the dragons that had left him to Shadow Light's clutches.

"I attempted to communicate with them," Fox laughed. "But the leader of their camp shoved a pouch of fragrant resin into my hands, my fingernails still stained with blood and ash. She told me to go *purify* myself."

"Ha ha," Owaen choked out. "Ha. I can only imagine."

With a sigh, Fox wiped his eyes with the heel of his hand. "I tipped it all into the fire of the inn that I allowed myself to stay at for a night. It smelt wonderful. But it wouldn't have helped me."

"You went to an *inn*?"

"Mm. It was near the public baths." Fox glanced at Owaen, his gaze serious. "I was in desperate need of one."

"Of course," Owaen said, his voice hoarse. "Of course you were."

Owaen let Blackthorn pick his way across a wide, shallow rivulet of clear water that cut into the once even pavers of the forest road. It was an obvious example of how much time had passed. Of how little people lived around this part of the world since the City of the Seers had fallen.

Had the town ahead changed, in the way time and chaos had changed them?

Last time he had been there, it was a simple quarry town, cut along and into the valleys of various coloured rocks, to house the workers who helped the dragons create the City of the Seers. He didn't really wish to see it, to witness how it may have changed. But at the same time, it meant a few more quiet days traveling together, before they had to really think about finding his brother.

Before the shit hit the trees.

"We need to stop there for the horses," Owaen said stubbornly as the animals in question made it to the far side of the stream.

"Fine," Fox muttered, his resigned sigh absorbed by the rustle of damp leaves whispering together in the frigid breeze. "Let's go to Baile Fuar."

19

Cas

Year 250, Cas at age 9
Baile Mara, City of the Sea

"Wane! Th-there you are," the man huffed, his cheeks pink. "Where's your brother?"

"He's looking for pirates."

"W-what?"

"Pirates." Hugging a miniature wooden ship, the blonde boy beamed up at the old man, young green eyes clear and amused. "He reckons we can spot them amongst the sailors and merchants down here."

Evreth Burns, head of the household at the Carter family estate, blinked hazel eyes rapidly. After giving the blonde boy a perplexed look, he assessed the bustling docks. The salt breeze mussed his woolly white hair. The only ships in port were fishing vessels and merchant traders.

"P-pirates?"

"Yep."

"I see."

"Why?"

"Your mother has sent me to fetch you both."

"Oh." The boy's smile faltered. He fiddled with the toy sailing ship in his little hands. "He's up there." Wane pointed a grubby finger upwards at the stack of oak barrels that he leant against.

A blonde head peeped over the rim of the highest barrel.

Evreth tilted his head back, one hand shielding his eyes against the intense sun directly overhead.

"Where...? Ah."

Caspian Carter, the oldest twin to the esteemed alchemists at the forefront of magical expansion, grinned down at Evreth and Wane. He reached a hand into his spotless linen shirt. He pulled it out with a dramatic flourish.

Cas' middle finger waved down at them.

"Oh." Evreth's shoulders slumped.

Cas was gleefully enjoying the mania amongst the creaks of cargo ropes hard at work, and sailors yelling at useless folk to get out of the way.

A newly arrived merchant ship, the largest Cas had seen all year, rode low in the calm waters of the bay at the closest pier. The great ship of barnacled wood was covered in swearing and shouting sailors, its three sails pulled in out of the brisk, cool breeze. Thankfully, the island in the middle of the bay wasn't smoking much, the sickly stink of egg scented gas was only a faint stain on the ocean air. A chaotic crowd had spread out around the boat, a mix of shouting sailors, red-faced crane drivers and a line of expectant merchants.

"Cas!" Wane cupped one of his grubby hands over his mouth. "Mother and Father want us home. Come down, okay?"

The eldest twin heard Evreth's announcement. Cas pretended to think.

"No thanks. You two go without me."

"Um." Evreth's shoulders sagged further. "But I have to make sure you go, you see..."

Cas snickered. Ever since he'd nearly burned down one of the barns a couple of years ago, a servant was never far away. He never thought about that incident anymore. At the top of the stack of barrels, Cas shrugged.

As a matter of fact, he *never* thought about it.

At all.

Ever.

Silver-flecked blue eyes, one dark, one pale, blazed.

"I don't need magic," the boy muttered, the words absorbed by the cacophony along the docks. "Magic can get," Cas double checked to make sure Evreth couldn't hear, "*fucked.*"

It was impossible that he'd ever grow into being able to use it, like Wane had done.

Except.

What had Rook once said?

Magic is more flexible than your parents realise, little shrimp. Perhaps there is hope for you yet.

Pretending not to see Evreth approach, Cas had been quite content to spot the foreigners amongst the new arrivals all along the docks. It was far better than being cooped up at home with Mother and Father. After watching a young serving woman carrying away a basket of limp lizards last week, Cas had stepped back, pressing himself against the wall as the dead reptiles had passed him by. The sight of a tiny clawed foot poking out from a layer of stained burlap had caused him to want to both vomit and shut his eyes tight. He did neither.

Not at first, anyway.

Forcing himself to watch, Cas had waited until the servant had shut his mother's study door and trekked down the cool hallway and turned right. Then he had run off to empty the contents of his stomach against a rosebush in one of the rear formal gardens. A peacock had eyed him strangely. Cas had apologised to the bird, staggering off to rinse the foul taste in his mouth at a fountain bubbling with cool water.

Strangely enough, Cas had told his brother about it afterwards. Tracking Wane down to where he was reading some musty old scroll an equally musty old tutor had supplied, Cas had expected Wane to laugh at him. Because that's what Cas would have done to Wane. Instead, his younger brother had nodded, his dark green eyes thoughtful. There had been a moment of solidarity between the twins.

Until Wane had opened his stupid mouth.

"Mother says it's for the greater good, though, Cassie."

Today, Cas was similarly dressed to Wane's white shirt and linen shorts, but where Wane was a sand-stained mess, Cas had kept his clothes spotless. Even during the climb up the stack of musty smelling barrels. He had wanted to see the wide expanse of the deep blue bay and its crowd of incoming ships on the high tide. All the docks were full. The air was alive with salt breezes from three different directions, fresh tar and oily food being hawked to the eager sailors freshly back to port.

"Caspian," Evreth called. "Your mother and father need you home now. P-please come down."

Above them, the boy tilted his head. Behind him, the sun turned his pale hair into an ethereal halo. "Why?"

Evreth pursed his lips. At his hip, Wane concentrated on straightening the sails of his little ship, but Cas could see his brother was clearly biting back a snigger.

"Because," said Evreth.

"Why?"

"Because they have some task for you both."

"Why?"

"I d-didn't ask them. But they sent me to fetch you —"

"Why?"

"Your mother is very busy working on some grand experiments. Hypatia needs you both —"

"Why?"

Wane was openly giggling now.

Evreth's cheeks went from pink to red. "Caspian Carter! Come down here right now!"

"Why?"

"You know why! You can't be... Um. Just come down. Right n-now."

"Why?"

Cas beamed at his brother, who was now laughing openly. Evreth's hazel eyes were wide, the old man clearly distressed. His wooly white and grey hair blew over his face, getting stuck in his mouth. The servant meant well enough, despite always being a bit of a bore. At a young age, Cas had become adept at tuning the man's voice out. Wane was also bored with the exchange, busy poking a dead seagull at the base of the barrel stack with a sandy boot.

A low hum interrupted the bustle of the crowd. The strange faces that Cas had been hoping to spot *finally* began emerging from the fantastically enormous ship. Most of the men and women were tall, with black hair long and in braids. All had delicate features foreign to Baile Mara, especially their beautifully almond-shaped eyes.

Cas whooped out a laugh.

Pirates!

At last.

Yet as he stood up to get an even better look, Evreth, still spouting nonsense below, said something that caught Cas' young ears. Eyes wide, the ship forgotten, the boy stared down at the pink-cheeked servant. Cas interrupted the man's sullen tirade.

"Mister Evreth?"

"I know they are busy! But why they send me, I don't know, neither of them pay any attention —"

"Mister Evreth," Cas repeated with more volume to make sure he was heard over the stirring crowd. "What did you just say?"

Taken aback, the man covered his eyes with his hand again and squinted up at the lad. "Huh?"

Cas' hands tingled. "Who is at home with Mother?"

"Oh." Evreth dropped his hand. "I said Morgan Rose has come. The librarian has brought some scrolls —"

Cas didn't wait.

Sparing only a vague thought for his white shirt, he jumped over the edge. Sliding down a rope along the barrel's edge, he landed on the stone dock with a light leap. Winking at Wane, he ran off, an exasperated Evreth behind. Sure enough, Wane's quick boot steps fell in behind as he started up the long ascent of warehouses, terraced gardens, cobbled streets, and boutiques.

As he sped past a public house with its patronage spilled out onto the front street, Cas spotted something that slowed him down, if only barely. Dodging a cranky donkey being led on a rope by a small girl, he hopped aside with nimble footwork. As quick as a seagull darting for a stray crust of bread, Cas' little hand slipped in and out of the back pocket of a passing scribe.

"Cas!" Wane panted, not far behind. "Wait for me!"

"No," Cas hollered.

Laughing to himself, the boy clutched the white feather quill to his chest and continued his untamed sprint home.

"Pirates..."

After his initial burst of speed, passing through the packed market district, the boy's progress slowed. He passed a street shrine built into a stone wall, a small square inset shelf about shoulder height, filled with finger-sized quartz points of different colours. A few elderly men with wrinkled faces, eyes closed, and all dressed in robes of pale blue, were chanting before a curl of incense as it drifted about. The fragrant smoke was battling with the sour stink of a bitter breeze welling up from the bedrock itself.

"At least I saw some," Cas huffed to himself as he jogged, internally scoffing at the worshippers and their blind devotion, "from afar."

He was almost disappointed, though.

Yet what had he expected?

An angry mob bursting forth from the bowels of the ship?

"*Yes!*"

The exclamation earned him a startled glance as he ducked under a shop awning; the rafters filled with a myriad of brightly coloured silk scarves, including flaming crimsons, hanging and flapping in the breeze. Cas stuck out his tongue at the shopkeeper as he passed. He didn't wait for her reaction as he headed uphill.

The foreigners he'd glimpsed for only a moment certainly appeared to be kin to those causing trouble along the coast. In all his years, Cas had certainly never seen their like before. They wore long tunics and short vests, mostly black, with sashes at their waist of rainbow hued fabric. One of them had worn a sash the exact shade of coppery red. A colour Cas liked best. That foreigner, a handsome woman with a black cape tossed over one shoulder, had also carried two long swords at her belt.

It had been worth the wait, even if he'd left sooner than expected.

Earlier that morning, the young twins had arrived at the wild, desolate beach of black sand south of the city. Both were intent on seeing if the ship that Illarion had built really would withstand the surf. Wane had been concentrating on making sure the miniature pieces of ballast were evenly spaced in their slots, his tongue poking out of his mouth, when Cas had called out in surprise. Sailing in from the west had been the merchant ship, The Southern Bruce, heading for the crowded bay.

From arguing with sailors about which boxer was the best down at the public houses when shirking his studies, Cas had learned two important things about The Southern Bruce.

First, it brought in heavy ingots of metal that the famous blacksmiths of Baile Mara used to craft beautiful swords and weapons, and delicate scientific instruments. Second, it was the *only* ship powerful enough to make the crossing to and from the distant eastern islands. Foreign lands that had names Cas couldn't pronounce.

With Wane close on his heels, Cas had dashed along the sand, over treacherous rocks with a boy's careless bravery, all the way to the empty wharf, eager for the colossal ship's impending arrival.

As the twins had caught their breath, a blacksmith had grinned at them as they staked out the stacks of cargo along the wharf. The middle-aged woman with sparkling eyes of hazel, brawny arms and her long hair in a thick braid over one shoulder had winked.

"Here for the Bruce, lads?"

"Yes!" Cas had shouted. Wane, still huffing, nodded. Cas bounced on his toes. "Pirates!"

The woman laughed, adjusting her thick leather apron, spotted and pockmarked with burns. "Ha. I'm here for the rare metals."

"Metals? What will you make with them?" Wane asked, coming to stand behind his brother. Cas was inspecting the closest stack of wooden barrels.

"Pretty knives," winked the blacksmith, "and even prettier swords."

Wane screwed up his nose, but Cas' ears perked up. "Swords?"

"Yes, lad, the finest in the city." A young man with yellow hair nearby snorted. By the look of his thick apron, he was in the same trade. The woman turned her back on the fellow. She held up a scarred hand, her index finger topped by a silver spark of energy, glittering brightly even in the sun's relentless glare. "Tested by one of the oldest bloodlines in the city."

"Ha!" the young man snorted.

The blacksmith sent him a frosty glare, flexing her arms. The young man swallowed and pointed his nose in another direction.

"You use your magic to test the metal?" Cas queried, eyes narrowed.

Turning back to face Cas, the woman nodded.

"I want it sharp, so it has to be the right blend."

"Can't you test it without?"

"Without magic?" The woman shrugged. "Sure. It would take longer and happen after this ship sailed off with my coins. So why would I?"

Cas bit his lip. It was his turn to shrug.

"Whatever."

"Magic is awesome," Wane said happily from behind Cas' shoulder.

"Aye, lad. Magic has its uses, that's for sure."

A flock of seagulls swooped overhead, the collective crowd ducking to avoid the rain of droppings and diving birds on the lookout for unsecured food.

"It can't do everything," Cas sulked. "Metal knives aren't always best. Father says the black glass from the island cuts cleaner than any silver blade. He only uses that material when working on his beehives."

"True. But there's always a use for a nice, heavy blade." The woman eyed the two boys curiously. "Bees, you say?"

"Yes, father —" Wane began, but Cas interrupted.

The elder twin crossed his arms over his small chest. "So?"

Throwing a quick glance to the grand estates overlooking the city, the woman's eyes narrowed. "You're the Carter boys, aren't you?"

"What of it?"

Bright eyes turned thoughtful. The blacksmith lowered her voice. "I know of your parents. We all do. There's a rumour they're working, spreading more magic further, not just for the dragons or arming the soldiers with the ability to hunt down pirates. But sharing more for us common folk too. Is that true?"

Feeling hot under his collar for reasons he couldn't explain, Cas grabbed Wane's hand. "I don't know," he scoffed. "I don't care. Come on, Wane, let's find another spot where we can see better."

Cas had dragged his brother to the far side of the crowded wharf, past the vaguely person-shaped amethyst statue representing some long forgotten god that watched over the ships arriving to the terraced city by the sea. Cas sent it a dry smirk, while Wane protested about his ship getting knocked about. Not caring, Cas held Wane's hand all the way to the tallest stack of barrels outside another warehouse, cheeks flushed and lower lip stuck out.

Yes, magic was useful.

If you had it.

"I... don't... need... magic..." Cas heaved.

Close to being winded, the blonde boy continued his focused race home.

As he climbed higher into the city, Cas turned the conversation with the blacksmith over in his mind, along with the image of the copper-red sash. Cas thought of the silk scarves he'd ducked under a few streets back.

Would *she* like one?

Cas stored that thought away for when he wasn't running up hills, back and forth along warm, terraced streets.

The city of Baile Mara was laid out in a vast half-bowl shape. It made for an astonishing vista from either the top or bottom. It also took one's breath away to traverse. In urgent situations like this, that required nimble feet and a knowledge of back streets in which to avoid the market day crowds, like today.

His younger brother finally caught Cas as he paused for a moment at the halfway point. This was at the mouth of a narrow back alley. The twins eyed each other.

Wane shook his head.

Cas straightened his shoulders.

"We should go," Wane puffed, "the longer way —"

"Shut up," Cas hissed.

Before Wane could protest, Cas dashed down the lane.

It didn't take long.

As their boot steps echoed along the cobbles of the winding street, an older boy stuck his head out of a third-story window up ahead. Cas rolled his eyes as the boy whistled three times, an evil smirk on his stupid face.

Further along, a group of kids stood up from their doorsteps, where they had been eating spiced candy. Even more stuck their heads out of upper-story windows.

Eyeing the far opening of the alley, Cas picked up speed. Wane would be fine. His magic would protect him.

Cas simply had to run.

Fast.

Because each child had pockets of stones, ready for the inevitable moment when two privileged boys were caught taking a shortcut up the city's middle terrace to their fancy estate.

It was possible to ignore the rocks, despite each one locating their target every time. Sharp stings struck his arms and legs, heated by the spiteful magic of children who should have known better, but didn't.

What outraged Cas were the words.

"Loser!"

"Son of the great Hypatia can't boil an egg with even a puny spark!"

"Weirdo!"

"Freak!"

The scratches and burns hurt, but they'd fade. They always did. It was the names that burned holes onto his heart.

Because compared to Wane, all of them were true.

Bursting out of the alley, Cas left the kids behind, eyes wide, chin trembling, lungs burning. He must have slowed. He hadn't intended to, as a brief moment later, Wane grabbed at Cas' shirt but missed, struggling to keep up. His younger brother had never learned to run this fast.

He'd never needed to.

The kids in the alley were a new breed of children. Offspring of the craftspeople of Baile Mara, living in the middle class part of the city where magic was spread more thickly amongst the population than down at the docks. Those gifted with special skills could further enhance their craft with magic earned for their dedication to the arts and technological advances they made.

Idly, Cas wondered if any of them belonged to the blacksmith. He wished he'd got her name, so as never to purchase any of her wares. Wane finally grabbed hard on Cas' sleeve as he struggled to keep up.

"Cas! Let me go back and take care of them for you!"

Pulling away from Wane's grasp, Cas raced ahead without a word.

It was his job to look after his little brother, not the other way around. Despite how spoiled his younger brother was, Cas was the eldest, if only by moments.

Cheeks pink and eyes welling with anger, Cas jumped over a startled ginger alley cat. It hissed. He hissed back and kept running.

The librarian never paid him much attention. She avoided him, actually, which he didn't understand at all. Occasionally, pale green eyes full of shifting unease would pass over him, gone before he could catch them. She never stayed long, running the occasional errand for Mother or Father. But when Cas glimpsed her coming and going about the strange vials and coloured vapors of Hypatia's study, the petite woman wore the same expression as Cas might wear today.

If he'd had the guts to face himself in a mirror after enduring the barbed taunts of spoiled children. When he never allowed himself to stop and fight.

Because against magic, as he was now?

He'd lose.

Lungs burning, blonde hair damp and his youthful heart bruised, Cas dashed on. The gods never listened, so he prayed to the cycles of destiny instead. He prayed he would be fast enough today as he raced onwards and upwards through the city by the sea.

Towards home.

Towards *her*.

20

Karlien

Year 367
Baile Mara, City of the Sea

Everything was not fine.

"Tiny princess."

Karlien's nostrils flared.

Nothing good came of dealing with Baek Hyeon while victim to a raging hangover. Especially considering the events of last night. Not just his dream. Perched on the delicate velvet stool by his makeup table with a crystal flask of morning wine chilling in a basin of cold water nearby, the prince contemplated the innocent-looking sphere. It remained on the desk across the room, a harmless bauble of sparkling clear quartz. Karlien's gaze followed the blue incense smoke licking along its smooth curve. Eyelids painted with shimmering copper lowered halfway over azure blue eyes.

The prince's thoughts darted from one vivid image to another. Last night had been startling and strange.

Above the confusion, however, paraded the image of Hyeon, bare for the world, or at least Karlien, to see.

Hmmm.

Copper eyelids drooped so much that one might think the prince was asleep at his desk.

Was it for better or worse that he no longer had to wonder what artwork lay beneath his bodyguard's clothes?

Beautiful, wild images of symbols, ships, and fantastical sea monsters filled his mind. He wondered if they had meaning? Like the illustrations in the few historical books that survived in the city to this day. Maybe —

The prince blinked the black patterns on glistening skin away. Examining his flushed cheeks in the gilded mirror at his makeup table, Karlien entertained the thought that the lustrous pink balm he normally wore might not be required today.

A soft knock from the doorframe was followed by a low cough. "Princess."

Inhaling the gentle aroma of cinnamon incense, Karlien took a languid sip of wine, chin raised. Squashing last night's events deep down inside, blue eyes blinked rapidly at themselves in the reflection down his straight nose. Perhaps balm was needed after all, a perfect disguise to hide his unexpected flush. Setting the glass down, the prince's slim fingers rearranged his makeup brushes, narrow to wide. That was nice. But too predictable. Ignoring a resigned wolfish sigh from the floor, Karlien rearranged the brushes again, by handle length this time, short to long. As he moved the delicate bone handles around on their golden tray, his mind wandered to other things.

A servant had come past with his wine and the prince had asked for his grandmama's schedule. The servant had shrugged.

And then left.

That was normal, that was fine.

What was *not* fine was the hulking brute by his door. A man that Karlien couldn't look at without thinking about the way the widest bands of black had travelled all the way down to *another* work of art hanging like a —

The prince's grip tightened on the longest brush, a lovely thing with a rounded head of soft bristles. His gaze rose back to the mirror.

Decision made, Karlien dipped a fine brush into a small glass jar. He spread the pink balm across his cheeks. From his side, the morning sun flowed through the windows, highlighting his otherwise unblemished skin. Eyes narrowing, he bit a still-swollen bottom lip.

Was it his mother whom he had to thank for his creamy complexion? Or his father?

The brush halted on his left cheek, the faint tremble of fine bristles barely visible.

"Oh," said the prince. "I don't remember."

The young man in the mirror tilted his head, eyes wide and staring. It had been a long while since his parents had gone to the Gods.

When everyone told him that everything would be just *fine*.

Until his parents died.

Eyelids fluttered, the image in the mirror appearing blurred for some reason. It was probably the spicily sweet incense. Karlien reached into his robe and pulled out a delicate wisp of creamy silk. He dabbed the annoying moisture away, careful of his perfectly applied eyeshadow. Discarding the cloth, he picked up a thin brush, applying black kohl with swift movements.

"Everything was fine… But…" Trying not to blink, Karlien peered down at his aligned brushes. "I don't remember either of your faces."

Another cough, louder this time, resounded from the doorway.

"Princess Karlie —"

Spinning on his stool, Karlien launched the exquisitely made brush across the room, hoping it impaled somewhere soft.

It didn't.

The brush bounced off a leather-clad, broad chest. It landed on a patch of the stone floor not covered by a rug with a ringing clatter.

The prince gaped.

The delicate handle was now in two pieces.

Azure eyes rose to the doorway, wide and accusing.

"Look at what you did!" Karlien screeched.

Pushing off the stool, he stalked towards Hyeon. Crouching with a resigned huff, the prince gathered up the remains of the brush. When he rose, he waved them in Hyeon's face.

"This was my favourite!"

Hyeon didn't move a muscle. Only his stupid crimson-flecked pretty eyes reacted, following Karlien's every move.

Nostrils flaring, the prince crossed his arms over his chest and studied the taller man. His long hair, sleek and partially braided, shone in the morning's bright sunshine. The two thick golden torques glinted beneath, their blunt ends dipping below the open collar of his white linen shirt and black leather vest. The hilts of two swords poked over his shoulders. A muscle twitched along the man's tattooed neck. Studiously ignoring Karlien's appraisal, Hyeon glanced past Karlien at the bed, his rigid gaze quickly shifting to the desk and the ephemera crowded across it.

"Great lady says bring that."

"What?"

"Great lady dreamt and sent word to me. Bring you. Bring sphere."

Eyes rimmed with kohl narrowed.

Of course his grandmama had dreamt about it. Hopeful she hadn't seen *everything* that had taken place here, though. Gods, was there any privacy at all? Although, it would be good to finally find out what the heck was going on. And he *had* wanted to see her, after all.

"Princess?"

"*What.*"

"You bring? Sphere?"

"Gods!" Karlien snapped, eyes rolling dramatically. "Yes! I bring. Ugh. Calm down."

The sharp crack of candy between teeth filled the otherwise silent bedchamber.

"*Heol*," Hyeon muttered, his rich voice restrained by his tense jaw. "*Heol*."

"Hmp." Karlien tossed his head. Hyeon sometimes used that word. Karlien didn't know what it meant. "Whatever."

Avoiding the dark gaze that pressed against him like warmth from glowing embers, Karlien stalked to his open closets and glanced at the two pairs of boots he'd pulled out. One style was made of supple, deep brown leather, laced, knee high to go with his new emerald green long pants of fine wool. The other pair were ankle high, shiny black, perhaps more fitting with the older black pants that went well with his navy tunic?

Snuffling, the grey wolf rose, stretched and wandered over, this time pressing its black nose onto the back of Hyeon's hand. Karlien pursed his lips in annoyance. It was Hyeon's wolf, yes. But last night, it felt like some of the beast's undying loyalty was for him, too. Tossing his golden copper curls over his shoulder, Karlien straightened. He examined the closest wall, following the patterns of fine cracks in the stone where they webbed in behind faded tapestries.

"So grandmama wants the sphere." Azure eyes slid to his bodyguard. Hyeon was also examining a patch of wall.

The tall man nodded, a curt bob, the single long braid over his shoulder shifting.

"Hmm." Karlien scrunched his nose. "You should learn more of our language, you... pirate."

Tapered, exotic eyes tightened.

"Then I can tell you that there are more horrendous mouse droppings in my room again." Karlien sniffed. "And you would finally do something about them. How are there so many? Especially that one with the black spot! Yech. Why do they keep following me?"

"Mouse? Hm." The bodyguard's bland expression was offensively annoying as he slid his gaze to the prince.

Was the giant pirate trying not to smile?

The longer they stared at each other, the more convinced Karlien became that Hyeon's expression was somewhat smug. He wanted to wipe it off the man's face, maybe with his

—

Closing his eyes, Karlien counted to three before opening them once more. Only to rake his eyes over the mysterious man before him. He was firmly *not* thinking about winding patterns of black ink, or how they followed the curve of golden flesh and toned muscles. When Karlien's gaze made it back to Hyeon's face, he realised that the smug expression had deepened.

Was that a *dimple*? How had he not seen that —

The prince cleared his throat.

Mice.

Think of the mice!

Sufficiently disgusted, Karlien flounced back across his chamber. Why didn't anyone else take those tiny, filthy creatures seriously? They were everywhere.

Choosing the ankle-high boots and navy tunic combination, Karlien stepped behind a screen of red silk to dress. He took his time, paying particular attention to adding rose oil behind his ears. He liked it on his wrists most days. Today, it seemed appropriate to apply it much higher.

When he emerged, Hyeon was where Karlien had left him, a neat figure by the ornate gilded door. The grey wolf sat on its haunches, one massive hind paw scratching a tufted grey ear.

"Well. Hurry up." Rings flashing, Karlien waved a hand at Hyeon and then the sphere. "Bring it along."

He swept past the figure to exit the room in a cloud of rose oil. The prince was pleased to note Baek Hyeon's smug expression had changed from smug to nice and stony.

Beaming, the prince skipped down the hall, hangover fading.

If Hyeon kept swearing under his breath like just now, the tattooed foreigner may finally get the hang of the common language.

The sun was close to its highest degree by the time the prince made his way through the ruined estate. Sweeping curved stairways had shifted out of their original position, the cracks covered over with wooden scaffolding. Sour smelling drafts permeated the extensive building.

Karlien, despite growing up amongst the ruins, offered a wistful sigh as he passed the decades-old damage.

After the chaos of years before, tradesfolk were hard to come by. On top of that, his grandmama insisted that those who lived in the city, amongst the sometimes toxic gases that blew in from the island, should come first. That was admirable, if a little irritating.

Karlien bit his lip. His grandmama would most likely cuff him upside the back of his head, if she'd known how he felt about that. He glanced through a large window to the bright day beyond. The weather was fair, with few clouds in the wide expanse of blue above. Servants bustled about, although far less than usual. He sniffed. The aroma of fresh bread was wafting up from the closest kitchen. Perhaps they were at their midday feast? No.

"They must be eating early," Karlien said waspishly, "because it's not *that* late."

Behind, Hyeon and the wolf sighed as one.

The prince pointedly ignored them both.

As they moved through the cracked halls and passages of ruined masonry, the prince paused by a floor to ceiling window. Outside, two large black horses were being walked through the courtyard. The animals were the tallest horses he'd ever seen, black with mane and tail tipped with reddish brown. At Hyeon's impatient exhale, Karlien rolled his eyes. But perhaps it was time for a ride? He hadn't been out with his favourite dappled pony for days. The highly strung animal would likely try to bite him next time he paid the adorable beast a visit. Smiling fondly, the prince sashayed past his glowering bodyguard, the stupid crystal sphere held firmly between powerful hands.

On arrival at the lowest level of the sprawling residence, Karlien approached the grand old door to his grandmama's humble reception chamber. His boot steps echoed on black flagstones, at odds with the two quiet, brooding presences behind. He stopped as a servant exited with an empty tray. It looked like the man had been involved in some sort of scuffle. A bruise was forming around one eye, and his lower lip marred with a fresh split. Avoiding the prince's gaze, the young man scurried off, giving Hyeon a wide berth.

"How childish," Karlien scoffed.

"Princess?"

The prince flicked a polished nail at the retreating servant.

"Getting into fights! I mean, really. This is the royal residence. Where is the respect?"

Silence followed his statement. The wolf shook its head, tall, pointed ears flapping. Karlien rolled his eyes and indicated for Hyeon to open the door with an impatient wave. Eyes on the cracked frescoed ceiling, the bodyguard knocked on the door. The giant man's annoying, shapely lips were pulled into an impertinent smirk.

At the soft 'yes' from within, Hyeon balanced the sphere in one hand and opened the petite door. As Karlien brushed past Hyeon, he sniffed, nose pointed high.

"Don't smile like that. You look like a fool."

The prince flounced into the chamber, half expecting another *Heol* from Hyeon as he ducked behind. This time, the man said nothing.

The space within was another rare one, like Karlien's bed chamber. A mostly intact room. It faced the bay, with floor to ceiling windows of thick glass open to the salt breeze. Smelling of incense to cover the sulphur gases of the city, the room was sun-bright and full of low couches and little tables. Along with the smokey incense, fresh fragrant rose blooms in all manner of glass vases covered the pale wooden shelves that lined the bare stone walls. It was a nice change to the stink that blew in from the smoking island of the bay some days, like some dragon still clung to the slopes, breathing out its toxic bad breath upon the innocent civilians in the terraced city of black stone across the water.

"Grandmama!" Karlien demanded, flopping to his knees before the Regent of Baile Mara. Eyelashes fluttering, he pouted at his great-grandmother. "Why have you been ignoring me? You've shut me out of every formal meeting this past week like I'm some spoiled child."

Before his grandmama could respond, someone coughed, stifling it almost immediately.

Karlien's azure eyes narrowed. Turning, he glared at a young man lounging with easy abandonment on a high-backed couch nearby.

"Torres," Karlien exclaimed. He hadn't seen his closest friend for ages. It had been *days*. "When did you arrive? Where have you been? What the heck are you doing here?"

"Easy, my prince," the youth beamed. He held up a highly polished fiddle. "I was merely amusing our most esteemed Regent, while her young charge took his sweet time waking up, getting up, and getting here. Your cousin will be here soon too."

Torres Hart, of the well respected Hart family, was dressed today in a dashing outfit of offensive yellow. With a mustard cape thrown over one shoulder in carefully positioned folds, the young man cut quite a figure. His tanned skin, visible above his low cut wool shirt, gleamed with lustrous oil. The colour was earthier when compared to Hyeon's golden toned flesh. But only slightly. Karlien dragged his thoughts back to the present as Torres pointed the toe of one leather boot at him.

With a grin, Torres *tsk-tsked* the prince.

"I came as quickly as I was summoned," Karlien insisted, cheeks flushing.

"Did you?" the young man drawled with a flicked glance at Hyeon, who stood nearby. Gold eyes glinted at the pink colour under Karlien's made-up cheeks. "You *are* easily distracted."

Twisting on his knees, the prince glanced behind him. With the wolf off exploring after an impressive leap out the low window to the grass outside, Hyeon was standing unobtrusively by the closed door, the quartz sphere in his hands, the hilts of his dual swords poking one over each shoulder. The man wasn't looking at them. Instead, he was staring at the sparkling horizon beyond the turquoise bay below, face unreadable. Karlien spun back to eye his great-grandmother, tossing his copper curls over a slim shoulder.

"Baek Hyeon took too long to tell me I was *finally* allowed to be let in on what is going on."

Bathsheba spared an amused glance over Karlien's shoulder before her gaze slid to Karlien's. He shifted on the thick green-toned rug beneath his knees.

"Um," said the prince. "I... dressed with care, wanting to look my best for you, grand-mama."

Bright blue eyes, their outer halo of iridescent azure, the same as her great-grandson's, twinkled. Under their piercing examination, Karlien cleared his throat.

"And... and I... made sure that I tidied my room before I left... the mice, you see..."

Twinkling blue eyes widened a fraction, the fine wrinkles drawing tight.

"The mice?" Bathsheba's voice, mistaken as weak by those who didn't know her well, was mild.

"Yes!" Karlien insisted with a dainty shiver. "There are mice everywhere. They keep following me."

"Oh." Eyes that had seen more than Karlien had imagined flicked a glance at the imposing figure by the door once more. "I see."

Ignoring the snigger from his *supposed* closest friend, Karlien dropped his head and clasped the frail hands folded before him. He kissed his grandmama's knuckles, then dropped his chin to her knees. Her thick wool dress of deep burgundy smelled faintly of honey and spice. He fluttered his eyelashes at her.

Her smile was wry as she extricated one wrinkled hand to pat her silver hair. A few wisps had escaped its elegant twist. There were only a few random wisps of copper left amongst the grey, these working well with the plain gold circlet she wore on some days. The pearl drop earrings hanging from her ears were just as simple, yet elegant. Even seated in the simple room, adorned only by flowers and the breathtaking vista beyond the open windows, Bathsheba was an imposing figure. The sheer centeredness of her presence more than made up for her lack of height. Seated primly in her burgundy dress, with no thick cape or cloak like most other citizens of Baile Mara preferred, her demure slippered feet rested upon a little three legged, velvet lined stool.

Even at a great age, his great grandmother was beautiful, and someone Karlien loved deeply and admired immensely.

At a nod from Bathsheba, Hyeon came forth. With a whiff of burnt sugar, he sat the quartz sphere on a modest table to Karlien's left. The bodyguard had thoughtfully brought along the stand, so the sphere wouldn't roll away. Karlien eyed it with suspicion.

"You heard it too, grandmama?"

Bathsheba ignored the sphere, her keen eyes on Karlien's face.

"I didn't hear all of it. There was..." at her delicate pause, the prince swallowed, "background noise."

"Ah." Karlien managed a weak chortle. "Was there now? Ha. Curious."

"Indeed. What did you hear, Karlien?"

"It was confusing at first, I —"

"Up studying last night, were you?" Torres snickered.

Beside him, his bodyguard made a soft, strangled sort of noise. Karlien side eyed him icily.

"Yes." The prince cleared his throat. "I was."

"While you were drunk, huh?" Torres smirked. "Did that tall, willowy creature show you how to cut your quill properly —"

"Torres Hart, by the gods, if you don't shut your —"

"Children, hush." That shut them both up. "What did you hear, Karlien?"

"Someone wanted help," the prince mumbled, wanting to sink into the floor.

Bathsheba's gaze lost focus for a moment. She nodded. "Yes. I think I heard all that was said. Enough, anyway. The timing *is* right."

"Oh." Karlien didn't know how to interpret her thoughtful look. "Um. Okay."

"And?"

"Ah. It didn't just speak, it glowed again."

Bright eyes narrowed. "What colour?"

"Blue, this time."

She nodded, thoughtful.

"Is that important?" Torres interrupted.

Karlien spared him a dark look. Unperturbed, Torres scratched an ear with his middle finger.

With a dainty huff, Karlien faced his great-grandmother. He should have called her that, but she'd protested at his use of 'great' on so many occasions, that simply 'grandmama' had stuck instead.

Shifting her feet to the floor in front of Karlien, Bathsheba's shrewd eyes appraised her kin as she sat up.

"For me," Bathsheba said quietly, "it was a dream, of course."

"Dream?" Baek Hyeon murmured.

Karlien eyed him. All knew of the strange dreams that plagued some of the Elphin royal line.

Didn't they?

Hm.

Ignoring the man's query, Karlien spoke directly to his grandmama.

"Were you okay when you woke up?"

"Not at all." Her resigned tone was upsetting.

"Oh, grandmama. The usual headache? Let me make you a cup of willow tea myself —"

"Hush, child. Sit back down."

"Oh. Yes, of course." The prince sank back to his knees.

"My dear great-grandson." Karlien straightened at the concern in her voice. Beside him, Hyeon tensed. A frail, time-worn hand reached out. The faint tremor of the inflammation which cursed her bones was evident as she caressed his curls.

"Karlien."

"Yes?"

"Karlien Elphin, prince of the royal blood."

"Y-yes, grandmama?"

"It's time."

"Time? For what?"

The bright blue eyes dimmed as Bathsheba's thin shoulders rose and fell with her studied exhalation.

"It's time to grow up."

In the silence that followed, Karlien's lips parted, his fluttering lashes frozen. In the corner of his eye, Torres coughed into a hand. Behind, Karlien sensed Hyeon shifting his stance.

"G-grandmama?"

The little woman straightened her posture, her head barely reaching over the top of Karlien, despite him kneeling before her. The scent of honey, burnt and not at all sweet, filled his nose. Outside, a peacock screeched, and the prince spared a thought for the bird. He hoped the wolf tore its beautiful plumage to shreds. Swallowing, he met Bathsheba Elphin's gaze.

"I fear I've let you play too long." Intense eyes bore into his. "I thought we had more time, you see, for you to enjoy what I could not. Your parents crossed the veil too young. But now for you, it's time to be a ruler. It's time to be responsible."

Responsible.

But no one listened to him!

"What?" Karlien said out loud. He attempted to withdraw his hands. Before they could escape, Bathsheba's wrinkled hands held his tightly. She squeezed his ringed fingers in earnest. He blinked, tears forming at the sting. "Now?"

"It's time to rule your kingdom. Blood binds us all to rule when required, Karlie."

Why would she quote that now?

"But... b-but you're still here! Baile Mara is doing just fine. I'm still busy with my lessons..." Karlien paused.

Except, he'd wanted this, hadn't he?

Less of the books and more of the practical nature of rulership. Yet, those yearnings were for the future, not now, but for when he was older. Weren't they?

The prince bit his lip. "My scholars have more to teach me about Baile Mara, about the people..." his voice faded at the serious look on his grandmama's face.

Bathsheba shook her head. "No, sweet prince."

"N-no?"

"Not the kingdom of Baile Mara."

"What..." The prince licked dry lips. "What kingdom are you talking about?"

"I am talking —" Bathsheba began, and paused.

Her hands, frail, but no one would call them weak, squeezed Karlien's fingers tighter. Bathsheba observed him as he flinched.

"Grandmama?" Lower lip trembling, Karlien shook his head, his voice hoarse. "What kingdom? Baile Mara, right?"

The regent's thin shoulders trembled as if each hard-won year was a heavy weight upon them today. Karlien just caught the glance she shared with Hyeon over his head.

"My little prince," Bathsheba sighed as her blue-ringed blue eyes bore into his. "I am talking about your other one."

21

Aurelia

Year 367
Aneirin Castle

The great fireplace of Aneirin Castle's library, centered along the wall of windows, crackled with dancing flames of glowing orange and fleeting flecks of blue. No other light filled the musty, cavernous space. There was no longer the scent of bonfires sending off the dead riding the frigid air, but fresh wood smoke, a welcoming fire burning to keep the living warm.

What was not so welcome was the uncomfortable silence.

Well, the *almost* silence.

Standing with her back against one end of the soothing heat of the hearth, Aurelia examined the expressionless librarian seated at the great table in the centre of the room. Neither spoke a word. But while flames licked over blackening logs with a merry crackle in the massive hearth at her side, accompanying that was a relentless, glassy tapping.

Tink, tink, tink.

Aurelia swiped a thumb over the cut above her right eye, which had stopped bleeding quickly thanks to a concoction of bitter oil made for such a wound.

Wyll had been so lost to his prejudice that while he may have been a skilled swordsman, he was shit at hand-to-hand. In this way, the wound irritated her for the fact it had landed by luck, not from any skill. Rhydian was still trying to get some sense out of him. The man had been put under watch, locked in his personal chambers.

Earlier, Aurelia had waited, seated on the steps below the thrones in the great hall, listening to the rising noise level of the preparations for the feast in the freezing courtyard. When the day's light had almost gone, Kyle had found her there.

Eyes solemn, voice soft, the boy had brought word.

"Lady Hywel would see the king."

It had taken a moment for Aurelia to place the name. Perhaps Merion had alerted the librarian that Rhydian was looking for her. The groom's uneasy admission, that he had seen Lady Hywel recently, had certainly startled the king from his weary anger earlier in the stables.

And so, with a placid smile at the boy, who had been staring at the wound on her face, Aurelia had sent him along to Wyll's chamber. To then promptly make her way here ahead of the king.

Who knew what this absent woman had been up to? One whom Rhydian placed faith in, for answers to his family and also for the location of his family's crown.

The impatient Elf had entered from the hall outside, lined with its marble busts coated with the dust of ages. Aurelia had paused a moment at the ornate double wooden doors, wondering at who might be waiting within. Feeling somewhat hesitant, her keen gaze had examined the doors carved with unusual motifs, beasts of unknown origin, stylised stars, and swirling organic shapes. Steeling herself despite the fatigue growing within her, not from the earlier fight, but from every damned thing, Aurelia pushed one of the doors open and entered.

The first thing she noticed was the lack of light.

None of the rainbow-coloured glass lanterns scattered about on side tables or hanging from above were lit, and the large floor to ceiling windows on either side of the massive hearth had little daylight to let in thanks to plunging temperatures and gathering clouds. The colours of the room were faded, the carpets dull, the shadows deep.

Aurelia's arrival had not had the desired effect that she'd hoped for. The librarian had looked up as Aurelia had entered without knocking. Her heart-shaped freckled face was at odds with whatever grand lady Aurelia had expected. The petite woman had assessed Aurelia with a single arched eyebrow, before glancing away to examine the ephemera cluttering the mantlepiece.

Fuming, Aurelia had stalked to the fireplace and crossed her arms to wait.

She had been waiting a while.

Outside in the frosty courtyard, a feast of food and drink had been laid out for all who could make it to partake of. Poorly timed perhaps, but a hopeful step to healing some of the unease that lingered from decades of divide between the two races. She hoped Rhydian arrived sooner rather than later, got his questions answered, and then they could be off to the gathering. Bindy was likely drunk already. Aurelia wouldn't mind catching up, but the thought gave her pause.

A spark of awareness, a sour ferment, flickered in her guts.

It was this feeling that had left Aurelia glad she had chosen to stand. At the fireplace with its grand stonework, she could watch the room while warming her back, instead of the old armchair by the fireplace where she and Rhydian had first shared a passionate kiss.

Gods, how long ago was that?

Not long at all.

Torn between duty and instinct, Aurelia had chosen her heart at a terrible cost to both her and Rhydian in the end. Eyeing the tiny figure at the table, Aurelia hardened her heart. It had been worth it.

Her lids lowered as she inhaled slowly, the potent smell of aged parchment and dust, along with fresh smoke, flooding her senses. Under it all was something sweet and unfamiliar, along with salt. She sniffed, scanning the shadowed space, with its three walls of books, the mezzanine above and the spiral stairs at two dark corners. Unsure of the source, Aurelia turned her attention back to the single occupant at the table, its great size large enough for a dozen, its smooth surface stained a golden brown.

Tink, tink, tink.

The Elf's green eyes narrowed, her arms tightening over her chest. Under her bandaged knuckles, her fingers flexed.

The sting was welcome, the cuts and bruises well-earned from earlier. Hoping Wyll was enjoying the pain she knew she'd inflicted, Aurelia's lips curled in a private smile. It faded quickly, as here, in the relative calm of the library, the urge to fiddle with her knives was strong as she waited, a deep throb of unease in her chest at being alone with the mysterious woman before her. The threat here felt different to the obviously volatile Wyll.

This woman was unknown, disdain and something indescribable taking up the space around her.

Aurelia's fingers twitched, calluses rasping against linen wrappings.

The librarian continued to ignore her.

With hair that even in the low light was as red as a fierce sunset, held off her face by a twist of colourless silk, Lady Hywel remained seated at the table. Her posture was straight as she sat upright and calm, her gaze now downcast. Aurelia examined the librarian openly, guessing that the top of that red head would barely have reached the middle of her forearm. The seated figure was clothed in a plain tunic of dark green, a matching cloak discarded over the ornate back of her chair. A pale wooden staff leant against the arm of the chair to Morgan's left. The woman paid no attention to Aurelia's assessment.

Aurelia's gaze drifted to the table.

The last time Aurelia had been here, the surface had been filled with scrolls, books, quills, and inkwells. Today, it was bare. Completely cleared except for a clear quartz sphere on a little metal stand in front of the Lady Hywel. Beside the sparkling object lay a faded velvet cushion of dark purple with a circular depression at its centre, as if the quartz orb had lately sat atop of it.

It was from this sphere that the source of the tapping came.

The librarian's gaze was focused on the transparent crystal, a sphere about the size of a fully grown Elf's head. One delicate hand rested palm down on the smooth wooden surface of the table. The other was clenched before her, the ridge of one fingernail tapping an endless rhythm over the curved surface of sparkling quartz.

Tink, tink, tink.

Exhaling with forced patience, Aurelia shifted her supple boots to keep the blood flow fresh in her toes.

Where in the hells was Rhydian?

Yes, it was fair that he had questions for his bastard of a friend. Aurelia knew the feeling. She had questions aplenty lined up for Fox whenever the fuck he made it back. But considering the growing unease of being in the presence of this strange person, Aurelia thought of another unusual woman. Somehow, Aurelia's own strength and spark of magic had been neutralised by another female of demure stature. Wearing a face not her own, the petite yellow-haired beast had thrown Aurelia off a ruined building, resulting in significant cost to Fox.

Her pale faced friend had explained some things, but many other mysteries burned in her guts.

Tink, tink, tink.

Nostrils flaring, Aurelia cleared her throat.

"Lady Hywel."

The librarian's consideration remained on the sphere.

Tink, tink, tink.

Aurelia uncrossed her arms.

"Lady Hywel." Spoken with a little more force than was perhaps required, it had the desired effect.

The tapping stopped.

Washed-out green eyes, flecked with firelight, slid Aurelia's way.

"Don't call me that," remarked the librarian coolly.

"Excuse you?" Aurelia snapped, tossing her dark hair over her shoulder. She took a step towards the table.

Pale green eyes scanned Aurelia from boot to nose before dropping back to the crystal ball.

"That was a name that I used while I was waiting."

"For what?"

The librarian ignored the question. "Call me Morgan."

Aurelia blinked.

Had she found the right woman?

Was the librarian in another room, waiting for the king?

No.

Aurelia eyed the small, freckled hands. Both were stained with black ink. Bright green eyes narrowed on the quartz ball with its flickering reflection of the crackling fire to Aurelia's right. She took another three steps, her split-leg wool skirt settling around the top of her boots.

"Well, Morgan. Let's get this over with. What the fuck is that thing? Where did you go? What were you waiting for?"

Looking at Aurelia like she was a part of the furniture, the librarian's eyes remained cool. "This thing is none of your business. I went where I went. Now I am waiting for the king."

All Aurelia could do was snort.

What in the freezing hells?

Did the woman not realise what was at stake?

Of what had happened here between the Elves and Humans, with more still to be settled?

And just who was she, called by one name, but preferring another? It seemed like Aurelia had been right to trust her unease.

Was the woman an Elf? Had some spark of Aurelia's magic responded to something deeper, wild within the flame-haired woman that she'd never met before? The appearance of the sphere suggested so. Along with her staff of washed-out wood topped by a massive faceted ruby, the quality of which Aurelia had never seen before.

Tink, tink, tink.

Calloused fingers flexed. Rubbing at the cut above her eye once more, Aurelia wondered what Rhydian would do if he arrived and his librarian, once lost, now found, turned up with a black eye.

She didn't have to wonder for long.

Heavy boot steps, growing rapidly louder, could be heard making their way along the hallway.

Soon after and with no ceremony whatsoever, Rhydian burst through the partially open door. He was dressed as before in casual riding clothes, his cloak discarded somewhere, one boot half unlaced, golden brown hair a wild mess, a reddish bruise from his fuckwad of a mate's wild punch forming on his cheek.

Halting, breathing hard, the young man took in the tense scene before him, concerned blue-ringed eyes snapping to Aurelia's face.

At the slight shake of her head, Rhydian frowned.

After taking a deep breath, he strode to the table while raking a hand through his tousled gold-brown hair.

"Lady Hywel, where have you been?" demanded the king, his voice thick with emotion. Arriving at the heavy wooden table, he grabbed the high back of the chair facing the librarian with both hands.

Aurelia made her way over, strides measured, examining both Rhydian's white knuckles on the carved wood, and the librarian's unruffled stare.

The only change in the seated figure was that the tapping ceased. The petite woman stared up at the king, making no move to stand as his rank required.

Aurelia knew Rhydian wouldn't care in the slightest. But that wasn't the point. As she came to stand by Rhydian's right arm, Aurelia casually rested a calloused hand on the hilt of her favourite dagger.

Not casually enough.

Morgan's eyes tracked the movement.

The first emotion that Aurelia had seen crossed the librarian's freckled face.

It wasn't fear.

Nor was it annoyance.

It was amusement.

Freckles shifted as a crimson eyebrow rose amongst the shadows on the side of Morgan's face. Blinking once, her amused expression cleared.

"I am here now."

Aurelia cursed under her breath. Pale green eyes slid her way. Scowling openly, Aurelia held the woman's stare until Rhydian spoke again. Pale green eyes slid from Aurelia's frosty glare to lock eyes with the king.

"*Now*? I wanted to see you long before now. Where have you been?" Rhydian demanded hotly.

"I left." Morgan withdrew her fingernail from the sphere. Small hands folded together and dropped to her lap below the edge of heavy wood.

Aurelia glanced to her left, watching the play of emotions over Rhydian's astonished face. A bead of sweat had broken out amongst the three-day growth along his top lip.

"Why? Why did you leave?" His voice had lost its heat, sounding small in the vast room as the fire hissed and popped.

The librarian made a dismissive noise.

"This particular mess isn't mine to deal with."

Aurelia grabbed Rhydian's arm as he reeled back as if slapped.

"Of course it isn't, but that doesn't —"

"Sit down."

"What?" Rhydian's arm tensed under Aurelia's squeeze. His normally gentle eyes hardened. "What is going on —"

"I said sit down."

"Lady Hywel —"

It was Aurelia's turn to interrupt. "That's not her name."

Sparing her a side-eyed glance, Rhydian frowned, clearly troubled.

"Your *librarian*," Aurelia commented, emphasising the title with a sarcastic drawl, "wishes to be called *Morgan*."

"Morgan?" Rhydian's voice was a suspicious murmur.

"Yes," Morgan affirmed, an impatient twist to her soft pink lips. "And now that you are here, I will share what I can. So," she added, "sit down." Red eyebrows rose as she exhaled impatiently at Aurelia's glare. "Please."

Rhydian and Aurelia shared a look.

Eventually, Aurelia shrugged.

They were here now, something Rhydian had desperately wanted for a while. The question of names could be worked out later.

Swallowing her pride a little, Aurelia pulled out her chair, then motioned for Rhydian to step aside. He stared at Aurelia, a kind of weary confusion marring his handsome face. Aurelia sat down first and nudged out another ornate chair with her boot. She pulled Rhydian down with a gentle tug of his hand. Silently, he obeyed.

Feeling somewhat petty at the satisfaction this gave her, that he would sit for her and not the other, Aurelia ignored the librarian's second sigh.

"Wyll?" Aurelia murmured to Rhydian. Not caring if she was heard by Morgan, Aurelia had lowered her voice in respect for Rhydian's clearly frayed nerves. "Any luck with calming him down or making sense of that fu —," she coughed. "Ugh, that fool?"

A muscle in his grizzled jaw twitched, his gaze darkening.

He shook his head.

Damn.

Inhaling the musty smell of old parchment amongst the waft of smoke, Aurelia faced the woman across the table. She bared her teeth in a bland smile.

"So. Sounds like you abandoned your king, huh?"

Morgan's lips parted as her eyes narrowed.

"Aurelia," Rhydian cautioned. He sounded more lost than angry, however.

"It's a valid question," Aurelia insisted. Her smile faded. "Do you know what he's been through? Yet you sit there like some ice queen from the pages of history, like you have the right to look down on him."

"What you think of me is of no consequence. This..." Morgan licked her lips, a furtive movement of the tip of her tongue. "This fight isn't my fight."

Leaning forward, Rhydian rested an elbow on the table and spoke through his fingers as his hand pressed to his mouth. Under the table, his other hand remained in hers.

"Why is it mine? Why do some of my people, my *friends*, why don't they see there is only one way forward?"

"Careful, my king." As Morgan added the title, her cool gaze met Aurelia's briefly. "Only one way forward? That sounds awfully like the one who came before you."

"Could you do better?" snapped Aurelia.

Morgan said nothing to this.

As the silence lengthened, unease had spread to Aurelia's hands, a kind of numb itch. There was danger here. Which was frustrating, because there was no focus to the threat. Apart from the staff by the librarian's arm, there were no obvious weapons. She assessed the other woman's unforgiving gaze. Physical weapons, anyway.

Unmoved by Aurelia's taunt, Morgan continued to sit in silence.

Absurdly, Aurelia wanted to shout, to clap, or break the tension. The calloused hand that held Rhydian's twitched. The involuntary movement of her hand repeated itself as she became aware of a new sensation against her skin. It was the hum of what felt like more than a simple heartbeat in his hand that throbbed in her grip with a concerning pulse. Inhaling carefully, tasting the musty air and no tinge of anything else bar the fresh wood smoke that hadn't been sucked up the great chimney, Aurelia bit her lip.

There didn't seem to be lingering magic here, where so much had happened. Yet the odd pulse under Rhydian's skin prickled the hairs on the back of her arms.

Could Rhydian sense anything amiss?

Was he feeling just as spooked as she?

The fingers that covered his mouth didn't tremble, but the strain of the battle and recent events had earned his expression a hard cast, his pretty eyes a red-tinged hue. Aurelia's heart yearned for him. Topped by the ridiculousness of his close friend's outburst today, the young king was certainly carrying too much for one man. Despite the blazing fire, Aurelia shivered.

Gently disengaging their hands, Rhydian sat upright and placed both palms flat on the bare wood in front of him. Perhaps noticing the quartz sphere for the first time, he jutted his chin towards it.

"The stories you told me," he said, hesitant. "About dark days ahead, a young king facing a trial, a tough journey. They were real, weren't they? Somehow, you were talking about me."

A shadow passed over Morgan's face. Aurelia watched the woman struggle for a heartbeat.

"Yes." Her voice was calmer than her hooded gaze.

Rhydian nodded, a considered bob of his head, and leant forward.

"Are you an Elf, then? You have magic?"

"Can't you tell?" Morgan replied instantly, her expression cunning for a moment.

One of Rhydian's hands twitched.

Aurelia frowned.

"Would it do any good if I did?" Morgan went on as she leant forward, echoing Rhydian's pose, palms down by the sphere. "Your duty as king is to use your own power."

Aurelia flinched.

Rhydian exhaled slowly. "I'm trying."

Morgan's voice was cold. "Try harder."

Rhydian inhaled sharply, his chair creaking as he leant back. With a slow exhale, he raised a hand and trembling fingers rubbed across his thick wool jumper, right over his heart. Morgan's gaze followed the movement, red hair shifting in a shining curtain behind the scarf as she tilted her head to the side. As Aurelia held herself back from launching across the table and tried to decipher the woman's dark expression.

Rhydian surprised her with his next statement.

"I think my mother and father did something to the original royals." He laughed softly, a sickening sound of hopeless amusement. "Perhaps I'm not the true king."

A charged silence followed his admission. Aurelia sat up straighter.

"Wait, wait. What?" she asked. For some reason, Aurelia felt relieved despite the tension in Rhydian's shoulders. "Wouldn't that be a good thing? You could... leave."

Rhydian shook his head.

"These are still my people. I believe that. But I don't feel... Considering the foul magic that my glorious parents used..." as he spoke, the hand pressed to his chest stilled as he looked past Morgan to the walls of loaded bookshelves beyond her. "I don't feel that I have the right to lead."

"You are," Morgan said carefully, not meeting Aurelia's fierce gaze, "the king they have for now."

Aurelia wondered about her choice of words while Rhydian ran his hands through his hair. He stared at them after examining them front and back, then dropped them onto his lap. Mulling over this odd conversation, Aurelia reached underneath to twine her fingers back with his. He gave her a weak smile, his warm hand squeezing hers for a moment.

Across from them, Morgan glanced at Aurelia.

"Where do you still fit into this?" asked the librarian, only mild curiosity lacing her voice.

"What do you mean?" Aurelia said sharply.

Two pairs of green eyes locked together across the table, the sphere between them like a ball of perfectly transparent ice.

"Your Elder is dead. You carried out that ridiculous plan. Why are you still here?" Morgan inquired.

Without a word, Aurelia lifted hers and Rhydian's joined hands out from under the table. Silently, she rested them on the faintly stained wooden top.

Morgan blinked at their entwined fingers.

With half her face in shifting shadows, she stared in silence.

So fleeting it was barely there, Aurelia was fascinated by the pain that crossed Morgan's otherwise expressionless face.

"I see," the librarian whispered, her lids lowering for a moment. "Of course. As blood binds all, love blinds all."

"I am still here," Aurelia began, compelled to talk for some reason by the shadow that crossed the mysterious woman's face, "because I am aware that I was cut off from the rest of the world, not just by geography and distance. I was cut off by lies." She gave Rhydian's hand a visible squeeze. "In my short time here, I have found more truth than the entirety of my life lived under the ice back home."

After quietly digesting her confession, Morgan's shadowed gaze bounced between the pair.

"But how did you get past the line of magic placed by his father?" she asked, her cool gaze holding a challenge.

Instead of going with the first retort that came to mind, Aurelia was silent for a moment, giving the question the serious thought it deserved. A shouted laugh sounded in the hall as multiple footsteps hurried past the library doors. Inside the library, no one moved.

"Fox was affected by it, but Flare wasn't," Aurelia finally admitted. "It was when Rhydian invited me across —"

"No," Morgan interrupted. She gave an impatient wave of a dainty hand. "Magic, any coiled energy, doesn't work like that. You say Fox was affected, but Flare was not? Think harder."

Angry but a little stunned at the idea forming, Aurelia sat back.

Fox was visibly sickened by the curse line.

As was Jessica, Shadow Light, she corrected herself.

Flare had —

She didn't have to think about it too long, did she? The idea had been tucked behind her bruised heart for a while now.

"Oh fuck," Aurelia breathed. "Flare was fine... I... Oh, fuck."

"Aurelia?" Rhydian turned towards her, alarm filling his troubled face.

Her emerald green eyes met Rhydian's bloodshot stare.

"Fox also met Flare in the forest when he first encountered your mother," Aurelia hissed. "Flare and she were together."

"I am not following," Rhydian admitted, fatigue written into the deep shadows of his face as he stared at her, "so I really wish you'd explain right now. Please," he added.

"I am going to fucking kill that scaly little shit!" Aurelia exploded. Yanking her hand from Rhydian's, she pushed her chair back from the table, ready to rise.

To... what?

What could she do?

"Fuck, where the fuck is Fox?" Aurelia muttered from her seat, hair falling over her face as she stared at her twisted hands bunched in her lap.

"What your... partner," Morgan interrupted, "is saying, is that the curse wasn't just your parents' doing, Rhydian. I am sure they were behind its inception. But they needed a lot more magic, dragon-sized magic, to make it happen. Considering your mother was found with Flare after shit went down in Aneirin, I'd say he had a lot to do with the magic that kept others away from your kingdom. While it kept you and your people within."

Whilst grateful for the explanation, Aurelia hated to hear the words spoken out loud.

How could she have been so reckless to think a dragon could ever be her friend?

Although... her thoughts came to Fox.

The complete opposite to Flare in pretty much every single fucking way, Fox was a genuine friend... wasn't he?

Unable to look at the others at the table, Aurelia chewed on her bottom lip. So much had come to light. So much was still hidden by the past. A past that this potentially dangerous librarian seemed to know more about than she cared to share.

Fuck.

Was there an end to the lies?

"Fuck," Rhydian said in an eerie echo of Aurelia's thoughts after digesting Morgan's statement. "Flare has got a lot more to answer for than what we thought. If I see him again, I'll kill him."

"Well," Aurelia muttered, raising her head as Rhydian, with a muted squeak of wood on stone, pulled her chair to face his, "you'll have to get in line."

After kissing her forehead, Rhydian pressed his own forehead to hers.

"I won't leave it up to you," he said, softly but firmly. "I owe you for everything that is good."

Morgan cleared her throat and Aurelia pulled back from Rhydian, wishing they had more time alone.

Would it be unseemly to drag him upstairs and miss the feast?

Aurelia frowned at the woman watching them from across the table.

Probably.

"I don't know everything about the why of it," Morgan said, her voice barely audible over the crack of the fire. "But I think they created the curse as merely a spell, to break free and protect them from the horrors of the past. But it didn't work. Sensing something amiss, some of the people here packed up and left Aneirin or either forgot who they were,."

"They felt it," Aurelia guessed. She thought of the odd hum in Rhydian's hand. "There is magic here, watered down, but blood remembers. Rhydian, when we first met, you didn't know what was going on. Instead, you *felt* something was off."

Morgan nodded, pale green eyes unreadable. "Yes. I would expect that of you."

"Explain that," Aurelia commented waspishly as she squinted a little.

The librarian shrugged. A fingernail tapped the clear quartz before her.

Lips pursed, Morgan considered Aurelia before replying.

"With their diluted Elven blood," said Morgan, "from Baile Mara ancestors, some of Aneirin's people realised something was wrong."

Rhydian rubbed his chest once more and remained silent. However, his jaw was clenched tight, a muscle twitching. He looked over at the fireplace. Logs shifted under his stare, collapsing with a dull thud. Startled, Aurelia glanced from the flames, back to Rhydian, catching the play of shadows across his tense jaw.

When she spoke, it was to Morgan.

"Are you aware of a man called Caspian Carter?" Aurelia murmured.

It was fascinating to watch Morgan's face.

Nothing changed in any obvious way, but the woman became so still she suddenly appeared like the ghost of herself, unreal, glassy, transparent. Aurelia's unease flared up like a call to arms. Even Rhydian must have sensed something. He didn't move, but the tension in his body could be felt like a thickening of the air at her side.

Aurelia forced herself to stay where she was as Morgan's eyes pierced her heart.

"Yes."

The librarian's single word carried the weight of a thousand.

Her heart dancing a wild rhythm, Aurelia chose what to say next with care. It seemed best not to ask how Morgan knew him. There was obvious history there. It may have certainly been important, yet Aurelia wasn't sure if this woman chose to show them her true self, that Rhydian could be protected from whatever that entailed.

"What do you know of him?" Aurelia hedged, wondering why the woman hadn't asked why Caspian's name had come up.

That was equally curious and worrying.

It was Morgan's turn to consider what to say. Rhydian leaned forward, his breath hitched. Aurelia kept her focus on Morgan, the wash of red and orange from the fireplace adding an ethereal tone to the woman's delicate beauty.

"He's maneuvering things," Morgan said eventually, her tone entirely too casual for the strain in the air. Her voice dropped to a whisper. "People, events, things. Always maneuvering."

"Like a game?" Aurelia asked.

"No," Morgan replied more firmly. Her lips formed something that wasn't quite a smile. "Not like a game."

"He sounds insane," Rhydian muttered.

Ready to throw herself in front of him, Aurelia inhaled abruptly. But Morgan shook her head, the uneasy charge to the air dissipating as she exhaled.

"He is quite sane. Which is potentially worse. He is maneuvering the world around him for survival. He likely knew both of your parents."

"Recently?" Rhydian's tone was sharp.

"I don't know. Perhaps." Morgan shrugged. She contemplated for a heartbeat. "More likely a long time ago."

"How old is he?" Aurelia queried, aware that magic combined with biological age was a tricky thing.

"We are both from a different time," Morgan said simply.

"What time?" Rhydian asked. Instead of answering, Morgan looked away, her gaze distant.

"When he was young..." Morgan licked her lips, "he was... in a position to observe the best and worst around him. That affected him deeply."

"The best and worst of what?" Rhydian asked.

"Of *whom*," Morgan corrected. "Of us."

At a loss, Aurelia glanced at Rhydian, exhaling in a long puff of air.

Was he thinking the same?

Of how the odd-eyed blonde man had lent her a cloak to keep warm, but left her to die?

Of how Caspian's glowering yet confident brother Owaen, calm and devoted to Fox, seemed to think his brother was completely unhinged?

"Maneuvering," Aurelia mumbled.

Morgan lowered her gaze to the crystal sphere, nodding to herself or them, but did it matter?

Tink, tink, tink.

Confused, and sick of being manipulated by others, it was to her shame that Aurelia felt she might have a faint understanding of how he may have felt. That didn't excuse him, though. Nothing would.

"You speak as if you approve of him," Rhydian commented, his voice was more curious than accusatory.

Morgan's fingertips stilled against the sphere. Her gaze swept over him and Aurelia both. She made no comment, but Aurelia felt the gaze like a ripple of snow ready to slide off a mountain. The feeling eased, but only a little, as Morgan's gaze moved away.

"My father," Rhydian began, then swallowed. "He said to me... that I knew what they had done."

Shocked silence from both Morgan and Aurelia filled the void left behind from the king's vulnerable words. The librarian sat up, her back rigidly straight.

"He said that to you?" Morgan hissed. She clicked her tongue.

"Yes," Rhydian's voice hitched. He looked like he was going to be ill. Aurelia scooted closer to him, sitting on the edge of her chair. "I don't quite remember when… but he reminded me that I once knew."

"Bastard." Morgan's disgust was written across her face with a scowl.

"When?" Aurelia whispered, as surprised as she was by Morgan's obvious distaste, she was more afraid of what Rhydian was going to say.

"When we were alone, on the battlefield," Rhydian admitted quietly, his voice thick.

Aurelia's eyes filled with stinging tears as Rhydian blinked his own away. It was obvious the only time they would have had a moment alone was after his father had been shot.

Shot by her night-black arrow.

"Rhydian, I'm sorry —" Aurelia mumbled, pulling him close, but he pushed back gently against her hands.

"No, don't be," he said with his face turned to the side. While he got himself under control, he laughed, weak and pitiful. "I know what I've sacrificed, that more is likely to be needed —"

"You've given enough," Aurelia commented stubbornly, her anger rising.

"So have you! Gods, what I asked of you? And Fox, too."

Aurelia sat back against the chair, watching Morgan return her focus to the polished quartz ball.

An idea struck her.

"He'll be back soon," Aurelia said clearly, watching Morgan's face. "With Owaen."

She wasn't disappointed.

Lips parted, Morgan sat up straight, washed-out green eyes wide.

"Skye… Fox?" Morgan demanded. "Fox is coming back? With *Owaen*?"

Aurelia watched the librarian's annoying, ever present calm evaporate like a puff of ash in a frigid breeze. The petite woman's green eyes hardened to a poisonous jade as her gaze danced wildly between them.

"Yes, to help once more," Rhydian answered hotly, as if her disbelief affronted him. "Because I need all the —"

"*Here*?" Morgan spat, interrupting him.

"Yes. To Aneirin. That was the plan. They should be here any day now —"

With an unanticipated movement, Morgan pushed back from the table and stood up, lips moving as she murmured something.

Once more, Aurelia placed her hand on a dagger at her hip. The librarian didn't notice. Instead, her wide gaze was distant, aimed at the massive hearth to her left.

"I didn't see this…"

Aurelia glanced from the fireplace with its crackling blaze, back at the flaming-haired figure across the table. Morgan had murmured something that she didn't quite catch.

"What was that?" Rhydian asked, his tone sharp. He had missed the mumbled words, too.

Pale green eyes flicked first to Rhydian, and then to Aurelia.

"I'm going to the crypts," Morgan declared, her voice far too casual for her strange expression.

Without another word, the librarian spun around and gathered both her cloak and ruby-topped staff. Not waiting for them to rise, she strode to the door, leaving behind a vague mix of aromas, a perfume like incense or sweet smoke.

Startled, Aurelia stood up, calling after the woman as she reached the door.

"Why the crypts?"

The tiny woman paused for a single heartbeat, but didn't turn around.

"To pay my respects to those who have come before me, before..." Morgan cleared her throat. "Goodbye."

Not waiting for a response, the librarian slipped out and was gone.

Aurelia stared after at the ornate doors with their flakes of peeling gilt. They were left slightly ajar.

What in the freezing hells was that?

She took a step towards them, but stopped. Morgan was a stranger, her cool exterior a clear mask to the wildfires that burned within. It felt best to leave that mystery alone for now, when the one who needed her the most trembled against her now.

Lips parted slightly, Aurelia dropped her gaze to Rhydian, letting her eyes fill with the deep affection she felt for this man, his positivity despite all that tried to pull him down.

He'd remained in his chair and his fascinatingly blue-ringed eyes were staring at the fire. With his haggard complexion and grizzled chin, Rhydian's appearance lent him the air of one who had seen too much.

With a frustrated puff of an exhale, Aurelia leant over and wrapped her arms around him. She pressed a kiss into his hair, inhaling the salt and musk aroma that was simply, sweetly him.

"What did you make of that?" she murmured, lips tangling in tousled golden brown locks before she pulled away a fraction.

"I make nothing of that. I just hope Fox gets back here, like you said." Rhydian leaned back into Aurelia's embrace with a prolonged sigh. Pale blue eyes with their outer ring of darker blue blinked once as he gazed up, the red mark on his cheek thankfully not darkening to a bruise.

"Like I said?" Aurelia murmured.

Lids drifted closed and Rhydian nodded, the top of his head rubbing against her chest. His reply was an exhausted sigh.

"Soon."

22

The Watcher

Year 367
Aneirin Castle

In a briskly cold corner of Aneirin Castle's great hall, the Watcher crouched on the chilled stone floor. It was relatively calm here, compared to the noise and commotion in the main courtyard.

From what the Watcher had gathered, a few guards from the Elves and humans had conspired together. An outdoor feast had been arranged, with the King's blessing. Despite the unease, all were welcome to celebrate the new, if uneasy, peace, and uncovering truths. A type of 're-uniting' an older servant had mused. Plus, it was also a meal to celebrate those wounded in the battle being moved into better accommodation. The massive effort of the recent days had meant the corridors of empty rooms deep within the castle had been aired out, ready for their unexpected occupants.

With their backside on their boot heels, arms around their knees, the Watcher sighed, the aroma of smoked meats and juices thick in their nose.

Outside, drums sounded, flutes played, folks laughed. Yet as the deep boom of the drums came, the Watcher wondered at the echoing thud of their confused heart. While most of those in attendance seemed happy enough with the free food and music, sullen faces at the edge of the crowd filled the Watcher with unease. It was still daylight, mid afternoon. Yet the expressions of those not taking part appeared like an apparition in the smoke from the bonfires, sparks at the edge of the weak daylight ready to catch.

The Watcher shook their head, eyes unfocused.

What was really happening here?

Not just amongst the people of Aneirin, a growing unrest felt as a low hum in the blood despite the delicate truce. It was also the way others had somehow used the conflict to learn and grow, opening up new possibilities about the outside world.

A world beyond the Watcher's experience or understanding.

Is this what the wider world was really like? Were those who had died here, some far too young, not lost to some preordained destiny... but lost to something else? Was each of them at the mercy of another, those greedy and full of lies?

Eyes surrounded by dark circles examined the drab colours of the hall.

Inside the nearly deserted hall, lofty arches soared above in shadow and shifting lantern light. It was mostly silent. The wounded, from the battle that should never have happened, had gone. They had left the hall either through healing arts, provided freely by some of the Elven healers, enabling the patients to find more comfortable accommodation in the freshly opened chambers.

Or they had been too mortally wounded, even with their strange arts, and left through death.

Eyelids slid closed and the Watcher's forehead sunk to their crossed arms.

Outside, the feast went on. Within, the last of the volunteers arrived with buckets and mops to clean any remaining stains from the cold expanse of the floor. The helpers were of both races, humans and Elves. The Watcher raised their head slightly, observing the cleaning work from their dark corner.

Humans, born to live and die the way nature intended according to the loudest voices. Elves, born with magic that they apparently used for beauty and skills, concerning fabric crafts and weaponry. Along with the healing arts, extending their years to decades beyond the human norm, if what was rumoured was believed to be true. The Elven healer's skill with the humans and their own certainly added weight to that.

The Watcher gnawed on a fingernail, tasting honey from lunch along the tip of their finger. If what had happened to —

Eyes snapped shut.

No.

"Don't think about what happened. Only what to do about it," the Watcher mumbled, "and to who..."

Nothing would undo what had been done. There was no magic strong enough for that. The Watcher hadn't dared to ask, but had seen enough unmoving figures with bloodied linens pulled up over their faces. Nothing had been able to bring them back from beyond the veil of death, where only the gods could traverse both ways.

In the courtyard, the pipes were joined by a mournful, lilting voice. The Watcher continued to chew a thumbnail, a pensive nibbling of teeth. They had excused themselves from the feast, their mind too full to eat despite the fare on offer.

Sullen glances were still exchanged from both sides of the divide at all shared activities, not just today's awkward gathering. Eating, repatriation of the farms, the organisation had been swift. Something to keep all busy. For the most part, it was clear the differences were blurring. In a short time, thanks to the massive effort of the humans that had opted to remain in the castle, and the Elven captains who deigned to assist. Wounded soldiers had been billeted to other parts of the draughty castle, even amongst the various levels of the city. King Rhydian looked like he was running on no sleep, his eyes red rimmed, cheeks pale. His new companion Aurelia, with long dark hair and as tall as the king, was never far away, hovering about and glowering at any of the guard captains who hesitated when given direct orders.

The Watcher frowned.

The Elven women were different from a lot of the women from home. Not better or worse, but perhaps more like men than some of the men themselves. They wore colours that the Watcher hadn't encountered in clothing before, apart from the occasional town councillor or well-to-do merchant visiting the castle. They also wore weapons, laughed loudly and swore as if being a 'lady' was of no concern to them.

Perhaps it wasn't?

Shifting, the Watcher peered into the hall, at the great expanse of smooth slabs that stretched the length of the space, to the stairs at the end, at the two empty thrones. Their arse was going numb from being so close to the frigid floor, but this out of the way place seemed as good a place as any to find time alone. Not to feel, simply to think. Feeling caused great hot ripples to shift about inside their guts, waiting to burst out.

Out of all the peculiar, heartbreaking and confusing things that had happened over the past couple of weeks, one of the most odd had happened the day before.

It didn't concern the death, fear or terror of a dragon overhead, or a chaotic, useless battle.

It didn't concern one of the many petty fights breaking out in the aftermath, past sunset, when guards from both sides of the mysterious divide changed their watch.

It didn't concern angry voices, although there were plenty of them on and off, even some right now, somewhere in the distance. Inside or out of the castle, it was hard to tell with the echoes. Occasionally, multiple pairs of boots running about sounded nearby as well. The Watcher wasn't concerned. They'd seen enough men and women running about to know it wasn't good. They wanted to stay clear and process what needed to be processed.

Because one of the oddest things, a minor thing really, concerned a subtle pink blush, playing across cheeks rounded with a stunned smile.

It also concerned a stolen kiss.

And a bunch of yellow flowers.

Alone with their thoughts, slack lips parted slightly. The Watcher shied away from the lightness in their heart at the memory. Because feeling light right now didn't seem respectful at all.

But the warm spasm of wonder, deep within the bone-weary ache of loss, refused to die away.

Earlier, the lukewarm sunlight and the chance to do some light duties had been a blessing after running a series of errands for the King.

The Watcher had been minding their own business, beating dusty mats against a gritty stone wall in one of the many lanes that wove around the castle's expansive grounds, some steep and breathtaking to climb. This narrow thoroughfare was relatively flat, running parallel to the side of the warm-coloured mountain range the castle butted against. Since seeing Davyn painting a day or so ago, the Watcher had tried to see what the man was keen on capturing. It must have been important.

Who knew a man like Davyn would ever have attempted such a pastime?

As they worked, the Watcher had become aware of blue shapes spaced around the towers that rose to the sky. Congruently, the soft light and shadows playing in shifting shapes across the cobbles, and empty, stacked barrels, caught their eye, wondering at the dappled play they had never noticed before. Dust motes caught the weak light, or soft flakes of soot, specks that winked in and out as they fell. They could have been sparks from some heavenly hearth beyond the clouds.

To be honest, it was rather pretty.

Almost done with the pile of musty mats from the chambers being aired, a muffled laugh had startled the Watcher. On turning, the Watcher spotted two figures emerging from the rear stable doors that faced onto the back pathway.

Neither Davyn nor Bindy had noticed the Watcher amidst the stacked barrels.

The couple's passionate embrace had assured that.

Extremely passionate embrace.

Cheeks had heated uncomfortably, but the Watcher hadn't looked away. Instead, they had stared, head tilted to the side as the kiss ended, mouths parting, shoulders rising and falling to muted, shared laughter. A donkey-drawn cart had come trundling along from the far end of the lane, laden with hay. Approaching the stable doors, the driver glared at the pair.

The Watcher recognised the woman on the cart. She was someone who had recently been spending a lot of time with Wyll.

Davyn apparently recognised her, too.

The pair had jumped apart.

Davyn abruptly, Bindy less so, her hand reluctantly dropping from his broad shoulder. Once the driver had hopped off her cart to stalk into the stables with her nose in the air, leading the animal by rope, Bindy and Davyn had shared one last tender press of their lips.

Then the towering Elven woman had slapped Davyn on the arse before jogging off down the lane.

"Later, Blackwood," the Elf sang out, not looking back.

Davyn had stumbled off in the other direction, grinning widely.

The dusty mat slipped from the Watcher's fingers.

Clutched tight to his chest, Davyn was holding a bunch of flowers, scruff-covered cheeks pink with pleasure.

Davyn had ambled past the Watcher, eyes a little glazed, petite yellow blooms pressed to his nose. The flowers had been held together by a twist of emerald green silk. The Watcher had to bite the inside of their mouth to stop the laugh of astonishment at the sight.

"She gave me flowers," Davyn said with wonder, beaming and blushing as he ambled away.

Now, sitting in the forgotten corner of the great hall, with the aroma of pine and orange oil lacing the hot sizzle of barbequed meat, the Watcher let their smile free. The sensation felt unreal, muscles moving to form something not seen for a long, long while.

"Elven scum," they murmured, the smile a fragile query as the words formed on hesitant lips.

Shifting to get their current crouch more comfortable, the Watcher snorted at the way things didn't seem to add up. A burst of laughter had their gaze rise from the shadows playing across the hard yet time-worn floor. A group of two gaily clothed Elves, a young man and woman, along with a human girl, were organising the last of the makeshift pallets of basic beds and blankets into neat bundles to be taken away.

"Yellow flowers," whispered the Watcher.

The group carried out their task together, competent, calm. When the human girl stood up, arching her neck to ease it, the young Elven man smiled at her. The Elven woman hummed under her breath as she bent over, a long braid of rich brown hair on either side of her face swaying gently in time to the soft beat of drums in the courtyard as she worked.

"What shall we do?" the Watcher mumbled, echoing words heard recently, spoken in secret. Their fragile smile faded.

Yet the picture of Davyn with cheeks the colour of berries persisted to fill their thoughts. Not wanting to disturb the peace of the hall, the Watcher bit into a worn shirt sleeve. It was to stop a snort threatening to break free at the memory of Davyn beaming like a lass. Almost immediately, the Watcher pulled their sleeve away, startled at the sweetness. Another spot of sticky honey marred the thinning fabric. They wanted to laugh at their own stupidity, but the Watcher's brow furrowed instead.

Another group appeared to their right, entering the hall from the base of the King's tower. As the new group moved past the various torches burning on the walls, their shadows made uneven, abstract shapes on the giant blocks of stone as they passed. The group of three figures working at tidying looked up, their soft chatter dying. Silently, they finished their work, moving quickly as if they too felt the change of air, as the new group moved through the grey light of the vast space.

Sweetness forgotten, the Watcher sat up on their heels anxiously, making sure to stay unseen. They had gotten good at watching people, and these newcomers to the hall were walking so casually it had attracted their attention, rather than the opposite. As they approached with steps silent and unhurried, the Watcher pressed back into the corner. The three were heading near to where they crouched.

Wait.

A mad laugh threatened to escape.

The Watcher choked it back.

Their confused gaze darted between two women, robed in homespun brown and green linen and wool, to the taller figure, stooped over, hooded in a dark blue cloak. The Watcher's intense gaze dropped to the hooded figure's boots.

The urge to laugh died.

The Watcher stared at the approaching figures, inhaling sharply, a gasp tucked behind their lips, struggling to burst free.

Three figures ambled on past the Watcher, so focused on not being seen that they didn't notice the single figure tucked into the corner at the rear of the hall. One of the women even peered furtively over her shoulder at the group cleaning up in the centre of the hall.

Her eyes passed over their hiding space.

The Watcher held still.

Her gaze passed on.

Eyes half closed observed the thick, heavy black boots of the central figure as they exited the hall via one of the main corridors, into the heart of the sprawling building. All that remained were the two Elves and the human girl, muttering softly amongst themselves as they worked. The Watcher blew out their breath very, *very* slowly, heart matching a more invigorating drum beat as the melody changed to something primal.

The Watcher pushed to their feet, the taste of honey on their lips gone sour, the wonder of a moment pondering yellow flowers gone stale. Behind their ribs, a sore heart beat with an odd, jerking rhythm. With their eyes on the archway into the heart of the castle, they paused. Only a few murmurs could be heard. Faint rays of grey light penetrated the still, chilled air of the hall, all the way to the stairs, dais, and empty thrones at the far end of the Watcher's position. If one squinted, it looked like rows of sombre figures facing each other across a space divided by nothing at all, really. Simply two Elves and a human doing what they could to make things right.

A burst of laughter from many voices filled the late afternoon outside.

The Watcher flinched.

Perhaps the uneasy populace, native and newcomer, were occupied now with enough distractions, that the Watcher could finally lay to rest the sorrows of their heart. Not through letting go, but by giving in to the rage that burnt bright within, deeper than their heart, into secret, unknown places that had no name.

"Elven scum," the Watcher murmured, thinking of the boots that had just passed them by.

Was this their chance?

Were they ready to take action to make things right as well, or if not right, then at least take action for lost companionship, gone forever?

Had the gods answered pleas for guidance, made to the dark in the silence of the night?

The Watcher raised a boot, ready to follow.

A firm grip over their neck from behind jerked them back.

"Oof," croaked the Watcher as they were swung about.

They froze.

Tawny eyes that missed nothing bore down from above.

"Can't... breathe..."

Thankfully, the painful grip was released.

The towering Elf didn't step away, however, staring down at the Watcher, her eyes serious.

"Why are you lurking here?"

"I'm," came the coughed reply, "not lurk —"

Bindy stepped close enough that the Watcher caught a whiff of leather and a floral aroma they couldn't name.

"Why are you lurking here? You've been following us. Why?"

The Watcher swallowed. "N-no..."

"Spying for Wyll, hmmm?" Distaste marred the Elf's remarkable beauty.

The Watcher gave a vehement shake of their head.

"What's that? Speak up." The Elf crossed lean arms over the front of her green fur cloak. Her leather pants creaked as she shifted her stance to cover the Watcher's view from the hall. There was no sword at her hip, only a set of two daggers with ornate hilts of yellow gold, each adorned with tiny emeralds throwing sparks the same colour as her richly coloured turquoise cloak.

"I..." The Watcher gulped.

"What's your name?"

"I'm not a s-spy —"

"Hmp. Prove it."

Biting their bottom lip, a single word emerged from the Watcher's trembling lips.

"Free?" Bindy asked, a line forming between her silver eyebrows. "*What*?"

"W-Wyll."

"What —? *Wyll*? That arsewipe is free? Are you serious?"

All the Watcher could do was nod.

"When?"

"Just now," the Watcher breathed, stomach twisting under the intense scrutiny. A soft whisper of sensation brushed against the inside of the Watcher's skull for a blunt, sickening moment. It was their first time encountering such a feeling, a direct contact of subtle power from someone with magic in their blood.

Thankfully, the pressure released almost as quickly as it came.

"You're telling the truth." Tawny eyes blinked rapidly as Bindy studied her disoriented companion.

"Y-yes..." The single syllable was barely a gasp.

Bindy uncrossed her arms, running a hand over her face, brushing away stray wisps from her thickly braided hair. After glancing at the hall, the Elf faced him once more. Her strange eyes glinted, the tiny flame of a far off torch a gold spark in each iris.

"Where?"

A shaking thumb pointed down the black, unlit passageway towards the library and inner chambers of the castle's courtyard level. A sudden laugh broke the silence of the hall, and the Watcher cringed.

The Elf did not.

Instead, her fierce grip returned to the Watcher's neck, this time as an encouraging squeeze, with a nudge in the direction Wyll had disappeared. No choice was offered.

A trill of high-pitched notes caused the Watcher to balk.

Bindy's voice, low and savage, tickled the Watcher's ear as the Elf leant close.

"Come on, 'Not A Spy', lead the way."

Bindy and the Watcher peered around the corner.

The Watcher hissed as their cheek made contact with the chilled stone wall. The warm hand on the base of their neck tightened briefly and Bindy's voice sounded directly against the Watcher's trembling ear.

"Hush."

At the end of an empty hallway that split left and right, the two women and the hooded figure in heavy boots conferred together in fierce whispers. They had stopped near a large yet grimy clear glass window. Their voices were low, yet one woman was practically hissing. The tall, hooded figure interrupted. The irate woman stepped back, flinching. Her back was to them, but the stiff set of her shoulders indicated what her expression may have been. Tugging urgently, her companion grabbed the angry woman's shoulder, dragging her to the right and up a small set of timeworn stairs, the steps worn down in the centre by decades of passersby.

The Watcher bit their lip, aware the winding stairwell led up, deeper within the newly opened chambers. Where the bulk of the Elven wounded were being housed.

With the two women gone, the figure dropped their hood.

A low hiss escaped Bindy's clenched teeth.

Wyll shook out his hair, stretching his neck. His face was in profile as he watched his companions disappear. In the weak light of the window, shadows broke the lines of his face, cool and transparent. The Watcher couldn't work out what the shapes were at first.

They sniffed.

From the bittersweet aroma of burnt meat, it seemed like the bonfires outside had grown. Their columns of smoke appeared to be causing the gentle sunlight to pass across Wyll's face in soft shapes, barely shadows at all, really. Unaware that he was being observed, Wyll took something out of the pocket of his dark blue cloak. The Watcher couldn't tell from this far away. It seemed like the Elf could. Bindy tensed beside them, the surrounding air crystallising into a stillness that had the Watcher's stomach feeling like it dropped away.

Down the hall, Wyll turned left, taking the passage that led to a smaller side door to the main courtyard. It would take him to the feast outside.

And the stables.

A prickling sensation curled along the Watcher's spine.

A brisk poke in the lower back had the Watcher stumbling down the hall, past the library's closed double doors to their right. When they reached the end, both Elf and Watcher paused on a faded rug centered over the large flagstone landing. The aroma of smoke and meat was abundant here. Two heads peered cautiously around the next corner, a thick braid of silver hair tickling the Watcher's cheek. They held back a sneeze.

Wyll had disappeared.

The eerie prickling grew worse. Beads of sweat broke out on their top lip.

The heavy, iron-bound door at the end of the passage he had taken was closed. There was nowhere else for him to have gone. Bindy rounded to face the Watcher, her full lips a thin line, eyes serious.

"The king," she said clearly, eyeing her trembling companion.

"What?" The Watcher squinted, trying to concentrate. It was becoming harder to find air amongst the scent of smoke and prickling sensation that had spread like questing ants over their chest.

"Find the king," Bindy urged. Her eyes ran over the Watcher's face, as if sensing what her guide was experiencing. "Tell him what you saw."

The Watcher nodded, wiping their nose with a sleeve. It was marginal, but Tawny eyes softened.

"It's going to be alright," the Elf said, soothingly. Her powerful hands grasped the Watcher's shoulders.

"F-flowers," the Watcher mumbled, eyes closed, heart racing at the Elf's touch.

"What?"

"Y-yellow flowers." Sad eyes opened, blinking away salt water.

Raising their gaze, they stared fully into eyes full of gold and grey shifting lights amongst the grey shadows of the hallway. After a moment, Bindy glanced away. She eyed the door Wyll had exited for a beat, then turned back. She nodded, a low bob of silver hair.

"Yes." Eyes unashamed, the Elf smiled, a wan thing, a gentle, sweet curve of pale pink lips. "I gave Davyn flowers."

"He b-blushed."

Silver lashes lowered halfway over golden eyes as Bindy bit her lip. Eventually, a single eyebrow rose. Her smile grew.

"I blushed too."

The admission startled the Watcher. They gasped. But all at once, the hesitant sound of quiet chuckling from the pair joined the murmuring voices and pipes from outside. Their quiet laughter faded, a gentle sharing of fleeting solidarity. The Watcher raised a tentative hand, but instead of reaching out, they stroked the dull fabric of their own homespun shirt.

Bindy tilted her head to the side. "We use bright colours," she said, understanding the unspoken question, "because our home is black rock or white snow. Our magic helps us chip away at the ice and stone, to reveal treasures us Elves use in many ways."

Her companion absorbed this in silence, shifting as they thought that over.

"Humans..." the Watcher mumbled eventually, "and Elves. We are different. But we are also the same..."

Bindy nodded, her eyes bright and solemn all at once.

"Elf is just a name for folk with a bit of spice in their blood. But in the end, it doesn't stand for much."

"Elf," the Watcher whispered. Reverberating through the wooden door at the end of the passage, leather drums beat low. Wood pipes rippled delicately.

"Elf," Bindy repeated once more with a bob of her head. "A name from some royal family I never met, who helped magic become what it is today." The brief smile reappeared, sad this time around. "I doubt this is what they had in mind."

"Elf," the Watcher echoed, firmer.

Bindy nodded, crouching down into a squat. "We're the same. Different bits inside. See, I can do this."

A muted rustle at their feet had the Watcher's lips parting in surprise.

Dust motes rose out of the tired old rug. The motes rose past their knees and congealed. What—

The mass came together in a rush. The specks of dust had formed into the shape of a giant wolf spider. It didn't do anything, like attack. It simply appeared, motes shimmering in the pale daylight. At the sight of it, the Watcher's throat heated. The Elf and the Watcher stared at it. Bindy, using a slight gesture of her long fingers, caused the eight-legged thing to dissipate after a moment of scrutiny. Grains dropped back to the old carpet like coarse rain.

"Wow," breathed the Watcher.

"It's just magic," sighed the Elf. "Sometimes it means naught. Only frivolities."

Outside at the feast, a woman laughed. Elf or human, the Watcher couldn't tell.

It didn't matter, did it?

Shaking hands reached out. Fingertips, hesitant at first, until Bindy nodded, brushed the thick strands of the Elf's hair beside her cheek. Up close, it was an intense mix of blonde and grey with the occasional hidden streak of shining gold. More confident now, fingers stroked the closest ray of gold, almost hidden amongst the thick weight of the silver braid.

"Elven scum, they said," the Watcher mumbled, their gaze filled with new light. "But the yellow flowers..."

Tawny eyes, close by to the Watcher's, filled with something that shone in only the way unshed tears could. Bindy nodded. She tried to speak. She swallowed, then tried again.

"I'm sorry for everything that has happened since we arrived."

The words bloomed between the two figures, tiny blooms amongst flecks of dust floating about in the muted light. Abruptly, Bindy pulled the Watcher close with lean arms, tight and sincere. Her voice was thick, heavy.

"Please forgive us, *all* of us... I'm so sorry."

Inhaling leather and musk, the Watcher hugged her back just as fiercely, scared and unsure yet no longer as angry or confused. But all too soon, the embrace was over as quickly as it had started. Bindy pushed away, her tawny golden eyes intense.

"The king," said the Elf, rising to her full height. "Go."

Getting up without another word, Bindy jogged down the passage Wyll had taken. The Elf's movements were quick, almost silent even as she drew a golden dagger from her belt.

The heavy outer door closed without a sound.

With a thumping heart set to burst forth from their chest, the Watcher headed back along the musty hallway toward the great hall. The merriment from outside faded as the windows gave way to solid stone walls decorated with soaring columns and iron sconces of unlit candles.

The Watcher gnawed at their bottom lip.

Where would the king be?

At the feast, surely?

Boot steps hurried along the lengthy stone passage, past the library door on their left. They were a few strides past the double doors when a hesitant plea reached their ears, barely audible above their shallow breaths.

Unsure what they'd heard, the Watcher stumbled to a stop, twisting to face the library's doors. They didn't have to wait long.

"Please help us."

The Watcher stared at the door a moment, shoulders rising and falling swiftly. They glanced back in the direction of the hall.

"Anyone, please help us."

The voice was soft enough that if it was male or female, the Watcher couldn't tell. But it was loud enough that the desperation could be felt as well as heard, a kind of weary hopelessness that the Watcher knew far too well.

Heart fluttering, the Watcher took a breath, retreated a few steps.

The library doors, a tall set of ornately carved wood, were in need of a polish. The carvings of trees and dragons were cracked, dry and split. Yet they were heavy and would surely make an obvious sound if opened. Noticing a keyhole amongst the flaking gilt around the handle, the Watcher knelt and pressed their eye to the metal.

"Anyone! Are you there? Gods, if you're listening, help us —"

Holding their breath, the Watcher adjusted their cheek against the cool metal. The room appeared blurry as eyelashes brushed against the flakes of gilt. Warmer air than the chill of the hallway seeped out against their flesh. In the vast room with its high ceiling, it was hard to see exact shapes against the gloomy shadows of the three walls of books, not through the keyhole anyway. No fire was lit, or if there was, the flames had fallen to embers, a red glow unseen amongst the pale light from the wall of windows beyond the Watcher's field of vision. An angry sob from the centre of the room sharpened their focus.

With their back to the library doors, a hooded figure stood at the central table, hunched over.

A hand flew to a wide open mouth. The Watcher had thought for a moment this was Wyll, here somehow slipped past them. But the shoulders, narrower than Wyll's, excluded that possibility. The figure was also taller than his companions had been. It was impossible to see much else about them.

"We've given enough." The figure's hiss was eaten up by the musty atmosphere.

Heart racing so fast they feared it would be heard, the Watcher breathed out carefully, swallowing with a throat gone dry. They couldn't see anyone else inside, but that didn't mean there wasn't. But the figure's attention appeared fixated on the table.

Or something on it.

"*He's* given enough."

Another sob from the hooded figure broke the stillness of the room. Around the hunched figure, the books were uncaring witnesses to the raw emotions on display before them. Not able to explain why, and despite the intense fear of being caught, tears filled the Watcher's eyes. They knew that rawness of feeling, the way words might burst forth at any moment, words of anger, fear, and grief.

Words of hopelessness.

Words of pain.

Holding their breath once more, the Watcher withdrew from the keyhole. They pushed up with care, making sure not to catch any cloth on the old doors lest they make a sound.

They didn't pause until they reached the shadowed alcove of the great hall. It was completely empty now; the cleaners gone. At the far end, two serious thrones sat at the top of the stairs, almost in mockery of the two monarchs and their despicable actions.

Would justice come for the victims of their crimes?

Was that what Rhydian was working towards, braving the ire of his people and the suspicion of an Elven army?

The Watcher rested for a moment in contemplation of all that had happened in the last short while. Hands trembled, heart sputtered. Here, where the shadows couldn't be reached by the tall windows, a few torches had been lit. Warm flames flickered, barely making a dent in the deepening cold and damp as night fell.

Was that how Rhydian felt? Lonely flames against the promise of wild fire if no solution to the building unease could be found?

Perhaps the feast would be enough.

Perhaps time would heal.

Perhaps the Gods would answer all the pleas from desperate mouths, eager for peace, eager for hope.

Would any help come?

Despite knowing there were no statues of the old Gods left in the city's vast temple, once beautifully crafted works of sparkling crystal, the Watcher closed their eyes. Maybe divine ears still listened despite having no place for worshippers to come. Music and voices from outside, rowdier now, echoed around the empty hall.

"Please," the Watcher breathed, "help me too."

Hands clenched so tight that blunt fingernails bit into sweaty palms. They could only pray, desperate as the figure in the library, for any help with the secret plans that burned within their grieving heart.

Wiping damp eyes with a sleeve, sniffling slightly, the Watcher straightened slim shoulders.

But first, there was the matter of right now.

Wyll.

The king.

Reaffirmed, the Watcher stepped quickly along the deserted passage, towards help, towards Rhydian, or wherever he may be.

The king would know what to do.

Outside, the piercing shatter of breaking glass burst violently above the joyful pipes and drums.

23

Rhydian

Year 367

Aneirin Castle

Was the feast worth it?

Taking a rare moment alone to digest the worrisome conversation with Lady Hywel, *Morgan*, he corrected himself, Rhydian observed the courtyard gathering from the top of his isolated tower.

Enclosed by the castle on nearly three sides, the sprawling yard below rippled with heads bobbing, lanterns and bonfires doing what little they could against the chill. The gates in the far stone wall had been thrown open for any to wander in or out, as they pleased. The daylight had slunk away, low clouds left in its wake. Aneirin's castle with its halls and towers had been built of the reddish stone that it crowded against. But the wan light with long shadows that seemed to deepen as he observed them had bleached the colours to flat, washed out greys.

As ash and smoke drifted in the now bone-achingly icy breeze, the king frowned at the crowd far beneath. Yes, all the guests ate and drank while pipers from both races took turns playing their favourite melodies. Laughter also made a good portion of the general hum.

But a vague line denigrated the two different races. Almost dead centre along the vast open space, on one side of the divide, a crowd of plainly dressed figures huddled in smaller groups. On the other side, further from the bonfires, a boisterous crowd of figures danced in three interwoven circles around smaller fires. They moved in groups of a dozen per dancing ring, turning different ways to each other. Close to the flames as they were, their richly made cloaks blazed with bright flashes of colour. It was fascinating to see everyone in the same space. There was progress here, yes.

But overall, the line was clear.

After the recent chaos of the battle, a desperate clash of lies on the fields once feeding the people he loved, here was another fight to win. Because below was another clashing as two races coming together, this time in peace, yes, but a peace but burdened by suspicion. Each person was unsure of their place in the grand play as Rhydian urged them forward, away from a fractured history to something filled with hope.

The troubled king inhaled the frigid air, cold enough that it was like layering the inside of his lungs with ice. Which was welcome, in a way. It distracted him from the insistent throb in his heart, the unsettling ache in one hand.

Cracking his neck, Rhydian's half shuttered eyes lifted from the sea of people and spread to the dark valley of his homeland. Was that deep ache from the cold? Or something else? Or the troubling words from a librarian he'd grown up with and thought he knew?

His weary mind shied away from such thoughts.

Tonight was for better things.

If better things were within reach.

"Fox," Rhydian whispered, the words escaping as a white mist, "where are you?"

It seemed shameful to pin his hopes for help once more on a mysterious man, an odd creature met only recently. But Fox had shown his true nature to him, that of protection for the ones he loved, however few.

Yet surely he had more information to share?

If one could pry it out of those cool lips.

Rhydian reached up, aching fingertips brushed his own frigid mouth, his hand trembling only a little as a sober drumbeat began below, accompanied by the single mournful drone of a low-pitched pipe.

The icy air caught in his throat.

It was clearly a funeral dirge.

The crowd quietened down, the general murmur lost to the forlorn music.

Stepping back from the stone wall that edged the tower top, his hand slipped from his face. As the song coiled upwards, Rhydian raised his gaze to follow the notes as they were offered to the night like a reverent prayer of loss and longing. As the steady melody and hollow notes flowed around each other, he closed his eyes to the night, feeling the pressure of the sky above as the clouds grazed the roof of the tower. The main three bonfires below were stacked with multiple logs of wood as thick as a man's waist. But the yellow glow didn't reach this high.

It meant that as he opened his eyes, the low clouds with their shadows remained mysterious and full of secrets.

The half seen swells of the low sky blurred as his eyes stung with unshed tears. It was an effort to hold them in.

"Surely enough tears have been spent?"

There was no answer to his sombre plea.

"Is it really my destiny to be king of... all of this?"

Again, there was no reply to his melancholy musing.

Turning from the courtyard to face the west, Rhydian's watery vision lent a dreamlike quality to the vista of other tower tops spread before him.

The various buildings, lit by bursts of lantern flame by the gates to ward off the deepest shadows, seemed surreal. Like stacks of giant pins in a child's game, propped up, ready to tumble. Beyond them, the mountain to which Aneirin clung was a colossal, looming black mass. Beyond the back wall of the castle complex, the half-seen mass disappeared into the hanging clouds, only marginally different in their suppressed tones of grey, charcoal, and shadowed black.

The air tasted bitter up here. With smoke from below and the occasional puff of ash, the aroma wasn't unpleasant, but seemed entirely fitting with the mournful wail of the pipe, and the steady, hollow boom, boom, boom of the drum. In a land with newly awoken magic, the weary king imagined the notes might become real, fantastical shapes, turning into part of the mist that rose from the crowd's heat to find equilibrium above.

Rhydian blinked.

He *could* see shapes.

Unsure if his vision or mind was playing tricks, Rhydian glanced down at the crowds of men and women, two races, mingling and not mingling. His blue-ringed gaze rested on one of the bonfires, its sparks rising in flashes of gold and red.

"What?" he breathed, his heart stuttering.

As the pipes rose in pitch, another drum joining in, Rhydian realised he could see *into* the fire, each burning log.

He could distinguish between the parallel grains of charring wood. Above them, blue and green flecks blended with fiery crimson, as faint minerals from the logs popped as the blaze consumed them.

Swallowing, Rhydian shifted his gaze to the faces surrounding the flames.

Two children with meat juice on their faces, above them two whispering women in matching grey cloaks, glancing furtively into the crowd as if gossiping about their lovers.

Fuck.

Rhydian knew he'd always had good eyesight. But to make out such fine details from a tower so high it was easy to imagine one could kiss the clouds?

No.

The only way that was possible was if —

"No..." the single syllable was uttered less like a word and more like a moan.

Eyes snapped shut.

"No!" hissed Rhydian.

Dread pooled in his sternum, spreading out to his limbs like an insidious fever.

"I don't want this!"

Rhydian grabbed the stone wall that circled the tower's roof to steady himself as his heart stuttered once more. He leant on the exact part of the roof from which Aurelia had been flung off into nothing by his father. He squinted through the darkness equal to his elevated height.

"What the fuck?" he breathed, swallowing around the fiery lump forming in his throat.

The clouds were moving.

Rhydian stared unblinkingly.

Or was it shapes shifting within them?

His frighteningly keen vision sharpened further, and the frigid air seemed to freeze completely.

It became hard to breathe.

Vast, nameless masses boiled and expanded amongst the clouds, not quite dipping any distinguishing features below their bottom horizon.

Wait.

Was that a —

"*Dragon?*" Rhydian wheezed.

Unsure whether to call out or run inside, the frozen king remained where he was, transfixed, not sure if the clouds and their shadows were about to reveal their secrets, or whether his mind was about to shatter from an intense hallucination. As his straining eyes followed a thin, ebony shape danced across the darker sky, too small to be seen really, the entire world appeared to alter.

A low hum, grinding and bone jarring, filled his ears, his skull.

Shouts erupted underneath the tower.

The music died.

As the clouds boiled above and the earth heaved, a wild, confusing force erupted from within Rhydian's heart.

He cried out, afraid, confused, agony in his chest.

Far above the crowd, no one was there to witness.

The night, already dim and full of ice, spun about as he collapsed.

"King Rhydian?"

Opening his eyes, Rhydian glanced up at the concerned, serious gaze peering down at him.

"King Rhydian?" The young lass repeated. In front of her soft blue apron, she wrung nervous hands together. "Are you okay? What should I do?"

Had he passed out?

Blinking to clear the grit and gum from his vision, Rhydian pushed himself up and examined his surroundings.

He was on his arse on the slate terrace of his tower, his back against the stone wall, legs out straight before him. Unsteadily, Rhydian tapped his boots together to bring the feeling back into his tingling toes. Heart throbbing, he coughed.

"Yes... yes, I'm fine..."

A delicate brow arched.

"Your name?" wheezed Rhydian as he cracked his neck.

"Orion." Shy, pink lips tilted upwards at their corners. "Orion Court, sire."

Rhydian peered at the figure more closely. Under their pale blue apron of clean linen, a deeper blue robe with an iridescent shimmer flicked as she crouched down by his side. Rhydian squinted. She was pretty in an unusual way. Her features were strong, with unblemished skin like she hadn't seen the sun in a year.

Deep gold eyes shimmered, the same colour as her long, neatly braided hair.

Ah.

By the light in her eyes, and the colour of her odd clothes, it seemed right to assume she was an Elf.

But Orion?

That was a boy's name around Aneirin, unless in Lolihud it was different.

"I'm okay, lass."

The smile deepened.

"What should I do?" The Elf hovered before him, her apron and shimmering skirts moving in the frigid breeze.

Waving one hand to show he was alright, Rhydian ran his other hand through his hair. His palm came a way damp. Bleary-eyed, he peered at his palm.

It was clear sweat, not fresh blood.

As he was thanking the gods under his breath, someone shouted far below.

With a jolt, Rhydian realised he was hearing the pipes and drums, the dull hum of voices.

Laughter.

The dull clink of tankards coming together.

Peering at Orion, the king frowned.

"What happened?" he queried, scraping his boots along the slate as he bent his legs to the side. He managed to get to his knees, biting back a groan all the while. A delicate hand wrapped around his own to steady him. Her grip was stronger than he expected. He nodded in thanks.

"Did it scare you?" she asked. "Before he went to calm the horses, the Master Groom said it was a bad one, but nothing to be scared of."

"Master... Oh, Merion? Wait... Did what scare me?" Rhydian queried as he glanced up.

The clouds hung in place as before, low and dark.

Calm.

No shapes rode amongst them, no shifting masses.

No threats.

Dragons were nowhere to be seen.

"The earth tremor, sire."

Rhydian's gaze flickered to the golden gaze of his unusual companion. Unable to comment for a moment, he rubbed his palm over his wool shirt to dry it. Beneath his fevered flesh, his heart was beating with surprising ease. The ache that had plagued him for the past few days was gone.

"Tremor," he repeated, staring at his hand. Flexing his fingers, the digits that had been throbbing before were feeling completely fine.

Had he been knocked out by falling masonry?

Looking about himself, Rhydian searched for loose rocks or stones. The low wall that ran around the tower was intact. Nothing lay nearby that may have caused him to black out.

"Is everyone okay?"

It was Orion's turn to blink. "Yes, sire. It was just a deep hum, then a rumbling jolt, but it was over quick. A few lost their drinks, but I think they were drunk already."

"I see." He licked lips caked with bitter soot and grit. Rhydian stood up with a barely concealed grimace. The Elf's gaze remained on his, so he forced out a smile. "How did you find me?"

"Aurelia sent me. Sire. She guessed where you were. People have been asking for you to join them in the dancing."

The music below had changed, Rhydian realised. It was upbeat, the funeral dirge long over. Clapping and cheers now accompanied the pipes and drums.

Inhaling the smoke curling amongst the icy breeze that lifted and cooled his damp hair, the king stared across the roof. It wasn't a large space, but it wasn't small either. Yet the door was clearly visible. Along with the finely made but rusting hinges, the thin sheen of ash and condensation forming around the frame. His vision honed in and the neat blocks of reddish stone grew in focus, speckles and flecks he'd never noticed before but had always been there, easily distinguishable. A minuscule spider with a white dot on its abdomen scurried from one barely there gap, where the doorframe met the masonry to another.

Fuck.

His enhanced vision remained.

Was this the beginning of all the things he had come to dread?

His mind protested at the scorching thought.

Calm down Rhydian, he urged. *Calm down.*

Surely, while the peace strengthened below, there was enough time to sort everything out. His kingdom, the divide, the fear of what hid in his heart, his ancestry.

There was time.

There had to be time before anything else went wrong.

"The tremor only just happened," Rhydian asked, as calmly as possible, "right? I think I fell asleep."

He attempted a weak laugh.

Eyes the colour of boiling honey stared at him, warily curious.

"No, sire." Orion bit her lip. "The tremor was hours ago."

Dressed in her usual wide legged riding pants and a deep green cloak she'd procured from somewhere, Aurelia handed him a steaming drink.

Cautiously, Rhydian sniffed the sweet and spicy vapors. He forced out a smile as a group of Elves crowded around them.

"What's this?" he mumbled out of the side of his mouth.

Lubricated by the free-flowing ale, wine and spirits from the royal cellars, the gathering had grown loud as the night passed. Noise bounced and echoed off the stone walls. Some laughed about the tremor. Others nodded sagely together, discussing the earth settling as the temperature dropped with the loosening of the magic that bound Aneirin. No injuries or damage had been reported. It had come and gone with a fleeting rumble, just as Orion had said.

Rhydian eyed the lake of people, taking in the sight with circumspect eyes.

Humans and Elves.

Down here amongst the revelry in the courtyard, it seemed that finally, the line that denoted two separate people had blurred. Taller than most, Rhydian observed the huddles of folk exchanging stories by the bonfires. More logs had been heaped upon the flames. Great conical blazes roared. A few of the Elves had produced coloured salts from various leather pouches as he had exited the castle a short while ago. Now the flames shone brightly, with blues, purples and even greens, amongst fiery red and brilliant orange.

"By the look on your face," Aurelia whispered as Rhydian took a suspicious sip, "you'd think I had handed you a cup of fresh horse piss."

Rhydian spared her a dark look.

"You looked miserable, so I thought this might help," she declared with a shake of her head. "I can't comprehend how overwhelmed you are, but this feast was your idea."

"I know," Rhydian mumbled.

He nodded as the jostling group of young Elven men laughed at something he hadn't managed to catch. He was fascinated with the play of rainbow hued light across their multi-coloured fur cloaks, wool hats and warm scarves. Averting his gaze, he half turned to Aurelia, concentrating on the slight cut that marred her otherwise perfect brow.

"Where have you been?" Aurelia stepped close, her arm going around his waist. Her wandering hands slid under his thick cloak, a dark grey wool with a narrow band of silver embroidery along its seams. She gave him a reassuring squeeze. Aurelia's voice was low against his lobe and he shivered, blushing as an Elf whistled at them. "You look miserable. Was it the tremor?"

"The tremor," Rhydian said. "Mm. Sure."

Not meeting her gaze, he knocked back the steaming liquid. It burned as it went down, tasting like burnt honey. Welcoming the fiery heat spreading in his guts, Rhydian's brittle smile relaxed as the Elves whooped around him. Another cup of the same was pushed into his hand. He raised it and they raised theirs. More clay cups were drained. He drank half of his in one go, swallowing the urge to cough.

Forcibly breaking his stare of the colourful lights and shadows playing off the clear, beautiful faces of the magic infused folk before him, Rhydian glanced up. The clouds seemed close by, even from the level of the crowded, noisy courtyard.

Was that an illusion of the bonfires?

Or his gods-be-damned vision?

As some of his guards joined the surrounding crowd, Aurelia pulled him to the side, backing him against a chilled wall beyond a circle of dancing figures, their bright robes swishing in time to complicated footsteps.

"Rhydian," she murmured into his neck.

Lost to the sensation as her lips filled him with warmth comparable to the fiery drink in his guts, Rhydian found himself swaying a little to the deep beat of the drums.

"*Rhydian*," she repeated. His name was affectionate, but her tone was firm. "What the fuck is wrong? Besides the obvious, I mean?"

"I'm concerned," he replied. Honeyed steam filled his nose as he hiccupped. "About Fox."

Pulling away, Aurelia stared at him with eyes flashing like living emeralds. "Fox?"

Using his free arm, Rhydian gathered her back to him and wrapped the loose end of his fur cloak around her. He inhaled the wild aroma of her long hair, spilling freely over her shoulders tonight.

"Mmm. I want to see my horse. What's taking them so long?" He drained the rest of the clay cup.

"Ah." A snigger rumbled against his chest. "I bet Fox and Owaen are getting *reacquainted*."

Rhydian spat out his drink.

Aurelia laughed, unaware of how close he'd come to spraying it all over her hair. She laughed louder as he cursed, a sound that freed his heart a little. Despite it all, he grinned.

While he wiped frantically at his dripping chin, someone called to him from the crowd.

"My king!"

He sighed.

"Yes?"

It was another request for insight into matters that he had opened for discussion. Ideas on farming, housing, the list went on. With a sigh, his genuine smile faded. The brittle one returned.

He hoped that tonight might be a break from it all. But some folks, aiming to place themselves first with a kind of hopeful optimism, were attempting to use the gathering to gain advantage. Well into their cups, suggestions and casual mentions of their merits were inserted into most of the few conversations he'd had since following the pretty little Elf downstairs to join the feast.

Were they tactless members of the court whom his father had kept around him?

Or were they townsfolk vying for possible new positions?

Despite the ache in his chest having disappeared since the tremor, a new tension was coiling up from the intense heat in his guts, snaking around his spine, teasing the base of his skull.

"K-king Rhydian?"

Rolling his eyes, Rhydian glanced about for another full cup of whatever the hells the fiery liquid was. He likely shouldn't, but he was determined to drink about a dozen more. Laughter burst forth from the crowds as a young lass began a bawdy drinking song. Other voices joined in with drunken calls and answers.

"Rhydian? P-please..."

A sharp tug on his cloak had him spinning around, ready to snap at the next vocal person daring to spoil his night further.

His curse, ready to be flung with as little care as he dared, died on his lips.

Above flushed cheeks, wide eyes met his.

It took Rhydian less than a heartbeat to size up the frantic gaze, the trembling hands clutched against a puffing chest. The closest bonfire flared blue as another handful of mineral salt was thrown into the flames. As the fire leered above them, the fear reflecting in the wide gaze stopped his heart.

Not looking behind him, Rhydian's hand reached out blindly, finding Aurelia's arm and tugging her close. Sensing his panic, she was by his side in an instant.

"What is it? Quickly, now," urged Rhydian, the cup forgotten in his other hand.

"It's W-Wyll..." came the stuttered reply.

"Wyll?" Aurelia hissed.

"He's free... with a weapon... and..."

Rhydian's stomach fell away with a lurch, the tension coiling around his spine now a spike in his skull. Pressed half behind and beside him, Aurelia swore under her breath.

"With a weapon, and..?" Rhydian urged, fighting the dread lacing the spiced drink in his guts.

"With a w-weapon... and... f-friends."

Staring off above the crowd, Rhydian nodded, unsure why it was hard to breathe.

There was time, his mind repeated, *there was time. Time before he admitted what he didn't want to about himself, time to get this chaos under control before the tinder of unrest was lit by a man with hate in his heart.*

Wasn't there?

"Oh," he managed, a dull mutter more than an audible word.

Aurelia grabbed his arm.

With the spicy, fiery drink making its way through Rhydian's blood, the faceless crowds appeared to spin, the smoke thick, the scent of meat and embers once a sign of revelry, choked his throat.

Surely, there was time to grow into his role and sort out the tangled web of uncertainty and decades long fears and resentment.

The unwelcome sound of racing, booted feet filled his ears.

Someone shouted, the noise shrill.

Not a laugh, not with joy, not a song.

"The stables," Rhydian snapped, giving the messenger an urgent shove. "Go!"

Another shout joined the first.

Directly after that followed a scream, accompanied briskly by the impersonal clank of metal clashing against metal rising above into the frigid night.

"No," Rhydian moaned. "No, no, no..."

Chaos still reigned in his kingdom, a fiercer tyrant than any curse.

There wasn't any time left at all.

24

Cas

Year 250, Cas at age 9
Baile Mara, City of the Sea

Would she still be there?

The haunting cries of wandering peacocks, residents of his family's estate, filled his ears as he entered the lush gardens.

Ever since Evreth had said the name that tormented his adolescent heart down by the docks as pirates came ashore, the boy had been racing onwards and upwards through Baile Mara.

Despite the cool ocean breeze, Cas' lungs were afire.

The boy pushed on.

It had been months since he'd glimpsed green eyes and red hair. He'd overheard Mother and Father talking about the library in the City of the Seers. There was some exchange of important works that had kept their librarian away.

Cas practically flew along the main track through the Carter Estate, with its great Oak trees lining each side. Vineyards, rose gardens and the occasional outbuilding covered the grounds, with pale wicker bee hives crowded together in humming conversation at various locations. It was a wild type of beautiful, every child's dream to live amongst the greenery. Away from the gaseous stink of the lower city, with its impressive yet imposing black buildings, up here was paradise.

It would be best enjoyed if you had wings too, as the gardens had some kind of pattern to them that Rook assured Cas was 'spectacular' from above. As with most things, great things could be achieved and experienced with magic.

I.

Don't.

Want.

Magic.

Cas scrunched his nose as he passed stretches of fragrant roses in full bloom. He imagined the bullies of the alleyway earlier decorating the thorny shrubs, crying as they struggled free. The fleeting image startled him and he laughed, half a gasp really, as he ran.

In the distance, the tips of gold-topped black towers loomed over the trees. Baile Mara's palace, home of the Elphin royal family, wasn't far off. Both constructions, the Carter house and the royal residence, were built of the same ebony stone at the top of the cliff. Thankfully, inside the Carter's home, some rooms and outdoor fountains were lined with pale limestone. The softer material was easier to etch than the volcanic rock.

It was towards one such collection of water gardens he headed to now, climbing over a stacked stone wall. The taller of the twins, Cas grinned. Wane couldn't climb this section easily yet. Furthermore, his brother was carrying the toy ship too, and wouldn't leave that behind. If he was lucky, Cas would have a few minutes before Wane raced around the gates, slipped through, and veered back to Mother's workroom.

Passing a peacock, the bright blue bird cawed at him.

"No crust today, sparkly bird!"

The call of the bird behind him sounded disappointed. Cas felt a moment's pity, but that was quickly forgotten. Cheeks flaming pink, he skidded through an archway into the wing he'd been summoned to.

A group of richly robed figures jumped off the flagstone path as Cas bounded amongst them, darting around them. A small figure with a golden circlet amongst their auburn curls frowned at Cas as he raced past. Something muttered, something like 'Elven brat', drifted after him.

The boy snorted, uncaring. They'd clearly confused him with Wane. Cas didn't have magic sponsored by the Elphin royals, therefore he was not an Elf.

Footsteps slapped loudly as he hopped up a set of stairs. He dashed down wide hallways, past arches and doorways, heading to the only door that mattered. Not able to moderate his wild pace, Cas slid on his feet, slamming the workroom door open as he careened inside.

Cas had a split second to appreciate that *Yes! Morgan was still here!*

Before he tripped.

Speed unchecked, the boy fell straight into the tidily stockpiled, massive worktable in the middle of the room.

Vials clinked.

Birds in wicker cages shrieked.

Reptiles in metal pens hissed.

And a clay bowl of steaming green liquid up-ended to smash onto the wide flagstones below.

The hot substance splashed everywhere, over the floor, the wooden drawers, under the bench.

All over the back of Cas' right leg.

Framed by a long curtain of copper hair, pale green eyes widened in shock.

About to curse at the searing agony, Cas flung his hands over his mouth.

"Caspian!" Morgan gasped.

Across the room, she was holding up one of the chunks of jagged blue-green crystals his father couldn't stop raving on about. Yet the tiny librarian dropped the crystal carelessly into its basket by the window and hurried over to the breathless boy.

"Are you alright? Don't move."

Cas, paralyzed with both pain and shame, shook his head. He swallowed a sob as the green substance seeped into his skin, burning.

Yet he must have made some small noise.

From her desk under the main window in the centre of the far wall, Hypatia Carter raised her head. Her quill dipped back into the little glass inkpot with a slight *clink*.

"Well done, Caspian," said the alchemist. "I'll have to make another batch."

Behind him, Wane skidded to a stop just inside the open door.

"Cas?" he exclaimed. "What did you do?"

Mutely, hands over his mouth, Cas shook his head. Morgan had procured a jug of water and a soft cloth. Without waiting for Cas to say or do anything, she began carefully wiping the goo off of his leg.

He didn't look down.

He choked back another sob.

Not daring to look at Morgan or Mother, Cas twisted around. Wane stared back, cheeks red. His shoulders were heaving, and the little ship was clutched tight to his chest. His brother's bright green eyes were full of pity.

Despite the pain, Cas glared.

Biting his lip, Wane retreated into the hall.

"Wane," Hypatia called, finally moving through the books, cages, and towering contraptions of metal and hanging plants. "Don't go. I sent Evreth to fetch you."

"I'm here, Mother," Wane mumbled, eyes on Cas through the doorway.

Eyes watering, Cas averting his gaze, finally glancing down at Morgan. She was a tiny person, like him, small for her age or something. Still, she was taller than he. Musing over how long it took to grow taller compared to a woman likely to stay young for decades, the boy assessed the puddle of green liquid staining the flagstones and the legs of the heavy oak table.

"Are you done?" Hypatia asked as she passed them, Wane following at her hip as she led him back to her desk by the window.

Cas got a good view of the look Morgan aimed at his mother's back.

"Nearly," was all the librarian said. Morgan glanced up at Cas, realising he'd seen her glare at Hypatia.

Cas stood up straighter, puffing out his chest. Morgan hardly ever looked at him, yet here she was, full of concern.

Maybe the pain wasn't so bad?

As the thought crossed his cunning mind, the pain lessened as his calf warmed under the wave of soft magic she unleashed over his protesting flesh. As her palm hovered over him, her stern gaze softened.

"It'll be okay," Morgan murmured. "Your leg will be fine. There may be a mark, but I don't think it will scar. If it does," she aimed another dark look at Hypatia before looking back to Cas, "I'm sorry."

"Like this?" Finding his voice, Cas reached out to touch the tiny sliver of a scar under Morgan's right eye that he couldn't remember seeing before. She flinched away. "I'll have a scar, too?"

Morgan shook her head, exasperated. "Worse."

"Oh," Cas swallowed. He smiled, warmed by her attention. "Okay."

Sitting back on her heels, Morgan frowned. "It's not funny."

He arranged a solemn expression. "Okay."

Pale green eyes narrowed.

At the desk, Hypatia was fussing over Wane. Over the top of the central worktable, Cas eyed the pair of them. The tall figure of his mother, her long golden brown hair done up in a bun to keep the strands out of her face, was studying the blonde lad propped up on the desk with a cushion before her. Cas took a moment to appreciate that from what he could see, Mother's apron was a fresh one, the old leather one, with its stains and scratches nowhere to be seen. The sound of glass clinking against glass from within the pockets of Morgan's sage green tunic reached his ears, as her freckled face blocked his view.

"All better?" Morgan asked, her voice low, eyes back to their cool aloofness.

Cas stood up straighter.

"You don't have to do that," he said solemnly.

"Do what?"

"Pretend everything is alright."

Morgan's face paled, the pattern of her freckles making an interesting collection of little specks. Petite hands pushed red hair away from her cheeks as she assessed him.

"When you are in your lessons, I am not sure if the priestesses love or hate teaching you."

Cas shrugged, chewing on his bottom lip. If he had to guess by their reactions to the drawings he made, when he didn't know the answers to their questions on history and philosophy, he'd say both.

Well, mostly the latter.

Ignoring the tingling stinging in his leg, Cas held out a hand.

In his fist was the white quill.

"Why do you look the same? The other priestesses look dried up."

As Morgan eyed the feather with its nib of yellow gold, her copper eyebrows rose.

"I am not a priestess."

"I know." Cas brandished the quill. "Take it."

"No. Keep it." Morgan's smile tightened. "It's too pretty for the likes of me. A priestess will likely snatch it."

"Oh." Cas scratched his head. "You could zap them if they tried."

"Zap... them?"

"Yes," Cas nodded. "Only a few folks and those who become dragons have it so far. The priestesses and some craftspeople. Yet you, Mother, Father and Rook haven't changed in all this time."

"All this time?" Morgan repeated, one eyebrow crooked up.

"Mm. Since I can remember, you look exactly the same, since I was a boy."

Morgan's other eyebrow followed the first. Cas examined the red welts across his leg.

"That means a lot of magic, right? So zap anyone who tries to take what's yours. That's why you're here so often, why Mother needs you. I know you've got a heap of magic, too."

The librarian sighed. "Yes, I do have magic."

Cas looked up. "More than them, though, right?"

Morgan eyed him carefully, her voice calm. "Yes, I have more magic than them now."

"Why?"

"Your parents and I..." Inhaling slowly, Morgan poked at a piece of smashed red clay with the toe of her boot. "Never mind, Caspian."

From across the room and not looking up, Hypatia called out. "Caspian? My librarian has finished for the day. Tidy yourself up."

Morgan gave the boy a grim look.

Cas shrugged, his eyes on hers. He held up the quill. Smiling a little, Cas snapped it in half and dropped the pieces to the floor.

"I'll find something better for you."

"Please don't."

Holding his stare, the librarian very deliberately kicked the two halves of the broken quill under the low base of the central wooden workbench. The corners of Cas' lips curled higher. After checking that his mother was still busy with Wane, he gathered up the shards of the smashed bowl with the toe of his boot into a haphazard pile.

Then he kicked the pieces under the bench as well.

The librarian and the boy eyed each other, pale green eyes sparring with blue, one light and one deep sapphire, both shimmering with flashes of silver.

"Can you stay?" Cas murmured, eventually.

Morgan's eyes closed. "No."

"Why?"

"Because."

"Why?"

"Because I can't bear to watch."

Morgan left the workshop without another word.

"Good day, my brilliant wife."

"Husband."

Entering the study, Illarion winked at Cas as he headed over to the row of windows. Bright sun poured in through the ceiling-high glass. The rays highlighted Hypatia's hair with spun gold, and Wane's blonde locks with pearl. Illarion passed by his oldest twin by the door without another glance, balancing a wooden tray of instruments as he navigated the crowded space.

Both of Cas' parents were tall and full of energy, perhaps magic, perhaps iron determination. Today, Illarion wore a beekeeper outfit, white leather overalls with full sleeves and long pants. His hood was down, and the scruff on his chiselled jaw had a piece of beeswax stuck amongst the blonde bristles.

"Wane, my son! Are you holding up alright?"

"Yes, father." Wane's voice was a whisper, thick with unshed tears.

Crossing his arms over his chest, Cas craned his neck to see better.

Through the faint grassy vapors of the workroom, Cas watched his father ruffle his youngest son's hair. Wane's cheeks were pale, his scrunched forehead covered with a fine sheen. Hypatia had him sitting on top of her desk, his back to the window, and his legs hanging over the front. Wane's watery gaze met his brother's mismatched blue-eyed stare.

Cas raised his eyebrows, head tilted to the side.

Wane looked away.

His twin's current state of distress was fair enough, Cas supposed.

Considering their mother was slicing his arm open with neat, precise cuts.

"Look at this one," Hypatia murmured to Illarion. "It heals much faster this way."

"I see! That's incredible."

"Hold still Wane."

"Yes, Mother."

His father's pale hair caught the same brilliant sun that touched his wife and youngest son.

Cas remained silent in the shadows by the door.

Along with whatever Mother and Father were working on that had the household whisper excitedly when they thought no ears were around to hear, the workroom was filled with all sorts of oddities. Shelves were stacked with scrolls, great vats bubbled away. The two giant chunks of jagged crystals fascinated him beyond all reason. Sometimes, not often, Cas dreamt of them, along with the cold, frothing ocean and the grainy black sands of the great southern beaches that the twins loved to explore. Cas actually liked it here despite what happened within its soaring stone walls, but the temptation to poke around was strong. So, considering what usually happened when he did, he was banned from entering, unless an adult was present.

Wane was allowed to come and go as he pleased.

Blowing hair out of his eyes, the restless boy sniffed at the mineral tinged gases tickling his nostrils. He wondered what Morgan was doing. He wondered when it was his turn on the workbench. There was an idea forming in his imagination, and the boy wanted to get back to the beach.

"Father," Cas said, breaking the tense silence across the room. "What are the two big, craggy, greeny-bluish crystals for?"

"Ah," said Illarion, his green eyes lit up. He winked at Cas. "That is our biggest experiment yet. We are going to expand magic. Not just for the dragons, but for all of us."

"Why?"

"Well, we —"

"Hush," said Hypatia, not looking up from the latest cut on Wane's arm.

The thin red line, looking small from all the ways across the study, faded as Cas watched.

He glanced down at his white shirt. When it was his turn, would he be allowed to remove it?

"One day," Illarion whispered loudly, sparing a grin for Cas. "I'll tell you one day." Dropping his voice, he spoke to his wife. "Rook seems to think he's found a way to help the lad."

"Ha," Hypatia scoffed. Peering at Wane's arm, she was holding up a thick piece of crystal to magnify the boy's inflamed skin. "He's delusional. The dragons are drunk on their abilities. We've tried. It won't work."

"It might if he —"

"Go join them, husband," Hypatia snorted, straightening. The crystal piece landed on her desk with a thud. Her tone was mocking. "If you agree with Rook, go."

"Don't be like that."

"Thanks to Morgan's latest insights, we know the likely results, anyway."

Illarion sighed. Cas met Wane's eyes briefly until their father's broad back blocked the view. He could still see Wane's small hand, fingertips brushing against the wooden toy ship at his hip amongst the implements and journals. Small yellow sparks flared between little fingertips and the wood, in time with each careful slice.

"Stop moving," Hypatia muttered impatiently. "If you reach for that toy again, I'll have your father take it away."

"But —"

"You're too old for toys," Hypatia went on. She glanced at Illarion. "Where is the gold scalpel?"

Cas bit his lip, waiting for his father to defend the wonderfully realistic ship. Father had built it himself for his sons to share. Illarion remained silent and passed his wife the next blade. Cas frowned. Their ship was a source of pride for both father and sons.

Why didn't their mother agree?

"I'll get going," Illarion murmured eventually. He planted a kiss on the top of Hypatia's sun-kissed head, at the wispy strands escaping her tight bun. She remained bent over Wane's arm, the crystal in her hand again. "I've got three new hives going in at the eastern rose garden."

"Good." The woman didn't look up.

"Bye, Wane," their father said, squeezing Wane's shoulder. Wane mumbled something. Illarion made his way back to the door, and smiled encouragingly at Cas. Cas stared back evenly, lower lip protruding slightly.

"That ship," said Cas, uncrossing his arms, "is not a toy."

Illarion flicked a glance back to his wife and son, lit by warm sunlight. He turned back to Cas. "Yes, it is." Illarion looked down. "Where are your shoes?"

"I took them off."

"How come?"

"I like the feel of the flagstones under my feet."

"Oh?" Illarion's blonde eyebrows rose. "Well, don't lose them, son."

Cas bit his lip. "Like I lost my magic when I was born?"

For a moment the only sounds were the muted caws of caged birds, restless feathers ruffling, trapped as they were behind wicker bars. Eventually, the resigned sigh from by the window had both Illarion and his oldest son sharing a long look. Illarion smiled gently with a shake of his head, but Cas lifted his chin.

"I know you think I don't have it. But what happens if I do? And somehow..." Cas flicked a glance at Wane, who was steadfastly looking at their model ship, "I lost it. Maybe I can get it back? I can re-absorb it somehow. Like how you and the dragons —"

"Caspian," Illarion interrupted. "We tried."

"But —"

"You failed."

Cas opened his mouth as if to protest. At the even more exasperated sound from his mother, the boy finally closed his mouth.

Failed.

Illarion smiled, a tight, uneasy expression that Cas had never seen before across his father's normally sunny face. Illarion looked away from Cas, sparing a glance at Hypatia. "Bye, my sweet."

It was Cas' turn to receive a shoulder squeeze, a gesture surely meant to be reassuring. Cas ignored his father, his gaze fixed without focus on the closest birdcage, a fluttering grey pigeon with red eyes within.

Hypatia murmured something under her breath as Illarion made his exit. The man bumped into a serving woman, on her way past the open door as he left, her arms full of folded linen. They both laughed at the near collision and walked off together down the hall.

"Mother?" Cas asked aloud, shaking himself off. He turned to eye his brother across the crowded room. Wane was still fixedly ignoring all of them. Of course. "Mother, can I —"

"Hush."

Fine nostrils flared.

Hush didn't answer Cas' question.

Stepping lightly between the central workbench and a set of shelves against the wall, Cas made his way down the room. Apart from Wane's sniveling, the space was filled with the sounds from caged birds cawing and restless, pacing lizards scratching in their pens on the worktable and on other benches.

Delicate glass globes containing various objects hung from the rafters above, suspended on fine chains. The globes varied in size. Some contained butterfly specimens, others bits of what looked like moss. The largest one contained a twisted piece of wood longer than Cas' arm, smoothed and bleached by the sun. Amongst the glass globes, metal orbs were suspended, copper, silver and iron. The iron ones were spinning slowly, the others were only swaying as the mineral scented vapor that hung about the air undulated through the various suspended items.

Cas reached the end of the central workbench. He was about to turn right and head towards the windows, but paused. On the end of the bench, amongst potted plants that were heavy with sickly sweet flowers, sat two great clay vats. They were shaped like great wine jars, perched on thick wool cushions. Each one was decorated with the same stylised design, a terraced city in black, above a curved bay of blue. In the centre of the bay was a small island. The basic shapes were an abstract form of the vista beyond the twin's playroom upstairs, facing the eastern sea. Beyond the room's floor to ceiling windows, the bay sparkled beyond the black and gold city far below. On clear days, ships like tiny white specks bobbed on the calm sea, with the island in the centre of the bay a black smudge, with its faint haze crowning the sheared away peak.

Cas stepped closer to the clay vessels. The images were interesting. He fancied he could copy the bold lines and abstract shapes next time he found a place to leave his mark on the stones somewhere. Yet what attracted his attention most, however, was the white smoke that occasionally bubbled from the top of each vat.

He sniffed.

Strange.

The aroma was rich, bitter and sweet all at once.

Mixed in amongst it was the spice of burnt honey, something hot and syrupy that made his eyes water. The jars also radiated both heat and cold at the same time.

Curious, Cas reached out.

"Get away!" Hypatia shouted from the windows, her eyes flashing.

Cas jerked his hand back.

"I didn't touch it!" he shouted indignantly.

Actually, he had.

Fingers tingling and going slightly numb, Cas stared from under low brows at his mother. Hypatia examined him without a word. Silently, she held up a finger. She crooked it.

"Come sit here. It's your turn now."

His chin raised, Cas made his way to the desk and hopped up next to Wane. His brother's tightly clenched eyes had leaked shining trails through the smudges of dirt on his cheeks. Wane shifted as if to hop down, but Hypatia pushed him back.

"Stay here. I need to compare."

"What are you comparing, Mother?" Cas queried as he settled amongst the papers.

Wane clutched the toy ship to his chest with one hand, avoiding Cas' gaze. His other hand now held a small glass bell jar. It was full of angry bees crawling over a peach-sized blob of dark orange honeycomb. It seemed at first as if Hypatia would ignore her eldest son, but eventually, she relented. Holding up a clean scalpel of silver so dazzling it was almost white, the alchemist pursed her lips.

"I thought both of you had been born... as intended. I am finding out what happened. Why both of you aren't..." She hummed for a moment. "Special. Like Wane."

"Oh." Cas glanced at the far end of the central workbench, past the oddities and implements, eyeing the two smoking clay jars. He wondered if it would be possible to sneak in later. His fingertips still stung. "Aren't I special?"

"No. Roll up your shirt sleeve."

The humming of angry bees filled the silence.

Cas obliged.

Hypatia poured some clear liquid onto a soft white cloth and wiped it along her oldest son's pale arm. It stung, much like making contact with the smoking jars. Hypatia eyed him, as if expecting Cas to flinch or cry out. His mother's eyebrows rose. The boy grinned. She nodded once.

His heart warmed. From Mother, that was silent praise.

"Do I get a jar of bees, too?" Cas asked. He liked honey, and the idea of owning a little hive thrilled him.

"No. Wane needs that to learn to control his magic. You don't have any. Lessons for you will be," the alchemist paused, frowning as she poked around the sharp knives on the tray, "unnecessary."

"Why?"

"You're broken."

The freshly awakened warmth in Cas' heart faltered. "B-broken?"

"You didn't work out. But don't worry, I can compare Wane to how normal you are."

The glow in his chest sputtered out.

Beside him, Wane's eyes widened, his green eyes imploring Cas to... what? Cas bit his lip and turned away, the chill in his young heart spreading to his limbs and tingling fingers.

Broken, Cas mouthed.

He wasn't sure he understood at first. But Morgan's face paling from its usual cream to sickly yellow told him as much. So he was broken, then? Less than his brother. He knew he possessed no magic.

But to be broken?

What else was wrong?

Hypatia turned back after selecting another gold scalpel.

"Oh no, Mother," Cas said, determinedly swallowing the sick feeling in his guts. "If you want to cut more neatly, father says the black glass is sharpest."

The alchemist froze, blade held at the ready.

"Caspian Carter," said Hypatia, smiling at him for the first time since Cas could remember. "Good boy." The silver blade was swapped for black glass. "Now hold out your arm."

Cas eyed the wooden ship in his brother's tight grip. Rubbing at the stinging flesh of his forearm, the boy's clear gaze shifted to the fireplace.

"Mother says we are too old for toys."

On the rug before the fire, Wane's wide green eyes, rimmed with red from spilled tears, stared at his twin's thoughtful expression.

"Father built this for us."

"Yes, but for when we were children."

"Cas," Wane hedged, his young boy's voice wavering, "I think we are still —"

"Besides that," Cas interrupted, shifting amongst tasseled cushions on the window seat. "We've played with it long enough. It floats. Woo."

"You love this ship!" Wane accused hotly. "We always play pirates with it."

At the window, bare heels rocked and kicked at the front. Cas stared thoughtfully at Wane, with only the crackle of the freshly banked fire and the dull thuds of heels on hollow wood. A mess of tiny long-haired figures with equally tiny metal swords was spread before Wane's crossed legs.

The pair of them were in their playroom. It was a long narrow chamber with high ceilings, heavy curtains, and two fireplaces. Only one was lit. Wane was settled close by the warmth, with a white wool shawl pulled over his shoulders. Cas still wore his white shirt and shorts. His boots were flung into a far corner of the room. Eyeing the red spots on his shirt, Cas frowned. His experience with the young bullies had taught him that the blood was quite difficult to get out. These latest stains were from a sharp blade, however, not rocks fuelled by small minds and cruel hearts. Turning his back to his brother, Cas peered outside at the twinkling lights of the evening city.

"I love other things now."

His brother said nothing, but Cas could hear the other boy sigh as he inspected the rigging on the charming ship. Illarion had built it for them to learn how to share. They were similar in many ways, Cas knew. But the older he got, the more he realised their differences were defining them. Their father had likely tried to keep them from drifting apart.

"We are too old for toys," Cas whispered to the shadows through the cold window. His soft words left a faint mist on the clear surface. He breathed out with force, adding to the condensation. A cock and balls would be funny, yes. But if they were too old for toys, what lay beyond that horizon of growing up?

Rolling his bottom lip between his teeth, Cas smirked.

After taking a deep breath, he added more damp breath to the glass. His small fingertip left a trail of fine droplets amongst the moisture. Sitting back, he examined the image. Considering the medium, the feather quill looked quite realistic. Yet...

Cas frowned.

It looked too pretty.

Too nice.

He wiped it with his shirtsleeve, leaving a smudge of fog and moisture behind.

"Hm," Cas murmured. His eyes focused on the miniscule points of light beyond the chilled glass. The city could have either been aflame with miniature bonfires, or somehow reflecting the indifferent stars above.

A loud pop from the fire caused him to bite his lip. Inhaling the fragrant smoke from the dried wood burning merrily, Cas didn't turn back around. His gaze dropped from the nighttime ocean beyond the city, with its tiny specks of light across rippling waves reflecting the thousands of lantern lights in the city above. Rubbing his thumbs across his still tingling fingers, Cas' odd blue eyes narrowed. It didn't hurt at all. It felt different. Like he'd touched lightning, just for a moment. Not enough to get fried like the sweet dough balls Beltane, covered in sticky syrup. But just enough to sense the immense power it contained.

Potential.

"Magic," he murmured. "Is this what it feels like?"

"What?" Wane queried from the rug.

"Magic," Cas repeated. He hopped off the window seat, his bare feet landing on the cold floor. "I hate it."

"Hate it? Why?" Green eyes, still shining and red-rimmed, met his. A thin frown line marred Wane's usually smooth forehead.

Ignoring his brother's question, Cas padded over to the rug by the fire and sat down next to his brother. Wane sat by his favourite soft animal, a white dragon. Cas disregarded the floppy thing and grabbed a pirate figure instead. Small fingers smoothed the long, black hair from the figure's menacing expression, faintly detailed in bright paint. The doll even had a bright sash, this of forest green silk. It was nowhere near as brilliant as the real thing had been. Cas' silver blue gaze flashed to the toy ship. It really was a marvel. It was too small to be to scale with the pirates. But it was perfect in most details, even down to the tiny specks of seagull shit Cas had added when no one was looking. His father had given him a long look when realising, but had only shaken his head. Wane was horrified. Cas had laughed.

"Why do you hate magic?" Wane insisted.

"Because."

"Because why?"

"Because it makes people…" Cas shrugged. He thought of the tiny stones whizzing past his ear as he raced home. "It makes people stupid." He thought of pale green eyes, and a heart-shaped face, framed by copper red hair that hardly smiled.

Cas didn't know why his heart ached to see that smile. He had no frame of reference for the tightness in his chest when the librarian appeared.

Or why it disturbed him when Rook teased her in front of him.

"It doesn't have to."

"But it does."

Chewing at his lip, Wane set the ship on the thick wool rug. Even with the dense insulation underneath them, the ever present cold of the dark stone seeped through. The radiant warmth from the fire was welcome, yet Cas liked the cold too.

"Magic can help people," Wane went on, enthused. "Mother and Father are making sure that more can use it, not just those with influence, like the dragons. The Royal family commissioned another experiment to help with that. Craftspeople, not just the important members of the city, and the council, have magic now."

"So they can build nice things that aren't necessary," Cas mumbled, crossing his arms over his chest, the pirate in one hand.

Something sharp bit into his soft flesh.

"Fuck," Cas hissed.

"Cas!" Wane admonished.

The sword, real metal as there was nothing but the best for the Carter twins, had pierced the soft skin of his palm. He held up his hand. A fresh red spot, bright red and shining by the yellow light of the fire, welled up.

"Fuck," Cas said again, louder. His brother glared. Not bothering to apologise, Cas pressed the doll's dark hair into his palm. The blood seeped into the black strands, horsehair, he assumed. His blood did nothing to change the ebony colour of the doll's long locks.

Realising Cas had hurt himself, Wane sniffed. Cas rolled his eyes.

"What?" Wane snapped. He held up his arm with a wet sniff. "It *hurts*."

"Are you serious?" Cas scoffed. He held up his own arm and waved it about with a sarcastic twist of his lips.

Not quite identical in appearance, the twins were certainly brothers. Cas was slender to Wane's slightly stocky boy's build. Their eyes were different, that much was obvious. Both were pale skinned and pale-haired. Yet the marks on their arms were in no way similar. Cas had seven lines of finger length cuts in neat rows from wrist to elbow, crusted and smeared with an antibacterial honey. In the same area, Wane's arm looked smooth at first. On looking closer, it was possible to see seven pink lines, neat and evenly spaced. The lines were clearly almost healed and very faint.

"You," Cas said, his voice thick with scorn, "have nothing to worry about. Magic will always heal your mishaps. But not mine."

Wane had the courtesy to look ashamed.

"Why did you tell her to use the other blade?" his brother eventually mumbled. The boy's cheeks were damp, his tears falling afresh.

"Because."

"Because why!"

"Because I knew it would hurt less, idiot."

"How!"

"Father said so once. That the black glass cuts cleaner than a dragon's tooth."

"He isn't always right."

"Isn't he? Mother is." Cas let the pirate drop from his bloody palm. He picked up the toy ship.

Wane eyed the ship as Cas tipped it upside down, green eyes flicking back to his older brother's face and then back to the wooden toy. Ignoring the flare of alarm from Wane's expression, Cas turned over four words in his mind.

"'*Caspian Carter*'," Caspian whispered. Unfocused blue eyes shimmered with both silver flecks and gold light from the crackling fireplace. "'*Good boy*'."

It was the first time that he could remember his mother looking at him with interest.

For a fleeting moment, anyway.

Wane cried out as Cas raised the ship. His shout was in vain.

"Little brother, magic can't do *this*."

As the ship landed squarely on the merrily crackling flames, the stink of burning glue, cloth, and lacquer filled the room. Feeling nothing, Cas retrieved the pirate figure from the rug. Without regret, the boy broke its arm off at the elbow. The mutilated toy slipped from tingling fingers to land with hardly a sound amongst the dense weave of wool below.

Cas held up the sword, with its pathetic doll's arm attached to the hilt. Mismatched blue eyes examined his younger brother's horrified face beyond the sharp edge.

"We are too old for toys," said the boy with a serene smile.

Wane burst into a fresh wave of tears as Cas slashed the toy sword across his waiting palm.

25

Merion

Year 367
Aneirin Castle

"Hush, sweetness," the groom soothed.

Keeping his voice low, Merion patted Aurelia's stocky pony with reassuring movements of his broad hand. The animal shook its head under his touch, ears well back. One tufted hoof stamped.

He frowned.

"Is it the party?"

Chewing on his beard, Merion peeked at the half-closed doors he'd slipped through when he hoped none of the revelers were watching.

He liked company, he truly did. Yet horses were definitely his preferred companions for quiet days, days of solitude and simple thoughts. The crisp aroma of clean, dry straw and even the aroma of horse waste was a comfort after all the turmoil.

Except...

Merion chewed his beard. Tonight, inside this haven of ancient but well-built stone walls, slate and horse, his beard felt like it twitched of its own accord as he listened.

The bonfires and merriment in the great courtyard continued, and likely would for the entire night. Bright shapes and deep shadows flickered through the slight gap between the open doors as dancers passed in front of the intense bonfires, pillars of flashing deep orange and brilliant crimson. A young woman's voice rang out as she laughed.

"Good on you, lass," Merion concluded after a moment's thought.

Perhaps this *was* a good idea.

Shaking off the dark cloud of his sorrows, if only for an evening, he wandered to his workbench and rubbed a hand over the latest saddle he'd been working on. As his fingers rubbed at a thick splotch of oil, he stared at the deep brown leather without quite seeing it. The gods only knew that everyone needed to let their tension out somehow, and dancing after an odd cup of ale or two might do the trick.

White teeth appeared behind the bush of his beard as he grinned. Plus, the fresh meat had been welcome, caught deep amongst the lush forest in the south by the Elves. It was their gift for the feast. As were their fragrant spices, added to the warm wines of Aneirin's open cellars. The fiery liquid was a welcome balm to his aching bones, as well as his exhausted heart.

The groom moved down along the stalls, deep in thought.

Absentmindedly, Merion hummed under his breath to the pipes as they picked up the pace, their melancholy dirge forming new, lighter melodies.

The tune actually sounded a little like something he half remembered as a wee babe. Stumbling over a stray tuft of hay left on the uneven slate, he chuckled as he righted himself. The lantern he'd brought inside was back at the workbench by the saddle. He knew his way along here, but Kyle seemed to have left some of his chores undone.

"Or too much wine, perhaps?" he snorted.

At the far end of the aisle, a horse whinnied.

"Ah," Merion sighed, a wistful exhale of spiced breath. "Is it Blackthorn you're missing? He'll be home soon to lord it over you all, don't you worry."

Moving towards the lesser used stable doors at the farthest end of the elongated building, Merion squinted.

"Eh?"

An out-of-place shadow waited amongst the other dark shapes, barrels and sacks stacked inside the closed doors. There was hardly any light here, and the meagre magic in his family's blood couldn't help him see what it was. It was likely there was more than one exhausted soul taking refuge here this evening.

"Kyle?"

Smiling a little, Merion continued down the stalls, the horses on either side of the central thoroughfare silent.

Not even a snuffle.

Coming to a stop, Merion hesitated.

"Hello?"

"Hello, Merion."

The languid acknowledgement emanated from the half-hidden shape.

A figure too tall to be his young nephew.

Startled, Merion cursed.

"*You!* What are you doing here, by the gods?"

"This is your chance, Merion," the voice drawled.

At the dry tone, a horse whinnied.

Merion's blood chilled as his fury rose.

"This is my chance to do *what*?" he spat.

Refusing to glance back to the nearly shut doors in the distance behind him, where merriment carried on none the wiser to the threat within, the groom's hands edged towards his apron pocket.

"Tsk-tsk," cooed the voice. A boot step broke the thick silence. The voice was closer next time the figure spoke. "You can help fix this travesty, Merion. There is still a chance."

"To what? I told you I want nothing to do with... whatever this is. *Nothing*." Blinking in the darkness, Merion held his ground, hands dipping between folds of thick leather across his chest.

"Magic is *unacceptable* —" the voice declared. It was nearer again.

"You know full well magic isn't to blame for what happened here —"

"Magic and magic-users," hissed the voice, malice twisting each syllable, "bewitched our so-called *king*."

"NO!" Merion roared, his eyes stinging with shame.

As hairs rose along his brawny arms under his wool shirt, fury expanded through his chest, kin to the flames of the bonfires outside, inflamed echoes burning within his frantic heart. Under the fury was exasperation at realising his pocket was empty.

All of his tools were on the bench by the door, at the far end of the deserted aisle at his back.

"*Yes*. You need to join us, Merion. You need to protect your home against *his* weak heart!"

"You're wrong! *None* of this is Rhydian's fault. I'll die first before I raise a hand against that lad."

The figure stepped forward, close enough now that Merion could see the wild passion in the man's eyes. Merion swallowed, his next protest stuck in his suddenly parched throat.

Wyll was clothed in an ankle-length dark cape, the gathered hood thrown back. A faint sheen like fresh dew covered his furrowed forehead. Now that he was nearer, there was just enough of the ambient glow to highlight his wide eyes.

The groom's heart stuttered.

Beneath Wyll's inflamed gaze, within a trembling white fist, was a knife.

Merion's chilled blood froze completely.

Had it really come to this?

Dread spread through his chest, following the icy rush along his dilated arteries.

Oh.

The blade was a beautiful thing. Delicate curls of yellow gold and jewels adorned the pommel visible beneath the heel of Wyll's hand.

Oh, no.

The blade was clearly Elven made.

"Tis a pretty thing," Wyll hissed, spit marring his bottom lip. "A pretty thing to incite another war, one where we can *clearly* place the blame upon the wicked, don't you think? No way to slip out of justice this time, eh?"

"What are you doing, man?" Merion gasped. He stumbled backwards, his hip hitting the stall door of an agitated horse, fresh horse manure acrid in his nose.

Wyll inhaled with a jagged, excited breath, his eyes bright, filled with an unearthly lust for something the groom would never understand. Merion swallowed at the blaze in the man's intense gaze.

"I gave you a choice," Wyll said, his gaze fierce, soft enough that Merion realised the comment was for Wyll's own ears.

The realisation was like a fresh shovel of frost down the groom's spine. Confused and at a loss, Merion blindly reached behind, unlatching the door of the stall at his back, hands reaching out amongst the shadows for anything at all to defend himself.

The horse danced sideways as the groom's hands grasped empty hooks, bare walls.

There was nothing.

As he spun around in the gloom, the horse kicked out beside him, a shrill whinny accompanying the dull thud of a nervous hoof against wood.

It was almost completely dark back here, but he could make out the only movement that counted.

"Wyll, how could you?" the groom cried out, his voice breaking. "Are you really threatening *me*, you daft bastard?"

Wyll raised his knife. "You're gods damned right I am."

He charged.

26

Cas

Year 253, Cas at age 12
Baile Mara, City of the Sea

Cas burst through the heavy door of the library.

"You're here!"

Glancing up from the workbench, Morgan eyed him, unease clouding her face. Pale green eyes narrowed, attempting to focus.

Cas held his breath, wondering if she would speak today.

Or ignore him.

A moment of silence passed.

"I am the librarian."

The boy's breath escaped with a loud puff while his cheeks turned pink at her sarcasm.

"I mean, you're here in Baile Mara, back from the City of the Seers," Cas clarified. He hurried on. "How was your journey?"

"The same as any other."

Despite the flat quality to her voice, the boy grinned. From behind, a briny wind pushed into his back, ruffling his freshly clipped blonde hair.

They were the same height now, a smug thought that filled Cas with the glow of pride.

Perched on her usual stool, worn leather boots swinging clear above slate tiles, it was clear to Cas that Morgan had stayed the same height as always. She was a fully grown woman, with magic to enhance her health or prolong her life, but her height would be the same. In the months that Morgan had been absent, however, Cas had grown. Hesitating by the open door, he straightened.

Or perhaps he was taller?

The thought filled him with a warmth that spread across his shoulders, along his rangy arms. His fingertips tingled.

Not looking at him, Morgan picked up a brown clay teapot. She poured steaming liquid into an equally plain cup. Lemon and rose aromas reached Cas' nose. Outside, waves crashing onto the ebony shore far below the cliff reached them while inside, the silence lengthened. Closing the door carefully, Cas sniffed appreciatively. The tea's rich, floral aroma was better than the stale, sickly sweet smoke he'd recently come to associate with Morgan, before she'd left to travel deep inland.

Even the bitter scent from the three flickering lanterns on her desk was better than *that*.

Cas took two steps closer to the central work table. He flicked a low hanging frond aside, glaring at the plant above his head, hanging from a cobweb-laden beam. One of his father's indoor hybrids was in need of a trim. Pursing his lips, Cas' studied the red-haired woman at the desk.

Mismatched blue eyes glinted.

"I thought you'd be off tending to your poppies."

The teapot landed on the bench top with a heavy thud.

"How did..." Morgan swore under her breath. "Rook," she muttered. Her messy bun wobbled as she shook her head. Irritated, she tore the scarf out of her locks. Flame-coloured locks spilled about her shoulders and down her back in a rumpled wave.

Smiling innocently, Cas pointed to Morgan's drink. "Is there enough for me?"

"No."

Cas sauntered forward another step, pulling an object from the pocket of his freshly pressed pants.

He held his treasure up.

The librarian took a noisy sip from the cup before placing it down with a dull thud. A drop sloshed over the edge, hissing against the side of a lit copper lantern by her right arm. Other splatters landed on an unrolled parchment held down with solid glass paperweights. Morgan eyed the mess. She flicked a glance to the boy, one copper eyebrow raised. He shrugged. Expression smoothed, Morgan picked up her quill.

And went back to studying the parchment.

"Um." Cas frowned. The object in his hand clinked gently as he waved it. "Morgan."

"No."

"I made another —"

"No."

"I made *this* one out of lost things."

"No."

"Discarded things. Like us."

Lifting her head, Morgan eyed him coolly. "No."

"But —"

"No."

"I'll just add it to the shelf, then?"

The metal nib of the librarian's quill tapped against the cup of steaming tea. Green eyes surrounded by deep shadows examined the object in his hands. They moved to his face. Cas' lips curled up at the corners. Without another word, Morgan shifted so her back was turned to the waiting boy. Without pause, the quill began adding notes to a massive burgundy leather-bound tome that looked like it had come from some children's story of spells and fairies.

The boy's smile wavered.

His right eye, with its iris of darker blue, flashed silver.

Was she ignoring him for the sake of it?

Or was she stoned again today?

The tea's aroma made it hard to tell.

Cas' hands tightened on the twine in his fingers. Taking another step, he studied the dark circles under the librarian's eyes. He could just see them from this angle, purplish green bruises. With another step, he eyed the table. Where was...

Ah.

There it was.

A silver smoking pipe, one end tarnished with sticky brown residue, lay on the table amongst the sheets of parchment and a collection of other books and stacks of notes. The floral tea had indeed covered it. She was taking a risk leaving her pipe out where any priest or priestess dropping by could see it.

Should he lock the door for her?

Giving the door a surreptitious peek, Cas' silver blue gaze paused on a staff propped next to the heavy door he'd burst through. About as tall as he, it was something he didn't remember seeing before. The bleached, smooth wood was similar to some of the items amongst the treasure he'd created for her return. Perhaps it would look better with a jewel of some sort at the top? A stubby fork of wood at its peak would house a recessed crystal prettily.

The boy stored that thought for later.

Not dissuaded, Cas headed to his left, towards a shelf of odds and ends that Morgan had collected.

All manner of polished shells, from miniature spirals of pink and cream to fist sized shapes of pearlescent peach, made up two of the wooden shelves. Cas' favourite was a spiked shell of brilliant white and purple so dark it was almost black. The other levels held fantastic shapes of bleached driftwood, chunks of black volcanic glass and coins found on the coarse ebony sands as well. Everything was immaculately arranged. About two dozen glass bottles, most missing the neck, of deep colours like forest green and cobalt, were displayed at eye level, cleansed and shined to catch the low light of the beeswax candle sconces nearby. Crouching, Cas focused on the bottom shelf. The dusty space was packed with the odds and ends he'd contributed to her collection.

Picking off the balls of dust, he wondered what needed to be moved to make room. The boy studied his latest creation, eyeing it critically as it lay across his open palm.

It was a necklace. Not of jewels or precious metals.

A fingertip traced the worn patterns across a bent copper coin.

The necklace was made of discarded fragments.

Oddities.

He'd made it himself from things found on the beaches of Baile Mara, like the other pieces stuffed into the bottom shelf. There was nothing pretty about it. Strange objects adorned the random twist of twine that Cas had pinched from one of his father's sheds. A pink crab claw made the centerpiece. Two different sized coins of copper flanked that. Holes had been drilled through each and Cas had cursed when one had gone slightly off centre. Small pieces of bleached driftwood were threaded along the rest of the twine.

He shifted some of the other items on the bottom shelf to the side, all of them other things Cas had collected for her. Morgan never accepted them, not directly. But she never refused them like the quill he'd tried to give her, as a foolish little boy, either.

"Perfect," he murmured, a small smile playing upon his lips. He had draped his hand-iwork over a triangular chunk of driftwood he'd found poking through the black sands last year.

He knew Morgan liked to wander along the shore at dawn. Sometimes Cas spotted her there at low tide when he slipped away from home. But usually, by the time he had raced to the sands from the city, Morgan had always disappeared. He hoped one day they'd peruse the beach together.

Pushing up from the slate floor, Cas turned back to Morgan. He cleared his throat as he passed through more fuzzy, low hanging fronds of some sage green plant. It smelled like mint, only more peppery. Before he could speak, the librarian's dry voice broke the muted silence.

"Where are those two..." She cleared her throat twice. "Where are Hypatia and Illarion, Caspian?"

Approaching the work table, Cas helped himself to a spare stool. Seated across from the librarian, he let his gaze wander.

Morgan was like a wild flower amongst the muted gloom of this place, with only the breaking waves below and gusts of salty wind outside for company. The library, solid and dark inside despite the lanterns, felt gloomy and musty most days when he slipped away from what he should have been doing to come here. Today Morgan was dressed in a tunic of dark indigo, over leggings of deep green. He'd spotted her usual knee length leather boots before she'd sat down. With her hair of dazzling red and deep copper, creamy skin and soft green eyes, the librarian didn't suit the place at all.

Apart from the resigned expression that adorned her beautiful face when she saw him. Cas smiled.

Leaning over to rest his elbows on the desk, Cas experienced a thrilled shiver down his spine. He was *definitely* taller than Morgan now. Both he and Wane had experienced a growth spurt that pleased Father and fascinated Mother this past couple of years. His joints ached every night, and he hoped it was still going. There wasn't much else going for him. Cas rubbed his palm over a patch of bare wood, his thoughts darting away from the aimlessness that scared him some days.

Would anyone notice if he carved something here?

Shapes?

"Caspian."

Names —

"Caspian Carter."

"What? Oh." Cas gathered up a tightly rolled scroll. He waved it about. "The usual. Father is making love to his bees. Mother is in the greenhouse today." He shrugged. "At least she was when I slipped out."

"Mm." Morgan's hum was noncommittal. "Perhaps you should lend a hand back home."

Cas snorted as politely as was possible.

Surely she wasn't serious?

He watched the quill moving with muted scratching across the pages of a notebook beside the larger open tome, the tall feather quivering with each mark. Blonde head tilted, he couldn't decipher what she was writing. Idly, he held the rolled scroll up and stared through its hollow length.

"I think Mother was checking her latest seedlings," he continued. He moved the circle of his vision to one of Morgan's freckled hands. "After that earth tremor last night, she wanted to make sure her precious babies had survived."

The hand paused. Cas moved the circle to the feathered quill. The soft ruff quivered. The circle crept along an arm, up to the librarian's face. Morgan was assessing his sour expression. She said nothing. Cas struggled to smooth the bitter twist to his lips. He discarded the scroll with a careless flick of his wrist. A finely shaped red eyebrow rose at the gesture.

"Thankfully, we don't get quakes as often as we used to," Cas said, attempting to smile.

"Perhaps."

The boy hummed. "We still get the gas from some of the cracks in the cliff face, though." He laughed. "When the wind dies and the gas collects in the Lower city, it smells worse than a sailor's armpit."

After a beat of silence, the scratching resumed.

"Charming," the librarian commented eventually, not looking up. "How is…" she cleared her throat once more, "their work progressing?"

Thinking of Father's growing field of angry beehives and Mother's study, Cas chewed on his bottom lip.

Hypatia's work room was overflowing with things he wanted to know more about. The cages of animals had been cleared to make room. The pots of plants had all been relegated to the green rooms that lined their estate. But the room was still stuffed full, with metallic instruments and trays of transparent crystals of all shapes, colours and sizes. Cas sighed. He wanted to go back and investigate the two bubbling clay vats wrapped in thick wool, one which he'd touched as a child. Rubbing his fingers together, Cas eyed the steaming cup as it was raised by a delicate hand.

"Ongoing. Long."

"Mm." The librarian blew over her tea, before taking another sip.

"Mother keeps banging on about needing more heat, like fires of the earth heat, but father —"

Morgan spat out her tea.

The liquid landed all over the notebook and parchments spread out on the desk, including the burgundy ancient-looking tome. The wet patches glinted in the lantern light from above. Gasping, she shifted the closest lantern of fragrant oil out of the way.

"Oh, here," Cas fished out a clean piece of cloth from his shirt sleeve. He hopped off his stool. With a hacking cough, Morgan waved it away.

"I'm fine," she wheezed. "Wrong pipe."

"What about these?" He attempted to wipe the ancient book down, but Morgan shook her head.

"Leave it."

Smirking at her disregard for the priceless book, Cas tucked the fabric away. He stayed where he was. It smelled nice just here. Perhaps it was the tea. While Morgan recovered, he sought for something to say.

"My parents have some new things to play with. A clutch of clear quartz spheres as big as my head, like giant dragon balls. Ha ha."

"Hilarious." Morgan picked up her quill. Cas eyed the ink stains on her fingers.

"Wane says if you look closely, each has a heart of gold, a tiny speck. I can't see it though. Some alchemist visiting from down in Verglass brought them. Treasures from Lolihud traders, or so they said." Realising he had Morgan's full attention, Cas paused. He blinked at her grave expression. "What?"

"Lolihud? They've been busy then. The caves have only been active for a few decades. It seems unlikely."

It was Cas' turn to eye Morgan strangely. "No. Lolihud has been producing materials for both the dragons and mother since the year one-four-zero. Or just after. So that's... hmm. One hundred years before I was born. Oh. You look like you're about to choke again, Morgan. Are you okay?"

"Y-yes... I..." Morgan put down her quill. Green eyes stared at the rows of gloomy shelves across the way. "Um. It seems I've lost track of the days."

"Are you sure you're alright?" Cas stepped forward, unsure about the fine coating of sweat breaking out on Morgan's creamy forehead. A loose strand of hair fell from the mess on her head and she swiped at it. "You look really ill all of a sudden."

Forcing a laugh, Morgan shifted away from him. "The priests say that sometimes."

"That you look sick?" At Cas' question she nodded, but avoided his searching gaze of uneven blues. "Are you?"

"No. It's just... the magic I've received... it makes people this way sometimes."

Crestfallen, Cas crossed his arms over his chest, hoping his white long sleeve shirt was tight enough to show his growing muscles. Wane's arms were chunkier, but Cas was pleased with the long toned shape of his own. Morgan was back to avoiding him, facing away, towards the back of the room. Odd blue eyes flashed both with silver and resentment. Why did she keep avoiding him? His bottom lip trembled.

He wanted her to look at him.

To *see* him.

"I've studied people," Cas said loudly. One hand dropped to the desk, and his finger rubbed a damp spot of tea on her notebook. "This past year I've learned a lot. And *you* seem emotionally repressed."

Slowly twisting to face him, Morgan's eyes were wide. "Exactly how old are you now?"

Cas stuck out his chest. "Twelve."

"For fuck's sake," the librarian muttered under her breath. She dropped her head into her hands. "What in all the hells am I still doing here?"

Alarmed, Cas stepped forward. "What do you mean? Why? Where are you going?"

"I need to get away from here." The librarian didn't raise her head, instead spoke through her ink-stained fingers.

"Why?"

"I..." Morgan swallowed. "I want to travel," she finished lamely.

Suspicious of her explanation, Cas leant over the bench to gauge her expression. Shooing him away, the librarian found her cup and drained it. Frowning, she patted about her tunic.

"Gods, I need a drink."

"Why?"

"Because."

"Why?"

"*Because.*"

"You can tell me, Morgan. Why do you drink? Why would you leave? Why —"

"For fuck's sake, Caspian," Morgan hissed, eyes flashing, "because here, this part of the world is going to fucking end."

Cas blinked at her. "Oh. Is that all."

"What? 'Is that all'? Hells. It's true."

Unperturbed, he rubbed his chest. "How do you know?"

"I dreamt it." Morgan appeared to be quite sick now, skin clammy, the scatter of freckles on her cheeks standing out in contrast to the cream.

"Well, I dream too. They don't come true," Cas said, not at all alarmed. He felt more wistful than anything.

"Caspian."

"Yes?"

"Mine do."

Despite the closed door, a sudden gust sent the lanterns and plants above swinging from the beams. Shifting shadows crossed Morgan's face, weary and a little sad.

"Leave, then." Cas bit his lip. "I'll come too."

"No."

"But —"

"No." Morgan's tone changed, the weariness gone. Her voice was firm. "Go."

"I can —"

"Leave, Caspian. I have work to do."

The boy blinked twice, three times, four. Jaw set, he stepped forward. Carefully to avoid her tea, he ripped the page from her notebook out from under her arm. It made a satisfying chewy sort of noise as it came free.

Morgan sat back, lips parted.

He held it up.

Pale green eyes stared at him, not wide or narrow. Bland, mildly curious maybe. The boy reached over the work desk, sleeve catching on a paperweight. His fingertips stung as he opened the copper door of the closest lantern and touched the edge of the page to the happily twitching flame.

Pulling it back, Cas dropped the torn-out page onto the desk amongst the other sheets and parchments. One corner of the burning sheet curled inwards as an orange flame grew into three orange flames, slowly consuming the rows of her tiny writing. Acrid coils of thin smoke reached his nose. The air between them seemed to charge with ozone, his skin itching across the back of his neck.

Was it her magic, ready to pounce in some way?

Or his own anticipation of seeing how many other sheets would catch the flames?

Cas was breathless to find out, to see what would happen.

Beside him, Morgan swallowed.

Above the licking flames of orange, he regarded her. The glow from his vandalism brightened the dark circles under her sad eyes, turning her expression almost sunny. She sat there, lit from a freshly kindled fire, without magic, watching her work burning without a sound. Petite shoulders rose and fell naturally as she inhaled the coil of smoke spiraling upwards. There was not an ounce of bother about her.

Impressed, Cas studied the soft shape of her nose, the swell of her top lip. He stared until the momentary brightness faded, the dark circles deepened, the spark gone.

The air between them lost its expectant charge.

His skin no longer itched.

The sheet he'd set alight had burned through. Unfortunately, the spilt tea had protected the rest from following.

Cas laughed out loud. An accident, preventing potential catastrophe. He didn't know why it was funny, but it was. He touched one of the wet spots with a curious fingertip. Clearly against her will, Morgan also laughed. Unlike his snort, hers was a soft noise that sounded like one of the faint waves crashing outside and far below the cliffs.

When she spoke, her voice was just as quiet.

"I thought the rest would burn. How strange."

The boy stood up straighter, odd blue eyes glinting. "Do you want that to happen?"

The librarian turned to him with a quick twist. Dark circles made her pale eyes stand out like wild, tortured peridots left too long in the sun. Cas flinched at the anger that hadn't been there a moment before.

"Go."

"But —"

"Go now."

"But —"

"I am sick, as you say," Morgan hissed, "so *go*."

"What? No! I can help," Cas insisted, one hand tugging on the ends of his blonde hair. "What is it? Why are you sick?"

The fury in her eyes scorched hotter than the flames that had died, their bitter aroma poisoning the air.

Morgan's voice was pure ice. "You."

Cas reeled back as if slapped. Except, a physical blow would have been more welcome.

He didn't have to wait long.

Before he could think of anything to say, Morgan shoved him away, her freckled hand petite, the blow to his chest immeasurable. Stumbling back, Cas retreated awkwardly to the door. At a loss, he stood there open-mouthed, his eyes wide. A momentary phantom, akin to a fleeting shadow, crossed her stern face before it was quickly smoothed over, like it had never been.

"What?" he whispered. The word was forced past his dry lips. His throat felt as if it was burning, as if it was being squeezed by delicate hands.

The librarian picked up her quill. Red hair fell across freckled cheeks as she leant back over the ruined remains of her work. Cas didn't need to see Morgan's face to feel the full force of her barbed, frigid words.

"It's you who makes me sick. I said *go*."

Mismatched blue eyes dropped to the hand that held the quill. Dainty fingertips, stained with black ink, clenched tight. Feathers trembled as if caught in a sharp breeze.

Choking with both shame and confusion, Cas did as he was told.

He fled.

27

Karlien

Year 367
Baile Mara, City of the Sea

"Hyeon!" Karlien shouted across the chaotic passage.

It was difficult to yell and not vomit at the same time, thanks to the fluttering in his stomach. Fanning himself with a soft pink silk slipper as servants bustled past, the prince took another breath.

"*Hyyyyyeeeeoon!*"

The solid wood door opposite the prince's chambers was suddenly yanked open with such force that it slammed back onto the wall inside. Outside in the hallway, a sharp piece of black rock fell away, landing with a delicate scatter of shards on the flagstones below. An older serving woman recoiled on her way past with a basket full of linen.

"Oh, *do* be careful," Karlien snapped. He adjusted his brightly coloured silk robe with an airy sniff.

The servant rushed off, her gaze averted from both the flushed cheeks of the prince, along with the gritted teeth of the scowling foreigner in the prince's doorway.

"Princess." The word was clipped.

"What took you so long? I was calling for *ages.*"

Ignoring the taller man's wet hair and damp shirt that revealed an intriguing glimpse of what lay beneath, including his two heavy gold torcs around his tattooed neck, the prince stepped past the bodyguard. Retreating into the safety of the hall and a few paces away from his chamber, Karlien pointed his slipper back to the open door. Squaring his shoulders and looking as regal as he could with one bare foot and only a silk robe of charming apricot, Karlien lifted his chin.

"Hyeon."

"Karlie."

Another servant bustled past, this time in the opposite direction with empty baskets. Avoiding the man's intense glare, the prince waited until the stone passage, a ruined echo of a once majestically appointed hall, was empty. When they were alone, Karlien raised his slipper, at the same time as lowering his voice.

"Hyeon."

"Karlie."

"The *mouse*."

"Ah."

From Karlien's right, a small errand boy emerged down the hall, carrying a silver message tube. Spotting the prince in the passage, the boy gulped, then fled. The prince eyed the silver tube clutched tightly in a small fist as it disappeared down the hall. He frowned at the boy's retreating form, then focused his frown on Hyeon.

"The mouse," Karlien hissed, "is *back*."

Rich brown eyes with their scatter of ruby flecks gazed calmly into Karlien's wide blue gaze.

The hulking man had somehow perfected the precise balance of sarcasm and amused politeness. The prince's frown deepened. Crossing his arms over his chest, Hyeon sauntered up to the prince in three long strides. He looked at the petite young man down his exquisitely shaped nose. The scent of musk and candy drifted between them. Refusing to be distracted, Karlien tore his eyes from Hyeon's lips. He arranged what he thought was a haughty glare.

"Baek Hyeon. Did you hear me?"

"Hm."

"There is a m-mouse in my room!" Karlien barely restrained himself from stomping a foot. "Again! The s-same one."

"Same?"

"Yes!"

"You know this?"

"There is a spot," slipper raised and trembling, Karlien pointed it behind himself. As the errand boy ran back the other way, hands empty, Karlien whispered in a furious hiss, "on its *backside*."

"Spotty arse?" Hyeon said loudly with perfect diction.

Unfortunately, this was spoken right as two young women in thick robes of green and gold ducked into the passage from an open archway a scant few strides away.

Giggling, their steps on the cold flagstones slowed a fraction as they rounded the corner. Karlien realised with horror one of them, the tallest, was the willowy girl from the other night.

Gods, had Hyeon noticed?

The prince risked a glance at Hyeon's profile. From the narrowed eyes and tense jaw, Karlien's heart flipped. It seemed the man had recognised her. Dark eyes, glossy and intense, slipped back to Karlien. From the sudden glint in their depths, Hyeon looked like he was trying not to laugh. Hyeon stepped close and the prince's eyelids fluttered at the creamy aroma of goat's milk soap, candy and musk. The man rolled his candy around against the inside of one broad cheek.

"Tiny mouse lives in big chamber. Shame to kill."

Heat crept up Karlien's neck. Nostrils flaring, Karlien's gaze, flinty and full of azure fire, narrowed.

"Get. Rid. Of. It." Each word was a clipped hiss.

"Hm." Hyeon pursed his lips as if thinking. His gaze made a lazy sweep over the prince's face. "Make mouse dead?"

Karlien had had enough.

"Yes, you fool!" he shouted, ignoring the latest crowd of bickering, oncoming servants and teetering baskets. The prince waved his now crumpled slipper at the damp figure before him. "Aren't you here to protect me? What else do they pay you for!?"

Even before Hyeon's eyes widened with shock, Karlien knew it was the wrong thing to say. His free hand fidgeted with the loose folds of his apricot coloured silk robe.

"Oh, um..." the prince stammered. "Oh no, I didn't mean..."

Wordlessly, Hyeon let him flounder on, words dropping like loose marbles from his trembling lips, eyes narrowing with each useless syllable.

"Obviously um, you are not paid to be here and look after my royal person, so of course that was incredibly insensitive of me, and ha ha, well now that I've... said it... I should..." the prince's voice faded to a breathless wince.

With silence around them like a cloak of ice, servants continued to hurry past with barely concealed amusement, interest and murmurs.

"*Heol.*"

Karlien had heard that word before. He still had no idea what it meant. Nothing good by the strangled tone, surely. Karlien cleared his throat with a dainty cough.

"Baek Hyeon, ah, what I said just now —"

"Not paid," Hyeon gritted out through clenched teeth.

"Yes, I know, that was cruel of me, ha ha, oops... ah, the mouse scared me, you see and..."

"Not paid," the bodyguard repeated.

Oh, heck.

Hyeon pressed forward, his hard body and damp chest forming a solid wall against Karlien's silk robed front. With his back pressed to the cold stone wall, the prince swallowed his squeak. Long, wet silken hair formed a dripping curtain around their faces as Hyeon stared down at the petite prince. Hyeon's breath was a heady cloud of musk, sugar and burnt honey, blown directly onto the prince's face. Making sure his faint accent was barely detectable, Hyeon spoke very slowly.

"*Blood*," the bodyguard declared, making the consonants pop against his lips, "*debt*."

"Hyeon," Karlien mumbled, his voice small. "I'm sorry. P-please..."

"'*Please*'?" The word was a gentle caress, a mocking reminder of desperate voices overheard the night before. When Hyeon had seen everything there was possible to see concerning his prince.

The air between them heated.

Oh gods, no!

Not now.

Karlien shifted his hips away from the charged air before him, his burning face twisted to the side. Hyeon's breath followed the movement.

"H-Hyeon, please..."

"Can't hear you."

"Hyeon," Karlien whispered, eyes shut tight against the searing heat that burned him.

"Yes?"

"Please... squash that mouse for me."

The man snorted. "Yes, princess."

The damp, fierce weight against his chest disappeared. A rush of blessedly cool air was left in its wake. As the prince's eyelashes fluttered wildly, he felt the last, wet strands of long black hair leave his cheek. Hyeon stopped in the centre of his room and glanced around. Without turning to face the prince, he called out.

"Where?"

Surreptitiously adjusting the folds at the front of his loose robe, Karlien peeked inside. Lolling on its back across the bed, the giant grey wolf was rubbing the top of his head on Karlien's pillow. Spotting the prince, the beast froze, amber eyes guiltily wide. Exasperated, the prince crept inside, careful to remain close to Hyeon. The man was his bodyguard, after all.

In response to the arched eyebrow, Karlien pointed his silk slipper at the window. With a sigh, Hyeon strode over to investigate. A trail of water dripping from his hair left spots of water on the floor in his wake.

With a drawn-out sigh, the man poked around, shifting the curtains and a potted miniature fig of muted green that was positioned just so to catch the morning light. Karlien made a strangled sort of noise as Hyeon bent over to peer under the bed. At last Hyeon rose, his wet hair dripping, toned muscles and tattoos showing beneath his damp shirt. His calm gaze assessed the trembling young man almost right behind him. His lips twitched as Karlien hopped away.

"Mouse gone."

"*What*?" Karlien squeaked. Eyeing the potted plant, he cleared his throat. "What do you mean?"

Smiling easily now, Hyeon returned the pot to its original position. That gesture pleased Karlien beyond words, almost enough to forget the current worry of setting out to a foreign kingdom.

But not quite.

Because there was a rogue mouse in his room.

Again.

Hyeon sauntered back to the doorway, Karlien scurried after him. The towering man paused just long enough to scratch the wolf's belly, smiling to himself and sucking on his stupid lolly. Clearly over being caught in such an undignified position, the great grey beast was now contentedly gnawing away at the corner of a white wool cushion, on its back, hind paws in the air. Pausing at the door, Hyeon shrugged.

"Gone," Hyeon repeated. The man's irritating smile widened to a smirk.

"Gone?" the prince echoed, incredulity lacing the single syllable.

"Yes."

"I... Hm. I see."

"Yes. Too bad."

Karlien stared at Hyeon, his gaze cool. His bodyguard was just a little too pleased with himself.

"Hyeon."

"Yes?"

Karlien dropped his gaze to his slipper. The silk was rumpled now from being clenched in his sweaty fist. Delicate knuckles tightened around its beautiful stitching. His gaze landed back on Hyeon and he judged the force necessary to cause the giant at least a fraction of the inconvenience and humiliation Karlien was experiencing.

Twinkling blue eyes with their own blue halo appeared within the prince's mind.

Responsible, his grandmama had said.

That meant think smarter, didn't it?

Hm.

"Yes?" Hyeon repeated. His mocking smirk faded into suspicion at the easy play of emotions across Karlien's face.

Instead of throwing it, Karlien dropped the slipper carefully to the floor. He held out his hand to the tattooed warrior. Hesitant at first, Hyeon clasped the offered dainty fingers within his. Thick knuckles marked by countless scars rippled. Using the bodyguard to steady himself, the prince slipped his foot into the crumpled silk. When satisfied, Karlien's smile was sweet as he glanced up. He tossed his copper curls over his shoulder.

"Grab my pillow," the prince instructed, eyelashes fluttering daintily.

Hyeon's answering blink was slow. He peered down at their joined hands. "Pillow?"

"Yes," Karlien beamed. "I'm sleeping in your room tonight."

"Ugh." The prince's nose scrunched. "Your room is so boring."

"Thank you, princess."

"Hyeon, that was not a compliment. This room is about as interesting as the basalt on which this city is built."

"Black rock strong."

Ignoring Hyeon, Karlien glanced around.

Hardly furnished, the room was functional at best.

As with the rest of the sprawling old estate, the room showed the black rock of Baile Mara in all its fractured glory. The naked walls and ceiling, with only a few tiles left of its original design, showed the violence of the city's distant past. No tapestries covered the various walls of the three alcoves, and only one thick rug of brown fur lay across the floor beside the bed. There was a simple weapons rack, made of sturdy wood, holding Hyeon's two swords and knives. A pair of boots sat neatly beside the rack of blades. There was a small doorway, similar to the one in the prince's room that he assumed, and hoped, led to a working water closet. Thankfully, the fireplace in this room hadn't been blocked with rubble. The flickering of a small fire to ward off the evening chill lit the room with a pleasant glow and woodsy aroma. A small table and two stools had been placed by the large window that faced westwards into the estate's terraced yards.

Karlien blinked, his eyes shifting back to the alcove where the modest four poster bed was situated. There was no canopy of lush fabric draped over the frame, yet the bed linens and thick blankets were neatly pulled up, their folded edges tucked *just so*.

"Hyeon."

"Karlie."

"There is," the prince paused for emphasis, "no couch."

Hyeon's grunt of agreement was noncommittal.

Sitting on the bed with his back to Karlien, Hyeon continued to towel off his still dripping hair. An occasional drop hit the single candle flame of the giant pillar candle, lit on a little table on the far side of the bed, a small hiss peppering the silence. Swallowing, the prince avoided examining the way that the loose strands stuck to his damp shirt. Karlien's gaze eyed the mattress. Unlike Karlien's mound of pillows and cushions of all shapes, textures and sizes, Hyeon only had one. Karlien's favourite pillow had been carefully placed neatly next to it. Delicate nostrils flared.

"Hyeon."

"Karlie."

"So." The prince expressed his displeasure with a dainty sniff. This was not *quite* how he had envisioned this to go. "Where are you going to sleep?"

There was another grunt from the far side of the bed. This time, it sounded amused.

Warmth pressed against Karlien's side, startling him. The prince spared a glance for the wolf as it brushed past to flop down onto the rug. It had Karlien's once white cushion in its lethal jaws. Karlien bared his teeth at it. The wolf went on chewing, amber eyes heavy-lidded. This was definitely not going according to the vague plan the prince had to wipe the smirk off Baek Hyeon's face.

With one last tousle of long hair, the towel was thrown on the weapons rack. It landed perfectly on a wooden hook that seemed likely to be made for such a purpose. Patting his curls, freshly scented and moisturised with a floral oil, Karlien spared a wistful thought for hair that could go to bed still damp and wake up smooth. Shifting to his back, Hyeon dipped his long legs under the covers, pulled up the rugs to his shoulders.

And turned his back to the gaping prince.

"Good night, princess."

Lips parted, Karlien stared at Hyeon's broad shoulders until the movement at his feet had him glancing down in fright.

It was just the wolf.

Cushion forgotten, the beast had risen. It gave the prince a quick look.

It looked back to the narrow bed, then back to Karlien.

"Hey, wait —"

Without a second glance, the wolf leapt up onto the bed and settled with familiarity and a canine sigh of satisfaction against Hyeon's back. Karlien's lips thinned. Amber eyes blinked at the prince with perfect contentment.

Really.

Gathering his robe tight to his chest, Karlien stepped out of his slippers. He placed them by the base of the closest bedpost. For no reason in particular, he sneaked a look underneath the bed.

It was hard to see in the low light, but apart from a few wisps of wolf fur, the space was empty. With a wistful look at the closed door, the prince sat on the bed, gingerly easing himself down. As his hands examined the linen sheet and thick blanket, the wolf's thick tail thumped an enthusiastic beat. Rolling his eyes, and taking a breath, the prince slipped beneath the sheets.

It took him a while to settle. Once he'd found the exact midpoint between the edge of his side of the bed and Hyeon's warmth, his eyes drifted shut. It had been a ridiculous idea to make such a decision while only wearing a thin robe. Feeling the heat from beside him seep into his chilled skin, Karlien was unable to muffle his own satisfied sigh.

Two noses inhaled deeply in unison.

Karlien's eyes snapped open, taking in the domed ceiling in the shadows above.

"Did you both just *sniff* me?" hissed the prince.

Neither the wolf nor his gods-be-damned bodyguard answered.

"*Well?*"

There was a pause.

"Too... flowery," came the muttered response.

Unsure what to say to that, Karlien twisted to his side. He stared at Hyeon's back. The wolf rose and moved around, standing on the prince's thigh. Unbothered by Karlien's exclamation, it settled with its head next to his. Amber eyes that appeared to glow in the low light stared into his, alert yes, but also extremely relaxed. As the wolf and prince continued to stare at each other, Hyeon pushed up onto his elbow and leaned over to the small iron table on his side of the bed. Hyeon took a breath.

"N-no! Don't..."

The wolf lifted its head, nose close to Karlien's chin. Annoyed, the prince pushed it away with a finger on its cheek. After a quick huff, the wolf settled down, eyes remaining open. Hyeon was still half up, weight resting on one arm, the flickering candle on the table not yet blown out. Hyeon twisted a little to peer down at the prince. Karlien avoided his questioning look.

"No?"

Karlien licked his lips. The embers would die down all too soon and he'd forgotten to get Hyeon to add more wood. The candle should burn for most of the night by the look of its size. Karlien adjusted his curls across his pillow, acutely aware that the floral oil he'd used to smooth his locks maybe was a tad strong.

"No?" Hyeon repeated.

"Um." Karlien kept his voice neutral. "Please don't blow it out."

One dark eyebrow rose. This close and with the single flame to illuminate him, Hyeon looked close to Karlien's age. In the bright light of day, the foreigner looked older, wise and smug, like he'd seen serious things. *Done* serious things. In the intimacy of his room, Hyeon just looked like a young man. Tucking a loose lock of long hair behind one ear, his bodyguard waited, eyes expectant.

"My dreams," Karlien began. Should he have brought some wine? He cleared his throat. "They wake me. Sometimes," he attempted to laugh, "they're not pleasant. Well, most of them. So when I wake, I need to see... that I am... here," he finished lamely.

Hyeon was silent for a moment more, his gaze inscrutable. Karlien avoided it, and stared at the ceiling, bottom lip rolled between his teeth.

"Need more?"

Karlien's gaze slid to Hyeon in confusion. The man's eyes had changed. An understanding shone there in such a way that it was as startling as it was unexpected.

"What?"

"More light?" Hyeon clarified, assessing Karlien's wide-eyed stare.

"Oh." The prince blinked, blue irises with their azure haloes shimmering. "N-no. Thank you. One candle is fine."

Hyeon turned to face him more directly, laying on his stomach, arms crossed as he rested on both elbows. He pondered Karlien. "Great lady dreams."

"She does," Karlien agreed quietly. His faint smile was brief. "I dream too."

"Of?"

"Oh. Ha ha…" the prince's feigned indifference disappeared as quickly as the warmth in Hyeon's gaze. A different light filled the man's mysterious eyes. Karlien flushed, realising the look was one he'd seen before, akin to 'don't try that shit with me, princess'.

"Karlie. Dream of?"

The prince attempted a weak laugh. He failed. He closed his eyes.

"Well. I dream of what happened."

"Here?" Hyeon's tone was cautious.

"Mm, yes. It isn't nice."

"Go on."

"Ah. There is…" Karlien's breath hitched. One eye at a time, his lids opened. "There is choking… rubble."

Hyeon waited, his eyes hooded, crimson sparks lost to shadows with only the single flame of the candle illuminating the chamber behind him.

"Piles of splintered flesh."

A muscle in the bodyguard's jaw twitched.

"A city once ruled by magic, all gone to ruin… And as it is happening, I am there. Watching. Witnessing."

"Ruin," Hyeon repeated carefully.

Karlien nodded, blinking rapidly. The ceiling had gone out of focus.

"I need a light left burning to see… that when I wake, it's over… I need to see that the air is cleared of gas, smoke and falling ash."

Hyeon studied the prince for so long that Karlien pulled the blankets up to his nose.

"Karlie…" The man's forehead dipped to his pillow. His voice was muffled, strangled. "I see."

His face now smoothed of any expression whatsoever, Hyeon lifted his head. In silence, he settled back upon the mattress, this time laying on his back.

Oh.

Was that it?

This was the most intimate conversation the pair of them had ever had in the few years they'd been thrown together, by events out of their control. Not sure what else he'd expected to talk about, Karlien wiped his eyes with the blanket.

An ember broke apart with a weak pop in the hearth, but otherwise, all was still. The servants had ceased their bustling past and likely the estate was in bed, ready for an early morning. Karlien didn't want to think about that at all.

The wolf kicked a paw into Karlien's shin as it adjusted its great bulk between them, but strangely, the prince didn't mind. He peered at Hyeon from the corner of one eye. The man's lids were lowered, his profile a glowing sculpture of pleasant lines and mellow shapes.

"Hyeon."

"Karlie." Hyeon's eyes remained shut.

"Why doesn't your wolf have a name?"

Hyeon's lips twitched. "It has name."

"Oh."

Silence. Karlien pursed his lips and counted to five.

"Hyeon."

A sigh. "Karlie."

"Well? What is it?" he demanded. Beneath the blanket, one hand waved dramatically. "I'm sick of the pair of you sharing secret looks across the room, like some kind of mythical beast straight out of a fairy story."

Another sigh.

"Well?"

"Well?" Hyeon mimicked. He still hadn't opened his eyes. Between them, the wolf rolled onto its back, its weight pressing firmly against the prince. From under the bedcovers, Karlien pushed back with a bony elbow. The wolf wiggled again.

"Ha ha *ha*. Well. What is it?"

"Don't know."

The reply was so immediate that Karlien couldn't help but laugh. "What?! That's ridiculous. All dogs have a name."

A low rumble beside him had Hyeon chuckling, a deep, velvet chuckle that had Karlien's eyes snap shut. He wanted to block his ears, too.

"*Wolf*," the word was said with emphasis, "hasn't told me."

What the heck?

It was Karlien's turn to be silent. He rolled to his side to face Hyeon. He pushed a tufted ear out of his way. It sprang back when he released it.

"I don't understand you."

This time, Hyeon's sigh was half a snort. "You tried?"

"Oh. Well, things are complicated, aren't they?" The prince slid a hand out from under the covers to wave it about more effectively. "We're different."

"Complicated," another snort. "Different. By the old gods, yes."

"Hyeon."

A low mutter punctuated the silence. Finally, dark eyes opened and Hyeon turned to face him. There was just enough light washing across his shadowed face for Karlien to make out the man's resigned expression.

"Do you..." Karlien licked his lips. Hyeon's eyes narrowed as they followed the movement. "Do you miss your family?"

Shadowed eyes, the shifting flecks of red appearing, snapped to Karlien's face. Unable to explain it, the prince's eyes welled. Blinking angrily, he sniffed.

"I don't remember mine very well, you see," Karlien went on. Hiding his face from the bodyguard's impassive stare, Karlien burrowed into the wolf's shoulder. Something, perhaps a wolf's nose, perhaps not, brushed his hair gently. Karlien was surprised he didn't mind at all. His voice was tiny. "I had an older sibling, too. They died. Everybody just... died."

"Karlie... Karlien. You miss them?"

This close, the wolf's thick fur had a pleasant, musky scent. Karlien hadn't expected that. He huffed, spitting out the fur stuck to his tongue.

"I... don't remember what my parents looked like. There aren't many of us left," the prince said instead of answering Hyeon's question. "The magic left in our bloodline is rotten, faded. It heals and helps with some things, but also causes us great harm. So unless you are one of the lucky ones," he snorted, "you die young."

"I'm sorry." Karlien peeked up at Hyeon at the quiet words. His bodyguard tilted his head. "Lucky?"

"A dreamer. If a member of the Elphin family dreams, you aren't likely to die so young."

"Ah." There was a pause. "Like great lady."

"Yes. Like grandmama. But it's a curse."

"Curse?"

"Yes. The price for a longer life is the curse of watching your home... crack open and people... lose themselves every night." Karlien paused, this throat hot, words thick and resisting the need to spill them. He tried harder. "We... My family must have done something terrible to deserve this."

Beside him in the almost darkness, Hyeon exhaled very slowly.

Unaware, the prince put an arm around the wolf and squeezed, breathing in animal musk and something spicier. The guilt in his heart at what had happened to his city could be felt as a heavy, uncomfortable pressure in his chest. It was twisted with the anger that he kept buried like lead weights in his guts. Frozen within his dream state, unable to shut eyes already closed, Karlien was forced to watch as the shining estate, an empire of magic, fell into ruin. Giant stone by stone, gilded tile by tile. A broken vessel of broken cages, cracked bowls, cobwebs and dust. The city torn apart, filled with muffled screams and thick smoke tasting of bitterness, ash and blood.

"Magic is a curse," was all he said of the desolation he witnessed each night. With half his face pressed into the wolf, a single azure eye blinked at Hyeon.

Absorbing this solemn proclamation, Hyeon rubbed a hand over his face.

"Magic... not always curse."

For some stupid reason, fresh tears welled in Karlien's eyes. Annoyed at how red they'd appear tomorrow, if this nonsense went on much longer, the prince blinked them away.

"Yes, it is. Think about where we are going. I believe you agree with me, too."

"That is why, with others, you... stay awake."

"Ha. Why I bed so many? Aren't you clever," Karlien muttered, his tone waspish.

"Does it work?"

"What do you think?" Annoyed now, the prince pushed the wolf away, dodging a warm lick on his hand. A change of subject was in order if he was to get any sleep. Aware he was pushing it, Karlien cleared his throat. "Hyeon."

"Karlie."

"Are you going to the temple tomorrow, to say your goodbye to your old foreign gods that you always pray to?"

As another ember popped. The wolf huffed. Karlien peered over the beast's furry chest. Calm, dark eyes met his.

"No. Can't."

"What? Why?"

"I... not allowed."

Karlien sat up, suddenly indignant at the man's unease. "Why not?"

It was Hyeon's turn to avoid the prince's gaze. "Blood debt."

"But... But we are going inland! I know what the sea means to you... I've seen your... um, tattoos."

Karlien expected a snort. There wasn't one.

"So you... really can't say goodbye to them?"

"No."

"Who says?"

"Law. Forbidden."

Hm.

"I see." The prince cleared his throat. "Well. Thank you for coming with me."

This time, the snort was a loud ripple of disdain.

"No choice. But..."

"But?"

"But I'd come if... had choice."

Karlien settled back down, eager for more information on the man's mysterious past. Only his grandmama seemed to know Baek Hyeon's full story.

"Why?"

"Because."

"Because?" Karlien urged, lips parted.

Hyeon turned away, his face to the ceiling and its shadows. In the fireplace, the embers were nearly out, the single candle a brave light in the gloom. The silence stretched. The prince let it, ready to find out more. He was disappointed.

Hyeon slid him an unreadable look from the corner of one delicately pointed eye.

"Because princess is weak."

As Karlien stared, mouth open wide, Hyeon rolled away completely. A metallic clinking as the two torques settled beneath long and damp, silky hair.

"Good night princess."

Upset beyond his understanding, Karlien stared at the ceiling, eyes wide, mind racing. His grandmama's shrewd voice was an unpleasant echo, deep within his lonely heart. Amongst the story she had told, a single word followed him like that blasted mouse.

Responsibility.

Eyes damp and throat burning, Karlien pressed his face once more into warm fur. All he had ever wanted was to be taken seriously. But did that mean a journey into the unknown? Leaving the only home he'd ever had, with no preparation at all?

Karlien listened to the beast's heartbeat for hours, wondering why it beat as fast as his own.

The next morning, Hyeon looked haggard and somewhat strained. This pleased Karlien more than he could say. He spared a glance for the wolf.

The grey animal was sitting patiently by a tall ebony horse, sniffing a shining hoof. The horse in turn eyed the wolf with suspicion, its ears flicked back. With a sigh, Karlien toed the flagstones with his new riding boots, made of dark brown leather. Hyeon had planted Karlien in this spot, told firmly to *stay*, and then strode off.

His thoughts shied away from the impending journey ahead, instead turning over last night. When the prince had finally fallen asleep, some dreams had plagued him as always, but overall, the night had been peaceful. Despite the troubling words of his mysterious bed companion, it had been a restorative few hours.

Perhaps having a warm body that was there for comfort more than anything else had something to say for itself.

The prince shivered, rubbing his chest absentmindedly.

"Get over yourself, Karlien," the prince muttered under his breath, watching servants readying pack animals, arranging sturdy wooden carts and bustling about with chests of supplies. None of them looked at him directly, only a few bobbed their heads on their way past. "No one wants that with you. They know you're just going to lord it over them one day. Nowhere near as gracefully as their favoured regent."

With a low whine, the wolf pressed against his side, the beast's enormous head rubbing against his hip. Absent-mindedly, Karlien slid his fingers over one of the dark grey ears. Enjoying its thick, silky fur, he tugged a little. This seemed to please it because the animal pressed closer.

"You don't count," Karlien said, rubbing between its amber eyes. He glanced across the terrace, out to the sparkling bay of Baile Mara, visible through the gap left behind from a partially collapsed outbuilding. "Neither do I. I'm just another Elphin prince, waiting to grow up and watch my family die. If I am careless enough to have one of my own."

With a sudden yank, the prince wrenched his cloak open. His chest was feeling far too warm. He'd dressed in sturdier clothes than normal, layers of burgundy wool and brown leather, rather than pale silks and delicate cottons. Despite being wrapped in so many layers, the fabrics he preferred needed a blazing fireplace nearby to keep one comfortable.

Karlien tossed his golden copper curls over one shoulder and closed his eyes to the sky.

I am being responsible.

Everything is fine.

Fine, apart from the incredulous look given to him on his way out the estate's front door.

Sheela, the stately head of the royal household, had been blustering about on the top step like some commander of a great theatrical performance. With her bright red cloak, she had looked like a rather heavyset rose atop the ebony stone stairs. But she had stopped long enough to listen to news about a recent shipwreck off the north headland from a passing group of servants.

"Wreck?" the prince had interrupted, stepping out of the grand entryway into the brilliant day. "When did that happen?"

Four pairs of eyes had looked him up and down. The youngest servant had hidden his face in a pile of oiled canvas. Sheela had offered a pitying look. That alone infuriated the prince. But no one had told him! It was her next comment which sent his blood steaming, however.

"Nothing to worry about, your highness."

"Of course I am worried," Karlien had snapped. "Was anyone hurt?"

"All made it to shore, helped along by another merchant vessel arriving from Port Town. But the trade goods were lost. Along with the ship."

One hand on his forehead, Karlien had grimaced. "Why don't they build a fire tower on the headland like I suggested last Imbolc? It is now Samhain."

Multiple pairs of eyes blinked at him. "'Fire tower', my prince?" Sheela enquired politely enough. But her expression said it all.

Karlien had been about to spit something about another useful fire somewhere more local, maybe down under her wide backside, when a determined hand had gripped his upper arm. The grasp had come from nowhere but had efficiently cancelled his retort as he was led down the stairs to a group of waiting horses.

"Hyeon!" Karlien had hissed as he was pulled along. "Let me go!"

"No."

Halting by a spectacularly enormous horse, Hyeon had whirled to face Karlien. He was warmly dressed as well, a thick cape suspiciously close in colour and cut to the one hung over Karlien's slender shoulders. Looking down his exquisite nose at the prince, the man's eyes were full of shifting emotions.

But mostly pity.

Of its own volition, one perfectly manicured hand rose on its own, swinging for Hyeon's cheek. At the last, Karlien jerked it back. Hyeon didn't move.

"How dare you," he had hissed.

"I dare," Hyeon had hissed back. Too hot under his collar, Karlien blinked and stepped back. Hyeon's eyes bored into his. "Fools."

"W-who? Me? But they —"

"I know, Karlie."

"You know what?" Stepping out of Hyeon's proximity, the prince bit his lip.

Hyeon's eyes shuttered, the muscles in his neck straining against his pair of golden torcs as he tilted his head back. Visibly forcing himself to calm down, Hyeon eventually lowered his gaze to the prince. "*They* are fools. Not you."

Struck by the foreigner's sudden grasp of the common language, Karlien had felt the angst rush out of him in an intense wave of released pressure.

"A fire tower would warn the ships of the rocks," he mumbled. Forcing himself to forget the unpleasant exchange, the prince tossed his curls over his shoulder. "Either way, I am ready."

"Really?"

"Yes. Of course."

A dark eyebrow rose.

"Okay, fine, no. Not really."

Hyeon's cheeks hollowed. "But you go anyway?"

The prince shifted in his boots. His nod was a hesitant bob of his delicate chin.

Averting his gaze, Hyeon whistled for the wolf over his shoulder. The great grey beast ambled over from marking a garden bed of trimmed rose bushes. Hyeon flicked a last look at Karlien, a measured appraisal from boots to curls. He glanced at the head of the household on the grand steps.

Dark eyes with bright spots of ruby flecks made their way back to Karlien.

They narrowed.

"Stay."

For some unfathomable reason, he had.

Standing in the warm morning sun *was* nice. The usual blustery ocean winds that rushed up the terraced city from the wide bay below, stinking of gases from deep fissures, had calmed. Today, the air was fresh and cool. Although the promise of lower temperatures and rain was there, by the look of the clouds gathering beyond the bay and its single, smoking island. The yard smelled like the freshly baked bread and hot clove tea that was being passed about to those assembled.

With the wolf at his side, the prince tilted his face to the sky as others bustled about, eyes heavy lidded. He wondered at what lay ahead as one hand continued to play with a thickly furred ear. At least the wolf was coming, a small piece of home. His pony too. That plucky little thing must have been milling about here somewhere. Baek Hyeon too, of course.

Clearing his throat, the prince concentrated on the growing hubbub.

The crowd of people was growing. It was noisy, full of loud, calling voices, carts creaking, horse snorting, and the salt breeze blowing through the trees that lined the largest courtyard. An armed guard shouted her orders at someone nearby, and Karlien's eyes opened. When his eyes had adjusted to the bright daylight, he could see more lines forming up through the large arched opening into the next yard.

Far off across the garden beds, a few pigeons pecked at the grass. Only one peacock could be seen through the shrubbery, clusters of wicker beehives, and blooming salt resistant bushes of a dry kind of green and furry silver.

The prince eyed the peacock with suspicion, glad for the distance and chaos between them. The thing *was* pretty. It was also a creature he'd like to see stuffed into the closest gaseous vent amongst the cracks in the broken ground. As it paraded amongst the gardens, jewel-bright and turquoise feathers shining, it called out. Karlien's hand clenched.

"Goodbye, you lice-ridden —"

"Prince Karlien!" a youthful voice called across the crowded terrace.

Quickly removing his hand from the wolf, the prince looked up. Torres Hart was practically skipping across the flagstones, jumping across a large crack. Puffing, the young man poked Karlien with the case of his fiddle.

"Cheer up, honeycup! We are *travelling*."

Karlien pursed his lips. "I am so excited for us. Yay."

"Ha! Don't look at me like that. I know you love this city despite all its *faults*." Torres winked at his pun, pointing a gloved thumb behind him to the smoking island that had apparently been partly responsible for cracking the city open. "My sweet prince, we are going on an adventure."

The prince sniffed. "I guess a chance to see the continent could be interesting."

"Pah! Interesting?" Torres' black eyes flashed, his teeth white against his bronzed skin. Lowering his voice, the excited youth stepped closer, the vivid reds and oranges of his robe making Karlien's eyes water. "You are going to conquer the *world*."

Paling a little, Karlien gawked at his friend. "Say what now?"

"What?" Torres blinked at the prince's confusion.

"'Conquer'?"

"Well." Torres waved his fiddle case at the lines of assembling figures.

Gut sinking, Karlien realised the crowd had grown to fill the courtyard. The servants were in the minority. Most of the newcomers were soldiers. Checking straps and their weapons, lines of men and women of all ages, had gathered in mostly tidy rows with horses, carts, and the occasional yapping dog.

"Oh." Karlien licked his lips, tasting salt left there from the damp breeze, his hand grabbing for the wolf. The beast pressed into his grasping touch. "Oh. Ha. Yes."

This was what he wanted, wasn't it?

A chance to prove himself?

After his grandmama's talk about their family, the past and the future, Karlien was expected to step up.

Blood binds all of us to answer the call, she had said.

Let me tell you a story.

The story had been some of what he had known, and some of what he had not. It turned out that there was more to the cut off kingdom of Aneirin than he had been taught. There was likely more.

So wasn't this his chance to find out? To possibly make some amends to the lives lost to the chaos of the past?

"I'm r-ready," whispered the prince. It seemed too loud suddenly, the courtyard too full, the sun too bright, the breeze too still.

Torres eyed him, a line forming between his eyes.

The wolf pressed closer.

Shifting from boot to boot, Karlien eyed the growing line of soldiers. After a while, the voices died down.

Bathsheba Elphin had appeared.

Dressed in a deep-green split-skirt to match her fur cloak, she strode along with her head held high, copper streaked grey hair in a single thick braid. Her eyes were focused, her expression proud. A burst of applause greeted her, many bowing their heads. After acknowledging them, the formidable regent of Baile Mara spotted her great-grandson and headed over. Her steps were light and as sure as ever as she navigated the uneven ground.

The woman was exceptionally petite. Despite Karlien's small stature, standing next to him, she was almost a full head shorter than he. Reaching them, she nodded at Torres and patted Karlien on the shoulder. But instead of addressing her great-grandson, she leaned over the wolf. As short as she was, and as tall as the wolf was, she didn't lean far.

"How's my puppy?" Bathsheba crooned, her voice full of mirth. "Is this lovely doggy ready to run free?"

A burst of nervous laughter escaped Karlien's mouth.

His amusement died quickly, however. He had expected the wolf to run off in a huff. Instead, the stupid thing quietly put up with the small hands pulling on its jowls, rubbing its chest. Amber eyes slid to Karlien's for a moment before sliding away. Karlien frowned.

Was that *guilt*?

The prince stared, dumbfounded, as the thing's dark, bushy tail thumped a few times on the flagstones. Greeting over, Bathsheba withdrew her hands from the animal and finally focused on her great-grandchild.

Her hands, frail yet firm, squeezed his. Attempting to smile, Karlien examined her time-worn face.

Their royal bloodline kept his family looking young, for the most part. Bathsheba had somehow ended up with longer years, but her body had not quite lived up to expectations. Would she leave him too? There was no way to know. Records of family living hundreds of years were dotted amongst his family history. Examining the web of intricate wrinkles, a cruel echo to the cracks in the black stones of his home city, Karlien swallowed. He embraced her instead of sharing the feelings that lay heavy on his heart. Hugging his grandmama felt like hugging a fierce sparrow. Normally, it gave him great comfort. Today, he could feel the frailty beneath her strength. Karlien's smile was watery at best as he pulled away.

"My dear child, why do you look like a peacock shat in your honey?"

Torres sniggered into a gloved hand.

The prince laughed, weakly. "Grandmama," he nodded. "Should you really be coming with us?"

Bathsheba gave him a long look.

"Well," the prince began, "by what Hyeon says it will be a hard journey, and you might... need to..." his words faded as her blue on blue eyes flashed. "I mean, I know I need you with me... but... well..."

Beside them, Torres coughed into his sleeve. Karlien shot him a narrow glare.

"Karlien Orion Elhpin, Prince of Baile Mara."

"Y-yes, grandmama?" His gaze found the bright eyed stare fixed on his face.

"I *will* see you to Aneirin."

With a brisk gesture, she released Karlien's hands and reached into her heavy fur cloak. A silver message tube was withdrawn. With no ceremony, she shoved it at a grey eyed young man in blue robes to her left. He looked startled, but bowed his fair head as he received the tube.

"Open that when it's time."

The man frowned. "Pardon me, your highness? When?"

Bathsheba patted the faded copper of her hair. "When your monarch returns."

The man bowed once more and retreated into the crowd. Karlien gave his grandmama's cloak sleeve a tug.

"Grandmama," Karlien muttered for her ears only, "do I need to make a speech?"

His great-grandmother appraised him, her bright azure eyes wide. Karlien swallowed. He had clearly taken her off guard.

But surely he should say a few words?

"You're right, Karlien. But I didn't factor that in," she acknowledged. "So let's skip that. Now, where is that towering hulk of yours? He was organising the carriage horses, as they were so spooked today."

"Oh, but —"

"Hush Karlien, I really must —"

"Bathsheba Elphin," Karlien enunciated clearly. The surrounding bustle died down. His grandmama gaped at him. The prince cleared his throat. But he lowered his voice and surreptitiously grabbed a furry ear for support. "Have you factored everything in for this undertaking, except for me?"

In the stillness, a wispy eyebrow rose. "I see I must take care to not make that mistake again."

Karlien sniffed. "Thank you, grandmama."

"Good. Is that why you look so pale?"

"What? No. It's the soldiers," he began and stopped. Ignoring the staring onlookers, he attempted to sound as casual as he could. "Are you sure there are enough?"

Both Bathsheba and Torres turned toward the growing lines of men and women with armour stashed in packs behind their saddles. Overhead, a seagull flew past, crying loudly above them all. The breeze had picked up, and the prince's golden copper curls waved about his face. Letting them obscure his pale cheeks, the prince kept his gaze on the family member he couldn't bear to lose.

"Soldiers?" Bathsheba queried, turning back to Karlien, eyebrows high above bright eyes.

"Yes," the prince replied, heart beating with a sickly, wild rhythm. It was something he hadn't quite allowed himself to think about. He'd studied strategy, of course. But this was real. The pieces of chalk and wood were now people of Baile Mara, not being moved around on maps displaying battles and military strategy. "The army."

"Army? What makes you think we will need an army, Karlien?"

"To take Aneirin. To take the kingdom back."

A cormorant flew overhead, dipping and wheeling with a lonely cry as the salt breeze strengthened. Karlien's cloak flapped about his shins, his boots shifting uneasily on the hard ground.

"My sweet prince, you won't need an army." Smiling, Bathsheba Elphin squeezed his hand. "Aneirin is about to fall apart."

$$28$$

Flare

Year 367
Baile Fuar, City of Stone

"I *need a priest,"* Caspian had sighed on the rocky outcrop earlier, collapsed under the weight of his own misguided grandeur.

Flare had known the forlorn man when he was a little boy, precocious, wild, sweet at times.

But always, *always*, wickedly cunning.

The dragon landed with a crash in a partial clearing amongst a meadow pocketed with aromatic cedar trees, far enough outside of the quarry city that little notice would be taken. The dragon grimaced.

Caspian hadn't wanted just *any* priest.

Confused, afraid, and his heart a shivering mess, Flare had obliged.

So they had come to Baile Fuar.

As they had soared through clouds of ash and nebulous vapors, the naked man had clung to the shining row of wickedly sharp spikes along the dragon's spine. Caspian hadn't moved much. That seemed to be due to a combination of things. He was clearly focused on keeping the egg safe, while also seeming to sink into some kind of delirium. From pain, or other, Flare wasn't sure.

It was deeply concerning though, because everyone knew you treated a wounded animal with caution.

Considering Caspian was a man of unknown magic at this stage, it seemed best to go with his immediate directive. For now, at least.

Despite not moving around much on their flight from the cave due east to the quarry town of Baile Fuar, Caspian had occasionally called out from his near dream state. Flare listened with wary ears over the wind at the nightmares, memories, whatever they were.

Morgan had been mentioned many, many times. Along with his fevered musings, Caspian had shouted out her name, begging for her heart, laughing hysterically into the frigid gusts and more forgiving thermals.

The dragon shivered.

Flare knew who Morgan was.

He had hoped to never see her again.

On the ground amongst trees, now missing some of their branches, Flare ruffled his aching wings, shaking off twigs and detritus from his ungainly landing. The air was damp and the aroma of moist earth was almost crushing in its intensity.

As his claws kicked up tufts of jewel-bright green moss and drab clumps of damp ash alike, the dragon cleared his throat.

"Caspian?"

Atop his back, the man shifted. By the vibration along Flare's scales, it felt like Cas was shivering.

"Flare…" A hacking cough sounded. "Are we there yet?"

"We are not far." Flare hesitated. He couldn't quite twist his great head around to view his passenger. Slitted purple eyes squinted at the patch of gloomy sky above. "It seemed best to land outside the town, as they have likely not seen a dragon for many years."

"Hmm," mused Caspian. A brief laugh broke above the wind behind Flare's crown of spikes. "Did you know that flames can always be extinguished?"

"What?" Flare frowned at a sprawling oak, senses tuned to the chuckling figure astride him.

"But no matter how quickly you put them out," Caspian continued, "they will always be left b-behind. As burns, seared into my heart like wildfire."

"Um. I —"

"Never mind. Lie down."

"But —"

"I am getting down, Flare. I said, lie down."

The fiery line of unseen magic that bound man to dragon didn't pulse or jerk. But the threat in the exhausted voice was there. Unable to do anything but comply, Flare maneuvered his great bulk around, one half extended wing knocking over a cluster of prickly tree ferns.

A scatter of roosting birds took off, cawing in a fluster of bright wings as they flew up into the dappled gray light.

Purple eyes clenched shut as Caspian slid his bare arse down the shining purple scales of Flare's flank.

The man landed in the moss with a muted thud.

"Fuck," Caspian hissed under his breath.

One purple eye opened.

Stepping into Flare's view, his cock right before the dragon's snout, Caspian had the egg clutched tight under one arm. His broken hand was held up before his face. Blue eyes, one light and one dark, examined the red, swollen mess.

Catching a whiff of flesh gone sour, the dragon grimaced.

Tearing his eyes away from the horrid mess, his gaze landed on the iridescent rash spreading not just along Caspian's arms, but outward from his chest now, too. Horrified, Flare's eyes snapped to Caspian's.

Silver-blue eyes shone back. There was obvious pain there, aching and deep.

Along with resolute determination.

"I am going to walk to Baile Fuar from here," Caspian announced, swaying just a little. His eyes narrowed. He cleared his throat with another hacking cough. "You shall become small once more. I assume your flight has digested your fine feast?" Not waiting for an answer, he rambled on. "You will meet me there in secret. Find the p-priest, as your leathery appendages will do better than I."

Flare nodded, unsure but willing to get some distance, at least for a little while.

"I will try. How will you find us?"

A gentle tug, almost lovingly, quivered along the binding that joined Flare's trembling tail to the man before him.

"Oh." Flare gulped. "Of course, ha ha…"

With a slight, pained smile, holding his ruined hand out before him like a tortured work of art, the bedraggled man pivoted towards a break in the trees, the direction into town.

A faint curse broke the gentle sigh of the trees as Cas nearly tripped over a crushed fern.

He kept walking, though.

Flare blinked.

"Caspian," the dragon called out, incredulity winning over fear. "You're still n-naked!"

The man didn't stop.

Dappled grey-green light painted his pale skinned bare arse with the spiked shadows of crisp ferns and bushy shrubs as he walked. His scars, countless pale circles and a mean discoloured patch along the lower half of his right leg, were on full display as he strode away.

"So?" Caspian called over his shoulder. "Don't forget, my mighty dragon, so are you."

The quarry town of Baile Fuar was almost a city, but not quite.

It was certainly situated to be an important destination. With the coastal settlement of Port Town an hour's flight east, and the inland City of the Seers to the north and west, Baile Fuar had one day held high hopes of growing into an imposing place.

But it never had.

With the fall of the two great cities decades ago, the City of the Seers and the port metropolis of Baile Mara, Baile Fuar had floundered.

Its original purpose had been to supply both cities with enormous blocks of native rock. The original quarry tapped into an unusual convergence of fault lines and subterranean activities that led to a unique mix of strata. The gigantic monoliths were hewn with both magic and dragon strength. Basalt and obsidian of the deepest black had helped Baile Mara grow into the shadowy splendor that had once been. Stone of paler hues, delicate quartz and breathtaking marble were flown to the City of the Seers, lending it the pearlescent shine the city was renowned for at the height of its glory.

Workers and their families arrived in the quarry town to assist. As the population grew, the encampment around the open cut depression of bare rock had spread. Trees were logged for huts, huts became stone buildings. The population had flourished as craftspeople, cooks, tailors and other traders came to enjoy the boom of an expanding populace.

And then one by one, first Baile Mara, then the City of the Seers, had fallen.

Survivors of both calamities had flooded the town of Baile Fuar, but sickness had decimated the native population and those seeking refuge alike. The town had taken a heartbreakingly long time to recover. But the growth hadn't spread outwards along the edges of the open cut quarry, or through the forest of the surrounding valleys.

Instead, the town had spread in a different direction.

Down into the abandoned quarry.

Then inwards.

The open cut of the quarry itself was extensive enough that it could take a good two or three hours to cross it by foot. The open air market complex took up most of the central quarry floor. Yet on non-market days, it was still a challenge to make one's way across. With the town making use of the unused sections of stone and transportation lanes, there was no planning or sense to the streets and lanes.

To reach the quarry floor, folk used one of the many bare rock ramps spiraling around from the town's rim. Radiating inwards from each of the multiple levels, hollowed-out spokes radiated into the raw and uncut rock walls. It was hard to tell how many true levels there were. Along with the ramps, staircases spiraled up through solid stone to join various junctures together. Glowing fungus and fragrant glass lanterns peppered the long interconnected tunnels, much in the same way ants created their underground nests. Businesses, the town council, and even religious sects all had at least one or two major warrens and halls to themselves, with smaller tunnels jotting out from them. People had made homes amongst it all, wherever there was enough rock left behind to create an insulated series of rooms, plus proper ventilation ducts as well.

It was common knowledge that, along with fresh air, sunlight was still a requirement for good health. No matter how thick the magic was in your blood. So all had access to the public parks dotted amongst the maze of market squares and streets.

Along with a segment of layers in the north wall, Bailey Fuar's council had their own building on the lowest level, the quarry floor. One of the very few buildings built, not carved out of unused stone left protruding from the bedrock. Accompanying the council building and market complex, public bathhouses tapped into the various hot springs that run under the once volcanic area. Drainage had been developed in underground channels to help with water management. There was even a modest sporting stadium in the south end of the excavated area.

Circling high above it all, Flare sighed to himself. The sound was a mere wisp of air compared to the frigid wind that his reduced wings flapped against.

Below him, despite the fading light, it was clear to see that the public parks were still a marvelous sight.

Endless cartloads of soil had been wheeled down by ox from the surface, creating vast swaths of green. Drought-resistant plants and lush ferns made up a microcosm of different climates. Depending on the time of year and clouds of ash that circled, some areas would be well illuminated and other parts would be in shadow all day. The townsfolk took their leisure time of daylight fresh air seriously. The midday sun was reserved for those who wanted to spread out on the grass, but it was not uncommon to see shepherds grazing their flocks through the parks morning and evening. At certain times in the life cycle of plants, it had been worked out that occasionally animal waste would be left behind to further enrich the imported soil. On those days, the parks were used far less by the populace. The air in the quarry was fresh compared to the tunnels, but strong breezes were scarce at the lowest level to clear the stink away.

It was for this reason that most of the more fragrant trades, leather tanning, were banned from the central market areas.

Although those around the base of the mine had access to the parks, it was cheaper to live in the middle levels. There was always more rock to be hewn, more tunnels to be dug. Eateries and public houses were more popular around the bottom of the quarry, where the bubbling hot springs provided mineral-rich water to daily life, as well as for leisure activities for residents.

The springs were also a welcome blessing for the few travelers who still passed through. Like Caspian and Flare.

The dragon assumed the man was headed towards the hot springs, considering the state of him. His blonde hair was now a dirty, windblown mess. Flare had gotten a good look at skin covered in cave dust, ash, and dry splatters of blood as Caspian had disappeared into the forest. Along with the countless circular scars of pale white and pink over his chest and back, the reddish-purple scar that wound around Caspian's calf and knee added to the ghastliness. The man's hand was also a broken, swollen appendage of pus and seeping blood. The little finger, and perhaps the ring finger next to it, were clearly broken and pointing off at whatever angle the remaining strands of tortured flesh and ligaments allowed.

Despite his shocking appearance, Caspian appeared unconcerned as he approached the noisy pub established around one of the wide boulevards that wound down into Baile Fuar. By the sounds of the loud chatter, it was after dinner. The patrons of this pub were well into their cups. Riotous laughter bubbled over the top of the fiddlers, all competing with the noise.

Flare, who should have been looking for Caspian's priest, unable to help himself, landed on the clay tiled roof next door with quiet wings and a gentle scrape of claws. The business within had shut for the night and the rooftops were bathed in dusk light beneath gathering clouds. Reeling from his horrific crystal feast, Flare ignored the enticing aroma of cooked meats and spiced vegetables.

Instead, he held his breath.

The blonde man had emerged from the tree line to limp along the dark road. He had headed for the closest open shopfront. When he arrived at the decoratively lit front yard of the bar, he stopped, observing the cheers and revelry before him.

No one noticed the naked figure, not at first.

Flare crept further to the edge of the awning, his snout a scale's-breadth away from the light.

Blinking at the bright lanterns with their flickering colours, Caspian clutched the egg to his chest with his good hand, his shattered one still held up like the spout of a broken teapot before him.

It wasn't until Caspian wobbled to the outermost table of the front yard, a table occupied by six burly tradespeople of some sort, that anyone noticed him.

Caspian swiped a man's tankard from his raised greasy fist, drained it in one gulp, broken fingers flapping, and then slammed the tankard down.

"What the fuck?" the man whose tankard Caspian had drained swore as he jumped up.

His companions remained seated. But their laughter died down as they registered what happened. Tankards came to rest on the tablecloth, a chequered yellow cotton laden with dried fruits and cheeses.

Eyes closed and swaying a little, Caspian belched.

The standing man, clothed in rough homespun wool pants with a grey wool shirt and thick, worn boots, blinked rapidly, his mouth agape.

Unperturbed, Caspian reached past the man, muttered a humble "excuse me," and grabbed a fresh fig. He took a dainty bite and chewed with obvious relish. The noise around the table fell into a fascinated hush.

"Thank you," said Caspian, licking his putrid thumb and forefinger. "That was delightful."

Shifting the egg under his other arm, he glanced around.

The standing man eyed him up and down.

With visible scars, dried and fresh blood and layers of grit, it was understandable that there seemed little to say at first.

"M-mate..." stammered the man eventually, thick brows lowered over black eyes.

"The first time I had a fig," Caspian declared, his tone conversational and sincere, "was after I lost my virginity, you see. They'll always hold a special place in my heart."

Despite the situation, from the table a young man with a wispy beard raised his tankard in solidarity.

"M-mate?" repeated someone at the table, this time as a question. "What happened to you?"

Swaying more obviously, Caspian turned his shining gaze to the man who had spoken.

"Oh." Caspian thought a moment, his brows furrowed. At last he smiled, a garish expression amongst the filth covering his face. "Drop bear."

There was startled silence, then all at once, the table erupted.

All the drinkers cheered and a couple more men stood up, pressing more fruit and drinks towards Caspian. He took another drink, politely refused the rest and asked which was the best inn down below.

From the immediate and other tables, the crowd argued with each other about which establishment was best and would take care of a traveler after such an epic ordeal. None remarked on the egg. It was a continental truth that another man's misfortune, no matter how ridiculous, was the most interesting topic to chew over.

Drop bears were mythical beasts of the forest, after all.

One drinker, with bloodshot eyes and his copper hair twisted into loops and braids, grinned from his stool.

"Crikey," he breathed. "Just how big was it?"

Despite his current state, Caspian didn't miss a beat. He flapped his broken hand at his flaccid, but clearly well proportioned, cock.

"Almost as big as that."

Cheers followed Caspian as he staggered away to the closest ramp. The chequered table cloth was wrapped around his narrow hips, the egg clutched close, as he followed instructions on where to go once he reached the quarry's lowest level.

The men at the table clinked their shining tankards together in his wake.

"Poor bugger," the copper haired man sighed wistfully.

"Poor *handsome* bugger," his companion on the left sniggered.

Another cheer was made.

As Flare flew off from his hidden perch, he wondered why the drinkers hadn't realised there was a more dangerous creature amongst them than a fabled forest beast.

Shaking his crown of spikes, the little dragon soared out past the rim of the town's curved edge, towards the area that, last time at least, held the religious sects.

Following his snout and listening to evening prayers, Flare's hunt took several hours.

Hovering about the temple for a few beats, he examined his options, and decided for the least refined.

After selecting this, he wiggled his tiny form through a cracked open window and glided across a rudely furnished sleeping chamber. There was no fireplace, and the room was cold, but warmer than expected. Lending the small room a pleasant fragrance, a lone beeswax candle was lit. The flame wavered with the faint draft caused by a small pair of leathery wings. A man with long, loose hair, white with great age, was propped up in the single bed. A frown marred his wrinkled face as he examined a scroll, its red binding ribbon the only pop of colour in the peaceful chamber.

The dragon, desperate with worry that he was taking too long, landed with an ungainly thud on the man's chest.

The scroll went flying to the side, and the man's frown disappeared as his eyes widened to comical proportions.

"Good evening," said Flare, his cold snout pressed against the old man's chin.

Grey eyes blinked rapidly above a nose marred with brown age spots.

"Well," said the man. "Hello."

Keeping his hands away from Flare's frantically flapping wings, the priest very carefully felt around for the scroll, his eyes leaving Flare's for a moment. The dragon watched the man's gaze soften a moment as he realised the parchment was intact. His startled gaze returned to Flare.

Inside the stone room, it was silent apart from the man's steady breaths and Flare's wild heartbeat.

"Reuben?" Flare panted, one purple eye slitted as he scrutinized the man. He looked familiar.

Wiry eyebrows arched high above his clear eyes at the fact that the dragon on his chest knew his name.

The priest nodded, and the dragon visibly sagged.

"Come with me," said the dragon.

The old man blinked.

Flare pulled away and reared up as regally as he could, considering their situation. "Now."

The man continued to stare, but his thin lips twitched.

"Please," Flare added.

Not waiting for an answer, Flare backed down the man's chest to hop onto the bedside table near the candle. Curling his precious tail around his legs as he crouched in readiness for the man to get up, to do anything.

The man simply observed his visitor, head tilted slightly to the side. As if the appearance of a long-lost creature of magic, in compact-form that had slunk through his window, wasn't enough to get out of bed for.

Flare nodded with encouragement, as if that was enough to get the man moving.

It wasn't.

"May I ask why?" enquired the man, his tone more curious than afraid.

The dragon shifted uneasily. The lone candle flame with its sweet honey scent lent a golden shimmer to his purple scales as his tail twitched.

"Caspian Carter."

"Oh," Rueben said, then grinned. He sat up, swinging thin, spindly feet out from under the covers to the slate floor. "Let's go."

It seemed Caspian had found the finest inn. It was a ground floor level establishment built into the western wall of the quarry, about halfway along its length.

Flare had followed the uncomfortable twist of thread that joined his tail to Caspian's bizarre blend of magic, leading Rueben from rooftop to rooftop. The old man was frail, but his gait was sure. As they navigated the market streets, peaceful and packed up for the evening, to one of the ground floor inns, Rueben kept up, following Flare's progress with an air of silent expectation.

Earlier, the priest had pulled on pale blue robes, grabbed a leather satchel after questioning Flare on a few points, and carried the dragon under his heavy navy wool cloak without fuss as he left his temple. He took them promptly through hushed halls of bare rock, lit pleasantly with more fragrant beeswax candles. They passed a few sleepy priests wandering about with strings of beads entwined in their fingers as they paced along, but no one stopped them.

As they slipped out and beyond the two statues of blue rock crystal by the main front doors, the dragon said a brief prayer of thanks as the decorative black wrought-iron gates closed with a grating squeak behind them.

Spotting the inn where the thread of magic led him, Flare landed on Rueben's bony shoulder and squirmed back into the man's cloak, smelling of fresh incense, before Rueben could protest.

The sleepy innkeeper let them in through an ornate iron door, decorated with even more sumptuous designs than the priesthood's plain gate. Examining the priest's blue robes with disinterest, the blonde woman yawned and pointed to the stairs.

"You're here for that sweet man that just arrived?"

Flare, barely able to see from Rueben's hood, bit back his gasp of indignation.

The priest's cloak shifted as he nodded.

"Top floor, love," the woman declared and went back to filing her pointed nails.

Rueben left a silver coin on the innkeeper's desk and stepped lightly up the stone staircase without a word.

There was only one door on the top landing. There were no windows here, just a flickering lantern of black iron, windowed with crimson coloured glass, lending a red wash to the space.

Rueben didn't hesitate.

He went straight to the single wood door and knocked once. The answer came in the sound of a man coughing his guts up. With a sigh, the priest opened the door and stepped through.

The priest paused just inside the open door, and Flare stuck his head out from the man's fragrant robes.

Sharp teeth glinted as his jaw hung open.

Caspian lay face up amongst tasseled cushions in the room's four-poster bed, an intricately carved creation of wood in a deep cherry colour.

A boisterous fire burned in the simple rock hearth, the chimney no doubt connected to the inn's warren of air shafts to take the smoke away. The few lanterns scattered about were unlit, but it was obvious Caspian was unwell.

A faint sheen had broken out on his forehead and fresh globs of blood coated his chin. What could be seen of his bare arms and chest showed the sickly looking copper shimmer, a mottled pattern of splotches in various shades as it followed the dips and swells of his muscles and bones. One bare foot hung over the side of the mattress. Thankfully, the tablecloth was still being worn as a skirt, a gathering of yellow material tied at the waist, the lower edge bunched up around his thighs.

Flare inhaled sharply.

But where was..?

Ah.

From the fireplace came a dull crack as a log settled, the warm glow flaring for a moment. Amongst the pile of cushions, a glint of iridescent blue and green flashed next to Caspian's dirty hair.

A loud click behind had Flare flinching as Rueben used his heel to swing the door shut.

"You look better than the last time I saw you," Rueben sang out with a laugh.

Despite his odd blue eyes straining to focus, Caspian pushed up onto his elbows. Teeth flashed, stained a dark crimson, both from blood and the fireplace's warm glow.

"Ha," the grinning man coughed.

After spitting out a fresh mouthful of gore down his scarred chest, he fainted dead away.

"What do you suppose is wrong with him?" Rueben mused from a pretty three-legged stool by the richly appointed bed.

Flare gaped at the priest.

What was *wrong* with him?

With *Caspian*?

After the obvious fact that the man was an unhinged maniac, the list seemed too endless to even begin.

"No, little creature," the priest said, his grey eyes kind. "I know what you're thinking. What has happened recently? Why is he here?"

The priest and the dragon were watching the sleeping man toss fitfully back and forth on the bed. Rueben reached over, his arms bared to bony elbows, to move the egg out of harm's way.

"Please, don't touch it..." Flare whimpered from the top of one of the bed's thick posts.

That got the first serious reaction Flare had seen from the man.

Withdrawing a spotted hand from the chunk of crystal, Rueben glanced up. The gaze that landed on Flare was shrewd.

"Hm," was all the priest said.

Thankfully, he left the egg next to Caspian.

Hours ago, after calling out the door for some supplies, two junior servants, a boy and a girl, both with hair so red that Flare couldn't wish them out of the room fast enough, had made a few trips back and forth from downstairs. Steaming copper bowls of water arrived, accompanied by a pile of warm towels. A tray with a silver kettle, tea strainer, and two glass goblets arrived soon after.

Along with clean clothes of white linen and wool.

Since then, the dragon, his tail wrapped around his fore-claws, watched Rueben administer herbal compresses, bandages and even prayers over the sick figure amongst the cushions and velvet blankets. Caspian remained unconscious, although his skin, including the area covered by the odd copper sheen, wasn't as slick with sweat. His broken hand was finally cleaned and bandaged, something Flare guessed Caspian would be grateful that he'd been unconscious for.

The dragon swallowed his gag reflex at the memory of the pus and black blood that Rueben had coaxed from fevered flesh.

"So what happened?" Rueben murmured, adjusting his robes over his knees.

"Um," Flare began, then stopped. Scales rippled along his flanks as he took a breath. "A lot," he finished lamely.

"I see," the priest sighed. "That's usual for the Caspian I know."

"And how do you know him?" Flare said with hesitation marring his voice.

Smoothing mostly clean blonde hair from Caspian's cheek, Rueben huffed a quiet laugh under his breath.

"I saved this man's life, and in return, he helped me save my own."

The words were spoken lightly, the emotions behind them were nothing of the sort. Grey eyes watched calmly as the purple gaze atop the bedpost widened.

"Liar," a voice rasped from the pile of cushions.

Flare flinched.

Rueben smiled, his gaze dropping to Caspian's squinting face.

"I told a lie?" the priest enquired, leaning forward to inspect the mismatched blue eyes that were open a fraction. He used his thumb and forefingers to check the whites of Caspian's eyes.

"Ouch," Caspian pouted.

"Don't be a baby," Rueben cooed. "Hm. I think you'll live this time."

"I hope so," his patient complained, wincing as he turned his head. His expression softened as he caught sight of the egg. "I've got too much to do before I die."

"Don't we all?" Rueben said. He grabbed a clean cloth from the fresh pot of water by his sandaled feet. "What did I lie about?"

"I never saved you," Caspian mumbled.

"Sure," replied the priest as he wiped Caspian's forehead.

"Is Morgan back yet?" the pale man mumbled, his eyelids fluttering.

Rueben pulled the cloth away. He flicked a glance at Flare, then back to his patient.

"Ah. It seems the fever is yet to break, after all. He's still delirious."

"I asked her once about why she never wanted to be a dragon," Caspian went on, his gaze searching blindly. "I can't remember what she said."

He was staring at the chamber's ceiling, stone cut to look like individual rocks. Flare inhaled carefully, keeping his wings still so as not to attract the man's burning, if unfocused, gaze.

The mismatched blue stare found him, anyway.

"I think it was because she realised dragons were something that scared her," Caspian whispered. No longer covered in blood, Flare could see his lips were peeling. "Do you know why she found them alarming? Here's a clue. It started with the letter *m*."

Silently, Flare shook his head.

His fear was there, but frustration was rising, overcoming his shame. How could he not retaliate, fight back, and break free? Caspian was a wreck before him, yet all Flare could do was sit still and hope his tail stayed where it was. Rueben sat back on his stool.

"Miracle?" he guessed.

"Ha," Caspian muttered. "You're such a good little priest. Can you guess, my sparkling, oversized amethyst?"

It seemed obvious from the wicked gleam in Caspian's eyes, but Flare said nothing.

"M-monster," Caspian snickered, followed by a heaving cough.

Flare groaned, a sound of pain and frustration.

"Stop talking," Rueben soothed, "hush now —"

"You know which Elves wanted to become dragons?" Caspian announced, lifting his head off the pillows as if that would help find Flare's gaze. The dragon turned away, and was staring at the flames as Caspian went on. "Elves who were already cold, who were already good at nothing but being greedy, people who only knew how to take, take, take, and leave terror and grief in their wake..."

It would be unseemly to cover his ears, so all Flare could do, like always, was pretend that there was nothing he could do.

Mumbling over Rueben's ineffective *shush*, the bedridden man wheezed as he took another breath.

"All of them, all of us," Caspian gasped. "We were defective to begin with and defective we remain. We take what we want and we leave. You're good at that too, Flare! Like how you left your family, how you left Skye with Shadow Light. We had a plan. With you too! Do you know what he did while I was stuck —"

"Stop it," Flare mumbled. He sniffled, hoping Caspian didn't hear.

He pushed himself up amongst his pillow and cushions, ignoring Rueben's ineffective protest.

"Now you can't even get me to Aneirin without grumbling, without cowering in fear! All you need to do is help me make this shit storm right! Or is all you're left with simply failed spells and curses? Shall we have an endless night fall across the land again? You stupid fucking —"

"Stop it!"

Flare erupted with a flurry of scales and wings as he took off from the bedpost and circled the room, hot tears leaking down his scales.

"I told you!" the little dragon shouted as he flapped about on trembling wings. "He had too much power already, thanks to you! I was afraid of him! We were all afraid of him. I had to leave her! There was nothing that I could do!"

Landing against the door, Flare flopped down, his head under a wing, weeping shining tears.

It seemed his words had fallen on incoherent ears. Rueben was urging Caspian to calm down with gentle words, but the man was muttering to himself once more.

"Night indeed fell," Caspian murmured with a wistful sigh. "It's her destiny to fix this... And mine to help... to take everything from everyone who doesn't deserve what they have... to let a new sun rise over us all..."

Flare's eyes shut tighter, his spikes catching on his wings. He shivered despite the relative warmth of the little chamber.

Suddenly, he felt a wave of frigid air pass over him, like Caspian was getting ready to squeeze him tight. Flare bit back his cry, shivering as the feeling swept over him. Daring to fight back a little at the ominous sensation, Flare imagined himself in a cocoon of shadows, an invisible shell of protection.

The feeling disappeared immediately, and Flare's eyes sprung open.

That icy feeling hadn't been Caspian at all, was it?

This feeling had been different, expansive.

Almost like —

"I was a monster too, Rueben," Caspian whispered, interrupting the frozen dragon's tumbling thoughts. The weakened man's voice sounded far younger than his many years of age. "But I had to be in order to survive. For hundreds of years..."

"Caspian," the priest said gently, "You are not old enough to have been a monster for that long."

"But I..." The man inhaled sharply. "When was I born? I thought I had wandered for centuries without magic, waiting, trying to heal, to become magnificent again? I'm sure someone told me what year it was, and I felt I was far too old to be hurt by the disappointment of others..."

Shaking off the earlier sensation of frigid air, the dragon wondered at Caspian's words. The man was obviously delirious, but at other times, his sense of the years seemed off.

"I'm confused, Rueben," Caspian sighed. "Many things confuse me. Especially time."

"There, there," Rueben crooned under his breath.

Caspian didn't seem to hear. He snickered abruptly.

"Once I had such pretty wings, but I lost them after fighting things..." The man half laughed, half choked, at his rhyme. "And now all I can do is cry, while everyone deserves to die..."

At that, Flare spun around, eyes wide, shining and damp.

Rueben was pushing Caspian back into the mound of pillows, leaving him sitting upright to help his lungs stay clear. The priest picked up the egg with care and placed it back next to Caspian's head. The man's eyes were closing, his face covered in sweat. Even as he sank back into delirium, he kept mumbling.

"Everyone except you, my two sweet peas, my lovely Morgan and Petrichor..." Silver and blue eyes clouded over like a storm filled sky.

As his words faded and his breathing evened out, the room was left silent apart from the dry crackle of flames licking over glowing logs.

Flare's gaze slid from Caspian's serene face to the priest.

"I didn't mean for any of this," he said to Reuben, eyes pleading for the man to understand. "I wanted magic to help, not to curse anyone..."

"Liar!" choked the dragon.

Flare blanched as blue eyes, only one reflecting silver, flashed his way. They stared at each other until Caspian's lids grew heavy. Blue slits shone for a single heartbeat.

Then his lids closed once more.

Rueben sighed, pulling the blankets up to Caspian's chin.

"Why do you care about this man?" Flare hissed, unable to tamp down the ire in his voice.

"Isn't it obvious, my noble dragon?" Rueben's expression was hard to read. "He's my friend."

Unable to think of a single thing to say, Flare's jaw swung shut with a sharp snap.

Oh.

A friend.

From the shivering heap of purple by the door, a shimmering, scaled tail twitched.

29

Cas

Year 253, Cas at age 12
Baile Mara, City of the Sea

It's you who makes me sick...

Cas stumbled out of the library.

I said go...

An organ that was supposed to be his heart but felt like a lump of lead beat ferociously against his ribs. Bile rose in his throat. The desire to vomit was a violent urge. He swallowed it as he ran, blind to the day that had turned from bright to brittle.

He wanted to... what did he want?

A strangled noise escaped Cas' throat as his boots slipped along the clifftop's edge. Of their own accord, they halted a step from clear air, as he fought the urge to wipe the shame in his heart away, with a leap into salty air, into the sudden gust.

To plunge towards the waiting darkness below, black sands, oblivion.

The boy raked claw-like hands through his hair as he shook, a mere slip away from falling.

Eyes of two different blues gazing without focus at the point where the blazing sky melted into the shifting, sparkling ocean.

"I don't know what to do," gasped the distressed boy. His blonde hair lifted in the brisk ocean breeze and filled his ears with a rushing ache. Gooseflesh rose along his neck despite the blazing sun directly overhead. "I don't know what to do!"

Morgan's guarded green gaze, brimming with a burden he didn't understand, filled his mind. His shoulders rose and fell without rhythm as he fought to stay upright, to stay alive. It cost all of his concentration to steady mad gulps of air and the restriction in his lungs. Eyes closed, he fought it, the down pull to nothingness.

Worn out green eyes filled his heart.

Was this what it was like?

Is this what Morgan felt?

Is this why she rarely smiled, rarely laughed?

Their fleeting moment of solidarity only a brief moment ago, her laugh —

Gods!

Her *laugh*.

Cas wanted to roar like he imagined Rook might in his dragon form when tearing apart a pack of wild bears.

He wanted to scream for him and Morgan both, locked into their current life for reasons the boy didn't understand, the helplessness to improve their lot felt as a physical restriction binding him cruelly with barbed rope.

Alone on the soaring clifftop, Cas breathed, wrangling his racing mind and body back to sensibility. It was a while before the sickening sensations crashing from toe to temple eased, although it didn't quite fade completely.

Grow up, Cas!

What to do?

Well.

Clenching his eyes wouldn't help, nor yelling at the wind.

Slowing his breathing, Cas opened one eye at a time.

First his right, deep sapphire. Then the left, washed-out aquamarine.

The boy blinked.

The sun burned his sensitive pupils, sealed tight for so long. Salt water pooled and ran down his flushed cheeks at the burn.

He kept them open.

"Morgan," Cas sighed to the ocean air that lifted his hair. "Morgan, I forgive you."

Sniffling, with one last glance at the looming ebony shore of coarse sand and fractured black boulders below, he stepped back from the pitiful end a long drop would bring.

No.

That was not for him.

The boy turned away from the horizon and began heading for the city.

As he walked, Cas kicked at the loose rocks along the path leading to the steps cut into the raw stone. He detested the footbridge leading to the city, so the cliff side stairs were his preferred choice.

Yet he stopped at the top tread, cut long ago into the bare rock. His stomach still roiled with emotion, unsettling and unbalancing. His hands tingled with pins and needles. At the thought of slipping by accident, not on purpose, bile rose in his throat and left him grimacing.

Spinning on his heel, Cas ducked around the length of the library, heading for the trees.

If he was going to vomit or fall over like some flightless baby chick, he'd rather do it where none could see, rather than on the cliffs for all to witness. Especially anyone watching him from nearby.

Reaching the tree line, Cas glanced back at the squat, low building of the library.

From this angle, all he could see was one narrow end and the back wall. No shadowed figures peered out from any of the windows of thick glass that faced his position. The building was as he left it, no smoke emanating from cracked windows or a caved in roof.

The fire was truly out.

Odd blue eyes flashed silver as they narrowed thoughtfully. Smiling a little, the boy turned his back to the building and ducked amongst the forest.

It was immediately cooler and quieter beneath the sturdy, salt tolerant pines. The sun barely made it through the wind twisted shapes of the outermost fringe. There was hardly what you could call a path. Wiping his cheeks with his palms, Cas headed for a brighter patch ahead, warm rays of sun piercing from the canopy above and painting the undergrowth with shifting shapes of gold. As he ventured further into the scrub, Sea Gums with ghostly pale, distorted trunks appeared, dotted about like phantoms of the wind-tortured forest.

With his mind on other things than where he was walking, his boot caught on an exposed root.

The boy cried out.

Cas tumbled to the ground with a startled curse and landed with a sandy thud. He lay on his stomach, panting, breathing in the scent of trampled pine needles.

It was disgusting against the dirt and detritus of the forest floor, but his revulsion snapped him from the mania within. Cas closed his eyes, imaging that the page he'd burned had indeed spread crackling flames across the desk, stools and beams following hotly behind. Maybe they would have spread to the line of trees as well.

Especially that blasted root that had tripped him over.

"Pity," murmured the boy.

Tiny legs crawled across his hand, spread out by his cheek.

One eyelid lifted.

A bug was shuffling across a scuffed knuckle.

He blew on it, and the multi legged grey creature vanished with the heated puff of his breath. After making sure it was not about to reappear with an army of its creepy little mates, he rolled onto his back, wincing faintly at the throb in his ankle. He stared at the soaring treetops above with their complex shifting patterns. Did their size come close to the massive trees of the west and north? He'd love to see them one day.

Especially if the experience was a shared one.

"*Sick*," mumbled Cas as he observed the separate shapes of the green canopy move as one creature.

After a while, he pushed himself to sit up in the dirt. It was awful to be amongst the grit, but he made himself stay where he was. The forest was silent here; the wind broken by the outer trees, the inner world here a sanctuary from the crisp chill and abrasive salt.

Dropping his gaze, Cas frowned at his grazed palms. He rubbed them together, wincing at the sting as sensitive flesh met sensitive flesh. There was nothing to wipe them on without staining his pants, which were likely ruined anyway. Gritting his teeth, Cas climbed to his feet. He trod heavily towards a lighter patch of green amongst the changing shadows. A few faint spots of red and yellow could be seen beyond velvet dappled leaves, coiled ferns and waist-high shrubs. Edging closer with more caution than before, he squinted as he pushed low-hanging branches away from his face and hair.

As he crept closer to the blurred shapes, changing crimson and yellow ahead, the light transformed. Before, at the edge of the forest high above the sea, the exposed trees had their colour sapped by the near constant winds of exposure at the top of the cliffs. Here, further away from the edge of the forest, the colours gradually grew richer, deeper. Then all at once, the light brightened to a painful intensity after the shadows beneath the gum and pines.

He stopped abruptly, not daring to step forward just yet, lest he break the spell of the unexpected glory at the sight ahead.

For Cas had come to the edge of an open meadow.

A meadow absolutely filled with poppies.

Her poppies.

Heavy heads of red and yellow bobbed gently on slender stalks of fuzzy green. Their crowded meadow was roughly square, absent of the towering, spicily scented pines. The blooms crowded the open area, clearly at home amidst the mineral rich soil. As Cas blinked stupidly at the meadow, thousands of thumb sized buds danced in worship to the life giving sun above.

The place was beautiful, peaceful.

Melancholy.

With barely a gust of wind, or roar of crashing waves this far inland from the ocean's might, it was simply the most tranquil place he'd ever been.

"*Sick*," Cas whispered around the hot lump in his throat. "*You make me sick.*"

Poppies had many uses, most of which he was aware of. He had spent enough time amongst the animals and experiments of Mother's study to know its potential uses. At the front of his thoughts, however, the sticky opium pipe came to mind. Along with the cloyingly sweet smell that lingered in long hair of burnished red, framing purple, shadowed circles around weary green eyes.

Swallowing, Cas rubbed his fingertips over his stinging palms. The absence of magic that filled others in his family had never felt more acutely like an organ missing from his body than it did now.

The poppy meadow was heavenly.

It was also a lock to a private hell.

Surprised with himself, Cas wished his brother were here. He wished that the sweet field of shifting flowers might be spontaneously razed to the ground. It would make a fantastic amount of smoke, a stunning funerary offering to the tomb-like building beyond the trees towards the edge of the cliff.

Visions of flames filled his eyes, as if each red or yellow bud burst into a tiny flame, a thousand tiny flames that morphed and joined to form a roaring blaze.

With his heart beginning to beat unevenly in a rhythm that had him close to retching, Cas took one step backwards, away from temptation.

He took another, stumbling from the vivid, hellish vision within.

Choking on the smoke and ash within his imagination, Cas scrambled back through the towering pines. He raced away from ash and bitterness, towards air tainted with salt and cold. Dashing past the library, the boy ran towards the cliff edge, towards the horizon, turning at the last moment to miss the uneven edge of jagged, ebony shelves to find the steps to lead him down to ferocious waves of chilly salt water. His pale hair lifted from his forehead in the wind, the sweat drying quickly on feverish skin. All about him, the roaring wind was joined by the pounding waves of the incoming tide as it crashed onto land.

"You make me sick," Cas repeated as he descended, the whirling wind numbing his ears. "You make me sick."

All at once, his boots touched sand.

Coming to an abrupt halt, Cas squinted groggily.

Pushing his boots into the ebony grains of the near empty beach, Cas spared a glance at the imposing cliff wall behind. Normally the descent took longer, didn't it? He couldn't remember traversing down gritty, weathered steps of rock. Perhaps it was because this time, the librarian's strained expression troubled his heart, a heart racing beneath the mark she'd hopefully left on his skin. It seemed unlikely that she was as affected by him as much as he was by the mystery she posed.

Only a short stroll away, the sparkling sea glittered as it beat upon the shore, crystal clear water crashing onto shadowed grains. Ahead of him, two men and three small children were in the process of laying a linen blanket close to the water's edge. The waves approached, then withdrew in a rhythm that heaved like the watery lungs of some mythical god, like the faceless statues of quartz points that had been placed as watching sentinels around his home city.

"Gods," Cas muttered, bitterness lacing his voice, "who left us long ago. Science and the lust for alchemy fill the heart of this city now."

Palm stinging, one hand clenched by his hip. The other pressed firmly to the bruise forming on his chest, a bruise he hoped was in the shape of a delicate ink stained hand. Cas swallowed against the hot lump in his throat. Despite her small stature, Morgan had shoved him with a strength that had startled, and pleased, him.

He stayed where he was while the sun beat down from overhead, golden bright and glaring from the blue sky. It was nothing compared to the brightness of the ache within. Not for the words hissed into his face, but for the expression in those soft green eyes. There was illness in her wary stare, a sort of unease, yes. But away from the gloomy library, with its shadowed aisles and yellowing books and scrolls, here in the fresh air, it seemed impossible that it could be him making her sick.

Surely it was the place she spent too long in?

Surely it was how often she shut herself off from the rest of the world?

Illness that bound her to the place she obviously detested, an illness that masked a deeper pain behind her jaded gaze. Something that he was sure he'd seen. Before he'd turned and fled like the coward he was.

Fear.

"Morgan," Cas said, eyes watering in the glare of the bright blue sky. He spared a glance over his shoulder, up toward the point where the switchback stairs disappeared over the top of the towering cliffs. "Why are you afraid?"

Blue eyes shimmering with sun turned silver across their mismatched irises shone brilliant, wild, serious.

Mulling over all sorts of wild possibilities, the boy started towards the south end of the city.

His steps no longer faltered.

As he passed the picnicking group, he ignored them. Voices brimming with joy and ease made their way to him. A little girl of four or five years tumbled over in the sand. Before she could cry out, one of her parents was there, swinging the girl up and around. Tears were avoided. Giggling resumed. Cas averted his gaze, focusing instead on the city of Baile Mara.

Not looking back, he marched on, navigating the shifting dunes of gritty sand with intense focus.

"Are you sick with fear?" Cas muttered.

The terraces of black stone, gold and white tiled roofs spilled down to the circular bay, partially obscured by a yellowing haze of smog. He sniffed, glad he wasn't able to scent the sour gases that seeped from fissures in the bedrock over the entire area.

"Or has fear made you sick?"

Who could he ask?

At present, Wane had no interest in things other than girls and lessons. That was no good. With their heads tilted, Mother and Father would simply examine Cas if he presented such a hypothetical to them. They would likely wonder at the odd thoughts and words their eldest offspring came out with. Cas strode on. Overhead, a flock of grey and white gulls swooped past, no doubt heading for the young family. The thought of their impending doom, regarding any picnic snacks at least, eased the spasm that twisted his heart.

With the glittering ocean on his right, and the sheer cliffs on his left, Cas could almost pretend he was caught between two massive forces or beings of nature. He loved his home, the city by the sea, or Baile Mara in the old language. The deep, curved steps of each level arched around the shape of the bay, a great bowl of levels that started at the docks on the water, stepping up all the way to the top of the cliff. A sheer chasm separated the top levels of the city from the cliffs where the library had been built. The deeply narrow black fissure shifted occasionally, coinciding with the large plumes of stinking yellow gases that wafted skywards from the bay's island with its wide, conical mountain. There was a bridge spanning the gap, yet Cas preferred the cliff steps. There were stories whispered amongst the students who sometimes shared classes with Wane and Cas down at the temple. Stories of children being blown off the stone arch that spanned the gap when the ocean roared and the salt gales gusted up with cutting force.

Why a person would be out during a gale and crossing the bridge, Cas didn't know. Anyone stupid enough for that deserved to be lost in the chasm below. That seemed fitting, really. Although when he'd mused out loud to a tutor banging on about the ancient architects and the dragons that helped them, the looks he'd received showed that perhaps that wasn't the best of thoughts to share.

He wisely kept further thoughts of that line to himself.

Trudging on, Cas shook his head, letting the approach and recession of the crashing waves wash close by amongst the growing hum from the city ahead.

Some things puzzled the boy, while others seemed crystal clear. But with his pale forearms covered in fine scars while his younger brother had none, Cas had always stuck to the steps up from the beach, huffing up the steep stairs. It seemed clever to refuse to tempt fate. No matter how clever the people of this city claimed Mother and Father to be, that was something their magic couldn't fix. Brushing his blonde hair from out of his eyes as the salty breeze chased him, Cas chewed on his bottom lip as he walked back towards the docks.

What could magic fix, though? What was it good for? Besides earning the city its name for beautiful crafts, longer lived, prettier people, and powerful dragons, of course, what was the point? Did Cas even want that much power, power to fly? To live longer?

Pale green eyes, distant and fatigued, made no case for it at all.

The shock of his encounter with the librarian was fading, the shame of having upset her replaced by intense curiosity. People who had magic could heal quickly and lived longer than those who, for whatever reason, had none. Morgan had magic. Yet she was sick.

Had Mother and Father done things to her as well?

Things that she couldn't heal from?

As Cas reached the first wooden dock of the lowest part of the city, his steps halted once more. The library was indeed like a tomb, inhabited by a ghost with flaming hair, eyes like lifeless peridots that glared at him from the gloomy circles that framed them. She was not well at all. But what kind of connection was it that bound her to the joyless life she seemed to accept with resignation?

Growing up as a young boy in an estate of servants and gardens and endless halls, Cas and Wane had the run of the place when not at lessons with tedious priests. Most staff and visitors adored the boys. Well, Wane at least. Yet the mysterious librarian used to avoid them whenever their paths crossed. He remembered the occasional tight-lipped smile when he was young. She'd even helped heal him when he'd ended up with a caustic potion down his leg.

A ripple of phantom pain ran down his calf.

"Morgan," Cas said, silver-blue eyes narrowing, chin lifting. "I think..." Nostrils flared. "I think it is *my* turn to help *you*."

There was no way of knowing how, but he would.

With his heart lighter, Cas hopped up onto the wide yet shallow stone steps that joined the end of the beach on the southern edge of Baile Mara.

To his left, a wide promenade rose from the docks to wind along the edge of the next higher terrace, soaring above and past the lower rows of warehouses. It led into various crafts and market districts. Straight ahead, warehouses had been built and rebuilt over the years, at first purely from wood, but now many had stone foundations built down onto the black bedrock. Their frontages varied from office shopfronts to thickly barred buildings, all with ornate doors and locks and hinges of iron and brass. Some, like the customs house where ship captains paid their port fees, were even gilded. It was as if the merchants wanted to share that they were particularly good at what they did. Or at least wanted their buyers to think so.

Despite the better view of the bay from the promenade, Cas chose the longer route to his right, along the waterfront. He slipped into the chaos and bustle of the midday docks. An audible wave of shouting, cursing, and occasional roars of laughter welcomed him in, drowning out most of his inner thoughts. Not all, but most. A few crafty food vendors had set up their wheeled stalls nearby, ready for sailors eager to taste fresh, or at least different, food after weeks or possibly months at sea. The aroma of fried pastries, sweet and honeyed, along with savoury spices, wafted above the briny air.

All berths of the busy docks, bar two, were occupied with a variety of vessels, coming and going as the city traded with other towns up and down the coast. Pungent aromas of newly arrived spices filled his nose as the cursing and shouting of sailors and traders assaulted his ears. Cas shouldered through the crowds, paying little mind to who he was squeezing past. He could see a group of boys his own age near a warehouse further along, known for paying a coin to those willing to run errands into the city above. One of the boys spotted Cas. The boy stopped mid conversation with a tall, black-haired man, and elbowed the young boy beside him. Cas waved his middle finger at them before ducking into the crowd. A curse followed his firm shove as he parted the sea of people. He laughed at the catcalls tailing his exit and pushed on.

The closest open dock was busy, in a way that expectant sailors and merchants could be busy. Some uncoiled ropes, some swore, some argued over the goods approaching on the ship, large, low and creaking as it slowly drifted in from the open bay. He brushed past the base of one of the welcoming 'Gods', a massive shard of deep indigo amethyst, there to welcome sailors home from their long stints at sea.

Cas halted, glancing over his shoulder.

Were the catcalls louder?

Shrugging, he turned back to the approaching ship, the aroma of hot oil and dough in his nose. Side-stepping a stack of wine amphora in crates packed with yellow straw, Cas whistled a single low note of appreciation for the ship coming to port.

He'd never seen this giant sailing vessel before. The galleon seemed like a mystical wooden beast out of the stories he read by candlelight after Wane had gone to sleep. The ship was so large that even in the calmer waters of the port; it groaned as it ambled through the bay, approaching the wooden pier with expert precision. On hand in the water were little stocky tug boats, manned by men with balls of lead, their tiny boats bobbing about the large galleons to steer them in safely with wooden poles. The occasional ripple of mist above the gentle waves showed that some of its sailors were using water magic to assist.

Ignoring the jeers of the kids above the crowd, Cas glared.

With no skill of any to speak of, what could he do?

Something soft bounced off Cas' back with a startled cry.

"Hey," Cas began angrily, pivoting around. He was about to swear like the surrounding sailors, but paused.

Sprawled on the ground was an auburn-haired boy of eight or nine years. His grey eyes were wide as they stared back up at Cas. Between the lad's snotty nose to his tear-stained cheeks, it was clear the boy was having the same kind of day as Cas. Possibly worse.

"Oh," said Cas. He reached out awkwardly, wincing at his stinging palms, to help the boy stand. "Um. There you go."

The noisy crowd jostled them about. Cas grabbed the boy's arm, pulling him away from a heavy cart laden with two large barrels. The boy steadied himself and wiped at his nose with a sleeve. Cas recoiled. He fished around in his pocket, offering the boy his spotless handkerchief.

"Th-thank you," the boy said, his voice surprisingly steady despite his bedraggled appearance.

"What happened?" Cas queried, eyeing the lad's pale blue linen tunic. He looked like a priest. But so young?

"Nothing." The lad straightened, holding up the soiled cloth.

"Oh, no." Cas grimaced. "You'd best keep that."

The boy nodded and went to move away. There was a small group of other young children dressed in muted tones of blue at the next berth over.

"Wait," Cas said. The auburn-haired boy looked over his shoulder, eyes wide.

"What?"

"Are you training to be a priest already?"

The boy shook his head at first. Then bit his lip. He nodded.

Digesting that, Cas dodged a seagull that swooped low, racing past to take off with a woman's fried bread. She squawked indignantly. Cas clapped at the sight. The young woman, minus bread, gave the pair of them a filthy look before heading back to the food stalls, her nose in the air.

Cas and the younger boy's gaze met. As one, they burst into fits of laughter.

"Hm," Cas mused once he stopped laughing. "Priest, huh? Good luck with that."

The boy attempted to smile. It looked like he was going to burst back into tears.

"What's wrong?" Cas asked, wary. His opinion of the temple priests that came to educate him was pretty low. There was no reason for it to get lower. He had a feeling it was about to.

"I don't want to go."

"Then don't."

"My parents are dead," the boy said so quietly that Cas almost missed it amongst the bustle.

"Oh. Oh!" Cas blinked. Morgan came to mind. He knew her parents had abandoned her at a young age. "You're an orphan."

Miserably, the boy nodded. More interested now, Cas rubbed a thumb along his bottom lip. He quickly pulled his hand away, frowning at the taste of pine and salt on his hands.

"How?" he asked.

The boy eyed him curiously. "Mine."

"Huh?"

"Mine collapse. Diamonds."

"Oh." Where...? Cas pictured the map of the coast in his mind. "Verglass?"

The boy nodded again, tears leaking down his cheeks. Cas shuffled on his feet and patted the boy's arm once, twice. It felt awkward but seemed the right thing to do.

"I'm sorry," he said. "Are you arriving or going?"

"Arriving," the boy said after clearing his throat. "There is a school here for... kids like me," he finished lamely.

Cas shivered, thinking of the priests and their toneless voices and boring lessons.

"I'm sorry," Cas repeated. "That's the last place I'd want to go if I had a choice." The boy's eyes widened. Cas added hurriedly, "But don't worry! I'm sure it'll be fine. Ha ha."

With a watery smile for Cas, the boy shrugged. He held up the cloth.

"Thank you for this," sighed the younger lad. "I should go back to the others. I just wanted to see this ship."

"It's a beauty, isn't it?" Cas said wistfully. He wandered nearer towards the dock's edge, the lad at his heels.

The giant vessel was idling onwards to the dock where the wooden planks met stone walls, creaking and moving at such a slow pace it was hard to tell that it was any closer. The increasing mania around them meant it was indeed getting nearer, men calling out to each other to hold the ropes steady. Not hearing the group of older kids approaching from behind, Cas beamed at the melancholy boy.

"I'm Caspian Carter. I live up there. Next to the castle." He pointed out the rim of the city's uppermost terrace. The boy's eyes widened. "Carter Estate. Find me if you need anything."

A new expression crossed the younger lad's features, not quite a smile, but lighter than his tears. The boy nodded, opening his mouth to say something. Cas missed it.

Without warning, a force like a hot whip snaked around his ankles.

It jerked once.

Hard.

With no time to prepare himself for the inevitable, Cas tumbled headfirst into the frigid saltwater. His mouth opened in a wordless cry as he fell, so he immediately swallowed water. There was just enough time to panic about both that and the steady approach of a giant sailing ship towards the wooden pier and its stone supports. Cas kicked sideways, spluttering, realising too late the high tide meant there was practically no clearance under the wooden pier.

It didn't matter, anyway. Whatever little shit had toppled him was also intent on forcing him back into the choking embrace of the sea. Shouting had erupted above Cas, quickly extinguished as water closed above his head, the force of villainous intent from above pressing him down with hands that didn't exist, in a way he wished he understood firsthand.

The intent was a potent balm for greedy hearts.

For it was *magic* that held him down.

The struggling boy attempted to kick his way up, legs and booted feet scissoring wildly. It didn't help at all.

He was pushed deeper into the inhospitable water, so deep he wondered at it. More water entered his lungs as he cried out at the pain from the force that weighed on him, at the shocking cold. There was no one to hear him, but his own ocean swamped ears, blocked by salt water, and the rushing, frantic bubbles along with the intense pressure from above.

As black spots appeared before his eyes like flecks of soot and ash, Cas wanted to scream at the injustice. He'd only just figured out what he should be doing, not how, but who for at least. He thrashed violently, fighting the force that bound him, wailing, inhaling more water for the effort.

Morgan, Cas attempted to cry.

The name was uttered without air or words or clear thought, his vision fading, limbs heavy, twitching as his muscles spasmed wildly. There was no cohesion to the movement of his limbs. They refused any order his brain sent their way.

As the light from above faded into the depths, it faded from his vision, too. The golden sun turned green, then blue, then was lost to gloomy purple and filthy grey, the murky waters at the bottom of the berth. The broad hum of the tide against the stones and wood, deafening at first, went quiet.

All went perfectly still.

All went completely silent.

Peaceful when compared to the chaos above. Apart from one thought that wouldn't fade like the rest of his body faded from sensation. This single thought beat hard and fast, stubborn and full of resistance.

Morgan.

How do I save you when I can't save myself?

Time slowed, slower than the casual approaching of the ship making its inevitable way towards the sinking boy. Cas couldn't move. His hands and feet had gone completely numb. His face too. There was no way to tell if his boots had touched the muddy bottom.

The last thing he could move were his eyes, shifting against the force from above, his flashing silver-blue gaze, not quite seeing but sensing the last bubbles rise past his sinking form.

They halted, their ascent interrupted.

One by one, they popped.

Lungs on fire with water and agony, Cas blinked at the space where the bubbles disappeared. The tips of his pale hair wafted about his face as if it were flaps of silk in a languid breeze. Astonished, he watched more bubbles burst, the pockets of air dispersing into the murk. He didn't know what it meant, but had no time to examine such a thing, for the crushing pressure from above remained. The last of the piercing light amongst the purple bruised water had faded to mere phantoms. At last, the stone and wooden pier bumped his back, the solid wall of tar-smeared planking bearing down.

All at once, an explosion of bubbles around a small shape appeared from above.

The drowning pressure eased, not fully, but backed off.

The stillness around him broke, his ears popped with a painful burst, water trying to find its way into his head, to drown his thoughts, his brain.

The new collection of bubbles grew larger, closer, and a frantic shape appeared before his fading vision. Small hands and arms searched for his, grabbing, jerking Cas towards the light that promised life and air above.

A hand blindly grabbed his shirt, twisted, and pulled.

It was seconds, hours; it was agony.

His boots brushed something soft. Cas gave a struggling kick, hoping he wouldn't get sucked into the mud. He didn't. With a prayer to whoever the fuck was listening, the boy kicked harder, furious, fighting now to rise.

It was he who dragged his frail saviour into glorious air, bursting up into violent noise, light, colour, sounds and yells.

His lungs heaving, Cas vomited salt water back to whence it had come. Gasping, choking on brine and bile both, Cas faced the boy against him, sea-slicked head barely above the waves. Grey eyes were wide, horrified, not triumphant at his successful rescue at all.

"Are you alright?" Cas rasped. Fuck, his limbs were refusing to move again.

"C-can't..." the boy gasped, "C-can't swim..."

Cas might have laughed if he wasn't drowning.

Together as one, they sank down, kicking fruitlessly.

It seemed fitting. Out of all the magic-abled citizens above who had seen the useless son of the city's eminent alchemists near drowning, the only one who was helping was an orphaned child who couldn't swim. Vomiting sea water, knowing he was about to be crushed by an approaching ship, or drowned, maybe both, Cas felt vindicated more than ever that magic was *wrong*.

As his heart spluttered, his lungs expelling air in fresh bubbles of barely swallowed air, he finally let his laugh free.

Not just at the vindication, but at the sensation of what death felt like. It didn't hurt. Had it happened? Water still blocked his ears, his nose too. Senses used to translate the nature of the world around him to his brain didn't work yet. But death felt a lot like flying, rising from water into nothingness.

Hang on.

Death felt like rising into... the sea air once more?

He held tight to the boy and let himself enjoy the unexpected floating feeling death had delivered.

"Fuck," Cas hissed, shocked into opening his eyes at the sudden, fierce impact of a hard surface against his spine.

Death *did* hurt.

Did it?

He blinked. The boy was crying against him.

As his own tears washed away water that was just as salty, Cas realized with a brain slowly kicking back into working order what had happened.

The two boys had somehow risen from the water to be unceremoniously dropped onto the wide wooden planks of the docks. As he rolled onto his side, groggy, he felt the pier shudder as the great ship made port. Along with the groan and creaking of the massive vessel as it came to rest, cries and furious yells assaulted his hearing as the water drained from his swollen ears. The boy rolled away from him and pushed up to his hands and knees, coughing, sniveling. The boy was quickly crowded by priests with stern faces.

Faces that glared at Cas.

His senses returning, Cas vomited more water. He had wits enough about him now to aim the filth as close as he could to the open-toed sandals of the priests.

Panting, he lay there, blinking, wondering, mind both full and blank.

"Fuck," Cas hissed, his lungs spasming.

A familiar shadow blocked the sun.

"Better get home, lad," Rook said, crouching down. His voice held no sympathy. "Get your lungs checked by Mother and Father."

"P-piss off," Cas mumbled, his lips starting to chatter.

The crowd edged closer, as if the soggy heap of two boys was made safe by Rook's approach. Next to him, the boy was helped to his feet. Cas helped himself to his knees. Struck by a sudden impulse, Cas reached out and grabbed the boy with a wet hand.

"Thank y-you," he mumbled, teeth chattering. "B-but you're an idiot."

The boy was shivering, too. "It was the r-right thing to do..."

He squeezed Cas' hand, offering a weak smile, eyes red, nose just as snotty as before. Rook took off his scarf and handed it to the boy. The man turned to Cas.

"You've got some enemies to watch out for, lad."

"Do I?" Cas muttered, wondering if it would be rude to ask the boy for his handkerchief back to blow his nose.

It likely didn't matter. Despite the crowd gathered around him, no one would meet his eyes. Long hair draped over Rook's shoulder caught the sun, gold and blue flecks flashing amongst the black locks. Beneath the locks, a red poppy peered from a small chest pocket. Cas squinted at it, in the right enough state of mind to feel a rush of white heat race up his spine. White teeth flashed as Rook smiled.

"Enemies mean you're important. Good thing I was here, hmm?"

"It was you." Heart still racing, lungs bruised, Cas stared. "You lifted us."

A casual smirk was his only answer.

"Th-thank you," Cas managed, water draining from his hair to his blue lips. "I owe y-you."

"You do."

"I..." Cas narrowed his eyes on the poppy. "I am in your debt."

"You are." With that, Rook rose. "Like I said, get home. You need to clear your lungs." Rook pointed to a pair of women perched on a two-wheeled cart. Their grey donkey was snuffling the cloak of the man in front. "You, take this boy home. You know where to go." He turned to Cas. "And you know where to find me when you need help. Again."

Not waiting for an answer, Rook dismissed the uneasy stares of the two women and melted into the crowd. The boy watched him go, the crowd parting for the man that ran the shadowed underlayers of Baile Mara. As the crowd merged and reformed in Rook's wake, a strange sort of understanding struck Cas deep in his saturated mind. It was a converging of things that both added up, but shouldn't. About light and dark, good and bad. What people did to achieve what they thought was best. He swallowed, the uncomfortable thoughts needing to be dragged from the dark corners of his subconscious another day. Today, right now, he needed to simply breathe.

In the background, sailors swore and life went on. Close by, whispers drifted around the pair of wet boys like the sour gases that rose from the coyote's stones after strong quakes.

Hissing at the offended priests, Cas pulled the smaller boy close. He hugged him tight, hating the rub of their wet fabric, yet welcoming the small, shaking arms that hugged him back.

"Your n-name," Cas stammered, freezing now. He ignored the gestures of the two impatient women, urging Cas to climb up onto their cart. One of them climbed up, resigned to wait. The other made her way over, eyes cautious.

"Ru —" the boy coughed, trying again. "R-Rueben."

Cas bowed his head, treasuring the name, wrapping it carefully with tenderness in his mind, placing it into the darkest chambers of his heart, like his favourite things stashed on Morgan's shelf of oddities, found discarded on the beach. It seemed fitting to think of himself like that.

Discarded, washed ashore.

Tripped up by bullies, kids who had no place to hold magic. Cas spared a moment's relief that his younger twin was such a sap and not a bastard.

But this boy had found Cas worthy, worthy enough to risk his life for. Cas, whom the boy could never have hoped to save, surely? Someone he had met only moments before. Cas glanced up at the black cliffs, curving around to where the top of the library waited, haunted by another soul discarded by society and found worthy by just one other.

"Rueben," Cas mumbled, dropping his gaze to the lad at his side. "L-like I said, I'm Caspian. But call me Cas."

The boy nodded, lips blue, eyes solemn.

Cas thought of them rising together, saved by magic.

Nearly drowned by the same force.

The push and the pull of magic was a dangerous battle of opposite ends of the same force. Ideas rattling in his brain, Cas released his hold on the boy. As they parted, Cas stared at his dirt-scraped, water-sodden hands. He marvelled at the uselessness of his current state. He wondered at magic in the hands of good, at magic in the hands of... not so good.

Magic, caught between those of opposing hearts.

Weak.

Like those able to swim or save him, like the shifting crowd who had stood by and watched as they either drowned or were crushed.

Strong.

Like the orphan who had dared to do something, anything, without any hope at all.

Just to try.

To do the right thing, against all odds.

Shaking uncontrollably, Cas smiled. Reuben bit his lip as Cas spat out more water, catching an approaching priest in the groin. The priest didn't swear, of course, but his gaze was murderous. Cas' smile widened to a grin, his hair plastered to his head, nose snotty, eyes stinging.

Admittedly, it *was* hard to breathe. Rook was right, he needed to get home. Cas tilted his head to the side. The feeling of water draining out of one ear and popping nearly had him vomiting again. Cas grit his chattering teeth as the woman from the cart reached him. Her brown eyes were still cautious but determined, ready to follow one of Baile Mara's oldest dragon's commands.

"Rueben," Cas said, making sure he got out each word without choking. "I apologise for your introduction to this city. Unfortunately for you and your new teachers, there are no gods to save us. Just us, and destiny. It isn't a good place at present. Baile Mara is sick."

With a sharp jerk, the priest pulled Rueben away.

"What?" gasped the boy over his shoulder. "What do you mean?"

Cas, ready to collapse, let him go.

"This place is sick," he declared.

Glaring, the priest gathered Rueben up in his arms and walked him bodily away. The boy poked his head above the priest's bony shoulder, his piping voice loud enough to make himself heard.

"How do you know? And what will you do?" Rueben called.

The brown-eyed woman caught Cas as he slumped. He let himself be dragged to the waiting cart and donkey by brawny arms. Above, on its platform of black bedrock, the watchful, faceless statue of an amethyst idol shimmered with mystery.

But with wisdom, with life?

No.

The boy managed a saturated wink as Rueben was carried into the milling crowd of nameless, careless faces.

"Don't worry, Reuben. I'm going to cure it."

30

Cas

Year 367
Baile Fuar, City of Stone

Considering all that he'd done, it seemed too much to ask any of the silent gods for a prayer to be answered.

Well, Cas thought to himself, his mind working about as fast as a bee stuck in a web of syrupy silk. *Those figures of myths weren't really gods at all though, were they?*

So it was pointless to pray for anything at all.

It was good to ask for what you wanted, though.

Before he opened his eyes, Cas shifted under the cool hand pressed to his forehead.

"Morgan," he murmured. "Move your hand lower."

The quiet laugh by his side definitely did not belong to a petite woman with flaming hair.

"My apologies, Cas," Rueben's gentle voice soothed. "I love you, my friend. Just not like that."

Cas' smile faded. He'd not let many people touch him like that.

Morgan, of course.

He refused to think of the dead king's groping hands and mouth.

Bloodshot blue eyes opened to clear the unwelcome recollection away, and he swallowed.

That had been a means to an end, one he would gladly go through again to claw back any of the magic he'd been without for too long.

Gladly.

Cas cleared his hot throat with a dry hack.

"Thank you for that grimace," Rueben added sarcastically. His wrinkled face looked haggard, but his sweet grey eyes sparkled with mischief. "I thought my hands weren't too bad for an old man."

The priest helped Cas sit up and to take a sip of cool water from a goblet that had appeared from somewhere.

"It's not your hands I'm worried about," Cas mumbled after taking his fill. "I wonder how much of a priest you have become."

When the cup was drained, Cas swatted away further help from Rueben and settled himself upright amongst the pile of pillows. With a grimace, he shifted weakly to get comfortable, keeping his throbbing right hand out of the way. Rueben ignored his protest and stood up, leaning over to stuff more cushions behind Cas' back.

"Careful now, lad," said the priest with a resigned sigh as he sat back down.

"Lad?" Cas huffed. "What's with that?"

"Ha."

After Rueben adjusted his robes over his knees, the priest and the patient stared at each other in silence, until Cas gave the room a cursory glance. The shifty little dragon was nowhere to be seen. A devious jerk with his mind, along the hot thread that bound them together, earned him a startled whimper from the floor by the fireplace below the end of the bed.

On his stool, Rueben arched his wispy eyebrows and crossed his arms over his thin chest.

Cas twisted his lips and shrugged.

His languid mind felt like it was starting to work, his sluggish thoughts beginning to make more sense. They still had to make it to Aneirin, but considering how close he'd been to sliding off a dragon mid-flight, the time for healing had been unavoidable. Thankfully, the inn was certainly living up to its enthusiastic recommendation.

The place was called "The Basalt Rose", which suited Cas just fine. Along with it being Morgan's last name, it was located on the lowest level of Baile Fuar. It was expensive too, which had Cas frowning.

Considering he had nothing on arrival, not even the clothes on his back, he'd have to send Flare out to procure coins somehow. The innkeeper's amused expression but closed lips on his arrival earned her at least a handful of the purest gold.

Mismatched blue eyes glinted.

Gold that would be taken from someone who had more than they needed.

Waving away Rueben's help as he coughed, Cas examined the room. He could see it more clearly, now he was not half-collapsed from whatever was making him feel like death was searching for him.

The tidy chamber was windowless. The three front-facing garden rooms had already been occupied when he checked in. Fresh air was still plentiful via the carefully planned system of air vents. The fire was burning brightly in the simply carved but elegant hearth, accompanied by a stained glass lantern to his left on the low table by the bed. All four walls were dark stone, flecked with shards of natural silica or something similar, reflecting the flickering glow like silver fireflies. His bed was a four-posted piece of heavy wood, the posts carved to look like twisted columns and stained a dark cherry. A gentle aroma permeated the air, woodsy but fresh.

Fresher than him, Cas realised with a flip of his stomach.

As a thought struck him, he glanced to his left in a moment of panic, but his heart eased almost immediately.

His treasure was right there, propped up on a plush pillow of turquoise velvet, which pleased him. All the room's soft furnishings were coloured in jewel-bright tones, burgundy, turquoise and gold. It was ostentatious but comfortable, flashy while not overwhelming.

His lungs were wracked by another cough and Cas cursed inwardly.

Just what had happened to him?

Was it the king's magic?

Or was it being caught in a collapsing tower back in the City of the Seers?

He frowned down at his hand.

It still hurt like the hells. Now it was bound up, the throbbing was mostly contained in the two smallest digits. Cas said another prayer to the non-existent gods that the pus had been cleared.

Blue eyes, one light and one dark, slid from the carefully wrapped bandage to Rueben. His old friend was certainly getting on in his years. Refusing magic his whole life, the man was now well into his one hundred and twenty-odd years, and certainly looked it.

"You look like a dried up version of yourself," Cas sniggered around the lump forming in his throat. "Weak, frail, lost. A poor man who refused more potent magic and will probably drop off his branch sometime soon —"

"Yes, yes," Rueben laughed. "Thanks for that. You know," he said, his voice sharpening. "I was thinking about you recently."

"Good things?" Cas asked with what was a nonchalant air as he cleared the welling of heat in his mouth. Rueben had likely saved his life.

Again.

"Good things, about you?" teased the priest.

"Of course," Cas replied.

A faint strangled noise sounded from below the end of the bed.

Cas ignored it.

"Ha. I was thinking about the boy who attacked me when I was almost finished my training back home," Rueben replied. With his head tilted and eyes narrowed, the old man looked like a white crow searching for a treat. "They never found him."

"Oh." Cas settled deeper into the fragrant pillow of plush pillows. It was difficult to not let a smug smile spread across his face, so he let it. "That's a shame."

"Then the next time I saw you," the priest went on, "you had just about choked on your own blood, too. You need to stop that."

Cas' smirk transformed from smug to a fond grin.

"Mmmm." He sighed, eyes closed. "I hadn't quite got the knack of crystal consummation. I still don't, not really." His eyes snapped open as a thought struck him. "Are the priestesses here still just as mischievous? I saw them on the road south, a while back. I wonder how they are doing."

Rueben spared him a saucy grin. "They're fine."

Cas rolled his eyes. "I'm sure they are."

Fidgeting with the edge of a cushion under his bandaged hand, Cas spared a glance for the end of the bed, where he knew Flare was still very much listening. It seemed inevitable that Flare would finally make a break for it. So as soon as he was able, Cas needed the room to cease spinning, his bones to stop aching and his lungs to end their desire to turn themselves inside out.

It had also been ages since he'd had proper food. Would his stomach tolerate that yet? The watery memory of a tankard of cool ale and a fig swam to the surface of his mind. Was that recently?

The priest cleared his throat, interrupting Cas' line of thought.

"Do you want to tell me about that?" he asked placidly.

Silvery blue eyes traveled from the end of the bed to the lump of sparkling crystal by his side.

Cas winced as his right hand rubbed against the blanket.

"A lot is riding on this beautiful piece of rock," Cas said seriously, his eyes sparkling as he examined the priest's lined face. "I just haven't quite worked out how to go about it, you see."

Rueben's eyebrows arched towards his receding hairline. "When have you ever known what you were doing, Cas, my lad?"

"I have a right to make things up as I go," Cas protested. "I want to wipe away the continent of chaos, I want everything..." Eyes flashing, his jaw tightened. "I simply want everything that I deserve."

The pair of them stared at each other until Cas could stand it no longer. He snorted and blinked lazily at the room, finding it difficult to focus. He wished his mind would stop spinning, and let him rest a moment, rather than plaguing him with images of scales and wings, spikes and teeth. The fire continued to crackle and hiss, lending more weight to the hellish vision that played in his subconsciousness.

"The royal family... the map," Cas muttered. "I've got to make all of this right..."

Rueben's gentle voice helped soothe Cas, the tone yes, the words not so much.

"Not by getting into too much trouble, though?" the priest inquired, not judgmental, but sincere.

"Mm," Cas hummed noncommittally. "I never wanted to be the grand architect of chaos... but someone must find a tolerable way for the world to find ease, clawing it back from those that leech off of the rest of us. I'll serve whatever penance comes after, if I survive."

"You did it, didn't you?" Rueben asked. Cas blinked at him. "I never really worked it out for sure."

"What?"

"You became a dragon."

"Oh." Swallowing, Cas nodded. He hoped Rueben missed the sudden twitch of his hand. "Yes."

Rueben sighed. "So where are your scales now, lad?"

Cas sighed at the shadowed stone above.

"I went to Mionlach," he murmured, lowering his gaze to watch the top of the flames licking into the low chimney above them. "It took me a while to get there. This was after the City of the Seers fell. I was damaged... My wings were gone. I was on two feet. Well, I had two skittish horses. I wish I'd had that fucking crystal sphere," he added under his breath. As a black log broke apart in the hearth, Cas winced at the sharp crack. Rueben waited patiently, as he always did. "I wanted to watch Skye do it, you see. I wanted her to become who she was supposed to become."

Mismatched blue eyes narrowed as little claws scraped against the slate floor out of sight. Rueben, by Cas' side, sat up straight, clearly enthralled.

"I was too late." Cas sighed. Without looking, he reached out with his good hand, grabbing the egg. Fingers caressed the rough exterior, tracing the crystalline surface of fractures and lines. Scooping it up one handed, Cas pressed it to his chest. With his bandaged hand, he pulled the edge of the blanket up to cover it. Cas glanced at Rueben from the corner of his eye. "I found what came after, though."

Rueben blinked calmly, his expression open and nonjudgmental. "What did you find?"

Not hearing the question, Cas leant forward. His lips caressed the egg, sensitive skin rubbing against the jagged curve.

"I was so proud of her," he whispered. "I'm sorry I missed it."

Another scratch of a twitching claw and a muted sob sounded from the floor in front of the fireplace. Cas' lips twitched against the ridges of glittering crystal. He let the soft sounds of the chamber wash over him, the solid rock a living presence amongst the three silent figures. Disappointed that Flare had yet to protest or stutter any excuses from his hiding place, Cas tilted his head, turning until his cheek pressed against the top of the egg instead of his lips.

On his stool pushed up to the side of the bed, Rueben waited, wavering shadows crossing his face. With its merry crackling, the glow from the fire made interesting shapes of the man's wrinkles. Almost as if the priest was standing in a dark forest, the canopy swaying under a burning sun.

Cas let out a dramatic sigh.

"Shadow Light had already had his way with Skye. It shouldn't have happened like that... but she had broken free. Then she had her way with the dragons," Cas mumbled. He maneuvered until his chin was propped back on the egg. After clearing his parched throat, he called out towards the end of the bed. "Did you hear that, Flare? They deserved it. She's going to hurt you, too."

Flare gave a tortured sort of squeak. But, to Cas' surprise, there was a rustle at the end of the lushly draped bed. A small scaly purple head poked over the edge of the mattress, the tiny crown of spikes backlit by the radiant fire behind.

"She'll never forgive me," Flare whispered.

Not sure if the little dragon meant Skye or Aurelia, Cas smiled.

It didn't matter.

"No, she won't."

Amethyst eyes shone with thick, dark tears. "We are monsters, aren't we?"

His bright expression fading, Cas nodded.

"Yes," he said, turning solemn. "Yes, we are."

Reuben cleared his throat, but neither Flare nor Cas flinched. Climbing up, so he crouched on the edge of the bed, it was the dragon who looked away first. Silver-blue eyes examined the creature's flaccid wings, the limp tail.

It wouldn't be long now.

"The gods might be absent from our continent after so long," the priest said primly. "But I truly believe that things can be forgiven. If we really mean it."

Cas faced the old priest. Solemn eyes, one dark blue, one light, both shining silver, flashed.

"Reuben, my friend. I'm not sorry for anything... Hm. Maybe just the things that I have failed to do thus far." Cas pressed his lips against the egg in another reverent kiss. "This is *my* god."

The priest's thin shoulders rose and fell with his delicate sigh. A sad but understanding smile lit his face, the age spots and wrinkles disappearing for just a moment, his face young and fresh once more.

Ignoring the reptile, shivering atop of the blankets by his feet, Cas reached out with his bandaged hand. The appendage throbbed, yet he bit back his cry of protest as he reached for Rueben's bird-like fingers.

"How long was I out?" Cas asked, forcing a smile to his lips.

Rueben took the offered hand in both of his. The glint in his eye told Cas the old priest wasn't fooled.

"A full day." Rueben spared a glance for the door. "It is night again."

Hm, Cas mused. *A day.*

It had felt like a while since Morgan's magic had flared like a bonfire. He needed to find her before she slipped away.

Out loud, he asked, "Are there any bath houses open this late?"

"No. They close as the sun drops," the priest replied. "These folk still have their superstition about water spirits that come out at night to drown the unwary bather."

"Ha. I shall go anyway, so let the beasts try." Cas' brittle smile widened into a rueful grin. "I stink."

Against his old friend's advice, Cas decided that the risk of passing out again was worth it to be clean.

Not just wiped over by a damp, clean cloth, but fully immersed in the steaming, mineral-rich waters of Baile Fuar.

At the eastern end of the city's elongated kidney shape, the hot springs had been tapped by accident during the extraction of stone for the City of the Seers.

Once the quarry was no longer needed, keen-eyed business folk had realised their potential. The hot springs had been expanded, glittering oases carved out of the once hidden bedrock to service both the workers who had stayed on in the town, along with travelers and merchant caravans.

The town received some of its fresh water from the underground system, while about a dozen businesses had set up to make coin from the natural resource as well. The townsfolk were not entirely welcoming to outsiders, which is why the baths were gated and accessible by a pretty fee for each use. Some of the luxurious baths were set into the cavernous tunnels radiating into the quarry walls, while others were out in the open, with the wide open sky above.

It was to one of these that Cas headed.

Bathing might not be popular after sundown thanks to the ridiculous myths, but the town was still awake.

Conversation and laughter echoed from the town's rim far above, following Cas through the more deserted streets that led to his preferred institution. Few businesses on ground level were late-night establishments, and most passersby that he encountered avoided his curious gaze as they passed each other.

That didn't concern him at all. He was exhausted, sore, and supremely heart sick. Whatever his body had been struggling with was still being overcome. His head was still feeling like it was full of viscous honey, and his eyes were struggling to focus on distances far away.

As he paused at a junction of two streets to catch his breath and reorient himself to the maze-like town, Cas lifted his chin and examined the sky.

Swaying a little, he squinted.

There wasn't much to see.

No treetops were visible as the forest didn't start until well back from the quarry's edge, and the stars were hidden behind clouds that appeared like murky shadows gathering in the gloom.

Inhaling thoughtfully, Cas could just make out the scent of minerals, the undertone of sourness of the night air implying that the sulphur-fed springs weren't far.

Shifting the egg on his hip with his left hand, he eased his right into the pocket of the new trousers that Rueben had sent for. They offered no warmth at all, only modesty. Despite the low temperature outside, with the promise of heat not far, Cas had scoffed at Rueben's use of his priestly robe to make the trip. The priest had also offered to come with him, but Cas had waved that offer too.

Being the man's unconscious patient was enough vulnerability for one day. Being naked while removing only the gods knew how many layers of filth was a step too far.

"Besides," Cas snapped through gritted teeth as his broken fingers poked at a collection of loose coins, "I am doing just fine."

A fresh bolt of pain sent a spasm of agony through his hand.

The loose coins in his shallow pocket slipped out, scattering about on the bare stone road with a metallic clatter. A few landed on their rims and rolled a few paces away, settling in the shadows of a large, unlit building facing the wider of the two streets. A set of heavy footsteps were headed his way from up the dimly lit street in front of him, but there was no one else around.

"Fuck!" Cas hissed.

Not wanting to set his crystal treasure down for even a moment, he sank down to his knees, his bandaged hand fumbling about the poorly lit street for his coins.

About a half dozen gold pieces, sourced by Flare when Cas was passed out, were strewn across the ground. It was likely he didn't need them, as he'd be breaking in anyway. But it would be nice to leave a token of his thanks.

"I just want a fucking bath!" he spat as the sky swayed above him.

On his knees, he closed his eyes and willed himself to calm down. Considering the wild, unhealthy rhythm of his racing heart, it was difficult. After a while, his gaze opened to the deserted street, appalled at what reached his nose. The town had never been one for piles of trash like some villages, the townsfolk keenly aware of the lack of strong breezes down this low.

The sour aroma that filled his nose was him.

Disgusting.

The coins in the shadows could fucking well stay where they were.

"I would kill to get clean right now," he muttered with a groan as he stood.

Not far off, someone clicked their tongue with a disdainful *tsk*.

Cas blinked.

A man in long robes had appeared at the junction where Cas was fighting to stay upright. Behind the stranger, a tall thin tower rose towards the sky, a single light of blue flame lit at one window towards its roof.

"That seems a poor judgement, on your behalf," the man exclaimed loudly.

Cas ignored the stranger, and with the egg pressed to his shirt, passed him without a second glance. The promise of hot water was too appealing, too close by, to stand there and discuss the merits of getting clean —

Behind him, the man called out with judgement fortifying his deep voice.

"Blaspheming against the gift of life is the same as ignoring your duty to the gods, young man!"

Cas halted, eyes closed as he debated whether to confront the ridiculous statement, or ignore it and carry on his way.

Nostrils flaring, he turned around.

It was a slow spin, looking over his shoulder first, body following. Mismatched blue eyes narrowed as they assessed the man's robes.

Pale blue.

Sighing, Cas spared a glance for the looming sky, outlined by colourfully lit buildings far above.

Of course.

Rueben, the gods bless him, was a definite oddity amongst his adopted kin. Humble and gentle.

Harmless.

Unlike most of those that chose the robes of faded blue.

Narrowed eyes, one dark blue, the other as washed out as the robes of the stranger on the street, lowered.

The man, about fifty if Cas was to guess, glared at him, his beefy arms crossed over a rounded belly.

"Blaspheming, you say?" asked Cas.

He took a step towards the priest.

"Exactly!" the man declared. He raised his chins to look down at Cas. Considering he was a head shorter, the effect was ridiculous. "How could you take the gift that the gods gave you so lightly —"

"Lightly?" Cas repeated, gawking at the angry man. He indicated himself with his bandaged hand. "No, good sir, I do not take this lightly."

Confused, the priest squared his shoulders. One hand dropped to his pudgy hip, the other to point an accusing finger at the unamused blonde man before him.

"Why would you dare say a thing like that, then? In this holy place?" The man demanded.

"Holy place? *This*?" Cas snickered, a pale eyebrow arching.

The priest, with his curly hair of black bobbing, nodded. Cas followed the man's fat finger as it pointed to the silent building that he'd just passed.

Cas waited as calmly as he could for whatever the man felt the need to point out to someone clearly desiring to be anywhere-the-fuck else.

"This is a holy sanctuary for those in need," the man scoffed, his expression prim, "run by priests for the good of those who are less fortunate than you or I."

"Huh." Cas took another step. "That's quite a talent you've got there, holy man."

"What?" The priest blinked through his glare.

"Judging by your girth, my dear priest, it's amazing that you've talked yourself into believing how righteous you are. Well done."

"What?" repeated the priest.

"The building for the needy," Cas jutted his chin at the silent structure, a three storied construction of white plaster and pale, native stones. "It looks in need of sustenance, while you have certainly had more than your fair share."

He took another three lazy steps. The streets spun a little, but Cas stayed upright by pure will as he stopped directly in front of the priest. Leaning forward, Cas sniffed the air near the priest's neck dramatically.

"Ambrosia and rose? Good taste. Expensive taste."

The man spluttered at Cas' blatant disrespect, his pudgy hands resting on his belly.

"Hold this," Cas said brightly.

Without waiting for a response, he shoved the egg at the gawking priest, tucking the egg into the outer flap of the man's voluminous robe.

"What the blazes —"

With both hands, Cas grabbed the priest's head without warning. His broken hand protested with a fiery burst of pain, but he willed it away. His working fingers probed the man's ears, thumbs pressing into fat cheeks. The man froze, both in sudden fear and the coil of magic Cas sent from his trembling fingertips.

"Hold on, holy man," Cas whispered, nose to nose. The man's eyes widened at what he saw in the gaze that flashed silver so close to his. Cas gathered what energy he could to his palms, his wrists, his arms. "Hold on *tight*. This is the closest you are going to come to your absent god."

Perhaps the priest understood what was about to happen, perhaps not.

Either way, his eyes clamped shut as Cas let out the surge of magic from within like a charge of lightning, not as a whip, but as a burst of strength.

He yanked with a twisting jerk.

Hard.

Despite the flare of scorching pain in his fucked-up hand, the loud *snap* of a neck parting ways with its spine was agreeable enough. Yet it was the wet, ripe tearing of over-fed flesh and sinews separating that pleased Cas the most.

The head, now free from its earthly tether, was left in his freshly soiled hands, the heavy body collapsing with an untidy fold to the street.

Cas blinked at the gaping expression on the bodiless head as he spat out the steaming, coppery spray that coated his face and mouth.

The burst of strength had surprised him, if he was honest. He thought it would take at least one more twist back the other way.

"Well. This is awkward."

He peered down.

A gasp escaped Cas' bloody lips.

The priest's head hit the ground with a wet thunk.

"My *baby!*"

On his knees in the street for the second time that evening, Cas scooped up his sparkling treasure from where it had rolled half out of freshly stained, pale blue robes.

He held it close after a quick examination, eyes bright with relief.

The egg was perfectly fine.

His nose scrunched at the stink of blood and the emptying bowels of the corpse as he stood up. Not far off, the aroma of the hot springs remained refreshingly intoxicating.

"I'm sorry, love, now you need a wash, too." Cas sighed dramatically, the priest in two pieces with his amusingly shocked expression forgotten.

He squinted up the widest street.

"Where are these fucking baths?"

By the time Cas had found his way, by sniffing at each intersection of dim stone road between buildings where only faint snatches of conversation could be heard, the two Keepers of the Waters were chaining shut a tall gate of ornate iron, spanning a gap between thick stone walls.

Cas sped up as fast as his current dizziness allowed.

"Good sirs," he began, but the two brawny figures turned.

Both were women with finely muscled arms showing out of their short-sleeved wool tunics.

"Good ladies," Cas corrected himself with a modest nod. "I must beg —"

One of the women held up a glittering lantern of thick, clear glass and copper.

"No beggars..." she began. But her voice, pleasantly deep, faded and green eyes widened under her cropped auburn hair.

Glancing down at his bloodstained clothing, Cas blinked. Holding the egg close to his heart, Caspian looked back up, clearing his throat.

"Pardon me," he said respectfully.

The pair gawked at him.

Using his right hand to carefully wipe hair damp with what he suspected matched his clothes, Caspian tried his best winning smile on them.

"Yeah... no," the younger of the two said with a slow shake of her head. "That's not gonna help."

Sheepishly, Cas fished out some coins from his pocket. He held them out on his bandaged palm.

The second woman by the gate, an older woman of perhaps seventy winters with white bobbed hair, stared at him, mouth open. Cas peeked past her, listening to the barely perceptible ripple of soothing water. He sniffed with longing as mineral salts teased his senses.

The first woman eyed the coins. Her glare turned shrewd.

"Is it yours?" the woman asked, eyes on the gold.

Dropping his gaze, Caspian glared at her.

"I fucking stole it, so fucking yes, it's fucking mine now."

"Oh," the woman said hurriedly. "Okay." She elbowed her older companion. "Open it up."

The other woman glanced between them. After a careful assessment of Cas' state, his fierce expression and the glittering object in his arm, she nodded. With an efficiency from well-practiced movements, the heavy padlock was unlocked, the gate opening with barely a squeak. After the younger woman handed her companion the warmly lit lantern, the lady with the keys skittered away a few paces, giving Cas a wide berth.

The auburn-haired woman examined the coins after swiping them from Cas.

"Ha. These are good. Almost pure quality."

"Of course they are," Cas snapped. "So may I pass? With your lantern for... my good manners and letting you go in peace, hm?"

"What?"

Cas arched his brows, letting his appearance speak for itself.

"Ah." The woman swallowed. She motioned for her companion to place the lantern on the ground.

Without hesitating, Cas stalked towards the lantern. The older lady backed away. After yanking the merry light off the street with a shake of his head, Cas headed to the gate.

"Okay then. Wait... hang on." The woman's eyes were lit with a cunning light. Cas stopped, sighing with impatience. "Where did you get these?"

Cas didn't even have to think. He opened the gate and slipped through, calling over his shoulder.

"My dragon."

After a startled silence, nervous laughter filled the dark street.

"Wait," the woman called. Cas rolled his eyes skyward, but paused once more and turned around. The woman was biting her lip. "Lock up the gate, yeah? Don't want any more beggars... ah, anyone else, messing up the place after you, sir."

Lips pursed, Cas bowed as best as his vertigo allowed.

Then he spun on his heel and headed into the open aired complex for a long, *long* overdue deep clean.

It was hard to see the full shape in the chilled, dim evening, but Cas thought he'd been to this bath before.

The shape of the single massive pool was similar to the kidney shape of the quarry itself. It appeared glassy black in the chilled night, springs bubbling gently from under the water, making only the shallowest of ripples under a soft, white mist. The entire complex was cut out of the native rock, with pillars joined by arches where shades could be hung to protect bathers from the sun during hotter months. Along the edge all the way around, a series of steps were carved, allowing folk to sit at different depths as preferred. Various animals and birds carved into the dark stone decorated each pillar, alcove bench areas and even a central platform of rock in the centre of one end of the pool. Bathers could take cool drinks into the water, resting them nearby on the shelf, while they themselves relaxed in the soothing warmth fed by the heated springs from below.

Grabbing a wooden bowl of pink salt from the canvas-covered seating area, Cas placed both that and the egg by a smaller separate plunge pool in one of the arched alcoves. With some cursing and some careful adjustments, he stripped off, and dropped into the deep, chilled water, bloody clothes discarded on a section of stone bench.

After enduring the pain of scrubbing away most of the dirt and grime that his friend had been unable to remove, Cas emerged, feeling almost reborn. He grabbed the egg, walked three steps, and practically fell into the main pool.

The bandage was a soaking mess around his hand, but he didn't care.

Floating on his back in the salty, steaming water, the egg on his chest like a young otter mum with her cub, Cas stared at the overcast sky.

It was heaven down *here*, no matter what the religious orders across Beinacoilia proclaimed about living well for your next life.

Chest heaving, hand on fire and his mind spinning, Cas slipped one arm around the crystal and ducked under the water, fully immersed.

He screamed.

Cursing, swearing, and letting the water absorb his rage and frustration rather than the echoing town beyond the surface, he kicked and yelled; the water bubbling like a freshly boiled kettle around him.

Hours later, floating once more on the surface, eyes stinging and throat raw, Cas cleared his sore throat. He felt a lot better... but there was just so much more to do.

"I need a drink," he croaked.

Balancing the egg, appearing dark blue black in the night, on his chest, Cas kicked backwards towards the steps. When the back of his head scraped the top stone just under the waterline, he sighed, rolling over. Catching the crystal with his bad hand, he winced. The thing was certainly as heavy as a man's head.

That could be verified with recent evidence.

Cas pulled himself up with his good hand, taking his time and dripped his way to his discarded clothes left on the rock hewn bench. The seating extended either side of him for quite a way. He wondered what it was like here in the day, full of laughter and life.

Did people still smile like they used to, even after all the death and chaos of the past decades?

This place certainly used to be a lively destination. And by the sounds of the few remaining public houses along the town's upper rims, perhaps it still was. But the threat was there, wasn't it? Even with the dragons gone, wild magic still roamed the continent. A few wily creatures amassing it for themselves at the expense of others.

Carefully looking about, making sure he really was alone, Cas placed the egg on the bench beside his clothes. His head was ringing, and his hand was stinging from the mineral salts and steaming water.

Swallowing his discomfort, Cas stood there, staring.

The egg glittered silently, ripples and jagged edges of deep blue and deeper green. A simple, inert rock.

But dead?

He refused to believe it.

"How can you be dead?" Cas whispered. "After all I've done to make way for you?"

A noise, barely perceptible, emerged from his left.

Raising his dripping head, Cas peered sideways into the shadows, aware a light rain had started.

The white mist above the glassy black pool was clearing beneath the drops, and the temperature plunged, earning him goosebumps along his flesh.

"Hello?" he called, bleary eyes blinking through the salt water streaming down his face.

Naked as that day he was born, with more scars both within and without, Cas glanced up, directly ahead of himself.

Thankfully, the crystal egg was nestled amongst his bloody clothes, otherwise it might have slipped from his fingers.

Water seeped from sodden, pale hair to an even paler face, obscuring his vision, but a small noise escaped his throat as the face came into focus.

Wet eyelashes fluttered in surprise.

"It's you," said Cas after some time. Salt water joined the mineral stream coating his wet cheeks. "You look different from last time we met."

31

Fox

Year 367
Baile Fuar, City of Stone

This was certainly not the town he remembered.

From his horse at the top of one of the stone ramps spiraling into the quarry town, Fox examined the elongated kidney-shaped quarry.

Gold-flecked black eyes narrowed as they traced the open-cut mine from end to end and side to side.

"Hm," he mused.

In the nighttime chill, the town looked like a vast pool of deep shadows, with bright lights like small, fragrant pyres floating around the edge of a black lake. A bottomless body of water, whose unknowable depths sank into cold shadows.

Time enough had passed for the town to expand along and down its various strata of rocky cliffs and cuts. But perhaps what was more poignant was that he was here, more in his right mind than the last time.

Which counted for a lot, considering the state he'd been in.

They had arrived not long after the setting sun, lost somewhere behind the roiling clouds. It would rain soon, possibly snow. It was certainly cold enough.

Fox nestled deeper into his thick cloak of wool and furs, wondering if he should get another one. For Owaen, too.

The blonde Elf had reined in his horse beside Fox, letting the vista wash over them. Along the quarry's rim, a few pubs and inns were still open. Their rainbow-coloured lantern lights welcoming beacons after travelling down dark roads that wound through aromatic cedars and restless shadows.

"Let me buy you something," Fox murmured, his gaze tracing Owaen's wide shoulders and firm waist beneath his own travel-stained cloak. Green eyes glanced his way.

"We have little coin —"

"Your lover has gold enough to spare," Fox scoffed.

Not waiting for an answer, he clicked at his weary horse, urging it to the sloping road where gravel transitioned into bare rock. Thankfully, the ramp was wide, its gradient shallow enough that the horse didn't kick up a fuss.

Muttering under his breath, Owaen urged Blackthorn to follow.

By the time they had walked their horses to the town's lowest level, Fox was ready for hot water, a soft bed and his lover's seeking embrace.

Fox's mind was preoccupied with these thoughts as Owaen headed Blackthorn to his preferred accommodation, when they passed a single story building of whitewashed stone, lit with candles in every narrow window. The tidy streets were almost deserted. Most other establishments were shut up for the night, both the standalone buildings on the quarry floor and the dwellings cut into the cliffs themselves.

Just inside the lit-up building's decorative metal double gates, a small group of women in washed out blue robes and cloaks of navy sang together. Their choir leader, a tall lady with a shimmering white scarf wrapped around her head and holding a fragrant candle, stood before them.

While his horse danced under him, snuffling the air with puffs of hot breath, Fox frowned at the candle.

The single flame was protected by a little shield of blue glass, in the shape of a crystal point set into the iron candle holder.

Unaware of the sour expression on the man beside him, Owaen called out a friendly greeting.

"Good evening, good Sisters."

Fox was quite prepared for the singers to ignore him, but their leader turned and smiled. It faltered a little when she noticed the figure with brooding black and gold eyes atop his inquisitive horse. But genuine warmth, and perhaps something else, returned as she spotted Owaen.

Black eyes narrowed, the gold lost in the shadows.

"Good evening," the lady with the white headscarf called. Her interest remained solely on the blonde rider on the proudly regal black horse. After a moment, her clear eyes widened. "It's you!" she gasped. "Back again at last? I think it's been nearly a decade at least!"

Her companion's song died off, the sweet melody replaced by giggles.

Fox's frown intensified, the fine line between his dark brows marring his pale skin.

Owaen shook his head.

"I haven't been here for many..." The blonde Elf cleared his throat with an embarrassed cough whilst avoiding Fox's seething glance. "It's been a long while since I've been through here. I think you've got me confused with another."

Licking her lips, the woman stared at him for a moment.

"Oh," she said eventually, clearly disappointed. "My apologies."

Unable to help himself, Fox urged his horse to press against Blackthorn's side. With a crafty swipe, he grabbed the black horse's bridle and pulled it with him as he squeezed his knees into his own mount's flanks.

Ignoring the murmur in their wake, Fox only let go of Blackthorn's reins when they were a fair distance down the isolated street. Counting his breaths to calm down, he hoped Owaen didn't sense the faint rumble of the earth following their progress into the sleepy town.

"Care to explain?" Owaen drawled, a broad hand making a sweeping motion at the angry stone below.

Fox's chin rose. "I might ask the same of you," he said icily as they came to an intersection of three wide avenues.

"I have no idea," Owaen hissed, coming alongside Fox, "but calm the fuck down with your pettiness. We don't want to cause a scene here. And if my suspicions are correct, it is likely Ca... my brother, whom that nun thought she was addressing."

Shaking his head, Fox walked Willow in the direction he hoped was the right one.

"She's a priestess, my love, so your jealousy is quite misplaced," Owaen called after him. It sounded like the bastard was trying not to laugh. "I only stand to attention for you."

Cheeks turning a gentle shade of pink, Fox battled with himself to calm down the rumbling below their horse's hooves.

It took more effort than he cared to admit.

Considering his delirious state after his revenge over the dragon homeland when Fox was here last, one thing he remembered was the way most of the more luxurious inns were tunneled into the solid bedrock.

Most likely there was plenty of fresh air through ventilation shafts, but it didn't change what they were.

Fucking caves.

And after his captivity by Shadow Light in a cave filled with pain and terror, Fox had had enough of the damn things by the time he'd dragged himself, and his former captor, to Baile Fuar. After that, he had wandered amongst greenery, vast trees and lush forests, under the open sky for many, many years before deigning to live under rock once more at Lolihud.

Fox was more than happy that Owaen didn't want to stay in one either.

Biting his lip, Fox had finally let the Elf take over and lead their small party of weary travelers to a freestanding building of multiple levels, about halfway along the open cut town. Faint laughter originated from the Inn's common room. After securing their own chambers however, Fox had headed upstairs to the top floor with their gear, Owaen to the stables with the horses.

Now, after making some suitable adjustments to the space to ensure it was extra cozy, Fox paced the room, wondering what was taking Owaen so long. He was also wondering why the back of his neck was prickling. A ripple of sensation that was neither pleasant nor unpleasant radiated down his spine like a line of determined gnats.

Wondering what it might be, Fox clenched and unclenched his aching right hand as he paced along the wide wooden planks. He kept one glittering eye on the door, ears alert for Owaen.

How hard was it to stable and feed two horses?

He was concerned, yes, but also hungry, horny and frustrated with how slow it was taking them to make their way back to Aurelia and Rhydian.

Surely they could leave the horses and he'd fly back?

Impatient boot steps halted.

Pale blue eyes with their darker ring of sapphire appealed to him within the recesses of his frigid heart.

"My horse..." Rhydian would sigh, crushed. "Fox... How could you?"

With a toss of black hair, Fox resumed his restless pacing.

A heavy boot step on the stairs was followed by a curse.

The faint scent of musk and salt on the air increased, alerting Fox that, at last, Owaen was on his way back.

The heavy oak door swung wide as Fox yanked it open.

Owaen flashed him a fatigued grin, dropping the fist he was making, ready to knock. He stooped to collect two buckets of hot water behind him and backed into the room as he balanced them.

"Before you ask," Owaen grunted as he turned around to face the room, "I was making sure the stable master understood that I wanted our horses looked after, considering the ridiculous amount of money I... handed over..."

As his words faded to a startled silence, Owaen blinked at the bed, then aimed his emerald stare at Fox.

"What the actual fuck?" breathed the Elf.

Fox flicked a piece of invisible fluff off of the shoulder of his shirt.

Speechless, Owaen crouched and placed the buckets on the floor, not looking as they splashed over the beams.

"What the fuck is this, Fox? A pillow fort? Does a dragon need a *nest*?"

Sparing a glance to the bed where Owaen was pointing, or to be more precise, at the mountain of pillows he'd paid a servant two gold coins for, Fox clasped his pale hands in front of him, and shrugged.

Owaen continued to gape, still lost for words.

Fox sighed and gestured at Owaen's crotch with his own accusatory finger.

"I am sick of a harsh forest floor when we fu —"

Cutting Fox off, Owaen crossed the room with a single stride and pulled the indignant man against his expansive chest with a hard squeeze.

"Fox, Fox," Owaen huffed into the silky black hair against his lips. "We are here…" He pulled back with a pained expression on his grizzled face. "We are passing through, trying to not attract attention."

"And?" Fox enquired unblinkingly.

Owaen pressed his lips to Fox's forehead.

"And it looks like you have stripped this inn, perhaps this entire town, of pillows. How did you do all that when I was seeing to the horses?"

"You took too long," Fox snapped.

Fox stepped back and grabbed a single pillow from the two dozen or so mounded on top of the wool blanket and shoved it at Owaen.

"There you go. Don't fret, little Elf."

"Oh my gods," Owaen muttered. He yanked the pillow from Fox and chucked it away, uncaring about how close to the fireplace it landed. "Are you still *jealous*? Of a priestess who said hello?"

"No."

"So why is your face like that?"

"Like what?" Fox huffed, trying hard to not lean into the heat that enveloped him as Owaen gathered him close against him once more.

Owaen's warm chest rumbled against Fox as he spoke.

"Like you just bit into a candy to find it a block of salt."

Fox bowed his head and said nothing.

Rubbing his cheek against Owaen's chest, he inhaled slowly, letting his lungs fill with the scent of the one he loved in an attempt to settle his nerves.

It was hard to explain in words the feelings that had him questioning his memory and the ability to think clearly. Last time he'd been here, after all, he'd just about massacred nearly a hundred dragons.

At the recollection, the room rumbled faintly, the bedrock shuddering at the energy seeping out from Fox's heart, the beats slow but uneven, and possibly missing a few. Of their own accord, cool hands crept under Owaen's shirt and around his waist, seeking the soothing warmth. Fox felt warmer some days more than others. Today was a day of chilled flesh.

"I apologise," Fox spoke directly against Owaen's chest. "Magic, and its use... I really think the world will be better off without it."

Owaen chewed that over for a while. Eventually, he nodded, the rasp of his chin scraping against Fox's black hair.

"I wonder..." Owaen hesitated, choosing his words with care.

"What?"

"Sometimes I wonder if your life would have been better if we'd never met."

Aghast, Fox jerked back, one hand reaching up to grab Owaen's chin.

"Don't say that! *Never* say that."

"I'm sorry..." Owaen rested his forehead against Fox's. "You have been hurt too much. Magic, like you said, might be better off gone."

"Hmm," Fox mumbled, eyes closing.

Hating to disturb the moment of warmth, Fox cleared his throat. But he bit back his next words, wondering how to broach the topic.

"What is it?" Owaen murmured, his lips brushing against Fox's hair with affection.

"You know me well."

"Not really. Please continue."

"I..." Fox licked his lips, tasting the journey there of the past few days. He frowned as he explained. "While you were out, I tried to look for Caspian."

Owaen stiffened against him, saying nothing. It felt like the Elf was holding his breath.

"I can sometimes see things... people... across a vast distance with magic and my mind."

"And?" Owaen's voice was carefully neutral.

"Nothing," Fox declared, his eyes narrowed. He blinked at the stone wall beside them. "I tried looking for that flighty wasp, Flare, too."

With a long, indrawn breath, Owaen relaxed a little. "And Flare?"

"I thought..." Fox began, then halted.

"Could you find him?" Owaen urged softly.

"I felt a ripple, but it was gone quickly. He hasn't the same amount of resources as I do. But he has a lot of magic, nonetheless."

After another moment of contemplating this, Owaen nodded.

"I see."

Grateful that Owaen didn't ask why he hadn't attempted this before now, Fox wrapped his arms tighter. It seemed like Owaen was already well aware.

Their time alone together, without care for others, was basically nonexistent. So the few days together, even with Rhydian's blasted horses and the urgency of their hunt, had been almost the best they had shared so far.

They held each other as the fire crackled and popped, simply breathing each other in.

Fox would have liked to stay like that, to hells with the outside world. Yet another ripple of particles slid along his spine with fingers of sensation that wasn't quite the power that he knew. It was hard to explain. The sensation wasn't unease, and he didn't even know how to begin explaining it to Owaen. It was akin to flying, when the winds tasted different from place to place.

"Are you hungry?" Owaen murmured finally. "I'll go."

"No." Pulling away with reluctance, Fox chewed his bottom lip. "I'll go. Stay here. Don't leave the room."

"What —"

"Promise me."

Owaen still appeared suspicious.

"Okay," came his sullen reply, his dark green eyes narrowed.

"I said wait here," Fox warned, black eyes flinty with yellow gold sparks.

A thick blonde eyebrow arched.

Fox coughed. "Please."

Brawny arms crossed over his chest, Owaen's narrow eyes examined Fox from boot to nose.

"How long will you be?"

With hands that had chilled rapidly despite the warmth of the chamber, Fox pulled Owaen's face back toward him. Their lips and tongues melded together in a lengthy and heated kiss. After catching his breath, Fox licked his slick lips.

He smiled in answer to Owaen's earlier question.

"I will be gone long enough to rouse the cooks for hot food and to find me some hotter water."

Owaen disengaged a hand from Fox's backside to point at the steaming pails of water.

"A bucket?" Fox scoffed. "No. Wait here, I am going to have a full, immersive bath. That is something I do remember that this town did rather well."

On foot, Fox walked along the street past a shadowy tower rising above a collection of unlit double story buildings. The area he had just emerged from was the outer edge of the principal markets. Where there were bustling stores by day, at this time all were shut tight for the evening.

Here at the cluster of orderly structures, he paused. They looked like they had foundations of solid rock with hand-cut stone blocks built on top. Near the tower's upper floor, a single flame shone in the window.

He stared at it a moment, not sure if the flame itself was blue, or the glass behind which it shone. His glittering gold-flecked gaze slid down the side of the tower, examining the emblem above the arched doorway, just discernible through the ivy covered gates. A bird? A peacock, perhaps. Either way, the aroma of salty, bitter water was getting tantalisingly close.

It was a sad fact that the inn they were staying at had no personal baths, just buckets. It was likely planned that way, some kind of racket with the bathhouse owners to split profits.

Why offer a hot bath for free when you could charge for it?

Fox inhaled, tasting the frosty night air on his tongue and in his flared nostrils.

He was searching for a hot spring, any bath really, following his keen sense of smell, trailing the closest mineral saturated breeze for the heat he craved. Owaen's arms offered that aplenty, but a bucket of hot water was not going to get him to the standard of freshness he required after traveling so long. With only frigid streams to deal with, endless hot water was now imperative.

And so it was, wandering the nighttime streets and not making eye contact with anyone, that he came at last upon a concentrated waft of steam and bitter mineral salts at a deserted crossroad.

Unfortunately, the inviting aroma was spoiled by the copper tang of freshly spilled blood.

Inhaling with more concentration, Fox turned about. The thick fur of his cloak was pulled down from his face just enough, as he debated if it was worth investigating the unexpected scent, with the temptation of a cleansing immersion so frustratingly close.

Fuck it.

"Not my problem," Fox muttered, with a severe shake of his head. "Bath it is —"

Something metallic grated on the stone street under the heel of his leather boot.

Cursing, Fox lifted his foot.

Gold shimmered from the shadows blanketing the rocky street.

"What —?"

He'd stepped on a ring.

In the centre of the street, the gold band was topped with a modestly sized, spectacularly coloured amethyst.

Crouching, Fox caught a more vigorous whiff of blood. His nose wrinkled as he picked up the shining jewel. Urged on by the curious sensation across his shoulder blades, as faint as the rustling of butterfly wings, he touched the object to the tip of his tongue.

Yanking it away immediately, Fox stared at the ring, glittering black eyes wide.

It tasted of blood, both old and new, along with salt and sweat.

But it also tasted of magic, that wild, ozone laced aroma of potential and aftermath. It reminded him both of Rhydian, oddly enough, and also of Shadow Light.

Along with something completely unknown, similar in a way to the shards of green crystal that hung about his neck under his clothes.

"Where the fuck did that come from?" Fox muttered under his breath as he stood up.

With a curious glance around, he let his enhanced vision pick out what didn't belong.

Sure enough, to his left, a splatter of blood, and beyond that, a misshapen lump in the shadows by a dark door step.

After checking there was no one else about, Fox stalked to the lump.

Lumps, he realised. *Plural*.

There were two.

The first was the headless corpse of a squat but wide person. Beside it was the second lump, a man's decapitated head. It seemed likely that one belonged to the other, and by the look of the fresh blood, were in fact united until recently.

Pale blue robes were stained from the neck down with a severe gush of blood, appearing purple in the dim light of the overcast night. The blood beside the body and the head's stump was still fresh. The syrupy liquid pooled in a shallow groove in the road, the edges only just starting to dry.

Fox stared at the ring in his limp hand.

"Curious," he whispered. "And yet... I still want a bath."

He'd tell Owaen about it later and let the Elf decide what to do. Their current aim was getting the horses to Rhydian first, and once that favour was made, onto Caspian. Which also meant dealing with Flare as well.

Fox slipped the ring into his leather pants that smelled strongly of horse and carried on, his mind turning over what to expect when they reached their first destination.

With a grimace, Fox realised Aurelia was more than likely putting on a brave face at present. Flare's defection to Caspian and whatever he was up to surely hurt more than anything. Anger would be there, justified, burning away just below the surface of her stoic calm. But just beneath that layer of fury would be a deeper well of grief, for the betrayal of the friendship she'd thought she had shared with a dragon.

Fox was mulling over the untrustworthy nature of dragons, self included, when he halted with an abrupt scrape of his boots.

Lips parted, he held his breath.

Had he spoken out loud?

Blinking rapidly, he twisted around, ears pricked for what he was sure had been words spoken into the frigid night air. He inhaled, tasting the hot water he craved, fresh from the earth, tantalisingly close.

Was it some drunkard out late, full of grog and regret who had spoken?

No. It was unlikely to be an inebriated citizen who had spoken, considering the word that had caught Fox's attention was an unlikely collection of two syllables hardly bandied about.

Dragon.

Someone, a man quite close by, had muttered the word.

A very light rain began, sprinkling his fur with tiny drops that might have sparkled if there was any light. Through it, Fox's keen vision caught sight of an iron gate set into a high stone wall. That was normal enough, the rich aroma alerting him to the fact it was the very place he'd been looking for. What was less normal was the fact that the padlock of heavy metal was unlocked, its latch not clicked away, as it hung on the gate's decoratively cast handle.

And through the rain and salt, that strange scent, picked up on the tip of his tongue not long before.

The ring in his pocket shifted as he took a step.

The faint caress of gentle wings surprised him again, his shoulders twitching with anticipation, excitement, and even disbelief at what, or whom, might actually be on the other side of the gate.

Taking more careful, muted steps, Fox slipped into the bathhouse without a sound.

Barely breathing, Fox first passed a covered area with shelves full of bowls of salt and glass bottles of unguents waiting for tomorrow's guests.

In the open air, he passed benches carved out of the native rock, terraced into the inner wall of the sprawling hot springs, the air laced with steam.

Silent boots halted as he came to one of a dozen pillars of single blocks of stone, joined by arches and set with various hooks. Some pillars had bronze mirrors on one side. For guests to check their hair or to reflect the light, Fox didn't know or care.

He pressed against the rock, this side without a mirror, grimacing at the feel of steam coating the smooth edge. Taking a shallow breath, Fox cautiously peered around the perfectly straight edge of slick, black stone.

It might have been more efficient to wrap himself in shadows and approach more openly, but considering the unease and strange flavour of the amethyst ring, prudence seemed best.

Owaen, Fox thought to himself, *you would be proud.*

I am choosing to not attract attention —

Through a cloud of hot, misty air, a man cursed.

Water splashed and wet footsteps sounded.

Fox blinked through the steam.

The shock of seeing who he thought was Owaen had Fox leaning so far out that if the wet man had turned right at that point, he would have no doubt seen a pair of wide eyes, gold sparks bright with surprise against jet black.

Except...

It wasn't Owaen, was it?

That arrogant Elf was back at their cosy inn.

This man was ever so slightly taller. He was less brawny as well, with slimmer shoulders and narrower hips.

Pale hands flinched against the wet stone.

Here, of all places, was Fox's prey.

Caspian Fucking Carter.

A slow smile spread across Fox's face, pale lips twitching with suppressed mirth.

Found you.

But...

His grin quickly lost its delighted, manic light.

We are not here to attract attention, Owaen had impressed.

Fox's hands quivered with indecision.

But surely *this* ridiculous coincidence overruled such caution?

Debating his approach, Fox observed the man, naked and dripping from his immersion in the steaming water that called to Fox even now. Caspian carried something, cradling it to his bare chest, head bent towards it as if he might touch it to his dripping lips.

Catching the light of the single lantern hanging by its hook nearby, the object glittered.

Fox squinted through the shifting mist as a cool breeze stirred the steam, clearing some of the air.

His vision was excellent, but the object looked decidedly odd. Or was that just how it felt to look at it? His stomach was feeling a little queasy, if he was being honest. That could simply be the uneven beat of his heart, throbbing with the possibilities of how this stroke of luck could be presented to Owaen in the most gratifying way.

Which meant the opposite of ripping out his twin's still beating heart and presenting it on one of Fox's plethora of cushions.

As his internal debate continued, Fox continued to watch, calculating, anticipating. Lips parted somewhat. His heartbeat fluttered, manic, full of the blessed buzz of revenge about to be had. A buzz that was equally welcome and disturbing.

Cas glanced to his left and right, checking all the benches were indeed empty. Fox assumed the man had decent eyesight as well. Between the cloudy night and mists of steam, the bathing complex was full of damp shadows. Satisfied, Cas set the shimmering crystal next to a pile of what appeared to be the naked man's clothes.

Letting his measured inhale barely stir the steam, Fox tasted the air.

Cas' clothes indeed carried the aroma of fresh blood, that of the decapitated corpse whence Fox had come.

Idly wondering what had occurred, Fox's muscles tensed.

Getting ready.

Not far past the pillar, Cas had gone still. He stared down at the crystal. Its ridges of deep green and blue glittering with faint, inert sparks from the flickering lantern on the metal hook above.

"How can you be dead..?" Caspian mumbled, so faint that Fox wasn't sure he'd heard it all.

Dead?

Fox stood up straighter, ears straining, wondering at what malicious intent this person was hatching.

"After all I've done to make way for you?" the man continued with intense emotion.

What?

Pale hands flinched of their own accord on the humid pillar.

"Hello?" Caspian's voice emerged as a scratchy croak.

The sodden head lifted, and bleary eyes blinked toward the sound made by the involuntary flinch of Fox's fingers against the rock, as the concentrated energy in his fingers allowed them to sink a little into rapidly heating rock.

Cursing under his breath at his own startled curiosity, Fox bit his lip, willing his greedy heart, racing with tension, to calm down. He wanted to catch the man unawares, not in a front on attack. He saw no foul play in being crafty as opposed to honorable. Fox took a deep breath, ready for Caspian to drop his guard once more, waiting for his attention to drop back to the thing he was talking to.

Instead, Caspian turned fully, facing the closest pillar to his left.

The one which Fox was waiting behind, one half of his face peering around the sharp edge.

Not moving a muscle, blinking or even daring to breathe, Fox remained frozen in the steam and shadows, cursing the cool breeze that shifted the clouds of wet air.

Caspian flinched.

Fox, wordless, halfway between pouncing or ready to jerk behind the pillar, mentally begged Owaen for his forgiveness for the oncoming clash. Sweat beaded his normally cool forehead as he strained with indecision on how best to go about it when the dripping man spoke again.

"It's you," Caspian whispered.

Fox watched the bitter water run in shimmering streams, out of soaked hair and through sodden brows. Eyebrows, more delicately formed than his younger twin's, arched high.

"You look different from last time we met," Caspian went on.

To Fox's utter amazement, as he was about to launch in a wild mass of claws, teeth and magic, Caspian took a step towards the pillar.

Fox's heart stopped.

Not from what Caspian was saying, but because black eyes shot with sparks of yellow gold, finally caught a good look at the full extent of Caspian's flesh.

Scars.

Beneath a coppery discoloration of the man's damp skin that Fox hadn't noticed at first, were hundreds of tiny, circular scars.

Too many to be a mere accident.

Stunned, Fox's mouth snapped shut.

What the fuck?

Owaen hadn't said anything about them.

Wordlessly, Caspian reached out towards the pillar, his right hand extended.

Instead of revealing himself, Fox's own right hand jerked with an empathetic spasm. Caspian's hand was red and swollen, the smallest two fingers clearly broken, torn flesh hanging, ready to give way.

Gold flecked black eyes widened at Caspian's arm.

Another set of scars ran parallel along the inside of his arm in neatly aligned rows. Each pink line was a finger's length. Here too his flesh carried the odd copper tinge, shimmering faintly.

Fox swallowed, his heart stuttering, a single beat, then two, then none, his body held upright by will alone as the night spun around him.

This is your destiny, Skye.

Blinking, his mind flashing with the image of dragon teeth, dragon claws, Fox bit back his cry, willing the phantom voice and memories away. He focused on the sheen of water on Caspian's face. Another frigid gust blew by, clearing more of the steam.

Arm raised, the dripping man was standing on the other side of the pillar, just enough to the side that his observer could see the mismatched set of blue eyes. One dark, like burning sapphires. The other a sun-bleached aquamarine. Silver flashed in each as the shadowed planes of his face moved, the lantern behind him making an ethereal halo out of the remaining steam still wafting about.

"It's you," Caspian repeated on another exhale.

And while Fox gaped, the man touched the far side of the pillar.

All at once, Fox understood.

Caspian was speaking to himself.

To his reflection.

Fox's gaze slid past the mumbling man, to one of the bronze mirrors on another pillar. There was still steam in the air, but the fresh night breeze had cleared some of it away. Meaning it was possible to make sense of the reflections on the highly polished surfaces.

The broken hand withdrew, trembling fingertips caressing the wet hair across his flushed forehead. The wandering caress fell to his bare chest, his light touch hesitating over some of the scars.

"What happened?" Caspian rasped. He blinked, eyes straining to focus as his croak increased in volume. "What happened to you? Why do you look like that? No answer, huh? Because you know you must endure until this is done with!"

You must endure, Skye, for the sake of all of us, the black dragon demanded.

Finding it hard to get the air he needed, Fox shook his head, eyes clenched shut for a moment. Thankfully, Caspian was too enthralled with whatever he was seeing to notice the top of Fox's head, his flashing eyes in the shadows only a pace away.

Caspian's parched voice rang out across the water, snapping Fox out of the unwanted memories.

"I may be broken, but have a use! And I will not be discarded!" Caspian announced, his voice breaking into a morbid laugh.

The skin across Fox's back rippled, itching, images of long gone events etched in bright colours, twin to the memories he needed to forget if he wanted a peaceful life. Images that he promised himself would never be forgotten. Black spots danced in his vision, his heart reeling, as Caspian whirled on his heel and staggered towards his bloody clothes, to the iridescent object on top of the pile.

Instead of stopping at the bench, the man collapsed to his knees by the water's edge, rogue streaks of mist parting around him.

Fox swore out loud, but the prostrate figure showed no sign of having heard.

The man's back was worse.

Double that of his front, Caspian's back was more scar tissue than skin. Below that, along his right leg, the calf was covered in a dark patch, winding around, in painful welts of red and purple.

Laughter rang out as Caspian crawled along and plunged his hands into the pool. Bent over, he mucked about, splashing water over his arms, his tortured chest.

Mesmerized with the man's unexpected frivolity, it took a while until Fox realised what he was doing.

Caspian was scrubbing.

At his scars, the copper rash, on both his arms and chest.

Or at least, attempting to.

"Oh," Caspian mumbled with a cracking laugh.

The sound crawled along Fox's skin like splinters of fractured crystal.

Chilled laughter broke over the sound of dying Elves, over the sound of a woman sobbing, crying for souls she'd never known, or have the chance to, while the blue glow of silent crystals watched on, cold, heartless as her captor.

Using the pillar to stay upright, rather than hide behind, Fox sagged against the stone. As his fingers twitched, the stone continued to heat and soften around them. It was a battle to remain grounded in the present and not horrific recollection, as the manic splashing by the dark water's edge slowed.

Then stopped.

"Oh... that's right... they won't come off..." Caspian sighed with a forlorn chuckle.

A chuckle that was instantly followed by a broken sob.

It was all Fox could do to hold himself up as Caspian's head dropped forward. Half laughing, half weeping, with the sound of a wild animal trapped in a snare, he pushed himself about, crawling to the bench.

Trailing fresh puddles of water on the ground, Caspian pulled himself toward the seat. Still kneeling, his broken hand grabbed the top of the blue green chunk of crystal. His other hand groped amongst his clothes. His face, barely seen from the side, was half obscured by wet hair, appeared stricken.

"Oh no," he wailed, his desperate words punctuated with wet sobs. "No, no, no... my ring...!"

Limp, shaking and unable to get the air he craved, Fox stared, transfixed by the man's mania, by his grief.

It was unexpected.

It was familiar.

Giving up on his desperate search, Caspian grabbed his glittering treasure with both hands, sitting back on the wet stone in a slump. A fresh cascade of tears ran down his face, leaking from his reddened eyes. Fox watched, his throat hot, tight, restricting his air intake.

"I was wrong," Caspian whispered, lids falling to close tightly. He hugged the crystal to his chest, rocking back and forth. "It wasn't the deep well of magic from that bastard king, was it?"

A pale hand crept unbidden to slip inside a travel-stained shirt, trembling fingertips brushing up against shards of jagged, green vivianite crystal dangling on cold metal chains. Fox's heart shuddered in time to the man's panicked rocking. Thoughts like golden threads spun out in all directions deep within Fox's crippled soul as he grasped the two shards against his chest.

As the possibilities of that jagged, blue-green chunk of crystal struck like a gong of ill omens in Fox's heart, Caspian stammered on.

"I don't need any other crystal. Now I have you, don't I? It was you, little one, my love, my saviour, here to save all of us..." Oddly coloured blue eyes opened. "Why won't you talk to me? I'm sorry for what they did to you..." He sobbed once, covering the object in his arms with wet, tear stained kisses. "I'm sorry for what they did to me."

You won't be sorry, the black dragon crooned, you will thank me.

Fox shut his eyes, hearing two conversations at once.

Long ago, the insidious voice of Shadow Light, here in the present with a man he should have dragged under the water and torn apart by now. His heart was a frantic muscle tapped behind his ribs, his brain a crazed cyclone of sensation, of remembered pain.

"It's not your fault. Don't be scared. Morgan will make it better. And I'll help you! You can come out and be free..."

Don't be scared, Skye, my wonder.

The freedom we will share will be endless.

"Don't let anyone tell you that you're nothing, to do their bidding," Caspian moaned, his words becoming more unintelligible. "Skye had to deal with that, did you know?"

Eyes almost completely black snapped open, the hand that clutched the tiny shards of pedants withdrawing, the icy fingers sinking deeper into solid stone.

Endless Skye, you will be endless! We will govern all of magic together!

"We can't let that happen again..."

Fox shoved his hands into his dry mouth to stifle his cry, trying to decipher reality from images and voices that threatened to drag him into unconsciousness. However, Fox needed to hear what this man saw as the truth, when under the impression none were watching and judging in the deserted night.

As Fox panted, shivering as the temperature fell, a new movement caught the corner of his eye.

The steaming surface of the once glassy pool was developing ripples, shallow but scintillating waves not caused by the wind.

Shifting his stance, Fox was horrified to detect a faint rumble below, deep in the solid bedrock beneath his boots. His gaze snapped back to the forlorn man by the water's choppy edge, his frigid heart splitting in two at the sight of the physical and emotional pain distorting the man's anguished face.

If Owaen appeared to Fox as an Elf bathed in warm daylight, his brother appeared to be trapped in the shadows of the deepest caves.

Fox bit back a desperate moan of his own, trying to convince his turbulent mind, his frantic heart, that he was here in the now, not trapped once more in a cave of his own hellish past.

"I know you'll find me, Skye," Caspian gasped, "And you will see. It's your destiny to undo all this chaos! Chaos that those fucking bastards caused! I let it go too far... I'm sorry..." He pulled away from the glittering weight, holding it up to eye level, strain apparent on his tear and snot streaked face. "Owaen still would forgive *them*, too! Would he forgive me for fixing their mess? Or their deaths? Ha!"

The laughter once more turned into strangling sobs, tugging at Fox's sanity, his thoughts afire with pain and unspeakable crimes made against himself, and gladly made by others.

"Morgan..." Caspian sniffled, rolling to his side. He ended up half submerged, dangerously close to drowning himself in his current broken state. "Morgan, where are you? I'm coming... are you still there, waiting in Aneirin? Please help me... it hurts... gods, it hurts..."

Heart beating so fast, in a way that no Elf or Human could survive, Fox lurched away, not knowing where he was headed, or if he was heard or seen.

Because the sky was falling.

Or was that the crushing weight of memory?

And the ground was crumbling.

Or was that his desolate heart coming apart?

Either way, he couldn't see.

He couldn't hear, taste or smell.

The only sensations were the fresh, hellish sensations of the earth shifting and buckling beneath his boots as his stumbling shifted into a panicked, terrified run.

PART TWO

Roots

"Many trees and plants are supported by roots that cannot be seen. Unlike Buttresses, most roots are hidden beneath the humus, deep within the soil away from the light.

Whilst also absorbing nutrients and water, the plant is anchored to the earth through this system. A plant or tree without stable roots can therefore be at risk of catastrophe later in its lifecycle."

Taken from 'Plant Lore on the Continent of Beinacoilia' by Hypatia Carter, commissioned for the Library of Seers.

Added underneath in an expressive scrawl:

'My dear wife, I am tempted to make some jest here. But the seriousness of this situation, rumours of our eldest finding some way to syphon magic for himself, leaves me cold and dark like the roots you speak of...

x Illarion'

Underneath lies another note, written with tightly restrained form:

'Husband.

It is not possible and I do not believe it.

Hypatia.'

32

Owaen

Year 367
Baile Fuar

Desolate and bone tired, Owaen stared at the ceiling of the inn's cosy chamber.

"Ah, fuck."

Green eyes like the deep forest, hooded by dark circles, examined old beams of dark wood spanning the ceiling over the bed. An exquisitely warm fire crackled in the hearth, lending interesting shadows to the spaces between the lengths above. Judging by the whorls and knots down their grainy lengths, it appeared the tree had grown up amongst turbulent seasons.

That's how Owaen felt right now.

Solid and dependable, yes.

Supportive to those he cared for despite everything, that too.

Full of scars and deeply ingrained marks that counted each hard won lesson, triumph and loss?

Abso-fucking-lutely.

He had given himself a basic wash, and now reclined on Fox's ridiculous, but admittedly comfortable, mound of pillows and cushions. With his long legs stretched out, the heels of Owaen's clean, bare feet almost hung off the end of the bed. He was dressed in a simple shirt and the cleanest pants he carried with him. The single pillow shoved at him hours ago was held tight to his chest with crossed arms. He nursed it like the thing could provide comfort as his mind lurched. He reached up to rub his thumb across his grizzled jaw.

"Fuck," Owaen repeated to the empty room.

There seemed little else to say.

Aware of his own expansive arrogance, Owaen wondered what else he had inherited from his family.

While washing away layers of dirt and horse, his thoughts had naturally led to the idea that perhaps he could refresh his soul as well. To cleanse his heart from Fox's latest admission, that the brilliant Hypatia and Illarion Carter had caused the death of most of the people Owaen had known. Not only was he dealing with a world that had changed dramatically since his long sleep, he was expected to deal with far too many unwelcome revelations for his stubborn heart to handle.

"Skye, my endless Skye," Owaen murmured gravely to the wooden beams overhead, "what else are you hiding from me?"

It wasn't just the news that had been shared that pained him; it was also the likelihood that his lover held more back. Not so much from dragonish arrogance, although that was certainly part of it, but a kind of wicked protectiveness, too. The kind of protectiveness that had landed Owaen bound inside a cave of glowing quartz, lulled to sleep with a magic fueled by both rage and grief.

Exhaling slowly, Owaen willed his clenched hands to loosen around the pillow.

"What the fuck is going on? The dragons are all but gone, Fox, because you did... whatever you did to them," Owaen muttered. "There is a new fucking king in Aneirin, practically a child at that. My parents are responsible for countless deaths. My brother is on some wild mission with a cowardly fool. What the fuck else is going on?"

Jaw set tight, Owaen shoved the pillow away, aware of how the fine linen had crumpled with messy wrinkles like deep scars.

Troubled green eyes shifted their gaze from the shadowy beams to his bare feet. The blonde Elf wiggled his toes. It was an effort, but Owaen began counting his breath to calm the fuck down. His heart was racing enough that it felt like the bed vibrated with a resonant hum.

"Shit. I should have gone to the baths. My heart is as worn out as my damned boots."

He had stayed behind with reluctance. But it was the first time Owaen had been alone since Fox had admitted what he knew of Hypatia and Illarion Carter.

Pioneers of magic, there was no doubt about it.

But now, one could add 'Destroyers of his beloved homeland, Baile Mara, City of the Sea,' to their accolades.

Pressing his damp hair into the pillow behind his head, Owaen closed his eyes.

Some of his tutors had called his home the 'Black City'. Those same folk had also called the City of the Seers 'The White City'.

Either way, both were gone.

The city of pale stone now dust and rubble in the north, lost to dragons and greed. The city of imposing black rock now ruined, lost to the sea, lost to a fathomless misuse of power.

"I'm sorry," Owaen whispered to the empty room.

Should he be crying?

No.

I feel numb.

The fire hissed with a modest spray of fiery sparks, the earthy spice of scorched wood filling his nose. That was normally an aroma that calmed him. Yet the hitch of his breath, along with the unpleasant thud of his heart, were unwelcome companions to the impatient wait for a refreshed dragon to return, ready to bask in the fire's orange glow.

Wet locks of blonde hair shifted as Owaen turned his head. On the bedside tables on either side of the mattress, a couple of fragrant beeswax candles flickered. Their pleasant smell would always remind him of a home that would never come back. He knew that. He felt that in his bones. But the memories of growing up there receded further into the depths of time. Memories that were being buried under painful layers of new truths come to light.

From the nest of pillows, Owaen frowned. He glanced at the heavily embroidered green and gold curtains across the room's single window.

Was that thunder?

The skies had certainly been threatening to piss down with icy rain, or possibly snow.

Next to his jug of spiced wine, one of the fragrant candles danced wildly for a moment.

Earlier on, after closing the thick drapes, Owaen had hollered from the landing. He had wanted wine and more light. The petite servant who had supplied the candles at his request had long hair wrapped under a red scarf. Owaen had been so tired that he hadn't realised it was fabric instead of crimson hair. Owaen had nearly had a heart attack, thinking that he'd stumbled upon the holder of Caspian's affection, here in the middle of one of the last great towns on the ravaged continent of Beinacoilia.

A distant rumble of thunder mimicked the sporadic beat of his heart.

The servant hadn't been Morgan, thank the bloody gods.

"Where did you go, by the way?" Owaen wondered aloud.

When he was young, she had always been there, calm and aloof when helping with whatever she had been called to do. Morgan had been the opposite of his sometimes overbearing mother, his overexcited father, both of them the centre of attention wherever they went.

Even while assisting them, Morgan had stuck to the corners, pale green eyes watching and observing from her petite, freckled face. She would bring over dusty tomes from the city's library to their estate. The books weren't supposed to leave their building atop the soaring cliffs, but with special dispensation from the royal family, the Carter Estate had held a fair collection of what should have been housed in the official public building.

That special dispensation had saved a decent amount of books when the library had burned down.

Owaen squinted at the wooden mantle above the fire.

How many years ago had it been?

He himself looked like he'd seen thirty or forty winters. It was hard to judge. Magic did that. It played with the body and extended life. Or slowed it down at least. But for him, it seemed to have affected his memory too.

Or was that because there was simply too much for his weary mind to handle?

"Fuck," Owaen hissed through clenched teeth.

He reached up to run a hand through his damp hair. The moisture was flicked off his fingers absentmindedly, the scattered droplets absorbing into the wool rug by the bed without a sound. His thoughts were on the lost books of the library, gone in a moment, victims to one of Caspian's wild tantrums.

The books that had been saved, safe in his parents' collection, had been important works, lifelong studies by a multitude of scientists. Records of experiments, linked to the great magical expansion that Hypatia and Illarion had been working on ever since Owaen could remember.

All the while overlooked by a demure woman of short stature, with flaming red hair and cautious, haunted green eyes.

Eyes that Owaen had caught radiating dazzling affection, just once.

Owaen, about sixteen, had been tending one of Illarion's various collections of hives near the western rose gardens on a crisp morning under clear blue skies.

He had been sitting on lush grass, laying out slices of sweet honey melon under the wicker hives. Hungry bees circled him with insistent humming. Most bees hibernated in the chilly months, but his father's bees were active all year round. But soon enough, the humming was interrupted by a low laugh accompanied by the quiet scuff of a boot on dry gravel.

Wondering if Caspian was about to sneak up on him, Owaen had looked up. Peering suspiciously through the thorny depths of pruned back roses, Owaen had indeed caught sight of his twin.

Caspian, lips swollen, was swaggering towards one of the estate's side entrances. Beyond his smirking brother, the younger twin had caught sight of a petite woman. Struck by a vision of unexpected beauty, Owaen hadn't realised who it was at first.

Leaning back against a wall built of rounded stones, Morgan was smiling. It was the first time Owaen had seen that expression on her face. After watching Caspian walk away, the librarian turned without a sound. With a flash of flaming red hair flowing loose over a green wool cloak, she disappeared through an arch framed by neatly clipped ivy.

Amazed, Owaen's unblinking gaze slid back to a slightly rumpled Caspian, just passing the hives along the gravel path.

Owaen sunk down abruptly into the grass with bees crawling over sticky hands, and held his breath. The crunch of boot heels paused on the other side of the clusters of rose bushes Owaen crouched beside. But after a moment, nothing happened, and Owaen rose to his knees.

Twinkling blue eyes flashed with wicked silver between the thorny stems in front of Owaen's face.

"You perv," Caspian announced with a dazzling grin.

Startled, Owaen fell back with a curse. He landed on his arse amongst slices of melon and annoyed bees. While he batted away the buzzing insects, the sound of a languid laugh resounded down the path.

Alone in the inn, Owaen stared at his hand. The faint sheen of dampness from his wet hair coated the callouses, highlighting the lines and whorls across his palm. Despite his meagre spark of magic, a mere sparrow's fart compared to Fox's well of power, Owaen would use whatever strength he had to protect his lover.

In the same way that Caspian would for Morgan.

With a groan, Owaen sat up, licking away a remnant of the spiced wine from his bottom lip. He glanced at the door, his gaze sliding to the decoratively dressed curtains with an impatient glare.

What was taking Fox so damned long?

Wasn't the reason they were in an inn with a bed, complete with a mountain of pillows, was so they could fuck? Without bruising his lover's bony —

A severe burst of thunder, intense in volume, cracked directly overhead.

Somewhat stunned, Owaen blinked, but kept his emerald gaze fixed on the curtains. More specifically, the top of them, to the gap between the wall. There had been no flash of white light preceding the violent rumble.

As another barrage of thunder split the night, even more intense than the first, Owaen swung his legs over the side of the bed. Bare feet touched the floor.

An ominous tremble reverberated through stone and wood.

"Fuck," Owaen breathed, his mouth drying.

He stood up.

Right as the inn jerked with a violence that had him staggering sideways.

Reaching for the wall, Owaen grabbed the clay jug of wine as the room shuddered again, the window rattling and the door shuddering. Alarmed voices could be heard from the streets outside, as the city woke to the series of violent tremors hitting the town as it settled for the night.

Owaen grimaced as his ears popped. The air pressure was changing, the temperature dropping. As the building trembled once more, he staggered to the door, the scent of ozone thick in his nose. Before opening it, Owaen glanced at the jug. To the sound of thunder increasing to a painful volume above, dust raining down from the ceiling, he drained it. Fighting for balance, he set the jug on the floor, then braced himself.

He opened the door with a jerk.

The hallway was dim, almost empty. Owaen's gaze dropped to his feet.

A dark shape huddled on the floor like a cowering child, white hands pressed to its ears, trembling fingers twisted in ebony hair.

The air left Owaen's lungs in a rush.

"Skye!"

The hulking blonde Elf dropped to his knees and rolled Fox over. Owaen cursed.

The man's face was a mask of terror, lids shut tight, mouth a wordless scream.

"Fuck! What happened?" Owaen roared. "Skye!"

As the world outside trembled, he gathered the limp figure to his heaving chest with trembling arms. Owaen gripped his lover's chin, looking for wounds, for anything. Far beyond its usual cool smoothness, Fox's skin was like slick ice. He hadn't appeared to have made it to the mineral pools to wash. He still carried the aroma of travel sweat, his clothes the same combination of travel-worn black shirt and stained leather pants.

"Fox!" Owaen pleaded desperately, his gaze bouncing around the grimacing face before him. "Talk to me!"

Eyes of the deepest black snapped open. No fleck of shining gold sparkled within their hollow depths. Pale lips struggled to form words.

"Owaen," Fox gasped. "I…"

"What! What is it?"

Fox's lids fluttered closed, lines forming on his normally smooth forehead. Icy fingers clutched at Owaen's arms with bruising force.

"Can't… it hurts… help me…. the egg… can't…"

"Skye! What are you saying? Please!"

"Owaen," Fox wheezed. His haunted eyes flicked open, wild, crazed.

"Skye!"

"...can't breathe..."

Fox's eyes rolled back into his head as he convulsed in Owaen's arms.

Not sure how he managed it while panicking, Owaen dragged Fox to the fire and stripped them both down of their clothes. He'd hooked a foot around a log and kicked it into the hearth, using a wildly aimed spark of his magic to ignite it straight away.

Fox was still convulsing with great shudders, his body temperature as cold as Owaen had ever felt it.

Owaen reached behind himself, searching blindly for the blankets on the bed, snarling until one stray corner was caught in his wildly grasping fist. With no finesse, he threw it over his own shoulders, gathering Fox to the length of him, heating the man from the fire in front and his own body heat behind.

Inhaling, closing his eyes to the tortured expression of the one he loved, Owaen slowed his breathing. Concentrating on each inhale and exhale, he searched for the connection that bound them in ways beyond his understanding. It took a moment, but... there it was.

In his mind, it appeared as a faint gold thread.

Catching sight of it between his eyes, in his mind, or nowhere at all, he couldn't say, Owaen imagined it thickening, the twist of gold braid becoming more elaborate. Knots forming, tightening, securing them together.

Knowing and not knowing what he was doing, Owaen held with a desperation that scared him to the shuddering figure in his arms.

All the while, as his magic coiled about them both, Owaen whispered, his breath misting between them as thunder boomed beyond the window and the floor rumbled beneath. Quietly, calmly, not allowing a hint of the panic in his heart to reach the ears next to his lips, he rambled on.

"Fox, my love, I'm here, it's Owaen," he murmured, hating the thumping behind his ribs, lest its crazed rhythm panic Fox further. "I'm here, my love, I'm here."

Kissing the man's forehead, Owaen nearly sobbed aloud. Fox's forehead was now clammy, rather than the winter's ache of earlier.

"That's right," Owaen soothed, lips bruising the feverish flesh. "Come back to me, beautiful creature, come back..."

Unable to bear the sight of Fox's tortured expression, Owaen closed his eyes.

"I love you," he mumbled. "I love you. I love you now, I loved you then, from atop that tower when you arrived, covered in gems with the sun shining on the world as it never shone before. Even then, I loved you…" Owaen choked back his sob. "I love you. Come back to me. You're safe, you're safe here, you're safe here in my arms…"

A pitiful moan reached Owaen's ears and his eyes flicked open, his deep green gaze searching Fox's face. The man's convulsing, the jerking of his hands and feet, was slowing, and the room's low hum of trembling earth far below eased.

More sweat beaded along the expanse of skin pressed against Owaen's.

"That's it!" Owaen sobbed, unable to hold back his tears. "That's it, my love. I'm right here."

Eyelids so pale they were a faint blue twitched, and long black lashes fluttered.

"Oh fuck," Owaen hissed, squeezing Fox so hard that a normal man might have fought him off. "Come on baby, wake up. Please wake up."

A tiny slit of black, peppered by a few sparks of gold, appeared.

"My love, yes my love, come back, come back to me," Owaen urged, holding Fox in his arms, holding the gold thread in his mind, sending what he could along the bond that held them intertwined.

With a heaving, final shudder, the convulsions stopped.

As the temperature of the room rose a fraction, Fox went limp.

Outside, the roar of thunder quietened, the ground stilled.

Not daring to move, Owaen counted to ten, feeling his heart race, waiting for another convulsion to start.

Fox shifted in his arms with a croaking groan.

All was still.

"Oh, thank fuck," Owaen sighed, sniffling. Straining his neck, he wiped his nose on one shoulder.

Concentrating on building the cocoon of warmth around them, Owaen stayed where he was, wrapped about Fox, instinctively pressing as much as he could of his heat and his magic into Fox as was possible.

Daring to move a little, Owaen leaned over, pressing his lips to Fox's, and exhaled.

Occasionally, he broke their kiss, inhaling softly, then resuming his measured breath into Fox's chilled lungs. There was no passion in the embrace, no wild fire that this creature normally invoked within him. The panic that Owaen was drowning in was receding a little like a lazy tide, but the fear remained.

Cursing inwardly, Owaen drew back, chewing the inside of his cheek.

"What happened?" Owaen whispered to the unconscious creature in his embrace. "Where did you go?"

Despite the man's flashy arrogance, Fox was obviously more affected by everything that he'd been through, much more than he had shared. The horrific tattoo across Fox's back was clearly a manifestation of the murky undercurrent deep within his soul. With the ego of a dragon, the creature would likely continue to react to disturbing events with an unbridled unwinding of his near-endless source of potential, a deep well of magic that was the backbone of his power.

A woman's shout echoed up the stairs beyond the door in the hall, and Owaen flinched.

Yet as he listened, he realised it was more of a relieved laugh than a yell. In the street, voices called, but the alarm was gone as the locals inspected the quarry town for damage.

"Owaen…"

Snapping his gaze from the door, Owaen peered down.

Fox stared back, his eyes still slightly wild. His gaze was back to its normal glittering gold and black.

"Skye!" Owaen cried.

Fox shifted weakly, and Owaen released his grip.

But not by much.

The man was trembling sporadically, and shivering could be felt down the length of him.

"Hush my love," Owaen soothed, hating the fact that his lover was too weak to protest at his use of Fox's previous name. "I'm here, it's okay. You're okay."

With a frustrated wince, Fox reached up to weave limp fingers into Owaen's sweat-slicked hair, as if he was checking Owaen was there, and that he was alright.

"I'm here, I'm safe, you're safe," Owaen murmured, dropping his forehead to Fox's. "I thought you were gonna bring this quarry down, my love —"

"Shut," Fox gasped, "…up."

Lifting his head, Owaen blinked.

"What?"

"Your b-brother…" Fox wheezed, his intense gaze searching Owaen's face from under furrowed brows.

"Caspian?" Owaen mumbled. "What about him?"

Fox's teeth were chattering now, but he forged on.

"I s-saw…"

Something unpleasant licked along Owaen's spine, similar to Fox's chilled fingertips against his scalp.

"You saw… what?" Owaen said carefully.

The frigid fingers slid out of Owaen's hair, past his ear to press into his cheek. An unreadable black and gold gaze roamed around his face. Both the chilled hand and scorching gaze held Owaen in place.

Even if he had wanted, he couldn't move for the strength in the hand that held him and the fear in his heart.

Fuck.

Fox wasn't checking to see if Owaen was alright. Instead, black irises with their golden stars studied the features of his face with untamed intensity.

As if comparing his face to another.

Which meant that —

"Owaen. Is Caspian a victim," Fox whispered, desolation veiling his parched voice, "just like me?"

33

Fox

Year 367
Baile Fuar

"Where is he?" Owaen rasped.

Unwilling to answer, Fox rested the back of his head against the stones behind.

Black eyes, burning with gold sparks, eyed the room. Most of it, including the heavy pieces of furniture, were intact. But the smaller pieces, the tables, candles, and a few decorations, were gone. A rogue feather drifted past his face.

Newly dressed, Fox stood against the wall beside the bed, gazing down the length of his nose at the assortment of shards and shredded fabric at his feet. Most of it had been kicked into a rough pile, the destroyed remnants of his untested mound of pillows, smashed pieces of wine cups and their jug.

"Where is he?" Owaen repeated with a hiss, struggling against his bonds from the bed.

The mattress was still in one piece, thank the gods.

With an expansive sigh, Fox padded barefoot to the bed and examined the Elf who held his heart.

Owaen had strong brows over dark green eyes, along with a square jaw that appeared brutish depending on his expression. He was marginally taller than Fox. He was broader about the shoulders, with far more muscle over the length of his limbs, a hefty strength contained within his solid frame. Yet when it came to his lover, Owaen's calloused hands contained a tenderness that effortlessly illuminated the darkest parts of Fox's restless soul.

Caspian had appeared to be the same height as his twin. But where Owaen was broad, it seemed his older brother was slimmer, his muscles longer and leaner.

"I've paid the innkeeper for the room," Fox murmured as his gaze roamed, "and a new pair of pants."

Owaen had been straining against the ripped bed sheet that held wrists and ankles together behind his back. They had been secured with a spark of Fox's magic. Owaen likely knew this. Yet he had still fought against his makeshift shackles. Still huffing from his mania just moments ago, dark green eyes narrowed on Fox and his struggling paused.

"What?" Owaen hissed, confusion marring his handsome features.

Raven black hair rippled as Fox tilted his head, his tone mild.

"I think the innkeeper shit hers at the sounds from inside this room just now."

Owaen blinked rapidly.

"I..." he began, then stopped. A pink flush crept along grizzled cheeks.

Anger or shame, perhaps both.

With careful movements, Fox sank to his knees beside the bed. He reached over Owaen's side, intending to loosen the Elf's binding. But Owaen shook his head, his blonde hair a tangled mess around his flushed face. Fox's pale hand halted midair above Owaen's hip.

"Don't," Owaen warned, lids shutting tight. A purple vein pulsed at his clammy temple. When he opened his eyes a few heartbeats later, his eyes were unsettlingly caustic. "I think I may need to just lie here for a while longer."

Dropping his hand to wipe a stray lock of hair off Owaen's forehead, Fox nodded solemnly.

It was still somewhat difficult to form words. Images and conversations whirled about his mind, almost audible whispers. Colours and shapes flashed behind his dark-circled eyes, scales, wings, scars.

"Did he..." Owaen whispered, his gaze fixed on Fox's face, "did he hurt you?"

As Fox shook his head, just once, a single tear slid from the corner of Owaen's eye to soak the loose feathers under his cheek.

"You have anger issues," Fox said. He immediately wished he hadn't.

The bark of Owaen's sarcastic laugh broke the tension. Bloodshot, damp, and slowly calming green eyes pulsed with intense emotion.

"Fox, my love," the bound Elf snickered from amongst the ruins of ripped sheets and torn up pillows, "you are one to talk."

Closing his eyes, Fox willed his scowl to smooth over, even as his mind filled with the roars of pain and fear as dragons were ripped from their wings, memories of his time amongst the hot black sands of his northern homeland.

Opening his gaze to the fireplace, where the last few embers pulsed with orange and deep red, he sighed, a quiet exhale compared to Owaen's ragged breaths. Outside, voices still called to one another, the occasional lantern from street level illuminating the ripped holes in the curtains. Hoping the horses were secure, Fox's cool gaze slid to the figure on the bed before him. Owaen's expression, amongst the rage, fear and confusion, could also be described as somewhat peevish.

"I cannot deny it," Fox allowed.

He refused to decipher Owaen's waspish mutter.

Taking a deep breath, Fox reached into his shirt. Left on the bed earlier, one sleeve had been torn free in the struggle to subdue Owaen from his wild mania. It was a mania born of protection for Fox, which Fox knew. But that was exactly why he had locked up Owaen all those years ago. Because the stupid oaf would have taken on the entire dragon race on Fox's behalf.

A white hand withdrew two small, green shards of crystal, each hanging on a metal chain. The gold and amethyst ring had been strung with shaking, chilled fingers onto one of the slinky lengths. Fox held up both chains. Just enough light from the fading glow in the hearth washed their uneven facets with curious sparks.

"There is something wrong with your brother," Fox said quietly.

"Something's wrong with Caspian?" Owaen yelled with a suddenness that had Fox flinch. Owaen blinked up at Fox from what was surely a painful position. "Are you serious? Tell me what the fuck is *right* with that fucking lunatic!"

Fox bit the inside of his cheek, holding the shards above Owaen's face.

Catching sight of them dangling above his face, Owaen's lashes fluttered with confusion. The crystals caught the low light with innocent flashes. They were relics of power used by an aggrieved queen, desperate to keep in contact with a loyal follower who Fox counted as one of only a few he loved.

Loved ones that needed protection from creatures like Fox.

Creatures who did what they wanted, at the cost to others.

Fox shivered, the scars across Caspian's body reminiscent of the scar tissue that enclosed his own undeserving heart.

"Tell me what happened, Fox," Owaen demanded, his voice sounding more like its normal smokey rumble. He cleared his throat. "Please."

His mind half in the past, half in the present, Fox let the pieces of snatched conversations from dragon elders come together amongst the memories echoing through time and his heart.

"It's worse than you can imagine," Fox murmured.

"What?" Green eyes darted back and forth between Fox's unblinking gaze.

"When you grew up, do you remember any unusual crystals?" Fox asked. He licked his dry lips.

"There were many." Owaen stared at him. "Why?"

"Do you remember your parents' experiments?"

"Huh?"

"Did you see them with a large crystal, like this colour, but more sapphire blue?" Fox lowered the shards and green sparks washed Owaen's flushed face with striking patterns. "About the size of a person's head?"

Owaen blinked, licking his own parched lips. He appeared to be thinking as he examined the crystals dangling above his face on their simple metal chains. When his eyes moved to Fox's face and then darted away, Fox knew.

He didn't need to see Owaen's reluctant nod, but the confirmation was validating. In a supremely fucked up way.

Sinking back to sit on his heels, Fox dropped the chains with their crystal shards and golden ring to the bed. He used both hands to brush more strands of blonde hair from Owaen's forehead.

"There were many odd things in Mother's study. But I remember them talking..." Owaen's throat strained as he swallowed.

"About hatching something?" Fox finished for him.

Turning back to Fox, Owaen stared at him.

Neither of them moved.

"Owaen," Fox murmured cautiously, "do you remember that there might have been more than one of them?" An ember cracked apart in the stone hearth at the side of the bed as Fox paused. "That perhaps there were ...two?"

"Two..." Owaen choked out, his voice breaking.

"Two eggs," Fox finished for him.

Trembling a little, it was Fox's turn to gather Owaen to himself. The hulking blonde Elf, bound and helpless, went limp, the fight gone at the scope of his parents' dark experiments.

"There were two eggs," Fox breathed against Owaen's fevered flesh, cool lips murmuring against cheeks slick with fresh tears. Silent sobs shook Owaen's body as Fox held him.

Strangely, the moment reminded Fox of Rhydian's mother. Of the young woman she might have been, had magic and greed not muddied the waters of her heart.

It's over, he'd said to her.

Then he'd fought with her, magic against magic, will against will. Both of them had died. Yet somehow Fox had come back, a cloud of particles, like crystal dust on a warm breeze, amongst trees so vast it was impossible not to think they had helped in some way.

Yet who or what could help him navigate this chaos now?

The simple answer was that there was no one. There were none left that could be trusted with the almost limitless possibilities that came with power. When there should have been temperance and wisdom instead.

As Fox fought acrid memories of the past to focus on the present, the image of the glittering, jagged chunk of crystal in Caspian's strangely discoloured arms rose to the forefront of his mind.

What kind of creature are you? Fox whispered against Owaen's damp flesh without a sound.

And how can I make sure you never encounter what I have?

There was only one way, of course.

I'm sorry.

But there is simply no hope for you.

34

Cas

Year 256, Cas at age 15
Baile Mara

“I must not accidentally expose myself at noontime prayer,” the wounded youth mumbled from the bed that was not his own. “I must not...”

A quiet laugh startled the figure out of feverish mutterings into semi consciousness.

Mismatched blue eyes opened haltingly, the blonde lashes gummed shut with dried salt, flushed lids coming apart with reluctance.

Cas gagged at the acrid taste in his mouth whilst blinking away the last vestiges of chaotic dreams. Echoes lingered, however. A whirling saga of malicious catcalls. Something about a blue-white pearl in the black sands of his favourite beach. A forlorn cry for help, with a pain like nothing he had experienced before. The chaos was accompanied by a frantic buzzing, along with the regal scent of damp roses in glorious colours.

Vaguely aware of his left hand clenched into a tight fist, Cas realised most of his body didn’t seem to want to obey any commands his brain gave it. Able to move his head only a little, Cas glanced about.

He stilled abruptly.

A sweat soaked tuft of blonde hair had fallen across his forehead, but it was gently smoothed away by a delicate hand. Accompanied by the faint perfume of citrus tea and sweet wine, it was a hand that also carried the scent of fresh ink.

Cas leant into the touch, his heart singing despite his current predicament. Not ready to face the petite figure seated next to him, lest they see the fever that burned not in his blood but deep within his fucked up gaze, Cas shifted his eyes to the room.

It was a small, spare chamber. There was barely enough room for the modest waist-high wooden chest and bedside stool, let alone the short bed Cas lay in.

He waggled his feet with a hiss as his swollen skin stretched. Despite the pain, it amused him that they dangled off the edge of the mattress. Yes, the bed was short, but his limbs and feet seemed to grow more every day. Spoilt by growing up in a sprawling estate of lush gardens and seemingly endless rooms filled with rich furnishings, this was the crudest place he had been in. Rook's establishments included. It was a foreign room, but the faint scent of parchment, ink and beeswax candles were exquisitely precious to him.

For all the dozen conscious heartbeats that Cas had spent here, he knew whose touch lingered on the feverish flesh of his cheek. So this bare and unlikely room became his favourite place in an instant.

He resisted the sublime urge to turn his head, but swollen and split lips curled up at the corners.

Still avoiding her gaze, Cas squinted at the wall opposite the bed. A scatter of bronze plaques adorned the pale plaster that covered the black stone beneath. Each plaque was a square or rectangle, made of what looked like thin sheets of metal pressed together of different sizes, framed in wood. The edges of each metal layer differed, and the lines made shapes. Some of which Cas recognised. Indeed, the central plaque was a map of Baile Mara, known by its deep, curving bay and island offshore.

Intrigued but saving further inspection for when he could rise, Cas glanced at the single window, not yet daring himself to meet the steady gaze of the one by his side.

There was no glass in the frame. A curtain of heavy white linen was pulled mostly closed and the blue sky seen through the gap showed it was late afternoon. A sliver of sunlight lazed its way across a faded carpet, all the way to the top of a bare staircase leading to the floor below. It wasn't bright, but it stung his eyes.

With a wince, Cas looked down the length of his body. He was completely covered by linen bandages that stank of pungent, antiseptic honey. Underneath them, he was naked.

Heh.

Finally, Cas faced her, breath hitching at her proximity. From between two crimson waves of long, loose hair, pale green eyes observed him coolly.

"Did you see it?" Cas mumbled through swollen lips.

On the bedside stool, Morgan stirred, hair rippling with a copper sheen across the green linen of her dress.

"Is that a no?" Cas urged.

With a grimace, he struggled to raise a limp finger, but he managed. Ignoring the angry pink and white circles over the sliver of flesh peeping through the bandages over the back of his hand, Cas pointed at the strips of linen over his groin.

"Don't move," Morgan eventually murmured, eyes narrowing. She sighed. "But yes, I did."

"Are there any scars there? Is it safe?"

Morgan's gaze was indecipherable. "You weren't stung there. You won't have scars." She paused, pale green eyes intense on his face. "I can't say the same for your back."

Unperturbed, Cas waved his hand, ignoring the agony of skin healing over tight flesh, thanks to whatever she had done for the countless wounds.

"And?" Cas demanded, blonde eyebrows arching, the shiny skin of his face tingling under cheeks flushed pink.

The diminutive woman by his side considered what to say in silence. Cas was pleased to think that she might have been speechless. However, after a moment, freckled cheeks twitched as she bit back a private smile. That restrained expression was to him brighter than any bashful smile by all of Baile Mara's ladies put together.

"And?" Cas repeated with a smirk, ignoring the stinging twinge in his cheeks.

"*And,*" Morgan replied with a pointed glance at his crotch, "I'm happy for you."

"And for you," Cas declared instantly, his tone tranquil despite the audacity of his statement.

"No," Morgan replied as she leant forward, red hair rippling and catching the sliver of light that lit the small chamber.

A pair of blue eyes, one light, one dark, sparkled with unblinking silver at the precious pale green gaze so close to his.

"One day, yes," Cas announced with certainty. His left hand unclenched and he glanced at his palm. He'd been holding on to a single bee, how he wasn't sure.

From his hair, perhaps? Cas struggled but held his palm close to his painful lips in order to blow the crushed insect, twisted bits of wings, legs, and thorax, away.

Watching calmly, Morgan slid a steady fingertip down Cas's splotchy cheek and pressed it into the largest bee sting until he hissed.

She smiled. "Never."

"*I must not accidentally expose myself at noontime prayer?*"

Wane straightened from leaning over his brother's shoulder, reading out loud as the fresh ink dried.

"Really, Cassie?"

At the desk, Cas placed his quill neatly back into its little onyx tray. He arched back, arms rising above his head in a languid stretch.

"No," Cas answered leisurely. "Of course not."

Wane pointed at the parchment where the same sentence was written over and over.

"You sure about that?"

"Are you blushing, Waney?" Cas teased as his hands fell back to the table. At Wane's horrified stare, he laughed. "Don't worry, the priestesses loved it," Cas assured his brother. "It gave them a much needed thrill."

Wane swallowed. "I highly doubt it." Deep green eyes narrowed. "It's because last time Morgan was here, she said to Father that the priests and priestesses are ridiculous, isn't it?"

"Maybe." Cas shrugged. "Dunno."

There was no point in admitting Wane was right. His brother didn't understand Cas' fascination with Morgan.

Which was fine.

Neither did Cas.

All that mattered was that *she* mattered.

She always had, and always would.

With a yawn, Cas pushed back from the desk and cracked out the kinks in his spine as he stood.

He had been in the study that he shared with his brother for hours. It was a large chamber with multiple windows, down the hall from their bed chambers on an upper floor. It was an elongated room with a fireplace at either end. Both were unlit, the fresh sea air flowing in through an open window at a nice enough temperature. Multiple desks of ornately patterned wood took up various positions to catch the best light at different times of the day. Lush armchairs were scattered between the shelves that lined the bottom half of every available wall.

Only half of them bore books and scrolls. The remaining shelves were crammed with odd pieces Cas had collected from the town markets and his favourite stretches of shoreline, plus an assortment of old-fashioned weapons and armour from the town blacksmiths. Wane filled some of them with models he had made of blocks of soft wood and plaster, dioramas of forests and temples built to scale.

Feeling peckish, Cas was about to head down to the kitchen for a post breakfast snack, when he halted. He turned back. Wane lingered by the desk with Cas' literary punishment, an ominous expression marring his handsome face.

"Did you want me?" Cas asked with a slight tilt of his head.

"Not quite." Wane bit his lip. "I came to warn you."

Interest piqued, Cas faced him fully from the arched doorway. "Ooh, what now? Rook's new whores have their tits back out down at the wharf to mock the latest pirates?"

"Huh?" Wane choked out, clearly affronted. "No —"

"Wait, wait, don't tell me." Cas pretended to think while Wane stared at him. One hand cupped his chin, the other pointing at Wane. "You found a precious girl to finally let you lift her skirts and I am to stay away when there's a stocking on your door?"

"What!" His brother's indignant splutter rose in pitch.

"Wait! I've got it, I've got it! You finally grew a hair on your co —"

"Caspian Carter! Shut your mouth right now! Or I'll..." Wane's roar faded at the twinkle in his brother's oddly coloured eyes. "You little shit."

"Heh," Cas said with a smirk, pleased to see Wane so riled up.

"Oh my gods," Owaen hissed. He pinched the bridge of his nose, eyes closed for a moment. "Just shut up, will you?"

The seriousness of his younger brother's voice had Cas stepping back into the study.

"What?" Cas' polished boots clicked on the smooth marble as he strode back to his brother. "Are you okay?" He grabbed Wane's arms with both hands. "Did someone do something to you —"

Wane's blonde hair was worn longer than Cas', the ends brushing his shoulders as he shook his head.

"Not me, you twit! Not me. *You.*"

Cas blinked at him, one corner of his top lip twisted.

"Huh?"

Wane lowered his voice.

"The Short Cut gang," he muttered, naming the bullies that had plagued Cas with insults, and sometimes worse, since they were little. "I heard them talking while taking a walk with Rhiannon —"

"Ah, so you *did* get a maiden to lift her skirts —"

With a growl of frustration, Wane shook his arms free. In the same movement, he backed Cas into the closest wall with one hand, the other slapping over Cas' mouth.

"Shut up and listen."

Cas nodded, eyes innocently wide.

Then he licked Owaen's palm.

"By the gods!" Owaen roared as he tackled Cas around the waist.

They collapsed in a heap of fists and limbs as they rolled across the lush carpet towards the centre of the room. Cas pummeled Owaen with strategically aimed jabs, while Owaen tried to use his brute strength to pin him down. Despite being stronger, he never let Cas win out of pity, which Cas appreciated.

After a mock fight that had landed a few not-so-fake hits, they lay panting on their backs side by side. Most of their fight had been contained to the thick rug, not the marble floor, and dust motes danced above the pair of tousled blonde heads.

Cas laughed at the fresh bruises blooming over his ribs while staring at the richly painted murals of wild beasts and shimmering dragons grappling on the ceiling.

Eventually, Owaen sighed.

"I meant it, Cassie," he said, serious once more. He rolled his head to examine Cas' profile. "They're planning something big this time, just for you. Ever since you evaded their tar and feather trap last harvesttime."

"If they want to play wicked games," Cas speculated aloud, "they'll win a delightful prize."

"This isn't a game," Owaen protested.

Cas shifted his gaze from the frescoes above to the wall of windows facing the sea. One couldn't see the horizon from the floor, just endless blue with a single wisp of white cloud, defiantly ruining the perfect sky as it soared past on brisk winds.

"Let them come," Cas said without fear. "I'm ready."

With the fickle clarity of fresh hindsight, it was obvious that Cas hadn't been ready at all.

As he was dragged along by bound wrists, a sack over his face, both heels catching on the gravel path, Cas was in sound enough mind to ponder the inflated egos of young men. Including himself and the pack of bullies that pulled him along to their whoops of triumph.

After Wane's warning that he should lie low for a while, Cas had done the opposite. After finishing up his thousand lines of punishment, he had raced off alone, ready to spy on those that dared to torment him and his brother. He had planned to slink down the backstreets where the gang dwelt, streets that Cas and Wane used when they were little to cut through the terraced streets. Hence the nickname of the spiteful kids.

But while Cas hadn't been ready at all, they had.

Trespassing where Cas had least expected, the clever little shits were waiting in the pleasant, sprawling parklands of the Carter Estate.

Cursing at his own inadequacy, Cas squinted through the cloth. It was a rough, itchy burlap, smelling of tar and chicken shit. An odd, humming sound was getting louder above the sound of the wind and jeers of half a dozen young men, and at least one girl. He laughed to himself despite the bruise on his jaw. He'd knocked one or two of them out cold before the others jumped him all at once, not even bothering to use their sparks of magic.

Cas' heart sank at that thought, and also at the odd noise as he realised what the humming sound was.

They were dragging him to some of Father's hives.

If plants and crystals were Hypatia's love, Illarion's pride and joy were his bees. Cas had no way of knowing which group of the countless hives they had dragged him to. None of them were ideal.

As he swore out loud, someone kicked him in the ribs. His own boot kicked out automatically, and it felt like it connected with someone's shin. The answering curse and slap to the side of his head was confirmation enough. Soon after, he was thrown to the ground. The buzzing drowned out the sigh of the parkland's many towering oaks and pines as the wind blew about them.

The nervous laugh of a girl met his ears as figures approached him on all sides, and multiple hands grabbed him all at once.

Cas was stripped, his well-made clothes ripped and torn away. Even his boots were pulled off. A hit of a wildly kicking foot almost broke it, as he scored a hit on what he hoped by the loud crack, and subsequent feminine wailing, was a nose.

"I'll get you back for this," Cas hissed vehemently, eyes shut tight against the indignity as his foot throbbed.

"Ha! Go on! I'd love to see you try!" a boy laughed, cruelty lacing his excited voice.

"Get his underwear!" shouted another.

The girl shrieked with fury. "Leave it to me —"

Cas kicked out again.

A feminine howl sung in his ears when he connected with something soft.

Unfortunately, that earned him a blow to the back of his head as a new scent reached his nose through the stinking cloth. It was smoke.

"Freak!"

"Loser!"

"Magic repellant snob!"

As Cas rolled over with his bound hands raised up and protecting his head as best as he could manage, the barrage of blows ceased. But before he could push up to his knees, he was held in place. A little sound, like the soft *snick* of a glass jar opening, punctuated the breathless laughs. Something cold, thick, and viscous was smeared over his back, and over the linen of his underwear that they hadn't managed to strip.

Under the hessian, Cas' face became an unseen mask of horror, his body rippling with a violent shudder as the seriousness of the situation dawned on him at last. Gasping, Cas fought for air as his heart began hammering in a panicked rhythm.

"I'm going to kill you fuckers —"

Without warning, the sack was yanked off his head, Cas was pulled to his bare feet, and let go with a vicious shove.

He stumbled, but stayed upright. As Cas' eyes adjusted to the sudden influx of light, he spotted two others, the eldest boys with golden hair, tossing a pair of merrily flaming branches into the closest hives. The wicker didn't catch immediately, but the smoke plumed thick and densely. The sudden increase in the volume of furious buzzing was a roar. Cas swore as his heart just about burst through his chest. He turned to run.

The girl was ready. She landed a painful kick to Cas' stomach.

Cas, smothered in his father's honey, was launched backwards into the closest hive of frantic bees.

Oh, no, Cas had time to think, as the bees closed in with thousands of stingers ready to defend the attack.

He closed his eyes, unaware that the ground was trembling.

Oh, fuck —

How he made it to his mother's study, Cas wasn't sure.

The massive house was usually populated by bustling servants, but the Carter Estate was oddly deserted. The aroma of honey and salt permeated the air, but under the salt breeze, the sour stink of ozone bit at Cas' senses. Whilst trying to discern what the fuck was going on, through swelling eyes, he'd spotted a crowd of people rushing down the estate's long drive. By both horse and foot, servants dashed off, armed with bundles and baskets. Their voices sounded frantic, but the pounding ache in each ear had obscured their distant words as they hurried. Cas had called out with a pitiful rasp for help, but none had heard.

By the time Cas reached the closed door of the study, his mouth had just about stopped working. His swelling hands failed to hold the iron latch. A low moan escaped his throat.

Over the rush of blood pounding in his ears, raised, angry voices accompanied by the shrill whine of a panicked animal came from the other side of the door. Cas hesitated, his bloody, weeping fist in midair.

The argument halted and impatient footsteps sounded. The animal's cry was quickly cut off.

Resting his throbbing forehead against the solid wood, Cas swallowed his pride and knocked, wincing as tiny wounds burst open from the impact. There was some scuffling, a curse, but eventually Illarion's voice called out, coming closer to the door.

"What is it?"

"F-father..." Cas wheezed. "Help... me..."

The door stayed shut, his parents' argument continuing.

"You can't be sure it was us," Hypatia hissed. "Ignore the door. Listen to me —"

"I am listening," Illarion replied, his voice firm. "But how can the collapse be a simple coincidence? The timing is too uncanny."

Cas gave another weak knock, eyes shut tight as the venom from countless stings spread through his shaking, sweating body. By the itching of his pained scalp, a few bees might even still be alive.

Hypatia continued. "We have crossed so many stages, surely some birthing pangs are expected. This is a long process. We knew that."

"Pangs? Half the old piers collapsed below the waterline, along with their warehouses." Hypatia swore.

"Husband. Don't get me wrong, I will not cease this work. But I do not want those Elphin royals poking their shiny little noses around here, telling us to back off. We will admit nothing of what caused the chaos today."

"Hypatia! Didn't you hear the message? Whole warehouses collapsed! They are digging people out of the rubble. Who knows how many drowned?"

The sound of a disdainful scoff had Cas scrunching his fevered nose.

"That volatile island out there has always created hazards, both with gas and undersea tremors," Hypatia said caustically. "And the pier was overloaded by the crowds. A crumbling city is not our fault, and the blame can easily be placed on these factors."

Illarion's sigh was long and drawn out. It sounded like he was moving away from the door. Their conversation continued, too low for Cas to make out. Reeking of honey, ash and blood too, he knocked a third time, ignoring the panic rising in his guts at the crawling sensation in his soiled, sticky hair.

"Mother..." Gritting his teeth, Cas raised his voice. "P-please... the d-door..."

"Not now, Caspian," Hypatia snapped.

"Not n-now...?" Cas whispered, incredulous. "W-when..."

He stared at the wood, concentrating on getting air into his lungs, and waited.

The door remained locked, those within giving no thought to beyond it.

Pushing away with a sickening lurch, Cas swallowed his sob. Instead, he called weakly for Wane. There was no answer from the empty hall, nor from the grand set of stairs rising to the floors above. The sob Cas had bitten back threatened to burst forth as a hysterical wail.

It was hard to shit without a servant passing by, so where the fuck was everyone today of all days?

Stumbling with feet that were refusing to work properly, Cas made it down the deserted hall and back outside. Nearly tripping down a set of steps, he came across a basket in a side ward and swiped the white bundle on top. It appeared to be a lady's tunic. Not caring at all, Cas somehow slipped it over his head, just about passing out as the luxuriously soft fabric whispered across his blistering flesh. Grabbing another piece of random cloth, and after picking out another dead bee from his sticky hair, Cas wound the fabric around his head. He hoped it looked like the modesty veil some of the sailor's wives wore ashore. Not ready at all for the long walk, he set off for the path back to the city.

With his body in agony, and lungs burning with an intensity that alarmed him, Cas set his thoughts to an unassuming wooden door. It was attached to the servants' kitchens of the expansive temple school where his tutors came from, tutors that he got into trouble with just about every day.

It was a simple door that he used to watch as a child. Hiding in the nearby magnolia trees, he hoped to catch a glimpse of crimson hair. Before he grew up, and realised maybe that wasn't the best approach.

But now, he had a reason to knock.

Smiling eagerly through tears of pain, Cas limped down the gravel on bare feet, hoping for a miracle by gods he didn't believe in, that the bullies had fled for now.

Now, in Morgan's bed, a place of both longing and refuge, Cas blinked away the horror of the day.

Dragging his thoughts to the present, his unblinking silver blue gaze landed on the precious, freckled face by his side.

His smile matched hers.

"Never," Morgan repeated as she straightened on her stool.

Not bothering to protest, Cas' grin widened. The honey soaked bandages were numbing the sting, but he was still sore and furious at being attacked.

He was also absolutely fucking delighted to be here.

Watching him observe her, Morgan chewed her bottom lip, the freckles on her chin and cheeks shifting in a decorative pattern. Cas was fascinated by her white teeth.

"I know what you're thinking," the librarian eventually murmured.

"I bet you really don't," Cas countered.

"Why didn't you go home for help?"

Cas' smile faded.

"Well, to be honest, you weren't my first choice. But no one..." Cas licked cracked lips. "No one was home," he finished.

Unexpectedly, Morgan nodded. "There was a holy festival in the city today."

"Ah."

"And there was also a quake."

"A quake?"

"It was a violent one."

Cas shook his head. The memory of words hissed behind a locked study door were too hazy to focus on.

"What happened?"

Morgan pursed her pink lips. "Parts of the old sections of the dock collapsed. Most of the crowd was fine, but a few were crushed or drowned."

"Did you go down to help?"

The librarian held his stare. "No."

Hardly able to question that since Morgan had been home to take him in, Cas nodded.

The festival explained his parents' careless focus elsewhere, and the lack of servants. The cleverness of the bullies in a successful plan on such a day had his lips curling with a sardonic twist. He wondered if they had ended up down by the water once finished with him.

"Why were you in a lady's dress?" Morgan asked curiously, interrupting his thoughts.

Cas gave a dainty sniff. "I refuse to be judged."

The librarian blinked for a moment, then shrugged.

"Fair enough. So why did you come here, Caspian?"

Swallowing, Cas thought about it. The question had been asked in earnest, sublime eyes intent on his face.

"Sometimes when we interact best with others," Cas explained, his eyes wide. "It's not with our hearts, it's with our scars instead."

Morgan's pink lips parted, and she blinked slowly. Bolstered by her speechlessness, Cas forged on.

"And I've got a fuckload of scars to share with you now."

"That's..." Morgan stared at him. "That's profound Caspian." Without warning, the librarian smiled and Cas' cock just about burst through his bandages, despite the agony where his blood pooled. Unaware, Morgan shook her head. "You could be a philosopher. You should write that down one day."

Shifting his hips, Cas shook his head against the pillows.

"Oh Morgan," he scoffed. "I don't have the patience or inclination to share my wisdom. Definitely not with the half asleep folk that clog up the world." His expression hardened at the memory of the boot connecting to his stomach. "No. The world simply does not deserve me."

Unimpressed by this statement, Morgan openly examined him. It was hard to tell when one was flush with magic, but she looked almost as young as he was right now. Her age was likely beyond his understanding. Either way, he couldn't care less.

Cas realised one red, fine eyebrow arched.

"Excuse me, what did you say?"

"I said," Morgan replied coolly, "what is the real reason you came here? And not to those that practice healing much closer to home?"

Looking away, Cas blinked at the window with its sliver of crisp light.

It was tempting to think of something inflammatory to say. He decided on honesty instead, aware of the truth behind his words about their scars connecting them in some way.

"I think," Cas began, his voice bitter. "I think Mother is right about me."

"What?" Morgan's single word contained enough anger that Cas flicked his glance back to her. Her cheeks were flushed. "How?"

"I can't do anything," whispered Cas. "I can't protect myself from those that scrape the barrel of this sick city! What am I good for? Why am I here? It's such a waste of my... potential talents. I wanted to do something when I grew up to fix the greed that sickens everyone, but I can't even win against *losers*. What does that make me? Mother is r-right." Embarrassed by his voice as it thickened, Cas turned his face away. "It's true. I'm broken."

To Cas' mortification, Morgan got up and disappeared downstairs without a word. But while he was cursing himself as the world's soppiest fool, soft footfalls sounded on the stairs as she returned.

"Morgan?" Cas called, hopeful.

Wincing as his body protested, Cas used what strength he could to push himself up into a seated position. His back was afire, but he kept that to himself.

Back in the modest room, the librarian approached the bed. Her pale green eyes were unreadable. In her hands was a long bundle, wrapped in layers of black silk. She sat on the bed, leant forward and peered into Cas' face. Aware that something momentous was about to happen, Cas cursed inwardly as his cock hardened further under her intense examination.

Satisfied or resigned, he wasn't sure, Morgan pulled back and began unwrapping the object in her lap. Wordlessly, Cas watched, her freckled and ink-stained hands moving carefully as the wrappings finally fell away. His breath caught as the object was freed.

It was a sword.

"What's that?" Cas breathed.

"A quill."

"Hilarious," Cas said serenely, unbothered by Morgan's dry tone. "Whose is it?"

Unsheathing the weapon from its worked leather scabbard, Morgan hefted the sword up with both hands wrapped around the hilt. It was beautifully made; the blade polished to a bright silver, the hilt decorative but functional, topped with a massive, faceted red jewel.

Morgan's eyes reached his over the sharp edge as she turned it sideways. She held it out, the point of the blade resting flat on her open palm.

"Yours."

Cas' jaw dropped open, his mismatched blue eyes wide.

"Why me?" His question came out as a parched whisper.

Morgan thought about it, then shrugged.

"Spite."

"Be more specific."

She smiled at that.

"Prove your mother wrong, Caspian." The librarian chose her words with care, her gaze on the brilliant weapon. "Find inner strength. Cut the ties to your weaknesses. Do that for me. I never could overcome mine."

"Do you..." Cas reached out, not at all ashamed to see his fingers trembling. "Do you truly mean that?"

"What?" Amused by his passion, Morgan laughed as her gaze rose to his. Cas almost forgot about the marvelous weapon in his shaking hands at the sound. "Of course."

"Um." Cas cleared his throat. He readjusted the blade in his hands. It was perfectly balanced from what he could tell in his current position. "I love it."

He rested the weapon very carefully on his lap beside his traitorous groin. Surprisingly, Morgan let him take her hands in his when Cas reached for her.

"Use it well," Morgan whispered.

It was impossible to think she hadn't seen the other scars on his body, the ugly patch from when he'd spilt that ungodly elixir upon himself when younger, or the lines across his forearms that had never faded. As their joined hands hung together in midair, connected for a brief moment, Cas wanted to ask a question that burned in his chest.

When was the last time someone reached out with kindness to you?

Instead, Cas raised his chin.

"Thank you. I will indeed use it well."

"I'm sure you will." Morgan pulled her hands free, and he let them go with reluctance. Her gaze hardened. "But you can't come here again."

"I will." Cas pointed at his lap, letting her interpret his next words as she wished. "This is a giant key, my love."

She didn't blink at his term of endearment. "No."

"I will."

"Please don't." The librarian's gaze became troubled. "Things might happen to you if we... if you..."

"Oh?"

"Terrible things."

"I see." He didn't. Blue eyes narrowed, but he wasn't put off in the slightest. "What a thing for one to say to another. Did you know that the tremor would happen today? Is that why you stayed away?"

Avoiding his gaze, Morgan rose, tossing the scabbard on the bed beside him.

"Now get up. Get dressed. Get out."

She headed towards the stairs, a hand waving casually towards the window. The curtain was yanked open by an invisible force, flooding the room with late afternoon sunlight.

Blinking and grimacing in pain as his eyes protested, Cas called out, grasping to keep her by his side.

"Morgan."

The librarian paused at the top step, one hand on the stone wall, her gaze on her feet. "Caspian?"

"I can predict the future."

Morgan flinched but didn't turn. "No, you can't."

"It's true." Cas' nostrils flared. "You have the power to destroy me, to undo me completely, and you will. Your smile is brighter than the brightest star, hotter than the hottest flame."

Still not looking at him, Morgan's voice was very soft. "Does that scare you?"

Cas scoffed with an arrogant puff of air. "I welcome it."

"Really?"

"Mm."

"But," Cas stroked the naked sword on his lap with a hand peppered by countless red welts. "I'm not sure what's worse. Wondering if you will. Or if you won't."

Morgan licked her lips and resumed her descent. "It doesn't matter, though."

"Oh. Why?"

"Like I said before," came the fading response. "Never."

The following morning, Cas made his way downstairs to the kitchens.

He'd slept fitfully, not quite able to get comfortable as his wounds healed with a soft infusion of Morgan's magic, plus the increasingly sticky bandages.

Still.

Despite, or perhaps because of the red welts already fading to scars all over his body, backside included, Cas was elated.

As he reached the bottom landing, a woman of great height emerged. Her attire consisted of tones of bronze and earth, her heavy plait of gold hair resting over one shoulder. He knew her as Dawn, one of his parents' greatest successes.

Cas gave her a polite nod.

Her footsteps, those of a surefooted fighter most of the time, faltered as he approached.

"Um, Caspian?" Dawn queried. "What happened to you?"

"Good day, warrior," Cas chirped as he breezed past.

He waved a blotched and swollen hand as he left her in the hall and stepped into the delightful smells and heat of the estate's main kitchen. He made sure not to swagger too obviously. It was hard, though, with his new sword hanging at his hip.

Following his nose, and guided by his grumbling stomach, Cas headed for the two figures wearing crisp white aprons leaning over one of the preparation benches.

"What are you making?" asked Cas, sneaking up behind Wane.

Wane jumped, flour going everywhere in a puff of white, and Evreth, the household head, screeched. They had been making a cake, apparently.

As the cloud of flour finally settled, Wane hissed.

"Caspian, what the fuck?"

"Master Wane!" admonished Evreth, but his eyes widened when he took in Cas' patchy face and swollen lips.

"What did you do this time, Cas?"

Cas sighed. Of course Wane thought it was his fault.

Wondering how to respond to a comment such as that, Cas ran a thumb over the faded lumps on his forehead, grateful that he hadn't landed face first. His back was a mess. Morgan had already seen it, though, which was a blessing, so she didn't get too much of a shock one day.

"How the hells can you smirk like that, Cas?" Wane demanded, his flour covered hands grabbing Cas' upper arms. "Look how swollen your lips are! What happened?"

"Oh," Cas laughed, peering over Wane's shoulder to see what bread had been baked for the day. "*That* wasn't the bees. That was my goodbye."

"Bees?" Wane's brow furrowed, an alarmed light filling his deep green gaze. He glanced down. "Where did you get that?"

"Hm? Ah, that's my new hobby."

Evreth stared at him, one of his grey eyes twitching.

Cas shouldered between them and swiped a bun baked with sweet spices and yellow fruit rinds. He took a bite. It hurt, but he was ravenous.

"You look like a wild person just come in from the deep forest," Wane managed at last.

Relishing the sting of his swollen lips, Cas stared at the spiced bread in his hand. His mind was elsewhere, on the half stolen kiss when he'd left Morgan's home the day before. His lids shuttered at the memory. When Cas pulled Morgan's mouth to his, Morgan had made a soft noise in her throat, a transcendent sound that words couldn't come close to describing. Right before she bit his bottom lip.

"Are you ill, Cassie?"

Odd blue eyes cracked open.

Wane was gaping at the expression on Cas' face.

"Little brother. I'm fucking fantastic."

35

Morgan

As the uprising raged in the castle and grounds above, Morgan's unhurried boot steps took her deeper into the relative peace of the deserted crypts.

Stopping at a sarcophagus topped with a bust of a man in red marble, the librarian yawned.

She poked at the man's timeworn face with the ruby in the head of her staff. No attempt was made to read which king or dignitary they had been. Not because the inscription was covered in limestone scale from moisture soaking through the natural rock ceiling above.

Morgan simply didn't care.

A king was only a man, after all.

Nothing more, nothing less.

Shaking her head, Morgan resumed her meander through the cavernous, gloomy hall of the dead.

Beneath the clash and yelling, a soft rustle of wings could be heard amongst the shadowy recesses of the cavern above. Her occasional exasperated sigh joined the bats chittering as they roosted amongst stalactites, along with the crunch of leather soles over pebbled, damp earth.

Earlier, after meeting with the latest king, Morgan had headed to where she knew would likely be untouched by the coming mania above. Passing a trolley being wheeled through the castle by helpers of both races, she had swiped a jug of crisp white wine by its handle of thick clay. She had drained it by the time the first angry voices and clashing had begun.

The jug had been discarded in the dust beside the most recent internments amongst polished stone. Young Chase and Lord Cyrus. More casualties lost in the endless jostling for power. Morgan's heart ached for both, truly. Even if it was only a little. She had purposely made no close friends during her time served here, having an inkling of what would one day come.

But sadly, it was the way of the world that innocents would always be the victims of misused power.

That was one reason Morgan had chosen to serve penance here. Biding time amongst the last substantial library on the continent of Beinacoilia. Amongst the books she hated.

It served her right.

After assisting two of the greatest murderers of all time, for the sake of coins and magic she had never got to spend, she deserved worse. And it would come for her.

There had been a plan in the depths of her heart for some while now, on how to welcome such a penance. But if Fox was returning to Aneirin at the same time as Caspian, the timeline had to be adjusted. Except, as to how Morgan was to persuade such an impossible creature like Fox to listen to her, with Caspian in the way, the librarian had no idea. If Fox and Caspian met, it was surely going to be a dangerously volatile encounter.

Morgan settled deeper into her cloak as the screams and cries of outrage echoed down the stairs, along the aisles of lonely busts and formally inscribed rock and stone.

Had any of her fevered dreams shown her who would prevail?

"No," Morgan whispered to the shadows after a moment's thought, slowed a little by the wine, "they hadn't."

The steady crimson glow from the ruby on her staff painted the busts as she passed with a faint, bloody light. The deeper her musing took her, the staler the air became. But it was a pleasant change from the fresh black ink that covered the walls of her tiny cell, and the dried ink that stained her fingers.

The air was also humid despite the coolness beneath the vast royal complex above. It was possible snow had started in earnest by now, something she hadn't seen for years here. Not since before King Aran and Queen Sophia had cursed the kingdom, in a bid for protection from the horrors of other magic users gone wild.

Because, with very few exceptions, power meant greed, the longing for more.

The thought had her wanting to roar at the absolute waste of time and life, those in the past, and those to come.

One of the last times she had been alone with Caspian before she had fled, he'd admitted to sinking beneath the waves to roar out his dissatisfaction.

"Dissatisfaction with what?" the librarian had asked, knowing it would be something grand.

"Everything," he'd answered her, tone mild.

Morgan had nodded to herself and pressed a hand to his cheek.

"You have quite *an ego, Caspian Carter."*

"No," he replied seriously after kissing her palm. "I merely have an allergic reaction to the egos of others."

A heartfelt roar underwater might help the unease in her guts. Yet her tiny chamber and her pitiful bowl of icy water would never be enough. A river maybe? At that thought, Morgan hiccupped into her delicate fist, the aroma of fresh wine and bitter ink thick in her nose.

Salt water crashing over black sands would be better, in a place that had almost been a home. The need to be back there, untethered to painful thoughts, was a longing that burned within her, almost as the need for something fiercer.

Despite the slow pace of her steps, her boot faltered on the next step.

It wasn't drugs that she ached for.

What was also needed was Caspian.

Calm soft green eyes examined where the crimson glow reached, the horizon of shadows along the dust and grit hiding the bulk of the subterranean necropolis beyond.

Were the dead listening to the crashing of metal against metal above?

"Perhaps," murmured the librarian as a tiny bat flittered past her unbound hair, "should I shout my dissatisfaction here and now? The dead might be truly asleep. But the living never listen to the burning hearts of others, do they?"

A mild snort filled the space.

The librarian's thoughts wandered to the new king.

After getting a chance to meet with Rhydian in the library, it was obvious there was a chance he was different. She had watched him grow up as a serious young lad, under the close eye of his father. Now Rhydian was king, young and thrown into the thick of things beyond his experience. For now, he appeared to have a heart large enough to make up for all those with only a muscle that beat to the tune of greed instead.

Time would tell if the dark bloom within him would find the light of day, or the shadows of night.

By then, hopefully, her penance would be served.

The librarian came to a dusty, grey marble bench at the cavern's edge. It was a formal seating area, built long ago, next to a pair of sarcophagi in matching stone.

She propped her staff against the waist-high wall of bricks built right into the natural rock wall. Marble arches met above in soaring carvings of ivy or some other vine in the same grey stone. If they were in a garden of lush green grass and rose bushes, the little marble folly would have fit right in. Yet here it served not to delight, but to provide a place of contemplation in the depths of the cavern of the dead. Morgan wondered which king or queen had built it, and for whom.

A parent?

A beloved?

A child?

A freckled hand drifted to rest on the thick wool of her tunic, directly over her flat stomach.

There was no desire for a child of her own, not just because Morgan had been a discarded one.

Wild dreams that chased sleep away, and the lingering resentment of sleeplessness while slaving at books during waking hours, were enough to contend with. Only one thing had come from them that had brought her any kind of joy, no matter how fleeting. Or how disastrous.

A lost creature like her had come into the world, Hypatia using Morgan's insights to engineer new ways to let magic bloom from generation to generation. Two babes had been born, but one had missed out on what should have been his birthright.

A boy, born with eyes of mismatched blue that flashed silver in times of joy, and times of the deepest pain.

With an amused twist of pale pink lips, Morgan wondered at his genuine smile, saved only for her. The other times his finely made lips curled?

Well.

His expression wasn't frivolous, but it was definitely malicious when he chose to be.

Sapphires laced with quicksilver, burning with a destiny that she had dreamt about for years before they had appeared in her lonely world. Eyes that scared her to no end. Their gaze focused on a destiny that made no sense, a destiny that had her drown the unwelcome visions with alcohol and opium whenever they became too intense.

"Magic."

The two syllables, whilst only softly spoken, seemed far too loud, down here as far from the violence above as she could get.

Magic was a blessing to some, a curse to others, like her damned bloodline and the visions during sleep that came with it.

A small spark in a few bloodlines originally, amongst the folk who lived close to nature and its bounty. Until its potential was studied, then mutated, tainted by casually nefarious experiments. As two alchemists pushed for more, more, *more*.

The only things Morgan had to thank magic for were a longer life, a face fresher than her years, and a heart that didn't know how to cope with what lay ahead.

With a beleaguered sigh, Morgan glanced down at her lap.

Just visible in the ruby glow of her staff, she bit her lip at what greeted her. Resting on her stomach by her belt, with its pouch of random coins, table dagger in its old leather scabbard, and leather flask, was her limp, freckled hand.

Stained with ink, it trembled like the aftershocks that had disturbed Aneirin since the last recent quake.

From fear?

A little.

The tremor in her bones seemed more likely from her icy rage at her part in the chaos that had veiled the continent for years. When as a naïve drunk, a lonely librarian had chased coins for wine, simply to drown her endless dreams.

Dreams that had allowed Baile Mara's eminent scientists to work out how to alchemize crystalline energy and blood transference.

Which had made her responsible, no matter how indirectly, for the disaster that was Caspian's birth into a cruel world.

And therefore his undoing.

Morgan's gaze slid from her stained hand to the hilt of her dagger.

"Caspian," murmured the librarian as the fighting above raged on. "Even after all this time, I'm sorry you got to Hypatia and Illarion before I did."

36

Merion

Year 367
Aneirin Castle

D ark eyelashes fluttered over bloodshot eyes.

What had woken him?

Beyond the wooden walls of the stables came strange sounds that made no sense. Voices raised in anger, metal on metal. And closer, a youthful voice crying out in an anguished wail.

Eyes, brown and normally full of life, blinked once more as the sensation came again. It was a soft tickle that disturbed the fading thoughts of the mind they belonged to.

It was desolately gloomy in the stables, and frightfully cold. A large shape moved nearby amongst smoky shadows. The velvet nose of a skittish pony nuzzled a bushy beard, trembling equine lips with coarse hairs probing closely.

Unable to move his body, all Merion could do was smile, with what the last working threads of his mind hoped was reassurance.

Aurelia's stocky pony, a magnificent beast with a fine bloodline, stomped on the hay by the groom's feverish face. A tufted hoof nudged Merion's out-flung arm, the long hairs coming away tipped with red. The pony grunted with a low whine of concern.

The animal's fear hurt the groom, more than the pain in his chest, which had faded into a blessed numbness.

"Hush," Merion gasped through blue white lips. "It's okay, my sweet..."

The pony whinnied, the sound a distressing cry that set the other horses to call out in response. Above the noise of weapons clashing with metal on metal, and voices raised with blood lust, the horse's worries bruised Merion's failing heart. He bit back a sob.

"It's... okay..."

The worried horse nudged him once more, velvet nose snuffling a bushy beard flecked with crimson.

"Hush, sweet... ness..." Merion breathed out as his eyes closed, the night fading into a soundless void. "Hush..."

37

The Watcher

Year 367

Aneirin Castle

The night had slipped from grudging merriment into a frightening pageant of violence and chaos.

As the Watcher scurried along the edge of the great courtyard of Aneirin's castle, they had no words horrific enough to describe what they witnessed.

Where there had been bonfires circled by dancers, each holding a tankard in one hand and the sleeve of the dancer in their other, now there were groups of armed soldiers fighting guests of the king's feast. Crimson and orange sparks flared high into the icy air above, mixing with the hot mist of those fighting to survive.

Tables piled with trays of juicy, steaming meat and jugs of ale were mostly overturned, the thick planks of stained wood used as barricades. Aneirin's finest alcohol pooled on slick cobbles, as assailants and innocent alike struggled to stay upright as they fought.

The crisp night air was no longer fresh or welcoming. Smoke bit at the senses instead of the homely fragrance of seasoned wood. The world seemed filled with the acrid stink of burning leather, singed clothing, scorched hair and worse, as figures tussled and cursed about.

And amongst the violent clashing of metal on metal or thuds of metal on flesh and bone, voices strained with hatred, calling above the shouting of the ambushed revelers.

"Humans! Down with the Elves!"

"Elven scum!"

Trembling, the Watcher slid along the inner walls of reddish stone, trying to escape attention. The long expanses of masonry were covered with ethereal figures engaged in desperate combat, looming above the fighters below in a mockery of the shadow puppets that appeared on market day. The Watcher bit their lip as weapons collided and people screamed in pain. Since the battle on the farmlands not long ago, they were no stranger to the hatred, to the building tension, or the threats of those that resented the way things had turned out.

But to see it firsthand?

It was a visceral experience that chilled their body beyond the ice that rode the air with bitterly sharp teeth.

With their guts feeling twisted into a dozen knots, the Watcher found a break in the groups of fighters. They ran from the wall to a heavily laden table still thankfully upright in a mad dash for cover. Skidding to their knees and sliding past the thick wooden legs, they panted, heart beating like a dragonfly's wings, breath so white and thick that they slapped shaking hands across their mouth to hide it.

From under the table, the Watcher peered through dripping globules of meat juice and overturned tankards of ale. The stables weren't far, but the clusters of folk fighting with swords, pikes, knives and whatever else came to hand, made them seem like the other side of the city.

Ignoring the dampness on their knees from the puddle spreading underneath them, the Watcher jumped as a jumble of shadows approached the table. It looked like two or three pairs of boots, accompanied by cursing. There was a struggle and then a dull thud above. Rubbing their bruised head after they jumped in fright, the Watcher risked crouching low enough to peer out and up.

They wished they hadn't.

A young woman dressed in dull grey fell to her knees before them, wide eyes filled with rage right before the Watcher's face. But thanks to the arrow head protruding out the front of her neck, soon enough the light faded from her gaze, her mouth slack. She slipped to the side, her last breath, a puff of red mist and crimson droplets, lost to the shouting around them. The young woman's corpse landed awkwardly, slumped in a twist to the side, red feathers quivering upright from between her shoulders.

The Watcher scrambled back with a cry.

Behind the body, a brightly dressed figure raced off, heading towards another jostling group of figures, waving their thanks at whomever had shot the woman from above. The Watcher ducked back under the table, wondering where to flee. Almost immediately, new boots appeared beside their wet knees.

With a sudden heave, the table was overturned with a crash of platters and the cracking of pottery.

"You!" yelled a man in armour whilst waving a sword, spittle flying, his face half obscured by a dented helm. "Get out of here!"

The Watcher moved.

Not knowing who was friend or foe, they sprung up, running off, dodging swinging swords and unknown projectiles that whizzed over their head. Tables and stools had been chucked onto the bonfires and by the towering blazes, it was possible to see Elves with long knives darting in and about the armoured assailants. Occasionally, a bright flash of sparks accompanied their strikes, followed by howls of pain.

As the Watcher skidded and slipped on the cobbles, catching themselves by scraped palms, they froze. It wasn't ale that dirtied their flesh, but something stickier, metallic and cloying even as it cooled. A strangled sort of noise escaped their throat.

Nearby, someone called their name.

Blinking, dazed, hands coated with blood that appeared black unless caught by the scorching fires as shadows crossed their intense glow, the Watcher looked up, and up, boots then long legs in bright green pants, bare arms, a heaving chest, and a plait of thick hair.

"B-Bindy..." the Watcher gasped.

"Up, up!" demanded the Elf, her face muddied and dangerously blank. "Behind me," she hissed, tugging the Watcher close and holding them to her back with a heavy hand twisted behind.

In her free hand was a long knife, stained dark and flashing deep ruby in the bonfires as they flared. The Watcher hid their face in the fur of her cloak, flung back off her shoulders to leave her arms free.

Letting themselves be led, the Watcher stumbled along behind, not knowing where they were headed as they were jerked about.

Bindy cursed and dodged, kicking anyone who appeared in her path with words the Watcher hadn't heard before but could guess their meaning easily. At one point, she halted abruptly. The Watcher peered around her side. A young man approached them with murder in his eyes, heavy broadsword held fast in both hands. Bindy laughed, a cruel cackle of fearlessness that had the hairs rising on the Watcher's neck. Without raising her knife, Bindy hissed something and the young man screamed, his sword hitting the ground with a clang as he grabbed his eyes and ran off.

As they found the relative safety of the courtyard wall again, closer to the stables now, a man's voice called out Bindy's name. Boot steps racing towards them had her spin around, knife raised, the Watcher tucked close.

Her weapon lowered a fraction when Davyn's sweating face appeared, his cloak gone, white shirt torn and bloody. He had no proper weapons, just a metal rod in each hand about the length of his arms. One of the iron lengths still held a piece of cooked meat by his knuckles.

The Watcher felt Bindy's tension ease as relief washed over Davyn's face at the sight of her and whom she'd found.

"Thank the gods!" Davyn cried, quickly gathering them both up in an awkward, and brief, hug.

While the Watcher choked at the stink of blood on Davyn's shirt, it sounded like the pair shared a brief discussion and an even briefer kiss.

"Traitor!"

Bindy and Davyn froze.

The Watcher swallowed around a constricted throat, eyes stinging from billows of thick smoke, ears ringing with shouts and cries of pain.

It was Wyll.

Firelight painted his scowling face with dancing black shadows and golden highlights. "You traitor!"

The low hiss caught the attention of a band of nearby fighters. Three armoured figures, all of them burly men, each with a sword, shield and expressions of cold fury, broke off and headed their way.

"Wyll!" Davyn called out, pushing Bindy behind him. "Was all of this *you*?"

Dressed in dark clothing, his cloak long gone, Wyll sneered with a baring of teeth, raising his sword in salute.

"It should have been you too!" he spat, eyes narrowed into thin slits of desolation. He took a step towards them, sword point lowered in accusation. "It should have been —"

"What are you saying?" Davyn shouted, skewers waving madly as the armoured men approached. "Stop this madness!"

Bindy snorted, and Wyll bared his teeth.

"Oh fuck," Davyn panted, pushing Bindy and the Watcher behind, trying to find cover as the four men advanced, swords glinting, raised, ready.

"You fucking cowards," Bindy jeered, standing fast despite Davyn's urging. "You're worse than the bat shit I scrape off my —"

As Davyn shoved the Watcher down by a leaking barrel made of old oak, the men charged, armour clanking. Bindy screamed a war cry, a second knife in her newly freed hand raised high, the other low. Davyn rushed to her side. As the figures came together, the Watcher cried out, covering their sweaty, grubby face with hands smeared with someone else's blood.

For a moment, there was the sound of metal on metal, a dark, feminine laugh, men cursing.

Then something happened.

The stink of something fiercer than lightning bit the Watcher's nose. At the same time, a flash of light so blinding it shone between their fingers, searing their eyes. They cried out, ears going numb as the air beat against their head.

All the violent sounds of the night ceased.

Then an earth-shaking boom split the silence.

With a fierce blow from unearthly pressure, the Watcher was thrown against the stone wall, nearly knocking them out. The barrel they had crouched against splintered into kindling. Across the courtyard, a wail of pain began.

As the after-effect of red pots and odd wavering shapes faded from their vision, the Watcher blinked up at the low clouds, dark grey once more.

The blast was over as fast as it had come, the night shockingly still.

The bonfires were out.

No voices, apart from panting nearby and the low sob of agony, filled the courtyard.

Aching all over, ears ringing, the Watcher sat up, squinting, face stinging with the bites of many splinters of wood. Something icy, delicate, and white settled on their eyelashes. The Watcher blinked.

It was snowing.

As they looked around while white flakes fluttered down from above, the Watcher's jaw dropped.

Most of the surrounding figures were no longer standing. A few clutched tables and stools to stay upright, but most were laid flat. Out cold or worse.

In the centre of it all, a figure stood alone, arms by his side, red sparks dripping from his fingers.

Around him lay those closest to the blast, or what was left of them.

But it wasn't just those who had come prepared, those with weapons and armour. Amongst the pieces of gore and charred wood, a torso with a bright cloak of yellow fur, or a leg in deep green leather pants, lay by his boots.

Mouth dry and tasting of ozone and blood, the Watcher gasped.

"M-my king," they gasped into the shocked silence.

Rhydian turned haltingly until he spotted the one who had spoken. Silvery flakes dusted the shoulders of his cloak along with his sweaty, golden brown hair. The young man's expression was indecipherable from this distance. But his eyes were easy to spot.

They were as red as the embers scattered about in the devastation around him.

38

Aurelia

Year 367

Aneirin Castle

A steady string of furious expletives fell from Aurelia's lips, like the bitter minerals dripping from ancient stalactites in the caves of Lolihud.

Her cloak was half-torn off, and her dark hair had come loose. The long strands stuck to her cheeks and neck with blood and sweat and some of her curses were of frustration, as there was no time to tie them back. She had dressed warmly in wool and fur for the feast, but her thin wool pants had nowhere near enough protection to turn away a sharp blade like her usual leather riding pants.

She had joined those fighting around the king. While she was resentful that she was battling with only a long Elven knife in one hand and a metal platter in the other, she was grateful for one thing. Rhydian had worn his sword to the feast in a symbolic gesture of command.

He was on her right near the steps leading to the main hall, facing away as he fought off an attacker in focused silence. Grunting, Aurelia aimed her boot at the young man snarling before her, landing a kick to his exposed knee. He had some armour on, a helm, and a short breastplate. Small pieces that could be worn under long cloaks and not discovered to be out of place until the last.

"You worm," Aurelia hissed and feinted one way, her blade swinging the other.

The man fell back and tripped over the dead woman at his rear. Aurelia felt no qualm about darting forward. She crouched, slashed and danced back with finesse, the blood on her knife refreshed.

The young man began wailing in agony. He released his sword, bloodied hands pressed to where his armour had failed him. His screaming went on as he tried and failed to hold in the long loops of intestines that spilled out in a steaming rush of crimson and pale pink.

Aurelia turned away, assessing the crowd that was thickest around the steps where they fought beside their king. Who was next? Wondering where the fuck Fox was and why he was taking his damned time to return, Aurelia's muttering continued.

"Aurelia!"

She whirled to Rhydian, the seriousness of his call. He was still fighting the same attacker, his focus severe. But he still managed to get her attention.

"Aurelia! Go!"

Aurelia hesitated as he snapped out her name once more. Only moments ago, she had been given a task by the king, but had yet not found a break to carry it out.

The chaos continued around them, and Aurelia spun about, trying to discern through the shouting and clashing of blows who was with or against the king.

Rhydian held his own, his training superior to most of those who had joined in the miserable uprising. His swinging blade landed each strike with enough force to maim and halt the attack, the upswing ready for a defending slash. Aurelia's heart, beating thrice its usual speed, heated at the sight. Those that came close to him had no chance. She prayed to whomever was listening that Rhydian could steel his heart against the deaths he dealt with shocking ease. It would be what came after that scared her the most. He would carry each one with him, of that she had no doubt.

Most of the traitors and loyalists alike fought with moves best left for the open spaces of battlefields. So here, amongst the overturned tables and bonfires, they struggled. But the attackers were armed well, and those come to the feast expecting an evening of peace fought with whatever was at hand. Tankards swung and blocked, along with platters that once held celebratory food, reflected the towering flames of the bonfires that had only just been coloured with hues of a joyful rainbow. The fires flared deep red and yellow as furniture was hurled in by those with a spare breath, allowing them to see who they fought. The air was still bitingly frigid, at odds with the flaming glow.

Spitting out ash and blood, Aurelia wheeled to face another attack. The newcomer was taller than her, and the man leered through the gap in his helm.

While she hadn't enough magic in her blood to harm him directly like some Elves, her tenacity made up for it.

Aurelia ducked.

The man swung his heavy broadsword low to follow her movement.

She was faster.

"Rhydian!" Aurelia yelled.

The king whirled to face her. Aurelia kicked at the man's knee from behind and he folded to one knee. Rhydian's expression was blank as he adjusted his grip on his sword mid swing.

The blade flashed.

Immediately after, the man's head rolled away into the scuffling boots with a thump, lost in the shouting that filled the chaotic night.

Aurelia and Rhydian shared a glance.

Before Aurelia could interpret the odd twinge in her guts at the glint in his eye, he twisted around, helping one of his loyal guards fend off the figures as they advanced.

She didn't have time to help him.

Someone yanked her hair and jerked her head up and back.

Trained by Bindy for such an occasion, where lengthy hair was seen as a weakness by those with violence in their hearts, Aurelia acted without thinking.

Wedging her knife between her teeth, she reached up at the same time as she collapsed her weight. She bit back the pain in her scalp. Her hands found the wrists of her assailant and she held tight. Like a lever, they were flung over her as she dropped and rolled.

The resounding crack of metal and bone on the steps of the castle filled her ears.

Aurelia laughed, a mad chortle, the only way to express her frustration and disbelief at the wicked scene unfolding around them.

Had everything she had fought for come to this, the possibility of death by traitors to their own king?

"Not a chance!" Aurelia roared, looking for a path through the mayhem.

Heading to a gap, she paused at a frustrated cry.

Where —?

There.

Two armoured young women pressed a young Elven man in a blue tunic stained with blood into a corner beside the steps.

Howling, Aurelia launched herself bodily into the air.

She landed with her knife in the neck of one woman. They fell together in an ungraceful tangle. Aurelia kicked at the boots of the dead guard's companion, her face a mask of shock as Aurelia pulled her knife free. The confused guard tottered, but didn't fall. The woman was about to charge at Aurelia, but she froze. Something in Aurelia's face gave the guard pause. She glanced at her intended victim crouched against the wall, then back to Aurelia, then turned and raced off, disappearing amongst the sea of those fighting for their lives.

"Here," Aurelia hissed, pressing the sword of the one she had just stabbed into the intended victim's hand.

The young Elf nodded his thanks as he fell back into the corner. He was clearly fighting to stay conscious. Aurelia checked no one was approaching from behind, whipped off her cloak and pressed it to where the blood was thickest on the Elf's tunic. He gasped, but his free hand was strong as he took over from Aurelia.

"Save your strength," Aurelia mumbled, grimacing at the foul stink of burning leather, "if you can heal it, do it. Or bloody stay down and pretend to be dead."

With that, she pushed up and reeled around. The guard she had just slain had landed with her boot in the closest bonfire. Aurelia scanned the mess close by. Finding what she wanted, she grabbed the jug of spirits and tipped it over the guard's legs, hoping it was flammable. Sure enough, encouraged by the spirits, the fire spread quickly over the woman's pants.

The last mouthful Aurelia saved for herself.

Taking a swig of the liquid, she swallowed it back through her parched throat.

A prickle of sensation along the hum of power in her blood was her only warning.

An arrow shot past her cheek, and Aurelia ducked with barely enough time to avoid it.

Yet, when she realised what had happened, she was desperately relieved rather than angry. Her breath misted white as she caught her breath, eyeing the new figure at her feet.

It was a man, someone who had been about to stab her while she had drained the jug, and the arrow had saved her life.

Now, yellow fletching protruding from his eye at a slanted angle.

Shouting her thanks to whomever had made it to a high vantage point to shoot down amongst the attackers below, Aurelia took her chance. She found a gap in the groups of fighters and set out to do what Rhydian had tasked her with when the fighting initially began.

Now that most attackers and feasters had squared off, this was her most likely chance.

"Protect the most innocent," Rhydian had tasked her as the assailants broke their cover and launched their treasonous attack.

She knew immediately who he had meant, but had yet to succeed in her mission.

Ducking and weaving, she slipped past Rhydian. He was holding his own. It was difficult to focus, as she still had to tell herself that those beside him knew what they were doing as they fought to keep him alive. She didn't look back, aware that he'd see her go and likely feel the better for it. She knew she fought dirty. Rhydian's kills were clean, hers were deliberately not.

Covering her face as she leapt past a smoking bonfire with a pair of legs sticking out, Aurelia continued to the stables, Rhydian's command clear in her mind. She choked on the sickly sweet stink of burning flesh, and was almost retching by the time she reached the stable doors.

As her free hand made contact with the stone wall of the stables, she paused, choking in the fresher air away from the burning corpse. But as she wiped her long hair out of her face, a fresh scent reached her nose.

It was the stink of lightning, ready to strike.

It was familiar, but in this quantity?

Looking up, Aurelia whirled, placing her back to the stables, her wide green gaze whipping about.

Surely it was Fox, here to wipe away the bastards who threatened the peace of the one she loved?

But there was no great winged shadow, no furious roar, not even a disturbance in the low-hanging, icy clouds above. Only the first flakes of snow, something that hadn't touched the grounds of Aneirin in the gods only knew how long.

"Rhydian," Aurelia whispered, the stink of ozone still puzzling her, "when this shit storm is over I'll take you —"

Her sentence was left unfinished.

The air in the courtyard shifted, the pressure expanding, then contracting in a rush.

It sped towards the steps of the castle in a cold surge that froze almost as quickly as it began.

There was a heartbeat of stillness.

Then, with a deafening explosion of roaring sound, blisteringly frozen air shot out-wards. Blinding blue-white light expanded with a crushing pressure, ear drums protesting with an agony that stopped the heart.

Aurelia had just enough time to close her eyes as she was brushed to the side like a cobweb stretched between the flimsy branches of a willow tree.

She landed on the cobbles with an impact that took the wind from her lungs.

As she passed out, the night went quiet.

"Do I have a shadow?"

It was her own voice, spoken from far away, in another time.

"Of course you do." Cool arms tightened around her, as words as cold as ice were spoken against Aurelia's hair. "Me."

Not sure how long she was out, Aurelia came around slowly.

Ominous words about shadows and desolate power echoed in her throbbing ears.

At first, it felt like someone was patting her face. But when Aurelia opened her bloodshot eyes, there was no one there.

Just the clouds high above, sending down crisp, icy flakes of snow coming to rest gently on her numb cheeks.

Aurelia tried to speak, but a thick coating of blood filled her mouth. When she rolled over with a groan and spat out a gob of filth, she realised something beyond the ringing in her ears.

The night was tranquil.

Aurelia pushed up, swearing at the throb in her head, and staggered to her feet. Her knife was gone, and when her gaze roamed about quickly for another, she froze.

"What in the hells..." she breathed.

She was one of the few standing.

The courtyard that had been filled with fighting figures of all kinds was silent. Those that had previously been upright were now laid flat like she had been, most still moving about weakly.

The smoke had cleared, swept away by whatever had detonated with a burst of power. Bonfires still burnt, but their flames were low, not quite out but nowhere near the roaring pillars of earlier.

Realising that she had been one of the first to gasp back to consciousness, Aurelia rushed forward a few paces towards the castle steps, then halted once more.

Rhydian stood alone by the castle steps.

"Oh fuck, no..." Aurelia choked out, her heart a block of ice.

His eyes blazed crimson, with tiny sparks dripping from his fingers in a fading cascade of red.

Someone gasped.

The king turned, no words leaving his lips.

But his face, his wide eyes as the eerie glow faded, said it all.

Rhydian was dazed, confused, blank.

His lost gaze rose to meet hers, and her frozen, astonished heart melted in a rush.

His expression changed as realisation dawned.

Rhydian blinked, the fiery heat of his gaze clearing as they stared at each other over the silence and devastation that filled the space between them.

He was about to fall apart.

Aurelia moved.

Not caring for herself or any other, she leapt over bodies, alive, dead, young or old. She didn't care. Aurelia dashed towards him, calling his name, over and over, hair trailing behind her as she ran.

She reached him as the wailing began. Soft groans, then cries for help, as some of those closest to him lost their shock and came to realise their dire circumstances.

"Rhydian," Aurelia gasped, her mouth parched.

She stopped at arm's length. Carefully. she held up her hands, palms out.

The glow had finally gone from his eyes, his pupils wide and round. He blinked.

"What happened..?" he mumbled, a line forming between his brows. "Who...?"

Calming her breaths by will alone, Aurelia edged closer. "Rhydian, it's me, Aurelia."

A little of the haze cleared in Rhydian's gaze and he held up his hands. He gawked at them a moment, then peered through his fingers at Aurelia.

"Aurelia?" he whispered.

Willing the nausea in her guts to calm down, she nodded.

"What happened?" he repeated, his voice sounding very small.

"You're alright," Aurelia soothed, wishing that he was. But her darkest suspicions had been confirmed. She took another step and anxiously grabbed his hands in hers. They were freezing. Bringing them to her mouth, kissing them despite the drying blood on her lips, she nodded. "It's going to be okay."

Rhydian stared at her.

It wasn't okay.

Nothing right now was okay.

They both knew that.

A muscle in Rhydian's jaw twitched.

But what else could she say?

Rhydian glanced over her shoulder, his gaze sharpening. Aurelia swallowed as his expression changed. It could be described as cold at best, glacial at worst. Turning, she followed his gaze, the icy breeze lifting the lengths of her hair.

The groaning and gasps of the wounded had grown. But under it all was a stunned wariness as astonished onlookers stared at the pair of them as they stood by themselves before the castle's main steps.

Aurelia licked her lips, gaze frantic as she surveyed the bloody bodies closest, and the pieces of what had once been people. Her heart flipped when she finally spotted a tall Elven woman by the courtyard wall. She was standing, but bent over. Beside her was Davyn, further easing Aurelia's panic. The pair of them appeared to be struggling with someone.

By some miracle, they finished what they were doing and Bindy looked up as Aurelia was glancing her way. Aurelia jerked her head vigorously in a certain direction.

Bindy nodded.

The towering Elf muttered something to Davyn, too low for Aurelia to make out as more people came to and sat up, crying out with shock or anger and fear.

Rhydian didn't move. Aurelia stayed by his side, one of his hands in both of hers.

They watched in silence as those who were well enough helped the injured around them. Aurelia glared at a guard who tried to crawl away, and the older man gulped, dropping his sword and holding up his hands. As she debated whether it was safe enough to let go of Rhydian and knock him out, Bindy and Davyn approached.

Both were bloodied all over, and Davyn had a bruise forming on one cheek. Between them, they were dragging a limp figure.

It was a man dressed in dark clothing, his hair a mess, arms tied to his sides with a leather belt, the same treatment done at his ankles.

They dumped him without ceremony on the cobbles, and Aurelia hoped that if he was alive that the force had broken his nose.

"Bindy," Aurelia said as calmly as possible despite the circumstances. "Organise the healers." Bindy nodded, grabbed Davyn's shoulder, and headed off to inspect who was awake. "Davyn, please organise those who you know are loyal, and round up all those still alive in armour, and see if you can…" her voice faded.

Davyn glanced at his king, then back to her. Not in suspicion, but with such trust and understanding that she nearly cracked.

"Of course," he said clearly. He bowed. "My king," he announced even louder and turned to do what he could.

Aurelia hoped it was enough, that whatever the fuck Rhydian had done had worked in their favour. That it had brought them time, not more enemies.

"Merion," Rhydian mumbled.

Aurelia, still holding one of Rhydian's hands, glanced at him. He was rubbing his chest, squinting across at the devastation with narrowed eyes. Snow had gathered in soft tufts in his hair. Aurelia reached over to wipe it off.

"What?" she mumbled.

"Where is my groom?" he demanded.

Without warning, he shook off her hands. He set off over the dead and the wounded with as little care as Aurelia had on her rush back to him.

"Rhydian," Aurelia called as she followed, "wait, you should stay here —"

"Merion!"

His voice was frantic as he raced over people, weapons, broken tables and stools.

Cursing once more, this time with fear instead of fury, Aurelia followed close behind.

When she made it through the stable doors, Rhydian was nowhere to be seen at first.

But a young man's terrified sob alerted her to a stall along the dark row of panicked horses.

Aurelia dashed towards the source of the noise and skidded to a halt, hay dust kicked up in her wake.

There were three shadows inside the stall.

Another sob broke the silence and tore at her heart.

One of the shadows in the gloom was Rhydian, on his knees in the straw.

Another was her pony, wild-eyed behind him.

The third was the groom, limp in his arms, eyes closed, a dark stain over his leather apron and pooling black in the straw.

"Aurelia," Rhydian cried, his face a mask of fear in the dim light.

"Oh fuck, no," Aurelia hissed.

She rushed in, wincing as her knees bounced on the slate beneath the straw. Not finding a pulse, she pushed up and stuck her head out of the stall. Hollering like a fiend, Aurelia spared a thought that if anyone had survived this chaos, it would be the figure in Rhydian's shaking arms.

Because if Merion didn't make it, she had no idea what he'd do.

39

Cas

Year 257, Cas at age 16
Baile Mara

"Did you get it?" Cas asked, breathless and feverish despite the crisp rain.

"Here you go," Rueben replied with a warm smile.

"Thank you," came Cas' half-strangled response.

Mouth dry, he received the small glass bottle with reverent hands. It was the priest's of Baile Mara's finest fortified wine. After checking the label, he slipped it into his leather overcloak. A bird chirped while Cas peered at Rueben after making sure the bottle was protected in his deep pocket.

Both of them were avoiding the heaviest of the downpour under the awning of a bakery, not far from the briny stink of the docks. The shop was closed this late in the day. They were still getting hit by some of the fat, icy drops. But it was shelter enough for Cas. He'd only be here a moment. The youth before him was clothed in simple pale blue and white, a wool tunic and a slightly thicker wool shawl. His feet were encased in open-toed sandals. The cheeky glint in his eyes told Cas that Rueben was comfortable enough, however.

The damp little sparrow on the priest's shoulder appeared just fine, too. It chirped under Cas' keen observation, head tilting back and forth as it hopped up and down. A thin red thread of fabric secured it to Rueben's shawl. Its tiny beak was clearly broken, but as it twittered happily and poked about Rueben's earlobe, its spirit was clearly intact.

"I bet that bird has seen some wild stuff," Cas acknowledged, unsure what else to say.

"It sure has." The priest paused, grinning. "Bet you're about to as well."

Cas opened his mouth to speak, but nothing came out.

"Ha! Look at you, all shy." Rueben laughed. "Good luck!"

Before Cas could think of anything to say, the young priest gave Cas a quick hug, then slipped back out into the rain. The sparrow squawked, facing Cas with indignant, shining eyes as Rueben's sandals slapped through deepening puddles. Cas blinked at the bird, then blew it a kiss before heading into the rain in the other direction.

As he drew his leather hood over his damp hair, the odd little bird remained foremost in his mind while he made quick work of the city's wet streets. Or rather, it wasn't the bird that had caught his eye, but the red thread. Like the crimson hair from his earliest dreams, a connection between two souls that were surely destined to be together. It was towards this other soul that the youth headed now, a little breathless, stomach giddy, heart full.

Glad for his new leather cloak, it had kept most of the rain off his brand new embroidered silk shirt and soft wool pants. His boots had been shiny on sneaking out from a side door of the Carter Estate, but they were soiled now. At his hip under the cloak, his sword was freshly polished in its scabbard. He was also sporting a fresh haircut. Now it was less of a single-length blonde flop. A few tasteful, rakish layers had been added by one of Rooks girls down at his latest establishment. As if aware of the occasion, the lass had winked, sending him off with a slap on the backside.

Normally, that would have offended Cas.

But today?

Today he wasn't a boy prone to react to such indignities, because today he was a man.

Or would be.

Soon.

Cas swallowed past the lump in his throat.

Heads turned as he dashed around most of the puddles, the rain falling heavier as he wove towards his favourite door. At sixteen, he was as tall as Father, the same as Wane, though less bulky. He was pleased with his slender figure and toned muscles from hours of sword work every day. Cas was good at badgering whatever warrior or pirate he could, down at the crowded inns. When he could sneak away from his tutors, that is.

As both young men and women catcalled him, a few older ones too, Cas grinned but kept to his path, both in the streets and in his heart.

That ripe organ was set.

There was only one for him.

As he passed by a temple full of people-sized crystal points of the deity that he always forgot the name of, Cas began rehearsing his carefully chosen words.

"Morgan, my goddess," Cas recited as he jumped over another puddle outside the front of the temple school, "you are the only goddess I will worship amongst these heathens, my love, my fresh strawberry, my sweet. You are a magical star fallen to earth from the heavens, full of mystery, and if you need more of anything, I shall get it for you.

"My beauty, my life, we will break free from those that use us, and I will cherish you in ways you never dreamed of, but that I do, every night."

Cas halted in the pouring rain, checking the street to each side of the corner was clear, before making a run down the cobbles.

"I know you best," he panted as he ran, "I can love you best. I *do* love you best. I... I... what was it? Ugh. Ah! I know. You collected the broken things, the unusual things down by the outgoing tides, preferring those to sparkly things that are never unique."

Arriving at the plain wooden door in the wall of black stone blocks, Cas' boots halted.

"Morgan," he wheezed, "I am the only man for you."

Straightening his shoulders, Cas patted his chest to make sure his gift was still safe, then knocked on the door.

While waiting, his fist stayed raised for some reason, like it didn't want to work, and a tiny part of his twitching brain registered that his wet hand was shaking.

Was he nervous?

Ridiculous!

The offending hand was about to knock again when the door was yanked open from within.

Above dark circles, frosty green eyes glared up at him, softening only a fraction when Morgan realised who was at her door.

The petite librarian was as breathtaking as always. Perhaps more so today. Warmth flooded out from behind her. The heat of the room might have explained the lack of any warm clothes about her top half. She wore a simple white linen shirt, its long sleeves rolled up to her elbows, the tails tucked loosely into relaxed trousers.

As frigid water dripped over the front of his hood, Cas' mouth dried up on realising that under the thin shirt, there was... nothing.

Nothing but two pale, pink spots of flesh that peaked in the cool air, their jaunty appearance immediately setting off a cacophony of fireworks in his brain.

Holding a steaming teacup in one hand, Morgan waited. Her cool gaze slid down to his muddy boots and back up to his flushed cheeks.

A single copper eyebrow arched.

"Yes, Caspian?"

The flush on Cas' cheeks deepened.

"Well?" Morgan sighed, impatience dusting her cool tone.

Cas opened his mouth.

Nothing came out but a squeak.

Blinking rapidly, Cas swallowed, gazing everywhere but straight ahead, and found himself glancing at the ground.

Fuck!

Her petite, exquisite feet were bare.

Bare.

Oh my gods!

As the youthful voice in his mind just about had a fit, the librarian watched unblinkingly.

No one else should see those lovely toes and nails like shimmering pearls! Cas wanted to rage out loud. *Along with her undershirt, where were her damned shoes?*

More importantly, where were his fucking words? His heartfelt, carefully considered poetic philosophy —

Morgan slurped loudly at the fragrant cup of tea.

Stomach somewhere below his knees, Cas' gaze jerked up. His odd blue eyes narrowed in suspicion.

Was she mocking him?

Cas straightened his shoulders, ignoring the pouring rain as it beat down upon his leather hood that deafened his throbbing ears.

Be a man!

An unsteady hand fumbled inside his cloak to present the bottle of rare wine. Unable to stand it, Cas closed his eyes to the glorious distraction of two barely covered, perfectly pink nipples whilst reaching for the only words that came ready and willing to his parched mouth.

"Morgan..." Cas croaked. "Fuck m-me..."

There was no delay.

The wine bottle was swiped from his grip right before the door slammed in his face.

40

Morgan

Year 257
Baile Mara

Afte slamming her door in Caspian's stunned face, Morgan stalked to the small square table of raw pine with its single, lonely chair.

The teacup banged down with a fragrant splash beside a plate of fresh figs. The bottle swiped from her persistent admirer was uncorked with trembling, ink-stained fingers. A generous dash of the precious liquid was added to the tea, filling the cup to the brim. Morgan drained the mixture immediately with a series of fierce gulps.

Keeping her back to the door where no doubt a soggy, blonde sixteen-year-old was sulking, Morgan wilted onto the chair, knees giving way.

"Get your shit together, Morgan," the librarian murmured bitterly to the empty cup. "This is the way it needs to be."

The sound of the chilled rain, falling heavier onto the cobbles beyond her resolutely closed door, swallowed her uncertain whisper.

It was difficult to regain her focus. She had smoked a great deal that morning after a blinding series of dreams. And, yes, most of their ominous images had faded. Not all, but enough that her day could be spent preparing for her travels.

Only a few paces across, including her bathing and toilet alcove hidden behind a heavy curtain of dark green wool, her home was livable enough.

The building was constructed with the city's native black rock. A squat iron stove filled with glowing embers heated the compact room. Its pipe to the roof warmed the single upstairs chamber as well. The way this home was built into the back of the temple, there was no room for a window on the bottom floor, only upstairs had the luxury of natural light. Magic had infused her eyes enough that this wasn't a problem, meaning she could work by the lone lantern on the table with its thick flame bobbing behind clear glass. This had led her to using a pale plaster wash inside.

So, despite the lack of a window downstairs, the space was reasonably light compared to most other public and private dwellings built of the same dark stone.

Inhaling deliberately and slowly, Morgan picked up the small square of copper sheeting off the table and continued. Precision was required, and yet the radiant spread of alcohol numbing her mouth and steadying her hands was welcome.

Her hobby wasn't really map making, so much as making contoured records of the city and the bay. They were the places that appeared in her dreams, chaotic and strange. Here, she had control over the images and could work them from her mind. The thin, flexible sheets of metal were expensive, along with the delicate tools to shape the layers and engrave further details. Her large influx of coins from the Carters, their compensation for Morgan sharing her bitter dreams and intuition, went a long way towards them.

Instead, she should have been saving to pack up and leave, heading to somewhere far away.

"Yet here I am," Morgan muttered, flexing her hand, the amethyst ring on her thumb glinting with reflected lantern light.

At the sound of a muted scrape on the roof above, Morgan grimaced at the stairs.

"Damn pigeons."

A freckled hand reached for the teacup, then grabbed the bottle of fine wine instead. Morgan drained half of it, hoping to quell last night's images of passionate dreams about the young man likely still staring at her door.

That way led to ruin.

Beyond that, there was only the barest possibility of something impossible that she had no reason to hope for.

Taking another swig, Morgan allowed the alcohol to soothe her aching heart and focused on the copper sheets.

In front of her was the unfinished map of Baile Mara and the shape of its wide, curving shoreline. It was one of many. There were different views, each from those washing across her confusing dreams. In the middle of this piece, minute layers of copper were being assembled to create the smoking island in the middle of the bay. Etchings covered the layers, symbols and words, a way of purging the troubling images from her mind, received into the metal in the hopes they would be forgotten.

Delicate tinsnips in hand, Morgan resumed trimming the outline of the next piece when another noise resounded from above.

It was not a scrape on the roof this time, rather it was a dull thud from directly overhead.

Inside.

"You fucking dirty pests," the librarian hissed.

Fresh air was well and good, rain and pigeon shit was not.

Wondering why she never shut the damned thing since installing the thick sheets of clear glass after a fierce rainy season last year, Morgan grabbed her broom, slipped on her sheepskin scuffs and stomped upstairs. It should be easy to shoo the filthy birds back outside. The upper room was as sparse and tiny as below. The difference was there was a compact bed, a stool with a few scattered crystals on top, a pale wooden staff propped in one corner, along with a cedar chest for her clothes.

But when Morgan reached the uppermost stair, she halted abruptly.

Both crimson eyebrows arched towards her hairline.

The blonde teenager, crouched on the stone sill of the open window, grinned at her astounded expression.

"What the fuck?" screeched Morgan.

Above her bed, Caspian sat folded up like a very large and very damp grasshopper.

His upper half was outside in the rain, and one socked foot was inside, toes gingerly searching for the mattress below.

The librarian blinked at him, then at the pile of sodden items in the middle of the floor. It was his sword, cloak, and a lone boot. Pale green eyes returned to Caspian.

As she watched, speechless, Caspian finally ducked his head through the opening with a curse. Sitting bent over and mostly inside, he tugged off his remaining boot. With a slick thud, it joined the pile of other wet items.

"What the fuck?" Morgan repeated.

Freckled hands tightened on the broom handle, her ring cutting into the spindly wood.

"I didn't want to get the bed dirty," Caspian explained as he landed crossways on the compact bed with a triumphant whoop. He'd obviously gotten over his hesitation only moments ago at her door.

Caspian rolled onto his back, long legs in the air, knees bent. His head hung off the bed, face upside down. He reached up to slide off his damp socks, and they landed one by one on his boots. He placed his bare feet on the wall beside the window, his dripping blonde hair stuck out from his head in wet spikes.

Eyes sparkling, Caspian grinned.

The young man pointed to his groin, or more precisely, at the obvious bulge behind the laces of his trousers.

"Here," he said, a little breathless. "Hop on."

Heat flooded Morgan's face.

The broom swung.

"You little shit!"

"Morgan, my lovely flame —! *Gah!*"

Caspian rolled away, the broom head missing his own by a wisp of air.

Morgan didn't stop.

Laying on his stomach with his hands protecting his head, Caspian's cries, as the straw broom head landed on him over and over, were muffled by her pillow.

"What. Are. You. Doing. Here?" Each word was punctuated by a *whack*.

He didn't reply, and Morgan halted her attack on realising his shoulders were shaking. Caspian looked up through the wild spikes of hair. He wasn't upset.

The bastard was laughing.

"You —!" Morgan hissed and charged.

That went as well as it could have.

The broom went flying as she slapped at him, vaguely aware that her fury was a distant thing.

She was more surprised than angry, really.

It didn't matter.

Caspian overcame her attack easily, the innocent fumbling of earlier at her door gone in the face of his bodily strength as he pinned her down. When she gave up with a cry of frustration, the sparks of silver in his eyes dimmed momentarily, then brightened. Without warning, he rolled onto his back, taking her with him, bringing her to sit crouched over his stomach.

He was breathing rapidly beneath her, but was in no way winded.

Eyes on her face, Caspian waited for Morgan to catch her breath, his hands light on her thighs.

Blonde lashes fluttered as the ends of her long crimson hair painted his damp face. Blue eyes, one light and one dark, turned solemn.

"Morgan." Caspian's voice was as gentle as the hands that wandered from her thighs to her heaving sides. "I love you."

The seriousness of his declaration was a side of him she'd never seen.

With a shake of her head, Morgan pushed at him to scramble back.

It was useless, though.

His grip tightened as he sat up, pulling her close. A hand cupped the back of her head as he pressed her cheek to his chest. Her cursing and resistance continued until she realised what he was doing.

As her ear registered the frantic rhythm of his heart beneath her cheek, Morgan went limp, hands crushed between them. A small noise escaped her throat.

"Listen to what you do to me," he rumbled.

"No," breathed the librarian, eyes shut tight.

"Yes," Caspian said quietly, his tone tranquil as his chest vibrated against her ear. "My wild flame, I love you."

"You're lying —"

"I love your fire," Caspian continued.

"No, no, no —"

"I love your dark humour."

"Please," Morgan said weakly, not knowing what she was asking for. Her hands slid up between them to push against the damp fabric over his chest, feeling the wild beat and echo of her own traitorous heart.

"I love your tenacity. I love your smile. I love your eyes." Caspian clasped gentle hands around her arms and shifted her on his lap, placing a lingering kiss on each part he mentioned. "Your cheeks, your ear, your hair..."

"Caspian," Morgan spoke through her constricted throat. "Please... *stop*."

Immediately, his hands fell away.

At the loss of their roaming exploration, Morgan glanced up at their absence. Dazzling, mismatched blue eyes shimmered with silver. His smile was a whimsical twist of flushed lips, not at all the expression she expected.

"Stop?" he asked. "I will if that's what you want."

Seated on his lap, fully aware of his ripe desire for her where it pressed against her backside, Morgan stared at him.

"I hate you," she whispered, the words the furthest from the truth that could be imagined falling from her lips with sickening ease.

Again, to her amazement, his reaction surprised her. The hard shimmer in the blue gaze close to her own softened.

"I know," he said with a sublime smile. "Me too."

His expressive gaze would always undo her, the intense light searing her heart.

"We can't," Morgan began, breath hitching. "This isn't right... I've seen it, the entire world... ruined..."

"I believe you," Caspian breathed, his forehead dropping to hers. His warm breath filled the minute gap between them. "And I simply do not care."

As their eyes exchanged a language spoken without words, the moment stretched between them like thick honey spreading across bare skin. But, unable to contain himself, Caspian's next statement ruptured the peace of the moment with the twitch of his groin beneath her.

"So, Morgan," he whispered, white eyebrows arched, "fuck me, hmm?"

Morgan reeled back. "Stop saying it like that!"

Laughing, Caspian bucked his hips. "*Ha!* Fuck me —"

Morgan slipped a hand into his pants and squeezed.

"Say. It. Again."

Caspian yelped as each word was accompanied by a vicious yank of his annoyingly and generously proportioned, most intimate self.

"Oh fuck, Morgan!" Cas exclaimed, rain drops scattering her face as he threw his head back. "Your grip is much stronger than I imagined —"

"Say."

"Nnngh…"

"It."

"Oh, *fuck…*"

"Again —"

What?

Morgan's movements stilled around the twitching member in her hand.

"Caspian… Did you just climax?"

She swore as he sagged against her.

"Use my shirt," Caspian murmured dreamily as he slipped her hand out of his soiled pants. He slid her fingers over his shirt, wiping the stickiness over himself. When he was done, he looked up. "Let's keep going, yeah?"

Morgan's lips curled upwards of their own accord, desire spreading through her body at the look in his eyes.

Caspian grinned in triumph. "Heh."

Carefully pushing her off his lap, Caspian reached over to the window.

"No."

Morgan pressed against him from behind, her small hand reaching for his.

"Leave it open," she murmured against the heat of his back. "I'll leave it open now, for… the rain."

As the deluge covered their slick hands with cool drops, they stilled for a moment, breathing in the crisp scent of wet cobbles and damp earth.

"I love you," Caspian sighed, his gaze on the clouds outside.

"I love… the rain," Morgan mumbled, inhaling the musk and dampness of his shirt. The feel of his snort was a pleasant buzz against her mouth, distracting her from the feel of countless little scars all over his back.

Withdrawing their hands inside, Caspian placed a heated kiss like fresh smoke on her fingers before dropping their clasped grip to his groin. Morgan laughed at the fresh swelling of throbbing flesh.

"It's your fault," Caspian explained, gathering her close as he turned around, a complicated shuffle on his knees considering her bed was about as small as a bed could be.

"What?" Morgan said as her head was lowered to the pillow with tender care.

"This." His hips rolled against her. "So take care of it, take care of all of me." Blue eyes with the lustre of quicksilver gleamed brightly. "And in return, I'll make it so you never doubt your hatred for me, and my love for you."

"Did you like that?" Caspian murmured, his lips busy over a responsive pink nipple.

He was on his knees leaning over her, one hand leisurely stroking himself, the other between her thighs. Morgan lay beneath him, limp, spent from his caresses that had fumbled a little at first, increasing with confidence as he considered her reactions, until their peak had swept her away to pleasure.

"Shall I do that again?" Blue eyes, normally sparkling, were heavy with lust as he raised his head for her reply.

"Don't look at me!" Morgan hissed. She reached behind her head to grab the pillow and mashed it into his flushed face.

Caspian's laugh was muffled. With a gentle tug, he tossed the pillow away with one hand, the other still attentive and languidly circling her core. He lent down to whisper directly against her ear, his low voice teasing, lips rustling the locks of damp hair over her cheeks.

"Show me," he murmured. "Tell me. Let me hear what you like."

Morgan made a small noise in the back of her throat as his long fingers summoned even more pleasure within her. His thumb circled just outside, where it was most sensitive, eliciting the same fevered response as earlier.

"You feel like silk and apricots. You taste like rose petals and honey," he breathed, continuing to lazily stroke the pink and violet folds of silk and heat between her damp thighs. "But I want to hear what you feel. Please. Don't hide from me, my love."

Lids shut tight, Morgan inhaled unevenly, tasting his damp hair on her lips, salt and sweat as his face moved to nuzzle the gentle curve where her neck met her shoulder.

"My... my body feels strange, light but heavy, like brittle stone..." Morgan hesitated. "Like I might crack, I might break..."

With one last caress like cool moonlight, Caspian withdrew his fingers. His hand slid along Morgan's thigh to her knee to calmly spread her legs. He glanced at her, judging her reaction once more. Swallowing, Morgan nodded, watching the smile she knew by heart grow wide with pleased mischief. Still on his knees, Caspian shifted, so he was between her legs, his cheeks flushed, his eyes on her face. That consideration alone would have eased the hardness of her resolve if she was not yet committed to their passion.

Lowering himself so that he lay over and against her, supporting his full weight on his elbows, Caspian closed the distance between their mouths. Morgan exhaled into him, her temperature rising, images and sensations drifting across her thoughts with barely coherent waves as the afterglow of her orgasm subsided.

Sunshine and blue sky, black sands and salt water, the simple sounds and aromas of her everyday life were magnified, made holy somehow. Along with the sensation of rough parchment, ink, dust, fresh flowers and cut grass, the sights and sensations of her tiny world seemed important, only by their comparison to this union and all that it meant.

It wasn't magic; it wasn't contained potential in the crystals that others worshipped; it was the power with which Caspian worshipped her now. There was fear on her behalf, mitigated almost entirely by his honest confidence. There was an arrogance to his demands, to his caresses, his kisses. But always, there was care.

Tender, exquisite care.

The hard heat of his throbbing flesh slid against her. Morgan sighed, her arms coming up, hands sliding over his slick neck to hold his mouth to her own.

"May I?" Caspian inquired politely, his tongue licking at her bottom lip.

Morgan's petite fingers curled into his hair, tugging a little as she smiled.

"You may," she whispered, her pale eyes full of wonder at the desire dripping from his gaze. She lifted her feet to wrap her legs around his bare backside, bringing the intense hardness of his cock directly in line with where it demanded to be.

At first, Caspian didn't move. He just stared at her. Eventually, he dropped his face to her damp chest.

"Caspian?" Morgan breathed.

"Give me a moment," came the muttered response. "It's about to be all over too soon."

He didn't seem embarrassed though, if the decadent laugh between her breasts was anything to go by.

"Mm. We *could* wait," Morgan said with a quiet laugh.

But, to tease him a little, she squeezed her legs. As expected, Caspian uttered another explicit curse as he was pressed against her everywhere that counted.

"I've counted all the stars while waiting to grow up for you," Caspian said as he raised his head, eyes narrowed with a teasing smile of his own. "Surely you can wait a breath or three until my body behaves itself?"

"No," Morgan said and leaned up to lick his neck.

And before he could protest, she reached between them and guided him home.

Caspian's wild curse and startled jerk were worth it, his gasp of wonder a sound that would linger in her daydreams for the rest of her life.

With a deep groan, he moved, sliding with immeasurable patience, a vein in his forehead popping with his restraint.

"Caspian," Morgan said, and grabbed his cheeks. "Let me hear you."

Biting his bottom lip, he shook his head, his eyes hidden from her this time.

"You felt me come apart around your fingers, beautiful boy," Morgan gasped, "so it's your turn to let it out."

And to her pleasure, he did.

Letting his cries of wonder free, Morgan was glad for the open window as Caspian's moans filled her room, their room, and echoing into the street outside. The wild sounds spoke of pent up fury and hidden fears. But as they moved together, Morgan wrapped all parts of herself around him, as fierce as was possible, reaching out, connecting, grasping to hold him close. Supporting each other with body and breath, in a way neither of them had been held before.

After minutes, days, hours or a breath, flames of heat and sensation exploded within each of them, Morgan first, Caspian not long after. Stunned by her as she first tensed, then melted beneath him, he followed her into oblivion, a sweet respite from the reality of their doomed home.

Did she care?

Yes.

No.

It didn't matter.

It was done.

Her haunting dreams showed her that at some point, after they came together, the world would come apart.

As Caspian climaxed, throbbing with deep spasms within her scorching, pulsing heat, he cried out with a relieved shout that gave her as much satisfaction as her own orgasm. Awed, he stared down at her, whispering her name, eyes wide, two fiercely blazing stars of sapphire and mercury shining just for her.

"Are you alright?" he panted, one hand wiping the sweat and hair away from her mouth and cheeks.

"Mmm," she purred, relaxed and limp. "Are you?"

Caspian swallowed, nodding. He opened his mouth to speak, seemed to think better of it, then shut it, lips pursed.

Pale green eyes narrowed. "What?"

"Oh." Caspian gave a sheepish grin. "I had a thought..."

"About?"

He shook his head at her tone. "Oh... no, it's fine."

Morgan grabbed his chin, eyes narrowing into thin, pale green slits like icy jade.

"Well," Caspian said with a nervous laugh. "I realised what you remind me of. You're tiny, surrounded by copper fuzz, but all soft inside."

"Keep going," she dared him.

"Sometimes there is a sting, sometimes there isn't," Caspian continued, then kissed the tip of her freckled nose. "You're like a bumblebee."

He cut off Morgan's agitated hiss with his mouth, laughing as he kissed her deeply, igniting their passion yet again.

The sound of a gratified sigh broke the silence of a room darkened by the late hour.

Naked, they sprawled together on the cramped bed, Caspian sitting up, Morgan laying by his side. They had refreshed themselves with cool water, Caspian having fetched the plate of figs from downstairs. He was feeding her bites of the ripe, sweet fruit.

"The plaques downstairs," Caspian asked suddenly, his voice obscured by chewing. "Are they maps?"

"Mm," Morgan replied lazily into her pillow, eyes closed. "I put my dreams into them, all of the chaotic imagery, making sense of it all."

"They're actual places then? Some looked familiar."

"Yes." Morgan rolled over onto her back, hands stretched above her. "Magic gathers in certain places in my dreams. I can make sense of them by doing this. Sometimes it helps the dreams fade a little so I can forget them." She blew out a long breath. "Sometimes not."

Sitting back against the wall, Caspian was silent. Morgan yawned, soft green eyes opening to glance up at his profile. He was a young man but his jaw, his cheekbones, were becoming more defined, a sign of the attractive man he would become. Ignoring the pang in her chest, Morgan rolled to her side and nuzzled his bare thigh. Silver blue flashed as Caspian glanced down from the corner of his eye.

"Maps to destiny then, hmm?" he asked, curiosity lacing his voice as he swallowed.

"Perhaps."

To the sound of a throat clearing, a hand touched her head, smoothing the hair back from her face.

"So," Caspian murmured casually. "How was I?"

Morgan reached up, tweaking his swollen nipple.

"You weren't terrible," she replied, laughing at his yelp.

With a beleaguered huff, Caspian slid down the wall with an awkward folding of long limbs and turned to face her, head propped on his hand. His blue eyes were wide. But after examining her face, a cunning light flashed across them. His gaze narrowed, glinting in the starlight shining through the open window.

"You must teach me then."

A small hand reached up to grab his chin.

"No," Morgan replied as she pulled his face towards hers, lips against lips. "Never."

Caspian nibbled at Morgan's chin, his mouth sliding down her glistening neck. The sweetness of his breath caused another lick of desire to flare deep within her core.

"Please? Share yourself with me. A breath shared with you is better than any sense of home," Caspian murmured against her skin, "better than anything, so may the gods forget me if I do you wrong."

Eyes welling at the words no one had ever said to her before, Morgan pushed him away while staring at the shadowed ceiling.

"Don't say that, Caspian."

He didn't reply.

Instead, a lock of long red hair was lifted out of the chaotic fan about her head. With great care it was used to coax unshed tears from copper eyelashes, painting the sparkling moisture over her cheeks. Caspian made no comment as Morgan slapped his hand away, then pulled it back almost immediately.

She said nothing, but quietly slipped her amethyst ring over his little finger.

The little jewel was one of only a few belongings found with Morgan when she was left with the nuns. A newborn baby with a soft wool blanket, a bunch of dried roses, and a ring tucked into her silk slipper. It wasn't much, nowhere near as valuable as the sword she had gifted, but what else could she give Caspian but pain and loss?

"For me? Thank you. This will keep me company when I think of you, my heart burning, my hand wrapped around my —"

The pillow whacking his face swallowed the rest of that statement. Laughing, Caspian pointed the last fig at a gloomy corner of the room by the end of her bed.

"A ruby atop that would match my sword."

Morgan tilted her head just enough to see where he was pointing.

Her staff?

"I'll get you a lovely faceted one," Caspian said seriously around a mouthful of fruit in reply to her snort.

"No."

"Tsk. So angry."

Morgan dropped her cheek back to his chest. The rain continued outside, the cool air a refreshing breeze over damp, salty skin.

"I'm not angry. I... don't feel anything."

"Nothing?" Caspian's voice hummed against her ear, his tone gently chiding. "You are at peace with the world, then, huh?"

The librarian scoffed, her lids drifting closed. Caspian continued, unabashed.

"All your scorn, my dear little firebird, sounds a lot like deeply suppressed rage."

Pretending to slumber, Morgan ignored him. But Caspian was determined to get whatever point across he was trying to make.

"Let me eat that rage for you," he murmured. A whiff of fig met her nose as his fingers brushed away a lock of hair from her face.

"You can't," she whispered, hating the catch in her voice.

"I fucking can. Because even if I die, my love for you will remain."

"Don't be ridiculous —"

"I'm as sure as there is salt in the ocean, as there is liquid rock bubbling away under that stinking island. My heart might dry out to a decomposed husk, but my love for you will endure."

Morgan was silent, digesting the youthful grandeur of his words.

A worried laugh rumbled against her. "Too dark, my love?"

"No," she said. "But speaking of dark..."

With a gentle groan, Morgan rolled onto her back, her free arm reaching behind to lightly tap one of the crystals by her bed on the stool. Her touch activated the chaotic charge inside its structure with a spark of her magic. The clear quartz sphere glowed an eerie lilac, the soft glow filling the small chamber.

"Huh. That's a fancy lantern," Caspian hummed.

Morgan cursed inwardly, aware of Caspian's intrigue with the magic that he was unable to possess. Hoping he wouldn't ask her about its use, she slid a hand down his bare abdomen.

"That's not a... Um. It's just a piece of charged quartz."

Thankfully, Caspian was easily distracted by her roaming fingers as they trailed through slick curls of hair below his navel.

"Either way," he purred, "it's beautiful. I'll be able to do that one day. Manipulate things. To fix... things."

Morgan licked her lips. "Why would you want to, really?"

Shifting about on his side, Caspian propped his elbow on the bed and rested his cheek on his fist. He appeared to be taking her question seriously. At first, anyway. His gaze shimmered as he grinned.

"I want wings to carry you, my ripe little strawberry."

"What?"

"I'll find a way," he said, his smile dazzling her. "And I will take you wherever you want."

"You're a clever fox," Morgan murmured quietly as her knuckles grazed his spent flesh. "If anyone can outsmart Hypatia, it'll be you." Her hand paused. "Caspian."

"Mm? Don't stop."

"I'll have to stop by the day after tomorrow."

"What? Why?" Eyes of blue, one light and one dark and clouded by lust, narrowed.

"I'm off to the City of the Seers. Even after all this time, the library was never finished. I've... been called up to help out."

Morgan hoped he missed the catch in her voice.

Would he realise she had asked to go?

As much as his devoted attention was a light that bathed her in its warm glow, it was also blinding. It could surely never last.

Besides, Rook had established a series of new entertainment venues in the City of the Seers, somewhere she could indulge in the substances that dulled her dreams. Without a pair of odd blue eyes watching her closely. Morgan still supplied Rook with poppies, and sometimes bought back the resin he refined from them in return, along with new and exotic substances he'd found. Because intoxicants could lift her from the weight of her sorry responsibilities, and dull her dreams. Sex, amazing as it had been just now, could not.

Caspian was silent for a time, a line forming between his pale eyebrows.

"No." His eyes narrowed into flinty slits of silver. "You can't go."

"Sure, Caspian." Morgan yawned, avoiding his gaze. A change of subject was in order. "Hey. What happened earlier? Before you snuck in like a thief?"

"Hm." After an annoyed sigh, he laughed softly. "I had so many words prepared for you."

"What happened?"

"I panicked."

Her fingers resumed their idle wander, her lazy gaze drifting to the window.

"Now you know how you make me feel, you beast," she muttered.

"Panicked?"

Morgan glanced away from the stars to the concerned blue gaze close to her face.

"Yes," she admitted. "Like the earth beneath will give way."

"I'll catch you," Caspian vowed, leaning down for a kiss. Morgan turned away.

"The earth won't crumble from beneath just my feet when it goes. It will disappear from everyone's."

"Then I'll catch them too."

"This isn't a game," Morgan said quietly.

"I know that."

Morgan kept her gaze on the cold stars beyond, pinpoints of cold light in a colder sky as her dreams crowded about her mind. Willing them away, she bared her teeth at them. Somehow, Caspian seemed to sense the direction of her thoughts.

"Do you dream about me?"

Not meeting his gaze, she gave a curt nod. Strangely enough, he dropped the topic and leant forward to nuzzle her neck once more. It was a while before she realised he was sniffing her hair.

"You've been frequenting Rook's dens more often, trying his latest imports. Isn't your poppy smoke enough, Morgan?"

Pale green eyes snapped to his. Their odd blue irises flashed silver and purple by the light of the glowing sphere behind her.

"My dreams, they... No. Not always, no," Morgan finished lamely.

A muscle in Caspian's smooth jaw twitched. "They tell you about some kind of ruin, yeah?"

She nodded. "Most of my dreams are true. I have no reason to doubt them."

"Delightful. When?"

"I don't know."

"Can we stop it?"

"No," Morgan said calmly. "Not anymore."

Caspian digested this in silence.

"The library?" he asked thoughtfully after a time. "There are no other dreams, or portents, recorded in your books from other seers?"

"I am not a seer!" she snapped, startling them both. Grimacing, she pressed herself against him, tucking her head under his chin, draping one leg over his. "And they are not *my* books. I hate those fucking books. I hope there will be none left one day, full of nonsense as they are."

"Really?" Cas laughed against her. "Fine. I'll take care of it."

"What?" Morgan frowned.

"Never mind." Caspian kissed her bare shoulder. "So can I eventually make it alright, afterwards?"

"After?"

"Whatever ruin is coming, can I make it right for you?"

"Caspian." Morgan pulled away to meet his dazzling gaze with calm eyes. "I haven't dreamed that there is one."

The purple glow from the softly glowing globe played over Caspian's eyes with sparkling flashes of amethyst and silver.

He blinked. "One... what?"

"An afterward."

41

Flare

Year 367

Baile Fuar

Rueben left not long after Caspian had staggered off to find a bathhouse that was still open.

Alone in the inn room, Flare stared at the fireplace.

He'd watched the logs burn down to embers, his shining amethyst eyes hardly blinking. Only an occasional crackle and hiss spoilt the weighted silence, the woodsy aroma of fragrant smoke fading as the wood burned away.

Hours before, and with a solemn bow to the dragon, the old priest had tidied up his belongings without ceremony and headed for the door.

"Won't you wait for Caspian?" Flare had called as the priest placed his aged speckled hand on the door handle.

Rueben had looked over his shoulder, wrinkled face lit with a genuine smile.

"No," said the priest. Grey eyes twinkled. "He and I no longer say goodbye to one another. Only hello."

Shivering and unable to get warm despite the heat that the embers still emitted, Flare sunk his head onto his fore-claws. They were stretched out before him, sharp nails shining as the orange and black embers pulsed.

Contemplating the nature of friendship in all its forms, finely scaled lids drifted closed.

He needed to add more wood to the fireplace. Instead, he stayed where he was, shivering. Every now and then, he let out a pitiful moan, his spiked tail jerking with involuntary twitches.

Flare, he tried to tell himself, *you need to choose.*

Another moan escaped his throat, so pitiful that he felt it rumble in his chest against the wool rug between him and the floor.

Sparks popped in the fireplace.

Amethyst eyes cracked open.

Was his moan that pitiful that he could still feel it?

Flare's head rose, infinitely slowly, as the embers shifted in the hearth and the rumble went on and on, increasing in both volume and sensation.

Just as he realised this was not his self wallowing moment of rumbling and groaning, a rock landed inside the fireplace from the chimney as the room experienced a vicious jerk. The great wooden bed creaked, the leftover tray with its discarded cups and jug rattled.

Scampering to his clawed feet, the dragon's jaw hung open as the untamed wild odor of scorching ozone reached his nose, rushing down the chimney and under the gap in the door.

Flare knew instinctively what this event was. It wasn't an earthquake at all.

When the earth naturally heaved and contracted, that wild stink didn't accompany such a calamity. As the floor shook and a jarring crack sounded near the door, Flare cried out. He rushed to the door. Scrabbling for purchase on the smooth surface, the little purple dragon sniffed at the gap with a trembling snout.

The stink was strongest here.

And underneath the fragrance of unleashed lightning was a wild bouquet, like a scatter of crushed jewels, bright and dark all at once.

A low moan escaped Flare's scaled lips.

"Oh... oh m-my..."

Booming noises echoed about the inn and its warren of rooms. And underneath the cacophony, barely perceptible footsteps resonated on the stairs.

The dragon scurried back from the door, as far as the modest room allowed, the great magic and might of his dragon heritage forgotten in panic. He backed into a wall, sliding into a corner, wings quivering, pupils wide with fear.

With languid casualness, the steps reached the landing outside. The ozone stink intensified.

The chamber door slammed open.

With eyes shut tight, Flare wailed, not at all prepared for the pain that would surely come.

42

Cas

Year 367
Baile Fuar

Cas stumbled into the room with an exaggerated belch stinking of strong liquor.

Catching hold of the handle, he paused in the doorway. Red-rimmed blue eyes squinted blearily. Flare had backed himself into a far corner of the chamber, his purple, leathery wings outspread, horrified eyes wide.

The drunken man blinked as the room swayed.

It looked like there were two dragons.

Blinking until the pair of winged creatures reconciled into one, Cas attempted to kick the door shut behind him. But he was more drunk than he'd realised. It was a challenge, considering the partying outside with their massive, booming fireworks, as if there was a kind of festival. On his search for their inn, people were everywhere, running about in the sleet and the snow, ignoring him while they danced and reeled from building to building.

Which was thankful, considering how much Cas had drunk and vomited as he'd lurched along. It was like the entire world was shaking, matching the careening tilt of his walk as he staggered away. Away from the baths, away from his pain, drowning it like the feisty librarian he would see one day soon.

Shifting his new satchel on one shoulder, Cas raised his near empty jug of spirits and pointed it in roughly the direction where Flare remained frozen, crouched in fright.

"What's with you, old man?" Cas hiccupped. "Find a grey scale? It looks like you've seen a fucking ghost."

One of the dragon's delicately scaled eyelids twitched.

As the room rumbled and spun with an offensive, sickening motion, Cas bared his teeth.

"What's got your spikes in," he belched once more, "a twist?"

In the corner, the dragon gulped.

Fighting the splitting pain in his head and willing the partying outside to shut the fuck up, Cas peered at Flare with genuine curiosity. Waiting for the dragon to respond, Cas wiped at his nose, swore as the jug jolted his fucked up fingers, then dropped his hand to his side.

Flare's wings drooped a little, but his amethyst eyes remained as wide open as Cas had ever seen them. As Cas watched, delirious, angry and also bemused, Flare flicked a glance to the door, then back to Cas. The dragon's jaw snapped shut.

"Um," croaked the dragon after a moment. "You d-didn't notice..?"

"Notice what?" Cas mumbled. He laughed as Flare gaped at Cas' next enormous hiccup. "This handsome lunatic is drunk."

"Ahhhh..." Flare squeaked as another deep rumble hummed from the festival outside. "Earthq-q-quake..?"

"*Earthq-q-quake..?*" mimicked Cas with prickly indignation.

The dragon nodded so slowly that Cas was fascinated. Flare kept his eyes on Cas' face, the spiked crown around his scaled brow quivering.

Cas glanced at the rug under his feet, then back at Flare. After an exaggerated blink, Cas tilted his head, still swaying in the doorway, and listened. Raised voices and multiple racing footsteps were still coming from outside.

"Are you sure? Well, *I* think it's," he burped, "a fucking awesome party."

"Umm. I'm s-sure, y-yes," Flare whispered, "perhaps a r-rather big one..."

Huh.

Of all times, now?

It seemed hilarious that while Cas felt as low as he had ever been after what was supposed to be an invigorating visit to the mineral pools, people outside were full of joy.

Finally getting the door shut, the gods only knew how, Cas trod an unsteady path across the room, the turbulence in his head as riotous as the revelry and booming outside, the room too hard to navigate. From the corner of his eye, Cas realised the fire had died to embers almost black.

Pausing just long enough to bend down, almost falling over, Cas kicked the basket of wood at the hearth. A sloppy kick sent the whole thing, logs and basket both, into the fireplace. Cas spluttered at the resulting cloud of ash peppered with a few sparks.

"H-how about I go out and investigate... w-would that work for you?" Flare mumbled from his gloomy corner.

"Well, it sure wouldn't," Cas drawled as he reached the bed with far too many steps than it should have taken, "but it's a fun thought. You just want to join the drinking, yeah? Cheeky fucker."

Missing the dragon's expression of complete incomprehension, Cas shook off the icy rain along with what felt like grit from who the fuck knew where. Struggling a little, well, a lot actually, he unhooked the strap of his newly acquired leather satchel off his shoulder and placed the bag on the blankets. He'd swiped the bag from someone running one way as he went the other. They had tripped and fallen. He assumed they were mostly fine. By then, he was on his second jug of alcohol. It was briskly cold and not at all good for the frigid weather, but it was dulling his heart and senses.

So that was fine.

Inhaling, he scented the rain on himself, the damp aroma just about giving him a hard on considering what the rain reminded him of. It normally soothed him as much as it turned him on. Yet while he was somewhat aware that he was drunk, he was also agitated for reasons that the same drunken stupor could not fathom.

The steaming waters of the hot spring had refreshed him, while also allowing him to release some of the pain that followed him with every broken dream that plagued his thoughts. He didn't normally drink so much either, especially after purifying his body, but the night called for it. His hand was a mess, although slightly less infected, thanks to Rueben. He'd lost a heap of weight, and was currently affected by some ungodly shimmering copper rash that had covered his hands, arms, chest and, by the old mirror back at the baths, could be seen creeping up his neck.

He was still in a sorry state, but clean.

And cold.

Spinning and just about collapsing against one bedpost, Cas raised his broken, trembling hand towards the fire.

The alcohol thrummed in his blood, but hadn't dulled his magic. With a sloppily focused thought, he aimed a curl of power at the logs of wood tumbled about in the hearth, slowly smothering the dying embers beneath.

Which was such an easy spend of magic, it was laughable.

What wasn't laughable was what happened instead.

Rather than the logs igniting with an explosion of sparks and heat, an explosion happened in Cas' head.

Or that's at least what it felt like.

Perhaps it was both.

A massive *whoosh* filled the room. Sparks flew and landed on the curtains and blankets. Flare yelped, a wave of coolness erupting from his scales as he cringed, the hundreds of tiny flames instantly dying as he scattered magic about with frantic intensity.

Collapsing to his knees, Cas grabbed his head with a wild cry. The acrid aroma of scorched fabric filled his nose.

"My magic! What the fuck?"

A dazzling pain whipped through his head, his face, his hands, and body. Unable to hold himself up, Cas toppled sideways before the extinguished hearth with its chaotic pile of logs, and gasped at the spinning ceiling as the world spun and roared. His face and neck hurt, even his hair, if that was even fucking possible.

Panting, Cas managed to lift his head. His different coloured blue eyes, both rimmed with red and flashing silver, found the dragon.

Flare was silent, his eyes shining with astonishment.

"What the fuck?" Cas shrieked.

Swallowing, the dragon shook his head.

"What did you do to me?"

"What?" Flare cried back at the hissed accusation. "Nothing!"

"That f-fucking hurt," Cas wailed as the agony faded, his ears popping.

"Um," Flare mumbled, taking one step forward. "Perhaps it is because you are s-sick... maybe just n-now," his wide eyes took in the rumbling room, then found Cas' once more, "oh, your hair is... um... maybe don't use your magic right at this moment..."

"Don't tell me what to do," hissed Cas from the floor.

The dragon shut up.

For some reason, his mother's face came to mind.

"She played at being a god," Cas muttered as he pushed to his knees. A belch followed this caustic declaration. "How ridiculous. But if she was, then so am I, and I will worship myself as one... my far seeing soul demands it."

Eyes shut tight against the fading agony of magic gone weirdly wrong, Cas crawled blindly to the bed. He felt like vomiting, but he swallowed it back. He wanted the alcohol to knock him out, not paint the floor of his room with sour aromas. Tomorrow would come soon enough, he thought sullenly, that he'd likely gotten himself into this pickle.

A pickle that included losing his ring.

His eyes opened at that sorry thought.

Biting back his sob whilst thinking he looked like a copper coloured pickle, Cas climbed onto the bed.

"It is up to the gods to decide," he mumbled. "I shall decide who gets to keep it... the rest is for me, for her and for you..."

Agonised fingertips slipped inside the damp leather of the bag, and Cas extracted the egg. Using one arm, he crawled under the top layer of the bedding with a shiver. It was cool under the cover, but foremost in his mind at that point wasn't about warming up. It was his sorry reflection, his haunted appearance back at the deserted mineral pools. Despite the weird copper rash encroaching along his flesh, it was a shock sometimes how much he looked like Wane.

"I wish I could hear the rain over the party," Cas sighed as his stomach heaved, "but here it is too much like a cave, locked away from the world."

Despite the thunder and the occasional tremor, despite the aches in his body, the lingering fever in his blood, and accumulating fatigue, Cas fell asleep almost straight away. He didn't even undress from his damp shirt and pants.

His sluggish mind had one last thought though before sleep took him under.

The iron gate of the mineral pools, had he locked it behind him?

He couldn't remember.

What a pity.

Apart from his emotional breakdown, it was the best damned bath he'd had in years.

Endless Skye, sang the lyrical voice.

Endless Skye, Endless Sky.

Endless Skye, so close by.

Exactly enough time later for most of the alcohol to be absorbed, mismatched blue eyes snapped open.

Cas sat up in bed, inhaling uneasily, and glanced around through gummed lashes.

He had been fast asleep in the same inn room that he'd passed out in hours before. An occasional muted voice could be heard elsewhere in the cavernous inn, along with the odd set of footsteps. The thunder and rumble of whatever the fuck had been going on had died down. The aroma of spiced breakfast tea wafted through the gap under the closed door. Which was odd, considering his senses told him it wasn't yet dawn.

Red-rimmed eyes squinted at first, before quicksilver pupils dilated, taking in the sight. The fireplace held no crackling flames, the glow that lit the room coming from cooling embers.

But there was enough for Cas to see something that hadn't been there before.

Behind the wooden door, a crack in the solid stone had appeared. It was about an arms-length, about waist height near the middle hinge. Multiple minor, web-like fractures led away from the main damage.

His wild gaze dropped to the jagged chunk of crystal, sparkling with tones of sapphire and emerald, pressed to his bare chest. A manic laugh threatened to escape his parted lips.

The name in his mind repeated without a sound, fading like blood drying under a noontime sun along with the taste of lightning on his tongue.

Cas released one hand from its deathlike grip about the egg and touched his forehead, his throat constricting.

Images, sounds, and sensations from the previous night bloomed like bright red poppies in his consciousness.

Well.

He was a total fucking idiot, wasn't he?

Eyeing the edge of the mattress at his feet for a few heartbeats, mind reeling, testing his stomach to make sure it behaved itself, Cas moved.

After twisting to place the egg into the warmth of his vacated pillow with tender care, Cas crawled to the end of the bed, spare pillow grasped in his good hand. Reaching the edge of the mattress, he stuck his head over the end, white blonde hair an untamed tangle about his head.

Then, with a flourish, he threw the pillow at the sleeping dragon curled up on the rug before the last of the embers.

Flare woke from fitful sleep with an aggrieved yelp. He looked wildly about until he realised Cas' upside-down face was less than a breath's span away from his. If Cas had been any closer, the blonde tips of his wild hair might have tickled the dragon's crown of spikes.

Wide reptilian eyes blinked rapidly at the blue eyes directly in front of them, each one flashing with tyrannical silver.

"Good morning, Flare, my precious jewel." Cas smiled with ominously restrained politeness. "Is there something you forgot to tell me?"

43

Karlien

Year 367
Travelling

It was Karlien's third night away from the only home he'd ever known.

Deep within his bedroll, the prince peered over the edge of his blanket at the silver stars shining above.

This was the furthest he'd ever been from the coast. The trees increased in height and girth the further along the road they travelled, in a long line of riders and carts. Occasionally, a crystal pillar representing some god or another stood by the gravel road, covered in mossy splotches. But the shrines became fewer as the days passed. Wondering when they would stop completely, Karlien poked his nose out and exhaled a puff of white mist.

The nighttime air of their latest camp had a surreal, ethereal quality about it. Lush aromas wafted about, reminding the traveller that during the day the world was a green place, full of oaks, cedars, flowering gums and towering pines, wet ferns and mossy boulders scattered about. Now that the sun had dipped behind the hills ahead, beyond the meandering road, a kind of sombre awareness had settled over the camp. The light had gone, but the wilderness remained.

Frogs croaked in ambient echoes of one another down by the creek amongst the trees. A pungent herb that grew in copious amounts amongst the camp filled the nose with the aroma similar to the lush crispness of ripe tomato vines. Clouds of wood smoke, blue and grey, curled about the camp, a tree-less, grassy meadow, with a dreamlike quality.

Here under the stars, the creak of gently swaying treetops and rustling leaves soothed the mind, the aroma of rich, damp earth filled the nose.

It was wild and beautiful, according to Torres.

Karlien hated it.

Azure eyes, turned stormy blue by the few fires still alight, narrowed.

No ocean crashed on black shores at the edges of his hearing. There was no taste of salt on the tongue. The prince was saddle sore, with no access to his face creams and scented oils to rid himself of the stink of horse and sweat, only hard soap and cold water. The ground, despite the moss and long grass full of who knew what, was awful. A thick fur coat, lined with red silk that had been an unexpected gift from his bodyguard, was an extra layer on his bedroll, but Karlien was still bitterly cold. A fire burned nearby, the wolf was pressed against him, but it wasn't enough.

Baek Hyeon had settled Karlien's bedroll on the outer edge of camp as usual.

The prince had queried this at first. Wouldn't the centre be more secure?

His bodyguard had muttered something about that being too obvious, and continued laying out their necessities. So now Karlien was under the outer edge of a vast oak, with who knew how many critters in the shadows above peering back at him with beady eyes and pincer-like teeth.

He hadn't seen any of the said creatures, but they were surely there. Karlien had spotted enough giant rats amongst the hills of volcanic ash and rock dumped outside Baile Mara's broken walls, where the rubble from the city was dumped, to know even more nefarious, hidden creatures dwelt in the unknown depths of the dense forest.

On top of that, the food was disgustingly basic. Why on earth did the cooks insist on preparing beans for a camp that slept so closely together? Karlien scrunched his nose at last night's particularly melodious experience.

Beside him, the wolf pressed into his side, half under the voluminous fur cloak. The great beast was so close that he had to spit out the animal's fur when an ear ended up in his face.

Hyeon hadn't made it to his bedroll just yet. It was handily close to Karlien's, and thinking about that, the prince chewed on his bottom lip.

Not that he needed his bodyguard this close on whatever backwater road this was.

Keeping his thoughts stubbornly away from where they were headed, the prince thought about the only thing that worked in his favour right now.

At the end of each day, the travelling party would take turns down by whatever watering place or river they encamped near. And that meant...

Well.

Since the pirate had rushed into his room after the last mouse incident before they'd left, Karlien hadn't quite forgotten that image. Neither had mentioned it since. To be honest, Karlien dwelled on it sometimes. Not just because of the man's incredible tattoos. But now bathing together had meant Karlien had managed to satisfy a lingering curiosity.

That, yes, he had in fact spotted a solitary brown mole in quite an interesting place.

Next to the magnificent trees that sighed in the chilly breeze and beneath the layers of bedding, Karlien cleared his throat with a delicate cough.

The wolfish ear next to his cheek twitched, and he slipped a hand out from under his blankets to swat it away.

Karlien had seen plenty of freckles in all sorts of places.

But that one?

"Hmmm," Karlien murmured.

His bodyguard hadn't been ashamed of his nakedness at all. He'd stood there in all his glory, two golden torcs around his neck and his plain but mean looking swords, one in each hand. The man was certainly attractive, his face stern but not threatening, high cheekbones and delicately shaped dark eyes that observed things with quiet dignity.

Aware that thought might lead to danger, Karlien inhaled slowly and tried to count peacocks in his mind as they pecked at imaginary manicured lawns, but his thoughts circled back to the interesting placement of a solitary mole.

Under the cloak that had been a gift, and suspiciously similar to the bodyguard's own cloak, Karlien rubbed his chest, wondering at the curious throb behind his ribs. As his fingers brushed against the fur cloak, he grimaced.

He missed his silken robes and soft bedding. He knew he was spoilt, not just because of the servants gossiping around him as he grew up. But he had taken none of it for granted. Knowing it was either pulled from rubble, or made with care from families trying to learn their old trades, the prince cherished every jewel, every lush fabric that made up his extensive wardrobe, most of which was back in Baile Mara.

Had the servants seen his resigned grace as he put up with the current inconveniences? He hoped so.

Stroking the warm fur under his chilled fingers, not realising it was the contented wolf and not his cloak, Karlien thought back to the last stop he'd made on leaving Baile Mara.

Like Hyeon's gift to the prince of a warm cloak, Karlien had a gift for Hyeon in return.

"Baek Hyeon. I have something for you."

His bodyguard, riding beside him, looked over, both of his handsomely shaped brows arched high.

"What?"

Karlien murmured something to the soldier on his other side. The woman looked past him at Hyeon, then shrugged.

"Don't be long," she warned. "I'll tell your grandmama if you fall behind."

With a prickly wave, the prince rode off, expecting Hyeon to follow. When he turned to check, the man had indeed followed. He sat on his horse like a gods-blessed warrior of olden times, a fur cloak and two hilts over his shoulders. Swallowing, Karlien dipped his heels into his horse's sides.

When they arrived at their destination, Hyeon reined in his horse. He stared at the building before them, a tall, narrow construction of shadows and columns with red and gold tiled roof over the black stone, then turned back to Karlien in silence.

"Well?" Karlien queried, hating the catch in his voice.

Hyeon blinked at him, his impatient horse dancing beneath. "The temple?"

"Yes." Blue eyes with their azure halo lit up with anticipation.

The bodyguard urged his horse closer to Karlien's, and when he spoke, his voice was gentle.

"Can't go in."

The prince sat up straight. "What? I'm the prince. I say you can. We are going inland, away from my home and further from yours across the sea."

"No." Hyeon actually looked a little uncomfortable. He cleared his throat. "I can't go. They aren't my gods inside."

Karlien looked at the impressive building, then at Hyeon.

"Oh."

"Karlie..." Hyeon coughed into one of his calloused hands. "Prince Karlien."

"What?"

"Thank you."

"Oh." The young man sniffed. "It's nothing."

Tossing his head and causing his golden curls to catch the weak light, Karlien desperately thought to find something else to focus on, anything but the disappointed heat in his face. The prince turned his horse back to the main road that led to the city walls and urged it onwards.

It was a magnificent animal, black with a reddish mane and tail. Sadly, his stocky little pony had to be left behind, something about first impressions or some other nonsense.

As he rode, he stared straight ahead, refusing the urge to cry. He didn't know why. Adjusting his new cloak carefully, Karlien sniffled. What was there to cry about? He was a prince. On an adventure.

A wild, big adventure.

His bodyguard had brought his horse alongside him and must have heard Karlien's pitiful sob.

"Karlie —"

"I said it's nothing. Don't look at me! I'll... I'll send you away."

Hyeon stared at him.

"You can't," said the bodyguard.

"What?"

"You can't send me away." Hyeon paused, a tiny smile playing about his lips. "Monsters."

Tears forgotten, the prince gasped. "Monsters?"

"Mmmm." Ruby flecked eyes sparkled under heavy lids. "Monsters out there eat princess if Hyeon sent away."

"Eat?" the prince repeated, his voice shrill.

"One gulp. Chomp. Princess gone."

"Chomp..." voice fading, the prince's eyes became unfocused.

Hyeon nodded, straight-faced.

"Well." Karlien cleared his throat. That wasn't ideal.

Wiping his eyes, the prince headed for the city walls. It was a great expanse of masonry, full of holes and cracks and gaps. The long line was still passing through the main gate, those ready to escort him somewhere he'd never been, to do something unknown with skills he'd never been allowed to use.

As they took their place at the rear, the prince tossed his head once more, glancing at Hyeon from the corner of his eye.

"I'm ready."

Hyeon's gaze was shining with heavy emotion.

"No," sighed the bodyguard after a moment. "Karlie not ready. But we leave anyway."

The pair of them rode through the threshold for the last time in who knew how long, out of the home of his birth. The shimmering heat of Hyeon's closeness as he passed was almost enough of a distraction to replace the fear. Not quite, but almost. Karlien shut his eyes as the walls were left behind.

Everything was fine.

Now, in the uncomfortable darkness of the camp, far from home in a place of strange trees, peculiar sounds and foreign aromas, Karlien thought of the wreck that was his home.

Despite the devastating eyesore that was The Scar, the great swathe of ruined terraces down the centre of the city, and the cracks that spread throughout its buildings of black stone, it was the only place he'd ever known.

Karlien wanted to make it into the place he knew it could be, and certainly had been once.

"What kind of place are you, Aneirin?" Karlien whispered to the cold sky.

He rolled to his side, grabbing for the wolf's soft ear, wishing it was a large, calloused hand instead.

The wolf didn't move when Karlien finally fell asleep, under the gaze of both the stars and dark eyes flecked with crimson sparks.

44

Cas

Year 257, Cas at age 16
City of the Seers

Alone on the roof terrace of the recently finished central tower in the City of the Seers, Caspian watched the hustle of a city unfolding block by block, letting his mind drift. All sorts of interesting puzzles twisted away in his subconsciousness.

Below, the stone city sprawled around him in twinkling pale stone. It was a marvel to him who had grown up amongst the black stones of Baile Mara's native rock. This unfolding capital was built of white, grey and pale pink marble, granite and quartz. A new quarry town had sprung up not far, the swoop overhead of dragons ferrying massive blocks of hewn stones to the new city. It had been in construction for the gods knew how long, funded by the Royal family along with their cousins and trading partners offshore, and also far, far inland. Dragons with their magic and might had a lot to do with it as well, wanting a place close to Mionlach, their scorched, self-proclaimed homeland in the north. It was to be a place of coming together, of learning, the sharing of knowledge.

Idly, Cas swatted away a curious cricket that had somehow found its way up here. It had possibly arrived up the long winding stairs with him, caught somewhere in the azure and gold thread embroidery of his white linen shirt, or on the matching velvet cloak that rippled in the brisk wind and tousled his hair.

Shouts caught his attention down below.

Cas squinted as a slab of pink marble, as tall as he, slipped out of the grasp of four workers hauling it off a wagon halfway along the courtyard. It missed crushing anyone as it fell, but cracked into three pieces.

Unable to hold it in, he laughed as a frantic shouting and scurrying commenced below.

It was likely Cas shouldn't be up here, but there was much to think about considering the past few weeks. In this up-and-coming metropolis dedicated to learning and magic, different cultures and races, few places were as free from noise as up here.

This tower was the first to be completed. The city had one on each of its corners, this fifth one was located in the city's heart. In the vast open courtyard below, a map of the principal cities of the continent of Beinacoilia was taking shape to the sounds of masonry tools. The tap and rasp of hammers and chisels were irritating. But dimmed a little when Cas turned from the work below to sit down on the tower's flat roof, adjusting his sword at his hip and placing his canvas bag of fresh figs nearby. Resting his head against the waist-high guard wall, he sighed.

Cas didn't really want to be here this long, but there'd been no choice. By the time he'd realised Morgan was serious about leaving Baile Mara, he'd taken steps.

He'd burned Morgan's hateful library down.

And yet, she had still left him for this strange place.

"Pity," Cas sighed, eyes closing as he turned his face to the noonday sun.

The light was different here, crisper. It stung his eyes; the stone reflecting and refracting rather than absorbing.

It had been tempting to simply follow her at first, unbidden. It would have been good to flee if anyone had suspected him of the arson of countless priceless books and scrolls.

But hilariously, an opportunity had arisen soon after.

In the following weeks, when the initial panic of the quake and destruction of the library died down, Illarion Carter had announced he would help where he could.

So Cas had joined his father, abnormally subdued, and Wane, leading a long line of displaced folk from Baile Mara to the new city. The plan seemed to make sense, helping those who had lost everything when the tremor had collapsed warehouses, workplaces and some of Baile Mara's busy docks alike.

Cas had his doubts about what seafaring ocean-side families would do in an inland city? But here they were, and so was he.

It had been a sombre journey on horseback, escorted by a contingent of guards provided by the Elphin Royals. They had led the slow caravan northwards inland, then west, a journey of weeks with the amount of families volunteering to leave their home behind. Hypatia had watched them ride out from their estate, blue eyes cold and unyielding.

For the first time in his life, Cas had seen Illarion look at his wife and turn away, the spark in his green eyes extinguished.

He had yet to delve to the bottom of it all, there being more important things to mull over when he first arrived in the City of the Seers.

Like where in all of the fabled hells was Morgan?

As soon as they had arrived in this massive city, with its work crews and craftspeople raising stones of bright white and soft pink, Cas had slipped away.

After dumping his gear, he had tracked down the street urchins, asking for directions. After an hour of searching, he had found the new library, an impressive circular building topped by a soaring dome.

Frustratingly, Morgan was nowhere to be found amongst the crates of scrolls. Nor at the chambers allocated to those tasked with making the library the greatest on the continent.

Slipping back through the alleys until the same urchins pointed him to the most luxurious and disreputable business, Cas had finally located her at last.

His worst fears had come true.

Far away from him, she had relapsed into her former self. Hateful, afraid, and thoroughly intoxicated, the fiery woman who held his heart had found new distractions to dull the fear that her dreams left her with.

Cas had laughed at the state of her as he'd carried her away, fighting him the whole while. Rook had been darkly amused, but let him whisk her back to her unfinished chambers.

"I'll clear her debts," Cas had called behind him while hoisting a petite but fiery woman over his shoulder.

"You will," Rook replied, his deep voice thick with his smirk. "You owe me twice now, Caspian Carter."

Like a wild beast from a mythical story, Morgan had raged at first.

She had spat many hateful words at him. He had snickered, amused, aware of who she was beneath the fierce anger as she detoxed. It had taken weeks of nursing, holding her down while she tossed and turned, or forcing water and honeyed bread down her throat. But at last, her pale green eyes had lost their fog and, finally, their fury.

Curled in his arms amongst the sweaty sheets, Morgan had raised her head to stare at him.

"I don't deserve you," she had croaked. "What we did was wrong. Why can't you leave me be?"

"No, my love," Cas had sighed, drawing her close, his hand entwined in long crimson hair to press her cheek back to his chest. "Never."

Once Morgan was well enough to walk around unaided, Cas had led her outside, both of them barefoot, both of them chewing on the figs that seemed even sweeter here.

The City of the Seers had been planned, so it was better laid out than the terraced city of Baile Mara that had sprung up in various levels over multiple dynasties. Hence, Morgan's chambers here were far nicer and larger. Thankfully, her bed was long enough for his now quite substantial height. She even had a private walled garden. The square, lush place was small, but one could still lay flat on deep green grass. The lawn was newly sprouted; and clear daylight filtered through ferns and vines that sent new tendrils up and around the marble columns of the arched opening.

When Cas brushed past the soft pink blooms, a sweet fragrance was released. It was a welcome change to the heady dust of the library. New as it was, the aged tang of dust and ink emanated from its openings, all the way down to the residences of the craftspeople and workers.

Lying on the grass together, they had let the sun drift overhead, illuminating the private space with a golden glow.

Morgan was atop him, stretched out and using him as a kind of rug. She had laughed as Cas wiggled his hips underneath her. It was more of a teasing gesture than anything. His heart was truly content to just be pressed close to her, whether or not there were clothes between them. Teasing him in turn, Morgan had slipped a hand between them to grab him with unexpected vigor through his pants. There was no delay in his body's eager response.

"Why are you so perfect everywhere, Caspian?" Morgan murmured, nuzzling his neck with sticky lips.

Cas laughed. "I'd love to say I was born perfect. But I was born missing a vital ingredient. So I can't."

"Magic isn't everything, you beast."

"Puh. What do you know? Magic is everything to me. Along with you."

"Why me?"

"Why not?"

"That's not an answer, Caspian."

Cas had laughed and pushed her away, his body too eager for her weakened state. Taking two steps into the furthest corner of the quiet space by a stone bench, he had turned to her and shrugged. Morgan lay on the soft grass, her refreshingly clear gaze on his smirk as he posed. Hands on his hips, Cas jutted a hip, mocking the statues of renown figures popping up in the public parks of the city.

"Caspian, stop that. You look ridiculous."

His smile widened, blonde eyebrows waggling suggestively.

"Fuck you, Caspian."

"Yes, please."

She threw the last fig at him. He caught it. Biting into its floral, sugar sweet flesh, he had waited for her nod, then laid back down by her side, unlacing his pants.

A crimson eyebrow arched.

But soon after, Caspian was panting with unhinged rapture as she pleasured him with petite hands and a hot mouth. It hadn't taken long, pent up as he was. Morgan had licked her lips, a line between her delicate brows.

"Why do you taste like the honey from your father's prized bees?"

Cas jerked Morgan's face away from his cock, dragging her bodily up and along his chest to meet his gaze. He lifted her chin.

"Stick out your tongue."

She did, and he bent forward to lick her tongue, tasting himself.

"Mm, I'm sweet aren't I?"

Huffing a laugh, Morgan dropped her forehead to his chin, muffled words pressed into the dip where his sweaty neck met his clavicle.

"I've wanted you for years," he breathed, eyeing the square of bright blue sky above them. "I'll take whatever you give me, even if it is a part of myself."

"Caspian," came Morgan's muffled voice, "don't make this more awkward than it already is. That was gross, even for you."

"Ha. I'm unashamedly in love with you, little jewel. Perhaps it's destiny. But I rather believe it was my fine brain and even finer body that helped."

"You're absolutely ridiculous."

Cas turned sombre, his pleasure receding as the perfection of the moment calmed his heart.

"Good things come to those who plan ahead. I expect nothing but what I'm owed."

Morgan twisted a little to glance up at him through red eyelashes, her cheek resting on his chest. He peered down at her, the sweet shape of her face, the freckles across her delicate nose. Doubt was the only thing that marred the perfection of her fiery beauty.

"I'm serious. Morgan, I've waited for you. I'll wait forever for you to see that. I'm yours. And you are mine."

Now, with Morgan cleaned up and calmer, their passion consuming them both, Cas had climbed to the top of the tower to be alone.

He idly scratched at a whitish, pale pink scar on the back of his hand.

It was one of hundreds that now decorated his body.

But he wasn't thinking about that, he was thinking about the dragons.

Specifically, three in particular.

The scaled, winged magic users had been overhead whilst Cas was searching for more fresh figs in one of the market squares. In a city built with the help of dragons, the scale of the place was truly epic.

The shopping district of the east quarter was no exception. Cas had been examining the wares of a fruit seller at the last booth near the open pits of clean sand where dragons could come and get a polish. Three were using it at that point, their conversation muted enough that Cas' keen, curious ears perked up.

Especially at the phrase *"sad but necessary risk of scientific experiments."*

"What are you talking about?" a copper coloured dragon had murmured, sitting upright and shaking sand off her violently sunburst coloured wings.

"The quake in Baile Mara," her companion, a dark green, petite reptile, had continued.

"What? Oh, I thought —"

"Hush," interrupted the third, their scales a combination of rippling sapphire and gold. "Not here."

Cas' hand had stilled over the mound of figs he was examining.

His wide-eyed gaze met the fruit sellers, a young man about his own age with a long braid of silvery gold hair over his slim shoulder.

The fruit seller shook his head slightly.

Confused, Cas had nodded, not quite sure what they had both overheard, or why it was unwise to ask.

As Cas handed over a few coins for the fruit and wandered away, the dragons continued to murmur in their massive pit of sand. Dismissive laughter followed him, somehow reminiscent of both his mother and the bullies that had thrown him into an angry hive.

Cas had slipped past the chatting city councilors overseeing the massive meeting chamber coming together at the tower's base, and climbed, ever up, step by step until he had emerged, blinking at the top.

He had stood there for what seemed like hours, mind spinning around overheard conversations, both here and from the servants back home.

"Hypatia and Illarion Carter," Cas murmured. "When will you stop dreaming of the future, and fix the present mess you both created?"

The bullies who had scarred him with the stingers of insects normally associated with sweetness had been dealt with. His sword, with its flashing ruby of sparkling crimson, had been used well.

But what for the bullies who had given him life, only to discard him, and subject his home to risk and ruin?

Fingers, calloused by long hours of practicing swordcraft, stroked the ruby winking in the overhead sun, the faint breeze stirring the tips of white blonde hair.

"Hmm," Cas mused, his mind turning things over like a hive of focused bees. "Broken..."

45

Fox

Year 367

The Forest

With the dense, damp forest on either side, the pair of them rode together on one horse, much to Blackthorn's disgust.

Rolling his eyes as Fox had attempted to mount up behind a sullen Owaen that morning, the horse had danced away on skittish hooves. Fox suspected it wasn't their combined weight that offended the animal, but more the fact that it was Fox joining his normal rider.

Owaen had simply stared out the stable doors, his exquisite green eyes dull.

Gathering his patience with extreme concentration, Fox had hoisted himself up without using his heels *too* firmly. Willow, ever obedient, followed its guide rope with no protest, loaded up with their meagre belongings.

Now, as they made slow progress down the south-western road leading away from Baile Fuar and all of its unwelcome revelations, Fox allowed Blackthorn to pick his own pace.

Despite the soothing heat against his chest, caught under the cloaks wrapped around them, an uncomfortable fact remained foremost in his mind. If they didn't have the horses to take care of, Fox wasn't sure exactly what he'd do.

What he had witnessed in the bathhouse at Baile Fuar, and subsequently experienced as traumatic waves of memory and sensation, hadn't left him yet. It never would, of course.

But seeing a man who had been the focus of his rage come undone, in much the same way Fox had at various low points, was unreal. Fox had no idea how he himself should feel at this point. Much the same as Owaen, he assumed.

Above them, expansive boughs of oaks and cedar arched over the road in swathes of green, yellow, and grey. The air was icy, the cobbled road slick with frost. There was less moss, and fewer uneven patches here, this road being more commonly used than its overgrown northern counterparts.

They had been riding for a few hours, Fox wasn't sure how long exactly. He was as unsure of that as everything else.

After an uneasy night wrapped together in their cloaks on the bed, the sombre pair had packed up with few words and exited the town without the fuss Fox had expected. It was obvious Caspian had known Fox was nearby and would have fled straight away, on sensing the earthquake emanating from Fox's breakdown. So the best they could do, without abandoning Rhydian's precious horse, was what they were doing.

Well, almost the best they could do.

Fox could get them to their final destination faster. He could have at any point.

But he didn't want to before, when it was Owaen and he travelling by day and making love by night.

And he sure as the icy hells were cold, he didn't want to get there faster now, considering things had changed.

Or had they?

Fox's arms, wrapped around Owaen's waist, twitched.

Owaen hadn't protested as Fox had packed all their goods on one horse and mounted up behind Owaen on the other. The Elf was lost in the revelations that kept coming, from his parents' role in the destruction of his home, to their experiments, which likely led to Fox himself being hatched. A new creature for the world, some kind of magical work horse to advance the misguided cause for magic to infuse the world.

As they rode on, the wind picking up and swirling little eddies of white flakes around them, Fox pressed his cold nose into Owaen's wide back. The blonde Elf was a ghost of himself. The easy arrogance that he exuded from his pores was absent, the fight in him gone.

"Aurelia," Fox mumbled, inhaling Owaen's musky sweat.

I need your cool head.

I…

I don't know what to do.

Wondering if this is how she felt on her misguided mission on behalf of Rhydian's jaded mother, Fox spared himself the luxury of thinking *why him?*

Hadn't he been through enough?

Hadn't his loved ones been through enough?

"Fox," Owaen croaked as their horses picked their way over a rivulet of sparkling water that ran across a low stretch of road.

Loosening his hold, Fox sat up and stretched his neck to prop his chin on Owaen's shoulder.

"My love?"

"Put me back to sleep."

"What?"

Owaen flinched at the word hissed next to his ear. Fox pulled away, staring at the back of Owaen's head with an ominous scowl.

"I've had enough," the Elf mumbled. "I can't... I'll kill Caspian when I see him. But I don't know that you want... that now... even after all the fucking crap he's done! My gods..."

As Owaen's voice faded into the swirling sigh of the icy wind and rustling trees, Fox half-laughed, half-sobbed against Owaen's warm back.

"I haven't decided how to proceed yet," Fox admitted, turning his head to watch the depths of the snow flecked midmorning forest pass them by. "But I'll never lock you away again. I will wrap my arms around you and *never* let you go."

A chilled hand found Owaen's warm fingers, tucked inside the front of his heavy cloak. He fought against Fox's hold at first. But, using his strength to overcome Owaen's pointless protest, Fox twisted Owaen's hand with careful movements and brought it over Owaen's shoulder to his lips.

A cool but firm kiss was pressed into the warm palm.

"Your absence was felt as a presence," Fox whispered, humbled by Owaen's devotion. "That's how much you mean to me. It goes without saying, but I shall say it anyway. If you were hurt because of the dragons... I... might have done worse."

Owaen was silent for a bit, and Fox had assumed his lover was dozing until Owaen's deep voice rumbled against his cheek sometime later.

"Remember everything you just said," Owaen mumbled. "And tell me often."

Startled from his thoughts of a crystal cave filled with the wails of Elven innocents combined with the scars that Caspian bore on his body, and likely his soul, Fox nodded.

"Always," he agreed.

Caspian's cries, echoes of the silent scream that Fox kept contained when the images became too much, throbbed in his ears.

What was this feeling called?

Where was his dependable cool ego, helping him get through the day with a glare and airy nonchalance?

"Don't let anyone tell you that you're nothing, to do their bidding," Caspian had moaned. "Skye had to deal with that, did you know?"

Fox bit his bottom lip.

Did Owaen know his brother at all?

His secret heart, not just his crazed actions?

Because if one judged Fox by his deeds, he deserved to be drowned into the liquid rock that burned below the ground.

The man had threatened Aurelia, amongst many other unforgivable things.

But...

But?

Fox exhaled a cloud of white mist. He was aware their progress towards a potentially cataclysmic meeting was hindered by his uncertainty, his cowardly choice of *not* deciding to act.

Blinking away a snowflake from black lashes, Fox glanced up with an unexpected shiver down his spine, his gaze unfocused. Pale lips parted.

He *had* to act.

He *had* to choose.

To turn away?

Or to follow the shadowy wings that just sped past far above, so high and fleeting that Owaen was too out of sense to realise which pair of troublemakers had overtaken them.

Fox's unblinking gaze fell from the barely there gust amongst the low clouds to the back of Owaen's head. A few flakes of snow had settled there, not pure white, but grey.

The delicate ice tainted with ash from Fox's own tyrannical rage years before.

He shuffled closer to Owaen, his arse numb from his awkward seat on the rear of the saddle. Caught between them, the two crystal shards under his clothes pressed against his chest. After seeing Caspian with the sparkling chunk of crystal in the bathhouse, Fox had finally realised what the fragments on his chain were.

Closing his eyes, Fox welcomed the sting as the shards rubbed against his chilled skin. They didn't hurt.

Why should they?

The shards were simply remnants of the shell that he'd hatched from, after all.

46

Owaen

Year 367
The Forest

"Stop," Owaen croaked the next day.

Fox, holding the reins with arms circling Owaen's waist, obliged immediately. Blackthorn tossed his head, ebony mane scattering flurries of flakes to the slowly disintegrating path below his hooves.

"I can't do this," Owaen said as he slid off the horse and nearly kicking Fox in the groin. Once on the ground, Owaen stumbled towards the line of thickly packed trees. Staring at the shadowed trunks and undulating pockets of deep green moss, he tugged at his ragged hair. "I can't... he deserves it... but I..."

A horsey snort accompanied by a muttered curse behind him indicated that Fox had dismounted.

Sure enough, boot steps approached cautiously on the mossy rocks.

A pale face, gilded, black eyes shining, appeared before Owaen. Even in the grey light of a frigid afternoon when a golden sun hung low beyond even lower clouds, Fox was a creature of ethereal beauty. Not his flesh, but the soul that peered at Owaen, intense, vast, and utterly unknowable.

Immeasurably powerful hands rose to hold Owaen's icy face with a gentleness that melted his skin. Thumbs caressed the rough hairs sprouting on his cheeks that he normally took care of, but hadn't bothered with since who the fuck knew when.

Fox leant forward, pausing at the last moment, their breaths mingling with a white puff of warmth in the cool air. At Owaen's simple nod, Fox closed the final space between them.

As the leaves rustled above, the frigid breeze and untamed birdsong filling his ears, Owaen sighed. The kiss was soft, lips as tender as any caress from any love, in any place, at any time. There was no fire or wild passion. As their tongues met, their lips sealed, there was only endless searing love.

Love from a creature that would do anything for him, including hide him away from the threats that roamed the continent.

Owaen reached up to place his hands over Fox's, pulling away from the tender kiss only when the need for air had black spots dancing across his blurred vision.

"Did I really ask you to do that to me again?"

Somehow, knowing what Owaen was mumbling about, Fox nodded as he pressed his face into Owaen's neck, their cloaks shifting in the wind as it picked up with icy gusts.

Owaen wrapped his arms around Fox and smiled at the connection they shared. While his aching heart beat weakly, his eyes remained on the trees, watching as a tiny black and blue bird, smaller than a walnut, flitted across the thinnest branches of a straggly pine. Its upright tail twitched as it rose, and tiny crumbs of snow fell from each twig as it landed.

"It comes down to only one choice, really," Fox said quietly against Owaen's neck.

"Hmm?" Owaen murmured as the little bird flew off into the bracken with a high-pitched chirp.

"Choosing myself," Fox continued. "Or choosing the one who would do anything for me."

Owaen tilted his head as Fox shifted against him, noses touching. Both were tall, Owaen only a little taller, but they were almost eye to eye. More snow was falling, a soft veil of purity amongst the darkness, causing the day to glow around them with a muted, if icy, harmony. Fox sighed against him, and Owaen pulled away to examine the black and gold eyes glittering so close to his.

"Shall I get us there quicker?" Fox asked calmly, a sad smile curling his fine lips. "I waited too long, perhaps. I don't know."

"What?"

"They passed us yesterday, you see."

"Who?" Owen replied, a line forming between his white brows. "Fox? What are you saying —"

"I'm sorry, I dawdled before we got to Baile Fuar, just to be with you. But I think the time for patience is gone. There is no point dragging out this unpleasantness."

Blinking slowly, Owaen looked up and around them as the noises of the forest dimmed with an expectant hush. His green eyes widened as the temperature dropped.

The road, the forest, and the surrounding air glowed.

But not with the muted daylight of a frigid day of increasingly heavy snow and ice.

"What is this?" Owaen breathed.

Swallowing, Fox pulled away, his scorching eyes shut tight.

"Grab the horses," Fox whispered as sweat beaded across his forehead. "Hurry."

As a sliver of fear blended with uncertainty wound up his spine, Owaen did the only thing he could.

Spinning, he dashed for the horses, both stomping with ears flicked back. Owaen grabbed the reins of each of them, gathering them up with one hand. With his pulse racing, and without looking, he reached behind. Sure enough, a cool hand gripped his with a reassuring squeeze.

Drawing Fox close as he turned around, Owaen wrestled with the fear in his heart, choosing to trust without expectation or understanding.

He was beyond that, wasn't he?

"Don't let go."

"Never," Owaen breathed against Fox's silky hair. "Never."

The crisp air soured with the acrid stink of lightning ready to strike. Around them, the falling snow stilled, flakes suspended in midair like insect wings in clear honey.

A horse whinnied. Owaen wasn't sure which one.

His stomach dropped.

"What —"

The world came apart.

47

Cas

Year 257, Cas at age 16
City of the Seers

Ail too soon, Morgan was gone again.

Freshly awoken in her chambers behind the new library, Cas stretched with a satisfied yawn aimed at the curved ceiling of smooth white marble overhead. Something sweet and crisp tickled his nose. Turning his head, he blinked at the squat wooden stool beside the rumpled bed.

Beside the unlit glass lantern sat a single fig.

Small, green and pink, the fig had a feathered quill embedded into the ripe flesh. The feather was a deep black with a single white spot at the top. A trickle of juice ran down the fruit's striated side, pooling on the stool.

Cas grinned, then frowned.

His hand reached for the warmth next to him, but even as he turned to look for a cascade of crimson hair, he knew.

Apart from his naked self, the bed was empty.

He was alone.

Sitting up, he swung his legs over the side of the feather mattress. His feet touched the cool floor and Cas rested his elbows on his knees, chin propped on clasped hands. Their conversation, a series of drowsy whispers as they had fallen asleep the night before, came back to him as he chewed the inside of his cheek, his heart already burning from Morgan's absence.

"Your quest for power," Morgan said quietly as the stars shone bright outside, "scares me as much as the ruin that is to come."

"My quest?" Cas chided gently. "*Our* quest. You fit into that."

"I don't want more than I have," she said.

Which was neither an affirmation nor dismissal of his vague plans. Eyes simmering with imagined grandeur, Cas held her close, draping his bare leg over her thigh.

"Well, that's well and good, little flame. But *I* want more than nothing at all."

Morgan pondered this statement as Cas idly stroked her back, his wandering fingertips marveling at the lustre of her skin by the warm glow of the single lantern on the bedside stool. After a while, when Cas was almost asleep, his body spent and his heart full, Morgan's whisper broke through the pleasant background hum of the nighttime city.

"If you had to choose, Caspian," she said, her tone serious. "Power or me?"

Speechless, Cas was wide awake at once, the stirring warmth in his heart ablaze in an instant. His voice was just as serious as hers had been.

"I choose the third option," Cas declared.

"Third option?"

Cas kissed the top of Morgan's head, inhaling the parchment dust and musk aroma of her unbound hair.

"I choose power and you. I will find a way to stop the arrogance of others, choosing you whilst fulfilling my own destiny."

"Destiny? There is no such thing." The petite librarian shifted against him, warm, languid, her voice thick with sleep.

"Your dreams then," Cas insisted. "What of them?"

"My dreams," Morgan murmured, "are simply future echoes. Coming back to me from the dark choices made by all of us."

Cas listened to the sounds of the deep night as Morgan drifted into unconsciousness, her own passion spent, hopefully enough that she would sleep deeply without the occasional dreams that plagued her.

He stared at the ceiling for hours, mind turning over his options.

Rook's words of long ago echoed deep in his bones, not from the future, but from the past.

Magic is more flexible than your esteemed parents realise, little shrimp.

"I will find that third option however long it takes," Cas vowed to the dimly lit room. His hand stilled on Morgan's back, gently rising and falling with each breath, Rook's words at the forefront of his mind.

Perhaps there is hope for you yet.

It was a frustrating ride back to Baile Mara.

He was grudgingly helping Owaen ferry three wagons of copied scrolls back to Baile Mara for the priests to fawn over. Which Caspian thought was hilarious. Morgan's books were gone thanks to him. Now Cas was fucking in charge of more to replace them.

Oddly subdued, Illarion stayed behind in the bustling city, settling the newcomers. Cas was relieved to depart his father's sour mood and head back to where he hoped Morgan had fled.

Yet when it came time to drop the scrolls off to the glowering priests in their soaring temple of black columns and massive chunks of crystal points, Morgan was nowhere to be found. In a snit, Cas rode home before the scrolls were finished unloading, ignoring Owaen calling for Cas to get his arse back and help.

Perhaps Morgan was at the Carter Estate helping Mother?

Unable to contain the hopeful grin on his face, Cas raced his fatigued horse up through the terraced streets of the city, hooves flashing on the cobbles of black rock, one hand on the reins, the other with its gold and amethyst ring on the hilt of his sword. It was soon apparent, however, that Morgan was not there either. His mother's workroom, full of plants, caged birds and reptiles, was deserted.

Frowning, Cas headed back outside and glanced around.

Avoiding the beehives with a shiver, Cas strode off towards the largest greenhouse, a structure of glass, iron and light. He would have preferred to change out of his stained riding leathers. Surely his pants could get up and walk by themselves by now. But he put up with the sweat and headed on.

He jumped over a cobbled wall, scattering three peacocks as he landed with a thump in the mulch. Uncaring for the bird's startled cries, he trod over a garden bed of young roses towards the largest greenhouse on the eastern side of the estate. The black and gold towers of the Elphin royal family's castle were visible just beyond the outermost grove of ancient oaks.

The light-filled space of the elegant greenhouse was a vast expanse of pungent aromas. The moist scent of ferns and exotic flowers was intense from the various vents in the glass as he headed along its expansive west side. Beyond the thick panes, a warm, dense, and intensely green indoor forest was crowded under the soaring arches of iron struts. As he rounded the corner to the front entrance, he noticed the doors were ajar, the aroma of wet earth and rich loam dense in his nose. The doors were built low for some reason, so that one had to duck down to step through.

Cas paused, his ears perking.

Along with the humid air came the sound of raised voices through the gap. It sounded like Mother and Father. But Illarion had stayed behind in the City of the Seers to help the refugees, hadn't he? Confused by the angry tones of each voice, Cas chewed on his lower lip, looking around.

Remaining outside, he stepped close to the crack between the doors, pressing his cheek to the iron frame, making sure he was concealed by the mass of tree ferns just inside the entrance. Inhaling the fresh aroma of humus and wet mulch, he listened.

"...boundaries were pushed, that's how the Elves were made, with the blood of the Royal family, that's how dragons came to be, Hypatia," the man's dry voice continued. "So why stop now? You're usually fearless."

"I am not afraid, Rook," Hypatia snapped, "merely cautious of the possibility that another quake could be triggered. But I am unlikely to stop now. We have come too far. You can thank the gods I am determined."

Blonde eyebrows rose.

So Mother was in there with Rook?

Wondering at that, Cas was about to open the door when Rook's next words caused Cas' breath to catch.

"The gods?" Rook laughed over the sound of a peacock cawing from nearby. "You and I both know there are no such things. They were only the first of all of us to experiment with magic."

Imagining the purple faces of the priests having an apoplexy at this blasphemous idea, Cas slapped both hands over his face to contain his nervous laugh. He'd had some suspicion himself about the lack of a divine origin for the local religion, but this was an idea he'd never heard voiced aloud.

The smart thing to do would be to leave and pretend he had never heard a thing.

Cas barged inside instead.

A creative architect had designed a series of pools off to one side, with a fountain of sparkling water flowing over mossy rocks, setting a humid but beautifully lush and idyllic scene of serenity and peace.

It was completely at odds with the horror of what Hypatia was doing.

The alchemist looked up from the low wooden table she was bent over, blue eyes blinking rapidly at the intrusion, lips parting in surprise above her blood-spattered leather apron. Her long brown hair was tied back from her face with a length of blue silk. Before her, a lizard was pinned down by four copper pins through its clawed feet, securing it to the tabletop.

On either side of it, each nestled on thick, soft grey wool, were the two jagged chunks of crystal. The pair sparkled with deep hues of sapphire and emerald, like two loaves of bread rising in the warmth of the bright sun that filtered through the glass and green canopy above.

Rook, in a matching set of white linen tunic and trousers, towered by her side, his long black hair loose. His shining black gaze examined Cas with a calm perusal. The man had a cloth held to his nose, no doubt to mute the stink from the lizard's guts and innards being laid out in neat rows away from its thrashing tail.

Cas gagged.

The thing was still alive.

His questions on their overheard conversation and his search for Morgan were forgotten at the grisly sight. One hand tightened on the hilt of his sword.

"Mother," Cas hissed. "Where is your mercy?"

Ignoring Rook's eyebrows arching, Cas kept his gaze on Hypatia.

Frowning, the alchemist straightened, bloody hands held before her, a freshly used scalpel dripping red to the reptile beneath.

"'Mercy'? There is no place for that here." The scalpel's wicked tip flashed in the sunlight shining through the glass overhead as Hypatia pointed to her work. "This lizard is sick, the tail rotten. I can see the blight has travelled through into the pelvis."

Cas' wide gaze dropped to the thrashing tail, whipping frantically side to side. His guts heaved and his gorges rising, Cas wanted to shut his mouth. But, confused by his own passion, he forged on.

"Why was it rotten to begin with mother?" he accused, the overheard conversation coming back to him, "what did you do? Did you play at being a god yourself? Is all of this a game to you?"

Hypatia stared at him while Rook choked back his laugh behind his cloth.

"Don't be a child, Caspian. This isn't *playtime*. We required stronger bloodlines for the people of this city. More magic means stronger bodies are needed, which means tests must be run," Hypatia replied, her tone scornfully incredulous. Her blue gaze narrowed. "And besides, my mind makes me godlike by default."

Edging away from the gore on the workbench, Rook pulled the cloth from his face, his hands held up before him.

"Don't either of you say that out loud near any of the temples, as much as I'd love to see a priest deal with that statement," he drawled. He faced Cas fully. "Let's keep the peace, hey? We don't want Hypatia's good work to get halted, do we?"

Ignoring Rook's warning glance, Cas took a step forward, still unable to stop his mouth. A disturbing heat was rising in his chest.

"We already have magic in the bloodlines of this magnificent city. Why increase it, Mother? Do the people of this city want what you are planning? Maybe you could help the ones who don't have it?"

Rook's eyebrows rose as Cas pointed to himself, steady in the face of Hypatia's glare.

"Oh, that's right," Cas went on, sarcasm dripping from his voice, "you failed."

As the tail whipped back and forth before the frozen alchemist, silence filled the greenhouse. After the count of ten, Hypatia's scalpel dropped with a flash of silver.

The lizard's head was severed from its body.

Cas stared at it, his wide eyes of mismatched blue focusing on the tail.

Horrifyingly, it still lashed about.

"Mother," Cas whispered, the heat, and the fury, rising to his throat. "Has anyone ever spent so much time achieving so little?"

Hypatia's hiss was a low wisp of breath, barely audible over the bubble of the sparkling fountain to Cas' left.

"Get out."

"Mother," Cas snapped back immediately. "For fuck's sake! I *tried*."

"What?" Despite the ice in her tone, the steely glint in her gaze, it actually looked like Hypatia was attempting to understand him. "What did you try?"

"To be more like Wane."

Hypatia spared him a chilling smile, and the scalpel placed with care beside the tail as its thrashing died down.

"I thought you were smarter than that, at least, Caspian. What's got into you?"

Jaw clenched, Cas replied with a serene smile of his own. "Not magic, that's for sure."

Rook coughed into his fist as rage crossed Hypatia's flushed face. It was thrilling to watch. But soon enough, the fury faded to a cool, impassive stare.

"Get out," Hypatia said once more. "There is no place for you here. Your disease is one I cannot cure."

Ignoring Rook's carefully blank expression, Cas opened his mouth, thought about it, then closed it.

With sudden clarity, Cas realised that beneath the scorching fury within him, he was disappointed. Even when provoked, he wasn't interesting enough to incur her anger.

With nothing further to add, Cas stumbled outside. Blinking at the sudden bright light, he wondered. How much did it hurt to cut away diseased flesh from a sick patient? What could be cut from him?

Or rather, how could it be added?

Wiping a layer of sweat from his eyes, the salty sting reminded him of being a kid, pushed face down into the waves of his favourite beach by a black dragon soaring just above him. Wondering what the hells Rook thought of the entire exchange, Cas grit his teeth and stalked back towards the main house. His brother's voice startled him.

"Cas!"

Rolling his eyes to the blue sky, Cas moved to dodge his twin, approaching along the gravel path. Owaen had taken the time to change. His blonde hair, longer than Cas', curled damply at the ends over his fresh shirt of creamy linen.

"You look like you swallowed some of Evreth's porridge. What's wrong, Cassie?"

Cas stopped, whirled around and grabbed his brother by the arms to shake him.

"What's wrong? Wake up! Do you know that for every animal Mother slices open, there will likely be an Elf created without their consent?"

"Only those who ask —"

"We didn't ask! I certainly didn't!" Cas huffed.

His brother blinked at him, confusion marring the handsome face that was like Cas', but also vastly different. Owaen was lit from within with a spark that had missed his older brother.

"What are you talking about?" Owaen squinted at him.

"Owaen!" Cas practically shouted in his brother's face. "Why are you so dense? Can't you see? They want to create a race of people just like them. Filled to the brim with energy from only fuck knows where!"

"They are going to protect this city," Owaen protested.

"From who?" Cas yelled. He shook his head, unable to calm the sickening twist of fury in his heart. "I am sure after witnessing that touching scene back there that our parents are the ones we need to protect this city from."

"But you don't have magic, Cassie," Owaen said, pity veiling his gaze. He drew Cas close, wrapping brawny arms around him. Cas stood there, stunned by his brother's calm statement. "It's not your fault! Like —"

"Wane," Cas began as he leant away from the embrace, hoping the nickname he hadn't used in ages would get his brother's attention, "I know —"

"— Mother said," Owaen continued earnestly, ignoring Cas' interruption, "you're broken."

Cas froze.

Broken.

The two syllables echoed and buzzed in his ears like angry bees.

Sensing the air between them change, Owaen's arms dropped away. A kind of red numbness crept up Cas' spine. Without even having to think about it, Cas stepped back and drew his sword, a graceful motion born of long hours of practice.

Owaen's pitying gaze widened.

But as Cas' raised hand quivered, a long arm reached around him from behind, a determined hand clasping his wrist.

Rook's voice sounded against his ear.

"Not like this, lad." Rook's superior strength forced Cas' hand back to his side, the point of the sword landing on the gravel with a grating clang. "Come on."

Cas made no protest as Rook pulled him away, his mouth drying to ash and words that would never be enough.

His brother was left gaping on the path behind, stunned, his hands loose at his sides.

"Caspian," he called, "wait!"

Rook dragged Cas away, taking a shortcut through the same garden bed that Cas had, not long before, the young roses crushed without thought underfoot.

With his heart fracturing at the stinging dismissal of both Hypatia and Owaen over Cas' apprehensions, his gaze drifted over the massive castle of black towers and golden domes further along the clifftop from their estate. The sun was directly overhead, beating down and giving life to the lush gardens, reflecting off the roof with a heated shimmer.

It was a marvel, really, that the light from a distant star warms him more than his home.

"Drinks are on me," Rook muttered as Cas blindly followed along, his wrist in Rook's grasp, the sword barely avoiding scraping along as they headed to the stables.

Numb, sickened and at a complete loss, Cas stood by as servants saddled his horse.

He blinked.

They were halfway down the city, his sword in its scabbard, his horse led by Rook on his own mount beside.

Cas blinked again.

Rook had led them both to his most flashy establishment yet, a three storied building of highly polished native basalt with balconies around all sides. It was many terraces up from the wide bay and black sands. The place was more sweetly perfumed than a temple, with incense burning thickly to hide the sour stink of the island with its low cloud of wafting sulfur.

Still in a daze, Cas stumbled after Rook, sights and smells of the brothel sliding over him in a pageant of coloured silk. He didn't know who the people were that smiled and waved, raising their glasses as they wound up the carpeted stairs. Their faces were blurred, unclear. However, by the time Cas had sunk his fifth shot of fire whiskey on the rooftop terrace under a starry sky so lovely it seemed a mockery, one thing *was* clear.

Morgan was nowhere to be found when he needed her scorching fire like never before.

"Broken..."

The legacy of his family was a series of inflated egos. And Cas had to pay for it with a broken body that had failed despite his mother's careful planning.

But why should he have to pay for it with his heart?

Eyes damp, Cas kept drinking, welcoming the spreading numbness, finally understanding for the first time why Morgan sometimes chose obliteration at the bottom of a bottle.

The searing pain in Cas' head woke him the next morning.

Cracking his eyes open carefully was a trial as the early morning sun was fully on his face, shining through a massive window, the white gauzy curtains no help at all.

As hazy images and sounds from the night before rose to his mind, Cas winced at the taste in his mouth.

It took him a few tries, but he sat up in bed, hair a tousled mess of floppy blonde spikes. His sword was propped neatly in a corner. But after spotting his travel stained pants on the floor, Cas cursed and yanked back the soft silk sheets.

It eased his heart immediately to see that his underclothes were still in place.

He must have drunk himself into a stupor, thanks to Rook's endless cups of liquor.

"Good morning."

Cas dropped the sheet, his bleary gaze snapping to the door.

"Think of the dragon," Cas croaked. "And the dragon appears."

"Oh, were you thinking of me?" Rook purred from the doorway. Dressed in his usual white, he leant on the door frame, arms crossed over his wide chest. "I'm touched."

"Fuck off," Cas muttered.

Rook laughed. "A fresh breakfast has been laid out to settle your guts. On the roof."

And with that, the tall man left Cas alone.

Cas thought about leaping out the window to end the throb in his head and twist in his stomach. Instead, he got up gradually, finding a set of fresh linen shirt and pants by the basin of cool water on the marble table by the window.

It took a while, but Cas made it to the richly carpeted hall, and followed a low, feminine laugh upstairs.

On the door to the roof terrace, Cas halted, blinking at the bright sun. Thankfully, layers of white fabric were stretched across the expansive space, from one side to the other and flapping in the fresh salt breeze. The view was spectacular, but it was the sight of the naked woman on a low divan filled with cushions in the centre that caught his gaze. She was posed seductively while a barefoot Rook sat nearby, an easel with a large sheet of yellow parchment before him slowly coming to shape with the voluptuous lines and curves of the woman's body in broad strokes of black paint.

The woman, an attractive figure of unknown age, winked at Cas from her curtain of silver hair.

Cas waved weakly.

"Where are we?" Cas managed after clearing his throat.

"My newest place," Rook said without looking up. "'The Stiff Mast'."

Not knowing what to say, Cas walked to the table nearby and sat down.

It was set with silver platters of steaming loaves of bread, a bowl of thick, creamy butter and platters of nuts, fruit, both fresh and dried pieces soaked in honey. A silver jug of fragrant tea, known for its energizing properties, sat in the centre, surrounded by multiple matching cups.

Cas poured himself some tea, wincing at the burn as he swallowed.

Like Mother said, you're broken.

With an angry wipe, he scattered the moisture from his eyes.

Past the city's edge with its bustling docks, Cas glared at the clear horizon, a stunning combination of bright blue fading to the dark sapphire of deep water as the sea met the sky.

Fuck.

Where the fuck was Morgan?

Unable to contain himself, Cas stood up, stalked to the wall of the roof terrace and roared over the side.

The sound was a furious, angry wail of desperation.

When he was done, panting, on the verge of throwing up his tea, Cas glanced down. The ache in his head made it hard to focus. But few people bothered to glance up from the busy streets below. It appeared most were unbothered by the usual activities at Rook's establishments.

Lips numb, Cas made it back to the table, sat down, and stared at the food. He reached for a slice of fig and glared at it.

"Feel better?" Rook's amiable tone made him want to chuck the fruit at the back of the man's shiny black hair.

"Fuck off. Why am I here?"

Rook turned his head to face Cas with a contented smile. "We are going to help each other."

"What do you want from me?" Cas dropped the fig and picked up a small loaf of brown bread. He took a bite. "I can't help you," he said through his mouthful of bread. "I'm not going back there."

Putting down his brush, Rook turned fully on his stool, smiling all the while. Remaining seated, the man who was sometimes a dragon rested his elbows on his spread knees, hands limp between them.

"You need to go back home for a little while, Cas. You owe me, remember?"

Chewing, Cas sat back, fully aware Rook was completely serious despite the ease of the man's expression.

"I know that. But why? There is no one and not one single fucking thing for me back there."

Rook grinned as the crisp breeze lifted the ends of his black hair.

"Yes, there is."

"What thing," Cas muttered after swallowing, "could there possibly be?"

Rook's dark eyes narrowed, glittering and unreadable. Spattered with paint, he brought his elegant hands together. His palms hovered away from each other, just wide enough that an object the size of a person's head could have fit between them.

His voice held a mysterious note of promise.

"Actually, Caspian, there are two."

48

Rhydian

Year 367
Aneirin Castle

The king stood beside the thrones at the head of the great hall and stared at the silent crowd before him, waiting for the prisoner to be brought forth.

His plain white linen shirt, dark brown leather riding pants, and worn boots were at odds with the ostentatious chairs. Two seats of power where his mother and father had once sat together, ruling over a kingdom where truths lay hidden under a veil of lies. The king's blank expression, hands hung limp by his sides, were at odds with the roiling upheaval within.

Multiple torches had been lit in their sconces along every wall, but their flickering glow did little to dispel the gloom. Glass lanterns hung above the crowd in great circular brackets suspended on chains and pulleys above, but these also lent no warmth to the vast hall. It was icy despite the heat of those gathered. Misted breaths mingled with the wisps of smoke that curled above the heads of those assembled. Outside, the strange white flakes of a rare snowfall continued to descend, covering the mess that had yet to be cleared in the great courtyard.

Despite the great hall being filled, the silence was profound. A cough occasionally disturbed the tension, as hundreds of pairs of eyes stared up at him. Many were on crutches, or on long wooden benches at the front of the hall below the dais. One of Rhydian's hands flexed as he counted the faces, noting that some were too injured to attend this morning's assembly. Or they were locked up in the dungeons below the feet of their kinsfolk.

Or they were dead.

A vein throbbed in Rhydian's temple as his bloodshot eyes assessed the crowd.

Halfway down the stairs and to the side stood Aurelia, with a few of the guards who had not been involved in the riot.

As far as they could tell.

Rhydian rubbed a hand at the ache in his stomach from being kicked at some point the night before, wondering at the word.

Riot.

Except last night hadn't been a riot, had it?

It was a rebellion. An uprising, a call to arms against a king who had been deemed unfit to lead by a substantial number of Aneirin's guards and other folk.

As the morning light, a weak, pitiful excuse of a day, broke through the glass along the great hall's vast wall, Rhydian glanced at Aurelia. The Elf wasn't looking at him. She was scanning the crowd, one hand on the knife at her hip, her other a clenched fist by the sword she had donned that morning. She had a bruise on her neck, but it was fading fast, much like the recent cut above her eye had healed with exceptional speed.

Magic worked that way, didn't it?

Or it was supposed to. Something that worked in harmony with the body, to be used for the benefit of oneself. The Elves amongst the native Aneirin folk had been born with it, the second or third generation of those with magic in their veins since birth, according to something Fox or Owaen had said.

But for Rhydian, it was different.

There was no gentle introduction to magic for him. No amiable companion since childhood. Instead of a spear of light sparking to life within his chest, growing, adjusting, unifying, he'd had the opposite.

The hidden power in his blood had been a throb behind his temples, deep amongst his ribs, waiting to uncoil. Then last night it had exploded into life, as if an extra limb had sprouted with a mind of its own. It had bloomed when he had faced another challenge that he had no training for, with no heart to weather the unexpected storm.

Thank you, Mother, thank you, Father, Rhydian whispered to himself as his throat constricted. *I hope you're both rotting in the deepest, icy hells.*

Wondering for the umpteenth time since the rebellion the night before, Rhydian cursed another figure, this time with impatience more than fury.

Fox, where in the hells are you? I need help... I need —

Muffled yelling interrupted his whirling thoughts.

The young king shifted his gaze from the faces before him. The sea of overwhelmed citizens, hoping that he had the answers, would be sorely disappointed if they knew the fears shifting around in his heart. Not fear for more cracks to appear amongst his people, but for the potential darkness in his blood.

A lot of the eyes that stared at him were wide, and strangely enough, were of pity. Rage he could understand, but to accept the sympathy of those who could see the weakness within him?

He'd rather take outright insults, words he could understand and reason with.

What he was experiencing now was beyond him. Considering about six people had died from whatever the hells had happened to him. Not a weapon, but something laying in wait in his blood. Five had been rioters, traitors to Aneirin. But one had been a young Elf, fighting at his side with a table dagger and a chair for what he had believed in. Justice, an end to lies, a hard won reconciliation between two races led astray by misplaced power.

Heat rose in Rhydian's throat.

The Elf had died for him, for Aneirin, away from home, at the hands of the one he'd been trying to protect. Another person deserving of a place in the silent hall of the dead in the royal crypts below.

I am going to throw my father's body to the crows, Rhydian vowed, his eyes closing for a moment. *To make room for an Elven warrior who should never have died in such a way.*

I'm sorry.

I caused this. The responsibility is mine to fix this.

I just... Rhydian sighed. *I don't know how.*

Murmuring among the crowd disturbed his dark thoughts. It came from the back at first, then along its centre as the waiting figures parted. From the rear, four guards, two men of Rhydian's choice and two Elven women directed by Bindy, dragged a resisting figure to the front of the hall. Bindy was stubbornly wearing her once offensively bright turquoise cloak. Its fur was grimy, bloody and torn, but Rhydian understood why she refused to take it off.

The prisoner wore a burlap sack over his head. His arms were bound, but his grubby bare feet were not. He wasn't walking, though. He was being dragged by his shoulders, sliding along the cold stone floor on his arse. Without ceremony, he was dumped at the foot of the stairs, landing in an ungainly sprawl on his backside.

All the while, the prisoner cursed. But when he realised he'd been let go, his sullen tirade ceased.

The murmuring increased in volume and below Rhydian, Bindy snorted.

Rhydian nodded at one of the guards, and he stepped forward to the edge of the dais. The sack was yanked off with little care and Wyll hissed as the light, weak as it was, flooded his swollen eyes.

Wyll had spent a few hours in the frigid dungeons, under watch, while the aftermath of his plan was dealt with. He looked like he'd been beaten about the head, his once shiny hair stringy with dried blood, his face a vision of purple and yellow flesh. Under the filth that caked him, Wyll's eyes were as bloodshot as Rhydian's knew his own appeared.

As soon as Wyll realised where he was, he aimed his glare at Rhydian, and his tirade began anew.

"How dare you!" Wyll spat. "You let these people handle your loyal citizens?" He jerked his head to the Elven women, only a sword's reach from his position. Neither of them said anything, but Rhydian was aware of Aurelia's tensing when he spared a glance from the corner of his eye.

Wyll went on and the king snapped his gaze back to the bound man at the base of the stone stairs.

"I guess it doesn't matter now though, does it? You've let one in your bed, infecting you —"

Rhydian remained silent and unmoving as Wyll continued. But one hand gripped the headrest of the heavy throne by his side, to remind him of who not to be.

"— and infecting your kingdom in turn! What the fuck was that last night?" Wyll pushed to his feet awkwardly as he huffed.

A woman yelled from the otherwise silent crowd. "You're mad!"

"Mad?" Wyll's laugh was bitter as he stared at Rhydian, his gaze blazing. "If it's mad to protect my family, our home, Aneirin, then yes, I'm mad! With how they've corrupted this so-called king, we need to make sure those dirty Elves don't get away with what they've done to us! And with what he will do to us to please them!"

"King Rhydian has always served his people," one guard by Wyll's side broke in. "What do you mean, what he'll do? His father was the one who led us to war, his mother leading the Elves, but him? He's the opposite. We've all seen him take care of others. You *are* mad."

The guard threw a guilty look over his shoulder at his king, but Rhydian waved the man's worry away. It was true, why deny it? He was the son of two brutal rulers. Continuing to hold his peace, although it was difficult, the king stayed where he was.

"*Mad?!*" Wyll spat and addressed the folk gathered in the gloomy hall. "*They* are the mad ones to think magic is the natural way of things, when it's the opposite! Magic users are the filth of the earth."

The shocked silence of the crowd had morphed into a low muttering, and Rhydian could not determine who was speaking and what was being said. His body was a map of aches and pains, and it was becoming harder to concentrate. Hardening himself, he merely listened, ignoring Aurelia's questioning glance.

"We saw what his father did! And Rhydian turned against him for it! Now look at him! How can we think that this is any different?"

Puffing, flushed red under his bruised, filthy cheeks, Wyll twisted with a grimace and faced Rhydian once more. He jerked his chin up, about to speak, when Rhydian released his grip on the throne and stepped forward.

"Was it you?" he asked quietly, stopping at the edge of the dais, the toes of his boots overhanging the step.

Wyll's jaw snapped shut. His eyes narrowed in obvious confusion.

"Was it you?" Rhydian repeated, his voice abruptly loud enough to fill the massive hall.

As the echoes of his demand receded, Wyll blinked upwards as Rhydian stared down at him, hands limp by his sides.

"Was it me?" Wyll snorted, his face twisted with disdain. "Sure it was me, along with quite a few dozen other —"

"No." Rhydian shook his head. "I'm not talking about your traitorous rebellion."

At this simple statement, delivered with a mildness that belied the fury rising within Rhydian's chest. Whispers and unease rippled through the crowd.

"What?" Wyll snapped, his top lip curling into a mocking sneer.

"I am talking," Rhydian replied as the fury threatened to erupt once more, "about Merion."

The whispering ceased at once.

The hall was still.

"What?" Wyll repeated, his filthy face going slack. "Merion?"

A few soft voices repeated Merion's name with confusion, but the young king spoke over them.

"I am talking," Rhydian said once more, his voice rising, "about the groom that served us with loyalty for his entire life." He descended the stairs with measured steps, his boots on the cold stone the only sound. When he reached the level where Aurelia waited, Rhydian paused. "I am talking about the fact that during a violent rebellion in my home led by *you*, Merion was attacked in the stables, alone, with no chance of aid."

Wyll shook his head. "Lots of people got injured last night in the quest for justice —"

"Justice?" hissed Rhydian, the two syllables rolling out between his teeth with the taste of hot iron. "What justice was there for an innocent, defenseless groom stabbed in cold blood and left to die?"

As the king resumed his descent, Wyll swallowed.

He took a step back, then halted.

A cunning light filled the prisoner's eyes.

In silent response, a wild tingling began in Rhydian's fingertips.

"How can you blame me for that? Merion was loyal to me! Not you." Wyll's dark eyes narrowed. "Why don't you check the facts? If it was an Elven blade that stabbed him, then —"

"Wyll," Rhydian said softly, fighting to keep his breaths even. "At what point did I say it was an Elven blade?"

Swallowing, the prisoner, still bound at the wrists, ground his teeth together, his jaw taught.

"The Elves are to blame," he insisted stubbornly.

"No," Rhydian said clearly, his gaze boring into Wyll's. "They are not."

"You don't know that!" Wyll declared, taking a step back. This time, Rhydian didn't stop the guards from surrounding him. Sneering as he struggled, Wyll raised his voice. "You don't know! The Elves are the devious ones, they —"

"I do know," Rhydian said, his own voice rising in volume, "because Merion told me himself this morning."

A few gasps filled those in the front rows of the crowd.

Wyll's eyes widened.

"Not only are you a traitor and an attempted murderer of a most loyal friend," Rhydian added with barely restrained venom, "you are an incredibly stupid bastard as well."

"Liar!" Wyll roared, spittle flying from his lips as his eyes darted about those closest to him. "It was the Elves! They're filthy liars with magic that comes from unearthly beasts and —"

Rhydian nodded at Bindy, standing close to Wyll and just about ready to commit murder by the set of her jaw.

The sack was yanked back down over his filthy hair and bloody face. When his face was covered, his cries muffled, the four guards grabbed Wyll's arms and roughly handled him back through the crowd.

The gathering parted to let them pass, voices raised with unchecked anger as they hissed.

Rhydian exhaled slowly, wondering what to do with the charge building up in his hands. The heat had travelled from his fingers to his palms, the unseen sparks licking at his wrists. He turned to Aurelia and Bindy, and the other guards gathered, waiting for his command.

He didn't know what to say. Davyn was with Merion in Rhydian's father's old chambers, along with the best Elven healers, their magic a blessing in this respect.

Ignoring the faces to his left, Rhydian swallowed past the taste of bitter iron in his mouth, his weary eyes on Aurelia's intense green gaze.

"What of Wyll?" she asked cautiously.

"Keep him alive," Rhydian replied, the blue rings around his irises flashing darkly. "For now."

49

Aurelia

Year 367
Aneirin Castle

"**I**'m yours, Rhydian," Aurelia murmured to her reflection, "no matter what."

In the mirror, a young woman with haunted green eyes stared back. Her cloak of dark fur was torn at one shoulder. Long, dark hair flowed in limp waves over her shoulders. Her face carried the faint flush of fading bruises. A smear of dried blood marred her neck, a stain that she'd missed when cleaning her face with a damp towel that morning before Wyll had been dragged before the king.

Did I look like this when I set out from home on this doomed quest?

The question hadn't been spoken aloud, but the fierce light in the green eyes of the woman in the mirror dimmed.

No.

I looked hopeful, believing in the lies I was told.

"Which means the glow of my naivety was worse," said Aurelia, her voice heavy with fatigue.

After the assembly where Wyll had been presented to the folk of Aneirin for a brief hearing, Aurelia had made her way up various sets of stairs. She had passed faded tapestries down a long hallway into a part of the castle that had few people about. After asking for directions, a young Elf with long hair of gold had silently pointed her to the previous king's bed chambers. Through the pair of ornate oak doors covered in peeling gold, Human and Elven healers alike were tending to Merion in the otherwise unused space.

Aurelia had slipped inside and made her way through those gathered at the bed. The groom was propped up on pillows of navy brocade, a thick blanket of burgundy wool pulled up under his limp beard.

Merion's face was ash grey. He was normally filled with life, positive and robust despite his recent losses amongst family and friends, cut down by her very own kinfolk. Sweat beaded on his cheeks and brow. He was breathing peacefully, though, his eyes closed. One of the Elven healers smiled gently at her questioning glance, a warm squeeze on her shoulder reassuring her he was out of danger.

Nodding her thanks, Aurelia headed back to the door. But rather than leaving, she examined the rest of the chamber. The vaulted ceilings overhead held little heat, and she was glad that two hearths had been lit. She pulled her torn cloak around her shoulders and took a seat at a table before a bronze mirror, staring at the dark circles under her eyes.

The pledge she made was a soft sigh as her lids shut for a brief moment.

"I'm yours, Rhydian," Aurelia repeated quietly, resting her chin in her hands, both elbows on the table. "But I'm not sure what help I can be."

Her green eyes blinked once, twice. She glanced down.

The table held a small set of golden bowls for holding various implements of grooming. It was hard to tell, because whatever had been placed here was now in fragments on the surface of the fine wood. A single comb of pearl was left in the closest bowl, a piece of luxury, visible in the serious craft of its shape and lustre. Aurelia's nose scrunched. She preferred her own wooden comb, carved by her father years ago. It carried the aroma of her floral soap and hair cleanser now after so much use. The comb before her was beautiful, but it was fragile, unlikely to last the use she'd put it through. Which was how she felt inside, like how Rhydian had appeared after whatever the fuck last night's show of power had been. It looked vulnerable, delicate. Too delicate to withstand constant use.

Half listening to the various Healers as they conferred, Aurelia dropped her face to her hands, wanting to slap herself.

How had she ever thought being dragged beneath a whirlpool in a raging river would be better than staying by Rhydian's side?

Protecting him in ways that he couldn't?

Unbidden, her mind wandered to thoughts of Flare and her misplaced faith in such a spineless creature. She rubbed at the ache inside her ribs with a pensive, absentminded gesture.

"Shit," Aurelia muttered to the shards around her elbows.

She would never let Rhydian down intentionally again. Yet, where was the help *she* needed in order to help him? Rhydian had been through so much by her own hand, and the schemes and falsehoods of others. Where was Fox, an unreliable dragon with a vast but icy heart?

Where had her pleas to the night been received, if at all?

Aware of her own failings, Aurelia bared her teeth, lost for a moment as the seriousness of the situation threatened to crack her shell. But that was impossible. It was important that Rhydian saw her as his rock, or shield. Yet inside, her confidence in being able to handle the situation felt as safe as a cave of brittle selenite crystals after a violent tremor.

"Aurelia."

With a jerk, Aurelia's head snapped up.

Rhydian's reflection had joined hers in the mirror, the pair of them framed by elaborately worked gold leaf.

His cheeks were pale, his chin grizzled and needing a shave. He was still dressed in the plain clothes he'd changed into the night before, after having a full bath. He was close enough that his warmth tickled the back of her head, but he didn't reach out.

Cursing herself for not paying attention, considering she'd just been telling herself about how she needed to be Rhydian's shield, Aurelia shared a weak smile. She leaned back, and his face softened, easing her heart. It wasn't much, but it was better than the shadows that seemed to hover behind him on silent wings.

There hadn't been any chance to speak alone, both of them running on little to no sleep since the fighting last night.

So, the appearance of his magic was a serious strain between them, an unbalanced weight left unchecked, without a safe place to land.

Rhydian eyed her in the mirror, the permanent line between his brows deeper than she had ever seen it. With a slight cough, he cleared his throat and held up one hand. His gaze broke from hers as he examined his raised palm.

"I'm lost."

Aurelia's lips thinned at the desolation in his voice. She kept her voice as calm as she could, despite the trembling in her bones at the potential power left unchecked in his blood.

"Lost?"

The king nodded, solemn eyes examining his hand. "Like a child wandering in the forest, alone."

Thinking of her journey to Aneirin, from caves of ice through trees as vast as hills, Aurelia considered her words with the levity that the current situation demanded.

"The forest can be many things."

Rhydian's eyes didn't meet hers, and she tried again, choosing her words with care.

"The forest isn't just a place of trees that go on forever, it's a place of hidden things, things that are yet to be uncovered. You are in the depths of a forest of choices and challenges, Rhydian." Aurelia shook her head, her gaze on Rhydian's face. "Challenges of which I don't doubt you'll triumph."

The pair of them were silent for a while as he digested this. Aurelia ignored the murmurs at the bed, aware of the serious line Rhydian was walking. It was impossible not to be aware of how underqualified she was to travel with him along it. She'd been born with magic, raised with it. It was like breathing. It came in handy for some things and made little difference to others.

The young man in the mirror behind her had no such privilege. For him, magic had until recently been a curse, a burden and something to run from lest it be wielded for ill gains.

"This isn't me," he said. Rhydian's voice was as ethereal as the cobwebs fluttering in the soft currents of air as the Healers moved around the bed.

Aurelia's voice was just as gentle.

"Rhydian."

His blue eyes, a soft shade ringed with darker tones, slowly rose to meet her gaze. Aurelia smiled.

"This isn't me," Aurelia murmured as she reached out to tap her fingernail on the edge of a golden bowl, its contents a range of personal items including a delicate comb of glistening pearl. "Yes, I'm here, in love with a king. It's a part of my current path, being here with you. But I am not a queen, and yet I will find my way through. You'll find your way, too."

Silently, she held his gaze. When he didn't look away, Aurelia reached behind, searching for his hand. After a moment, his warm grasp found her fingers and squeezed.

Eventually, he leant over and reached past her, his breathing gentle in her ear. Not letting go of the hand behind her back, Rhydian picked out the delicate comb of mother-of-pearl. It winked in the low light with a lustre that was as pretty as anything Aurelia had seen. It was one of the few items not smashed to pieces.

The grip of his fingers changed, and Aurelia swallowed her sharp exhale as Rhydian snapped the comb in two.

The brief snick of breaking shell was pitiful, hardly a puff of displaced air.

"This is neither of us. Yes, we'll find a way through. I just wish…" he dropped the pieces to the table as he searched for the words he needed. "I just wish we knew what path to take."

Without another word, Rhydian made his way to the pair of faded, golden doors. He paused and turned as if to say something more, but his gaze snagged on the bed in the far alcove, on the groom who lay there in a serious condition.

Aurelia watched his face change, his expression morphing from wearily burdened to a shuttered chill.

Without a sound, he turned and left.

Aurelia exhaled with a rush of held breath, shoulders slumping.

Her calloused fingers brushed over the two pieces of comb, pressing them together, willing a little of her inner spark, weak compared to Rhydian's wild eruption, and tried to meld them together.

It didn't work, of course.

At the moment, her magic was too weak. It was all she could do to see into the shadows come nightfall.

Meeting her own haunted gaze in the mirror, Aurelia sighed, wishing she could see into Rhydian's secret, inner heart instead.

A couple of muted thuds, like a pair of boots dropped to the stone floor, woke Aurelia from a fitful sleep.

After sitting with Merion, who had drifted in and out of lucidity during the afternoon, she had done what she could outside with others intent on braving the chill. The bodies had been taken away. But in the wan light of the new, icy day, workers still focused on clearing the courtyard of the violence left behind. Broken furniture, discarded weapons, spilled food and crushed tankards had frozen together in a disorganized jumble.

Despite the nature of their work, being part of a team amongst the snow had reminded her a little of working in the ice caves of Lolihud. Unexpectedly, a longing had overtaken her. Not so much for the chill and the snow, but for the simple way of things.

Yes, their community of Elven miners had been slowly subverted by Rhydian's mother, parading herself as a hard-done-by member of the magical community. But everyday life had been simple. Hard at times, but without most of the politics of Aneirin.

Although that didn't seem entirely fair. There was still politics, as Elders of the Lolihud community bickered about evenly distributed food supply in the coldest times of the year. Or when certain clan parties got too out of control and merriment echoed throughout the entire underground settlement for days.

But there had been seemingly endless days of relative peace. Whereas here, there had been lies, dissent, and now a gods-damned rebellion against a king put in an untenable position by his parents, and by certain members of the city folk.

In bed, under the covers, Aurelia's fingertips brushed the frayed family crest of the cushion at her side, the faint aroma of dust tickling her nose.

It was likely past midnight when she'd finally dragged herself to Rhydian's chamber, the winding stairs a trial on her fatigued limbs. Aurelia was used to long days and nights of walking, climbing, or fighting. But crouched over and sweeping away snow and ice to retrieve bodies and other ephemera from the courtyard had left her aching for rest.

Alone in Rhydian's bed now, her eyes fluttered open. A faint rattle sounded closer to the bed, followed by another dull clank. A discarded belt?

She inhaled carefully in the dark, and the familiar scent of Rhydian filled her senses. Man and soap, along with something hot and metallic. The heavy drapes covered the window, but Aurelia guessed he'd finally made it to his bed a few hours before dawn. No more voices echoed from the courtyard outside. Even the wind had died down. The peace that a soothing night like this would normally bring, however, was nowhere to be found.

"Merion?" Aurelia whispered.

"Stable," Rhydian replied, his voice muffled as he stripped. "The snow has ceased for now." His tone changed from resigned to amazement. "Snow! Here, of all places." His brief laugh was bleak. "I wonder if it can cover all the stains left behind outside."

"If only," Aurelia replied, hating that it couldn't. "When the freeze melts, the stains will remain."

Yawning, she twisted under the wool blankets until she could see the unlit candle of sweet beeswax on the wooden table beside the bed. Focusing the faint spark in her mind, Aurelia let it go. With a faint pop and hiss, a single flame ignited. That didn't always work for her, and she wondered at what had bloomed to life in Rhydian.

The mattress dipped behind her.

"I didn't need that," Rhydian murmured, his mouth hot on her exposed shoulder.

"Hm?"

Aurelia rolled back over to face Rhydian as he slipped under the covers against her, his bare skin chilled against her breasts. He pulled her close, nuzzling her hair, still damp from its quick wash by the fire, before dragging herself under the layers of wool and furs.

"I could see well enough without it." Rhydian's lips kissed under her ear, his lips as soft as his quietly spoken admission.

Aurelia slid her hands into his hair, tugging the silken strands to slow down his amorous attention. This earned her a hiss.

"We need to talk about what happened."

"No."

"But —"

"Aurelia," Rhydian lifted his face from her chest, grabbing one of her hands. He kissed her fingertips. "I can't talk about it. Not now. Let me have just this one moment. Please."

Aurelia tugged harder, and something flashed in his eyes.

"Alright," she allowed, pulling his face down to hers. "But at least tell me, do you feel..." *Okay* wasn't the right word. Nothing about this was okay. Overcoming her hesitation, Aurelia forged on, forcing calmness to her words that she didn't feel at all. "Do you feel well? People died, Rhydian. Not just because of Wyll."

His eyes, their unique colours lost to the low light and shadows between them, darted between her own. His lips parted, and when he spoke, his gentle tone belied the painful weight of his words.

"I am angry." Avoiding her assessing gaze, Rhydian held her close, lips tangling with her hair. "And I am... hurt."

As his knee nudged her legs apart, his hands wandered down her back to cup her backside. Aurelia let herself melt into his embrace, whilst speaking the words held back for some time.

"I asked for help, Rhydian. I'm sorry, nothing has come of it."

Not pausing as he rolled her onto her back, Rhydian's voice came from deep under the blankets as he shuffled down the bed.

"Fox? I'm wondering if that would be better," he paused to bite the inside of her thigh, "or worse."

"Mmm," she gasped, warmth spreading inside her core as his hot mouth roamed between her legs. "I know. But not him. Elsewhere."

He made no reply as his fingers and hands worked in unison to spark her desire. It flared immediately, almost shaming her with the sudden urgency she felt for his touch. Despite everything, the chaos and the horror of the day before, he was here to sink into pleasure for a little while, like he himself yearned for. As he softened the delicate folds of her core, she arched her back, fingers tangling in his hair. This time holding him there, guiding his probing caresses deeper within.

And when she was ready, he met her heat with a desperate thrust that sent her mind and body spinning as one. It was deep, astonishing, and severe. It was a side of Rhydian that Aurelia had never seen before. He was thorough in his attention though, adjusting his tempo to the sounds she made, the angle of her hips. As she panted beneath him, wrists held above her head, his teeth found her breasts and bit hard.

Aurelia cried out, coming apart around him, heels digging into his backside. Rhydian took his time, nowhere near done. His wide eyes were on her face, his gaze scorching as he moved within her, over her, around her, his own voice hushed. Limp, Aurelia received it all, almost at her second peak when he followed into his own spiral of pleasure, allowing himself a relieved grunt as he came.

They lay together, spent, sweaty, sated for now, neither letting the other one go.

Aurelia's calloused fingers moved over the back of Rhydian's hair with soothing strokes, and eventually she spoke.

"Things will be better eventually," she murmured. "I just don't know how."

Rhydian lifted his head. When he met her gaze, she watched the tiny points of light in his irises flicker, a single reflected flame from the sweet candle burning down to the last of its wick. His smile was brief, his words solemn.

"Whatever happens," he replied, "I'm choosing you."

At that, he rolled off her to the side, adjusting the cushions and pillows to get comfortable. The one he finally rested his cheek upon was the tired cushion with frayed threads, the crest of the royal household coming apart.

Aurelia swallowed, blinking away the shadow that crossed her vision. Not yet ready to get up to grab a cloth, she pressed closer to him, feeling the quick beat of his heart through his chest against her breasts. Under the covers, his hand found hers and she brought their clasped fists to her lips.

"I choose you, too," she said, watching the flames dance in his gaze. "Whatever happens, I choose us."

50

Karlien

Year 367
Travelling

“**M**y dear cousin, have you met the lovely brother and sister doling out today's bread?”

Karlien's normally bright eyes of blue, with their azure rings, were dull as he spared a waspish glance at Torres.

His cousin rode beside him, lazily strumming his fiddle with a polished fingernail. In Torres' hair, a red ribbon flapped in the frigid wind. With a noncommittal shrug, Karlien shifted in his saddle and looked away.

They had spent another two miserable days along roads of moss, dirt, and the occasional stretch of cracked cobbles. A kind of expectant air hung about the travelers. Except for Karlien.

As they moved further inland, the land had broadened, faint mountain tops in the distance just visible through an icy mist hanging above low hills and forest. The infrequent boulders that broke through the moss and ferns along the roadside were now of a reddish stone, one that Karlien hadn't seen before. A chilled rain had fallen during the day, churning up a muddy slush under their horse's hooves. Ahead, Baek Hyeon rode with some guards, the two swords across his back accentuating his broad shoulders.

Wrapped in his cloak of thick fur, the prince was grateful that despite the clouds hanging ominously close by, the rain had ceased. But he was bitterly uncomfortable and was looking forward to a wash. Even icy water would be better than the stink of horse and sweat that somehow accrued despite the chill.

"Hey."

"What."

Karlien's flat reply was disinterested, lost as he was in daydreams of copper tubs, rose soap, and perhaps a bathing companion to scrub his back. Blue eyes narrowed at the pair of swords gracing broad shoulders among the riders up ahead.

"Can you keep a secret?" Torres hissed, his horse coming alongside the prince's without warning.

Instantly alert, Karlien sat up.

"Absolutely not," said the prince, eyes widening. He leaned over. "Tell me!"

Torres urged his horse even closer and the two young men glanced ahead to check no one was listening.

"Did the regent tell you what was in the message tube she left behind?"

Karlien blinked. "No. Why?"

"I heard she had *another* prophecy dream before we left," Torres whispered. "About when you go to Aneirin."

His flamboyant cousin paused dramatically.

"And?" Karlien snapped when Torres dragged it on for too long, his dark eyebrows arched.

"And," Torres whispered, his ribbon fluttering, "while you are there, a native ruler will return home, to Baile Mara."

The prince stared at his cousin, a prickly expression marring his delicate features. *Why had grandmama told others and not him?*

"Who?" he sniffed. "There is no one else left."

Sitting back and waving his fiddle airily about, Torres shrugged. "Don't know."

Karlien wished he had something to throw.

"That's it?" He shook his head, eyes drifting to Hyeon's back. The man was wearing his hair in a single braid that hung between the hilts of his two swords. "That's not helpful at all. A dream like that could mean anything."

Not that he wished for more dreams. He certainly didn't want to wake the camp by crying out in the night. But Karlien had only had one last night, just before dawn. Perhaps because when he'd woken up, on either side of him had been a beast? One beast had fur, the other long black hair.

"That had nothing to do with it," Karlien muttered, uncomfortably aware of how safe he'd felt for a moment. Safe, despite the unknown road ahead.

With the memory of burnt sugar and wolf in his nose, the prince thought back to breakfast that morning.

Sitting on a rock covered with lichen by his campfire under a wide, gnarled tree of snow and bare branches, the prince sniffed his dry bread.

There was no trace of salt, just wood smoke and bitter ash. At his knee lay the wolf, its solemn amber gaze fixed on Karlien's breakfast. The prince ignored it, crouched in layers of wool and fur as he tried to wake up.

His fading dream lingered in his subconscious. It had been about a serious-faced boy burning down a building on sheer cliffs of black basalt that reminded him of Baile Mara. Unsure of what it meant, Karlien glanced across the haze of smoke over the fire, wondering why Hyeon was adding little pieces of food to a small leather pouch around his neck. The bodyguard was dressed in riding leathers, his normally white shirt replaced by a black one. The rolled-up sleeves of both his shirt and wool jumper revealed the whirling patterns of black ink over his golden skin.

Before Karlien could ask what the pouch was for, Bathsheba Elphin wandered over, sprightly as ever despite their journey. She was dressed in layers of purple fur and wool, hair tucked into a burgundy snood, with split riding pants despite travelling in a covered carriage of oak and iron.

Karlien jumped up to embrace her. Thin arms squeezed him back. He hadn't seen her this close for days. When they were settled back on Karlien's rock, Bathsheba on a folded blanket, her bright eyes examined his face.

"My little prince," Bathsheba queried. "Are you coping?"

"Of course, grandmama! Why wouldn't I be?"

Not missing the awkward smile of her great grandson, the regent sighed.

"Don't lie."

"I am just fine," Karlien declared hotly. A grey eyebrow arched.

"Blood Binds All. Remember."

Karlien yanked his bread away from a cold, wet nose. "Why now?"

"Why do you think?"

Ignoring the dark stare flecked with ruby across the fire, Karlien thought of home.

Did his fading dream have anything to offer? He had heard tales of a library long lost to arson decades before his birth, not too long before the chaos that struck the city. Occasionally, books and scrolls were still found amongst the rubble. Karlien's gaze dropped from the thick forest around him to the fire. What was still to be uncovered? And what lay ahead in a kingdom set to crack from within?

Biting back what he wanted to say, about what was the point of all his training on strategy, warfare and history, if no one told him anything, Karlien tore his bread in half.

"Are we answering the call for help, Grandmama?"

Bathsheba nodded, glancing briefly to Hyeon, then back to Karlien.

"Yes. Amongst other things."

"How can I help them?" Karlien was ashamed by the catch in his voice. Not caring if Hyeon saw, Karlien let the larger half of the bread disappear between a set of sharp canine teeth.

"That's unclear," Bathsheba replied, not at all concerned by Karlien's trembling lower lip. "But I am sure you'll do just fine. We shall see tomorrow. My secret is to be brave, be bold, even in the face of uncertainty."

A strangled sort of noise escaped the prince's throat, and he missed the second glance shared by the regent and the bodyguard.

"Oh," Karlien said, swallowing past the lump in his throat. That didn't really answer anything at all.

With a gentle pat to his golden curls, worse for wear in the icy sleet, Bathsheba hopped up and headed off to where a pair of servants were arguing about how to pack something in a cart. Aware the noise of the camp was increasing with the rising sun, the prince handed the last of his bread to the wolf. The beast's great bushy tail thumped as it chewed, amber eyes bright.

"Everything is fine," the prince whispered to the animal. "Simply because grandmama said so."

Yet why did his throat feel so tight?

"Heavy thoughts?"

Startled by the deep voice by his side, Karlien blinked.

Hyeon had somehow sat down next to him without him realising. The tall man's expression was unreadable, the red gleam in his dark eyes subtle in the grey morning light. Wordlessly, Hyeon handed Karlien the last of his own bread. Without thinking, Karlien took it with a murmur of thanks.

"You can't speak this language well," Karlien commented quietly. "Yet you always speak politely to me."

Hyeon went still. "What?"

Taking a bite, Karlien waved the hunk of bread in front of him at the servants bustling about, ignoring him.

"You listen to me, even when..." Karlien paused, then forced himself to keep going. "Even when I am being a brat. You listen to me more than my kinsfolk do. It overwhelms me sometimes."

Not at all sure why he admitted that, the prince shifted under Hyeon's unblinking stare.

"Don't go near river."

"The river?"

"Monsters. Princess stay away."

Snorting, Karlien narrowed his gaze at the man by his side. Hyeon was close, his warmth felt even through the layers of fur wrapped around the prince.

"Are you trying to distract me from my troubles?" Karlien demanded.

"Is it working?" Ruby flecked eyes twinkled with mischief.

Karlien stared at the rarely seen smile that had his stomach flip over.

He sniffed, turning away. "A bit."

"Everything is fine," Karlien repeated, eyes on the riders ahead.

"What?" Torres asked, back to strumming his fiddle. Under his dark, floppy hair, golden eyes were deep in thought amongst the handsome, warm tones of his skin.

"I said I need a wash," Karlien replied, rubbing his chest.

He eyed his cousin, and the dust and mud on Torres's garish outfit of navy blue leather pants and bright green wool jumper under his pale fur cloak.

"We really can't, though."

The prince's eyebrows rose as he scoffed. "Why?"

Torres, looking anything but scared, grinned with a flash of white teeth.

"Apparently, there are strange creatures along here."

Karlien remembered Hyeon's offhand comment earlier.

Could he have been serious?

Getting a whiff of horse as the chill breeze lifted the reddish mane before him, the prince shook his head.

"No. I shall bathe tonight."

Torres laughed. "You're braver than me, my prince." He spared Karlien a sly glance. "I doubt you can get away."

Thinking of a bottle of fragrant rose oil at the bottom of his pack found while looking for his tooth stick at lunch, Karlien aimed a crafty look at Hyeon's broad shoulders, eyes narrowed.

Be brave, be bold.

Heart racing, Karlien slipped through the snow-laden trees.

His golden curls were hidden under his cloak, and he was attempting to step lightly over the layer of fresh white draping the moss amongst the undergrowth. Torres was off flirting with the serving folk, and Baek Hyeon had left the wolf with Karlien to tend to their massive horses himself.

Unfortunately, the wolf wasn't as silent as the prince had hoped it would be. Each time Karlien checked he wasn't being followed, the animal would whine. Amber eyes reflecting the soft glow of the overcast evening shone with concern.

"I am being brave," the prince protested. "And I don't want to smell like you."

With that, Karlien ran for the next wide trunk of nubbly, gnarled bark, heading towards the river. Fragrant resin combined with the crisp bite of ash and snow, a refreshing change to the mud and sweat of the camp somewhere back amongst the trees. After walking for a bit, the determined prince found a break in the trees, soft willows overhanging a shallow inlet where the river curled about with the gentle lap of calm water. Further out, the water's surface reflected fractured clouds amongst the ripples of the faster current.

Standing at the water's edge, the wolf eyed him warily. It sniffed the water, lapped it once, then stared at the prince. It whined again.

"I'll stay in the shallows," Karlien murmured, his eyes intent on the clear water as one of his boots landed on the pebbles below the moss and roots of the bank. His soft towel of fine cotton and oil lay nearby.

Despite the frigid first dip of a bare toe, Karlien sighed with pleasure.

Amongst the floating green fronds of willow above him, a few small grey birds with black heads and yellow beaks protested loudly. The group was annoyed by a large orb spider threading its web close to their nest. Karlien shuddered. Not just from the watery chill as he waded into the river up to his knees. The birds were flitting about with such vigor that the peacocks of home seemed tame compared to these flashy little maniacs.

Ignoring the whine behind that increased in pitch, the prince stepped carefully over slippery rocks to his thighs. As the icy water touched his balls, Karlien hissed.

"Bold," he gasped through clenched teeth. "B-brave."

Blinking through frosty tears, the prince raised his gaze from his shivering genitals and stared out across the river as it cut through the sprawling forest. The open space was welcome, and despite Karlien's fears of the unknown, it was a beautiful place. It wasn't the same wilderness as home, of course. For one, it smelled different and there was no background crash of surf onto shore. But the ripple of water and distant mountains with a faint spot of light behind the fog held a kind of awe, of foreign grandeur and alien majesty.

"B-b-brave," Karlien stammered, sinking to his neck in the waist deep water with a squeal, his eyes on the distant patch of light. "I can do this! I c-can get clean —"

A massive splash behind had him jump up.

He lost his footing on a slimy rock.

Karlien yelled in fright, earning himself a face full of icy water. Emerging with a wet cough, the prince aimed a scorching gaze over at the wolf who had dived in and was bounding towards him with mad barks.

"I didn't want t-to get my hair wet —" Karlien yelled, but the words died in his throat.

As the wolf just about reached him, amber eyes round with alarm, it yelped.

Then swiftly disappeared beneath the thigh deep water, a ring of ripples expanding in its wake.

"NO!"

Karlien's shout echoed across the icy river, and not hesitating, the prince took a breath and dived.

At first, there was nothing but pain, the freezing water so cold that it burned.

As Karlien flailed about in the bubbles with panicked cries that made no sound, he slipped about on the rocks, on all fours, kicking about and lunging.

The lonely current was all that met his grasping fingers.

Kicking harder, the prince felt himself caught in a stronger rush of water. He let it take him, not bothering to come up for air, letting himself be pulled deeper.

A mad thought crossed his mind, barely coherent as the freezing temperature slowed his brain.

If the wolf was under, surely he'd been caught in the current too?

Eyes stinging and with little air left, the prince arched about below the surface, the overcast sky above making the subterranean world a place of shadows, thick glass and trapped air.

Sobbing, his tears of frustration joining the river, ready to surface with the catastrophe of his actions already weighing his heart down, Karlien's fingertips brushed against something.

Thick fur.

Yelling wildly, the prince kicked closer, hands reaching, grabbing, slipping at first, then holding firm.

The wolf was twisting about, and as Karlien found the animal's tail, he screamed underwater with almost the last of his air.

Something cold, hard and scaled, with a long row of teeth, was clamped firm around the wolf's thickly furred appendage.

Close to passing out, the prince punched at the scales, screaming, bubbles obscuring the thing that held fast. Karlien held tight to the dense fur with one hand, and raised the other, fighting the thick water as he swung.

The pain was instant as his fist connected to hard scales.

He kept going.

Karlien punched and punched, each one weaker than the last.

Blood soon joined the swirl of froth, fur, foam, and chaos about his face. It was likely his own hand, cut on sharp teeth, and the wolf's.

Not stopping, the prince punched until the row of teeth finally let go.

At the same time, something grabbed his ankle.

Only a few pitiful bubbles escaped as, held deep underwater, Karlien screamed with the last of the air in his lungs.

51

Fox

Year 367

Northern Aneirin

Panting and in pain, Fox lay on his back in the fresh snow at the base of a low rise of frosted hills, the earth below his cheek protesting with a deep, rumbling groan.

The concentration required to move himself, his lover, and two horses from one place to another had sapped his strength and sanity. The feeling of pressure building to unbearable proportions within could be compared to reaching orgasm. But instead of a pleasurable climax, there was only incandescent pain and confusion rippling along the filaments that bound his form together.

"Shit," Fox groaned as icy waves of agony fled his trembling limbs.

The light was dim; the landscape glowing an ethereal silver. Black eyes flecked with gold stared at the occluded sky, wishing the setting sun and the vast expanse of stars behind the frozen clouds were visible.

Stars that had elegant names written out in ornate letters in the City of the Seers library.

Or would have been, if it weren't decaying into dust.

So many things, places, people, dreams, lay in ruins behind him. Before him there was a chance to prevent another disaster, depending on what plans Owaen's brother was ready to hatch.

Literally and figuratively.

Fox blinked away the icy powder coating his lashes. While contemplating the exceptional purity of the flakes, a cough nearby had him roll his head to one side.

Owaen was next to him in the dirt and shadows. Instead of flat on his back like Fox, the blonde Elf was on his hands and knees, the reins grasped in one hand. Thankfully, he hadn't let go, considering Blackthorn was snorting and pulling wildly.

"Stop," Fox hissed, his gaze ominously raw.

To his amazement, the snow covered black horse rolled its wide eyes his way, ears back, but quietened.

Despite the pain splitting his head open, Fox spared the arrogant animal a vicious smirk. Willow stood next to it, shivering. They'd been through a lot, he'd give them that, and were dealing well, all things considering. Even as the thunder underneath their hooves rolled into a fading hum, leftover from their condensing of the distance they needed to get here, both animals seemed to bear up alright.

Owaen hacked out a mouthful of phlegm and swore. He spared an ashen glance to Fox, averted his face, then threw up the meagre contents of his stomach over the slush to one side. Thankfully, the place they had arrived at with a sickening lurch of power was somewhere in the northern part of the crescent-shaped valley of Aneirin, and was filled with old growth pines. Their pungent, spicy aroma covered most of the sour stink of vomit.

"You're adorable when you're not being an overprotective oaf," Fox declared, unable to help himself.

A thick mumble came between coughs, sounding something akin to '*fuck off, my love.*'

Fox pushed himself up with sweaty hands, the moisture cooling abruptly in the frigid evening air. He wasn't sure what time it was; only that it was late, the light near dark and the snowfall increasing in intensity. He spared a thought for the vulnerable parts of a man that caught the cold more easily than a woman and rose on shaky legs, his body filled with an untamed agony that spiked along his limbs as feeling returned.

He brushed off the snow from his pants and shook out his cloak, turning about to get his bearings. All at once, Fox's nostrils flared, his footsteps pausing, his ears straining over the low hum of the earth as the quake from his magic faded to occasional throbs deep below his boots.

He sniffed.

It wasn't an aroma that stood out over the rich pines and fresh vomit, but a trace of magic.

Was it his?

Or was it the trail of those who had passed overhead the day before?

Fox inhaled carefully, blinking away the icy flakes landing on his equally frigid lids.

It was hard to decipher the untamed aroma. Scorching pain hadn't quite faded from his extremities, his mind still pulsing with the after-effects of great magic that he'd burned through to get them this far. It reminded him of the mineral pools, where a blonde man covered in scars had broken down, loneliness and longing in his voice, a substantial chunk of jagged crystal in his arms.

The raven haired man ran a hand through his hair, eyes closed.

He'd never had his bath, and the longing for it now was an annoyance that he didn't need, because it was time to act. The low rumble under his boots diminished, along with the agony in his body, and the fear that came with tearing himself open to get them here. He had been concerned that this use of his power would take him longer to come back together, considering what he'd been through. Yet the wild thump of his heart was returning to its strange beat. Like the horses, he seemed to have borne the use of his powers well. The thought brought him no comfort though, as it meant he was getting used to using the magic that had never been meant for him.

Self satisfaction at getting all of them here relatively unscathed was replaced by a sharp pang of resentment in his chest.

Owaen wandered over, boots crunching on snow, with the two horses trailing behind. The blonde Elf wiped his mouth with a hunk of frozen grass. With a grimace, he chucked it away.

"My love, now that I can speak without hurling up my guts, explain that to me," Owaen muttered, eyebrows low over his emerald green eyes.

Opening his eyes, Fox peered into the trees past Owaen, marveling at their beauty.

The land here appeared serene, untouched, unblemished. Virgin forest sprawled as far as the eye could see on either side of the silvery white road they had arrived on. Gentle hills undulated over the land of frost, the light dim, the air thick with silence and a serenity that only fresh snowfall could bring. It was reminiscent of Lolihud, the aching cold bearable for the wonderful stillness of the heart and mind that only a frozen landscape could evoke.

Completely opposite to the heat and ash of Mionlach, home to dragons and their greed.

"Explain what?" Fox murmured, aware he was delaying his departure. "I offered to help. And we have come."

He had brought them here, and now it was time to act.

The *how* was still a mystery.

With a frown, ignoring the snuffling nose of Blackthorn at his ear, Owaen checked the trees behind himself. His gaze returned to Fox.

Under the emerald stare, Fox sighed for the handsome, masculine beauty of his lover, at ease in the landscape, while Fox himself felt like a walking wound that had yet to heal.

He wondered if he ever would.

"What is it?" Owaen asked urgently, the line between his brows deepening.

With arms of immeasurable power held in check by love, Fox stepped forward and embraced Owaen with an urgency that pulled at his heart in much the same way a whirlpool of dark water had pulled his closest friends under. The Elf grunted in surprise, both of his powerful hands, one holding a pair of reins, immediately pulling Fox close.

"I'll do my best, my love," Fox murmured into the warmth of Owaen's neck, the heat of him welcome to the ever present chill that filled Fox from the inside. "I'll try to be worthy this time, so that none we love are hurt."

"Fox," came the low growl in his ear. "*Explain.*"

Shaking his head, Fox peered along the road, up to the rolling hill. There was a slight bend towards the crest as the road wound its way up and over, heading down into the valley of Aneirin.

He frowned.

As he watched, the wan, muted light of the wintry night changed.

Was the setting sun behind the clouds bright enough to lend the silent valley beyond the hills such an abundant display of glowing, reddish warmth?

As realisation dawned, Fox hissed, the thunder that had faded from their arrival rumbling once more below his feet.

There, in the far distance, was where the terraced city of Aneirin spread out over one of the reddish mountains, forming the outer edge of the sweeping valley. Fox's lips parted as he examined the city that he shouldn't quite have been able to see just yet. But the unnatural glow was clearly visible. There was no mistake.

Caspian had shown his hand.

With Aurelia at risk once more.

And Rhydian now, as well.

After Fox had destroyed Rhydian's mother, a woman twisted by fear and greed, Fox had been torn apart in turn. He had drifted for a time in a place that was nowhere at all.

But he had chosen to fix the mess left behind, originating all the way back to creatures with scales and wings, fuelled by the ambitious, if misguided, vision of two brilliant alchemists. So when Fox had come back to life, into a body instinctively gathered from ethereal, scattered particles, after a sacrifice that had cost him everything, he had a question burning deep within his dark soul.

What did spending time with bright hearts do to a black one?

Now he could answer.

It made you want to be better, do better. Or at least, not do the worst, which was to do nothing at all.

Fox stared at Owaen, at the illuminated soul staring out from emerald green eyes, a soul that grounded Fox like nothing else in this chaotic world ever had, or ever would.

How many bright hearts had Caspian spent time with?

Yet, considering how much pain he had caused, why did Fox care?

And should it matter?

He eyed the menacing red glow pulsing over the low clouds in the distance.

"I was going to show you mercy," Fox hissed, the gold flecks in his eyes flaring.

Owaen pulled away from him, frowning in confusion. The pair of horses shifted uneasily, Blackthorn snorting with a white puff of hot air. Without a word, Fox grabbed Owaen's arms over his fur cloak, and turned him to face the direction Fox was glaring. It took Owaen a moment longer than Fox. His Elven eyesight was respectable but not as sharp as Fox's. As Fox felt the tension in Owaen's body increase to a dangerous stillness, Fox knew that Owaen understood.

"Is that him?" Owaen gasped, his voice thick with all the turbulent emotions that Fox was experiencing as well. "Is that my brother's doing?"

Fox nodded, aware that Owaen couldn't see, but that didn't matter. He let go of Owaen and lifted a foot without taking his eyes off the glowing city.

"I'll meet you there," Fox announced, his voice icy, as he dropped the first boot and began unlacing the second. Owaen whirled to face him, green eyes wide, his silhouette outlined by the deep glow on the horizon.

"Skye! Don't you dare —"

Fox darted forward and planted a fierce kiss, chilled lips pressed together for a moment that would never be enough, but would have to do.

Before Owaen could react, Fox tore off the chains that held the green crystal pendants, along with the amethyst ring, from his neck. He yanked them over Owaen's head. Then he spun and sprinted up the rise of the hill, discarding the rest of his clothes as he ran, ripping them away.

Closing his eyes, Fox centred himself, bracing for the searing pain that came with transformation, calling on the energy of potential, of the sparks that blazed in his arteries and veins.

It hurt, it always did.

He bit back his cry. Leaving Owaen alone would hurt the Elf enough. Hearing Fox call out in agony was something that could be prevented.

And yet Owaen cried out anyway, as he and the horses were thrown back by an explosion of rippling energy, displaced snow, pine needles and frozen clods of dirt.

With wing beats that threatened to burst the eardrums of the Elf knocked down into the snow, the magnificent golden dragon, its shimmering gold and green hue lost in the darkness, rose into the night.

With a furious roar that displaced the snowflakes suspended around it, the dragon whirled about, claws at the ready, heading for Aneirin.

52

Cas

Year 261, Cas at age 20
Baile Mara

Cas kicked at the charred remains of the old library along the cliffs, wincing as a puff of ash soiled his shining black boot.

The wind had died down, a salty breeze barely ruffling his hair. Judging by the scattered remains of cracked shells and oddly shaped rocks under the toe of his boot, Cas realised he'd found the location of the shelf that once held a delicately strung necklace of debris washed up on the ebony shore below.

A necklace made of the things he found, stuck on a shelf like Morgan had lived her life, held in place for others to admire or make use of as they wished.

Morgan had gotten craftier as time went on in avoiding him.

Simultaneously amused and bereft at her absence, Cas had kept himself busy. He followed Rook's orders. So, much to the surprise of his family, Cas was now a model of gentlemanly learning and respect. With his focus on the first stage of a protracted plan, he had studied meekly under the gaze of suspicious priests. He continued the art of swordcraft, paying the foreigners who grew increasingly impressed with his blooming skill.

And he listened with rapt attention as Rook shared all that he had garnered about magic, information that Hypatia and Illarion had never shared with Cas.

Only with Owaen.

It seemed inevitable that Cas now treated Owaen like a relative whom he had little in common with. They lived in the same grand house, but in different wings and levels now.

The aging head of the household occasionally pleaded with him to come back into the fold of the Carter family.

"*Come back in?*" Cas had laughed as he breezed past, dressed in green velvet and black leather, intent on a morning ride. "I was never *in* this family to begin with. You know that, Evreth."

Evreth had been left speechless, his white hair a wild halo, his grey eyes wide as Cas had made a beeline to the stables, pretending he cared for nothing but the open sky above.

Patience, he would repeat to himself as the days of holding in his disgust as the city championed the work of the two brilliant minds that happened to belong to Cas' parents.

Because, out of all the things Cas had learnt in the past few years under the incredulous stares of those who thought they knew him, patience was the most important lesson of all.

Blue eyes, one dark and the other light, rose from the wind-blown ruins to the hazy horizon, where the grand arch of azure sky met the choppy arch of the sea. Far offshore, three dragons soared above the ocean on thermals rising in the heat of the warmest days of the year, newest members of the exclusive collection of those with wings. Their scales reflected the light as they twisted, like colourful flames burning in midair.

With heart throbbing at the magnificent sight, Cas smiled.

The fire that had destroyed the library was years ago, the acrid stink of smoke diminished. Yet the flames in his heart still burned for both his absent lover, and the power that was about to be his after years of longing.

"Wish I'd burned this place down sooner," Cas mused to the gulls circling directly overhead.

At the entrance to Hypatia's workroom, Cas' hand hesitated.

The door was closed, but not locked.

He lifted the iron latch, heart beating a tad faster than usual, and opened the heavy door. Inside was no longer the place of wonder and mystery to his younger self. Instead, it had become a place where pitiful creatures came to be studied.

And then to die.

With a wistful sigh, Cas stepped through.

Striding past the central table, he headed to the work bench where the sun poured in through the wall of windows. His boot heels were the only sound, the space was empty apart from him. The bench was tidied today, stacks of notes neatly to the side, a tray of large uncut gemstones of all colours by his elbow. The study was remarkably quiet, no birds squawking in their cages or reptiles thrashing about in their pens.

The long anticipated experiment of Baile Mara's prime alchemists was coming to an eagerly awaited close.

Plans were hushed. So, however that would unfold, Cas had only a faint idea from what Rook had garnered from his time here, and Morgan when she had been around. Ignoring the pang in his chest, Cas dropped his gaze from the neat rose gardens outside to the sight in front of him. Beside the twinkling gemstones were two golden trays, lined with soft wool, bathed in golden light. Each tray held a glittering crystal the size of his head, their surfaces crossed with jagged ridges of deep green and sparkling blue.

Cas knew they weren't just crystals, stolen from a land across the sea to the east.

They were eggs.

A trembling finger reached out and touched the surface of one, the aroma of ozone teasing Cas' nose. He caressed the egg carefully. He wasn't checking their weight like Mother had been, but their temperature. The thing was warm, far too warm for the sunlight pouring in through the windows.

Silvery blue eyes narrowed.

If one squinted at the space just above the one he touched, a haze could be determined, distorting the air. Beside it, the air above the slightly smaller of the two was clear. When Cas touched that one, it was cool.

"Curious," he murmured.

He and Rook sometimes stayed up at night when the others at his parties had passed out. Only then was it safe to talk about the world and the way these eggs could help. Not only were the topics of their conversations fascinating, Cas felt more welcome amongst the folk of the underworld, who shunned the political nonsense of the city and made the night their own. His heart beat only for Morgan, but it was a relief to lose himself amongst the gaiety of late night parties, before he trekked back home to sleep until playing at obedience the next day.

But that was all over now, because this was the last day he would wake up here.

Cas lifted the slightly smaller of the two, the cooler one, and held it up to his face.

It wasn't as green as the other, but just as craggy. Both the sharp and dull edges of its ridges that followed the curved surface all the way around sparkled, a cascade of twinkling reflections scattering over himself, the bench and windows as he turned it about. Various memories shimmered in his mind, shimmering like the sparks painting his face from the crystallised surface.

A woman's soft laugh.

The curve of the Baile Mara's shoreline with its smoking island in the bay.

The noise, smells and sounds of his home city, a city that was perfect as it was.

A city that was at risk, according to all the signs, both Morgan's dreams and Rook's deep talks with those who visited his pleasure dens, those who had magic from faraway places.

Mismatched blue eyes, both shining silver, rose to stare at the windows. Beyond his shimmering reflection, the manicured gardens and woodlands of the Carter estate sprawled all the way to the golden-roofed black towers rising above the royal residence.

From the city's scientists and to its rulers, an imminent threat loomed. Perhaps Morgan was trying to prevent it by keeping her distance? But in her own words, it would happen. Cas gathered the egg to his chest, wondering at the hopelessness of the situation, how a mad plan to not simply prevent the chaos but redirect it could unfold.

"Put that down."

It was still an effort not to flinch like a guilty child at his mother's brisk tone.

Smiling faintly, Cas turned around.

At the door stood Hypatia and Evreth. His mother was without her apron, dressed in a velvet robe of deep magenta, her arms crossed over her chest. Hovering behind and dressed just as formally in a black tunic with the Carter crest in gold thread upon his breast, the housekeeper stared at Cas with shocked grey eyes. Evreth bit his lower lip, fingers clenching around the wicker basket in his hands.

Smirking at his mother's glare, Cas lifted the substantial crystal away from his chest.

Then, with a crafty fumble, he pretended to drop it.

A glass vial shattered on a shelf just inside the door to Hypatia's right. Evreth stumbled back into the hallway. Hypatia glared as Cas gathered the egg against the pristine linen of his white shirt.

"Careful mother," Cas laughed. "Don't make a mess."

With an arrogant toss of blonde hair, Cas returned the egg with care to its resting place with a casualness he hoped fooled those behind.

"Why are you here?"

Cas tilted his head as if deep in thought, blinking at his reflection in the glass.

"Hm. I felt like I needed to give you some kind of last warning, I guess. About the arrogance of ego and misplaced power." Odd blue eyes widened with feigned innocence as he faced his mother once more. Cas shrugged. "But I simply can't be bothered."

"That old nonsense?" Hypatia murmured as her caustic gaze scanned the room, checking for any disturbance, then settled her intense gaze back to Cas.

Evreth remained frozen at the tension between mother and son.

"*Nonsense,*" Cas repeated, strangely enough, a little sad. While he wondered at that, Hypatia straightened her shoulders.

"Yes, Caspian. I have set things in motion to instigate change for the greater good. You know magic will improve the order of things and increase efficiency," Hypatia stated coolly. "It is the only way to progress what has stagnated for long enough."

Cas knew his mother was tenacious, but at the look in her eyes, it was still a shock to see she was perfectly serious with her overbearing, arrogant view of the world.

"You're mad," Cas breathed.

"Mad?" Hypatia's laugh was thick with scorn. "You're wrong about that. You are continually wrong about a lot, even after all these years of steadfast study. But you were right about something. There was one thing I failed at."

A muscle in Cas' jaw twitched at the words he knew would come.

His mother looked serenely thoughtful as she spoke. "You're my greatest failure."

The tension in the room thickened.

Eventually, Cas nodded.

"Thank you, Mother," he said calmly, and offered her a mocking bow.

Then, an eyebrow arched in challenge, he scooped up a large uncut diamond from amongst the gemstones on display, and slipped it into the pocket of his shirt.

Hypatia said nothing, but her blue eyes narrowed.

Cas simply smirked at her, his gaze sliding to the old housekeeper with his wild tuft of wispy white hair. Evreth swallowed, stepped back with a mumble, then dashed off like the coward he was.

Unbothered, Cas' boot heels clicked as he walked to the door. He halted before the alchemist, a figure in whom so many had placed their hopes and resources.

Hypatia was a towering woman, but Cas rose above her by a decent amount. He wasn't trying to intimidate her as he stared down; he wasn't a chauvinistic prick. But it was hard not to feel a little pleased at her having to look up to meet his gaze.

"Goodbye," said Cas after a momentary pause. Not waiting for her to reply, he brushed past the woman who had given life to him, but not much else.

Goodbye, Mother, goodbye Father, Cas thought, his lips curling upwards at the corners. *Goodbye for now.*

Cas cleared his throat with a sarcastic cough.

The knock on the doorway at the top of the stairs had failed to get the attention of those on the rooftop terrace. Four, or possibly five, figures, were having an orgy in broad daylight, only shielded from the surrounding buildings by numerous flapping swathes of gauzy silvery cloth.

Naked and buried balls-deep in a groaning man on his knees facing the door, Rook was in the midst of the sweaty action. Perched on the man Rook was fucking, a woman had her heaving bosom in his face. Black eyes rose from the breasts to Cas' unmoved expression.

"I'm ready," Cas announced.

The other figures, whose number was still in question, continued on the pile of cushions, their moaning and undulations rather comical, while Rook assessed Cas in silence.

Cas chewed the inside of his cheek.

Was this what prey felt like when leathery wings of inky black circled above?

Hairs on his neck rising, Cas held his ground and fought to keep his hand away from his sword, instead forcing himself to stare straight ahead, fists by his sides.

Holding their locked gaze a heartbeat longer, Rook nodded.

Ignoring the disappointed gasp, Rook pulled out of his partner, stood up, and snagged a jug from a table of ebony wood and gold metalwork.

Pushing through layers of white gauze, Rook halted in front of Cas and took a long swig of whatever the jug contained. The aroma of poppy smoke pooled in Cas' nose. He knew Rook didn't partake in its stupor inducing haze, but had most likely been covered in it from his partners.

Wistfully, Cas wished he was covered in it too. Not from the writhing figures on the cushions, but from Morgan, who still hovered beyond his grasp.

"I'll get ready, too," Rook said softly, interrupting Cas' thoughts. "Get some rest."

With a stoic nod, Cas whirled and headed downstairs.

"It's going to hurt," Rook called behind him.

This time, Cas allowed his hand to grasp the ruby in the hilt of his sword.

He shrugged, the time for caring long past. When he spoke, it was for no one but himself, his voice indifferent, flat.

"Of course it is."

At nightfall, Rook led Cas from the city.

Neither of them spoke. Both were dressed plainly. In little more than a plain linen shirt and soft wool trousers tucked into shiny boots, Cas felt exposed. He cracked his neck in an attempt to ward off the sensation.

Rook had made him leave his sword, along with his jewelry, including his amethyst ring, back at the inn. Cas had his own lushly appointed room there now. He'd sleep there some nights when the facade of a reformed son became too much.

Overhead, the stars were out, the moon waning, the city alive below. Not as noisy and hectic as the day, nevertheless, people were out and about. Late night restaurants traded noisily with the aroma of freshly cooked spiced fish, and groups of sailors and other revelers made their rounds to the various bars and taverns. It was familiar to Cas, but also surreal.

His mouth had dried, his throat constricted. Saying nothing, he followed where Rook led.

The pair took the main roads back and forth along each terrace, all the way to the south end of Baile Mara. When they reached the end of the docks where the hand-hewn stone blocks met the black grains of the beach, Rook hopped onto the sand with an easy jump.

Dressed in white, with a bleached leather satchel slung over one shoulder, Rook looked like a prince of the night, his clothes glowing a little by the light of the moon and stars. His finely muscled arms showed under his rolled-up sleeves. Rook had the same handsome facial features reminiscent of the pirates that visited occasionally, with their finely curved eyes of delicate beauty and regal cheekbones.

Cas cleared his throat as he paused on the last stone step.

"Do I need to thank you for this? I know this is just to help yourself," Cas queried, hoping the catch in his voice wasn't detectible.

Rook ignored him and pointed to Cas' feet.

"Leave your boots here," he said.

"Why?"

Rook's black eyes narrowed. "Because I'm not fucking carrying them back for you."

"Oh."

Cas hopped down with a dull thud, slipped off his boots and socks, and found a gap in a pile of black boulders to leave them in. Rook nodded and took off down the beach without a word. Cas followed, inhaling the wet salt air, letting the briny aromas of low tide wash over him as he padded barefoot after his guide.

The rippling unease in his guts wasn't as simple as nervousness. So much of his vague plans of grandeur hinged on this moment. His heart was beating rather wildly, his mouth was dry, and his fingers were tingling.

But he was ready.

The pair walked for an hour or so, around the first curve of soaring black cliffs to their right, the old library's charred remains up top long behind them. They were far from the city and completely alone, apart from the ocean and the sky.

Rook stopped and turned to Cas.

"Why here?" Cas croaked.

Instead of answering, Rook, with efficient movements, unslung his satchel, undressed quickly and stuffed everything in the bag. It wasn't until he put the leather strap between his teeth that a prickle of unease slid along Cas' brow.

His dark-haired companion smiled.

Before Cas could jump back, the air changed with a violent heave.

He had just enough time to turn his face as the sand flew up and about, and the air pressure dropped. A sudden cloud of black mist rose, and the stink of ozone filled Cas' nose. As his ears popped, he fell on his arse with a startled grunt.

Before Cas opened his eyes, a set of enormous claws scooped him up. Their chilled temperature nipped at his skin and his stomach dropped with a sickening lurch as he became airborne. Forcing himself to keep his wits about him, Cas opened his eyes. He was clutched to the chest scales of an enormous black dragon, face down over the dark waves of the choppy ocean speeding by beneath them.

All at once, Cas knew their destination.

After a short flight, the dragon's black leather wings flapped in graceful arcs, and they landed on the tide line of the bay's mountain, topped with its usual crown of sickly fog and gas.

Named in an exotic language Cas could never pronounce but admired, it was simply referred to as Smoking Mountain by the locals. He'd never been here, and no one else he knew had either. It was an arid place of black basalt without soil. Boats couldn't land because of the dangerous reefs and rocks around the island's edge. Despite the deep water beyond those, the gases escaping from both the mountain and fissures in the rocks off its shores were too toxic to dwell near for too long.

He was released from the dragon's clutches with an ungainly drop onto damp sand. Dusting himself off, Cas wandered away from the shoreline a few paces. The top of the mountain, a dark, clouded shape against the night sky, was high enough that he needed to crane his neck.

The mountain was basically the entire island. It consisted of great folds of ancient rock, burnt orange and dirty black. Sour yellow pockets of mineral build-up bloomed across the jagged, sloping sides, increasing to a sheer point. From this vantage point, it was just possible to see through the gas that the peak was a sliced-open cone, sheared off at a steep angle by some great cataclysm long ago.

Eyeing the mountain uneasily, Cas swallowed past the lump in his throat. Behind him, a deep whoosh of air blasted his back with an explosion of sand and sea. The dragon had transformed. Rook came to stand by Cas' side.

"Why here?" Cas muttered.

"It's poetic," the man sighed. Cas turned to face him. "Morgan dreamt of this place many times. She'd moan about it in her stupor," Rook continued, a small smile playing about his lips visible by moonlight, his long loose hair reflecting the stars with streaks of silver. "You should be pleased."

"Oh."

Morgan dreamt of it? Hating the fact that Rook had seen her so vulnerable, Cas wasn't sure if that filled him with ease, or the opposite.

Cas thought for a moment. "Tell me why."

In the dim light, bare skin smooth, his muscles lean, Rook rummaged around in his bag as he spoke.

"You know why."

"No." Cas rubbed his bare feet into the damp grains of sand, inhaling the sour aroma that teased his nose along with the salty air. "I know *what* we are doing. *Why* do you want this? Why do you want the eggs?"

"I wish to be at the top of everything." Rook stared at Caspian as if it was obvious. "Power is required. And they have it."

"You have so much magic already. Why do you need more?"

The other man appraised Cas without expression, his eyes mysterious enough that they appeared fully black.

"I do it because I can," Rook declared eventually as the sea breeze ruffled his hair.

"What does that even mean?"

As the dark ocean lapped at the black sand in a soothing, watery rhythm at odds with what was about to happen, Rook's white teeth flashed brightly as he grinned.

"Why shouldn't I? Just because it's wrong? Pah." Rook shrugged. "There's no difficult backstory here, no poor me. I grew up with parents that loved me. But I want what I want. I want more."

"More..." Cas mumbled. That longing was something he understood.

Rook nodded. "And with you, I have the means to get it, in the most efficient way possible. I don't want an obvious trail behind me. I don't wish to be hunted down. We will play the long game, and we will win."

"This isn't a game to me," Cas snapped, silver flashing in his odd blue eyes.

Rook ignored Cas and pulled out his pants from the bag, then dropped it onto the sand. After dressing, he crouched down and pulled out a flask. From his crouch, he stared up at Cas with an ominous expression. Cas clasped his hands behind his back to hide their tremor.

"It's not an easy procedure," Rook murmured.

"How many times have you done it?"

Black eyes narrowed. "I haven't."

The test subjects in his mother's study came to Cas' mind as he mulled this over. *Fuck*.

"I see," Cas said.

Rook appraised him a little longer before beckoning Cas to settle in the sand before him.

Pretending his heart wasn't about to break through his ribs and escape into the deserted, beautiful night, Cas made his way over and knelt on the damp shore. The flask was offered. Cas stared at it, a silver vessel about the size of his hand with a tightly closed lid.

"Drink it."

Taking it without question, Cas unscrewed the lid, tossing it into the bag. He raised the flask to his lips, inhaling the vapors of an unknown liquor. He paused, his eyes watering from the fumes. Rook's eyebrows arched.

"What is this?" Cas gasped.

Rook's voice was matter of fact.

"Crushed gemstones, including that diamond I asked you for. Diamonds are suitably potent," he added.

Cas stared at him.

"Oh," Cas mumbled, his gaze on the flask. His oddly coloured eyes, more silver than blue by the cool light of the moon, returned to Rook's steady gaze. "Um. Rook. I'm not a dragon yet."

Shuffling forward on his knees, Rook reached out to rest his hands on Cas' shoulders.

"Remember, Caspian, I said this is going to hurt."

Of course.

With that thought, Cas raised the flask, tipped his head back, and drained it in one go.

He held Morgan's face in his mind as his mouth, then his throat, followed soon after by his stomach, started to burn. The vapors of the acrid alcohol filled his nose as the shards of crushed gems filled the rest of him.

Rook's voice seemed far away and close all at once as he spoke over the roaring in Cas' ears.

"When you can't take anymore, hold tight to the knowledge that the night is darkest before the dawn..."

Mismatched eyes snapped open.

"That's a fucking lie," Cas choked out around his bleeding tongue.

Rook laughed and as Cas' stomach boiled and burned, he realised the man was nervous. For some reason, that made him feel a little better.

"Hold it in," Rook warned, and edged closer. Their knees touched at first, followed by their foreheads. Rook's was cool against the sweat beading upon Cas'. When he spoke again, his voice dropped to a whisper. "There's a doorway here," Rook breathed, one of his hands sliding up to tap the junction of their joined flesh.

Struggling to stay upright as his guts burned with searing agony, Cas slapped the cool hand away.

Rook shook his head against Cas', pressing closer. The spice of the man's breath blended with the liquor that burned Cas' senses and seared his insides.

"Caspian."

The call of his name was a whisper, but echoed with eerie resonance as the sea beside them lapped at the ebony shore. A gentle probing, more indistinct than a coil of thin incense, tickled the flesh between Cas' brows with cold tendrils. He stared at the black eyes, a breath from his own, intense and focused.

"Caspian, let me in."

The gentle pressure strengthened, the cold changing to a pleasant coolness, taking the focus off the scorching burn in his mouth and his guts. But all too soon, as Cas panted, supported fully by Rook now, the coolness became a warm haze over his face.

Then the warmth became heat.

And then it burned.

Cas went to cry out, but he couldn't move. It was all he could do to swallow the bile rising in his throat, shredding open his innards once more as the fine shards of gems moved back the way they came.

"Hold it down," Rook urged, his voice coming from further off than before.

The stars disappeared, the moon went out.

Or was that because he'd clamped his eyes tightly shut?

As a roaring filled his ears, not the crashing shore but voices or air or wind, Cas had no senses left to tell.

It was all Cas could do to clamp his eyes shut. The tingle in his fingers was now in his toes, his arms and legs, crawling along his spine, warring with the agonizing scorch of the power releasing within, as Rook somehow wormed his way inside Cas' entire being.

It went on for a heartbeat, a thousand heartbeats, who knew?

But all at once, when Cas thought dying might be preferable to the agony that terrorized his soul, all sensation halted.

Cas sagged, spent, sweaty and heaving. Rook held him up.

"Oh, no, Caspian," Rook sighed, his voice strained. "It's not over yet."

Unable to speak because of his swollen tongue, Cas inhaled one last gasp of air when the world came apart in pain, an agony so unspeakable that Cas really wished he *would* die.

His heart beat increased with a sinister rhythm, as stabbing pain and boiling anguish became the entire world.

Morgan, the last part of Cas' sanity screamed into a starless void, as all that he was made up of descended into flames and agony.

I love —

The unpleasant feel of grit against a fevered cheek was the first sensation to return.

Next came breath, filling aching lungs, the salty air caustically sour thanks to the sulphur haze seeping through along the sand. The brine of the sea breeze coating his lips was soon followed by sound, the noise of the waves soothing his bleeding ears.

Finally, there was sight.

A single blue eye cracked open, staring at the horizon, the first rays of the sun teasing the predawn greyness. From amongst the gathering clouds, the stars still out, their new positions showing Cas had been out for some time.

He lay on the sand facing the east. When he could finally shift his head, gasping at the coldness along his spine, he spotted Rook in much the same position not far away. The tide had come in, and it lapped at Rook's out-flung hand.

They were both alive, but something was different.

As his mind slowly came back together, Cas realised what the something was.

It was as if his body had grown a new organ.

But rather than located in one place with sinew and mucus, it was unspecific, and all-encompassing. The new organ was just beyond his senses, but there nonetheless.

An unknown part of him had been born.

It also felt like every hole in his body was bleeding, but the fact that he could feel anything at all was a sign he was alive.

With a groan, Cas rolled onto his back.

The peak of the massive mountain smoked lazily, catching the first rays of dawn.

"Fuck."

Cas turned back to Rook. The man sat up and blinked groggily at Cas. They eyed each other warily.

"You survived," Rook croaked eventually.

Cas pushed himself up, confused by how his body moved. It was the same, but it was not. He was extremely dizzy and unstable, but he made it to his feet.

"No. Yes." Cas shuddered. "Maybe."

Rook appeared pleased. "Good."

"Excuse me," Cas mumbled.

Then, with no grace whatsoever, he shuffled on his knees and collapsed into the bracing water.

Rolling about, Cas washed away the sticky coating of blood, tears and sweat. When he was done, still marveling at the feel of his skin and the additional part of him that tickled his senses, Cas staggered to his feet and joined Rook above the tide line. The sun was making its first appearance, illuminating the sulphur haze as the gas thickened with billowing puffs of acid yellow from the sheared-off mountain peak. Flickering golden light licked at the dawn horizon, like flames that gave life, beginning their new journey across the sky.

With his heart lurching at the sight, Cas reached into his damp shirt and pulled out a black feather with a white spot. It was sodden and ragged, but it would do.

Cas held it up, his pulse increasing.

Silhouetted against the first rays of the sun, the spiked edges of the feather looked like they were afire. He concentrated, and soon enough a humming, zinging flash sped through his inner world, like bees had once done around him with countless stingers against his flesh.

Breathing calmly, focusing on the hum, Cas smiled.

The feather twitched, then stilled.

It twitched again.

Tiny curls of smoke appeared along its matted edges. With the stink of burning hair insulting his heightened senses, the feather burst into light.

Not from the sun behind it, as it rose with breathtaking majesty, but with fire.

Actual fire that *burned*.

His heart roared, all the while a dazzling stillness settling about his mind.

"Ah," said Cas, his voice as soft as the gases pooling about his bare feet. "So that's how it's supposed to feel."

He was pleased that his hand trembled just a little, barely at all, as the feather burned to its shaft. Cas opened his fingers, letting the ashes scatter, the soot joining the black sand.

Magic.

It was his.

"At last," Cas breathed.

As he pondered the endless scope of daring prospects, patting down his chest and arms with saltwater stinging his eyes, Cas realised something else. Black spots lingered in his vision and he realised he was hungry.

Not for food, but for something more.

Cas frowned.

Below the fresh glow of power within him, a shadow bloomed.

Now that he realised it was there, the hunger flared to life with a silent roar, overcoming the bright thrill of ecstatic possibilities within.

"Fuck," Cas hissed, wincing and grabbing his chest. "What the fuck is this?"

Rook, naked again, was smiling, but his eyes were dark.

"Rook," Cas snapped. His voice sounded absurd to his own ears. "What did you do?"

The man was silent at first, then shrugged. "What I had to."

"What?"

"You received my own special blend after all," Rook drawled. "I'm a deviant, you knew that. So I suspect you might develop certain appetites, too."

"You fucking —"

"They don't call me Shadow Light for nothing, so enjoy." Rook held up the leather of his strap, about to slip it between his teeth.

"Where are we going?"

"What?" Rook looked surprised. "*We* are not going anywhere. *I* am going back to sleep."

Cas blinked at him. "What the fuck am I supposed to do?"

"Oh," Rook pursed his lips. "Of course. We made a bargain, remember, the eggs, hm?"

"Of course I fucking remember," Cas hissed. But under his bravado, a sickening fear was creeping up his spine.

Rook wouldn't, would he?

"Good." The rising sun broke over the horizon more fully, illuminating Rook's grin. "So when I know you are strong enough to find me, we can proceed to the next stage."

Oh fuck, Cas realised, *yes, he fucking would.*

"Don't you dare!" Cas shouted, stumbling forward.

Rook danced out of his reach with a laugh, instead kicking out to trip Cas over.

Cas, wobbling like a newborn foal, collapsed to his knees in the sand with a curse. Afraid he was going to pass out, Cas glared up at the smirking man just out of his reach.

"All you need to do," Rook crooned, "is picture it in your mind."

"What?" croaked Cas, soggy hair a wild mess above his silver-blue eyes that flashed with poison at the man who had potentially given him more than he bargained for.

"Scales," Rook called as he backed away. "Scales and wings. Then let the hunger out."

"What!"

It was no use.

Cas covered his face to the sudden black mist, the roar of sound that popped his aching ears. There was another wild suction of displaced air and an explosion of black grains of damp sand. Thrown back into the rising water, Cas opened his eyes in time to watch the dragon rise above him with great flaps of wings that beat at his ears with a deep booming, a sickening pressure pushing against his sodden chest.

"Rook! What the fuck! Don't leave me here!"

With a deep laugh, the dragon headed back to the city. It called over its wings to Cas in a deep rumble.

"Remember, Caspian, let the hunger out."

Furious, Cas rose to his feet and lowered his gaze to the expanding gas.

No one else knew he was here. No one would find him for a long, long while. If he stayed, the sulfur would kill him in hours.

Unless he could get himself off the island.

"Well played, Rook, well played."

Only a single gull passing overhead, awake earlier than its peers, was close enough to hear. Cas watched it pass, in awe and full of grudging respect.

For who wanted a business partner that could not wield the power that they had gained?

That was the very reason Cas had embarked on this path in the first place. Heart pounding, but not with fear, Cas stared at the rising sun, eyes clear, daring the rays of gold to burn him.

Let the hunger out, Rook had said.

Alone amongst the poisonous gas that would choke him if he lingered, Cas closed his eyes.

And concentrated.

A creature of shining scales and silver light circled high above the city of Baile Mara.

It flew too high to be spotted by those below, even those with enhanced vision fueled by magic. Below was the Elphin Palace, a gloomy castle of pitch black towers and golden domes.

Not far along the cliffs from the castle sprawled the rambling Carter Estate, the grounds actually comparable to the royal estate when viewed from this height. A crowd of people gathered on the green grass, their hair and gaily coloured clothes pops of jewel toned colours as they celebrated.

Risking being seen, but unable to help itself, the dragon dipped. Hoping the flash of the sun would help disguise it, the creature glided into a low patch of fluffy cloud and peered through the dampness.

Slitted silver eyes could just make out a tall blonde figure being presented with something by a tiny figure with red hair.

Despite knowing it was one of a multitude of royal figures, the dragon's heart, now many times its usual size, beat erratically for a moment.

While experiencing a deep pang of longing, the creature missed spotting the other tall blonde man standing off to the side, glancing up at the sky, his mouth hanging open, green eyes wide with amazement.

By overhearing the servants a few days earlier, the dragon knew what the ridiculous pomp was all about.

Amidst the garlands of flowers and flapping ribbons strung up around the trees, Owaen was being presented with a symbolic key to the city. He was being rewarded for his "tireless work between Baile Mara and the City of the Seers, working with the refugees." He had also designed new ways of growing crops in small plots of land, with magic and ingenious compact canal systems scaled down for stone fences.

The tall woman next to him in a robe of deep magenta was being presented for her exemplary work in "furthering the reach of magic". A lot of expectation was growing for the end of the decades long experiment, regarding the ability to be born with power in the blood. An experiment that the dragon knew was a misguided hope to extend life indefinitely, and to cure the disease of simply being a normal human.

"I found it," the creature laughed with a great rumble of expansive reptilian lungs as it rose from the clouds.

The cure for all of this chaos was simple.

"The cure is me," the dragon roared as it flew off, scales flashing quicksilver blue in the rays of the rising sun.

53

Morgan

Year 367
Aneirin Castle

A sense of foreboding lingered over the hushed city. The riot had come and gone, but the unease remained.

Back in the library, where she knew he would eventually come, Morgan sat alone at the table. Every single lantern and candle was lit, bright flames echoes of the beacon that was her heart.

On the table before her rested two treasures.

One was the crystal sphere. Its transparent depths were layered with delicate mineral inclusions, along with a myriad of rainbows from the multiple flames that danced around her.

The other item was a symbol of power. Morgan eyed its golden sheen and swallowed.

A pot of tea, heavily laced with a pilfered liquor, steamed beside the two treasures. The fiery brew lent just enough unreal quality to the icy night. Beside that sat a loaf of fresh bread. A lump of butter on the cracked wooden tray, the hilt of her table dagger protruding from its soft side. It was the wrong utensil for that purpose, but for another, it would do.

As the alcohol spread through her veins, the librarian shuddered. Her body was used to it, her heart was not. In much the same way that the night was interrupted by visions and sounds that came and went like the tides of an endless ocean, they beat forward, then receded from her consciousness. Her dreams came, her dreams went, ebbing, flowing.

Leaving behind the detritus of a washed up consciousness that demanded to be deciphered with the dawn. Fragments of moments yet to come, always scorching in their intensity, but never clear. Now the most important moment in what felt like a lifetime, multiple lifetimes, was here.

Had she interpreted the right way forward?

Morgan shifted her unblinking gaze to the night beyond the windows.

Outside, flakes of snow fell past the frosted glass, but it was hard to tell. She suspected it carried the taint of bitter ash, leftover from a lone dragon's rampage in the north, many, many years before. Either way, it mattered little. It was bitterly cold outside and frigid within, the hearth unlit and silent.

The only warmth was supplied by her cloak, the candle and lantern flames barely sufficient. As her breath misted before her lips, Morgan's thoughts drifted to the only one she cared for, one of the few who had seen her, and helped her.

Even when it was against her will.

Born without magic, unlike his twin, Caspian with his iron will gained magic somehow, in a way that he'd never explained, from Rook. An unholy alliance between two outcasts.

As her fingernail tapped the teacup with its steaming brew, the librarian mused over the fact that Caspian had come into magic with a natural grace that both intrigued and alarmed.

He had never used it to lord it over people. Instead, he had paraded with arrogance, never to be a victim like the days of his youth.

Magic had infested the hearts of most people, as if it worked like the beetles that ate away dusty manuscripts. The City of the Seers had once had a serious insect problem, until bats had been introduced to live within its towering shelves, consuming the beetles one by one. The sad analogy was that the bats here, the greedy dragons that craved magic, were part of the problem, and needed a predator of their own.

Morgan's gaze dropped from the frosty glass beside the cold hearth and examined her stained fingers.

When would her magic finally fade? Long after the ink, one would assume. She never made it to dragon hood, by choice. So would she one day wake up a crone?

A delicate snort broke the thick silence of the library.

If so, that would be a test of Caspian's loyalty.

Amused by the thought, Morgan stirred her honey tea with a swirling finger just about the surface of the liquid. A single spark of her magic agitated the steaming brew, the mist above it a twin to her breath.

"Beast."

The word was a murmur from delicately curled lips, a gentle stirring of air and floating dust motes.

Caspian would likely be so turned on by anything that she did that she'd beg him to leave her alone. His fearless nature as a teenager when dealing with Rook, along with his patience as he helped her overcome a reliance on intoxicants, was testimony enough. Especially when she'd been wickedly horrible to him.

Caspian would never get enough of her, of that she was certain. That didn't scare her.

His unquestioning devotion only spurned her on, to move forward in the only way that she could see as best.

For *everyone*.

At the thought, scorching water sloshed over the edge of the teacup as her hand jerked.

"Caspian," she whispered. "Do what you must. I am finally ready to atone."

Sitting in silence, Morgan turned her thoughts inward and examined the dark hook sunk deep into her heart. There was a thread there, joining them across whatever distant place she dwelled in loneliness. At the other end was Cas.

She'd had the chance to summon him, with whatever spark he'd used to bind her to him after he'd used his sword with brutal finality, severing the ties to his family forever. But she never had. So this meant her world was dulled by his absence. Yet it was no less than what she deserved.

Her pale green gaze drifted down to the Aneirin crown, sparkling quietly next to the quartz sphere. The heavy gold of its design was supposed to symbolise power, when it actually had come to represent the weight of a chaotic legacy.

Next to the royal jewel lay a note. A square of crisp parchment was held down by the precious weight, addressed not to Rhydian, but to Owaen.

"*Owaen.*

Don't judge him, they deserved it.

Morgan."

The librarian read her words out aloud, but the words got stuck as her throat constricted.

Under her thick wool jumper, the hairs rose along both arms.

"Oh, shit."

Beyond the frosted panes on either side of the unlit fireplace, a weighty shadow soared past.

As the dark flash of glittering amethyst scales whooshed by, the alarmed call of a guard on the watchtower sounded out over the resting city.

Morgan stood up, her heartbeat an exquisite mix of fear and longing. She hadn't seen everything that would happen, and the news that Skye was coming back was a new thread to weave into the plans that would result in her atonement.

And his.

"Caspian," Morgan whispered. "I'm ready."

54

Karlien

Year 367
Travelling

On his hands and knees, Karlien heaved violently, vomiting bile and river water onto the icy mud and rocks by the waterline.

As he coughed, the sodden prince was vaguely aware of, high above the trees, a soft, warm light painting the clouds upstream, amongst the mountains on the western horizon. His frozen lungs were desperate for air, however, and he dropped his head to bring up more green foam and filth from his guts.

It took a while. When he was done, the panicked gasping easing somewhat, Karlien reached out with trembling fingers. Despite his misery, his terror eased a little when his fingertips brushed the drenched fur at his side. The saturated wolf paused in licking at the bloody teeth marks on his thankfully intact tail, just long enough to run its hot tongue over Karlien's shaking hand.

Above them, a man's ominous growl had both the young man and the animal flinch.

Showing great wisdom, the wolf pretended not to notice the scorching glare of Karlien's bodyguard standing over them, his hands clenched at his sides. Water streamed from his long black hair on either side of a glower as blistering as the river had been frozen. After a brief glance, the animal bent its dripping head back to poke at the row of wounds along its rump with its pink tongue.

Wrung out and half-drowned, Karlien was grateful that the amber-eyed wolf was fine. Unfortunately, Baek Hyeon was not.

Risking a look, the prince peeked up through the wet hair plastered over his face.

The towering man's dark eyes, flecked with ruby, glared back. Without warning, Hyeon moved.

Tattoos rippled through his soaked shirt, and Karlien let out a squeak as he was yanked up. But instead of being shaken about in anger, heavy fur was draped over his shoulders, and two powerful arms wrapped around the prince, holding him close. Their heat was as startling as it was welcome. A firm hand cupped the back of the prince's head, pressing his face into Hyeon's heaving chest.

"I'm f-fine," Karlien stammered, lips crowded in the fabric of Hyeon's sodden shirt. The man smelled of mud and musk.

Since pulling both the prince and the wolf from the river, the bodyguard had yet to say a word.

Until now.

He leant down to place his lips by the prince's ear. His voice was dangerously rough.

"What in the fucking hells was that, you spoilt little brat?" Hyeon whispered clearly.

Karlien's sodden eyelashes fluttered in surprise.

Hyeon lifted his chin from Karlien's hair and leaned back, his hands sliding up to cup Karlien's cheeks. The prince blinked, head tilted back to examine the taller man's expression more accurately, his sluggish mind slowly turning over what Hyeon had said.

Or more precisely, *how* he'd said it.

"Would you c-care to repeat that?" the prince said as calmly as possible despite the ache in his lungs. His tone was as icy as the frigid air, astonishment flaring.

Not answering directly, Hyeon's glowering face loomed close as he held Karlien in place.

"You brat," the bodyguard hissed, his breath a white mist that bloomed between the slight gap between them. "You absolute clueless, brainless, airheaded brat! How could you?" His voice increased with volume with each snapped out word. "You're a prince! The hope of three kingdoms! How could you be so stupid? What if you had drowned? Did you think of Bathsheba at all? For fuck's sake, did you think of yourself?" The hands that held Karlien around the upper arms clenched tighter, and Karlien winced.

Not caring or noticing, Hyeon continued his mad tirade. Hyeon's eyes were wild, the black tattoos under his two golden torcs slick with water, his shirt stuck to his skin, the golden tone flushed red, a white curl of heat escaping about his shoulders in the icy air.

"What the fuck was a mischievous brat doing by himself, in a land he doesn't know, with no one by his side, swimming alone in a river full of carnivores? Do you have any idea of the risk you just took? And for what?! Torres laughed when he said you'd snuck off to have a wash! *A wash!* I can't believe you! What the fuck have you got to say for yourself, Karlie?"

Hyeon's eyes were as wide and expressive as Karlien had ever seen as he huffed. Held immobile in Hyeon's iron grip and fighting the trap of their ruby speckled beauty, the prince tilted his head to the side in a jaunty angle. Water streaming down his face, Hyeon blinked at the prince's caustic expression.

Ignoring the pins and needles in his fingers and toes, Karlien peppered his reply with as much waspish acid as he could muster, despite the chill to his entire body.

"Well." The prince forced his chattering lips into a dazzling smile. "I especially liked your p-pronunciation of '*mischievous brat*'."

"What?" Hyeon snapped.

"And," the prince went on, his azure blue gaze flinty as his eyes narrowed. "Your fine delivery of expletives really showed a much m-more well-rounded feel for my language than I gave you credit for."

As Karlien fumed, a small part of him was pleased when Hyeon's mouth formed a silent *Oh*.

"*Oh*," Karlien hissed.

To his credit, Hyeon held Karlien's gaze, even as his high cheekbones bloomed pink under the water that ran down his face. He swallowed, lips pursed.

"Later," Hyeon mumbled through his strained jaw, as if that explained anything. The prince's eyes widened.

"You deceitful —"

"Karlien." As he spoke, the single word full of barely restrained grief, Hyeon crushed Karlien back to his heaving chest. "Losing you is not an option."

Pressed to the man's soaked shirt, Karlien's eyelids fluttered at the soft rumble against his ear, the heated promise of each word whispered into his hair. The prince cleared his throat, his shivering returning as his rage deflated like an empty bladder of the finest wine.

"Y-you," the prince managed through chattering teeth as the pins and needles formed into shivers, "are a lying p-pirate! A b-brute!"

"Yes," Hyeon agreed, his arms firm enough that Karlien wondered if they would ever let him go. The man's tremble was felt more than seen as he held the prince as close as it was possible to be. "Yes, I am. I am all of those things, and much worse."

The iron grip loosened and Hyeon held him at arm's length.

"What happened?" The bodyguard's dark gaze was intense as he wiped Karlien's wet curls from his forehead. Rising to his feet, he pulled Karlien with him and they stood there on the bank, the wolf licking noisily beside them on the shore as the light all but faded.

"I was b-being brave," Karlien muttered, avoiding the man's stare. "My rose oil... then a m-monster... and the wolf..."

A muscle in Hyeon's jaw tensed amongst the shadows on his face as the prince snuck a glance his way.

"The wolf?"

"The monster g-got it," Karlien mumbled. "I couldn't leave it."

"*Heol...*" Hyeon crushed Karlien back to his chest.

In doing so, the prince just about slipped on the mossy, muddy rocks under his bare feet. Hyeon held him up, then turned him about so he was facing the trees. There were no lights seen anywhere, and with a guilty flush, Karlien realised how far from camp he'd come.

Hyeon brushed his fingers over Karlien's forehead, wiping away the damp curls. At the intimate touch, warmth flared within, at war with the chill rolling over his skin. He was faintly aware of a low booming noise, some far off drum at camp perhaps as he sunk into Hyeon's fierce embrace.

At their feet, the wolf lifted its head.

"You tried to rescue the wolf?" Disbelief filled Hyeon's voice in the prince's ear, the words vibrating against Karlien. Stepping around the prince to face him, Hyeon leaned down and pressed his forehead to Karlien's, damp skin to damp skin. "Princess. Rescuing others is not your job. That's mine. Let me take care of that and everything will be fine. Did you consider my feelings at all?"

"There was no time —" Karlien began with a mumble, then paused, frowning.

Fine?

"Don't..." Hyeon's voice was a hot whisper in the prince's face. "Don't do that to me again."

Despite the pleasure of being pressed against all sorts of hard muscles and interesting shapes, instead of guilt, rage flared within the prince's chest. His muscles tensed, the safety of the warm embrace forgotten. As the low drum beat loomed closer, blue eyes ringed with azure narrowed, unaware the wolf stood up and began to pace back and forth, eyes on the dark sky above the break in the trees over the inky waters of the icy river.

"Excuse me," said the prince. Hyeon looked confused, and Karlien smiled sweetly. "Are you implying that I should simply obey everyone right now despite this mad convoy to a place I've never been and only heard sarcastic whispers about? That I should continue to act as if everything really is just *fine*?"

Baek Hyeon opened his mouth.

Karlien cut in first.

"Everything is not *fine*!" Karlien yelled, words erupting like steam from his blue lips. "Everything was not *fine* when my parents died, and no one could tell me why! It is not *fine* that I have to be taught all these particular skills and have no practical use for them! I'm sleeping on the ground instead of listening to peacock sh-shit outside my window while a mouse hides in my room and you and your stupid wolf—" at this the wolf whined, "—wait outside my door for me to slip up and get drunk again! Because everything is *not* fine! And you have just explained to me that everything will be fine in your p-perfectly fine grasp of this fine language!" Inhaling with a frantic breath of frigid air, Karlien grabbed Hyeon's face and dragged it down to his. "So no! Everything is n-not *fine!*"

The wolf growled.

The prince's nostrils flared as he huffed, the rage deflating, the bodyguard's expression a complicated play of emotions. As the moment stretched, the drumming growing louder nearby, the tension grew thinner in the slight space between them. Breaths mingling, the two young men held each other's gaze with stubborn intensity.

"Well?" Karlien demanded, puffing angrily at the river water dripping from his wet hair over his lips.

Deep black eyes speckled with red sparks lowered to examine Karlien's open mouth. The pink tip of Hyeon's tongue appeared as he licked his bottom lip. A slight noise escaped the prince's throat, and his fiery words faded to the background as a roaring filled his ears.

"Baek Hyeon..." the prince breathed.

Hyeon closed his eyes for a moment and shook his head. When they opened, they were full of heated things the prince was keenly aware he had no experience of, no solid ground to stand on in the face of the man's scorching gaze. With his own eyes full of challenge, Karlien leant in, his heart wild, lips parted, ignoring the wild backflips of his stomach.

Slowly, very, very slowly, Hyeon's hands slid up Karlien's arms, over his graceful neck and cupped the prince's flushed cheeks.

"Karlien Elphin," Hyeon murmured, a low purr that had Karlien's stomach feeling like it flipped back the other way.

Lips parted and ready, Karlien reached up and wound his fingers into Hyeon's shirt.

At the last moment before their mouths joined, Hyeon's gaze snapped to the clouds behind Karlien's raised face.

The bodyguard froze.

"Fuck," he breathed.

"Yes?" Karlien murmured, hopeful.

"That's..." Hyeon murmured, his gaze widening.

Confused, Karlien frowned, his expectant lips parted impatiently.

The wolf paced around them, growling louder now.

"What —" the prince began.

Powerful hands grabbed Karlien's cheeks and Hyeon turned the prince around so the pair of them faced the same direction.

Up the long, wide and winding river in the northwestern sky, to the dark mountain peaks earlier lost in the mist, Hyeon forced Karlien's gaze to where only a dull warm glow had been before. It had spread.

A fierce bloom now scorched the horizon.

With the chill of premonition, he knew where that ominous glow originated.

Aneirin.

Karlien inhaled sharply, the promised kiss forgotten, his mouth hanging open.

As he stared, the deep booming that had prickled his senses grew loud, and a great shadow appeared over the rustling trees across the river. With the low beat of leathery wings, the massive creature passed over them, heading for Aneirin.

They watched it in shocked silence; the wolf pressed against Karlien's leg.

A spine chilling roar reached them, wild and fierce.

Karlien grabbed onto Hyeon, his legs trembling.

"Oh."

Transfixed, Karlien stared until the winged shadow became a tiny speck, lost to the night, the sinister clouds and mist, as it headed for the glowing horizon.

"Princess?"

The prince inhaled, a remarkable sensation spreading through his numb limbs.

"Karlien?"

The prince attempted to speak, heat rising in his throat. The rage and terror in his heart changed to something deeper.

Responsibility.

"How dare you," Karlien spat.

Hyeon's eyes widened.

"What —"

"How dare that thing show itself now?" hissed the prince, clothes and hair dripping. Smacking Hyeon's hands away from his face, Karlien swept cold water away with an angry gesture of a bloody hand. "I had to leave my home for this wretched place! And a fucking reptile is heading there to destroy it first? After what dragons did to Baile Mara? Ha! Over my dead body, you great big —"

"Karlie —"

"Let's go!"

"Wait —"

"Baek Hyeon!" The prince barked, blue-ringed eyes flashing. "Save your words, you pirate!"

Admiring wonder crossed Hyeon's astonished face as the prince raged.

"We are leaving right this moment," Karlien sniffed with majestic arrogance, "before that f-fucking dragon messes with my other f-fucking kingdom!"

55

Cas

Year 367
Travelling

"**Y**ou fucking idiot!" screamed the man on the dragon's back, his cheeks pink with icy gusts and fury. "You useless worm!"

The deep leathery beats of Flare's massive wings cut the frigid air as Cas raged. As the curses burst from his dry lips, even Cas didn't know if he fumed at himself or Flare.

Both, probably.

He had wanted to meet with Skye in person after all these years, now that Cas finally had his magic back. An explanation was necessary on the unfortunate fuck up with Shadow Light, and to share how the world was meant to be. It needed to be presented carefully, so it made sense to the one Cas had been after for some time, a powerful creature who could ease the chaos of misused power across the continent.

But the opportunity had come and gone while he'd been taking a fucking bath.

On realising Flare had failed to share the fact that Skye had been nearby, Cas had sobered immediately despite the agony that still plagued both body and mind. After making a mad dash to dress, stuffing both the egg and a squawking dragon into his satchel, Cas had fled the inn, and with it, the old quarry town of Baile Fuar.

The last sane fragment of his mind had him throw a gold coin at the innkeeper as he rushed out with a stolen fur cloak thrown about his shoulders.

Breathless amongst the falling snow, Cas' diatribe faded to a fuming disbelief.

His eyes streamed from the icy wind, his hands were not quite numb enough to have lost their occasional twitch, nor the hot splices of agony in his ruined fingers. They had been flying for hours all day, without stopping. Flare was likely exhausted. Cas didn't give a shit.

How the fuck had it come to this?

He'd retrieved the egg, yes, but Aneirin was still in front of him, as were Morgan and the map. An unassuming artwork of lines and whorls in copper, the last key to lock together all the threads, that would enable him to coax Skye to his side, to the only side that mattered, and put an end to magic.

With the majority of it left for him, of course.

"I'll take it back," Cas hissed, teeth chattering. "You lot never earned it."

Flare flew on. The occasional yelp reached Cas' windburned ears as Cas urged him to make haste, with a loving twitch of pain down the red thread that bound them, man to spiked tail. It should have been a pleasure to be back in the air, high above the ethereal, sparkling forest of white treetops below. But his dreams were stuck on the ground in mud and shit.

Unless he could get his wings back, get Morgan back, and get Skye on his side.

Skye, who he had fucking missed.

But why had she fled?

Why didn't she at least launch some kind of attack?

Was it because Owaen had been there, and Skye had worried for his sake?

And Cas had drunk himself to a fucking stupor instead.

In his agonised rage, Cas gathered his power, the dragon's booming wings flapping on either side. Focusing wildly, he attempted to slice off another sharp spike, one of many before him and amongst which he was crouched.

But instead of the sharp appendage shearing off and dropping away, a searing pain scorched Cas' mind.

"What the fuck!" Cas screeched, acutely aware of how ridiculous he sounded.

A gasping cry reached his ears from the dragon as the great crown of purple spikes shuddered.

"Why the fuck are you crying, you cowardly little tit? What have you got to cry about? Is your world too dark, my innocent jewel?" Cas inhaled, not giving Flare a chance to interrupt. "Think about how dark my world is compared to yours. I should be filled to the brim with magic! That bloody perverted king! What happened to our bargain? And Rueben's magic wasn't enough of a balm to smooth over any real illness, so what the fuck is happening right now? Why is everything stacked against me?"

As Cas took another breath, it seemed Flare was at last unable to keep his snout shut tight.

"Stacked against you?" Flare shouted over his own wings. "*You* made it that way ever since you were a boy!"

"What?" Cas laughed like a fiend. "Even though you were there, you still think that? *Pah!*"

Cas wasn't offended that the dragon was trying to maintain his dignity. That was a pointless exercise. With a wry twist of his top lip, Cas hunched into his cloak, bottom lip quivering as he hugged the bag with its precious contents to his chest.

"I am like the new king of Aneirin," Cas announced over the wind and angry beats of dragon wings, "born into a fucking magic-sodden family without any of his own!"

"That's not true —" The dragon's declaration was as quickly cut off as it had been delivered.

Cas blinked as Flare's horrified gasp was absorbed by a fierce gust of wind. His broken fingers twitched.

"Excuse me. What the *fuck*?"

The scales under Cas thighs trembled.

After counting to ten, Cas cleared his throat and waited for the red wash across his vision to fade to the frost filled night.

"Could you repeat that?"

When there was no answer forthcoming, Cas jerked their bond.

Flare yelped.

"I don't know!" screeched the dragon, his wings faltering. "I don't know anything!"

"You don't know —?"

Cas sat back, mismatched blue eyes wide, lashes coated with ice build up as his stomach lurched, until Flare got a hold of himself and maintained an even path amongst the icy winds.

How unexpected.

The late king's magic had been absorbed by Cas with relative ease once their bargain had been made. And Cas' body had gobbled up the rest when the last of the fucking spell that bound Aneirin had been broken. But considering whatever the fuck was happening now, the magic had gone too deep within him to call forth. The result seemed to be some kind of allergic reaction to its use.

As his skin tingled where it had grown its weird copper sheen, Cas bit his lip, his silver blue gaze unfocused.

Could the king's son be of use in coaxing it forth?

Above the wailing of the wind came the pitiful sound of deep sobs.

"Shut it," Cas muttered.

There was no way he could describe the entirety of his vision to one such as the creature he rode. The only dragon who could was Skye, damaged at the hands of dragons in an experiment that shouldn't have happened the way it had.

"Well, of course she's mad," Cas sniped to himself. "That's fair. I admit I played a small part too, when things went wrong with Shadow Light and trying to get her to reach her potential." A thought struck him. "Flare," he called, "how fast can Skye fly? I can't remember, was she quick like you or I?"

There was no answer from up front.

"Tsk." Cas shook his head to clear his face of hair from the frozen tips whipping at his face.

Either way, he knew where Skye was headed.

There was nowhere else to go.

The same place as he.

Out loud, Cas shouted to the sulking dragon.

"Well, fuck. Hurry up! She's rightfully pissed and may go off at me before I can clear up any misunderstandings. Fuck, especially if Owaen is still with her..." His hands tightened around the satchel with a painful spasm, his mind spinning.

Morgan, Cas hummed under his breath, *catch me if I fall.*

His stomach lurched as the exhausted dragon dipped below the bottom layer of clouds, soaring away from the freezing whiteness, into the open air.

Cas was about to test his magic against Flare's spikes one last time when he realised how far they'd come. Instead of just the crisp scent of snow assailing his frozen nose, the pungent aromas of farmland and livestock greeted him.

Below spread a sprawling, expansive crescent valley, the faint crimson rock of the mountains to their right covered with fresh layers of snow.

And ahead, a weak blur of light could be seen from the city terraced into the tallest peak of all, its dark red heights plunging upwards into the underlayer of the clouds.

Aneirin.

"Shit," Cas cursed as he slid off Flare's near frozen scales.

Hardly able to stand, he spun about, eyeing the lower city of Aneirin where they had landed. Guards were shouting and calling to one another. People screamed, gathering their children and livestock and fleeing the moderately sized public square where Cas had directed the still upset dragon to touch down.

It was still bitterly cold at ground level, but less so than on dragon back amongst the clouds. As his extremities thawed, Cas realised his broken hand was as fierce a throb of agony as it had been before Rueben had tended to it. It was difficult to keep one hand on the strap of his bag, and one holding his cloak closed to the breeze.

The dragon's massive head swung towards Cas as he cursed again, the massive crown of spikes covered with thick frost. Flare winced as Cas stalked towards the closest giant eye. The purple iris was fixed on him, the slitted pupil contracted not just with fear, but something deeper.

Rebellion.

Considering his last directive to Flare before they had arrived in the surprised city, that angered Cas even more.

"You ungrateful beast," Cas scowled. "I'd eat you if I could, just so I could shit you back out."

"I won't do it —"

"I SAID DO IT!" screamed Cas directly into Flare's eye.

The vicious jerk along the magical leash from Cas to Flare's tail was hardly needed. He yanked it anyway. Cas was rewarded with a loud whimper over the shouts and screaming townsfolk.

With a flurry of wet snow, Flare took off with a great gust and Cas just about fell on his arse. Staggering, he wiped his eyes. He turned on the spot, picked a direction that looked somewhat familiar, and set off. No one approached, but even if they had, it wouldn't matter. They would be busy soon enough.

He stalked along the frosted lanes and streets, ever upwards, breathing heavily with misted breaths. Snowfall and ice blinding him as he tramped past rows of cottages, some stone, some of wood and plaster. A few larger ones were dotted about amongst the rest, most two stories high, some three or four. Their thatched and tiled roofs were thick with the snow, and icicles had formed under the eaves like rows of glassy dragon's teeth.

With the returning pain and fatigue, Cas was just about experiencing sensory overload when he found the cobbled street he was after.

And sure enough, a lone figure crouched on a stone step in the alcove of a closed door. It was shut tight against the weather that hadn't been seen in Aneirin for decades.

Why the figure sat shivering outside, playing with a broken fork, Cas didn't dare to guess.

"Boy," Cas called as warmly as he could, despite his world of pain.

Dressed in a cloak that barely covered the worn out knees of his shabby pants, the boy with the harelip flinched and raised his head. He blinked, and Cas smiled despite his discomfort as the boy's face broke into an astonished smile.

"Sir? *Sir!* What happened to your hair?"

Scrambling up, the boy raced over, the boy's bright expression illuminating his differently made face with a pure glow.

"Little thing," Cas sighed, shaking off his cloak. He draped it with awkward movements over the youth's shoulders. "Where are your parents? Why are you outside? And what do you mean about my hair?"

The boy let Cas arrange the thick wool over his thin shoulders as they rose and fell in a shrug.

"Inside, sir. An important visitor came a while back. So they t-told me to leave. Your hair is…" The boy blinked and pointed his fork at Cas. "Your hair is *pink*."

Cas stared at the boy, an unsteady hand brushing the hair back from his forehead. "Pink?"

Wondering what in the hells had happened back with Flare and the exploding pile of wood in Baile Fuar, Cas put it to the side for now. It was all he could do to concentrate on staying upright. His hand dropped to his side, and he frowned.

"So. You have been told to wait outside in this weather?"

Silently, the boy nodded. Above lips blue with the chill, fervent brown eyes peered up at Cas keenly.

After a moment of internal debate as he eyed a fading bruise on the boy's cheek, Cas sighed.

"Show me where."

The boy led him to another doorway along the street, thankfully not too far around the back alley of the building he had been sheltering against. After a moment's thought, Cas carefully unhooked his satchel and handed it to the boy. He gave the lad a long look. Wordlessly, the boy took it and slung it over the oversized cloak, dark eyes solemn.

Nodding once, Cas relieved the boy of his utensil and bade the boy stand behind him.

Without knocking, Cas grabbed the handle with his free hand, opened the door, and charged inside.

Well, it was almost a charge; he was quite unsteady on his feet. Either way, it was better than collapsing like a frozen fish in the snow as it piled up in the alley outside.

Chilled lids fluttered over mismatched blue eyes as a warm, cosy room of delicious smells and cheery light greeted him.

"What? Is that you — Hey! Who are you?" A red-haired man with bloodshot eyes slurred from the pleasant room's central table. He looked up from pouring a jug of steaming liquid into a clay cup, slamming the jug down onto the wood.

Cas halted on the threshold, assessing the situation. A woman in a long wool tunic appeared from a narrow doorway beside a chimney of red bricks. Her clear cheeks and shining hair showed Cas that she was as warm and at ease with herself as the man at the table.

His thawing lips thinned.

"Who are you?" The woman, about thirty winters, edging into the room warily. She glared at Cas, and the silent boy behind him. "You have no right to barge in here!"

"This is true," Cas said thoughtfully, his blonde lashes dipping in a languid blink. When his eyes opened, their gaze changed direction from the woman to the man. "Yet here I am."

It would have been cleanest to use his magic. But of course, that option was currently unavailable.

With a beleaguered sigh, Cas swallowed his dizziness and strode across the room in two quick strides. His broken hand yanked the jug from the table. Not giving the surprised man time to react, Cas swung.

The jug smashed directly into the man's face, and he was knocked out immediately. His face a torn and bloody mess, the man toppled sideways. His unconscious form landed on the floor with a crack.

Wondering if a cracked skull had saved him from further trouble, Cas spun to face the woman as she rushed him with a shriek.

What she expected to do, Cas had no clue.

His plan, however, was simple.

And supremely effective.

His broken hand lashed out, and Cas bit back white fiery agony as he grabbed the woman by the front of her tunic, in effect holding her in place. His other hand brought the boy's fork up in a smooth arc and plunged it into the side of her neck.

The woman stumbled away, gurgling noises escaping her throat. Her shoulder knocked through cooking implements suspended from the wooden beams above before she hit the wall. Collapsing into a heap near the man on the ground, she grabbed at her neck. Her boot heels wildly slid about in the spreading, steaming puddles of liquor and blood, unable to call for help.

Cas turned to his young companion, spitting out a few stray drops of blood.

"So. That's settled. I need your help."

He held up his ruined hand, the copper tinge competing with swollen, pink flesh. The broken digits stood out at odd angles, barely held on with agonised flaps of dying skin.

"Of course, sir," said the boy with a serene smile. "Anything."

"There's a lot of people out there that I know who have been going through some shit, and people that I don't know who are going through the same."

Rambling, Cas knew he had to hurry, but the pain was making it hard to think. He hoped Flare was doing what he was told.

At the table in the boy's cosy home, or home of the folks that should have been caring for him, Cas raised the cup of spirits to his lips and drained it in one swallow. In his lap perched the sparkling egg. Out of its bag, with ridges of deep blue and green, it was a reassuring weight. The bodies of the man and woman lay where they had fallen.

Both the man and the boy paid them no mind.

A series of pops sounded in the hearth as the boy added fresh logs to the crackling blaze. The boy had mopped up the sticky puddles as best he could, before pulling the freshly vacated chair out for Cas to sink into. The pleasantly spiced smoke covered the stench of blood-soaked rags as they burned.

Gasping as the sting of potent alcohol constricted his throat, Cas shook his head at the boy's concerned look.

"In my case," Cas mumbled, "a lot of my... trials... have been good. Because what has been stripped away leaves me with the inescapable fact that there is a part of me that just knows things. I can see around corners. Things just make sense. I can hear an invisible chime that rings true or untrue, depending on the matter at hand. Like when Morgan dreams, you know?"

Next to him on a little three-legged stool, the boy shook his head, scruffy hair damp with melted snow.

Untroubled by the boy's incomprehension, Cas gulped down another cup. He was hoping he could get drunk faster for what he needed, and that the following pain would sober him up immediately.

"There are big things in the world going on, and little things in the world going on, too. But the fucking only thing that matters is the luxury of being able to acknowledge these things." Sweat beaded Cas' upper lip, and he licked it away, grimacing at the copper tang. "By pausing for a single moment in time and reflecting on these big and little things that make up our lives, *that* luxury is peace. That luxury is mindfulness. Which, unfortunately, is a luxury that can be taken away at any point."

Breathing hard, Cas gave the boy a long look.

"Taken by who, sir?" came the boy's anxious murmur.

Perhaps the boy was understanding more than Cas originally thought. Pleased, he continued.

"By those who don't see self reflection as a luxury at all," Cas whispered. Inhaling the cleansing aroma of fresh wood smoke, he cleared his throat. "By those who see a moment taken by others to appreciate the world as something subversive to their agendas."

Silence stretched between them until Cas averted his eyes from the faded bruise on the boy's cheek. The boy shifted on the stool, his small fist tightening around the handle of the heavy knife in his grip.

"Their subversive agendas, compiled by greedy minds, greedy hearts, and greedy mouths," Cas hissed at the ceiling with its soot stains and cobwebs, hardly able to focus because of the scorching agony throbbing in his hand.

Letting the fire warm his back, Cas' good hand slid away from his freshly drained cup and came to rest on the top of the chunk of crystal in his lap. His breathing was erratic now, and he closed his eyes. The sound of the three-legged stool sliding back from the table indicated that the boy had stood up.

"Like I told you, lad," Cas cautioned from between clenched teeth. "Hard and swift."

There was a sharp intake of breath.

"Yes, sir," said the boy, his voice surprisingly firm.

Cas' good hand twitched on the egg as a faint disturbance of air came from his side.

Just before the boy swung down, Cas' eyes snapped open.

Oh shit —

Multiple unexplainable things happened all at once.

From not far off, somewhere in the city skies above, came a sudden jerk. It was a recoiling thread of power, snapping back to Cas with abrupt violence like a stretched piece of leather giving way.

Mismatched blue eyes widened as the cleaver swung down past his face.

"Flare you fu —"

With a fresh rush of displaced air, the heavy blade sank into the tabletop, through the last bits of flesh and sinew connecting Cas' shimmering, copper-toned hand to his broken fingers.

There was the thunk of metal sinking into wood.

Then a beat of silence.

Then a blinding, white flash of searing light.

The boy was flung across the room by an unseen blast of energy that popped Cas' ears and sent his chair tumbling backwards towards the fire. As he recoiled both from the returning leash that the fucking dragon somehow disconnected, a pain in Cas' head exploded.

A vicious spasm jerked his hands, and the egg went flying from his lap towards the hearth.

Blinking groggily, Cas rolled over, spluttering nonsensical words. He pushed himself to his knees, ears roaring. Disoriented, he somehow located and yanked the waiting wad of cloth off the table to tightly wrap his bleeding hand with the shaking fingers of his other one. That done, he rose, the throb in his ears fading, spinning wildly, trying to spot the egg.

It was nowhere to be seen.

What he found instead, however, was the boy.

The boy was slumped on the floor behind the door in a sorry heap, arms and legs folded awkwardly, his eyes closed.

With a cry, Cas pushed away from the table and skidded to his knees. Pressing around the slight frame gently, Cas ignored the fresh sting in his hand and checked the boy over. There didn't seem to be broken bones.

Thank fuck!

"Child, l-little thing, w-wake up," Cas stammered through numb lips, bringing the boy to his chest.

The lad weighed nothing at all and Cas was horrified to realise he didn't know his name. Or had he forgotten it?

"Please, wake up," Cas urged, eyes stinging from the fading flash and unashamed tears of panic.

At first, there was nothing, but a few wild heartbeats later, the limp figure in Cas' arms stirred.

Cas held him close and rocked him while he came to.

When the boy coughed, Cas sobbed out loud.

"What happened?" gasped the boy. A shaking hand rose to clasp Cas' arm.

"*I* happened," Cas sobbed and laughed with a kind of glum certainty. "It was me, I don't... I'm sorry, I'm sorry..."

Hugging the boy as he caught his breath, rocking gently back and forth, Cas willed his mind to focus.

What the fuck had happened, indeed?

What had Flare done to escape from Cas' thread that bound them?

There was only one way to find out.

Cas shifted to sit on his heels, the boy in his arms, then pushed up with a loud groan. Straining, he rose and carried the boy to the fire. He lowered him before the hearth, sitting him up against the warmed stones of the chimney surrounds, wrapping the cloak tight about him.

"I'll come back," Cas murmured as he fussed.

The boy blinked at him, shining brown eyes a little glazed.

"Promise?"

"No." Cas grinned weakly. "But I'll try my best."

The boy laughed at that. It was a pathetic huff, but it was something. Thanking the gods who didn't exist, Cas bent forward and rested his feverish chin against the top of the boy's head.

"Don't go outside," he urged seriously.

Hair shifted against Cas' jaw as the boy nodded.

"Good boy." He paused. "I'm Cas."

"Cas..." The boy sighed. "Thank you for coming back, Cas," mumbled the boy. His voice was muffled when he continued. "I don't have a name."

"Ah," Cas glared at the bodies beside them. He cleared his throat. "We'll find a good one for you."

After ruffling the boy's hair, Cas was about to rise when a faceted flash caught his eyes from the hearth.

The crystal egg was in the embers of the fire.

The thing had settled amongst the last remaining wisps of bloody, burnt rags.

It seemed an appropriate moment to panic.

Instead, Cas felt a strange sort of calm as he stared.

The chunk of crystal looked perfectly at ease, if such a thing could be said.

Huh.

"Come here, you," he sighed. He lifted an iron poker from its hook near the boy's head and used the tip to roll the thing out of the embers and ash.

Cas poked it too hard, and it sped towards him with a wild tumble, coming to rest against his knee. His shout of pain fizzled to a confused hiccup.

No acrid aroma of burnt flesh and fabric reached his nose, no sizzle of hairs crisping on his skin.

The egg wasn't hot at all.

It wasn't cold, either.

"Well, fuck me," Cas managed.

Reaching out carefully, he picked it up in both hands. The offending digits had been removed in far more of an explosive ceremony than expected, but strangely enough, his head was clearing. Standing up, Cas kicked more wood into the fire, got the innocent-looking chunk of crystal back in its satchel, and made his way to the door.

Before he opened it, Cas looked back.

From his seat against the warm stones, the boy gave Cas a limp wave.

Cas waved his bandaged hand in return.

Then he turned and stepped out into the night.

Carefully latching the door behind, he paused.

His head hurt, Flare had fucked off, his hand throbbed, and the weird rash on his arms and chest itched a little, but he was here.

Ready to complete a lot of careful planning.

Shivering at the icy wind, Cas set off, lost in thought as his brain seemed to shake off a little of the fog that had bogged him down.

He hoped the boy stayed warm, and he hoped that there was enough time to deal with the bodies of the two people who may or may not still have been alive. Horrific, truly, when you thought about it. But the boy seemed to be made of tough stuff.

The *real* horror was not so much the chaotic aftermath of Cas' required violence. It was the life lived by a boy who deserved no less than a caring home. Instead, because of a minor difference to his face, the boy had lived a life under carelessness that had failed and devastated him at every turn.

Hypatia and Illarion had been no better, of course. In fact, they had been much worse. In the name of science, they had destroyed lives, cities. Their sins must be atoned for, cured in the only way Cas knew how.

As cries of terror broke around him, Cas headed to the main street, boots crunching on fresh snow.

Would they be proud of him now?

He learnt from them, didn't he? So how should he feel, grateful or damned?

After all, they broke a city apart in an attempt to do what they wanted.

So why shouldn't he?

"Morgan, my love, my life," Cas called into the snow and the shadows as he began his ascent to the castle at the top of the terraced city while frantic people screamed and raced around him at the new threat blooming with soaring flames in the freezing night.

So Flare had done some of what he was ordered.

Breath misted before Cas' face as he sighed. He wished he had clothes that fit well, shining boots and his beautiful sword by his side. Instead, he was in borrowed garb from a town known for its fine stone rather than fine cloth, with a copper rash and pink hair. But at least the egg was safe in the bag held tight to his chest.

Through the city folk yelling as they dashed around looking for water that hadn't frozen, Cas trudged onwards and upwards.

Towards her.

"Morgan, wait for me. I'm here."

EPILOGUE

The Alchemy of Light

"The wonder of exactly how plants ... trees take the warm light of the sun within ... eludes us. Somehow, along with water, nutrients ... suitable climates, foliage feeds on daylight. The energy is consumed and absorbed.

This mystery led to the discovery of ... crystals can be used ... same way, as we evolve from Human to Elf, and then to ... pinnacle of all intelligent life: Dragon."

Taken from 'The Mystery of Matter and the Energy Within' by Hypatia Carter, commissioned for the Library of Seers. The volume is soiled with scorched edges, the parchment cracking and brittle, the ink flaking away in places.

Added underneath in a smudged scrawl:

'My ... wife, ... eldest competes in vain with those who shine, flickering like fractured light reflecting off our pair of vivianite eggs.

You say I worry needlessly, but what will become of him, ... development, his life's purpose? I wonder, ...truly do. What if another comes along ... snuffs out what little light he has?

x Illarion'

Underneath lies another note, written with tightly restrained form in flaking ink:

'Husband.

Any creation of mine, no matter ... broken, will radiate brightly ... some way.

Perhaps whatever light ... eldest might have ... simply not meant to last.

Hypatia.'

Rhydian

Year 367
Aneirin Farmlands

On the second day after Wyll's bitter, failed rebellion, Rhydian rode alone towards the river.

The rushing water was cloudy, the mossy banks frosted. Beyond it, the massive wall of trees that grew impossibly tall the further south one looked, was covered in a fresh downfall of snow.

It was a beautiful, if chilled, evening. Rhydian had wanted to work alongside the others as they cleared the courtyard well into the night, but Aurelia had given him a long look.

"Get some fresh air," she had said with a tentative smile just for him.

Considering there were enough workers doing what they could, Rhydian had grudgingly agreed. A ride would allow him to digest all that had happened.

The vision of Merion lying in a pool of his own blood, skin pale as death itself, in the stables he loved... that was an image that would never leave his soul.

The king's hands clenched, an ominous heat building in his fingertips.

The groom had been bleeding from three wounds. Two major ones, a furious gash along the ribs, another deep in his abdomen. And the third, a serious slash across his palm and fingers. This was likely the first wound, when Merion had tried to defend himself by catching hold of a naked blade with his bare hands.

The king pulled his horse to a standstill.

Inhaling deeply, Rhydian stood in the stirrups, closed his eyes, and roared.

"You bastard!" the king yelled at the frozen world surrounding him, his mouth drying as he sat back down in the saddle, slumped like a sack of grain.

With his heart racing, he sat still for a moment, eyes slowly opening to the landscape, not really seeing it as his mind worked through the tumult within.

Wyll was rotting in the icy depths below the castle until Rhydian chose what punishment fit him best. For Aurelia, there was no question, death, in as painful a way as possible. Wyll certainly deserved something harsh, and Rhydian preferred the man think about what was coming long before it happened. It was petty, cruel even, of a king to think such a thing.

Justice should be served swiftly and unerringly.

But after all Wyll had done?

Rhydian's pale blue eyes with their darker ring of blue narrowed, his jaw tense.

Perhaps Aurelia was right.

After checking the pole resting in the stirrup by his boot was secure, his hands tightened around the reins, and Rhydian urged his horse onwards. His heart felt as if it had been dipped in lead.

The air was bitingly cold, the threatening clouds so close by it seemed that if he reached up, he could disturb their drab underbellies and earn himself a face full of snow. It had fallen all day, blanketing those that came to carry away the last of their dead friends and family from a feast that had ended in violence.

Each person had been handed coins for burial or burning, whatever the families wished. Rhydian was unsure of the idea, but Davyn had suggested it awkwardly. It made sense; the people having been through so much. If they didn't look at it as blood money, and it brought some comfort and ease, who cared?

I do.

Rhydian let the horse pick its way through a field once lushly green, now frozen silver.

His sad gaze eyed the vast expanse of the valley, the low hills in the east to his left, the jagged mountain range to his right. The continent of Beinacoilia was still a place of mystery to him. Was that because of the curse? Was that why he had grown up so close to one place? What was life really like in Lolihud in the south, or how many folks lived in the wild lands of the north? He knew now there were a few towns, not just ruins, but the opportunity to see them for himself seemed impossible.

Would he ever get the chance? So far it had been fleeting, glimpses of strange wildernesses only in passing on a desperate mission to find the one he loved.

Fury surged in his chest.

Owaen's brother was still loose somewhere, scheming who knew what, with power stolen and misused. Rhydian had to breathe through his nostrils to calm down. The frustration that Aurelia had been caught up in all of this was felt as a twisting in his guts. Beneath him, the grey horse tossed its head.

What had his librarian, newly returned but in no way forthcoming with any information that helped them, had admitted?

Maneuvering.

Caspian was a man affected by the best and worst of people around him.

"Like me?"

Rhydian shivered as the unbidden words left his lips in a puff of white mist, a wave of unease rippling down his spine.

No.

He had nothing in common with that unhinged man.

The weary king forced his gaze from his clenched hands to the obscured sky above, searching for who knew what. Cracking his neck, Rhydian turned his horse towards the ring of ancient stones.

Downstream from the old bridge that he wanted to burn down, the land here was wild, untamed. Its beauty had been renewed, mysterious with its covering of crisp snow, the occasional spikes of green turning brown poking through. Chunks of ice bobbed downstream, to either melt or be sucked down into the maelstrom of the whirlpool that had almost taken the one he loved.

When he had left the city gates, the calls of supportive townsfolk had followed him. But were they really on his side?

Who would dare to speak against him now, after what he had done?

As he reined in his horse beside the stones, snow capped and covered in lichen, Rhydian swallowed past the lump in his throat.

His chilled fingers had tingled at the hidden thoughts of the people he had sworn to serve. If not formally, for the official crown was still missing, but in his heart ever since he was a boy.

A vision of Lord Cyrus, speaking out against Rhydian's father, crossed his mind.

The man's needless, violent death was most likely a shared whisper amongst the city now. The curse had broken, people had welcomed their senses returning, reestablishing interactions with an outside world long cut off.

"I'm sorry," Rhydian mumbled to the fields of snow.

The people thought he had the answers. But instead of solutions, the sinister power that had lain dormant within him had roared to life. It had struck out blindly to those around him, friend and foe alike.

"I'm sorry," he repeated, his gaze on the ring of snow-capped stones.

The lump in his throat threatened to break, his mind shying away from the stunned fury that had overtaken him when his magic had let loose beyond his control.

"I'm sorry," he sighed, his voice hoarse.

I am not my mother.

I am not my father.

I am a good king.

And a king must endure.

"My first duty as king was to lay my bastard of a father to rest. Why must I endure that?" Rhydian coughed at the bitter chill. "Why does he get to rest, and I must suffer for it?"

There was no answer forthcoming, of course.

Wiping his eyes, Rhydian dismounted, unhooked the pole from the stirrup and planted it in the snow for now. He hobbled the horse with efficient movements brought on by years of training. The animal would be cold, but it would hopefully occupy itself by nuzzling about in the snow for what was left of the grass.

He lifted the pole and examined the faded pennant at its tip. Taken from the old armoury, the weathered wooden spike was about as long as he was tall. The pennant was a triangle made of frayed green silk. The design was of a simplified sun in gold thread. Rhydian had spotted it that morning, whilst dumping weapons that no longer had owners.

In a corner filled with cobwebs, the thing had caught his eye and the idea of installing it out here amongst the vague border appealed. It could help centre him, a symbolic gesture of working towards a new beginning, new life, new hope.

Hope that was sorely needed.

A velvety nose nuzzled his neck. Expression grim, Rhydian strode away from the curious horse.

The hem of Rhydian's cloak lifted in the breeze, his boots crunching on the fresh snow as he passed through the ring of stones without pause. He inhaled the raw air.

Did he feel anything?

A chill along his shoulders, yes. But surely that was the ice suspended on the currents that passed in lazy puffs of cold air. There was no more magic here, the curse broken, lies uncovered.

The king pinched the bridge of his nose with numb fingers, his lungs stinging as he inhaled. Spread about him was the landscape of mystery, hidden under the fresh snow. Luckily, they had decent grain stores because the farmers, and the crops, weren't used to this weather. His chilled lips formed soundless words.

Did you plan for this, Father?

In case your magic was one day broken and Aneirin joined the natural ways of the rest of the continent once more?

Halting in the centre of the ancient circle, Rhydian kicked at the snow with a boot encrusted with ice.

There was no sign of the hole dug to find the cursed crystal dagger that had opened his throat, causing the kingdom of lies to crumble.

Steadying his heart, Rhydian lifted the pole and rammed its base into the near frozen ground. Thankfully, the tip broke through. At the same time above, a lone ray of setting sun burst through a break in the clouds towards the bridge.

Rhydian blinked.

Stripes of coloured light shone down, glittering among the ice crystals that disturbed the chilled air. The sight humbled him, and he smiled, a brittle twist of lips, but a smile nonetheless.

"There must be healing here," he said as the clouds reformed and the rainbow of glittering light faded. He glanced at his boots, at the pole where it sank into the disturbed snow and earth. "There must be a way."

As he twisted the wood to secure it deeper, he blew the ice off his lips.

Could the way be as simple as leaving Caspian to Fox, to Owaen? Allowing Rhydian to attempt to rebuild, once again, the uneasy peace of two races, enemies not long before?

The horse snorted nearby, and Rhydian shook his head. The ends of his hair were stiff. He pulled up his hood, eyeing the valley to the north from where he had come, the castle at the top of the terraced city to his left.

He brushed ice and dust off the pennant. It hung limply, the golden sun too heavy to be lifted in the breeze. Perhaps he should take a moment, considering he felt the same way.

Rhydian gathered his fur cloak under his backside, then sunk into the snow with a crunch. He wrapped his arms around his bent knees, resting his cheek on one hand. He wasn't content inside, but despite that he sat in silence in the hope contentment would come.

Blinking at the ice on his eyelashes, Rhydian gazed out at the once familiar vista around him.

The silent valley was covered in an unexpected freeze, its battlefield covered with grey ashes, topped with snow.

Was Fox experiencing such a chill?

And how was Blackthorn? Was he coping?

The next time his eyelids fluttered, they stayed closed.

Barely awake, Rhydian spared a thought to examine his inner world.

Underneath the rage, hurt, and confusion was fear.

During Wyll's short hearing in the hall the day before, his hands ached to lash out, a hot lick of power desiring to reveal itself and tear the man and what he stood for into shreds of red —

No.

"I don't want that," Rhydian mumbled inside his fur hood. "That is not the way. Not violence, but peace."

Peace.

I must at least show others peace, even if I don't feel it.

Head on his knees, Rhydian fell asleep in the snow, a king's fake smile on his face, while inside fear, like a shadow, crept silently across his heart.

The snapping of fabric flapping woke him, along with the sensation that he was falling, as if the earth had shifted on its axis deep below the snow and rock.

Blinking against the thick layer of flakes off his lashes, Rhydian cursed at the numbness on his limbs, his feet, hands and frozen arse.

"F-fucking hells," he stuttered.

Rhydian unhooked his arms from his knees, wincing, shaking off the snow from his wool jumper, and blew on his hands. The effort earned him a hacking cough of misted breath, his lungs protesting at the oddly bitter air.

When the feeling returned enough that he could stand, Rhydian staggered to his feet. This horse had wandered in between the ring of stones. It shivered nearby, eyeing him with obvious disdain.

He was about to apologise when a fresh gust of wind whipped about him, his cloak lifting, the pennant wildly flapping back and forth. The grey light of earlier had faded to an eerie twilight. It was dark, to the point it seemed the sun must be dipping towards the horizon behind the clouds. Sometimes during heavy rain, the sun setting behind the mountains generated the raindrops to ripple in a cascading mix of colours.

This night seemed no different at first. The intense colours were a wondrous sight for his weary gaze, relief lifting away from his shoulders like a feather rising in a warm breeze.

Wait...

Rhydian squinted more intensely at the odd reddish glow, the snow partially obscuring his sight.

Blue eyes widened.

"Huh?"

To the north, something flew over the valley from the east to his right. It wasn't a bird; it was far too big. The strange orange and red glow reflected off the creature's sides as it sped towards the mountains to the west. It was too distant to make out its colour or hear the deep beat of leathery wings, but Rhydian's heart eased in an instant.

"Fox!" Rhydian shouted.

Whooping through numb lips, the young king turned and jogged over to his sullen horse. After unhobbling the animal, he planted a boot in the stirrup, not quite registering the pink tinge to the horse's grey coat. He squeezed his knees, and the animal stepped between the stones, heading home with an anxious snort.

Rhydian swore at the chill when he wiped away the ice on the thick mane. He glanced up as the horse whinnied.

"Hush, it's okay. We're heading home. Everything is going to be alright..."

The king's voice faded to a wisp of fog, his heart stalling.

His throat tightened, as if he was breathing the ash that would surely fall in the coming days.

The terraced city, built into the side of the mountain, blazed with a sinister crimson glow, flickering orange and gold points of light blooming on various levels in multiple places all at once.

"Oh," Rhydian choked out, his throat constricting. "Actually, I don't think it is."

Aneirin, the city of his people, was burning.

The Nightfall Series
Book 4

Keep turning for an exclusive preview of Book Four (2026),
concluding the first part of The Nightfall Series

Shop The Nightfall Series
and sign up to The Nightfall Newsletter:
www.lorentuxford.com

Nightfall in the Forest of Burning Hearts

The Watcher

Year 367

Aneirin Castle

Deep within their hood of thick wool, the sound of ragged breathing filled the Watcher's ears as they ran.

They welcomed it, for it helped to cover the sound of flames crackling, desperate cries for help and incredible deep beats of massive leathery wings swooping over the city of their birth.

The uprising of discontent had passed, but an additional threat had emerged. This time, instead of angry townsfolk, afraid of the unknown as hearts struggled to mend, someone, something, had brought a scorching fury to Aneirin. And with it, the perfect opportunity had presented itself.

Get to Wyll.

He was someone the Watcher had known all their life, but who had since become a stranger with twisted thoughts that had resulted in a traitorous rebellion. An uprising against the king, his friends and the good folk of Aneirin, who had welcomed an uneasy peace with ears ready to listen, hearts ready to welcome and understand.

Despite their terror of the surrounding chaos, the Watcher sped onwards through the castle. It took everything they had to race towards the castle from the city, towards the thickest patch of heat and chaos. It was mad, and it would likely end poorly. But their heart was set. It was right; it was just. And they could get it done.

The Watcher skidded around groups of panicked soldiers with their face to the frozen sky, low clouds lit golden by flames that reached as high as the castle's outer walls. What burned, the Watcher had no clue. The heat was real as they leapt up the main stairs into the castle hall. The acrid smoke stung their nose as they headed inside.

A great sweeping shadow passed the great hall's windows, the smoke, flames and wings patterned on the far wall with stunning clarity. The Watcher inhaled sharply, but raced on. There was only one destination left, their heart was set.

Sweating despite the frigid air, the Watcher slid to a stop on time worn slate floors and turned towards the back way to their goal, lest anybody see. They didn't really care who found out after.

But not before it was done.

Harsh breathing filled their ears as they turned again, this time heading along a hall that had filled with hot curls of grey smoke towards the rear of the castle, a hallway of flickering iron lanterns lighting old tapestries, towards the library with its —

The ragged breathing hitched to a gasp, and the Watcher almost tripped as they came to a sudden stop.

At the far end of the short hall, kneeling amongst the smoke, was the king.

Above him stood a man, with a palm on either side of the king's jaw.

The scene was shocking, not just for the oddness of finding King Rhydian on his knees at such a time, but for the quiet air and the odd calm that filled the hallway while chaos reigned outside.

It was hard to tell from this far away by the flickering flames of the lanterns and gloomy shadows. But the king appeared stunned as the man above leaned down. The man had pale, almost pinkish hair, his gaze intent on the king's upturned face.

The Watcher's free hand covered their mouth as they bit back a scream.

Neither man looked his way as they stared at one other.

"My apologies in advance," said the man to the king kneeling before him. His bright laugh merged with the smoke, like bitter honey stirred into hot milk. "This is going to hurt."

Nightfall in the Forest of Burning Hearts
Book 4 of The Nightfall Series (2026)
Pre Order: www.lorentuxford.com

The Continent of Beinacoilia

Aneirin: Human Kingdom of Beinacoilia, built into the side of red mountains. Farmlands follow the curve of the valley, surrounded by forest. The trees in the south are many times the size of those found elsewhere.

Baile Fuar: Began as an open-cut quarry, supplying stone to the City of the Seers. The town is in three parts, along the rim, on the quarry floor, and tunnelled into the bedrock. The townsfolk are a mixture of races and are generally suspicious of outsiders. It features multiple hot springs.

Baile Mara: The City on the Sea, east of Aneirin. The city and its surrounding beaches comprise black volcanic rock. To those who live inland, the city is thought to be completely lost beneath the waves, after a fatal cataclysm in the mid 200s.

Lolihud: A series of vast caves in southern Beinacoilia, where most Elves live. Burrowed under the icy mountain ranges, the Elves mine crystals and rare minerals for the Dragons, who have all but disappeared. Magic amongst the Elves is fading. The name 'Lolihud' is derived from the old language, roughly translating to 'magic candy'.

Mionlach: Where the Dragons preferred to dwell, in the northern part of Beinacoilia. It is the warmest location on the continent due to volcanic activity.

The City of the Seers: Built to house scholars and record their works. Dragons were active in the design and construction, hence its impressive scale. This city was the meeting place of the Council, consisting of Humans, Elves and Dragons. In ruins since the early 300s, the first foundations were laid in the year 0, and left alone for many decades.

Notes and Pronunciation

Notes

Magic: The process of absorbing concentrated forms of energy, mainly from crystals and pure minerals. Its potential is then harnessed by the cells of the body, and through the mind, it is unleashed as energy in action. It is by no means an exact science, although some alchemists believe it is.

Humans: Those without magic, although there is some in a watered-down state within the general population.

Elves: Human with magic, some born with it, others through a painful process of assimilation.

Dragons: Elves who have gone further with magic and can transform into massive, winged creatures.

Beinacoilia: The major continent on which most known races live, however, there are vast swathes of unexplored lands further west, and also a variety of established islands across the Eastern Sea.

Dates: Year 0 – the official establishment date of Baile Mara, the first major city on the continent of Beinacoilia.

Pronunciation

Baek Hyeon: Baek – *ae* as in *hat*. Hyeon – *H* is silent; *yeon* like *young*.

Rhydian: *Rid – ee – ehn*.

Aurelia: *Or – ee – lee – ah*.

Acknowledgements

Compared to Books One and Two, writing was different this time around. Life was weird and my mind and body chose not to work some days. Yet here we are, thanks to the heavens above, and also to the following golden souls around the globe.

First up, The Order of Oodies. The Nightfall Series would simply not exist without your keen eyes and humour. I say thank you a lot, and each time I mean it. Middle sis and biggest sis, thank you for keeping my heart full. Mum, thank you for your support. To all my friends and family who were part of this journey, thank you. I'm not sorry for the rude bits.

My Editors, Beta Readers and ARC team, indie authors around the world will never be able to thank you enough for your enthusiasm. For your encouragement: Jess K, Meredith E, Aiva J, Vasudha C, Linda T, Leanne T and Tomi. To my fellow authors for sharing the journey: Ivana L. Truglio, Heather Leighson, Bellamina Court, Meghan E McComb, Kim Galliher and C.Z. Reeves. Thank you to all the authors that inspired me. To Isla S. in Tech support for SqSp: thank you for saving my digital backside.

The following are Instagram handles, by the way, so go look. For your exceptional portraits: @yka.11 For your wisdom and good vibes: @jayk_creates @crowandcauldron_ & @badluvevents For your supreme cookies: @sugarbowsco For giving authors a voice: @bookfairaus @emwigstersbookshelf @boysfromthebookshelf and @library_lioness

Finally, to my dear readers, and all who listened to me talk about crystal penises and complicated dragons within a world contained entirely inside my imagination, thank you.

Loren x

About the Author

After making her own books as a small child, Loren decided it was time to share her stories with the world, much to the delight of her dark sense of humour. With multiple books published, the capricious dialogue of Loren's chatty imagination is finally settling down... sort of.

Born in Australia, Loren enjoys writing, stargazing, birdwatching, strong coffee, wild places, overgrown cemeteries, reading and daydreaming.

www.lorentuxford.com

* 9 7 8 0 6 4 8 6 3 6 7 5 5 *